PENGUIN BOOKS

FROM INK LAKE

Michael Ondaatje was born in Ceylon (now
Sri Lanka) in 1943. In 1962 he moved to Canada, where he now lives, teaching at Glen-
don College, York University, in Toronto. He
is the author of a fictional memoir about his
family, *Running in the Family*, and several
novels, including *In the Skin of a Lion*, *Coming
Through Slaughter*, and *The Collected Works of
Billy the Kid*, all available from Penguin. His
collections of poetry include *There's a Trick
with a Knife I'm Learning to Do* and *Secular
Love*. He has twice been given the Governor-
General's Award for Literature.

From Ink Lake

CANADIAN STORIES SELECTED BY
MICHAEL ONDAATJE

PENGUIN BOOKS

PENGUIN BOOKS
Published by the Penguin Group
Viking Penguin, a division of Penguin Books USA Inc.,
375 Hudson Street, New York, New York 10014, U.S.A.
Penguin Books Ltd, 27 Wrights Lane,
London W8 5TZ, England
Penguin Books Australia Ltd, Ringwood,
Victoria, Australia
Penguin Books Canada Ltd, 10 Alcorn Avenue, Suite 300,
Toronto, Ontario, Canada M4V 3B2
Penguin Books (N.Z.) Ltd, 182–190 Wairau Road,
Auckland 10, New Zealand

Penguin Books Ltd, Registered Offices:
Harmondsworth, Middlesex, England

First published simultaneously in the United States of America by
Viking Penguin, a division of
Penguin Books USA Inc., in Canada by
Lester & Orpen Dennys, and in Great Britain by Faber & Faber 1990
Published in Penguin Books 1992

1   3   5   7   9   10   8   6   4   2

PUBLISHER'S NOTE
These stories are works of fiction. Names, characters, places, and incidents
either are the product of the authors' imagination or are used fictitiously, and
any resemblance to actual persons, living or dead, events, or locales is entirely
coincidental.

Pages viii-xii constitute an extension of this copyright page.

THE LIBRARY OF CONGRESS HAS CATALOGUED THE HARDCOVER AS FOLLOWS:
From Ink Lake: an anthology of Canadian short stories/edited by
Michael Ondaatje.
p.   cm.
ISBN 0-670-83339-8 (hc.)
ISBN 0 14 01.1832 2 (pbk.)
1. Short stories, Canadian.   2. Canada—Fiction.
I. Ondaatje, Michael, 1943–
PR9197.32.F76   1990
813'.0108971—dc20   90–50115

Printed in the United States of America
Set in Palatino

For Ken Adachi (1928–1989).
True believer.

Contents

Acknowledgements

I would like to thank Sarah Harvey, who helped me with the original research for this book. And the following for their advice and help: Kirsten Hanson, Stan Dragland, Anne Fullerton, Sheila Fischman, Germaine Quintas, and Don McKay for the memory of a poem of his named "Ink Lake". Also Robert McCrum of Faber and Faber, Kathryn Court of Viking Penguin, and Antoine Boutros of the El-Basha restaurant. Most of all, I'd like to thank Louise Dennys.

For permission to reprint the stories and excerpts in this anthology, acknowledgement is made as follows:

Atwood, Margaret, "The Boys' Own Annual, 1911", from *Murder in the Dark* by Margaret Atwood, © 1983 by Margaret Atwood. Reprinted by permission of Jonathan Cape Ltd., and the author. "The Man from Mars", from *Dancing Girls* by Margaret Atwood, © 1977 by Margaret Atwood. Reprinted by permission of the Canadian Publishers, McClelland and Stewart, Toronto, Simon and Schuster, Jonathan Cape Ltd., and the author.

Birdsell, Sandra, "Night Travellers", from *Night Travellers* by Sandra Birdsell (Winnipeg: Turnstone Press, 1982) © 1982 by Sandra Birdsell. Reprinted by permission of Turnstone Press Limited, Winnipeg.

Blais, Marie-Claire, "An Intimate Death", © 1989 by Marie-Claire Blais. Translated from the French by Ray Ellenwood, translation © 1989 by Ray Ellenwood. Reprinted by permission of the author and translator.

Blaise, Clark, "I'm Dreaming of Rocket Richard", from *Tribal Justice* by Clark Blaise, © 1974 by Clark Blaise. Reprinted by permission of the author.

Bowering, George, "Bring Forth a Wonder", from *Burning Water* by George Bowering, © 1980 by George Bowering. Reprinted by permission of the author.

Brand, Dionne, "Photograph", from *Sans Souci* by Dionne Brand, © 1988 by Dionne Brand. Reprinted by permission of the author and Williams-Wallace Publishers.

Clarke, Austin, "Leaving This Island Place", from *When He Was Free and Young and He Used to Wear Silks*, © 1971 by Austin Clarke. Reprinted by permission of the author.

Cohen, Matt, "The Sins of Tomàs Benares", from *Café le Dog*, © 1983 by Matt Cohen. Reprinted by permission of the author.

Ferron, Jacques, "Chronicle of Anse Saint-Roch", from *Selected Tales of Jacques Ferron*, by Jacques Ferron, © 1984 by Jacques Ferron. Translated from the French by Betty Bednarski, translation © 1984, The House of Anansi Press. Reprinted by permission of Stoddart Publishing Co. Limited, Don Mills, Ontario.

Ferron, Madeleine, "Be Fruitful and Multiply", from *Coeur de Sucre* by Madeleine Ferron, Editions Hurtubise HMH, Montreal, © 1966, latest revised edition, 1988. Translated from the French by Sheila Watson, translation © 1974 by Sheila Watson. Reprinted by permission of Editions Hurtubise HMH, and Sheila Watson.

Findley, Timothy, "Dreams", from *Stones*, by Timothy Findley, © 1988 by Pebble Productions Inc. Reprinted by permission of Penguin Books Canada Limited and the author. Published in the United States by Dell Publishing Company.

Fraser, Keath, "The History of Cambodia", from *Foreign Affairs*, by Keath Fraser, © 1985. Reprinted by permission of the author. "Roget's Thesaurus", from *Taking Cover*, by Keath Fraser, © 1982. Reprinted by permission of the author.

French, Alice, "Spring and Summer", from *My Name is Masak*, by Alice French, Winnipeg: Peguis Publishers Ltd., 1977. Reprinted by permission of author and publisher.

Gallant, Mavis, "The Moslem Wife", from *From the Fifteenth District* by Mavis Gallant, © 1979 by Mavis Gallant. Reprinted by permission of Georges Borchardt, Inc. for the author, and Macmillan of Canada, a Division of Canada Publishing Corporation.

Gould, Glenn, "The Search for Petula Clark", © 1967 by Glenn Gould. Reprinted by permission of the Estate of Glenn Gould and Glenn Gould Limited.

Harvor, Elisabeth, "Foreigners", © 1980 by Elisabeth Harvor. Reprinted by permission of the author.

Hébert, Anne, from *The First Garden*, © 1990 by Anne Hébert. Translated from the French by Sheila Fischman, © 1990. Reprinted by permission of the author, translator, and Stoddart Publishing Co. Limited.

Hodgins, Jack, "The Concert Stages of Europe", from *Barclay Family Theatre*, by Jack Hodgins, © 1981 by Jack Hodgins. Reprinted by permission of Macmillan of Canada, a Division of Canada Publishing Corporation.

Hood, Hugh, "Ghosts at Jarry", from *None Genuine Without this Signature*, by Hugh Hood, © 1980 by Hugh Hood. Reprinted by permission of the author.

Kelly, John P., "We Are All in the Ojibway Circle", © 1977 by John P. Kelly. Reprinted by permission of the author.

Kogawa, Joy, from *Obasan*, © 1981 by Joy Kogawa. Reprinted by permission of David R. Godine, Publisher, and the author.

Laurence, Margaret, "The Rain Child", from *The Tomorrow Tamer* by Margaret Laurence, © 1962 by Margaret Laurence. Reprinted by permission of the Estate of Margaret Laurence.

Leacock, Stephen, "L'envoi. The Train to Mariposa", from *Sunshine Sketches of a Little Town*, by Stephen Leacock, © 1912 by Stephen Leacock. Reprinted by permission of the Canadian Publishers, McClelland and Stewart, Toronto.

MacLennan, Hugh, "The Halifax Explosion, 1917," from *Barometer Rising* by Hugh MacLennan, © 1941 by Hugh MacLennan. Reprinted by permission of the author and his agent Blanche C. Gregory, Inc.

MacLeod, Alistair, "As Birds Bring Forth the Sun", and "The Closing Down of Summer", from *As Birds Bring Forth the Sun* by Alistair MacLeod, © 1986 Alistair MacLeod. Reprinted by permission of the Canadian Publishers, McClelland and Stewart, Toronto.

Marshall, Joyce, "The Accident", © 1976 by Joyce Marshall. Reprinted by permission of the author.

Mistry, Rohinton, "Condolence Visit," from *Tales from Firozsha Baag* (in the United States: *Swimming Lessons and Other Stories from Firozsha Baag*) by Rohinton Mistry, © 1987 by Rohinton Mistry. Reprinted by permission of Penguin Books Canada Limited, Houghton Mifflin Company, and Curtis Brown Limited. Also published in *Canadian Fiction Magazine*, no. 50/51 and *Coming Attractions*, #4, Oberon Press.

Moses, Daniel David, "King of the Raft", © 1987 by Daniel David Moses. Reprinted by permission of the author.

Mukherjee, Bharati, "The Management of Grief", from *The Middleman and Other Stories*, by Bharati Mukherjee, © Bharati Mukherjee 1988. Reprinted by permission of Virago Press Ltd., and Penguin Books Canada Ltd.

Munro, Alice, "Miles City, Montana", from *The Progress of Love* by Alice Munro, © 1986 by Alice Munro. Reprinted by permission of Alfred A. Knopf, Inc., Chatto and Windus, and the Canadian Publishers, McClelland and Stewart, Toronto.

Richards, David Adams, from *Blood Ties*, © 1976 by David Adams Richards. Reprinted by permission of Oberon Press.

Richler, Mordecai, "Some Grist for Mervyn's Mill," from *The Street* by Mordecai Richler. © 1969 by Mordecai Richler. Reprinted by permission of the author.

Ritchie, Charles, from *My Grandfather's House*, © Charles Ritchie, 1987. Reprinted by permission of Macmillan of Canada, A Division of Canada Publishing Corporation.

Rooke, Leon, "The Only Daughter", from *A Bolt of White Cloth*, by Leon Rooke, © 1984 by Leon Rooke. Reprinted by permission of the author.

Rosenblatt, Joe, "The Lake", © Exile Editions and Joe Rosenblatt, 1985. Reprinted by permission of the author and Exile Editions.

Ross, Sinclair, "The Painted Door", from *The Lamp at Noon* by Sinclair Ross, © 1939 by Sinclair Ross. Reprinted by permission of the Canadian Publishers, McClelland and Stewart, Toronto.

Roy, Gabrielle, "The Well of Dunrea", from *Street of Riches*, by Gabrielle Roy, © Fonds Gabrielle Roy. Translated from the French by Harry L. Binsse, 1957. Reprinted by permission of Fonds Gabrielle Roy.

Shields, Carol, "Scenes", from *Various Miracles* by Carol Shields, © 1985 by Carol Shields. Reprinted by permission of Stoddart Publishing Co. Limited, Viking Penguin, a division of Penguin Books USA Inc., and the author.

Smart, Elizabeth, from *By Grand Central Station I Sat Down and Wept*, © 1966 by Elizabeth Smart. Reprinted by permission of Grafton Books, a Division of the Collins Publishing Group.

Stegner, Wallace, "The Medicine Line", from *Wolf Willow* by Wallace Stegner, © 1955, 1957, 1958, 1959, and 1962 by Wallace Stegner. Reprinted by permission of Brandt and Brandt Literary Agents, Inc.

Thomas, Audrey, "Kill Day on the Government Wharf", © 1981 by Audrey Thomas. Reprinted by permission of the author.

Vanderhaeghe, Guy, "The Watcher", from *Man Descending* by Guy Vanderhaeghe, © 1982. Reprinted by permission of Macmillan of Canada, a Division of Canada Publishing Corporation.

Virgo, Sean, "Arkendale", from *White Lies and Other Fictions* by Sean Virgo, © 1980 by Sean Virgo. Reprinted by permission of the author and Exile Editions.

Watson, Sheila, "Antigone", from *Five Stories* by Sheila Watson, © 1984 by Sheila Watson. Reprinted by permission of the author.

Wiebe, Rudy, "The Naming of Albert Johnson", from *Where is the Voice Coming From?* by Rudy Wiebe, © 1974 by Rudy Wiebe. Reprinted by permission of the author.

Wilson, Ethel, from *Swamp Angel*, © 1954 by Ethel Wilson. Reprinted by permission of Macmillan of Canada, a Division of Canada Publishing Corporation.

Introduction

*"The one-armed explorer
Could only touch half of the country"*

W. S. Merwin's lines about a nineteenth-century geologist seem an apt warning to anyone who would try to represent the best writing of a whole country in one book. An anthologist goes mad trying to be fair and dutiful and must at some point relinquish that responsibility. My intent in this collection is to give instead an angular portrait of a time and place.

When I began work on this anthology there was the challenge that it would have two purposes. It would be a book published abroad, where it would in many cases introduce writers to a new audience. But it would also be published at home – as an interpretation for Canadians who are already familiar with many of these writers, though perhaps not with these particular works. Who was I supposed to aim the book towards? Was this collection a cargo cult? Was it to be some strange structure on our beaches for passing planes from abroad to interpret? Or to establish a firm and distinct border between ourselves and the United States? Or was it to be the pleasure of mapping that the explorer George Vancouver performed on the West Coast?

In Europe, as the Canadian poet Ralph Gustafson says, "you cannot move without going down in history". Pablo Neruda, speaking of South America, said, "there are rivers in our countries which have no names, trees which nobody knows, and birds which nobody has described. . . . Our duty, then, as we understand it, is to express what is unheard of. Everything has been painted in Europe, everything has been sung in Europe." Canada, too, is still documenting and inventing itself.

This is a country of metamorphosis, where we have translated ourselves. *"Here was Beauty and here was Nowhere"*, as the poet Dionne Brand writes. The landscape the early explorers of Canada found was surreal and brutal. We brought with us the old wounds of Europe and Asia and we completed old feuds and battles here. We put on new clothes here. We came as *filles du Roi*, "daughters of the king" – those girls of marriageable age, most of them Parisian beggars and orphans ill prepared for the hardships of life in Canada, who in the seventeenth century were shipped off to New France to provide the French army with wives. We came as exiles, or sometimes thinking Canada was just a conduit to the riches of the Orient or, later, a conduit to the United States – just "Upper America". We named fabulous mountain ranges and rivers after ourselves or the wives of English kings, labelled the landscape without any sense of irony.

The roughness and brutality of the land instead created irony about our worth. There was never a true sense of political or social or, until recently, literary confidence within our country. (Our vainglorious Prime Minister's idea of status is still to be photographed beside British or American leaders.) We make good horror movies. We tend to be known for our hockey players.

This is the surface image of the country. We must turn to our literature for the truth about ourselves, for a more honest self-portrait. Alistair MacLeod's Maritimes or Alice Munro's Ontario or Sandra Birdsell's Manitoba, Mordecai Richler's Montreal, Glenn Gould's Northern Ontario – these make up the true portrait of the country, which was what I wanted to catch in this collection.

The historical scope of the book ranges from a story by Sinclair Ross in the 1930s to the present. But even a contemporary story such as Alistair MacLeod's, which opens the book, reaches far back into the past, into fable and the roots of a curse in another country. The mythology of a place does not evolve chronologically. The past invades us. In Canada we attempt to rewrite it satirically, as George Bowering does, or we evoke it painfully, like Anne Hébert in *The First Garden*. The past is still, for us, a place that is not yet safely settled.

Our early novels had strange plots. In *Wacousta*, by John Richardson, a spurned Scottish lover follows a married couple to Canada, and, turning himself into a "firebrand Indian Chief", leads a bloody attack on the fort that houses them. Two hundred years later, in the early 1900s, Archibald Belaney turned himself into the legendary "Grey Owl" and claimed to be and was accepted throughout the world as an Indian. We wished romantically to become "Indian". Meanwhile we deprived the native peoples, the indigenous peoples of Canada, who already had distinctive cultures and mythologies, of their own voices, tricking them into treaties that took away their lands and traditions. It is only in recent years that the First Peoples have represented themselves, told their own stories to the world – through writers such as Jeannette Armstrong, Minnie Freeman, Alice French, and the playwright Tomson Highway in his two wonderful plays *The Rez Sisters* and *Dry Lips Oughta Move to Kapuskasing*.

I have tried to present more than the usual Anglo-Saxon portrait of this country that gets depicted in the official histories and collections of fiction. In the second half of this century new immigrant writers have painted a different image of Canada that is also outside the Anglo-Saxon tradition. It appears in important and fine novels like *The Sacrifice* by Adele Wiseman, and continues among writers like Austin Clarke, Harold Sonny Ladoo, Josef Skvorecky, and recently Dionne Brand and Rohinton Mistry. From French and Scottish settlers to Englishmen to Europeans and Asians and South Americans, immigrant writing is a familiar and continuing tradition. The drama of entrance into a new land is central in our writing, as is the desire to get *out* of a social structure – comically portrayed in this collection by Mordecai Richler and Jack Hodgins. This tense rubbing together of two distinct worlds is perpetual in our stories – in Atwood's "The Man from Mars", in Keath Fraser's "The History of Cambodia", and in Chief John Kelly's haunting speech to the political and financial establishment about native land rights.

I chose stories rather than authors. I chose stories that in some way mapped the geographical, emotional, and literary range of the country, from fable to chronicle to intimate moment. And while I agree with William Trevor's description of a Chekhov short story as "the art of the glimpse", I am drawn also to stories that seem to have whole novels contained within them. (Mavis Gallant's "The Moslem Wife" has more going on in it than five novels.) Or stories which descend deep into a psyche – like Leon Rooke's "The Only Daughter" or David Adams Richards' "Blood Ties". I chose what I felt was wonderful writing. These stories stand, first of all, as good literature, as part of what I think of as the best writing of our time. We are contemporaries of John Berger and Anita Desai and Peter Handke and Toni Morrison and Russell Banks and Graham Swift and Marilynne Robinson. These stories are the work of writers truthful both to themselves and to a subtle, believable country.

The book is a collage. I wanted to present an historical mix, a diverse assembly of forms and techniques and voices. Perhaps because I have never written a short story, and probably never will, I wanted a collection that was more relaxed in its rules of entry. I wanted to suggest a wider social context, to consider a larger literary range. Non-fiction – from the journals of the first explorers to the recent writing of Farley Mowat and Marshall McLuhan – has been a central and essential literary form for this country. It is the twin of fiction. We are a country swamped by British books and American movies and media and their version of history, and the non-fiction writers help us to hold on to our truths.

So I have included several works which are "outriders", to give the more traditional stories a context and to help place them within a real map. I have included a chapter from Wallace Stegner's *Wolf Willow* – a seminal book in its influence on our fiction writers – as well as part of a memoir by the Inuit writer Alice French, and Chief John Kelly's speech which is a stunning piece of writing and moral argument.

Memoir and history and fiction blend in many of the works. The documentary quality in the novelist Hugh MacLennan's description of the Halifax Explosion in 1917 is there thirty years later in Joy Kogawa's horrifying fictive memoir, *Obasan*, about being Japanese Canadian during the Second World War. In such works the barrier between fiction and document has been erased, creating an even more powerful form. And what *is* fact and what *is* imagining in Stegner's reconstruction of the surveying of the US–Canadian border? Where is fiction and where is memoir in Gabrielle Roy's "The Well of Dunrea", which to me has the power of that other great memoir novel – Willa Cather's *My Antonia*?

And as for Glenn Gould's comic deconstruction of Petula Clark, it seems to me as fictionally playful and literary-wise as the fiction of Julian Barnes in *Flaubert's Parrot* or the "Drover's Wife" stories by contemporary Australian writers. Gould's fictional critique is not that far away in intent and style from George Bowering's outrageous version of the explorer George Vancouver – who in his travels is surrounded by Indians who speak like eighteenth-century Englishmen.

And when we look at the stories, from Rudy Wiebe to Alistair MacLeod to Austin Clarke to Leon Rooke, there is the preoccupying image of figures permanently travelling, portaging their past, still uncertain of where to settle in this country which, in Elizabeth Smart's phrase, is "waiting, unselfconscious as the unborn, for future history to be performed upon it". We are all still arriving. From the *filles du Roi* to Dionne Brand's new Canadians is a minuscule step. Here was Nowhere, a terrifying new place:

> Shanti Narine spat food into her napkin ... It was what white people ate and she wanted to get the taste for it, but it made her ill. It was the kind they put on aeroplanes to confound immigrants and third world people ... They never let up, did they? If you thought you had their lingo down, they gave you spinach quiche to remind you that you didn't know anything. Then they threw in something with whipped cream on it so you couldn't tell whether to eat it or shave your armpits with it.   (Dionne Brand)

*

After two years of reading many books and stories and making this selection, I realize, looking back at the table of contents, that it is still only just half the country, possibly no more than a third. There are well-known writers I very much admire who do not appear here, and there is a burst of writing by talented newer writers, some of whom are already admired abroad, who have been left out unfairly because of space and an imposed time-period that was needed to contain even this large selection. If the title hadn't already been used I would have called the book *The Story So Far*. What is probably needed now is a sequel, a follow-up. As I emphasized at the start, this anthology is more a reader, a sampling, than my attempt at an official canon.

In a beautiful story called "Voices in the Pools" Gabrielle Roy talks about reading and writing:

> All round me were the books of my childhood which I had read and re-read, in a dancing beam of dusty light ... And the happiness the books had given me I wished to repay. I had been the child who reads hidden from everyone, and now I wanted myself to be this

beloved book, these living pages held in the hands of some nameless being, woman, child, companion, whom I would keep for myself a few hours.

In the end, as all irresponsible anthologists discover, with only one hand I could hold on to just some of the things that I loved.

Michael Ondaatje
January 1990, Toronto

From Ink Lake

As Birds Bring Forth the Sun

ALISTAIR MACLEOD

Once there was a family with a Highland name who lived beside the sea. And the man had a dog of which he was very fond. She was large and grey, a sort of staghound from another time. And if she jumped up to lick his face, which she loved to do, her paws would jolt against his shoulders with such force that she would come close to knocking him down and he would be forced to take two or three backward steps before he could regain his balance. And he himself was not a small man, being slightly over six feet and perhaps one hundred and eighty pounds.

She had been left, when a puppy, at the family's gate in a small handmade box and no one knew where she had come from or that she would eventually grow to such a size. Once, while still a small pup, she had been run over by the steel wheel of a horse-drawn cart which was hauling kelp from the shore to be used as fertilizer. It was in October and the rain had been falling for some weeks and the ground was soft. When the wheel of the cart passed over her, it sunk her body into the wet earth as well as crushing some of her ribs; and apparently the silhouette of her small crushed body was visible in the earth after the man lifted her to his chest while she yelped and screamed. He ran his fingers along her broken bones, ignoring the blood and urine which fell upon his shirt, trying to soothe her bulging eyes and her scrabbling front paws and her desperately licking tongue.

The more practical members of his family, who had seen run-over dogs before, suggested that her neck be broken by his strong hands or that he grasp her by the hind legs and swing her head against a rock, thus putting an end to her misery. But he would not do it.

Instead, he fashioned a small box and lined it with woollen remnants from a sheep's fleece and one of his old and frayed shirts. He placed her within the box and placed the box behind the stove and then he warmed some milk in a small saucepan and sweetened it with sugar. And he held open her small and trembling jaws with his left hand while spooning in the sweetened milk with his right, ignoring the needle-like sharpness of her small teeth. She lay in the box most of the remaining fall and into the early winter, watching everything with her large brown eyes.

Although some members of the family complained about her presence and the odour from the box and the waste of time she involved, they gradually adjusted to her: and as the weeks passed by, it became evident that her ribs were knitting together in some form or other and that she was recovering with the resilience of the young. It also became evident that she would grow to a tremendous size, as she outgrew one box and then another and the grey hair began to feather from her huge front paws. In the spring she was outside almost all of the time and followed the man everywhere; and when she came inside during the following months, she had grown so large that she would no longer fit into her accustomed place behind the stove and was forced to lie beside it. She was never given a name but was referred to in Gaelic as *cù mòr glas*, the big grey dog.

By the time she came into her first heat, she had grown to a tremendous height, and although her signs and her odour attracted many panting and highly aroused suitors, none was big enough to mount her and the frenzy of their disappointment and the longing of her unfulfilment were more than the man could stand. He went, so the story goes, to a place where he knew there was a big dog. A dog not as big as she was, but still a big dog, and he brought him home with him. And at the proper time he took the *cù mòr glas* and the big dog down to the sea where he knew there was a hollow in the rock which appeared only at low tide. He took some sacking to provide footing for the male dog and he placed the *cù mòr glas* in the hollow of the rock and knelt beside her and steadied her with his left arm under her throat and helped position the male dog above her and guided his blood-engorged penis. He was a man used to working with the breeding of animals, with the guiding of rams and bulls and stallions and often with the funky smell of animal semen heavy on his large and gentle hands.

The winter that followed was a cold one and ice formed on the sea and frequent squalls and blizzards obliterated the offshore islands and caused the people to stay near their fires much of the time, mending clothes and nets and harness and waiting for the change in season. The *cù mòr glas* grew heavier and even more large until there was hardly room for her around the stove or even under the table. And then one morning, when it seemed that spring was about to break, she was gone.

The man and even his family, who had become more involved than they cared to admit, waited for her but she did not come. And as the frenzy of spring wore on, they busied themselves with readying their land and their fishing gear and all of the things that so desperately required their attention. And then they were into summer and fall and winter and another spring which saw the birth of the man and his wife's twelfth child. And then it was summer again.

That summer the man and two of his teenaged sons were pulling their herring nets about two miles offshore when the wind began to blow off the land and the water began to roughen. They became afraid that they could not make it safely back to shore, so they pulled in behind one of the offshore islands, knowing that they would be sheltered there and planning to outwait the storm. As the prow of their boat approached the gravelly shore, they heard a sound above them, and looking up they saw the *cù mòr glas* silhouetted on the brow of the hill which was the small island's highest point.

"M'eudal cù mòr glas" shouted the man in his happiness – *m'eudal* meaning something like dear or darling; and as he shouted, he jumped over the side of his boat into the waist-deep water, struggling for footing on the rolling gravel as he waded eagerly and awkwardly towards her and the shore. At the same time, the *cù mòr glas* came hurtling down towards him in a shower of small rocks dislodged by her feet; and just as he was emerging from the water, she met him as she used to, rearing up on her hind legs and placing her huge front paws on his shoulders while extending her eager tongue.

The weight and speed of her momentum met him as he tried to hold his balance on the sloping angle and the water rolling gravel beneath his feet, and he staggered backwards and lost his footing and fell beneath her force. And in that instant again, as the story goes, there appeared over the brow of the hill six more huge grey dogs hurtling down towards the gravelled strand. They had never seen him before; and seeing him stretched prone beneath their mother, they misunderstood, like so many armies, the intention of their leader.

They fell upon him in a fury, slashing his face and tearing aside his lower jaw and ripping out his throat, crazed with blood-lust or duty or perhaps starvation. The *cù mòr glas* turned on them in her own savagery, slashing and snarling and, it seemed, crazed by their mistake; driving them bloodied and yelping before her, back over the brow of the hill where they vanished from sight but could still be heard screaming in the distance. It all took perhaps little more than a minute.

The man's two sons, who were still in the boat and had witnessed it all, ran sobbing through the salt water to where their mauled and mangled father lay; but there was little they could do other than hold his warm and bloodied hands for a few brief moments. Although his eyes "lived" for a small fraction of time, he could not speak to them because his face and throat had been torn away, and of course there was nothing they could do except to hold and be held tightly until that too slipped away and his eyes glazed over and they could no longer feel his hands holding theirs. The storm increased and they could not get home and so they were forced to spend the night huddled beside their father's body. They were afraid to try to carry the body to the rocking boat because he was so heavy and they were afraid that they might lose even what little of him remained and they were afraid also, huddled on the rocks, that the dogs might return. But they did not return at all and there was no sound from them, no sound at all, only the moaning of the wind and the washing of the water on the rocks.

In the morning they debated whether they should try to take his body with them or whether they should leave it and return in the company of older and wiser men. But they were afraid to leave it unattended and felt that the time needed to cover it with protective rocks would be better spent in trying to get across to their home shore. For a while they debated as to whether one should go in the boat and the other remain on the island, but each was afraid to be alone and so in the end they managed to drag and carry and almost float him towards the bobbing boat. They laid him face down and covered him with what clothes there were and set off across the still-rolling sea. Those who waited on the shore missed the large presence of the man within the boat and some of them waded into the water and others rowed out in skiffs, attempting to hear the tearful messages called out across the rolling waves.

The *cù mòr glas* and her six young dogs were never seen again, or perhaps I should say they were never seen again in the same way. After some weeks, a group of men circled the island tentatively in their boats but they saw no sign. They went again and then again but found nothing. A year later, and grown much braver, they beached their boats and walked the island carefully, looking into the small sea caves and the hollows at the base of the wind-ripped trees, thinking perhaps that if they did not find the dogs, they might at least discover their whitened bones; but again they discovered nothing.

The *cù mòr glas*, though, was supposed to be sighted here and there for a number of years. Seen on a hill in one region or silhouetted on a ridge in another or loping across the valleys or glens in the early morning or the shadowy evening. Always in the area of the half perceived. For a while she became rather like the Loch Ness Monster or the Sasquatch on a smaller scale. Seen but not recorded. Seen when there were no cameras. Seen but never taken.

The mystery of where she went became entangled with the mystery of whence she came. There was increased speculation about the handmade box in which she had been found and much theorizing as to the individual or individuals who might have left it. People went to look for the box but could not find it. It was felt she might have been part of a *buidseachd* or evil spell cast on the man by some mysterious enemy. But no one could go much further than that. All of his caring for her was recounted over and over again and nobody missed any of the ironies.

What seemed literally known was that she had crossed the winter ice to have her pups and had been unable to get back. No one could remember ever seeing her swim; and in the early months at least, she could not have taken her young pups with her.

The large and gentle man with the smell of animal semen often heavy on his hands was my great-great-great-grandfather, and it may be argued that he died because he was too good at breeding animals or that he cared too much about their fulfilment and well-being. He was no longer there for his own child of the spring who, in turn, became my great-great-grandfather, and he was perhaps too much there in the memory of his older sons who saw him fall beneath the ambiguous force of the *cù mòr glas*. The youngest boy in the boat was haunted and tormented by the awfulness of what he had seen. He would wake at night screaming that he had seen the *cù mòr glas a' bhàis*, the big grey dog of death, and his screams filled the house and the ears and minds of the listeners, bringing home again and again the consequences of their loss. One morning, after a night in which he saw the *cù mòr glas a' bhàis* so vividly that his sheets were drenched with sweat, he walked to the high cliff which faced the island and there he cut his throat with a fish knife and fell into the sea.

The other brother lived to be forty, but, again so the story goes, he found himself in a Glasgow pub one night, perhaps looking for answers, deep and sodden with the whisky which had become his anaesthetic. In the half darkness he saw a large, grey-haired man sitting by himself against the wall and mumbled something to him. Some say he saw the *cù mòr glas a' bhàis* or uttered the name. And perhaps the man heard the phrase through ears equally affected by drink and felt he was being called a dog or a son of a bitch or something of that nature. They rose to meet one another and struggled outside into the cobblestoned passageway behind the pub where, most improbably, there were supposed to be six other large, grey-haired men who beat him to death on the cobblestones, smashing his bloodied head into the stone again and again before vanishing and leaving him to die with his face turned to the sky. The *cù mòr glas a' bhàis* had come again, said his family, as they tried to piece the tale together.

This is how the *cù mòr glas a' bhàis* came into our lives, and it is obvious that all of this happened a long, long time ago. Yet with succeeding generations it seemed the spectre had somehow come to stay and that it had become *ours* – not in the manner of an unwanted skeleton in the closet from a family's ancient past but more in the manner of something close to a genetic possibility. In the deaths of each generation, the grey dog was seen by some – by women who were to die in childbirth; by soldiers who went forth to the many wars but did not return; by those who went forth to feuds or dangerous love affairs; by those who answered mysterious midnight messages; by those who swerved on the highway to avoid the real or imagined grey dog and ended in masses of crumpled steel. And by one professional athlete who, in addition to his ritualized athletic superstitions, carried another fear or belief as well. Many of the man's descendants moved like careful haemophiliacs, fearing that they carried unwanted possibilities deep within them. And others, while they laughed, were like members of families in which there is a recurrence over the generations of repeated cancer or the diabetes which comes to those beyond middle age. The feeling of those who may say little to others but who may say often and quietly to themselves, "It has not happened to me," while adding always the cautionary "*yet*".

I am thinking all of this now as the October rain falls on the city of Toronto and the pleasant, white-clad nurses pad confidently in and out of my father's room. He lies quietly amidst the whiteness, his head and shoulders elevated so that he is in that hospital position of being neither quite prone nor yet sitting. His hair is white upon his pillow and he breathes softly and sometimes unevenly, although it is difficult ever to be sure.

My five grey-haired brothers and I take turns beside his bedside, holding his heavy hands in ours and feeling their response, hoping ambiguously that he will speak to us, although we know that it may tire him. And trying to read his life and ours into his eyes when they are open. He has been with us a long time, well into our middle age. Unlike those boys in that boat of so long ago, we did not see him taken from us in our youth. And unlike their youngest brother who, in turn, became our great-great-grandfather, we did not grow into a world in which there was no father's touch. We have been lucky to have this large and gentle man so deep into our lives.

No one in this hospital has mentioned the *cù mòr glas a' bhàis*. Yet as my mother said ten years ago, before slipping into her own death as quietly as a grown-up child who leaves or enters her parents' house in the early hours, "It is hard to *not* know what you do know."

Even those who are most sceptical, like my oldest brother who has driven here from Montreal, betray themselves by their nervous actions. "I avoided the Greyhound bus stations in both Montreal and Toronto," he smiled upon his arrival, and then added, "Just in case."

He did not realize how ill our father was and has smiled little since then. I watch him turning the diamond ring upon his finger, knowing that he hopes he will not hear the Gaelic phrase he knows too well. Not having the luxury, as he once said, of some who live in

Montreal and are able to pretend they do not understand the "other" language. You cannot *not* know what you do know.

Sitting here, taking turns holding the hands of the man who gave us his life, we are afraid for him and for ourselves. We are afraid of what he may see and we are afraid to hear the phrase born of the vision. We are aware that it may become confused with what the doctors call "the will to live" and we are aware that some beliefs are what others would dismiss as "garbage". We are aware that there are men who believe the earth is flat and that the birds bring forth the sun.

Bound here in our own peculiar mortality, we do not wish to see or see others see that which signifies life's demise. We do not want to hear the voice of our father, as did those other sons, calling down his own particular death upon him.

We would shut our eyes and plug our ears, even as we know such actions to be of no avail. Open still and fearful to the grey hair rising on our necks if and when we hear the scrabble of the paws and the scratching at the door.

The Well of Dunrea

GABRIELLE ROY
Translated by Harry Binsse

I

His strange life, so beautiful upon occasion, yet so hard and exact-
ing, my father kept locked from our curiosity. He never said much
about it, either to my mother or to me, even less to our neighbours.
But he did talk about it to Agnès, on the syllables of whose name his
voice lingered lovingly. Why and at what moment did he unburden
so much of his heart to this young daughter of his, who was already
oversensitive? She long kept as her own secret what my father had
certainly told her not without considerable reticence. One evening
she began repeating it to us . . . Perhaps it was because we had just
been complaining that Papa was none too companionable. "He was,
indeed . . . he was . . . Oh! if only you knew!" protested Agnès. And
it was another strange thing that, while he was still alive, we spoke
of my father in the past tense, perhaps thinking of another aspect of
his personality, long since disappeared.

At the time in question, Papa was especially well pleased with the
colony of White Russians or Ruthenians established at Dunrea. For a
reason unknown to us he called them his "Little Ruthenians". Of all
the groups he had settled, this one prospered best. It had not yet
been established for a full decade; a short enough time in which to
build a happy settlement out of a handful of suspicious and illiterate
immigrants, let alone clear the land, build houses, and even make
God feel at home with icons and votive candles. Yet all this and
much more had the Little Ruthenians accomplished. They were not
a people absorbed in vexations, like the Dukhobors. Agnès seemed
to remember that they, likewise, were Slavs, probably from
Bucovina. Certainly the past counted for something in their lives – a
past deeply wretched – but it was in the future, a wonderful and
well-founded future, that the Little Ruthenians above all had faith
when they came to Canada. And that was the sort of settler Papa

liked: people facing forward, and not everlastingly whining over what they had had to leave behind.

Agnès told us that Papa had described his Dunrea settlement as a sort of paradise, and that was precisely the word he used – a paradise.

He had to traverse ten miles of scrub, of swamp, of badlands, constantly swept by the wind, to reach Dunrea. And suddenly there came into view well-shaped trees – aspens, poplars, willows – grouped in such a way that they seemed to constitute an oasis in the bareness of the plain. A little before arriving at this clump of greenery you could already hear, my father said, water flowing and gurgling. For among the trees, so verdant and so healthy, almost hidden beneath them, ran a shallow little stream called the "Lost River". Could it indeed have been Papa – so close-mouthed and sad – who had furnished Agnès with all these details? And why her? No one but her? "Is it surprising that Papa so deeply loved this Lost River?" said Agnès. "Just think: he himself created it, in a sense."

One day he had chanced to miss his way in the course of his rounds and had stumbled on the dried-up bed of this river; polished pebbles along its bottom and the placement of a few trees showed that here there had been water. And Papa fell in love with this nook of ground, once grassy and certainly charming, which with little care would recapture its former loveliness. He promised himself to settle some hard-working colonists here, good colonists, intelligent enough to glimpse what they could make of it with patience and a little imagination. Now the Little Ruthenians, when he brought them and showed them the bed of the Lost River, grasped at once what Papa liked about it, what he so clearly saw; they decided to remain there. And when Papa urged them to plant many trees near the Lost River, so as to hold the dampness in the soil, his little Ruthenians had followed his suggestion. Thus from year to year the river yielded more water, and in places reached a depth of six feet. Thereafter, of their own accord, all sorts of other little trees began to grow along its shores and interlaced their branches and created a kind of tunnel of verdure through which flowed and sang the Lost River. For, even when rediscovered, it continued to be called the Lost River.

And it seems Papa told Agnès that what he liked best for his settlements was water. In that Saskatchewan, so lacking moisture, the resurrection of a river was a major business. "Fire," he had said, "and drought are my settlers' worst enemies; running water their greatest friend."

The Little Ruthenians, having placed their confidence in Papa's prediction that water would return here, had built their houses along the dry stream bed, to such good effect that ten years later, all their houses lay within the soft and murmurous protection of the trees and the water.

Papa, when he clambered out of his wagonette and hitched his mare Dolly to the edge of the well of Dunrea, beheld a ravishing landscape: scattered in the greenery lay a score of half-hidden little white houses with thatched roofs; there were as many outbuildings, equally clean, whitewashed every spring; and besides all this, bee-hives, dovecots, lean-tos of leaves and branches where in the heat of day the cows came for shelter; throughout the village there wandered freely flocks of white geese which filled it with their amusing clatter. And yet, Papa said, the houses were not really white; you realized that their gleaming colour was softened by an extremely delicate tint, almost indiscernible, and due to the Ruthenian women's covering their walls with a thin lime wash to which they had added a dose of blueing. In the windows, which were small and low, they had red geraniums in pots. And Papa said that after having jogged for miles through a dismal countryside of stiff grass and wild vegetation, nothing could be more attractive – yet more surprising, too – than Dunrea. Each time he saw it, he had to rub his eyes before he could credit them and thank God.

Maybe, also, when he set foot in Dunrea, Papa felt the great joy of having been right on that day when the future of this small corner of earth had revealed itself to him; and maybe his joy sprang even more from the fact that his Little Ruthenians had so well fulfilled his dream.

The moment he stepped down from his rig, Papa found himself surrounded with children; he patted their cheeks, tweaked their ears . . . a strange thing, for with his own children Papa never did such things. Yet perhaps those children, more than we, had confidence in Papa; after all, we often enough saw how tired and disappointed Papa looked; we knew he did not always succeed in his efforts;

whereas these people believed him endowed with an almost supernatural power. Who can ever know what peace of mind, what
certitude Papa felt among his Little Ruthenians? Isolated, far from any
other village, not yet even speaking their neighbours' language, they
must have relied wholly upon Papa, and the trust between them was
total.

The geese, the hens, the young turkeys scattered in front of him as
Papa walked along through the mass of flowers. He always said that
when settlers planted flowers, it was a sure sign of success, of
happiness. And among his Little Ruthenians sweet peas clambered
on the fences, rows of tall sunflowers slowly turned their enormous
faces; pale poppies spilled their smooth petals to be scattered by the
wind. The women even set out flowers along the paths that led from
the houses to the little privies; and it seems that Papa had laughed at
this excess of adornment.

Papa, however, was a serious man, and his first concern was to look
after the crops. Now for miles around the village it was always
uniformly beautiful; the lands of the Little Ruthenians were free of
weeds and well tilled; wheat, the various grains, alfalfa, lucerne,
clover – all did splendidly. In their methods, too, the Little
Ruthenians had followed Papa's ideas: he had advised them not to
overburden the soil by trying for continuous heavy crops, but to
rotate, to be patient, and they had heeded him. And maybe that is
why he called his Dunrea settlement paradise. Was he not obeyed
there as God had once been in His Eden? He was confident and had
never yet been mistaken in all the things he had ordained for his Little
Ruthenians. Yet these Little Ruthenians, Agnès elaborated, were not
at all small; on the contrary, they were almost all of average stature,
some of them even very tall and sturdy. Papa called them the Little
Ruthenians for a reason unconnected with their size, but Agnès could
not remember precisely what it was. Though, said she, it seems that
in their intensely blue eyes there lingered something of childhood.

Papa made the rounds of the kitchen gardens, for he was interested
in the rare vegetables the women raised there; there were garlic,
cabbages, and turnips, as in all such gardens, but also dill, very large,
succulent black beans, cucumbers, Papa said, as sweet as nuts, and a
great many other things – melons, for instance; the Little Ruthenians
were very fond of melons. Papa went here and there surrounded by

an activity which hummed from every direction and yet remained invisible. He would go into one house, then another. On each threshold, the women came to kiss his hand, but Papa pulled it back; he was embarrassed by this gesture of submission. Followed by his interpreter, then, he was among his own. "For I forgot to explain," Agnès added, "Papa had had time only to learn a score or so of words in their dialect, and their English was not much better. Despite this, how well they understood each other! How they trusted the interpreter when he said: 'The gentleman sent by the government informs you that such and such measures should be taken . . .' or else, 'Boris Masaliuk respectfully inquires whether . . .' "

Then the meal was ready. While the men talked business, the women had prepared the food in so great a silence that, each time, Papa was startled to hear soft words spoken near his ear: "If you please, Mr Government, do us the great honour of coming to our table . . ."

The men sat down; not the women, whose role now was to remain standing behind hosts and guests, attentive to pass them the various dishes. Was Papa sorry for them, was he fond of them, these silent, shy women, who hid their lovely tresses beneath kerchiefs and murmured, as they served the men, "If you please"?

He had told Agnès that Ruthenian women's voices were the same as a murmuring of water and of silence. It is certain, though, that he would have preferred to see them seated at the same time as the men at their own table. This was the only fault he found with his Little Ruthenians – that they were absolute masters in their own families. Several times he was tempted to speak to them about this, to invite the women also to sit down at table . . . but he was not entirely at home.

Papa often spent a night at Dunrea. There he slept like a child. The women's voices were never high or screeching. They seemed happy. "But what does that prove?" Papa wondered. "The slaves of other days were certainly happier than their masters. Contentment is not necessarily the servant of justice." So the lot of the women at Dunrea was the only thing that upset him. He listened to them humming their babies to sleep . . . and soon he himself slipped into slumber as into a whole and deep submission. When he awoke, it was to the good smell of strong coffee which the women were preparing for him downstairs.

*

All that was too beautiful to last, my father would have said.

How did it happen that here alone peace and plenty reigned? Everywhere else settlers encountered obstacles. Look how it was with the Dukhobors! Among them the Devil's malice borrowed the very teaching of Christ the better to sow confusion. Indeed, in their effort always to act as Christ would have done in our epoch, to fathom the meaning of His acts, of His parables, the Dukhobors committed folly after folly. Had they not decided, on the eve of winter, to set free all their domestic animals, because, said they, "Did not our God create all creatures free, beasts as well as men?"

But how were we to know what God wished us to do with the so many little lives committed to our care? thought Papa, and he had said this to his Dukhobors, that one must not too greatly rack one's brain over this subject, that the important thing was not to mistreat any animal. None the less, the Dukhobors remained tortured by the idea that they must not infringe any of God's wishes . . . and they set free their flocks; which meant that they had to drive them out of their stables and pens.

The poor animals, upset and troubled, wanted to return to their captivity. But they were prevented. The snow came. The animals found nothing to eat; they almost all perished; in the spring only a handful – and they were no more than fearful skeletons – came back toward the dwellings of men. Thus among the Dukhobors the young children suffered a series of illnesses for lack of milk. Among the Mennonites it was folly of another sort. Many were the misfortunes in Saskatchewan in those days . . . and almost always through excess of good will, through eagerness to understand God perfectly.

And why was Dunrea alone spared? The men there were well behaved, true enough; they believed in God. Perhaps, even, they believed that God loved them better than He loved the Dukhobors and the Mennonites; this notion apart, they seemed to dwell in wisdom.

And Papa himself began to wonder why God seemed to love the Little Ruthenians better than the others. He was careful not to confuse their simple, naïve minds; he did not too severely try their good will. And from then on Papa felt a kind of anxiety. He blamed himself for having certainly been too proud of Dunrea.

Whenever influential government people, top men from the

Ministry of Colonization, asked to visit settlements, Papa always took them to Dunrea. And Dunrea helped his career, earned him consideration. The railroad companies sent photographers to make pictures of the Lost River; and the Canadian Pacific Railway produced a large number of Dunrea photos, sending them to places all over the world, to Poland, to Romania, to attract immigrants. For the CPR made a great deal of money from the transportation of immigrants. My father one day met a poor Czech who confided to him that he had come to Canada only because he had seen a very tempting poster: a river, golden wheat, houses "just like those at home . . ." and now this Czech was working in a mine.

When Agnès told us this, we understood why Papa hated all lies, and even lies by admission; why he suffered so much because Maman dressed things up a bit; but that is another story . . . At Dunrea, despite Papa's fears, the wheat continued to grow, the fine cattle to multiply. And since they prospered, the Little Ruthenians believed themselves better and better loved by God. They thanked Him for rains that came when they were needed, for sunshine in due season. They had no least expectation that God's gentle hand would ever weigh heavily upon them.

II

Delicate and sweethearted as she was, how could Agnès have kept to herself so long the spectacle she at last described to us? In those days, Papa had told her, prairie fires were always smouldering somewhere in Saskatchewan. This province, so lacking in rainfall and so windy, was truly the land of fire. So dry was it that the sun alone, playing on straw or a bottle shard, could set the prairie aflame! And if the slightest active breath of air should then make known its presence, at once the fire began to run like the wind itself. Now the wind in this part of the world was already a furious, mad thing, which beat the harvests to the ground, uprooted trees, and sometimes tore the roofs from buildings. Yet satanic as it was, it still left behind it the grasses cropped close to the soil, some living thing. But behind the fire, there remained nothing save the carcasses of young fawns, of rabbits pursued by the flames, overtaken by them, sometimes fallen dead in full flight . . . and for a long time these carcasses poisoned the air, for in the place where fire had passed, even the birds of prey took care not to come to eat the eyes of the dead animals. This was a not uncommon sight in many areas of Saskatchewan, and a man's heart could little bear to see a ruin so complete.

The Little Ruthenians had always been very careful of fire; when, from time to time, they had to burn stumps or weeds, they waited for a very calm day; and once the fire had done its work, they put it out by scattering the coals and then covering them with moist earth. Moreover, in their ever-damp oasis, within earshot of the murmuring Lost River, how could they truly have feared fire?

Now that particular summer was burning dry. Even in the Lost River the water level went down several feet. And a fire started, probably ignited by nothing more than the sun, twenty miles north of Dunrea. At first the wind drove it in another direction. My father was camping eighteen miles further on, in a region he was looking over with a party of surveyors. During the night he awoke. The wind had changed. It was stronger and laden with an acrid smoke which hurt his eyes and throat. A little later a messenger arrived on horseback. He said the fire was moving toward Dunrea. My father jumped into the wagonette; he made no attempt to follow the road, which was far from straight in that part of the country; as much as possible he took short cuts through the brambles and small, dried-up swamps. Dolly obeyed him faithfully, even though she was wounded by the sharp point of the briars. Behind him, as he crossed these gloomy stretches of scrub, my father saw the fire following him from afar, and he heard its rumble. He prayed for the Lost River. He hoped for another change in the wind, which would sweep the fire elsewhere, no matter in what direction save toward Dunrea. This sort of prayer, he admitted, was perhaps not a good prayer. Indeed, why pray for his Ruthenians rather than for the poor, lonely farms along the Lost River road? Is the misfortune that strikes those one loves greater, my father asked himself, than that which strikes those unknown to us?

Arriving at Dunrea, he ordered the men to take their horses and ploughs and quickly to turn under a wide belt around the village. He set other men digging ditches. The sky had become bright red . . . and that helped along the work, since one could see by it as though it were broad daylight. But how strange a daylight! What a dreadful glow silhouetted the terrified animals, the running men, each gesture and attitude of every moving shadow, but without disclosing their features, so that all these living beings looked like black cutouts against the horizon! Then the fire grew more intense; it divided and came from two directions at once toward the settlement. Papa ordered the women to leave, taking with them the children and old people. "The fewest things possible," he cried out to them. "Quick! Leave your furniture . . . leave everything . . ."

How astounded he now was at these women he had believed to be so docile! At first they did not want to leave the trenches they were digging alongside their men. Papa ran from one to the other, even grasping a few of them by the shoulders and shaking them a little.

Oh, those stubborn women! Once in their houses, they began collecting a hundred useless articles: mattresses, quilts, saucepans. "Is this the time to think of such things?" Papa angrily called out to them.

But they kept going back into their houses, one to collect her coffeepot, another a fine porcelain cup.

The farm wagons, the small two-wheeled carts, the buggies were piled high with domestic goods; upon these were perched the children, torn from their sleep, and now crying miserably, and hens that kept flying off, and young pigs. Women were hitching cows to the wagon tails. Never, so long as there remained a single movable object, would these insubordinate women have agreed to go. Papa ran about, whipping the horses at the head of the caravan. Terrified, they rushed toward the gap to the south, between the columns of fire which little by little were closing in on each other. Then Papa had the idea of setting fire to the crops to the north of the village. In this way fire would advance toward fire, and perhaps it would burn itself out. Such tactics had already succeeded on other occasions. He called Jan Sibulesky, one of the Little Ruthenians in whom he had always placed the greatest confidence, a man of judgement, quick to grasp what was sensible and make a rational choice.

"Quick," said my father to Jan Sibulesky, "take with you three or four men and, as soon as you can, set fire to the corners of all the wheat fields."

This was the moment when the Little Ruthenians gave every semblance of no longer understanding Papa. Jan as much as the others! Oh, the obstinate, greedy, silly men! In their own country they had possessed nothing – or so very little: a skimpy acre or two on the arid slopes of the Carpathians to feed an entire family; and they had left that behind them without too great pain. But now that they had all sorts of things – hay, sugar beets, wonderful wheat, full barns, really everything – they would not part with the least trifle.

"But if you want to keep everything, you'll lose everything," Papa told them.

And my father turned into something like a madman. He waved his arms, he shouted insults, thinking perhaps that the Little Ruthenians would at least understand those words. But the foolish wretches through all the thick smoke madly concentrated on pushing their ploughs around the settlement. Others carried water from the river to the houses to wet down the walls; still others drew pailfuls from the communal well, in the centre of the village, which was deep and almost icy. Did they think that this water, so cold it clouded the outside of the pail, would serve better to cool the atmosphere than the water from the river? Then Papa tried to go by himself to set fire to the harvest, but the Little Ruthenians forcibly prevented him. Thus Papa realized that they had perfectly well understood his orders, that henceforth he was alone among his own people, as they were on their own against him. This loneliness in the face of danger made him despair. The heat was increasing. Occasional brands of fire flew over the village. A powerful roar filled the air. And everything was in fearful disorder; no longer was there anyone in charge, any obedience. Each man was wearing himself out in individual effort; a few simply awaited the fire, axe in hand. Then the flames at a single bound cleared one of the trenches; they took hold of a thatched roof; in an instant the house glowed with inner light. All was lost.

"Go, go!" Papa cried to the men. "You've only enough time to save yourselves!"

I have often envisioned Papa as he must have appeared that night, very tall with his arms stretched toward the sky, which outlined him also in black. What a terrible silhouette!

But now the Little Ruthenians were trying to save the burning house. So Papa moved toward them threateningly. He raised his hand, showed them the glowing heavens, and, in their own tongue, he asked them: "Don't you know what that means?"

All equally bewildered, they raised their heads toward the night-mare glow above them. Papa said that they looked like stupid birds turning their heads in unison toward an incomprehensible sign. And in their own tongue Papa told them what the sign meant: "The wrath of God! Do you understand? It is God's wrath!"

Then there took place something infinitely cruel. Understanding at last, all the men made ready to go – all except that Jan Sibulesky whom father had loved and often singled out as an example because of his never-failing judgement. Abruptly Jan rushed toward the chapel and emerged from it holding an icon of the Virgin. His icon in front of him like a shield, he walked toward the burning house. Papa at once understood what Jan was going to do. The flames illumined his face, his mouth, his forehead hardened in unshakeable purpose, his blond beard, his blue eyes; in the full light big Jan marched forward, utterly visible; just as visible was the icon he carried, the icon of a Madonna with tender, childlike features. Thus brilliantly lighted, the eyes of the image shone as though they were alive.

"Stop, you idiot!" my father cried out to Jan.

But it was now a long while since anyone had obeyed him. His great mistake, obviously, had been to speak of God's wrath. All his life my father believed that there had lain his crime: to have inter-preted God, in a sense to have judged Him. Jan continued toward the flames, singing a hymn and holding the holy image just below his harsh face.

"You're going to die," Papa told him. "Stop him! Stop the poor fool!" he begged the others.

But they all stood like spectators, in a living hedgerow, and probably at that moment they were very curious about God and about Jan; so avid with curiosity that they were stripped of all other thoughts. The words of the canticle resounded for another moment above the crackling of the flames; then suddenly they changed into an appalling cry. Never could Papa erase from his memory, right upon the heels of the tones of prayer, this roar of horror. A blazing beam had tumbled upon Jan Sibulesky. The men who had been so intense upon miracles at last made up their minds to leave – and in a stampede. They sprang astride their horses, urging them on with sharp cries; they clambered on to the seats of the two-wheeled traps; they dashed out of the village, jostling each other. Papa begged them, as they passed him, to call out their names, for he could no longer recognize faces in the smoke, and he wanted to reassure himself that none of the Little Ruthenians would be left behind. "Get south," he yelled at each outfit as it passed by. In that direction, between the walls of fire, there was still a gap which, minute by minute, was visibly closing.

At last Papa jumped into his wagonette and, by the sound of the galloping horses, he tried to follow the caravan now hidden in the smoke. His vehicle, however, was too heavy to make enough speed over the stones and clods of earth. Papa at a bound put himself astride Dolly; then he got out his penknife and began to slash at the leather traces that attached the wagonette to the mare, reducing her speed. The traces were tough and hard to sever, but at last one came free, and then the other. Dolly went faster. The fire, though, was already raging here and there on the only route still open. Papa saw that Dolly by herself could get through quickly enough not to be burned, but that, burdened with a man, she certainly could not. From far up ahead one of the Ruthenians cried out to him to hurry. Papa called back that he needn't worry, he was coming. That was the last human voice he heard that night. Standing beside Dolly he gave her his orders: "Go . . . go . . . As for me, I still have the well of Dunrea; there – if I can get back to it – I'll be safe . . . And I'm too tired, really too tired to go much further . . . The well will give me a bit of rest . . ."

But that night no one was to obey him, not even his gentle, his obedient Dolly, for whom Papa, whenever he left Winnipeg on the way to his settlement, always took with him titbits and lump sugar.

So he raised his whip and struck Dolly a blow, on her most sensitive part, over the eyes. She went off neighing with pain and reproach. And, running, bending double to avoid the flames, Papa regained the centre of Dunrea. His hair, his beard, his eyebrows were singed from the heat. He breathed as little as possible, holding a damp handkerchief over his mouth. He reached the edge of the well. Grasping the rope used to haul up the pails of water, Papa slid down into the deep, cool interior. He lowered himself to the level of the water. Almost at once the roar of the flames surrounded everything. All around the well the grass was afire. The rope likewise began to burn; Papa saw it come apart, strand by strand, in little spirals of ash. Quickly he pried out bricks, which were only loosely embedded in the lining of the well; he dug himself a sort of niche, where he succeeded in finding a certain support. Then he cut the rope as high as he could. At just that moment he saw a shadow over the well opening, in perfect outline. He was greeted by a long-drawn-out neigh. "Oh Dolly!" cried my father, "Go . . . Go!" He ripped free a brick which he hurled at Dolly's head. Papa said that she leaned in to see whence came the furious voice and projectile. Then she reared and raised herself to a great height, head and mane erect. Papa began to smell the odour of burned flesh.

And he told how the inside of the well became broiling hot, the air so unbreathable that he had to go lower yet. He did it with the help of the rope, which he had tied to a stone projecting from the inner wall. He slipped into the water up to his knees, then to his waist. Half his body was freezing and numbed, while upon his head rained sparks of fire . . . and he thought that the end had really come. Papa said that he had been sure he was dead because suddenly nothing mattered to him any more. This was what gave him the deepest anguish when he thought back afterward: that everything, in the depth of the well, had become so dismal, so smothered, so extraordinarily silent. He had not thought of us; all he felt was quiet, so great a quiet that it was beyond resisting. These were his own words: "Neither regrets, nor hope, nor desires; a state of complete quiet." At the bottom of the well he barely could succeed in remembering life, having been alive. And how could he have the least taste for any return from so deep an indifference! Papa, believing himself dead, was a trifle astonished that death should be so gloomy, glacial, empty . . . and so reposing . . . that in death there should no longer be any affection possible. Within him there was a desert, just as above his head – in Dunrea – there was also a desert.

Papa said that then, in this absence of life, he had seen Agnès, come to wait for him as she always came to meet the tram that brought our father back from Winnipeg. He said that he had seen her at the trolley stop, at the end of our short Rue Deschambault, and that close to her stood our old collie dog, which always

accompanied Agnès. Such was the vision that in the end had penetrated so far to find Papa, in his quiet; regret at seeing the child and
her dog futilely waiting day after day, for weeks and months – here
was what brought his dead soul back to life. He had rediscovered
the language of other days, faraway words. "Go home, you and the
dog – back to the house!" he had tried to tell Agnès. And this word
"house", which his lips pronounced, none the less only awakened
an extreme astonishment in the depths of his brain. "The house!
Whose house? Why houses? . . ." And again he tried to persuade the
stubborn child, standing at the street corner, despite a cold winter
wind, and shivering, to go home. "There's no use waiting for me;
I'm already dead. Don't you understand? To be dead is to have no
more love – at last!" But Agnès answered Papa in the bottom of the
well: "You'll come back; I know it . . . maybe even in this next
tram . . ."

And Papa had been startled at hearing himself speak; the sound of
his voice made him understand that he was not dead. Because of the
child at the end of the street, he made an enormous effort to fasten
himself with the rope to the wall of the well. He had fainted.

The next morning the Little Ruthenians found him in the well.

When Papa opened his eyes on the desolation that was now the
Lost River, he believed in Hell. Curiously, it was not with the
furnace of the night before, with the outcries, with the unfollowed
orders, that he was to associate Hell, but with this – a thick silence,
almost inviolable, a dismal land, black everywhere, a dreadful
death.

Raising himself up on the charred soil where they had laid him,
Papa tried to give courage to his Little Ruthenians; since they had
not lost their lives, they had not lost the essential thing. Neither he
himself, however, nor the Little Ruthenians, had much further use
for this essential thing. They said that they had, all the same, lost
their lives, at least ten years of their lives . . . And Papa remembered
to ask about the women: "Are they all safe?" "Yes," the Little
Ruthenians replied, "they are all safe, but weeping for their dear
houses, their oaken chests, their chests full of fine linen . . ."

Papa returned among us . . . and yet did he ever return? Appalled at
his appearance, Maman asked him, "Has something happened to

you, Edouard? What on earth has happened to you?"

But Papa merely put her off with an inconsequential account of what had taken place, how he had lost a settlement. For a long time that was all he ever admitted. Only to Agnès, when one evening she came and sat close beside him and looked at him tenderly – she was not afraid, never was afraid of his half-burned eyebrows – only to Agnès did he tell how he had once meddled with the business of explaining God to men; perhaps it was a day when he regretted not having remained in the depths of the well . . . When Lazarus emerged from the grave, we have no knowledge that he was ever gay.

Still, there remained this most curious thing: Papa, become, as it were, a stranger to joy, so far removed from it that he was almost unable to recognize it in a human countenance, was, nevertheless, sensitive to suffering.

Oh, here indeed was something that troubled us: when we laughed, when on occasion we succeeded in being happy, Papa was astounded! But let a misfortune, a sorrow strike one of us, then we saw Papa come alive . . . return to us . . . suffer all the more!

The Medicine Line

WALLACE STEGNER

. . .that a line drawn from the most northwest point of Lake of the Woods, along the forty-ninth parallel of north latitude, or, if the said point shall not be in the forty-ninth parallel of north latitude, then that a line drawn from the said point due north or south as the case may be, until the said line shall intersect the said parallel of north latitude, and from the point of such intersection due west along and with the said parallel, shall be the line of demarcation between the territories of the United States, and those of His Britannic Majesty, and that the said line shall form the northern boundary of the said territories of the United States, and the southern boundary of the territories of His Britannic Majesty, from the Lake of the Woods to the Stony Mountains.

Article 2, *Convention of London*,
20 Oct 1818

The 49th parallel ran directly through my childhood, dividing me in two. In winter, in the town on the Whitemud, we were almost totally Canadian. The textbooks we used in school were published in Toronto and made by Canadians or Englishmen; the geography we studied was focused on the Empire and the Dominion, though like our history it never came far enough west, and was about as useless to us as the occasional Canadian poem that was inserted patriotically into our curriculum. Somehow those poems seemed to run to warnings of disaster and fear of the dark and cold in snowy eastern woods. My mind is still inclined at inopportune moments to quote me Tom Moore's "Canadian Boat Song" (Row, brothers, row, the stream runs fast / The rapids are near and the daylight's past) or tell me, out of Charles Dawson Shanley,

> Speed on, speed on, good Master!
> The camp lies far away;
> We must cross the haunted valley
> Before the close of day.

The songs we sang were "Tipperary" and "We'll Never Let the Old Flag Fall" and "The Maple Leaf Forever" and "God Save the King'; the flag we saluted was the Union Jack, the heroes we most

revered belonged to the Canadian regiment called the Princess
Pats, the clothes and the Christmas gifts we bought by mail came
from the T. Eaton mail-order house. The businesses whose names
we knew and whose products we saw advertised were Ltd, not
Inc., the games we played were ice hockey and rounders, the
movie serials that drew us to the Pastime Theater on Tuesdays and
Saturdays were likely to retail the deeds of Mounted Policemen
amid the Yukon snows. Our holidays, apart from Thanksgiving
and Christmas, which were international, were Dominion Day,
Victoria Day, the King's birthday. Even the clothes we wore had a
provincial flavour, and I never knew till I moved to Montana and
was taught by the laughter of Montana kids that turtle-necked
sweaters and shoepacs were not standard winter costume
everywhere.

But if winter and town made Canadians of us, summer and the
homestead restored us to something nearly, if not quite, American.
We could not be remarkably impressed with the physical differences between Canada and the United States, for our lives slopped
over the international boundary every summer day. Our
plowshares bit into Montana sod every time we made the turn at
the south end of the field. We collected stones from our fields and
stoneboated them down into Montana to dump them. I trapped
Saskatchewan and Montana flickertails indiscriminately, and
spread strychnine-soaked wheat without prejudice over two
nations.

The people we neighboured with were all in Montana, half our
disc of earth and half our bowl of sky acknowledged another flag
than ours, the circle of darkness after the prairie night came down
was half American, and the few lights that assured us we were not
alone were all across the Line. The mountains whose peaks drew
my wistful eyes on July days were the Bearpaws, down below the
Milk River. For all my eyes could tell me, no Line existed, for the
obelisk of black iron that marked our south-eastern corner was only
a somewhat larger version of the survey stakes (the Montana ones
had blue tops, the Canadian not) that divided our world into uniform squares. It never occurred to us to walk along the border from
obelisk to obelisk – an act that might have given us a notion of the
boundary as an endless, very open fence, with posts a mile apart.

And if we had walked along it, we would have found only more
plains, more burnouts, more gopher holes, more cactus, more
stinkweed and primroses, more hawk shadows slipping over the
scabby flats, more shallow coulees down which the drainage from
the Old-Man-on-His-Back hills crept into Montana toward the Milk.
The nearest custom house was clear over in Alberta, and all the
summers we spent on the farm we never saw an officer, Canadian
or American. We bought supplies in Harlem or Chinook and got
our mail at Hydro, all in Montana. In the fall we hauled our wheat,
if we had made any, freely and I suppose illegally across to the
Milk River towns and sold it where it was handiest to sell it. Even
yet, between Willow Creek and Treelon, a degree and a half of
longitude, there is not a single settlement or a custom station.

We ignored the international boundary in ways and to degrees
that would have been impossible if it had not been a line almost
completely artificial. And yet our summer world was a different
world from the Canadian world of town. The magazines to which
we now subscribed were American magazines, the newspapers we
read were published in Havre, Great Falls, even Minneapolis. The
funny paper characters to whom I devoted charmed afternoons
were Happy Hooligan, the Katzenjammer Kids, Hairbreadth
Harry, Alphonse and Gaston – all made in the USA. Our summer
holidays were the Fourth of July and Labor Day, and the *pièce de
résistance* of a holiday get-together was a ball game. In summer,
when we bought anything by mail, we bought it not from T. Eaton
but from the lavish and cosmopolitan catalogue of Sears Roebuck
and Montgomery Ward. We learned in summer to call a McLaugh-
lin a Buick.

Undistinguishable and ignored as it was, artificially as it split a
country that was topographically and climatically one, the international boundary marked a divide in our affiliations, expectations,
loyalties. Like the pond at the east end of the Cypress Hills, we
could flow into either watershed, or into both simultaneously, but
we never confused the two. Winter and summer were at odds in
us. We were Americans without the education and indoctrination
that would have made us confident of our identity, we were Canadians in everything but our sentimental and patriotic commitment. Whatever was being done to us by our exposure to Canadian

attitudes, traditions, and prejudices – an exposure intensified by the strains and shortages of the war in which Canada was a belligerent through four of my six years there – we never thought of ourselves as anything but American. Since we could not explain why the United States was "too cowardly to get into a fight" against Germany, and since we were secretly afraid it was, we sometimes came to blows with the uncomplicatedly Canadian boys. It used to agonize me, wondering whether or not the Canadians really did defeat the Americans at the Battle of Lundy's Lane during the War of 1812. It did not seem possible or likely, and yet there it was in the history book. Perhaps I reached the beginning of wisdom, of a sort, when I discovered that Lundy's Lane, which loomed like Waterloo or Tours in the Canadian textbooks and in my anxious imagination, was dismissed as a frontier skirmish by histories written in the United States. The importance of that battle depended entirely on which side of the frontier you viewed it from.

That was the way the 49th parallel, though outwardly ignored, divided us. It exerted uncomprehended pressures upon affiliation and belief, custom and costume. It offered us subtle choices even in language (we stooked our wheat; across the Line they shocked it), and it lay among our loyalties as disturbing as a hair in butter. Considering how much I saw of it and how many kinds of influence it brought to bear on me, it might have done me good to learn something of how it came there. I never did until much later, and when I began to look it up I discovered that practically nobody else knew how it had come there either. While I lived on it, I accepted it as I accepted Orion in the winter sky. I did not know that this line of iron posts was one outward evidence of the coming of history to the unhistoried Plains, one of the strings by which dead men and the unguessed past directed our lives. In actual fact, the boundary which Joseph Kinsey Howard has called artificial and ridiculous was more potent in the lives of people like us than the natural divide of the Cypress Hills had ever been upon the tribes it held apart. For the 49th parallel was an agreement, a rule, a limitation, a fiction perhaps but a legal one, acknowledged by both sides; and the coming of law, even such limited law as this, was the beginning of civilization in what had been a lawless wilderness.

Civilization is built on a tripod of geography, history, and law, and it is made up largely of limitations.

The angry American wolfers, who, in the spring of 1873, pursued Assiniboin horse-thieves northward, undoubtedly knew that they were carrying their gun-law in Canada, but the fact would not have troubled them. For one thing, Canada was still only a name, hardly a force; it had as yet made hardly a move to carry its authority into the North-West Territories. For another, there was enough Fenian sentiment and enough Manifest Destinarianism around Fort Benton to persuade most of its citizens that the northern Plains were a natural and inevitable extension of the United States. For a third, the boundary was less a boundary than a zone. There was no telling where the precise line lay: wolfers and traders did not carry astronomical instruments. Even such prominent landmarks as Wood Mountain and the Sweetgrass Hills might lie in either nation, and though the Convention of London in 1818 had established the 49th parallel as the boundary from Lake of the Woods to the Rockies, and the Oregon Treaty of 1846 had extended that line to the Pacific, neither the Indians who stole the horses nor the wolfers who pursued them recognized any dividing line short of the Cypress Hills – a line which had nothing to do with international agreements, but had been established by tradition, topography, and a balance of tribal force.

But even while the wolfers were riding northward across the unsurveyed boundary zone, the first line of the geometry of law was starting west from the Red River settlements. By October 1873, it would be at Wood Mountain; by the end of the following summer it would reach to the crest of the Rockies, to connect with the line that had been run that far eastward from the Pacific in 1861. Only a little more than a year after John Evans's men poured their murderous fire into Little Soldier's charging Assiniboin, the cairn-marked line of the border would be drawn accusingly across their track, making very clear the international implications of their raid. The series of trials and extraditions by which Canada would attempt for two years to convict and punish the raiders would so publicize the boundary that thereafter no one could cross it, for any purpose, in ignorance.

*

Surveyors are not heroic figures. They come later than the explorers, they douse with system what was once the incandescent excitement of danger and the unknown. They conquer nothing but ignorance, and if they are surveying a boundary they are so compelled by astronomical and geodetic compulsions that they might as well run on rails. Among the instruments of their profession there is none that lifts the imagination and achieves grace or weight as a symbol. The mythic light in which we have bathed our frontier times, when decision was for the individual will and a man tested himself against wild weathers, wild beasts, or wild men, and so knew himself a man – that light does not shine on the surveyor as it shines on trapper, trader, scout, cowboy, or Indian fighter. Surveyors do not even acquire the more pedestrian glamour of the farming pioneer, though they make him possible, and though their work is basic not merely to his conquering of the frontier, but to some of the mistakes he has made in trying to break it.

Among the chronicles of long Canadian marches, it is the march of Col. Garnet Wolseley from Toronto to Fort Garry in 1870, and that of the Mounted Police from Fort Dufferin to Fort Macleod in 1874, that have become folklore. But when the used-up Mounted Police stopped, 590 miles out of Dufferin, to repair equipment and shoe horses and oxen and to rest men and animals in a burned-over dreary plain within sight of the Cypress Hills, the surveyors were there ahead of them, having made, with practically no fanfare, practically the same march. It was from the survey depot at Willow Bunch, on Wood Mountain, that Assistant Commissioner Macleod begged surplus oats and provisions for his tired command. By that time the surveyors were close to completing a journey that might have been called epic if it had not been so well planned, so successful, and so utilitarian.

They may as well all be nameless: there were no heroes among them. And they do not need to be separated by nationality, for it was of the essence of their work that it was international, co-operative, mutual. But they need credit and remembrance for a job finished swiftly and efficiently – a job of immense importance. And though they have never struck anybody as glamorous enough to be written up in a western story, a young man in search of excitement in 1872 could have done worse than enlist with them.

Until the transfer of sovereignty over Rupert's Land to the
Dominion government there had been little need for defining the
boundary established in 1818. The scare which Louis Riel's rebellion threw into both Canada and Great Britain in 1869–70 hastened
the inevitable. The actual transfer took place in November 1869,
while the Riel situation was waiting for the spring weather that
would let Wolseley's expedition start west to settle it. But the sup-
pression of the Red River *métis* could not by itself solve much, for
there was nearly a thousand miles of unmarked and unwatched
border where trouble could erupt. The Dominion government, no
matter what local difficulties might arise, was clearly committed to
a swift survey to fix the bounds of its jurisdiction and deter the
raids and excursions, unofficial and semi-official, from the United
States. The initiating cause for the survey might have been almost
anything; in fact, it was a hasty American claim that the Hudson's
Bay post at Pembina, on Red River, was actually on American soil.

It took two years and a half, political action being what it is, for
agreement to be reached between the United States and Great
Britain on the terms of a boundary survey. An American Boundary
Commission was authorized, with a customarily inadequate appro-
priation, by an act of March 19, 1872. The British commission,
composed of a commissioner and five officers and forty-four men
of the Royal Engineers, augmented by a Canadian party made up
of a geologist, surgeon, veterinarian, and a group of surveyors,
was organized in June. By September the British outfit had made
its way to Duluth and thence across Minnesota by rail to St Paul.
On September 18 they met at Pembina an American party made up
of the commissioner, four officers from the Corps of Engineers, a
body of civilian surveyors, and Company K of the 20th Infantry as
escort. There their first act was to determine just where the 49th
parallel did cross the Red River. The disputed Hudson's Bay post
was demonstrated to be a few hundred feet north of the Line, but
the Canadian custom house was south of it. When the American
and British surveyors came up with a discrepancy of thirty-two feet
in locating the Line, the Joint Commission set a precedent in international relations by amicably halving it.

Not all problems could be solved by dichotomy. After being baptized by an equinoctial snowstorm immediately on arrival, they had

a month of fine Indian summer weather in which to survey the line through the almost impossible terrain from the north-west corner of Lake of the Woods, where the 1826 survey had ended, to the 49th parallel. There they encountered difficulties both political and topographical. The earlier negotiators, confused by an imprecise map, had allowed the border to drift a long way north of the 49th parallel, and it was clear now that to run a straight line south to that parallel would leave an isolated peninsula of American territory deep in Canada. Captain D.R. Cameron of the Royal Artillery, the British Commissioner, had orders not to recognize the north-west angle monument left by the 1826 survey, since the British hoped to eliminate the angle by further negotiation, but he did consent to having a sight line cut from it due south, in order to expedite the rest of the work. But the terrain almost rendered their political agreeableness an empty gesture, for they found that any land which was not soggy with water was under water, and they had a bad time even locating the monument that Cameron's orders forbade him to accept. Finally they did find it – a post surrounded by a crib of logs – several feet under water in a swamp, and started hewing their southward line. Indian axemen laboured in water above their knees, surveyors floundered across bogs whose mossy surface gave way to let them down to their waists in cold slime, supplies came in on men's backs, the camps were dreary quagmires. Sixteen miles of that, continuous swamp heavily grown with birch and tamarack, before they cut off the disputed American peninsula; then ten miles across the open lake, where they located the 49th parallel on the ice. From that corner they turned west, marking the first station on solid ground just at the west shore of Lake of the Woods. Again the instruments could not agree as readily as the commissioners; an overlap of twenty-nine feet in the observations was halved. As for direction, once they turned the corner on the ice they would not need to deviate again: straight west would serve them all the way. They were almost at the eastern edge of the Plains; across that oceanic land a boundary line could run as straight as an equator or a tropic, serene, almost abstract.

After the establishment of the joint astronomical station on the shore of the lake, the American party was forced by its inadequate

budget to retire to St Paul and fold up for the winter. It left to the
British, on a shared-cost basis, the hewing of a thirty-foot swath
through ninety miles of swamps, timber, and prairie to the Red
River. The British crews, finding the work easier after the freeze-
up, decided to go on with their astronomical and chaining work
through the winter; the American party would not finish its share
of that stretch until 1874.

The experiences of the British party in 1872-3, and those of the
American party a year later, differ only in degree, though it seems
likely that no American officer ever served his country under more
severe conditions or with more devotion and endurance than Lt
Greene of the Corps of Engineers when he completed the American surveying between Lake of the Woods and Red River. If he was
not an explorer, he had all the discomforts, difficulties, and
dangers of one; and the life of the British group was comparable.
All of them, here at the ecological boundary between Woods and
Plains, were in process of becoming plainsmen while having to
retain many of the skills of the woods. With modifications, they
were in the position that the Saulteaux, Cree, and *métis* had all
found themselves in, and the machinery of their daily lives was a
bizarre mixture of two cultures. They alternated between mules
and dogteams, carts and sleds, skin lodges and brush shelters.
Broken up into small parties for maximum efficiency, they were
caught out in blizzards that neither horse nor dog would drive
against, and fought their way in after days of exposure, half
starved, half frozen, and undismayed. Along with the boundaries
of their countries they surveyed the limits of endurance. Sometimes in the still cold their thermometers dropped to forty-five,
fifty, fifty-one below. In their icy camps they lay and heard the
gunshot reports of willows bursting as the sap froze, and on those
nights of windless cold they saw the Northern Lights in their
splendour, "vapour-like and yet perfectly transparent, so that even
the small stars could be distinctly seen through the illuminated
mist", or spreading in bands and streamers so bright they lighted
the sky like dawn. They learned how eyelashes could freeze
together on a trail, and how a muffler moistened by breathing
could freeze fast to a man's beard and threaten to smother him.
They learned to be wary about turning a tangent screw with the

bare fingers, for the brass burned as if it had been white hot; if the hand that touched it was moist, the metal froze fast and could only be removed with the skin. Tenderfeet who made the mistake of drinking out of unwarmed metal cups in the morning left the skin of their lips on the rim. The eyes of all the surveyors were painful from the constant dangerous contact with the eyepieces of their instruments, whose lurking frost could seize an eyelid and hold it fast, "as experienced by Russian officers in Siberia". After long exposure the eye would leak tears that froze instantly into beaded ice on the lashes, "and gave the face a comical look, somewhat like that in children's pictures of Jack Frost".

It was not a game for children. They had cause for pride in their work when they brought the line out of the Woods and into the Red River valley. Now before them lay the Plains, through which they were to sight a beeline for eight hundred miles.

April and part of May, during the spring breakup, were not surveying weather. The British commission spent six weeks under roofs at Red River planning for the season ahead, and they were already in the field when the American party reassembled on June 1, 1873, complete with an escort of one company of the Twentieth Infantry and two of the Seventh Cavalry under Major Reno. The cavalry would make lurid history three years later when the bankrupt Indian policy of the United States combined with official and unofficial corruption to bring Sitting Bull and Crazy Horse and a thousand Sioux warriors boiling down on Custer's centre column on the Little Big Horn. Here, though considered indispensable, they would prove to have no fighting to do. If they had had, the arrangement was that they were to protect without distinction both the American and the British party, though in practice the British and Canadians, beneficiaries of a sounder Indian policy and a less pugnacious history, were undoubtedly less in need of protection than their comrades on the other side of the Line.

Working alternate stations, each commission divided into several parties, they closed the Line from monument to monument. As far as the western border of Manitoba they would plant eight-foot hollow iron pillars four feet in the ground at mile intervals; in the empty country beyond all settlement their progress would at first be marked every three miles by a cairn of stones or a mound of earth. Ahead of them, thirty *métis* scouts commanded by an engineering officer reconnoitred the country for camp and supply-depot sites in the boundary zone. The measuring worm lengthened out, chaining itself toward buffalo country, toward the Blackfoot country, toward the lost hills where, only a few weeks before, the conflict of cultures had burst into brief and bloody war on Battle Creek.

The climate of the Red River valley is cold, and spring comes slowly, but when it comes, when one warm day is followed by a single night without frost, the whole prairie is misted with sudden green. Out of the same abrupt loosening of winter come mosquitoes in fogs and clouds to drive men and animals wild. The tender skin around the eyes of horses and oxen gathers moving crusts of torment; a rider rubbing a hand across his mount's face brings up a pulpy mass of crushed insects and blood. And horseflies, the savage things called bulldogs: a horse will flinch from the bite of one as if he has been nicked by a knife blade. His dung is full of bots. Even the strongest animals under these conditions are kept thin, and when one is too poor or overworked the constant attacks of the flies and mosquitoes may literally kill him.

Chain by chain, stake by stake, mound by mound, they measured their true-west Line, each party surveying as it went a belt five miles wide on its own side. The Red River valley's fertile prairie was back of them, they mounted the ridge known as Pembina Mountain and were on the Second Prairie Steppe, one mighty grassland marked by the skulls and bones and unused wallows of the vanished buffalo, and by the mounded burrows of innumerable badgers. Crocuses gave way to wild roses, but the mosquitoes and flies did not disappear as the summer heat came on. They ceased their biting only for an hour or two during the blaze of noon, and that was precisely the time when work could not go on because "over the whole prairie surface the air was in constant agitation, and in looking through the telescope at a distant flagstaff it was seen to dance with persistent contortions, and no observations on terrestrial objects could be made from point to point with accuracy, except in the early morning or late in the evening." They learned to like cloudy days; they blessed their luck when they were sighting across a valley, for only the lower thirty or forty feet of air did the heat dance.

Seventy miles of plains brought them to Turtle Mountain, straddling the line. Here was relief from heat and glare, plenty of wood for fires and smudges, plenty of water more potable than the sloughs of the prairie. But Turtle Mountain also brought a sharp increase in difficulty of another kind. One group of British axemen and surveyors was all summer cutting a fifteen-foot way through twenty-four miles of Turtle Mountain to meet an American party which worked ten miles in from the other side. In the thirty-four miles of their mutual effort, before they met on opposite shores of a mile-wide lake, they had crossed sixty-five pieces of water, across many of which the line had to be surveyed by triangulation. Also they discovered what havoc a sudden hailstorm, with stones as big as bantam eggs, could create in camp and among the horses. More than once they hunted cover and watched the violent winds that brought these squalls level every tent in camp. Nevertheless, Turtle Mountain was a place they left with some regret, its advantages of wood, water, and shade more than balancing its disadvantages. They established a supply depot there and chained on to catch up with an American party that had set up a depot on the Souris or Mouse River, still farther west.

Now plains again, interrupted by the winding floodplain of the Souris, with good camping and good grass, and past Les Roches Percées with their badlands erosional forms. For 138 miles the plains swept on without a major lift or break, until after many days the west showed a faint low line of blue. This, which faded almost out of sight as they approached and mounted it, was the Great Coteau of the Missouri, angling south-eastward from the Thunder Hills, on the Saskatchewan, to a point east of the Great Bend of the Missouri in what is now North Dakota. This was another distinct step in their measuring-worm march. It brought them to the Third Prairie Steppe, the highest and driest part of the northern Plains, where the flow of streams was uncertain and often alkaline. For many miles west of the Coteau they encountered salt lakes, alkali sinks, creeks that trickled off feebly to one side or other and died in brackish sloughs. They suffered for decent water, and sickened on what they had, and chained on.

Late in September, when the westernmost American party was quitting work at Astronomical Station No. 12, just west of the 106th meridian, 408 miles from Red River, and preparing to start for the Missouri and a steamboat ride to Bismarck and thence home, the British parties were still strung out across 400 miles, and they and their commissariat wagons were caught in various postures of unpreparedness by the first equinoctial snowstorms on September 23. They corralled their wagons into a horseshoe and lashed canvas sheets on the inside and huddled their tents into the frail shelter. For seven days and nights they could do little but stay in their blankets. Their horses, turned loose to graze in the lulls of the storm, came back and stood in the shelter of the wagons and did not eat for a week. That the first storm was almost always followed by several weeks of mild Indian summer weather did not much console men who had anywhere up to 400 miles to ride, across prairies swept bare of forage by fires, and who had to watch helplessly while their horses turned to scarecrows before their eyes.

A few days after the storm had ended, the most advanced British party was near a fly-by-night whisky post called Turnay's, on the Frenchman River just below its crossing of the 49th parallel. There was still snow on the ground. They were looking for a *métis* village supposed to be on Wood (or Woody) Mountain. For that matter, they were looking for Wood Mountain, which rumour said lay somewhere near the Line. Only the passing of a party of Sioux hunters heading south gave them the clue that let them find it: the Sioux said there was a hunters" camp a long day's journey north. Following the Sioux tracks backward across the snowy plain, the surveyors after 25 miles found the village at what is now Willow Bunch, hidden among the ravines of the high land, with good wood, water, and shelter. A few hours of bright sun let them take a shot with the sextant and determine that the village was actually 22 miles north of the Line. Balmy weather made the "rude and desolate huts" of the *hivernants* look attractive enough so that the surveyors selected Willow Bunch as their supply depot for the work of the next season. That was on October 8, 1873. By the end of that month they had ridden, almost casually, all the 450 miles back to Red River and closed up for the year.

The next May the advance commissary train of twenty wagons started west again, accompanied by a road-making and bridge-building party. At the same time a mounted reconnaissance party with Red River carts for its baggage pushed clear on out to Wood Mountain to build depot buildings; when they had those completed, they were to scour the country for a hundred miles to the west to spot water, fuel, and campsites. Two weeks behind the advance groups came the main body, 160 officers and men and 70 wagons, and so efficient had the road-builders been that the main party went 200 miles, clear to the Souris, without a difficulty or an interruption. There the river was in flood. They sank pole cribs loaded with rocks in its channel and in three days built a bridge. At the Great Coteau the astronomical and chaining parties broke off south to follow the boundary track to their stations; the wagons kept on the easier cart track toward Wood Mountain, where they arrived on June 22, thirty-two days out from Red River. At Willow Bunch they found that at least one element of the American frontier system was sound. The trader they had engaged in Fort Benton had already delivered across country sixty tons of oats, bringing them in a train of huge, broad-tyred double wagons, each pair drawn by nine yolk of oxen and carrying a payload of eight tons of sacked grain. The British were quite capable of matching American plainsmen in fortitude and more than able to match them in discipline, but in enterprises of this sort Americans would out-perform anybody in the world.

The survey crew had trouble crossing the deep gorge of the Frenchman, and found its water unpalatably salty, and on its plateau in early June they made the acquaintance of the crawling locusts whose swarms, growing wings, would shortly fly east to devastate for the second year in a row the crops of the Red River valley.

And out on the scabby plains beyond the crossing of the Frenchman, out on the flats where exactly forty years later my father would hopefully hunt up the survey stakes marking his half section of land, they met the buffalo for the first time. They chased him and hunted him and blessed his beef and cursed his habit of filling every slough and waterhole with mud and excreta. Once their wagon train, headed for a depot 150 miles west of Wood Mountain, was all but run over by an enormous herd being driven by Sioux. The commissary's *métis* scouts fired into the onrushing herd and

split it, and they watched the terrified bison gallop past on both
sides, and like apparitions the stripped brown Sioux on strong
buffalo horses emerged from the dust and were gone.

In Fort Benton men during those years were confidently saying
that the buffalo were getting more numerous because of the killing
off of the wolves, but a herd like that was already a thing of the
past in all the five hundred miles of plains eastward, and after
another seven years the buffalo would be gone from this last desolate prairie too – gone as if the earth had opened. The surveyors
witnessed one of the reasons: encountering hunting camps of *métis*,
they noted that every day each hunter would kill six or eight buffalo, from which his women would take the tongues and hump ribs
and leave the rest, even the hides. Across this "arid cactus plain"
between the Frenchman and the Milk the boundary line was
pushed through the carrion stink of a way of life recklessly
destroying itself.

In seventeen days they surveyed 108 miles across the cactus flats
where we would later homestead. They held their noses against
the smell of carrion, they gagged when they drank the brackish
water full of wigglers or nauseous with buffalo urine. With
undiminished speed they moved on toward the Three Buttes, or
Sweetgrass Hills, a natural divide like the Cypress Hills and Wood
Mountain, but on the south side of the 49th parallel. A few miles
from their depot camp they came upon the bodies of twenty Crow
Indians, scalped, half mummified in the dry heat – one more mani-
festation, belated like the spendthrift camp of *métis* buffalo hunters,
of an ecology still furiously vital on the very eve of its extinction.
As a power, the Blackfoot in 1874 were almost as dead as this Crow
war party they had killed, but they did not yet know it, and neither
did their enemies. Neither did the surveyors. The escort in these
dangerous longitudes included not only the customary two companies of cavalry but five companies of the Sixth Infantry based
upon Fort Buford, and Major Reno had issued orders that not even
that substantial command was to be divided too much – a precau-
tion that his superior would ignore, to the sorrow of many widows
and orphans, on the Little Big Horn.

Perhaps because of the big escort, perhaps because of their own
lack of belligerence, the survey parties of both sides moved on

without trouble from the Blackfoot. In the last week of August 1874, they jointly located the last monument of the 1861 survey that had carried the boundary from the Pacific to the Rockies, and on a remote ridge above Waterton Lake they completed the Line that now ran from sea to sea. Behind them, evidence of their personal contribution to international policy, stretched 388 cairns and pillars and forty astronomical stations. They could all go back to civilian jobs or to their normal army duties, leaving behind them that very open and penetrable fence; yet their work had drawn a line not merely between two countries, but between two periods of history. The final signatures of representatives of the two governments would be affixed to the official documents in London on May 29 of the next year. By that time Crow and Gros Ventre and Sioux and Blackfoot and Assiniboin would already know that the "Medicine Line", as they called it, was something potent in their lives.

Frontiers are lines where one body of law stops and another body of law begins. Partly by reason of that difference of basic law, and from the moment the boundary is drawn, they also become lines of cultural division as real for many kinds of human activity as the ecological boundaries between woods and plains, plains and mountains, or mountains and deserts. Likewise they have their inevitable corollaries. They create their own varieties of law-breakers, smugglers particularly, and they provide for the guilty and the hunted the institution of sanctuary.

The coming of the precise international boundary in the neighbourhood of such good hunting and trading ground as the Sweetgrass Hills, Cypress Hills, and Wood Mountain, made lawbreakers out of the whisky traders who until that time had only been lawless. Along the western reaches of that lonely border, whose entire 800 miles were patrolled in the 1870s and 1880s by no more than two or three hundred men (some newspapers spoke of their being "massed" along the boundary), it remained easy to slip in and out. For whisky or guns there was always a seller's market, and the excitement of successful rum- or gun-running was comparable, probably, to the Indian excitement in horse-stealing. And so there began in the Cypress Hills area a tradition of border-jumping that was still very much alive during my years there. The unmarked trails past our homestead, mere wagon tracks across a sea of grass, witnessed during 1918 and 1919 a remarkable lot of traffic in Marmons and Hudson Super Sixes, tightly side-curtained and so heavily loaded that their rear springs rode clear down on the axles. They drove mainly at night or in foul weather. We could see their lights far out across the plain groping toward Montana over the wracking burnouts, and we met them sometimes in the rain, travelling when no one else would risk the gumbo. Their tracks were often eight inches deep in the sod, ground down by the small hard tyres, the heavy loads, and the constant low gear, with periodic wallows patched with sagebrush where they had bogged down and dug out again. It is astonishing how some unrecognized professions can last. The history of that country practically began with whisky runners, and whisky runners were using the same trails nearly half a century later, only this time they were running whisky from wet Canada into dry Montana, and their customers were not Indian and *métis* hunters but Montana businessmen, mechanics, politicians, and housewives. Any real inequality or disparity between the laws of Canada and those of the United States starts a flow of contraband in one direction or the other.

But the most immediate effect of the completion of the boundary in 1874 was upon the Indians. It turned out that the Line which *should* not be crossed by raiding Indians literally *could* not be crossed by uniformed pursuers, and generally wasn't crossed even by the un-uniformed ones. The medicine of the line of cairns was very strong. Once it had been necessary to outrun your pursuing enemy until you were well within your own country where he did not dare follow. Now all you had to do was outrun him to the Line, and from across that magical invisible barrier you could watch him pull to a halt, balked, helpless, and furious. Sometimes raiders calmly camped, in plain sight but just out of gunshot, and jeered the cavalry foaming on the other side. The red coats of the Mounties, too, came only to the Medicine Line, like stars that rise only a certain distance into the sky. Altogether, a new and delightful rule was added to the game of raiding: there was a King's-X place.

It became clear very soon that the Canadian side was safer than the American, that the Mounted Police had more authority and were generally more to be trusted and easier to get on with than the blue-coated American cavalry, and much more to be trusted than Montana sheriffs or marshals or posses. The seethe of excitement on the American side – miners and cattlemen and army detachments and all the commercial complex of steamboats and stores and wagon trains that supported these – had as yet no counterpart on the Canadian side, where in the 1870s only a few Hudson's Bay Company posts, the random *métis* villages, a mission or two, and a handful of whisky forts like Whoop-Up and Stand-Off and Slide-Out foretold white civilization. It was inevitable that, being emptier and having a more responsible law force and no irresponsible free settlers, western Canada should become a refuge for hostiles from the States. Well before the surveying of the Line or the formation of the Mounted Police, the Sisseton and Yankton Sioux set the precedent when they took refuge in Manitoba after the 1862 Minnesota Massacres. Farther west, as similar crises came upon them, Teton and Hunkpapa and Brulé Sioux, as well as Cheyenne and Nez Percé, would all take the same road, and request the protection of the Great Mother. The establishment of the Medicine Line let them know precisely, as they already knew approximately, where they could step across and be safe, and they took pains to avoid trouble north of the border because they did not want to jeopardize their sanctuary. That combination of facts helps to explain why the Boundary Commission surveyors who encountered Sissetons on Turtle Mountain in 1873, and the Mounted Police who ran into some Tetons east of the Cypress Hills in 1874, found them extremely friendly and apparently willing to believe that both the survey and the police were meant for the protection of the Great Mother's red children against their enemies. Four years before Black Hills gold hunters crowded the Sioux nation to desperate war, there were eight hundred lodges of Tetons camped in the Cypress Hills looking the place over as a possible new home.

This is all to say that with the coming of the first line of law on the prairie's face, responsibilities and problems that were not new, and not created by the line, were sharply clarified and brought within the possibility of control. The international boundary was the first indispensable legal basis of that control. The instrument, the Mounted Police, was being created at the same time as the

survey, and arrived at the foot of the Rockies almost simultaneously with the completion of the border.

. . . From Fort Walsh, which was headquarters for the Mounted
Police from 1878 to 1882, the men in red coats watched over the
death struggles of the Plains frontier.

Bring Forth a Wonder

GEORGE BOWERING

Whatever it was, the vision, came out of the far fog and sailed right into the sunny weather of the inlet. It was June 10, 1792.

It could have been June 20 for all the two men who watched from the shore could care. The shore was rocks and scrubby trees right to the high tide water line. The two men were Indians, and they knew enough to blend in with the rocks and trees, for the time being at least.

"It is the first time in my life that I have seen a vision," said the first Indian.

"A vision?" said the second Indian.

"The old folks told me about them. They said you went alone to the woods with no food for a week or two, and you would see visions. Well, maybe I have not been eating much lately."

The second Indian, who was about ten years older, a world-weary man with scars here and there, sighed.

"You have had no particular problem with eating," he said. "You eat more than I do, though I carry more than you do."

"I am still growing. Surely you would not deny me the nourishment I require to take my place as a full man of the tribe?"

These young ones could be pretty tiresome. Full man of the tribe. Talk talk talk. The second Indian looked over at his companion, who was now leaning back on a bare patch of striped granite, idly picking at his navel. And now he is seeing visions.

"I will make certain that I give you half of my fish tonight, before you start hinting for it this time. Meanwhile I might as well tell you about this vision you are seeing."

The first Indian looked up from his belly as if he had forgotten about the vision. He held his hand up, palm downward, sheltering his eyes as he gazed out over the silver water, where another vision or whatever had joined the first. When it got close enough it would be seen to be larger than the first one. The first Indian put his fishing gear down on a flat rock and climbed a little closer down to the

water. Much further and he would fall in and the second Indian
would have to rescue him from drowning for the second time in a
week. I am an artist, he had said the first time, what do I know about
swimming? To which his lifeguard had replied: or about fishing?

"Okay, what do you see?"

"I see two immense and frighteningly beautiful birds upon the
water."

"Birds?"

"Giant birds. They can only be spirits. Their huge shining wings
are folded and at rest. I have heard many of the stories about bird
visions, the one who cracks your head open and eats your
brains . . ."

"Hoxhok."

"And others who alight from the mountains and the skies and
take away unsuspecting children and people with bad personalities.
Also the one with the hopelessly long name who eats eyeballs. But
never anything quite like this."

"Maybe, then, it is a vision that rightly belongs to another people
entirely," suggested the second Indian.

"An interesting thought, but the fact is that it has been revealed,
in the present case, to *us*."

"Then you do think there is something to facts?"

"Of course. But the facts can only lead us to visions. Some of us, at
least, were born to see visions."

"That is perhaps why you have so much difficulty getting a fish to
leave the sea and come home with you. He is a fact whether he is
hidden under the surface, or changing colours on the rocks. To
make this fact your fact, you need skill and a well-made hook."

"But a vision is not a fish, my old ironic friend."

"I was perhaps making that very point in its opposite order," said
he.

"But look yonder, how the late afternoon sun has picked out the
true aspect of those wings at rest. Now they are revealed to be gold,
and we are two lucky men to have seen this. We will camp here
tonight, and while the visions remain I will watch them . . ."

"You'll be asleep a minute after it gets dark."

"I will watch them until they have flown back into their sky or
heaven or homeland up in the air. Then I will open my mind to the

Great Spirit, and create a song, and the song will reveal the meaning of the vision, and I will take it back with me to the tribe, where I will be accepted and welcomed as . . ."

"A full man of the tribe."

He stopped writing and went out for a while in the Triestino sunlight. When he came back this all seemed crazy.

"Yes, a full man of the tribe. You should not sneer. That is perhaps more than you think I am, but it is also perhaps more than you feel need of for yourself."

The second Indian spat in the direction of those two giant swans or whatever they were.

"You see those visions of yours?"

"Yes, I see them. Oh, I get it. Very clever. But I do see them and so do you, so that takes care of your precious facts, too."

"Not quite." Now he was going to get the brash little squirrel. Little prick. "Those are boats."

"Haw haw haw!"

"Two large dugouts from another people, as I said."

"Oh sure, dugouts with wings."

"Those wings are made of thick cloth. They catch the wind as we are supposed to catch fish in our nets, and travel far out to sea."

"You are only trying to discredit me."

"No, I am discrediting only your fancy. Your fancy would have the fish leap from the water into your carrying bag. But the imagination, now that is another matter. Your imagination tells you where to drop your hooks."

The first Indian looked from his companion to the contraptions and back again. He turned full around, and looked at the second Indian as suddenly as he could, fishing for a truth perhaps swimming in the shadow of a rock.

"You know, I do not want to believe you, but I find it hard not to. I have been bred to believe you."

"Though you were born to see visions."

The artist turned from his older friend with hurt pride and feigned derision. His friend put his hand on his deerskin-covered shoulder and turned him around.

"They are boats. Your fancy cannot dissemble that much. You must allow your senses to play for your imagination. Now, look at the highest point at the rear of the larger dugout. What do you see there?"

The first Indian looked with his very good eyes.

"It looks like a man."

"Yes?"

"In outlandish clothes. Like no clothes ever seen on this sea. He must be a god, he . . ."

The second Indian squeezed tight on his shoulder.

"That is your fancy speaking. That can be very dangerous for people such as us. You must never believe that you have seen a god when you have seen a man on a large boat."

"You have perhaps seen them before?"

"I have."

"Up close?"

"Closer. The vision is made of wood. Hard, smooth, shiny, painted wood. The figures wear peculiar clothes, all right, and some have hair on their faces. Can you imagine a god with hair on his face?"

"Did you hear them speak?"

"No, my imagination did not take me that close. A friend who did hear one speak a year ago said these people come from far in the south, and they call themselves *Narvaez*."

In Trieste, it was raining most of the time, and he would bump other umbrellas with his own on his way down to the piazza, where he would look out at the fog that had drifted in across the northern end of the Adriatic.

It was his idea, crazed in all likelihood, that if he was going to write a book about that other coast as it was two hundred years ago, he would be advised to move away in space too.

It was a neat-sounding idea, but it didn't hold any water at all. In fact it was probably informed by the malaise that had been responsible for a decade of waiting around for a shape to appear out of the fog.

And while there were certainly some people who cared very much whether George Vancouver came back over the ocean with his maps, there wasn't anyone who cared whether *he* ever showed up in Vancouver with a novel written there or elsewhere.

He had thought he would write the book nine thousand miles east because there the weather would be too poor to promote lying on a beach, the city so dull that one day's walk would take care of the sightseeing, and he didn't know a soul (or body) within a thousand miles, and knew only a close relative of the language. He would be ineluctably driven to the manuscript because there would be no telephone to summon his voice for a lecture in a prison, no mail to petition his name for a young writer's attempt to secure a grant to go and write a novel somewhere else, no pub to call for his anticipation Thursday, his body Friday night, and his aching head all day Saturday. No distractions, he said, meaning partly that *she* couldn't get him to change a light bulb or listen to a dream while he should be, as he habitually put it to himself, sitting down in that chair in that tax write-off study, producing.

. . . The name of the larger of the two dragon-bird-visions was HMS *Discovery*, that of the smaller was HMS *Chatham*. Thirteen years earlier, HMS *Discovery* had appeared at Nootka, under the command of the yet uneaten Captain James Cook. Captain Cook has come down in the British historical imagination as a great seaman and superior Englishman. This is so because he told the Admiralty a lot of wonderful things. On one occasion, after the boats had spent days and days in a large inlet far to the north, he said to young Vancouver, his twenty-one-year-old pre-officer, "You see how far we have proceeded inland? This is clearly the largest river in the New World."

"It looks like an inlet, sir."

"You are inexperienced, George. It is the great river we have been waiting to find."

"Shouldn't we wait a little longer to make sure, sir? I mean to say we have been mistaken before now. We thought the strait between the great island and the mainland might be the way east. We called it the Great Inland Sea, you remember?"

. . . It had been Cook's purpose and responsibility to claim whatever lands he found for the British Crown. Vancouver had no such mission. He was supposed to chart the coast, be friendly but firm with the Spanish, and if he had any time left over, keep an eye open for gold and the North-West Passage.

But Vancouver loved to jump out of a boat, stride a few paces up the beach, and announce: "I claim this new-found land for his Britannic Majesty in perpetuity, and name it New Norfolk!"

Usually the officers and men stood around fairly alertly, holding flags and oars and looking about for anyone who did not agree.

Vancouver thought about Champlain and de Maisonneuve, who got to climb hills with big crosses and plant Christ in the soil of a new world. He wished that there were some Frenchmen around to fight. It had looked, when they left home, as if there would be another colourful war with the French navy, and a great military career was what he wanted to leave behind for his family.

Instead, they sent him as far away as they could, exploring, serving science.

The only Frenchman around had been Etienne Marchand, that little pecker, in the *Solide*. Marchand had taken one look, had seen no way of getting the beaver from the Russians and the Spanish, and gone on home.

. . . Well, that's the way he was. He thought and knew that he was the best surveyor around, the best navigator in the world. So he hated a lot of people, as the best often do. He hated fakers, as we have seen. He hated people who were satisfied with sloppy jobs. He hated Frenchmen and all other republicans. Yet he was not all that taken with the king, though he himself was the king, and that was something.

Most of all, on this trip, he hated the scientists. Especially Menzies, that godforsaken Scotchman. Oh yes, he wasn't very strong on Scotchmen.

The little fucker has the deck cluttered up with his stuff, and he is taking over more and more space every day. First there were those contraptions of wood and glass, through which he was going to advise the captain on longitude! Then there were the plants, bushes and trees and weeds from New Holland, New Zealand, the Sandwiches, the Societies, and now the North Coast. I cannot set anchor but the little porridge-eater is off in one of my boats, having commandeered two of my men, to dig up another obnoxious weed, to make a home for it upon *my* planks, and to sequester yet more canvas to make it a roof from the rain, as if it had never felt the rain in this desert!

The vessel is ninety-nine feet long, and he hopes to cover all of it, I'm certain.

. . . In Trieste there was no mail. Vancouver, BC, was proceeding day by day independent of his help or even knowledge. Was his wife alive? Was his daughter? Did his house stand?

James Cook spent his time at home with Mrs Cook and their three sons, an excellent salary and praise every day in the *Gazette*. After his strange and distant death there was a family as well as a nation to mourn him, publicly and in the dark hours after windows went dim along the street.

Who would have remembered longer than the news if George Vancouver had been cooked and eaten somewhere in the other hemisphere? This moment he could quietly slip his legs over the side and let his body fall into the retreating tide, and the world of affairs or the parlours of Albion would never notice the splash.

Even that wouldn't make much of a story.

He wanted to be a famous story very much, the kind of story that is known before you read it. He wanted his name and exploits to be a part of the world any Englishman would walk through.

So he wrote all over the globe. He laid the names of his officers on mountains at north 50° and south 40°. That was a kind of love. He put the names of his sisters on New Albion. He inscribed the names of every officer he had ever respected or needed up and down the coast. But most of all he loved to give abstract names to coves and headlands and passages. They would perhaps write his feelings, so seldom displayed any other way, all over the long-living geography of the southwestern half of the world. Being aboard the *Discovery* probably helped him decide upon Port Discovery, as well as Port Conclusion, Port Decision, Cape Quietude, Hesitation Harbour, The Straits of Inconsistency. He never wrote down on his charts any names that were there before he got there. He didn't imagine that one should.

And certainly (for novelists have the privilege of knowing every-thing) he thought a great deal about readers far in the future, as far as London and Lisbon, about what they would read when they uncovered his charts. They would read the depth of water, the true configuration of the shoreline, and the name that pressed through his exact head at the exact time that he was required to set ink to surface.

If they did not love him they would not be able to avoid him.

He had even allowed his own name to be affixed to a rock in the antipodes and a mountain in New Norfolk, as far from the common eye as possible, of a certainty.

. . . "Did you notice something odd about the *Mamathni*?" asked the first Indian the next day.

Mamathni was the Nootka word for the Europeans. In the Chick-liset tongue it meant "their houses move over the water". The Indians plied canoes just about as long as the *Chatham* but they had never conceived the notion of placing chairs and tables and beds in them. Of course in their circumnavigation of the watery globe, the Englishmen, as well, one supposes, as the Spaniards, the Russians, and the French, were accustomed to being called many varied and fanciful names. A hundred miles north of here they were called *Yets-Haida*, which translated as Iron Men, a way of calling them very rich, not quite gods, but certainly permitted by the gods a favoured position in life.

"Of course," replied the second Indian now. "One cannot help noticing many odd things about them. They have, for instance, a profusion of hair upon their faces, which suggests their relationship with beasts such as the bear and the wolf. Yet they have magic glasses that make the distance near."

"Well, I mean something more basic, something one has never noticed about any other distant tribes."

"They have, of course, that thin transparent skin. I remember many years ago or when I was even younger than you are now, my friends and I seized one of them and scrubbed him till the blood came. We thought they were painted pink, you see, as the norther-ners paint themselves grey. We got into serious trouble, but at least we found out. They are real inside and pink on the surface. It is perhaps as if their exterior skin has been removed from them, and they are compelled to face the world with their inner skin. How they must suffer in a cold wind! It is an explanation of why they wear those heavy garments covered with pieces of shining metal."

All the while these words were being said, the first Indian was fidgeting, his fingers and toes moving out of sequence, and his mouth slightly open. At last he was able to get some Nootka words in edgewise.

"In my own short lifetime I have seen over a hundred *Mamathni*. You have seen many more than I have. Our people have seen them every summer for twenty years at least."

"There are stories that our great grandfathers saw them. At least that is the most common interpretation these days of their stories about flame-bearded gods who sailed here from the sun."

The second Indian loved being middle-aged. It meant that he could be the one who passes on the stories from the old people to the young people, while still being able to pursue most of the young people's duties and pleasures. One also was credited with a certain store of wisdom. He thought he knew what his young friend was going to point out.

"What I would like to point out, if it has to be left to me," said the first Indian, "is that the *Mamathni* are all male."

That wasn't it. The second Indian was really taken aback. But it was true. There were boys on their houses that moved over the water, and there were men as old as himself. But there were no old men, and there were no females at all. It was a thought very difficult to assimilate.

"Now that you mention it, I see it. The pink people are all men. In that regard, the strangest race of people we have ever encountered. Nowhere else in nature have I ever met such a thing."

He was a truly disoriented middle-aged man for the moment.

"How do they make more of themselves, then?" asked the first Indian, as they sat on the rocks looking toward the cove where the buttoned people had last been seen.

"Perhaps they fall from the sky with the rain, as frogs do," said the second Indian.

"One of their number is often in the forest or the meadows, drawing pictures of plants, and taking plants to their floating house," said the lad. "Is it possible that they have in some way learned to mate with the plants to produce more of their kind?"

"Such a thing seems too fanciful for the imagination."

The second Indian was a little bashful for some reason, but he continued. "I have been thinking about it, and it seems to me that we should cleave to the simple line of reason."

"So you always say."

"Facts are facts."

"But the large winged craft on the sea bring us new facts in great numbers."

"Logic demands that we begin with these facts: the *Mamathni* are men, not gods; men like to fuck, but the *Mamathni* have no females in their species. Therefore, it seems plain that they fuck each other."

"Thus producing children?"

"So it would seem. You said yourself that their floating houses bring countless new facts. If a people can live with no permanently fixed home but rather houses that are nearly always in motion, they can probably produce children in their own way too."

The first Indian was playing with the scissors that had been part of the deal for the dream of the large eastern sea. He cut the leaves one by one from a salmonberry bush.

"We have our own men who like to fuck each other," he said at last.

"But they are not many. They are a minority, an exception to our ways. They are usually artists and designers and sometimes teachers. The *Mamathni* are presumably all that way."

"Maybe when men fuck men all the time it makes their skin turn pink."

"Maybe when men fuck men all the time they learn the lore that takes them great distances on winged homes filled with useful objects made of iron."

The First Garden

ANNE HÉBERT
Translated by Sheila Fischman

They are all there with Raphaël on the café terrace, Maud's friends –
Flora's daughter's friends – the ones from the commune. They've
pulled two tables together. They are drinking milk or orange juice.
They've seen her coming from a distance, with her shoulder bag and
her haircut, like Joan of Arc at the stake. Raphaël makes the introductions. He looks at Flora Fontanges's hairdo. He says:

"You look younger."

This glorious summer. Only, don't breathe too deeply, and be
careful to expel the air after it has revived the blood. Just live in the
moment. Confine herself to the present only. As if she were one of
Maud's friends at the table on the narrow terrace of a café on rue
Saint-Jean. She has already looked as far as she can, the full length of
the street, as far as the Eglise du Faubourg. As if to make sure that
nothing threatening could come from that direction.

They are all talking at once. Trying to explain about rue Saint-Jean
on summer Saturday nights. Groups of young people piled on to the
terraces. Passersby all on the same side of the street, no one's ever
figured out why. Cars pass at ten miles an hour. There's plenty of
time to shop, to select without getting out of the car the girl or boy
you want.

They laugh. They are giving Flora Fontanges a warm welcome
because she's an actress and she's come from Europe. They decide
to show her around the city. They treat her like a model tourist. The
usual sites. Montcalm's house, the treasure-houses of the Ursulines
and of the Hôtel-Dieu. At the Maison de la Fort someone in the
shadows, among the mock-ups all in a row, gives an account of the
1759 battle, scarcely a few minutes long, in the course of which the
city and the entire country were lost . . .

It's no use trying to explain to American tourists why so many
anachronistic cannons are aimed at them, here and there in the city.
Raphaël talks about the fortifications that took a hundred years to

build and have never been used. Ever since the English conquest, history has been filled with false alarms, and it makes a fine Tartarean desert, an awesome Syrtic shore for the soldiers at the Citadel perched high above. In their red coats and fur bonnets, they guard the beauty of the landscape and watch over the river and the clouds, awaiting a prodigious attack that has been delayed for two centuries now.

Sometimes Raphaël, the scrupulous guide, recalls that the birth of the city was a misunderstanding, the founders believing they were on the path to the Orient, with its wealth of gold and spices . . .

A thousand days had passed, and a thousand nights, and there was forest, another thousand days and thousand nights, and there was still the forest, great sweeps of pine and oak hurtling down the headland to the river, and the mountain was behind, low and squat, one of the oldest on the globe, and it was covered with trees as well. There was an unending accumulation of days and nights in the wildness of the earth.

"Only pay attention," said Raphaël, "and you can feel on your neck, on your shoulders, the extraordinary coolness of countless trees, while a roar, loud yet muffled, rises from the forest deep as the sea. The earth is soft and sandy under our feet, covered with moss and dead leaves."

Is it so difficult then to make a garden in the middle of the forest, and to surround it with a palisade like a treasure-trove? The first man was called Louis Hébert, the first woman Marie Rollet. They sowed the first garden with seeds that came from France. They laid out the garden according to the notion of a garden, the memory of a garden, that they carried in their heads, and it was almost indistinguishable from a garden in France, flung into a forest in the New World. Carrots, lettuces, leeks, cabbages, all in a straight line, in serried ranks along a taut cord, amid the wild earth all around. When the apple tree brought here from Acadia by Monsieur de Mons and transplanted finally yielded its fruit, it became the first of all the gardens in the world, with Adam and Eve standing before the Tree. The whole history of the world was starting afresh because of a man and a woman planted in this new earth.

One night, unable to sleep because of the mosquitoes, they went outside together. They looked at the night and at the shadow of Cape Diamond which is blacker than night. They realize they are not looking at the same sky. Even the sky is different here, with a new arrangement of the stars and the familiar signs. Where are the Big Dipper and Canis Major and Canis Minor, Betelgeuse, and Capella? The sky above their heads has been transformed like the earth beneath their feet. Above, below, the world is no longer the same because of the distance that exists between this world and the other, the one that was once theirs and never will be theirs again. Life will never again be the same. Here in this night is their new life, with its rough breathing, its sharp air never before inhaled. They are with that life, they are caught in it like little fish in black water.

The children and grandchildren in their turn remade the gardens in the image of the first one, using seeds that the new earth had yielded. Little by little, as generations passed, the mother image has been erased from their memories. They have arranged the gardens to match their own ideas and to match the idea of the country they come more and more to resemble. They have done the same with churches, and with houses in town and in the country. The secret of the churches and houses has been lost along the way. They began floundering as they built houses of God and their own dwellings. The English came, and the Scots, and the Irish. They had their own ideas and images for houses, stores, streets, and public squares, while the space for gardens receded into the countryside. The city itself laid out, more and more sharply defined, more precise, with streets of beaten earth racing against each other up and down the cape.

Flora Fontanges is struck by the early days of the city as Raphaël evokes them. He becomes animated. Thinks that the old life is there waiting to be recaptured in all its freshness, thanks to history. She says that time recaptured is theatre, and that she is prepared to play Marie Rollet then and there.

"A headdress from the Ile de France, a blue twill apron with a bib, earth under my nails because of the garden, and there is Eve who has just arrived with Adam, the King's apothecary. And Adam, Raphaël dear, is you."

She laughs. Shuts her eyes. She is an actress inventing a role for herself. She manages the passage from her life today to a life of the past. She appropriates the heart, the loins, the hands of Marie Rollet. Seeks the light of her gaze. She opens her eyes. Smiles at Raphaël.

"Am I a good likeness, Raphaël dear?"

He asserts that the creation of the world was very near here, and that it is easy to go back to the first days of the earth.

She goes through the motions of adjusting an imaginary head-dress on her short hair. She has been transfigured, from head to foot. At once rejuvenated and weightier. Laden with a mysterious mission. She is the mother of the country. For a moment. A brief moment. Before declaring:

"That's all mimicry. I'm a chameleon, Raphaël dear, and it's terribly tiring."

Suddenly she goes numb, like someone regaining her foothold in everyday life. She wants to go home. Says again that she's very tired. An ordinary woman now, lacklustre, on her son's arm, walking through the city streets.

That evening, Maud's friend Céleste assumed an injured look and declared that this whole story Raphaël and Flora Fontanges had made up about the city's founders was phoney and slanted.

"The first man and the first woman in this country had copper-coloured skin and wore feathers in their hair. As for the first garden, there was no beginning or end, just a tangled mass of corn and potatoes. The first human gaze that lit on the world was the gaze of an Amerindian, and that was how he saw the Whites coming down the river, on big ships rigged out with white sails and crammed with rifles and cannons, with holy water and fire water."

Raphaël talks about a bygone time, long before the English conquest, at the very beginning of the world, when every step that was taken upon the naked earth was wrenched from the brush and the forest.

They are all there on the shore, waiting for the ships from France. Governor, Intendant and gentlemen in their Sunday best, bedecked, beplumed and covered with frills and furbelows, in spite of the heat and mosquitoes. A few nuns resist the wind as best they can amid a great stirring of veils, of wimples, scapulars, cornets, and neck-cloths. Newly disbanded soldiers, freshly shaven, following orders, wearing clean shirts, eyes open so wide that the sun looks red to them, waiting for the promise that is marching towards them along the vast river that shimmers in the sun.

Below, at the top of the cape, is the sketch of a city planted in the wildness of the earth, close against the breath of the forest, filled with the cries of birds and muffled stirrings in the suffocating heat of July.

This time it's not just flour and sugar, rabbits, roosters, and hens, cows and horses, pewter jugs and horn-handled knives, lengths of wool and muslin, tools and cheese-cloth: this is a cargo of marriage-able girls, suited for reproduction, which is the matter at hand.

New France has a bad reputation in the mother country. People speak of a "place of horror" and of the "suburbs of hell". Peasant women need coaxing. They have to turn to the Salpêtrière, that home for former prostitutes, to populate the colony.

Now they are crowded here on to the bridge, huddled together like a bouquet too tightly bound. The wings of their headdresses beat in the wind and they wave handkerchiefs above their heads. The men, in ranks on the shore, stare at them silently. The decency of their costumes has been observed, at once and with satisfaction, by the Governor and the Intendant. Now they must find out, even before the women's faces can be distinguished, whether they are modest and their persons carefully tended. The rest of the meticul-ous, precise examination will be carried out at the proper time and place, little by little, even as they make their way towards us with their young bodies dedicated unreservedly to man, to work, and to motherhood.

In the absence of peasant women, they must now be content with these persons of no account who have come from Paris, with a dowry from the King of fifty *livres* per head. Though they already know how to sew, knit, and make lace (this they have been taught at the Salpêtrière, "a place as ignominious as the Bastille"), we'll just see the looks on their faces when they have to help the cow to calve and change its litter.

Now their features can be seen clearly in the light, framed with

white linen and wisps of hair in the wind. Some are red and tanned
by the sun and the sea air, others are bloodless and skeletal, consumed by seasickness and fear.

The men stand on the shore, on this splendid day, as if they were
seeing the northern lights. Now and then cries burst from their
heaving chests.

"Ah! the pretty redhead! That lovely one in blue! The little one
with curls!"

When men have been without women for so long, save for a few
squaws, it's a pleasure to see such a fine collection of petticoats and
rumpled linen coming toward us. It has been arranged, between
Monsieur the Governor, Monsieur the Intendant, and ourselves, the
marriageable boys, that we would take them as they are, these *filles
du Roi*, fresh and young and without a past, purified by the sea
during a long rough crossing on a sailing ship. Thirty passengers
died along the way and had to be cast overboard like stones. The
survivors will long be haunted by the lurching and pitching, so
deeply does the ocean's great flux still inhabit their bodies, from the
roots of their hair to the tips of their toes. They are like a procession
of drunken girls as they make their way to us along the gangplank.
Their lovely shoulders straining under shawls crossed on their
breasts sway like sailors on a spree.

Monsieur the Intendant is categorical. *All discharged soldiers, some
of them dealing as brigands, will be barred from fur-trading and hunting and
the honours of the Church and the religious communities if, within a
fortnight after the arrival of the* filles du Roi, *they have not married*.

The fattest ones were chosen first, during brief visits in the house
lent for that purpose by Madame de la Peltrie. It is better that they be
plump, to resist the rigours of the climate, so they say, and besides,
when you've consumed misery through all the pores of your skin in
the King's armies for years, it is comforting to sink your teeth into a
good solid morsel, for the time God grants us in this land that has
been a barren waste since the creation of the world. In reality, only
hunting and fishing are possible here. The condition of *coureur de
bois* would suit us well enough, although it is the King's will that we
be fettered to a piece of land covered with standing timber, with a
woman who talks on and on, claiming that she has emerged from

between our ribs to take her first breath here, in the earthly paradise. What answer is there, then, to that expectation, that desire for absolute love which torments most of the women? Only the succession of days and nights will win out over their fine ardour. That's because it wears you down in the end, to withstand the fire of summer, the fire of winter, the same intolerable burning from which the only escape is a wooden shack fifteen feet square, covered with straw. In the dwelling's only bed we take each other, and then again, and give birth and accumulate children, it is where we spend our dying days, then breathe our last. Sometimes it resembles a pigsty, and tears mingle with sperm and sweat, while generations pass and life constantly remakes itself, like the air we breathe.

Standing on the pier at Anse aux Foulons, surrounded by the smell of tar and the falling night, Raphaël and Flora Fontanges have started to recite the names of the King's girls, the *filles du Roi*, like a litany of saints, names hidden away in dusty archives forever.

Graton, Mathurine
Gruau, Jeanne
Guerrière, Marie-Bonne
Hallier, Perette
d'Orange, Barbe
Drouet, Catherine
de la Fitte, Apolline
Doigt, Ambroisine
Jouanne, Angélique
La Fleur, Jacobine
Le Seigneur, Anne
Salé, Elisabeth
Deschamps, Marie

In reality, it concerns her alone, the queen with a thousand names, the first flower, first root, Eve in person (no longer embodied solely by Marie Rollet, wife of Louis Hébert), but fragmented now into a thousand fresh faces, Eve in her manifold greenness, her fertile womb, her utter poverty, endowed by the King of France in order to found a country, who is exhumed and emerges from the bowels of the earth. Green branches emerge from between her thighs, an entire tree filled with birdsong and tender leaves, coming to us and casting shade from river to mountain, from mountain to river, and we are in the world like children struck with awe.

One day our mother Eve embarked on a great sailing ship, travelled across the ocean for long months, making her way to us who did not yet exist, to bring us out of nothing, out of the scent of a barren land. In turn blonde, brunette, or auburn, laughing and crying at once, it is she, our mother, who gives birth in the fullness of life, mingled with the seasons, with earth and dung, with snow and frost, fear and courage, her rough hands running over our faces, scraping our cheeks, and we are her children . . .

They must all of them be named aloud, all of them called by their names, while we face the river whence they emerged in the seventeenth century, to give birth to us and to a country.

Michel, Jaquette
Mignolet, Gillette
Moullard, Eléonore
Palin, Claude-Philiberte
Le Merle d'Aupré, Marguerite

It is nothing for Flora Fontanges and Raphaël to recite a rosary of girls" names, to pay homage to them, greet them as they pass, to bring them on to the shore – their light ashes – to have them become flesh again, just long enough for a friendly greeting. All, without exception: fat and lean, beautiful and plain; the brave and the others; those who returned to France because they were too terrified to live here with the Indians, the forest, the dreadful winter; those who have had ten children, or fifteen; those who have lost them all one by one; she who was able to save a single infant out of twelve stillborn – a little girl called Espérance, the name meaning hope, to ward off bad luck, although she died at the age of three months; the one who was shaved and beaten with rods at the town's main crossroads for the crime of adultery; and little Renée Chauvreux, buried in the cemetery on January fifth, 1670, who had come from France on the last ship and was found dead in the snow on the fourth day of January of that same year.

For a long time Flora Fontanges has been convinced that if she could one day gather up all the time that has passed, all of it, rigorously, with all its sharpest details – air, hour, light, temperature, colours, textures, smells, objects, furniture – she should be able to relive the past moment in all its freshness.

Of little Renée Chauvreux, there are very few signs: a mere three lines in the city register and the inventory of her meagre trousseau. This *fille du Roi* died in the snow. Her first winter here, her first snow. White beauty that fascinates and kills. Starting with her own childhood in the snow, we should be able to approach Renée Chauvreux, who lies under three feet of powdery snow, if we move stealthily, as lulling and numbing as death itself. But how to awaken the little dead girl lying stiff under ice and time, how make her speak and walk afresh, ask for her secrets of life and death, how tell her she is loved, fiercely, like a child who must be revived?

Margaret Atwood

THE BOYS' OWN ANNUAL, 1911

was in my grandfather's attic, along with a pump organ that contained bats, rafter-high piles of Western paperbacks, and a dress form, my grandmother's body frozen in wire when it still had a waist. The attic smelled of dry rot and smoked eels but it had a window, where the sunlight was yellower than anywhere else, because of the dust maybe. This buttery sunlight framed the echoing African caves where the underground streams ran, lightless, haunted by crocodiles, white and eyeless, guarding the entrance to the tunnel carved with Egyptian hieroglyphs and armed with deadly snakes and spiky ambushes planted two thousand years ago to protect the chamber of the sacred pearl, which for some reason, in stories like this, was always black. And when the hero snatched it out of the stone forehead looming bulbous and idolatrous there in the darkness, *filthy* was a word they liked, for other religions, the goddess was mad as blazes. Sinister priests with scimitars abounded, they could sniff you out like bloodhounds, their bare feet making no sound, until suddenly there was a set piece and down the hill went everyone, bounding along, loving it, yelling like crazy, bullets thudding into bodies into the scrub, into the surf, on to the waiting ship where Britain stood firm for plunder.

The issue with the last instalment had never come; it wasn't in the attic. So there I was, suspended in mid-story, in 1951, and there I remain, sometime, waiting for the end, or finishing it off myself, in a booklined London study over a stiff brandy, a yarn spun to a few choice gentlemen under the stuffed water buffalo head, a cheerful fire in the grate, or somewhere on the veldt, a bullet in the heart, who can tell where such greedy impulses will lead? Such lust for blind white crocodiles. In those times there were still chiefs in ostrich feathers and enemies worth killing, and loyalty, or so the story said. Through the attic window and its golden dust and flyhusks I could see the barn, unpainted, hay coming out like stuffing from the loft doorway, and around the corner of it my grandmother's cow. She'd hook you if she could, if you didn't have a pitchfork. She was sneaking up on someone invisible; possibly my half uncle, gassed in the first war and never right since. The books had been his once.

My Grandfather's House

CHARLES RITCHIE

The streets of the town were steep as toboggan slides up to the granite Citadel and down to the harbour wharves. People were accustomed to walking on the perpendicular. The houses clung at odd angles to the spine of the hill, so that a roof or a protruding upper window showed out of alignment, as in a crooked drawing. The effect was disturbing to the sense of balance. The houses were of indeterminate age – some eighteenth-century, others Victorian, built of wood or stone beneath their coating of dun-coloured shingle. They were narrow houses, bigger than they looked from the front, with an air of reticence, almost of concealment. Nothing was for show. One sees such houses in Scottish towns. The poor lived in squat, bug-ridden wooden boxes, the windows sealed tight, winter and summer. A charnel whiff of ancient dirt issued from the door-ways where the children thronged.

The Citadel crowned Halifax. It was flanked by army barracks built from London War Office blueprints, oblivious of climate or situation. Toy-sized cannon made a pretence of protection. Neat paths of painted white stones spaced with military precision and planted with a straggle of nasturtiums led to the officers' quarters. Barracks and brothels, the one could not live without the other. The brothels were at the foot of the hill near the waterfront and the naval dockyard. One could fancy that these rickety old structures would one day collapse from the vibration of the rutting that went on within their walls. From the wharves the stink of fish was wafted up the streets and the fog rolled in from the harbour, bringing with it a salty taste to the lips. The sound of the fog-horn was the warning melancholy music of the place.

Past my grandfather's house the trams rumbled, in front of it were three elm trees, behind it was a garden ending in abandoned stables. It was a tall, dark house. Inside, steep stairs went up and up; it made one gasp to look down from the top-floor landing into the hall-well far below. The stair banisters were narrow and dangerous to slide on. The house was lit by gas; pop! went the jets when lighted, and they gave off a pungent smell.

Each year my mother came to spend a winter month with her father in Halifax, and she brought me with her, first when I was six, then seven, then eight. My grandfather was a few years short of a hundred. When my mother was out shopping or visiting friends, I would be left playing with toys or reading in my grandfather's sitting room while he fussed and fumbled about his desk. He was a small, cheerful, impatient man, with the white mutton-chop whiskers of another era, his hands mottled with brownish spots.

The sitting room was hot and airless. Affixed to the panels of the door were strips of canvas on which bloomed sunflowers and lilies painted by my aunt Geraldine in an outburst of aestheticism in the 1890s. Over the mantelpiece were arranged photographs sepia with age. Some were groups of officers in which my uncle Harry figured boldly in his Highland uniform.

At times my grandfather seemed to have forgotten that I was in the room. The hours slid by unnoticed. Then, as though by a common impulse, we would both pause in what we were doing, he would subside with a sigh into his leather armchair before the fire, and I would break off my game or book. It was as though we were listening for something scarcely audible in the distance, but the only sounds were the shifting coals in the grate and the intermittent plashing of the snow as it slid from the window-panes to the ledge outside. Abruptly he would explode into talk: "When the Fenian raids threatened this country I led my boys into action. I charged up the hill waving my sword" (here, seizing the poker, he made to charge at me across the hearthrug) "and the Irish ruffians fled before us." My mother said that there was no charge and no hill; that my grandfather had raised a company to fight the Fenians but the raids were over before he could take to the field. I preferred my grandfather's version; his stories were like the stories I told myself or the games I invented. They were rambling and repititious, and depended on the imagination.

When my mother came into the sitting room, her cheeks flushed from the cold, she would fling off her sealskin coat and say, "Oh, how stuffy it is in here, what have you two been doing? Charlie, you ought to be out playing in the snow, it is a lovely sunny day. Father, you just have time for half an hour's rest before lunch."

There were many empty rooms in my grandfather's house, empty but furnished. The emptiest of all was my grandmother's bedroom, which had been left as it was when she was alive. The bed was made up; her hand-mirror, her hairbrush, and her Bible with a marker in it were on the table beside her bed. No one but my grandfather was allowed to enter the room. Once I looked in and felt a breath of cold enclosed air on my face.

Mt grandfather's bedroom I visited every morning while he was still in bed in a flannel nightshirt, and he would give me a dusty lemon-drop out of a circular wooden box. The room smelled of old age – and of other things. He kept a ham and a bottle of stout under the bed, to conceal them from the doctor who had put him on a diet.

My grandfather had had twelve children. But he had outlived all of them but my mother and her brother Charlie. What had become of all those children? Most of them had died young, some in infancy, as so many used to in those days. Except for my mother, those who did grow up were not long-lived.

Of all the children who had played and called to each other in those rooms, two were to be met with at every turn. As soldiers they marched and countermarched along the garden paths, as Red Indians they put each other to the torture, as horses they galloped or trotted up and down to the stables. All their games and exploits were more real to me than my own. They were my mother and my uncle Charlie. These were the tales my mother told me, "Charlie and I, Charlie and I". He had been bold and adventurous; feats of nerve and truant defiance were his, and my mother had been his accomplice and his imitator.

What was he really like, Uncle Charlie? I still tease myself with the question. But he is nearly seventy years dead, killed leading his regiment at Bourlon Wood in 1918, against real enemies, not like my grandfather's phantom Fenians. The letters from the regiment after his death read, "The men would follow him anywhere; he seemed to bear a charmed life." Yet what was his life until the war gave him his chance? A life of adventure wearing down into plain middle-aged failure. Expelled from the Royal Military College for gambling, dismissed from the Mounted Police for striking a bullying corporal, disappearing for months into the Yukon, drifting into jobs and bars in Calgary or Edmonton, eking out his earnings by his gains at poker, he left a trail of legends and stories. A few old men still recount them, but his magnetism has evaporated and the point is gone.

His women were come-by-chance encounters doubled with romantic entanglements, for he had the attraction of the undomesticated man, restless and susceptible. He made husbands and other aspirants seem tame. The women who knew him felt they had a card up their sleeves. He never married. In a letter to my mother on the day before the battle in which he was killed, he wrote, "You are the only one I have ever loved." On the night that she was handed the telegram telling her of his death she saw, or thought she saw, him at her bedside. He wore a torn scarf knotted around his neck and there was a button missing on the left pocket of his tunic. Afterwards my mother wrote to the sergeant who had been with him when he was killed and he confirmed these details.

To my grandparents my uncle Charlie had always been a worry and a disappointment, sharpened by contrast with his elder brother Harry. Harry was their idol, a dashing soldier, startlingly handsome, cutting a figure in fashionable London, married to an Earl's daughter. But the idol was expensive to maintain. They paid his debts and waited for his letters, which came rarely – except when he needed money.

My grandparents were old-fashioned, innocent snobs. Innocent, in the sense that they never thought of themselves in this way. They believed that they had a Position to keep up (though what that Position was it would be hard to say). What made it more difficult to keep up was that my grandfather all his life drank in bursts of drunkenness, when he vanished from his wife and home for days at a time. My grandmother covered and concealed the outrage in the Victorian manner. Sometimes it was not easy. Once when she was presiding over a dinner party for some legal dignitary, her husband, "unfortunately ill" upstairs, appeared at the dining-room door in his nightshirt, pleading for whisky. She rose from the table and majestically swept him away. He was smaller than she, and she so enveloped him in her amplitude that the guests could hardly believe, when she resumed her place, that he had ever been there.

Never in the course of nearly a century had my grandfather done a day's work. This, and his heavy drinking, may have accounted for his healthy old age. Although he was always prone to fits of gloom, his spirits revived quickly. The gloom was usually associated with money. He had inherited what used to be called "private means" from his father. Being generous and hospitable, he overspent his income. He and my grandmother found it difficult to retrench. My mother as a girl had no patience with their financial forebodings. "Why give dinner parties when we are in debt? Why import a spotty English boy and call him a footman?" My grandparents did not take these probings in good part. "Your father and I," my grandmother announced, "are pained, grieved, and disappointed in you, Lilian."

When I came to my grandfather's house as a child all this was long in the past. My grandmother's drawing room was shuttered, its armchairs and sofas under dust-covers. The little papier-mâché chairs, almost too fragile to sit on, were pushed to the wall. The room was crowded with objects which seemed to me of inestimable rarity and strangeness. There was a picture of a boy in peasant costume holding an alpenstock; a souvenir from Switzerland, it was painted on cobweb. I held my breath when looking at it, believing that the picture would dissolve if I breathed on it. There was a silver horse trotting over a field of silver grass and flowers. In one corner of the room, enclosed in a large box, was a pile of old daguer-reotypes. I would cautiously unfasten the rusty clasps of their black cases and bring to light a whole shadowy population. Men with fan-shaped whiskers and top hats, leaning gloomily against card-board balustrades, behind which hung a drop-curtain of majestic parks and castle towers out of proportion with watch-fob and frock-coat; women voluminously robed, bent pensively over a family album, one arm gracefully arched to support a languid head. All the denizens of this ghostly world wore the same expression of grave impassivity; even the children looked unnaturally solemn in their strange garb. They might have been the priests and priestesses of some fantastic and forgotten cult, the secret of which had perished with them. When I snapped the clasps of their cases to once again, it was as if I enclosed these dim beings in their tombs.

A marble group of the Three Graces stood on a red velvet pedestel under a glass case. Once when alone in the drawing room I lifted the glass case with guiltily trembling hands and ran my fingers over the cold breasts of the Graces. I knew that I was committing sacrilege, but the desire for the unattainable was too strong for me to resist.

Over the drawing-room fireplace hung the portrait of a lady, her hair parted in the style of the Empress Eugénie, her dark eyes smiling, her pink scarf floating away from her shoulders into an azure sky. It was my grandmother. But not the stout old woman in a black silk dress whom I could just remember. This was she as a young bride, painted in Paris on her honeymoon in the 1850s.

Beyond the drawing room was a small, damp library, also now disused. Here stood a desk, its drawers brimming with packets of letters yellowed by age, tied with faded ribbons. They were the letters of my great-grandfather to the girl he was to marry, written during their courtship. They folded inward on their broken seals of red wax. I unfolded them one after another. In one was a pressed mayflower that they had picked together in a wood. It was odourless and almost colourless. In another was a twist of hair, a living chestnut colour, leaving an oily stain upon the paper. The writing scrawled and hurried in haste or excitement, as though the nerves in the writer's hand were still alive. Bursts of feeling, scoldings, secret endearments, zigzagged across the pages. These letters were not meant for me. I was spying out of childish eyes.

Under the hall stairs swung a green baize door leading to the kitchen. Roxie was the cook. She had been with my grandparents all her grown-up life. She saw through them and she served them with cross-grained fidelity. She was red-haired and rough-tongued. When she finally retired to her family farm in Stewiacke, Nova Scotia, my brother and I used to spend a week with her there each year. She had no high opinion of me. "That there Charlie, when he is with you you would think butter would melt in his mouth, but just wait till your back is turned." They did not mince their words on the farm – "pee or get off the pot" was a favourite expression (and one which in later life I found to apply to many situations – social, political, and even amorous). Once when I returned from our annual visit my language surprised my mother. She was walking restlessly up and down in her bedroom smoking a cigarette when I suddenly said, "Why don't you sit down on your arse?" She came to a standstill, staring at me in disbelief. "What did you say?" "Well, that's what they say in Stewiacke." My mother was not genuinely shocked; she had little use for the genteel, and what she despised most, apart from cowardice, was what she called "affectation".

How far can one reach back into the past? Further than the sound of a voice? My mother was a natural mimic. Her ear was a tuning-fork for voices and accents; the least actressy of women, she had a face as mobile as that of an actress. She could bring before you not only the absent, but also the dead – those whom she had known in her childhood. They might just have left the room, and one could catch the inflections of their voices, hear their laughter just before the door closed on them. So, I saw and heard those people of the past not as they might have been described in books, but in the flashes of her mimicry.

There was still a handful of survivors of my grandfather's genera-tion living, among them Mr and Mrs Lorrimer. They were no favourites of my grandfather, particularly Mrs Lorrimer, who had been a leading light in teetotal circles. She was one of the innumer-able Queen Victorias who once peopled the Empire, modelling themselves on the Great Original. She had the lost Victorian art of putting one not at one's ease, but at one's unease. She dressed her part: a white cap perched on her severely parted white hair, and she was encased in an armature of whalebone. When she approached, there was a rustle of skirts, and the tap of her ivory-handled stick on the floor. She trundled rather than walked across a room; there appeared to be no leg action involved. She had a chilly little laugh, miles away from mirth.

The Lorrimers lived in the country not far out of town. I remember as a child going there once with my mother to lunch with them. We arrived somewhat late. "Dear Lilian," Mrs Lorrimer greeted us with the little laugh. "I hear you were delayed by rain. How *very* extra-ordinary that we have had no rain here only a mile away, but it is no matter. Here you are at last." We went in to lunch preceded by a very old and smelly Newfoundland dog. Mrs Lorrimer turned to my mother: "How is your father? Always so cheery. I am sorry your brother Charlie should be causing him so much concern. Your dear mother was always so indulgent to him, too much so, I fear." At that moment the dog growled and stirred under the table where he had crouched, and on a sharp note of rage my mother cried out "Damn!" There was a pause as if the clock had stopped. "He nipped my ankle," my mother explained. "Ha ha," guffawed Mr Lorrimer, "she said a big D, she said a big D." Our hostess's laugh was like the rustling of dry leaves. "I am sure she said nothing of the kind, but if," turning to my mother, "you had said 'poor doggie' instead of the expression which you did employ, it would have been preferable." In front of my place at the table was a glass of milk. "We had it brought straight from the barn for you as a treat. It is warm from the cow." With revulsion I downed a swallow of the milk. It had a distastefully intimate taste.

The luncheon-table conversation continued. "So dreadfully sad," observed Mrs Lorrimer, "for the poor Brumleys that their only son should have become a pervert" (the reference was not to his sex preferences but to his conversion to the Roman Catholic Church), "but our own High Church so often leads the way to error." We rose to depart. "Dear Lilian," she said, "I remember you so well as a child and what a naughty little thing you were!" and, bending down to me, "Bonnie Prince Charlie, you didn't drink up your milk." A boy of six cannot suffer from the menopause, but my symptoms were those since described to me; a surge of heat flushed through my veins, and embarrassment dripped from me like sweat. Even today the words "Bonnie Prince Charlie" set up a queasy sensation in me as of the taste of warm milk.

My grandfather and his remaining contemporaries belonged to a breed now long extinct. They were Colonials. The word carries a whiff of inferiority, but they were not to know this. They thought of themselves as belonging to the British Empire, than which they could imagine nothing more glorious. They did not think of themselves as English. Certainly everything British was Best, but they viewed the individual Englishman with a critical eye. If the English patronized the Colonials, the Colonials sat in judgement on the English. The Colonial was an ambivalent creature, half in one element, half in another; British, but not English, cantankerously loyal. These were Nova Scotian Colonials. The earthly subsoil of Nova Scotia gave a tang to their personalities and an edge to their tongues. For many years they and those like them had managed the colony under the rule of British governors whom, in turn, they managed. It was a comfortable arrangement as long as it lasted, and not unprofitable. It enjoyed the blessings of the Church – the

Church of England, of course. They were men of standing and standards, honourable men within the bounds of their monopoly. They were kind to their poor relations and moderately charitable to the poor who were not their relations and who lived in the slums. They began to think of themselves as an aristocracy, since there was no aristocracy on the spot to tell them differently. But they were small-town people, and they never escaped from the miasma of the small town. They woke to the apprehension of what the neighbours would say; they knew that, as always in Nova Scotia, ostentation was made to be undermined. There would be a dozen who would doubt the crests on their silver or the sources of their fortunes. So that they never achieved perfect complacency, a commodity hard to come by in that rocky land where misfortune revives friendship and where the worst word is "in trouble he let me down"

Halifax had been a garrison and a naval base for 150 years. Had not Kipling celebrated it as the "Warden of the honour of the North"? British regiments and sailors of the Royal Navy had come and gone in all those years and had set their stamp upon the town. No ball, picnic, or sleighing party was complete without them. They carried off the prettiest girls, and many a local man resented and hated them. They brought with them rumours of wars in the days when wars seemed an adventure, an honourable escape for the spirited and restless from home-grown tedium. Some found forgotten glory in those wars of Empire. Theirs were the tunes that went whistling up and down the steep hills of the town. "We're the soldiers of the Queen, my boys, the Queen, my boys, the Queen, my boys," and there were boys, like my uncles Harry and Charlie, to listen and serve.

When I came to my grandfather's house the British soldiers had marched down the streets for the last time and the little world in which my grandfather had grown up had long ago vanished. "I have lived too long, I have lived too long," he used to declaim in melodramatic tones. Yet all the sorrows and losses, the drinking, the fathering, the loving, and the talking (and he was a great talker) had not worn him out. He had been born in 1817 and was already a middle-aged man when Nova Scotia ceased to be a colony and became a province of Canada, an event that did not seem to have penetrated very far into his consciousness. He had never set foot in

"Upper Canada", as he called it. His journeys had been those taken from Halifax to England, weeks spent in rolling, pitching, smelly little steamers, with shipwreck off the Grand Banks or Sable Island an accepted risk.

My grandfather never reached his hundredth year; he died ten days short of it. It was his impatience that killed him. Rather than waiting for help, he seized the heavy copper coal scuttle in his sitting room and, in trying to pour the coal into the grate, he staggered, hit his head against the marble mantelpiece, and never recovered consciousness. My mother, my brother, and I were staying in the house at the time. By then it was 1917, and I was eleven years old. To me it was not the same house as it had been on my visits as a small child. I saw it with different and disparaging eyes.

On the day of my grandfather's death I was sent to the local cinema, I suppose to get me out of the way. When I went to bed that night in my bedroom at the top of the house I was not thinking of my grandfather. His death had not much moved me. He had come to seem no longer quite real to me, but like an old man on the stage who dies when the curtain falls.

At some moment in the night I woke to an intensity of listening. I got out of bed and stood at the top of the stairs, looking down to the gully where the banisters curved. The dense night silence reverberated around me; then there swept over me the tide of the past rising from the sleeping house below me. A constriction choked my throat. Had I heard a muffled sigh like a warning? What was it? Some signal from the frontier between childhood and old age where my grandfather and I had shared those timeless hours? When I went back to my bed it was to fall into a sleep as deep as the stairwell where the dead children had played.

The Halifax Explosion, 1917

HUGH MACLENNAN

Eight fifteen

There was now only one vessel moving north toward the upper harbour, the French munition ship *Mont Blanc*. An ugly craft of little more than 3,000 tons, she was indistinguishable from thousands of similar vessels which came and went during these days. She was inward bound, heading for Bedford Basin to await convoy. Moving very slowly, she had crawled through the opened submarine net and now was on her way up the Stream, past the breakwater, George's Island, and then the South End docks. She had been laded a week ago in New York with a cargo consigned to a French port, but only her crew, the Admiralty authorities, and the captain of the British cruiser in port to command the convoy, knew what her main cargo was.

Men on the motionless ships in the Stream watched her pass and showed no interest. The previous day they had all received orders not to move until further notification, but none had been told they were giving sea-room to a floating bomb.

The cruiser's captain came back on deck to watch the *Mont Blanc* pass and estimate the speed she would be able to produce. He was about the only person in the vicinity of Halifax to take any overt notice of her passage up the harbour.

The *Mont Blanc* moved so slowly that her bow seemed to push rather than cut the water as she crept past the cruiser. The pilot was proceeding cautiously and the cruiser's captain observed this with satisfaction. What was not so satisfactory to him was the manner in which the cargo was stowed. Her foredeck was piled with metal canisters, one on top of the other, held down with guy ropes and braced at the sides by an improvised skeleton of planks. The canisters and visible parts of the deck glistened patchily with oil. The after-deck was clear and some sailors in dungarees were lounging there out of the wind.

"I wonder what she's got in *those* things?" the captain muttered to his Number One. "Petrol?"

"More likely lubricating oil, I should think, sir."

"I doubt it. She's not a tanker, after all. Might be benzol from the colour of it. How much speed would you say she's got in her?"

"Ten knots at the most, I'd say."

"Doubt if it's even that. I wish they'd realize that a munition ship ought to be faster than the general run of ships. I can't have a cargo like that keeping station with the rest of them. She's got to cruise on the fringe, and she needs about three extra knots to do it."

But the *Mont Blanc* glided on up the harbour with little sound or evidence of motion except for a ripple at the bows and a thin wake. She was low in the water and slightly down by the head. A very sloppily laded ship, the cruiser's captain decided. She passed awkwardly onward, the pilot pulling her out to the exact centre of the channel as the harbour narrowed. The tricolour flapped feebly from her stern as she floated in, and as she reached the entrance to the Narrows, bells sounded in the engine-room calling for a still further reduction in speed.

Eight forty

The *Mont Blanc* was now in the Narrows and a detail of men went into her chains to unship the anchor. It would be dropped as soon as she reached her appointed station in the Basin. A hundred yards to port were the Shipyards and another hundred yards off the port bow was the blunt contour of Richmond Bluff; to starboard the shore sloped gently into a barren of spruce scrub. During the two minutes it took the *Mont Blanc* to glide through this strait, most of Bedford Basin and nearly all its flotilla of anchored freighters were hidden from her behind the rise of Richmond Bluff.

Around the projection of this hill, less than fifty fathoms off the port bow of the incoming *Mont Blanc*, another vessel suddenly appeared heading for the open sea. She flew the Norwegian flag, and to the startled pilot of the munitioner the name *Imo* was plainly visible beside the hawse. She was moving at half-speed and listing gently to port as she made the sharp turn out of the Basin to strike the channel of the Narrows. And so listing, with white water surging away from her fore-foot, she swept across the path of the *Mont Blanc*, exposing a gaunt flank labelled in giant letters BELGIAN RELIEF. Then she straightened, and pointed her bow directly at the fore-quarter of the munitioner. Only at that moment did the men on the *Imo's* bridge appear to realize that another vessel stood directly in their path.

Staccato orders broke from the bridge of the *Mont Blanc* as the two ships moved toward a single point. Bells jangled, and megaphoned shouts came from both bridges. The ships sheered in the same direction, then sheered back again. With a violent shock, the bow of the *Imo* struck the plates of the *Mont Blanc* and went grinding a third of the way through the deck and the forward hold. A shower of sparks splashed out from the screaming metal. The canisters on the deck of the *Mont Blanc* broke loose from their bindings and some of them tumbled and burst open. Then the vessels heeled away with engines reversed and the water boiling out from their screws as the propellers braked them to a standstill. They sprawled sideways across the Narrows, the *Mont Blanc* veering in toward the Halifax shore, the *Imo* spinning about with steerageway lost entirely. Finally she drifted toward the opposite shore.

For a fraction of a second there was intense silence. Then smoke appeared out of the shattered deck of the *Mont Blanc*, followed by a racing film of flame. The men on the bridge looked at each other. Scattered shouts broke from the stern, and the engine-room bells jangled again. Orders were half-drowned by a scream of rusty metal as some sailors amidships followed their own inclination and twisted the davits around to lower a boat. The scurry of feet grew louder as more sailors began to pour out through the hatches on to the deck. An officer ran forward with a hose, but before he could connect it his men were ready to abandon ship.

The film of flame raced and whitened, then it became deeper like an opaque and fulminant liquid, then swept over the canisters of benzol and increased to a roaring tide of heat. Black smoke billowed and rolled and engulfed the ship, which began to drift with the outgoing tide and swing in toward the graving-dock of the Shipyards. The fire trembled and leaped in a body at the bridge, driving the captain and pilot aft, and there they stood helplessly while the tarry smoke surrounded them in greasy folds and the metal of the deck began to glow under their feet. Both men glanced downward. Underneath that metal lay leashed an incalculable energy, and the bonds which checked it were melting with every second the thermometers mounted in the hold. A half-million pounds of trinitrotoluol and twenty-three hundred tons of picric acid lay there in the darkness under the plates, while the fire above and below the deck converted the hollow shell of the vessel into a bake-oven.

If the captain had wished to scuttle the ship at that moment it would have been impossible to do so, for the heat between decks would have roasted alive any man who tried to reach the sea-cocks. By this time the entire crew was in the lifeboat. The officers followed, and the boat was rowed frantically toward the wooded slope opposite Halifax. There, by lying flat among the trees, the sailors hoped they would have a chance when their ship blew up. By the time they had beached the boat, the foredeck of the *Mont Blanc* was a shaking rampart of fire, and black smoke pouring from it screened the Halifax waterfront from their eyes. The sailors broke and ran for the shelter of the woods.

By this time men were running out of dock sheds and warehouses and offices along the entire waterfront to watch the burning ship. None of them knew she was a gigantic bomb. She had now come so close to the Shipyards that she menaced the graving-dock. Fire launches cut out from a pier further south and headed for the Narrows. Signal flags fluttered from the Dockyard and the yardarms of ships lying in the Stream, some of which were already weighing anchor. The captain of the British cruiser piped all hands and called for volunteers to scuttle the *Mont Blanc*; a few minutes later the cruiser's launch was on its way to the Narrows with two officers and a number of ratings. By the time they reached the burning ship her plates were so hot that the seawater lapping the Plimsoll line was simmering.

The *Mont Blanc* had become the centre of a static tableau. Her plates began to glow red and the swollen air inside her hold heated the cargo rapidly toward the detonation point. Launches from the harbour fire department surrounded her like midges and the water from their hoses arched up with infinate delicacy as they curved into the rolling smoke. The *Imo*, futile and forgotten, was still trying to claw her way off the further shore.

Twenty minutes after the collision there was no one along the entire waterfront who was unaware that a ship was on fire in the harbour. The jetties and docks near the Narrows were crowded with people watching the show, and yet no warning of danger was given. At that particular moment there was no adequate centralized authority in Halifax to give a warning, and the few people who knew the nature of the *Mont Blanc*'s cargo had no means of notifying the town or spreading the alarm, and no comfort beyond the thought that trinitrotoluol can stand an almost unlimited heat provided there is no fulminate or explosive gas to detonate it.

Bells in the town struck the hour of nine, and by this time nearly all normal activity along the waterfront had been suspended. A tug managed to grapple the *Mont Blanc* and was towing her with imperceptible movement away from the Shipyards back into the channel of the Narrows. Bluejackets from the cruiser had found the bosun's ladder left by the fleeing crew, and with flesh shrinking from the heat, were going over the side. Fire launches surrounded her. There was a static concentration, an intense expectancy in the faces of the firemen playing the hoses, a rhythmic reverberation in the beat of the flames, a gush from the hose-nozzles and a steady hiss of scalding water. Everything else for miles around seemed motionless and silent.

Then a needle of flaming gas, thin as the mast and of a brilliance unbelievably intense, shot through the deck of the *Mont Blanc* near the funnel and flashed more than two hundred feet toward the sky. The firemen were thrown back and their hoses jumped suddenly out of control and slashed the air with S-shaped designs. There were a few helpless shouts. Then all movement and life about the ship were encompassed in a sound beyond hearing as the *Mont Blanc* opened up.

Nine five

Three forces were simultaneously created by the energy of the exploding ship, an earthquake, an air-concussion, and a tidal wave. These forces rushed away from the Narrows with a velocity varying in accordance with the nature of the medium in which they worked. It took only a few seconds for the earthquake to spend itself and three minutes for the air-expansion to slow down to a gale. The tidal wave travelled for hours before the last traces of it were swallowed in the open Atlantic.

When the shock struck the earth, the rigid ironstone and granite base of Halifax peninsula rocked and reverberated, pavements split and houses swayed as the earth trembled. Sixty miles away in the town of Truro windows broke and glass fell to the ground, tinkling in the stillness of the streets. But the ironstone was solid and when the shock had passed, it resumed its immobility.

The pressure of the exploding chemicals smashed against the town with the rigidity and force of driving steel. Solid and unbreathable, the forced wall of air struck against Fort Needham and Richmond Bluff and shaved them clean, smashed with one gigantic blow the North End of Halifax and destroyed it, telescoping houses or lifting them from their foundations, snapping trees and lampposts, and twisting iron rails into writhing, metal snakes; breaking buildings and sweeping the fragments of their wreckage for hundreds of yards in its course. It advanced two miles southward, shattering every flimsy house in its path, and within thirty seconds encountered the long, shield-like slope of the Citadel which rose before it.

Then, for the first time since it was fortified, the Citadel was able to defend at least a part of the town. The air-wall smote it, and was deflected in three directions. Thus some of its violence shot skyward at a twenty-degree angle and spent itself in space. The rest had to pour around the roots of the hill before closing in on the town for another rush forward. A minute after the detonation, the pressure was advancing through the South End. But now its power was diminished, and its velocity was barely twice that of a tornado. Trees tossed and doors broke inward, windows split into driving arrows of glass which buried themselves deep in interior walls. Here the houses, after swaying and cracking, were still on their foundations when the pressure had passed.

Underneath the keel of the *Mont Blanc* the water opened and the harbour bottom was deepened twenty feet along the channel of the Narrows. And then the displaced waters began to drive outward, rising against the town and lifting ships and wreckage over the sides of the docks. It boiled over the shores and climbed the hill as far as the third cross-street, carrying with it the wreckage of small boats, fragments of fish, and somewhere, lost in thousands of tons of hissing brine, the bodies of men. The wave moved in a gigantic bore down the Stream to the sea, rolling some ships under and lifting others high on its crest, while anchor-chains cracked like guns as the violent thrust snapped them. Less than ten minutes after the detonation, it boiled over the breakwater off the park and advanced on McNab's Island, where it burst with a roar greater than a winter storm. And then the central volume of the wave rolled on to sea, high and arching and white at the top, its back glossy like the plumage of a bird. Hours later it lifted under the keel of a steamer far out in the Atlantic and the captain, feeling his vessel heave, thought he had struck a floating mine.

But long before this, the explosion had become manifest in new forms over Halifax. More than 2,000 tons of red hot steel, splintered fragments of the *Mont Blanc*, fell like meteors from the sky into which they had been hurled a few seconds before. The ship's anchor soared over the peninsula and descended through a roof on the other side of the North-West Arm three miles away. For a few seconds the harbour was dotted white with a maze of splashes, and the decks of raddled ships rang with reverberations and clangs as fragments struck them.

Over the North End of Halifax, immediately after the passage of the first pressure, the tormented air was laced with tongues of flame which roared and exploded out of the atmosphere, lashing downwards like a myriad blowtorches as millions of cubic feet of gas took fire and exploded. The atmosphere went white-hot. It grew mottled, then fell to the streets like a crimson curtain. Almost before the last fragments of steel had ceased to fall, the wreckage of the wooden houses in the North End had begun to burn. And if there were any ruins which failed to ignite from falling flames, they began to burn from the fires in their own stoves, on to which they had collapsed.

Over this part of the town, rising in the shape of a typhoon from the Narrows and extending five miles into the sky, was poised a cloud formed by the exhausted gases. It hung still for many minutes, white, glossy as an ermine's back, serenely aloof. It cast its shadow over twenty miles of forest land behind Bedford Basin.

The Painted Door

SINCLAIR ROSS

Straight across the hills it was five miles from John's farm to his father's. But in winter, with the roads impassable, a team had to make a wide detour and skirt the hills, so that from five the distance was more than trebled to seventeen.

"I think I'll walk," John said at breakfast to his wife. "The drifts in the hills wouldn't hold a horse, but they'll carry me all right. If I leave early I can spend a few hours helping him with his chores, and still be back by suppertime."

She went to the window, and thawing a clear place in the frost with her breath, stood looking across the snowswept farmyard to the huddle of stables and sheds. "There was a double wheel around the moon last night," she countered presently. "You said yourself we could expect a storm. It isn't right to leave me here alone. Surely I'm as important as your father."

He glanced up uneasily, then drinking off his coffee tried to reassure her. "But there's nothing to be afraid of – even supposing it does start to storm. You won't need to go near the stable. Everything's fed and watered now to last till night. I'll be back at the latest by seven or eight."

She went on blowing against the frosted pane, carefully elongating the clear place until it was oval-shaped and symmetrical. He watched her a moment or two longer, then more insistently repeated, "I say you won't need to go near the stable. Everything's fed and watered, and I'll see that there's plenty of wood in. That will be all right, won't it?"

"Yes – of course – I heard you –" It was a curiously cold voice now, as if the words were chilled by their contact with the frosted pane. "Plenty to eat – plenty of wood to keep me warm – what more could a woman ask for?"

"But he's an old man – living there all alone. What is it, Ann? You're not like yourself this morning."

She shook her head without turning. "Pay no attention to me.

Seven years a farmer's wife – it's time I was used to staying alone."

Slowly the clear place on the glass enlarged: oval, then round, then oval again. The sun was risen above the frost mists now, so keen and hard a glitter on the snow that instead of warmth its rays seemed shedding cold. One of the two-year-old colts that had cantered away when John turned the horses out for water stood covered with rime at the stable door again, head down and body hunched, each breath a little plume of steam against the frosty air. She shivered, but did not turn. In the clear, bitter light the long white miles of prairie landscape seemed a region alien to life. Even the distant farmsteads she could see served only to intensify a sense of isolation. Scattered across the face of so vast and bleak a wilderness it was difficult to conceive them as a testimony of human hardihood and endurance. Rather they seemed futile, lost, to cower before the implacability of snow-swept earth and clear pale sun-chilled sky.

And when at last she turned from the window there was a brooding stillness in her face as if she had recognized this mastery of snow and cold. It troubled John. "If you're really afraid," he yielded, "I won't go today. Lately it's been so cold, that's all. I just wanted to make sure he's all right in case we do have a storm."

"I know – I'm not really afraid." She was putting in a fire now, and he could no longer see her face. "Pay no attention. It's ten miles there and back, so you'd better get started."

"You ought to know by now I wouldn't stay away," he tried to brighten her. "No matter how it stormed. Before we were married – remember? Twice a week I never missed and we had some bad blizzards that winter too."

He was a slow, unambitious man, content with his farm and cattle, naïvely proud of Ann. He had been bewildered by it once, her caring for a dull-witted fellow like him; then assured at last of her affection he had relaxed against it gratefully, unsuspecting it might ever be less constant than his own. Even now, listening to the restless brooding in her voice, he felt only a quick, unformulated kind of pride that after seven years his absence for a day should still concern her. While she, his trust and earnestness controlling her again:

"I know. It's just that sometimes when you're away I get lonely . . . There's a long cold tramp in front of you. You'll let me fix a scarf around your face."

He nodded. "And on my way I'll drop in at Steven's place. Maybe he'll come over tonight for a game of cards. You haven't seen anybody but me for the last two weeks."

She glanced up sharply, then busied herself clearing the table. "It will mean another two miles if you do. You're going to be cold and tired enough as it is. When you're gone I think I'll paint the kitchen woodwork. White this time – you remember we got the paint last fall. It's going to make the room a lot lighter. I'll be too busy to find the day long."

"I will though," he insisted, "and if a storm gets up you'll feel safer, knowing that he's coming. That's what you need, maybe – someone to talk to besides me."

She stood at the stove motionless a moment, then turned to him uneasily. "Will you shave then, John – now – before you go?"

He glanced at her questioningly, and avoiding his eyes she tried to explain, "I mean – he may be here before you're back – and you won't have a chance then."

"But it's only Steven – we're not going anywhere."

"He'll be shaved, though – that's what I mean – and I'd like you too to spend a little time on yourself."

He stood up, stroking the heavy stubble on his chin. "Maybe I should – only it softens up the skin too much. Especially when I've got to face the wind."

She nodded and began to help him dress, bringing heavy socks and a big woollen sweater from the bedroom, wrapping a scarf around his face and forehead. "I'll tell Steven to come early," he said, as he went out. "In time for supper. Likely there'll be chores for me to do, so if I'm not back by six don't wait."

From the bedroom window she watched him nearly a mile along the road. The fire had gone down when at last she turned away, and already through the house there was an encroaching chill. A blaze sprang up again when the draughts were opened, but as she went on clearing the table her movements were furtive and constrained. It was the silence weighing upon her – the frozen silence of the bitter fields and sun-chilled sky – lurking outside as if alive, relentlessly in wait, mile-deep between her now and John. She listened to it, suddenly tense, motionless. The fire crackled and the clock ticked. Always it was there. "I'm a fool," she whispered, rattling the dishes in defiance, going back to the stove to put in another fire. "Warm and safe – I'm a fool. It's a good chance when he's away to paint. The day will go quickly. I won't have time to brood."

Since November now the paint had been waiting warmer weather. The frost in the walls on a day like this would crack and peel it as it dried, but she needed something to keep her hands occupied, something to stave off the gathering cold and loneliness. "First of all," she said aloud, opening the paint and mixing it with a little turpentine, "I must get the house warmer. Fill up the stove and open the oven door so that all the heat comes out. Wad something along the window-sills to keep out the draughts. Then I'll feel brighter. It's the cold that depresses."

She moved briskly, performing each little task with careful and exaggerated absorption, binding her thoughts to it, making it a screen between herself and the surrounding snow and silence. But when the stove was filled and the windows sealed it was more difficult again. Above the quiet, steady swishing of her brush against the bedroom door the clock began to tick. Suddenly her movements became precise, deliberate, her posture self-conscious, as if someone had entered the room and were watching her. It was the silence again, aggressive, hovering. The fire spat and crackled at it. Still it was there. "I'm a fool," she repeated. "All farmers' wives have to stay alone. I mustn't give in this way. I mustn't brood. A few hours now and they'll be here."

The sound of her voice reassured her. She went on: "I'll get them a good supper – and for coffee after cards bake some of the little cakes with raisins that he likes . . . Just three of us, so I'll watch, and let John play. It's better with four, but at least we can talk. That's all I need – someone to talk to. John never talks. He's stronger – doesn't need to. But he likes Steven – no matter what the neighbours say. Maybe he'll have him come again, and some other young people too. It's what we need, both of us, to help keep young ourselves . . . And then before we know it we'll be into March. It's cold still in March sometimes, but you never mind the same. At least you're beginning to think about spring."

She began to think about it now. Thoughts that outstripped her words, that left her alone again with herself and the ever-lurking silence. Eager and hopeful first, then clenched, rebellious, lonely.

Windows open, sun and thawing earth again, the urge of growing, living things. Then the days that began in the morning at half-past four and lasted till ten at night; the meals at which John gulped his food and scarcely spoke a word; the brute-tired stupid eyes he turned on her if ever she mentioned town or visiting.

For spring was drudgery again. John never hired a man to help him. He wanted a mortgage-free farm; then a new house and pretty clothes for her. Sometimes, because with the best of crops it was going to take so long to pay off anyway, she wondered whether they mightn't better let the mortgage wait a little. Before they were worn out, before their best years were gone. It was something of life she wanted, not just a house and furniture; something of John, not pretty clothes when she would be too old to wear them. But John of course couldn't understand. To him it seemed only right that she should have the clothes – only right that he, fit for nothing else, should slave away fifteen hours a day to give them to her. There was in his devotion a baffling, insurmountable humility that made him feel the need of sacrifice. And when his muscles ached, when his feet dragged stolidly with weariness, then it seemed that in some measure at least he was making amends for his big hulking body and simple mind. Year after year their lives went on in the same little groove. He drove his horses in the field; she milked the cows and hoed potatoes. By dint of his drudgery he saved a few months" wages, added a few dollars more each fall to his payments on the mortgage; but the only real difference that it all made was to deprive her of his companionship, to make him a little duller, older, uglier than he might otherwise have been. He never saw their lives objectively. To him it was not what he actually accomplished by means of the sacrifice that mattered, but the sacrifice itself, the gesture – something done for her sake.

And she, understanding, kept her silence. In such a gesture, however futile, there was a graciousness not to be shattered lightly. "John," she would begin sometimes, "you're doing too much. Get a man to help you – just for a month –" but smiling down at her he would answer simply, "I don't mind. Look at the hands on me. They're made for work." While in his voice there would be a stalwart ring to tell her that by her thoughtfulness she had made him only the more resolved to serve her, to prove his devotion and fidelity.

They were useless, such thoughts. She knew. It was his very devotion that made them useless, that forbade her to rebel. Yet over and over, sometimes hunched still before their bleakness, sometimes her brush making swift sharp strokes to pace the chafe and rancour that they brought, she persisted in them.

This now, the winter, was their slack season. She could sleep sometimes till eight, and John till seven. They could linger over their meals a little, read, play cards, go visiting the neighbours. It was the time to relax, to indulge and enjoy themselves; but instead, fretful and impatient, they kept on waiting for the spring. They were compelled now, not by labour, but by the spirit of labour. A spirit that pervaded their lives and brought with idleness a sense of guilt. Sometimes they did sleep late, sometimes they did play cards, but always uneasily, always reproached by the thought of more important things that might be done. When John got up at five to attend to the fire he wanted to stay up and go out to the stable. When he sat down to a meal he hurried his food and pushed his chair away again, from habit, from sheer work-instinct, even though it was only to put more wood in the stove, or go down cellar to cut up beets and turnips for the cows.

And anyway, sometimes she asked herself, why sit trying to talk with a man who never talked? Why talk when there was nothing to talk about but crops and cattle, the weather and the neighbours? The neighbours, too – why go visiting them when still it was the same – crops and cattle, the weather and the other neighbours? Why go to the dances in the schoolhouse to sit among the older women, one of them now, married seven years, or to waltz with the work-bent, tired old farmers to a squeaky fiddle tune? Once she had danced with Steven six or seven times in the evening, and they had talked about it for as many months. It was easier to stay at home. John never danced or enjoyed himself. He was always uncomfortable in his good suit and shoes. He didn't like shaving in the cold weather oftener than once or twice a week. It was easier to stay at home, to stand at the window staring out across the bitter fields, to count the days and look forward to another spring.

But now, alone with herself in the winter silence, she saw the spring for what it really was. This spring – next spring – all the springs and summers still to come. While they grew old, while their bodies warped, while their minds kept shrivelling dry and empty like their lives. "I mustn't," she said aloud again. "I married him – and he's a good man. I mustn't keep on this way. It will be noon before long, and then time to think about supper . . . Maybe he'll come early – and as soon as John is finished at the stable we can all play cards."

It was getting cold again, and she left her painting to put in more wood. But this time the warmth spread slowly. She pushed a mat up to the outside door, and went back to the window to pat down the woollen shirt that was wadded along the sill. Then she paced a few times round the room, then poked the fire and rattled the stove lids, then paced again. The fire crackled, the clock ticked. The silence now seemed more intense than ever, seemed to have reached a pitch where it faintly moaned. She began to pace on tiptoe, listening, her shoulders drawn together, not realizing for a while that it was the wind she heard, thin-strained and whimpering through the eaves.

Then she wheeled to the window, and with quick short breaths thawed the frost to see again. The glitter was gone. Across the drifts sped swift and snakelike little tongues of snow. She could not follow them, where they sprang from, or where they disappeared. It was as if all across the yard the snow were shivering awake – roused by the warnings of the wind to hold itself in readiness for the impending storm. The sky had become a sombre, whitish grey. It, too, as if in readiness, had shifted and lay close to earth. Before her as she watched a mane of powdery snow reared up breast-high against the darker background of the stable, tossed for a moment angrily, and then subsided again as if whipped down to obedience and restraint. But another followed, more reckless and impatient than the first. Another reeled and dashed itself against the window where she watched. Then ominously for a while there were only the angry little snakes of snow. The wind rose, creaking the troughs that were wired beneath the eaves. In the distance, sky and prairie now were merged into one another linelessly. All round her it was gathering; already in its press and whimpering there strummed a boding of eventual fury. Again she saw a mane of snow spring up, so dense and high this time that all the sheds and stables were obscured. Then others followed, whirling fiercely out of hand; and, when at last they cleared, the stables seemed in dimmer outline than before.

It was the snow beginning, long lancet shafts of it, straight from the north, borne almost level by the straining wind. "He'll be here soon," she whispered, "and coming home it will be in his back. He'll leave again right away. He saw the double wheel – he knows the kind of storm there'll be."

She went back to her painting. For a while it was easier, all her thoughts half-anxious ones of John in the blizzard, struggling his way across the hills; but petulantly again she soon began, "I knew we were going to have a storm – I told him so – but it doesn't matter what I say. Big stubborn fool – he goes his own way anyway. It doesn't matter what becomes of me. In a storm like this he'll never get home. He won't even try. And while he sits keeping his father company I can look after his stable for him, go ploughing through snowdrifts up to my knees – nearly frozen –"

Not that she meant or believed her words. It was just an effort to convince herself that she did have a grievance, to justify her rebellious thoughts, to prove John responsible for her unhappiness. She was young still, eager for excitement and distractions; and John's steadfastness rebuked her vanity, made her complaints seem weak and trivial. She went on, fretfully, "If he'd listen to me sometimes and not be so stubborn we wouldn't still be living in a house like this. Seven years in two rooms – seven years and never a new stick of furniture . . . There – as if another coat of paint could make it different anyway."

She cleaned her brush, filled up the stove again, and went back to the window. There was a void white moment that she thought must be frost formed on the window-pane; then, like a fitful shadow through the whirling snow, she recognized the stable roof. It was incredible. The sudden, maniac raging of the storm struck from her face all its pettishness. Her eyes glazed with fear a little; her lips blanched. "If he starts for home now," she whispered silently – "But he won't – he knows I'm safe – he knows Steven's coming. Across the hills he would never dare."

She turned to the stove, holding out her hands to the warmth. Around her now there seemed a constant sway and tremor, as if the air were vibrating with the shudderings of the walls. She stood quite still, listening. Sometimes the wind struck with sharp, savage blows. Sometimes it bore down in a sustained, minute-long blast, silent with effort and intensity; then with a foiled shriek of threat wheeled away to gather and assault again. Always the eave-troughs creaked and sawed. She stared towards the window again, then detecting the morbid trend of her thoughts, prepared fresh coffee and forced herself to drink a few mouthfuls. "He would never dare," she whispered again. "He wouldn't leave the old man anyway in such a storm. Safe in here – there's nothing for me to keep worrying about. It's after one already. I'll do my baking now, and then it will be time to get supper ready for Steven."

Soon, however, she began to doubt whether Steven would come. In such a storm even a mile was enough to make a man hesitate. Especially Steven, who was hardly the one to face a blizzard for the sake of someone else's chores. He had a stable of his own to look after anyway. It would be only natural for him to think that when the storm blew up John had turned again for home. Another man would have – would have put his wife first.

But she felt little dread or uneasiness at the prospect of spending the night alone. It was the first time she had been left like this on her own resources, and her reaction, now that she could face and appraise her situation calmly, was gradually to feel it a kind of adventure and responsibility. It stimulated her. Before nightfall she must go to the stable and feed everything. Wrap up in some of John's clothes – take a ball of string in her hand, one end tied to the door, so that no matter how blinding the storm she could at least find her way back to the house. She had heard of people having to do that. It appealed to her now because suddenly it made life dramatic. She had not felt the storm yet, only watched it for a minute through the window.

It took nearly an hour to find enough string, to choose the right socks and sweaters. Long before it was time to start out she tried on John's clothes, changing and rechanging, striding around the room to make sure there would be play enough for pitching hay and struggling over snowdrifts; then she took them off again, and for a while busied herself baking the little cakes with raisins that he liked.

Night came early. Just for a moment on the doorstep she shrank back, uncertain. The slow dimming of the light clutched her with an illogical sense of abandonment. It was like the covert withdrawal of an ally, leaving the alien miles unleashed and unrestrained. Watching the hurricane of writhing snow rage past the little house she forced herself, "They'll never stand the night unless I get them fed. It's nearly dark already, and I've work to last an hour."

Timidly, unwinding a little of the string, she crept out from the shelter of the doorway. A gust of wind spun her forward a few yards, then plunged her headlong against a drift that in the dense white whirl lay invisible across her path. For nearly a minute she huddled still, breathless and dazed. The snow was in her mouth and nostrils, inside her scarf and up her sleeves. As she tried to straighten a smothering scud flung itself against her face, cutting off her breath a second time. The wind struck from all sides, blustering and furious. It was as if the storm had discovered her, as if all its forces were concentrated upon her extinction. Seized with panic suddenly she threshed out a moment with her arms, then stumbled back and sprawled her length across the drift.

But this time she regained her feet quickly, roused by the whip and batter of the storm to retaliative anger. For a moment her impulse was to face the wind and strike back blow for blow; then, as suddenly as it had come, her frantic strength gave way to limpness and exhaustion. Suddenly, a comprehension so clear and terrifying that it struck all thoughts of the stable from her mind, she realized in such a storm her puniness. And the realization gave her new strength, stilled this time to a desperate persistence. Just for a moment the wind held her, numb and swaying in its vice; then slowly, buckled far forward, she groped her way again towards the house.

Inside, leaning against the door, she stood tense and still a while. It was almost dark now. The top of the stove glowed a deep, dull red. Heedless of the storm, self-absorbed and self-satisfied, the clock ticked on like a glib little idiot. "He shouldn't have gone," she whispered silently. "He saw the double wheel – he knew. He shouldn't have left me here alone."

For so fierce now, so insane and dominant did the blizzard seem, that she could not credit the safety of the house. The warmth and lull around her was not real yet, not to be relied upon. She was still at the mercy of the storm. Only her body pressing hard like this against the door was staving it off. She didn't dare move. She didn't dare ease the ache and strain. "He shouldn't have gone," she repeated, thinking of the stable again, reproached by her helplessness. "They'll freeze in their stalls – and I can't reach them. He'll say it's all my fault. He won't believe I tried."

Then Steven came. Quickly, startled to quietness and control, she let him in and lit the lamp. He stared at her a moment, then flinging off his cap crossed to where she stood by the table and seized her arms. "You're so white – what's wrong? Look at me –" It was like him in such little situations to be masterful. "You should have known better – for a while I thought I wasn't going to make it here myself –"

"I was afraid you wouldn't come – John left early; and there was the stable – "

But the storm had unnerved her, and suddenly at the assurance of his touch and voice the fear that had been gripping her gave way to an hysteria of relief. Scarcely aware of herself she seized his arm and sobbed against it. He remained still a moment unyielding, then slipped his other arm around her shoulder. It was comforting and she relaxed against it, hushed by a sudden sense of lull and safety. Her shoulders trembled with the easing of the strain, then fell limp and still. "You're shivering," – he drew her gently towards the stove. "It's all right – nothing to be afraid of. I'm going to see to the stable."

It was a quiet, sympathetic voice, yet with an undertone of insolence, a kind of mockery even, that made her draw away quickly and busy herself putting in a fire. With his lips drawn in a little smile he watched her till she looked at him again. The smile too was insolent, but at the same time companionable; Steven's smile, and therefore difficult to reprove. It lit up his lean, still-boyish face with a peculiar kind of arrogance: features and smile that were different from John's, from other men's – wilful and derisive, yet naïvely so – as if it were less the difference itself he was conscious of, than the long-accustomed privilege that thereby fell his due. He was erect, tall, square-shouldered. His hair was dark and trim, his lips curved soft and full. While John, she made the comparison swiftly, was thickset, heavy-jowled, and stooped. He always stood before her helpless, a kind of humility and wonderment in his attitude. And Steven now smiled on her appraisingly with the worldly-wise assurance of one for whom a woman holds neither mystery nor illusion.

"It was good of you to come, Steven," she responded, the words running into a sudden, empty laugh. "Such a storm to face – I suppose I should feel flattered."

For his presumption, his misunderstanding of what had been only a momentary weakness, instead of angering quickened her, roused from latency and long disuse all the instincts and resources of her femininity. She felt eager, challenged. Something was at hand that hitherto had always eluded her, even in the early days with John, something vital, beckoning, meaningful. She didn't understand, but she knew. The texture of the moment was satisfyingly dreamlike: an incredibility perceived as such, yet acquiesced in. She was John's wife – she knew – but also she knew that Steven standing here was different from John. There was no thought or motive, no understanding of herself as the knowledge persisted. Wary and poised round a sudden little core of blind excitement she evaded him. "But it's nearly dark – hadn't you better hurry if you're going to do the chores? Don't trouble – I can get them off myself –"

An hour later when he returned from the stable she was in another dress, hair rearranged, a little flush of colour in her face. Pouring warm water for him from the kettle into the basin she said evenly, "By the time you're washed supper will be ready. John said we weren't to wait for him."

He looked at her a moment, "You don't mean you're expecting John tonight? The way it's blowing –"

"Of course." As she spoke she could feel the colour deepening in her face. "We're going to play cards. He was the one that suggested it."

He went on washing, and then as they took their places at the table, resumed, "So John's coming. When are you expecting him?"

"He said it might be seven o'clock – or a little later." Conversation with Steven at other times had always been brisk and natural, but now all at once she found it strained. "He may have work to do for his father. That's what he said when he left. Why do you ask, Steven?"

"I was just wondering – it's a rough night."

"You don't know John. It would take more than a storm to stop him."

She glanced up again and he was smiling at her. The same insolence, the same little twist of mockery and appraisal. It made her flinch, and ask herself why she was pretending to expect John – why there should be this instinct of defence to force her. This time, instead of poise and excitement, it brought a reminder that she had changed her dress and rearranged her hair. It crushed in a sudden silence, through which she heard the whistling wind again, and the creaking saw of the eaves. Neither spoke now. There was something strange, almost frightening, about this Steven and his quiet, unrelenting smile; but strangest of all was the familiarity: the Steven she had never seen or encountered, and yet had always known, always expected, always waited for. It was less Steven himself that she felt than his inevitability. Just as she had felt the snow, the silence and the storm. She kept her eyes lowered, on the window past his shoulder, on the stove, but his smile now seemed to exist apart from him, to merge and hover with the silence. She clinked a cup – listened to the whistle of the storm – always it was there. He began to speak, but her mind missed the meaning of his words. Swiftly she was making comparisons again; his face so different to John's, so handsome and young and clean-shaven. Swiftly, helplessly, feeling the imperceptible and relentless ascendancy that thereby he was gaining over her, sensing sudden menace in this new, more vital life, even as she felt drawn towards it.

The lamp between them flickered as an onslaught of the storm sent shudderings through the room. She rose to build up the fire again and he followed her. For a long time they stood close to the stove, their arms almost touching. Once as the blizzard creaked the house she spun around sharply, fancying it was John at the door; but quietly he intercepted her. "Not tonight – you might as well make up your mind to it. Across the hills in a storm like this – it would be suicide to try."

Her lips trembled suddenly in an effort to answer, to parry the certainty in his voice, then set thin and bloodless. She was afraid now. Afraid of his face so different from John's – of his smile, of her own helplessness to rebuke it. Afraid of the storm, isolating her here alone with him. They tried to play cards, but she kept starting up at every creak and shiver of the walls. "It's too rough a night," he repeated. "Even for John. Just relax a few minutes – stop worrying and pay a little attention to me."

But in his tone there was a contradiction to his words. For it implied that she was not worrying – that her only concern was lest it really might be John at the door.

And the implication persisted. He filled up the stove for her, shuffled the cards – won – shuffled – still it was there. She tried to respond to his conversation, to think of the game, but helplessly into her cards instead she began to ask, Was he right? Was that why he smiled? Why he seemed to wait, expectant and assured?

The clock ticked, the fire crackled. Always it was there. Furtively for a moment she watched him as he deliberated over his hand. John, even in the days before they were married, had never looked like that. Only this morning she had asked him to shave. Because Steven was coming – because she had been afraid to see them side by side – because deep within herself she had known even then. The same knowledge, furtive and forbidden, that was flaunted now in Steven's smile. "You look cold," he said at last, dropping his cards and rising from the table. "We're not playing, anyway. Come over to the stove for a few minutes and get warm."

"But first I think we'll hang blankets over the door. When there's a blizzard like this we always do." It seemed that in sane, commonplace activity there might be release, a moment or two in which to recover herself. "John has nails to put them on. They keep out a little of the draught."

He stood on a chair for her, and hung the blankets that she carried from the bedroom. Then for a moment they stood silent, watching the blankets sway and tremble before the blade of wind that spurted around the jamb. "I forgot," she said at last, "that I painted the bedroom door. At the top there, see – I've smeared the blankets."

He glanced at her curiously, and went back to the stove. She followed him, trying to imagine the hills in such a storm, wondering whether John would come. "A man couldn't live in it," suddenly he answered her thoughts, lowering the oven door and drawing up their chairs one on each side of it. "He knows you're safe. It isn't likely that he'd leave his father, anyway."

"The wind will be in his back," she persisted. "The winter before we were married – all the blizzards that we had that year – and he never missed –"

"Blizzards like this one? Up in the hills he wouldn't be able to keep his direction for a hundred yards. Listen to it a minute and ask yourself."

His voice seemed softer, kindlier now. She met his smile a moment, its assured little twist of appraisal, then for a long time sat silent, tense, careful again to avoid his eyes.

Everything now seemed to depend on this. It was the same as a few hours ago when she braced the door against the storm. He was watching her, smiling. She dared not move, unclench her hands, or raise her eyes. The flames crackled, the clock ticked. The storm wrenched the walls as if to make them buckle in. So rigid and desperate were all her muscles set, withstanding, that the room around her seemed to swim and reel. So rigid and strained that for relief at last, despite herself, she raised her head and met his eyes again.

Intending that it should be for only an instant, just to breathe again, to ease the tension that had grown unbearable – but in his smile now, instead of the insolent appraisal that she feared, there seemed a kind of warmth and sympathy. An understanding that quickened and encouraged her – that made her wonder why but a moment ago she had been afraid. It was as if the storm had lulled, as if she had suddenly found calm and shelter.

Or perhaps, the thought seized her, perhaps instead of his smile it was she who had changed. She who, in the long, wind-creaked silence, had emerged from the increment of codes and loyalties to her real, unfettered self. She who now felt his air of appraisal as nothing more than an understanding of the unfulfilled woman that until this moment had lain within her brooding and unadmitted, reproved out of consciousness by the insistence of an outgrown, routine fidelity.

For there had always been Steven. She understood now. Seven years – almost as long as John – ever since the night they first danced together.

The lamp was burning dry, and through the dimming light, isolated in the fastness of silence and storm, they watched each other. Her face was white and struggling still. His was handsome, clean-shaven, young. Her eyes were fanatic, believing desperately, fixed upon him as if to exclude all else, as if to find justification. His were cool, bland, drooped a little with expectancy. The light kept dimming, gathering the shadows round them, hushed, conspiratorial. He was smiling still. Her hands again were clenched up white and hard.

"But he always came," she persisted. "The wildest, coldest nights –

even such a night as this. There was never a storm –"

"Never a storm like this one." There was a quietness in his smile now, a kind of simplicity almost, as if to reassure her. "You were out in it yourself for a few minutes. He'd have it for five miles, across the hills . . . I'd think twice myself, on such a night before risking even one."

Long after he was asleep she lay listening to the storm. As a check on the draught up the chimney they had left one of the stove lids partly off, and through the open bedroom door she could see the flickerings of flame and shadow on the kitchen wall. They leaped and sank fantastically. The longer she watched the more alive they seemed to be. There was one great shadow that struggled towards her threateningly, massive and black and engulfing all the room. Again and again it advanced, about to spring, but each time a little whip of light subdued it to its place among the others on the wall. Yet though it never reached her still she cowered, feeling that gathered there was all the frozen wilderness, its heart of terror and invincibility.

Then she dozed for a while, and the shadow was John. Interminably he advanced. The whips of light still flickered and coiled, but now suddenly they were the swift little snakes that this afternoon she had watched twist and shiver across the snow. And they too were advancing. They writhed and vanished and came again. She lay still, paralysed. He was over her now, so close that she could have touched him. Already it seemed that a deadly tightening hand was on her throat. She tried to scream but her lips were locked. Steven beside her slept on heedlessly.

Until suddenly as she lay staring up at him a gleam of light revealed his face. And in it was not a trace of threat or anger – only calm, and stonelike hopelessness.

That was like John. He began to withdraw, and frantically she tried to call him back. "It isn't true – not really true – listen, John –" but the words clung frozen to her lips. Already there was only the shriek of wind again, the sawing eaves, the leap and twist of shadow on the wall.

She sat up, startled now and awake. And so real had he seemed there, standing close to her, so vivid the sudden age and sorrow in his face, that at first she could not make herself understand she had only been dreaming. Against the conviction of his presence in the room it was necessary to insist over and over that he must still be with his father on the other side of the hills. Watching the shadows she had fallen asleep. It was only her mind, her imagination, distorted to a nightmare by the illogical and unadmitted dread of his return. But he wouldn't come. Steven was right. In such a storm he would never try. They were safe, alone. No one would ever know. It was only fear, morbid and irrational; only the sense of guilt that even her new-found and challenged womanhood could not entirely quell.

She knew now. She had not let herself understand or acknowledge it as guilt before, but gradually through the wind-torn silence of the night his face compelled her. The face that had watched her from the darkness with its stonelike sorrow – the face that was really John – John more than his features of mere flesh and bone could ever be.

She wept silently. The fitful gleam of light began to sink. On the ceiling and wall at last there was only a faint dull flickering glow. The little house shuddered and quailed, and a chill crept in again. Without wakening Steven she slipped out to build up the fire. It was burned to a few spent embers now, and the wood she put on seemed a long time catching light. The wind swirled through the blankets they had hung around the door, and then, hollow and moaning, roared up the chimney again, as if against its will drawn back to serve still longer with the onrush of the storm.

For a long time she crouched over the stove, listening. Earlier in the evening, with the lamp lit and the fire crackling, the house had seemed a stand against the wilderness, a refuge of feeble walls wherein persisted the elements of human meaning and survival. Now, in the cold, creaking darkness, it was strangely extinct, looted by the storm and abandoned again. She lifted the stove lid and fanned the embers till at last a swift little tongue of flame began to lick around the wood. Then she replaced the lid, extended her hands, and as if frozen in that attitude stood waiting.

It was not long now. After a few minutes she closed the draughts, and as the flames whirled back upon each other, beating against the top of the stove and sending out flickers of light again, a warmth surged up to relax her stiffened limbs. But shivering and numb it had been easier. The bodily well-being that the warmth induced gave play again to an ever more insistent mental suffering. She remembered the shadow that was John. She saw him bent towards her, then retreating, his features pale and overcast with unaccusing grief. She re-lived their seven years together and, in retrospect, found them to be years of worth and dignity. Until crushed by it all at last, seized by a sudden need to suffer and atone, she crossed to where the draught was bitter, and for a long time stood unflinching on the icy floor.

The storm was close here. Even through the blankets she could feel a sift of snow against her face. The eaves sawed, the walls creaked, and the wind was like a wolf in howling flight.

And yet, suddenly she asked herself, hadn't there been other storms, other blizzards? And through the worst of them hadn't he always reached her?

Clutched by the thought she stood rooted a minute. It was hard now to understand how she could have so deceived herself – how a moment of passion could have quieted within her not only conscience, but reason and discretion too. John always came. There could never be a storm to stop him. He was strong, inured to the cold. He had crossed the hills since his boyhood, knew every creekbed and gully. It was madness to go on like this – to wait. While there was still time she must waken Steven, and hurry him away.

But in the bedroom again, standing at Steven's side, she hesitated. In his detachment from it all, in his quiet, even breathing, there was such sanity, such realism. For him nothing had happened; nothing would. If she wakened him he would only laugh and tell her to listen to the storm. Already it was long past midnight; either John had lost his way or not set out at all. And she knew that in his devotion there was nothing foolhardy. He would never risk a storm beyond endurance, never permit himself a sacrifice likely to endanger her lot or future. They were both safe. No one would ever know. She must control herself – be sane like Steven.

For comfort she let her hand rest a while on Steven's shoulder. It would be easier were he awake now, with her, sharing her guilt; but gradually as she watched his handsome face in the glimmering light she came to understand that for him no guilt existed. Just as there had been no passion, no conflict. Nothing but the sane appraisal of their situation, nothing but the expectant little smile, and the arrogance of features that were different from John's. She winced deeply, remembering how she had fixed her eyes on those features, how she had tried to believe that so handsome and young, so different from John's, they must in themselves be her justification.

In the flickering light they were still young, still handsome. No longer her justification – she knew now – John was the man – but wistfully still, wondering sharply at their power and tyranny, she touched them a moment with her fingertips again.

She could not blame him. There had been no passion, no guilt; therefore there could be no responsibility. Looking down at him as he slept, half-smiling still, his lips relaxed in the conscienceless complacency of his achievement, she understood that thus he was revealed in his entirety – all there ever was or ever could be. John was the man. With him lay all the future. For tonight, slowly and contritely through the day and years to come, she would try to make amends.

Then she stole back to the kitchen, and without thought, impelled by overwhelming need again, returned to the door where the draught was bitter still. Gradually towards morning the storm began to spend itself. Its terror blast became a feeble, worn-out moan. The leap of light and shadow sank, and a chill crept in again. Always the eaves creaked, tortured with wordless prophecy. Heedless of it all the clock ticked on in idiot content.

They found him the next day, less than a mile from home. Drifting with the storm he had run against his own pasture fence and overcome had frozen there, erect still, both hands clasping fast the wire.

"He was south of here," they said wonderingly when she told them how he had come across the hills. "Straight south – you'd wonder how he could have missed the buildings. It was the wind last night, coming every way at once. He shouldn't have tried. There was a double wheel around the moon."

She looked past them a moment, then as if to herself said simply, "If you knew him, though – John would try."

It was later, when they had left her a while to be alone with him,

that she knelt and touched his hand. Her eyes dimmed, it was still
such a strong and patient hand; then, transfixed, they suddenly
grew wide and clear. On the palm, white even against its frozen
whiteness, was a little smear of paint.

Swamp Angel

ETHEL WILSON

Ten twenty fifty brown birds flew past the window and then a few stragglers, out of sight. A fringe of Mrs Vardoe's mind flew after them (what were they? – birds returning in migration, of course) and then was drawn back into the close fabric of her preoccupations. She looked out over the small green garden which would soon grow dark in evening. This garden led down a few steps to the wooden sidewalk; then there was the road, dusty in fine weather; next came the neighbours' houses across the road, not on a level with her but lower, as the hill declined, so that she was able to look over the roofs of these houses to Burrard Inlet far below, to the dark green promontory of Stanley Park, to the elegant curve of the Lions Gate Bridge which springs from the Park to the northern shore which is the base of the mountains; and to the mountains. The mountains seemed, in this light, to rear themselves straight up from the shores of Burrard Inlet until they formed an escarpment along the whole length of the northern sky. The escarpment looked solid at times, but certain lights disclosed slope behind slope, hill beyond hill, giving an impression of the mountains which was fluid, not solid.

Mrs Vardoe had become attached to, even absorbed into the sight from the front-room window of inlet and forest and mountains. She had come to love it, to dislike it, to hate it, and at seven-fifteen this evening she proposed to leave it and not to return. Everything was, she thought, in order.

Behind her unrevealing grey eyes of candour and peace she had arranged with herself that she would arrive at this very evening and at this place where, on Capitol Hill, she would stand waiting with everything ready. There had been time enough in which to prepare. She had endured humiliations and almost unbearable resentments and she had felt continual impatience at the slowness of time. Time, she knew, does irrevocably pass and would not fail her; rather she might in some unsuspected way fail time. Her look and habit had not betrayed her although she had lived more and more urgently through the last few weeks when an irrational fear had possessed her that she, or he, would become ill, would meet with an accident, that some car, some fall, some silly bodily ailment would, with the utmost indignity and indifference, interfere; but nothing had happened to interfere. The time was now half-past five. It was not likely that the unlikely – having so far held its hand – would happen within two hours, but, if it did, she was armed against revealing herself and she would build in time again, or again, like the bird who obstinately builds again its destroyed nest. So strong was the intention to depart.

She had been most vulnerable and desperate when, more than a year ago, she had taken a small box of fishing flies to the shop known by sportsmen up and down the Pacific coast.

"May I see Mr Thorpe or Mr Spencer?"

"There's no Mr Thorpe. I am Mr Spencer."

"Here are some flies, Mr Spencer."

He picked up each fly and scrutinized it. Turning it this way and that he looked for flaws in the perfection of the body, the hackle, the wings. There were no flaws. He looked up at the pleasant young woman with less interest than he felt in the flies. There were small and large flies, dun-coloured flies, and flies with a flash of iridescent green, scarlet, silver.

"Who made these flies?"

"I did."

"Who taught you?"

"My father."

"Where did he learn?"

"At Hardy's."

Mr Spencer now regarded the young woman with some respect. She was unpretentious. Her grey eyes, rimmed with dark lashes, were wide set and tranquil and her features were agreeably irregular. She was not beautiful; she was not plain. Yes, perhaps she was beautiful. She took no pains to be beautiful. The drag of her cheap cloth coat and skirt intimated large easy curves beneath.

"Would you like to sell your flies?"

"Yes, but I have no more feathers."

"We can arrange that. Have you a vice?"

"Yes, my father's vice."

"We will take all the flies you can make. Would you like to work here? We have a small room at the back with a good light."

"I would rather work at home."

"Where do you live?"

"Out Capitol Hill way."

"And you come from . . . ?"

"I have lived in Vancouver for some time."

"Oh. You were not born . . . ?"

"I was born in New Brunswick."

"Will you come to the desk? Sit down."

He took up a pen. "Your name?"

"Lloyd." The word Vardoe died in her mouth.

He looked at her large capable hands and saw the ring.

He smiled. "You won't mind me saying, Mrs Lloyd, but I always back large hands or even short stubby hands for tying flies."

She looked down at her hands as if she had not noticed them before. "Yes," she said, "they are large," and then she looked up and smiled for the first time, a level easy smile.

"Your telephone number?"

"There is no telephone."

"Oh, then your address?"

"I'd rather call on Mondays."

He pushed his lips out and looked at her over his glasses.

"Oh," she said, "I know. The feathers. Please trust me the first few times and then I'll pay for my own."

"No, no," he protested. "Oh no, you must do whatever suits you best."

"It suits me best," she said, colouring a very little, "to call on Monday mornings and bring the flies I've made, and see what you want done for the next week and take away the material."

"That suits me too. What do you know about rods?"

"Not as much as I know about flies. But I can splice a rod, and mend some kinds of trout rods."

"Would you want to take the rods home too?"

She hesitated. "No, if I do rods, I must do them here. But I would like to do all the work you can give me . . . if I can arrange to do it."

That was how it had begun and she had been so clever: never a bright feather blew across the room; vice, hooks, jungle cock and peacock feathers were all ingeniously hidden, and Edward had never known. The curtains, drawn widely, now framed her in the window as she looked out and over the scene which she had loved and which she hoped not to see again.

In the woodshed by the lane was her canvas bag packed to a weight that she could carry, and a haversack that she could carry on her shoulders. There was her fishing rod. That was all. How often she had lived these moments – which had now arrived and did not stay – of standing at the window; of turning; of walking through to the kitchen; of looking at the roast in the oven; of looking, once more, to see that her navy blue raincoat with the beret stuffed in the pocket hung by the kitchen door, easy to snatch on her way out into the dark; of picking up the bags and the rod inside the woodshed door as quickly as if it were broad daylight because she had learned their place so well; of seeing the light in the Chinaman's taxi a few yards up the lane; of quickly entering the taxi on seeing the slant face of the Chinese boy; and then the movement forward. She had carefully planned the moment, early enough to arrive, too late to be seen, recognized, followed, and found.

Now she advanced, as planned, along these same minutes that had so often in imagination solaced her. When, in the night, as had soon happened after their marriage, she lay humiliated and angry, she had forced her mind forward to this moment. The secret knowledge of her advancing plan was her only restoration and solace. Often, in the day and in the night, she had strengthened herself by going over, item by item, the contents of her haversack and bag. She would, in fancy, pack a sweater, her shoes . . . the little vice and some flies . . . How many scores of times, as her hands lay still, she had packed these little bags. Each article, as she in fancy packed or discarded it, comforted her and became her familiar companion and support. And last night she had lain for the last time beside her husband and he did not know that it was the last time.

She had once lived through three deaths, and – it really seemed – her own. Her country had regretted to inform her that her husband, Tom Lloyd, was killed in action; their child was stricken, and died; her father, who was her care, had died; and Maggie Lloyd, with no one to care for, had tried to save herself by an act of compassion and fatal stupidity. She had married Edward Vardoe.

Mrs Vardoe raised her left hand and saw that the time was now a quarter to six. She turned and went through to the kitchen. She took her large apron from the chair where she had thrown it, tied it so that it covered her, opened the oven door, took out the roast, put the roast and vegetables back into the oven, and began to make the gravy in the pan. These actions, which were familiar and almost mechanical, took on, tonight, the significance of movement forward, of time felt in the act of passing, of a moment being reached (time always passes, but it is in the nature of things that we seldom observe it flowing, flying, past). Each action was important in itself and, it seemed, had never been real before.

The front door opened and was shut with a bang and then there was silence. As she stirred the gravy she knew what Edward was doing. He was putting his topcoat on its hanger, turning his hat in his hand, regarding it, re-shaping it, and hanging them both up – the good topcoat and the respectable hat of Eddie Vardoe – E. Thompson Vardoe. It's a good thing I'm going *now*, she thought as she stirred the gravy. I'm always unfair, now, to Edward. I hate everything he does. He has only to hang up his hat and I despise him. Being near him is awful. I'm unfair to him in my heart always whatever he is doing, but tonight I shall be gone.

As he walked to the kitchen door she looked up from her stirring. He stood beside her, trim, prim, and jaunty in the little kitchen. He was in rare good humour, and excited.

"Well," he said, "I pretty near bought it. Guess I'll settle tomorrow. Four hundred cash and easy terms."

She straightened herself and looked mildly at him. What was he talking about? Was it possible that what she was about to do was not written plain on her brow?

"If you gointa show people reel estate," he said, "you gotta have the right car. Something conservative but snappy. Snappy but refined. See."

"Yes, oh yes," she agreed. She had forgotten about the car.

He took off his coat, revealing a tie on which athletes argued in yellow and red. That tie, and other ties, were new signs of Edward's advancement and self-confidence. What a tie, thought Mrs Vardoe, stirring mechanically. When Edward took off his coat a strong sweet-sour smell was released. He took a paper from an inner pocket, went to the hall and hung up his coat. He came back to the kitchen and held out the paper to her.

"Take a look at that, woodja," he said with a smile of triumph. " 'E. Thompson Vardoe' – sounds all right, doesn't it!"

"Just a minute till I put the roast on the table," she said, picking up the hot platter.

He turned and followed her into the room. "Well," he said, aggrieved, "I'd think you'd be interested in your husband starting in business for himself!"

She went with her usual light deliberation into the kitchen again, brought in the vegetables, gravy and plates, took off her apron and sat down at the table.

"Let me see it," she said.

Mr Vardoe, sitting down in his shirt-sleeves before the roast, passed her a piece of paper with a printed heading. She read aloud "Webber and Vardoe – Real Estate – Specialists in Homes – West End, Point Grey and Southern Slope – Octavius Webber, E. Thompson Vardoe."

"Oh, it does look nice! I hope that . . ."

"*Say*!" said Mr Vardoe in an affronted tone, holding the carving knife and fork above the roast of beef. "Whatever got into you, buying this size roast for two people! Must be all of six pounds! Is it six pounds?"

"No," said Mrs Vardoe, with her wide gentle look upon the roast, "but it's all of five pounds."

"And solid meat!" said Mr Vardoe, striking the roast with the carving knife. His voice rose shrill with anger. "You buying six-pound roasts when I gotta get a new car and get started in a new business! Bet it wasn't far off a dollar a pound!"

"No, it wasn't," admitted Mrs Vardoe. She gave a quick look down at her watch. The time was twenty minutes past six. It seemed to her that time stood still, or had died.

"It'll be nice cold," she said, without self-defence.

"Nice *cold*!" he echoed. "Who wants to eat cold meat that cost the earth for a week!"

If you only knew it, *you* will, thought Mrs Vardoe.

Edward Vardoe gave her one more glare. In annoyed silence he began to carve the roast.

As Mrs Vardoe put vegetables on to the two plates she dared to give another downward glance. Twenty-five minutes past six. The roast was delicious. When Edward Vardoe had shown enough displeasure and had satisfied himself that his wife had felt his displeasure he began eating and talking of his partner Octavius Webber, a man experienced – he said – in the real estate business.

"Octavius's smart all right," he said, with satisfaction and with his mouth full. "Anyone have to get up pretty early to fool Octavius. I guess we'll be a good team, me and O.W." He at last pushed his plate aside. He continued to talk.

Mrs Vardoe got up and took away the meat course and brought in a pudding. Her husband looked at her strangely. He took his time to speak.

"Well, say," he said at last, "you got your good tweed suit on!"

"Yes. I have," she said, looking down at it. The time was twenty minutes to seven. She had to control a trembling in her whole body.

"Cooking a dinner in your good suit!"

"I had my apron."

"Well, what you got it *on* for! You never sit down in your good suit like that before! Wearing that suit around the house!"

She could conceal – how well she could conceal – but she could not deceive and she did not need to deceive.

"I wanted to see Hilda and her mother. I went there and they weren't in. So I walked around for a bit and went back there and they weren't in, so I came home."

"*And* never took that suit off, and went and cooked dinner in that suit!" (That suit, that suit, that suit.)

Yes, but, her mind said, if I didn't wear my suit I hadn't room to pack it. That was all arranged. Long ago that was arranged, arranged by night, arranged by day. I won't tell him any lies. I can stay quiet a little longer whatever he says. She ate her pudding mechanically, hardly knowing what she did or what he said. It all depends on me, now, she thought. If I can manage the next quarter of an hour, I'm all right. What's a quarter of an hour? Oh God help me. Just this quarter of an hour. Time could kill a person, standing still like this. A person could die.

"Any more pudding?" she said.

He shook his head. Ill temper made his face peevish.

"Gimme the paper," he said sourly.

"It's here." She passed it to him and her heart beat like a clock.

He turned himself from the table and seemed to settle to the paper. A weight lifted a little from her. She took out the plates, cleared the table, and went into the kitchen, closing the door behind her. She ran the water into the dishpan. Water makes more noise than anything but crumpling paper, doesn't it, she thought. I must have things quiet, so that I can listen both ways. She piled the dishes, one by one, very quietly. It was seven o'clock. She began to wash the dishes, silently enough. The moments became intolerable. A person could die, waiting for a minute to come. She could not bear it. She dried her hands on her apron and threw off the apron. It dropped to the floor. She snatched the raincoat off the peg by the door. She slipped on the raincoat and went out into the dark. If it's not there, she thought in her fluttering mind, what shall I do? If he comes into the kitchen and I have to go back in, what'll I do? I'll have been to the garbage, that's what I'll do. The taxi might be two or three minutes early. It *might*. She walked quickly down the little back garden path to the lane where the woodshed stood. The air, cool and fresh and dark after the warm lighted kitchen, blew upon her face. She saw up the dark lane a car standing, its engine running. The absurd fear nearly choked her that this might not, after all, be her car. Some other car might be standing there. Ducking into the woodshed, she picked up the two bags and the thin fishing rod in its case, slung the haversack over her shoulder, and began to run. She reached the taxi and looked eagerly in. She saw the Chinese face. Before the driver could reach the door handle, she wrenched the door open, sprang in and closed it.

"Drive," she said, and leaned back in the car with a relief that made her for a moment dizzy.

Spring and Summer

ALICE FRENCH

Listen, listen my children.
And I'll tell you a story of where I was born and
where I grew up.
About your ancestors and the land we lived on.
About the animals and the birds.
So you can see.

The coming of spring was looked forward to by everyone. From 15 March until 15 June was the ratting season in the Mackenzie Delta. During this time of year the trappers made the bulk of their money. If the market was good and the muskrats were plentiful life would be just that much easier during the coming year. Some of the boys and girls left school at this time to help their parents. Most of their families lived in the bush beside good muskrat lakes and channels. Even in school we were given two traps each and taught how to use them. So, in the spring our walks included lakes which had muskrat houses. The pelts we sold to the Hudson's Bay store and the meat was roasted for us to eat at the school.

In the spring, the Mackenzie Delta was beautiful. It was a land of muskeg, rivers, lakes and trees. It had mountains and hills on some parts of it. *Amauligaqs* – the snowbirds – came first in the spring. It was a joy to see them after a season with few birds. It signalled that spring was on the way. The ptarmigan fed on the pussy-willow buds and we children gathered tender young willow leaves to eat. We stripped the bark off the branches and sucked them; the juice tasted sweet and good. During our spring walks we looked for sorrel, which tasted like rhubarb. The liquorice plant, which we called *mussu*, was gathered, washed, and eaten raw. Sometimes we dug in the ground and found edible roots, shaped like almonds, which we called truffles.

Soon the land was filled with birds. Mallards and other ducks paired off to nest by our rivers and lakes. Most of the geese flew on to the coast to mate and bring up their young on the tundra. By mid-July whistling swans, with one or two downy cygnets, would be paddling proudly up and down the channels of the Mackenzie, as if to say "Look what beautiful children we have." Terns, gulls and skuas went to Gull Island near Kiklavik Bay to have their young. If we went anywhere near the island we would be scolded and attacked. Eider ducks went farther north, but some of the loons stayed in the Mackenzie. If we happened to come across one of their nests we did not stop to examine the eggs. We would have been dive-bombed. Loons were very fierce in the protection of their young. Young ptarmigan were fluffy and round but very fast on their feet, especially when being chased by a kid who wanted them for pets. Cranes did their mating dance before pairing off. If we saw one feeding on the ground, we would sing to it and it would flap its wings and jump up and down, doing its dance for us.

Songbirds came in thousands. Horned larks woke us up with their glad morning songs. Robins were busy gathering twigs and bright pieces of cloth to build their nests. There was a weird bird, probably the common snipe, that flew up in the sky until we could see it no more. Then with its wings against its body, it plunged towards the ground, singing, until we thought it was going to crash. At the last minute it would unfold its wings to fly up and begin all over. We called it the rain bird, because after one of these displays it always rained. There were waders of all kinds; turnstones and plovers that fooled us with their broken-wing trick; many curlews and whimbrels and birds of prey: hawks, owls and falcons.

The countryside was soon bright with colour. Pink fireweed sprang up everywhere. The marshy ponds were covered with yellow marsh marigolds. Certain small streams, rippling through the bush, had watercress along their banks. We gathered this to eat instead of *mussu*, whose root was stringy and tough by the time the purple vetch flowers came out. In the settlement dandelions, yellow buttercups, and green grass covered the ground around the houses and sidewalks. They made a scene that had been dreary and dirty, pleasant to look upon. The green leaves against the white bark of the birch trees and the light green tips of the spruce branches made our after-school walks a pleasure.

On the tundra the delicate white pink of the blueberry blossom and the white flowers, edged with deep red, of the cranberry plant, told us where there would be an abundance of berries for later picking – unless a late frost came to kill them while in blossom. The bells of the arctic heather showed white among the green leaves of the Labrador tea and made a delightful scent when we walked on them. We watched for the star-shaped flower of the delicious akpik berry along the lakes and valleys of the tundra and noted where they grew the thickest; we would be back later in the summer to pick them.

Shortly after the river was clear of ice we watched for the paddle-wheeler, the *Distributor*, to arrive from the south ... It carried mostly fresh fruit and vegetables for the settlements along the river. The people were hungry for the taste of apples, oranges, potatoes, onions and eggs, after eating canned or dried ones all winter. Before leaving to go back up river the captain took the children from both schools for a boat-ride.

A few days later other boats arrived with food supplies and dry goods for the Hudson's Bay and for Mr H.E. Peffer who was a free trader, and owned a store and a hotel in Aklavik. Mail orders from catalogues, sent out to be filled the past winter, also arrived on these boats. When we opened the crates and parcels we found that a lot of things had been substituted. Notes were attached from Eaton's and Simpson's saying that the items enclosed were of better make or material and more expensive than the original order; if goods were not satisfactory they could be returned and the money would be cheerfully refunded. No one ever sent back an order – the article would have taken until the following year to return. No liquor was brought up on these boats so far as I knew except, perhaps, a few cases the white people had ordered.

*

That summer in the second week of July grandmother decided it was time to be on our way to the whaling camp. My father took the schooner over to the Hudson's Bay store to load up with provisions for the trip down to Whitefish Station on the coast of the Beaufort Sea. By the time he was back we had the tents down and all the household things packed and ready for loading. The women and children carried the bags and boxes on board while the men loaded the 45-gallon drums which would be used for storing the whale blubber and dried meat.

Then came the hardest job. Between all the hunters in our family there were about forty dogs that had to be loaded on board. I loathed this task, mainly because I was scared to death of the dogs and they sensed this.

It was a beautiful evening as we pushed off and headed down the Mackenzie River bound for the coast. We turned off into one of the many channels; the water was clear and calm, like a mirror reflecting trees, banks and sky. Clumps of reddish-pink fireweed and yellow buttercups were everywhere and we could smell the faint scent of wild roses and the strong earthy smell of the forest. As I sat on deck that evening I felt content and happy. Later I went down to bed and fell asleep listening to the sounds of the schooner swishing through the water.

The next morning we were underway again. As we got closer to the coast the landscape started to change. The trees got fewer and smaller. Soon there were no trees, just gently rolling hills, gravel beaches, and clear blue water. The muddy waters of the Mackenzie River were left behind and we sailed along on the clear, clean-smelling sea.

Our destination, Whitefish Station, was about twenty miles from Tuktoyaktuk on the Beaufort Sea. For many years my people had gone there every summer for whaling. For me, the whaling camp had only happy memories. There was not a tree to hamper the vision of sea and sky and land. On a clear day we could see the mirage of Tuktoyaktuk hanging upside down in the sky and Kiklavik Bay, ten miles across the ocean.

While we were living on the coast we depended on the sea for our food and we had to be very careful not to anger the sea spirit. This meant that we could not work on the skins of land animals. There was rivalry between the sea and land spirits in providing man with his livelihood. Should we be so foolish as to forget this rule, the sea spirit would cause storms to keep us from going out to hunt on the sea. She might also lead all the sea creatures away in her jealousy.

Our whaling trip included all my grandfather's family. There were my uncles Michael, Harry, Colin, and Donald, and my aunts Olga, Agnes, and Mary. My grandma's married sister and husband were with us, and then there was our own family of six. In all we had five tents. The whaling camp, as a whole, was made up of some thirty to forty families. A freshwater creek flowed into the sea and made a good harbour for our boats.

Once we had settled in, my grandfather went up the hills with his binoculars, and soon sighted some whales. The men launched the boats and headed out to sea. They could be gone a few hours, or all night, so we supplied the boat with enough food to last for two days. When a boat returned we looked at the mast to see how many banners were flying. Our boat had two on the mast when it came in. This meant that they had two whales. Everyone rushed to the beach to help pull the white whales to shore. The children, with their jack-knives and small ulus, cut bits of muktuk off the tail flipper and ate it raw. Then the women began to work and within an hour the whale was just a skeleton. The meat was sliced into big slabs and hung up on the racks to dry. The blubber was stripped off the hide, sliced into narrow strips and stored in the 45-gallon drums we brought with us. The first layer of the hide was made into muktuk. It was cut into nine-by-nine-inch squares, hung on racks in bunches of ten and dried for two to three days. Then it was cooked and put into the same barrel as the blubber. This preserved it for eating through the winter months. The middle layer of the hide, called ganek, was stretched, dried, and used for shoe leather.

Grandfather was kept busy making ulus and sharpening them. My grandmother's job was to teach us the art of cutting up the whale and making use of every bit of it. She taught us how to make containers from the stomach, but first we had to practise separating the layers of skin on the throat. Until we could do this without putting a hole in the skin, we were not allowed to start the more serious task of container making. There were three layers to the stomach and it took two hours to take them apart. Only the middle layer was used. This was blown up and dried for use as a container for whale oil, dried meat, dried fish and bits of muktuk for the winter. The containers were also used for storing blueberries and cranberries and for floats to mark the position of a harpooned whale.

At the whaling camp the girls learned to make waterproof boots. The top part was made of canvas or of seal skin; the sole of the boot was made from whale skin, crimped with the teeth. I was not good at this, much to my grandmother's dismay. As a result my value as a wife went down.

By September most of us were back in school. I was glad to see some of my old friends back again – Betty, Peanuts and Connie among them. Some of the older girls had left school for good and there were a few new faces. We had our routine coal-oiling of the hair, our school uniforms were issued, and our personal clothing and identities were put away for another term. We became just the Anglican School kids once more.

Chronicle of Anse Saint-Roch

JACQUES FERRON
Translated by Betty Bednarski

I

Between the Madeleine lighthouse and the harbour of Mont-Louis an unmistakable line separates land and sea. Because of the height of the cliff the only access to shore is through one of four gullies, three of them visible from the water, one quite hidden from view. They are, travelling from east to west, Manche d'Épée, Gros-Morne, Anse-Pleureuse. They cut deeply into the cliff, but the coves they feed are small and exposed to wind and weather. "From Madeleine to Mont-Louis, pay no heed to what you see and sail right on," the old-timers used to say. The fourth gully, situated between Gros-Morne and Anse-Pleureuse, is not easily detected. Narrow and winding, it runs at a sharp angle into a deep and sheltered bay. It was christened the Valley of Mercy. "Don't depend on it," the sailors would say. "When you look for it you never find it, and you're sure to find it when you don't." As a result of this reputation, and also because of the fact that the larger sailing vessels could only enter it at high tide, its discreet harbour was hardly used. It was forgotten. And though today you might hear talk of a Valley of Mercy, no one would be able to tell you where it was. It has become a legend now.

The sailor judges the coast from a distance, aware only of the rise and fall of the land. The fisherman, who sails close to it, concentrates on the shoreline and ignores all that lies beyond. Accordingly, each has his own terms to describe what he sees. Mont-Louis, Gros-Morne bear the mark of the sailor, Manche d'Epée and Anse-Pleureuse are a fisherman's names. When the Valley of Mercy was rediscovered the place was christened Anse Saint-Roch, because the fishermen who spent their summers there came down from Saint-Roch-des-Aulnaies.

In November 1840 a typhus epidemic brought over on an emigrant ship, the *Merino*, swept through the parishes of the Lower St Lawrence. The Abbé Toupin, the young and conscientious curate of l'Islet, was not in the least surprised, for he had long anticipated this kind of vengeance from Heaven. The epidemic lasted well into February. He had plenty of time to explain it. His preaching gained him immense popularity. People came from neighbouring parishes to hear him. However, as time went on, the Abbé Toupin's sermons grew gradually more sombre. One Sunday he rose in his pulpit, a strange expression on his face. "Dearly beloved brethren," he cried, "the end of the world is at hand!" And he fell down dead. The epidemic died out soon afterwards. But its effects were to be felt for a long time. The following spring most of the boats stayed drawn up on the shore. Fishing had lost its appeal. The spirit of adventure had worked itself out at home. From Saint-Roch, only Thomette Gingras and Jules Campion went down to the Gulf.

II

After *brecquefeste* the Reverend William Andicotte asked his wife what she felt about Canada. Intrigued, she looked down at the table, but there was nothing there to explain the question.

"William, have you had enough to eat?"

The clergyman pushed his plate aside. He was serious. He expected a reply. Canada, Canada . . . Well, really, she hadn't the slightest idea.

"God be praised!" he cried. "Then you have nothing against my project?"

"Your project, William?"

"My mission, to be precise. I believe, dear, that Canada has need of us."

Reverend Andicotte was vicar of Liverpool Cathedral. A mournful looking man with red hair, he could, if occasion demanded, leave off his mournful mien and laugh. Though thin, he had the appetite of a band of fat friars, and while he preached asceticism, he hardly practised it. He was a man of contrasts, unintentionally disconcerting, an eccentric and quite forbidding in his way, yet a good minister for all that, and an astute theologian. The Lord Bishop had named him his successor.

His wife loved him. He loved her in return, as much and even more. For this her love grew stronger still, and time, thanks to this steady increase, had brought them both together. As they never had been very far apart, they were now extremely close indeed. This did not prevent them from having separate worlds. He lived for his church, she for her home. They had three daughters. The eldest resembled her father, without quite managing to be ugly. The others were like their mother. All three were accomplished young ladies.

"But what about the episcopate, William?"

Reverend Andicotte had been waiting for this episcopate for ten years. The Lord Bishop had promised it to him. When the old man died it would go to him. Only for ten years now it had not been the Lord Bishop's pleasure to die. In fact he was looking fitter every year and, if things went on this way, he would soon be celebrating his centenary.

"Fie on the episcopate!"

"Let's wait a little longer."

"The old boy will bury us. No, believe me, dear, it's best we go to Canada."

She believed him, just as she had always done. Besides she was still young enough to find the fervour of mission life more appealing than episcopal decorum. It was with a deep thrill of emotion, wholesome and utterly commendable, albeit unrecognized by the Church of England, that she gave him her consent. She had once been as ignorant of marriage as she now was of Canada, and marriage had not disappointed her.

"Shall I wash the dishes?" she inquired.

"No, no. Just break them, dear."

She did not dare. After twenty years of frugal living some actions were unthinkable. In the end she washed them. It was a bad omen.

III

One month after the fateful *brecquefeste*, the minister, his wife and their three daughters boarded the *Merino*. The day before, on hearing of their departure, the Lord Bishop had died of rage. They were still laughing about it. Seagulls darted above the girls' heads with shrill cries. The Reverend himself showed more restraint. He was escorted by an old and taciturn gull, with neck drawn in and wings starched stiff, belching from time to time just to prove it had a voice. The mother followed behind, slightly dazed by all these birds.

The captain was shaving. He heard the commotion. "What's all that?" He was told it had to do with some clergyman. He rushed out of his cabin and stood in their path, one cheek pink, the other black, his razor in his hand. Against the pink, the black stood out, and the razor became a scimitar. The seagulls fell silent. The old gull, hearing the laughter fade, thought he had gone deaf. Holding back the sound he would no longer hear, he hung there, motionless, above the silence.

"Who are you?" the Reverend asked the apparition.

"And who are *you*?"

"I am the Reverend Andicotte."

"And I am the captain of this ship."

The two men looked each other up and down, then, wheeling suddenly about, the captain disappeared again inside his cabin. Followed closely by his females, the clergyman carried on to his.

"What did you think of him, William?"

"Dear," he replied, "we'll meet with worse than that in Canada."

The *Merino*'s captain was not a church-going man. He had a strong dislike for clergymen, believing that they never laughed. And now it seemed they did. His curiosity was piqued. When he had finished shaving, he went to the Reverend's cabin. His appearance was much improved. They listened to him. He explained himself, and everyone was happy.

"But what were you laughing about?" he asked.

"About the Lord Bishop dying," explained Mary, the youngest.

The captain slapped his thighs. From now on, he decided, he would be an Anglican.

IV

The *Merino* was a former slave ship. Once the emigrants had boarded, the anchor was weighed. The emigrants forgot their woes and set their sights on the promised land. They left behind them a trail of human wreckage, of torn bellies, petrified children, demented souls and severed hands. The sails were hoisted. They were white. The ship left Liverpool, a black hulk borne on by hope.

"I'm the one who gives orders around here," the captain grumbled.

Her Majesty's regulations prevented him, at least while in England, from taking on more than two hundred passengers. Gracious Majesty, perhaps, but stupid regulations; he had already taken two thousand negroes across.

"We might as well sail with no cargo at all, just to amuse the crew."

They set sail for Hamburg. There, another three hundred emigrants embarked. The captain's mood improved: with any less than five hundred passengers on a vessel built to carry a hundred, he would have felt lonely.

"I like having souls, lots of souls, in my charge," he confided to the minister.

The minister praised his zeal, although the overcrowding it occasioned did seem to him decidedly un-Anglican. He did not wish to complain, however. It is advisable not to press a convert too hard. "Besides," he thought, "we'll meet with worse than this in Canada."

v

Jules Campion and Thomette Gingras sailed out at the beginning of May, and two weeks later they reached Mont-Louis. The next day dawned on a sea of infinite calm. It was no good hoisting the sail: it takes more than a piece of cloth at the end of a mast to get a boat on its way. The two fishermen waited for high tide before moving out of the bay, then, when they were in open water, they shipped the oars and let the ebb-tide carry them east. Below Anse-Pleureuse they came closer to shore. A few huge icicles still hung from the cliff, a sure sign that they were too early to fish for cod. They were in no hurry to get there. They got there just the same. A long bright streak, like a shadow cast by the jutting cape above, stretched before them out to sea. Here and there the swirling waters warned of submerged rocks. The tide, though ebbing, was still high. They moved in among the reefs. The hull of the boat scraped a flat rock. Campion stood at the bow and pushed with an oar. The rocks dropped suddenly out of sight beneath them, and they were in the harbour. The valley came into view. Then a single detail caught their attention: from a cabin near the shore, a pale whiff of bluish smoke rose up and disappeared without a trace into the still air.

"Christ!" shouted Thomette Gingras. "They're burning our store of hardwood!"

VI

The joy of departure lasted only as long as the departure. As soon as land was out of sight they began to be sick.

"Bah!" said the captain. "No one dies of seasickness!"

On the fifteenth day of the crossing four emigrants died. They were Poles. The captain shrugged his shoulders: they had paid their passage.

"They're not negroes. They can die when they like. After all, they're free men, aren't they?"

Besides, they had no doubt died of some Polish malady that would not affect British subjects.

VII

In her comfortable cabin on the upper deck, Mrs Andicotte was overcome by a malaise that seemed to rise up from the hold. If she ventured out, the reeling sky descended on her with harsh, discordant cries, and she was obliged to go back inside and lie down. Elizabeth and Mary stayed with her. She wept for their youth. Jane, the eldest, accompanied her father. She put the word of God before all else and paid little heed to proprieties.

VIII

Typhus is better than the plague. It brings with it a gentle resignation. Violent shivers, with scarlet spots, grip the patient. His tongue is paralysed. He can no longer articulate his pain, but sings it, softly, sadly, without resisting. He can be thrown overboard before he is dead.

IX

Jane learned one day that Tom, the captain's negro slave, was dying in the hold. She went down to talk to him of God and fell into the hands of four sailors, who left her, bruised and streaked with tears and grime, alone with the negro. He crept over to her and, with a trembling hand, wiped her face. Then Jane, observing his charity, was touched. The captain found them together.

X

The spotted shivers took hold of the minister's wife. The *Merino* had been tacking back and forth in the Gulf for a week. She died off Gros-Morne. Her body was brought out on to the deck. Above it Tom the negro hung from a yardarm. The captain placed a lifeboat at the disposal of the bereaved family, and the *Merino* sailed on without them to Quebec.

XI

At the sight of the smoke Thomette Gingras was seized with great indignation. He threw himself down inside the boat, rummaged about in the gear, reappeared with a loaded shot-gun and shouted to his mate: "Bring 'er in, Jules!"

Jules worked the oars and the boat ran up on the beach. Gingras jumped ashore. Campion got up to follow him. A girl came out of the cabin, young, red-headed, well-built, but very scantily clad. Campion froze in the bow like a figurehead. The girl, just as taken aback as he was, stared, her mouth agape, forgetting to do up her bodice. This oversight by no means worsened things. Campion caught up with his mate.

"Don't shoot," he said. "She looks pretty tame to me."

"What'll we do?" asked Gingras, whose gun was getting him excited.

"Go take a closer look," suggested Campion.

They made as if to step forward. But at that very moment two more girls suddenly rushed out of the cabin, leaving them completely hamstrung.

Gingras, now mightily impressed, shook his gun. "Christ! I'll shoot! I'll shoot!" he yelled, so as to keep himself from shooting. Campion did his best to calm him down.

"Easy now, Thomette! Easy now!"

Just then the girls, who were clustered in front of the door, parted, and a huge figure of a man, dressed all in black, with a shock of red hair, stepped out, a Bible in his hand.

"Christ! What's that?" The figure advanced. It was coming straight for them. Gingras fired. The man opened his mouth, as if he had swallowed the bullet, then pitched forward and fell to the ground, his nose buried in his big book.

XII

At Saint-Roch-des-Aulnaies autumn came and went. The village had waited in vain for the two fishermen. They were presumed drowned. Two years later a boat from Cap Saint-Ignace brought back news that they were still alive, healthy in body but in peril of their souls, consorting with three she-devils. The following spring fishermen in great numbers sailed out from the Lower St Lawrence to fish the Gaspé cod. On their return they all confirmed the news. Gingras and Campion had settled in Anse Saint-Roch, each with the girl of his choice and the children born to them out of wedlock, happy, healthy, and perfectly disposed, should the opportunity arise, to take the holy vows of matrimony, and not, by any means, in peril of their souls. Their women were two magnificent creatures, with skin as white as milk and flame-red hair, distinguished ladies, who spoke English like fine society folk. As for the devilry, it was all the work of the eldest sister, a strange, thin girl, red-haired, but without the milk, who spent her time reading from a big black book, while around her hung the black child she had had by Satan before the fishermen had come.

XIII

A single bird a sea-lit day
One lone gull wheeling low
It spins and dives to skim the spray
What you are I do not know.

Yet surely it is a sign to me
This ocean rose this stemless bloom
Showering its petals over the sea
And your love makes my senses swoon.

A shimmering veil this dizzy flight
As tenderness reveals its fate
And a wing-tip traces in the light
Your own emerging shape.

You rise new-born from the water's motion
Wrapped in a mantle of silent wings
Bearing the mark of the ocean
And your name my heart now sings.

Let the lone bird still spin and turn
While God trembles far above
I glimpse your body's nascent form
And know you, Goddess of Love.

XIV

Man is a wanderer. Woman holds him back. A land without a
woman, fit only for passing through, a country uninhabited because
it lacked a place to plant the stake the restless animal is tethered to.
Such, for many years, was the north coast of the Gaspé. Fishermen
from Montmagny, from Cap Saint-Ignace and l'Islet went down
there every spring, but they returned home at the end of the season.
No one ever wintered there. The adventure of Gingras and Campion
marked the end of an era. The French Canadian woman who
triumphed over the squaw, her rival, in whose arms lay a whole new
continent for the taking, was not the kind to give up her men. She
would let them go as long as she could be sure of their return;
otherwise she would go with them. And this was what the women
of the Lower St Lawrence did. Since the Gaspé was no longer safe,
they said farewell to the older parishes, to their serene and Catholic
countryside. They came down with their men, not for one summer,
not to live out some dream of late afternoons beside the sea, but,
bundled up to the neck, prepared for all seasons, to give life to the

country. Before long, from Méchins to Rivière-aux-Renards, every cove was settled.

XV

Under the cliff, facing out to sea, your house is not large. Your man is brave, but he is not the master. Giants hover over you at night. At dawn the wind cuts down in all its force from the cliff-tops. It passes over your roof like a thousand shrieking birds. You shiver, even in normal times, when you have nothing to fear. But when a child stirs in your womb, you are filled with dread. Why did you leave the old country, where man is master, where the houses are large and the lands small? Why did you follow the fisherman's call to this wild, forsaken bay?

XVI

Jane came to a stop on the beach. She hesitated, her own question taken up for a moment in the harsh cries of the gulls and the unsteady motion of the air. Then she recovered. She had caught sight of her son, playing with shells, surrounded by a flock of ragged and familiar crows. She had arrived here in great distress; then a child had been born and with its angry cry had reassured the whole world.

When the little black boy saw his mother, he left the shells and crows. She took him in her arms and rocked him. She was tired. She would have liked him to go to sleep, but his laughing eyes never left her. Soon afterward his uncles' boat came in. The men threw their catch up on to the shore, then climbed out themselves, happy as children. Jules Campion picked up a stone and threw it. To his surprise it hit a crow. The bird stayed where it was, its wing outstretched, its neck drawn in, its beak half open.

Jane had cried out in an attempt to stop Jules. She jumped up now, but it was too late. Misfortune had already struck. She took the bird in her hands. It stared at her fixedly. She tried to say she was sorry, but she knew that she would never be forgiven. So she let the bird go, and it hobbled off, dragging its broken wing.

Jules and Thomette laughed at her distress. Two days later the little black boy cut his foot on a shell. The cut festered, the woolly head was soaked with sweat. All night the fever raged, and at dawn the shrieking birds swept down from the cliffs to carry off his soul.

Several weeks passed and Jane did not recover from this final blow. One morning as the sun came up, she was sitting on a log, holding in her lap the huge Bible she no longer read, when she saw the wounded crow. She got up. The bird ran off toward the path that leads to Anse-Pleureuse. She followed it. Every now and then she lost sight of it, but whenever she stopped it would reappear. The path is steep; it veers up over the mountain to avoid the jutting capes. Jane was soon exhausted; her knees gave out. She had come to a burnt clearing that stretched across the path. She looked around her and saw the entire crow nation assembled there to judge her.

XVII

The Abbé Ferland, a professor at the college of Sainte-Anne-de-la-Pocatière, a giant man with a heart of gold, spent that summer ranging up and down the north shore of the Gaspé, baptizing, confessing, marrying, bringing with him the peace of God. At Madeleine, with a single stroke of an axe, he silenced the Brawler who had been terrorizing the village. When he left Anse Saint-Roch, Jules Campion and Thomette Gingras had each one taken an English girl, with skin as white as milk and flaming hair, to be his lawful wedded wife. They were the happiest men alive. And they had many more children. As for Jane Andicotte, the Abbé found her half-dead on the footpath to Anse-Pleureuse. He took her back with him. She found her final rest in the convent of the Ursulines in Quebec.

This chronicle records facts that may appear unseemly, but life itself is not always seemly. What counts is that in the end events all fall into place, and around the wild, forsaken bay, little by little, the gentle customs of the old country triumph over pagan fear, softening the cries of the birds that pass in the gusts of wind that sweep down off the land.

The Lake

JOE ROSENBLATT

A powerful wind whips over Eagle Lake causing chops of water to lick through bays and inlets. The moaning and writhing along the shore, an aquatic dirge. Fed by a chain of neighbouring lakes and rivers, the waters of Eagle Lake are chilling with eerie currents at different depths, so that even in July it seems some wild joker is dropping ice cubes into the drink. The black water connotes a sunless freezer; only the hardiest of fish survive.

At mid-lake the water is deeper, darker and colder, the light lost with each layer of icy water. It's as if a glimmer from a small pen-light had forced its way through an inkwell. The depth at the centre strikes the imagination; you begin to think you are privileged to be at the point where several ounces of lead and fishing line keep falling until you yawn or think the line has struck bottom, but then there is a sudden jerk and the line continues to fall. Everybody loves to brag about their favourite lake, and as it happens, it is the deepest lake on the planet and usually a northern lake, a forlorn lake, ignored.

At the dark centre, I kept hoping my fishing line would disappear into another dimension, an aquatic twilight zone where one meets souls of the departed. That notion tickled the fancy of a fourteen-year-old: the lake of death; and maybe some hand would surface with a mighty sword . . . or at very least, a prehistoric monster, half fish and part beaver, would surface to see who the violators of the sacred silence could be. And were there swimmers foolish enough to go skinny-dipping in the frigid soup? I like to think I was the first person who saw a giant squid glide past a canoe in that lake. Perhaps sunlight played against the surface of the water, distorting anything that passed my view, but I had seen the *thing* and I didn't press the point, fearing ridicule. I didn't mention garfish or a creature with an elongated serrated narrow mouth lurking in the coldest depths; it wasn't a good idea to float about on the darkest water.

An aquatic mood, as opposed to a human one, a minnow or a pod of minnows, are cells skittering like thoughts below the lips on the body of water. I thought of minnows as flecks of thought pursued by heavier thoughts in a chain of cannibalistic renewal: the smaller diminish, the larger fatten. The losers, those slow dim-witted life forms – minnows – are soon devoured, and others who are sick, too weak, or who can't adapt to a more rigid existence, vanish, food stock to larger fish thoughts. The result of this purge – not a molecule of fat wasted. No fat floats around the heart of the lake, and sometimes if one listens to a dreadful silence, you are conscious of the pulsating beat as the canoe is swept to one side or the other.

I believe poetry is often revealed in the evening, at midnight on a day in July. I am staring at the expensive crystal-ware in the sky, and see bits and pieces of silver fall toward the lake; fireflies sizzle and dissolve. It's dry ice, splinters and shards of frozen carbon dioxide at absolute 'zero ... falling into black water, devoured ... a soul becomes gas ... I see the lake as a body in deep sleep; the bed in which that body turns is a basin and denotes the outline of a bowl composed of volcanic matter, igneous buckshot from the explosion at birth ... a basaltic bowl filled with bone-chilling tears and restless fish population, or impulsive thoughts. Collectively, they form a conduit, or psychic telephone line to the other world above the surface of the lake, or the dream outside the dream where somebody answers all unrecorded messages. My thoughts fall into the water and if I concentrate on just one pore on the surface, somebody or something will answer. A silence forms a skin over the lake, not a ripple or breeze present. The surface is glassy. The lake is pretending to be dead but I don't trust the lake. The lake can think, it absorbs thoughts because it stores energy from sunlight, from fish life, motion in the currents, from thought. The lake is breathing, filaments of thought move through its entire system, and then that brain explodes. The water heaves, picking up momentum, inhaling, exhaling ...

The light dims in the sky and the lake appears dark and brooding before a summer storm and that mood moves like a viscous substance filling up the eyeball of its own sadness; and then the sky allows a sheath of light to touch the water and sunlight ripens, not at the centre of the lake, but closer into the shore before the water darkens and you are aware that the light has gone into the *drop*, and from the drop the whole widens and falls further into some psychic abyss where fingers of currents drag the luminescence down and devour it. Near the shoreline, the water is transparent, not a residue of impurity there, no foreign matter, and an illusion takes hold. The swimmer feels that he or she is above the purest substance on the planet, resting on a liquid eyeball and staring directly through to the pebbles at the bottom. You could stare forty or fifty feet down and pretend you are resting on a magnifying glass. You can see every pore, every detail, a sunbeam of fish darting behind a rock form-ation. The creature dissolves inside a private condominium. A few bits and pieces of gravel go up in its wake and then fall. There is so much clarity here you begin to feel that any light ray would instantly cauterize the slightest contamination. A few minuscule strands of algae fall away, burnt by a light beam . . . or has a goldfish nibbled at it? A dark sliver flees across the floor and I wonder how that sliver of intelligence can flee from joy.

The sun is warming my body. I do a dead man's float face down, hands in front, feet straight as a log . . . and soon my skin begins to itch from the heat of the sun. I dive as deep as I can, pushing a fluttering sunfish out of my way, but dive as I may, I still can't match the magnificent penetration of a sunfish jabbing through the water, having its fun, or sex, with the elements. A cold current catches the roof of my spine and I strike up to the surface with the cold trailing me. I'm stabbed by an invisible finger of ice. No wonder minnows enjoy this form of coitus with mother water. I watch them thrive around the current. It revitalizes them. Born again minnows. I realize how they feel when they are sent into exile, into the holding tanks of Uncle Nathan's fish emporium. Fresh Fish. They craved and worshipped that cold current, one of many deities in the polter-geist establishment. How painfully lonely they must have felt in Nathan's limbo, his fish tanks, and what a poor substitute that cold water proved . . . that man-made current . . . not enough vigour to wash away the staleness of their spiritual decay. And soon they'd be united with a stronger current in a darker world. But in the midst of my dark forebodings I have this sensation: either I or the lake is a bulbous dream, a see-through dream, and both of us are trying to empty ourselves of all thought. The lake forces out its minnows, I expel my thoughts. Boo, I cry, blowing bubbles at golden hordes. Boo, they reply, before they evaporate into the cold deep ink.

Blood Ties

DAVID ADAMS RICHARDS

February 1968

In the evening the sky was slate, coming down to touch the earth, the snow in the fields. He sat in front of the window, watching nothingness, with the chair tilted on two legs and his feet against the small paint-chipped ledge, with his cigarettes and whisky beside him – watching nothingness. She had gone out again – Irene's probably, with Ronnie; "And I won't be home tonight," she said. "Fuck ya," he said.

It was not cold anymore – not like with the wind the day before, yet there was a chill in the house always there – always. It came in from the windows, up from the cellar underneath. He drank from the pint. If she wanted to leave he'd certainly let her – if she wanted to leave and take the kid he'd certainly let her.

Now and then a car on the highway. "I'd certainly let ya, ya goddamn bitch, ya goddamn bitch," he said under his breath, then laughed. "As if it'd bother me, as if it would, as if her goin away would bother me – fuck bother me, here's the ticket, get on the Jesus train and go – and I suppose –"

He stopped short – there was nothing in the house save his voice or the lack of it in the air, the tilted clock silent on the wall above the sink, the clock he had bought her for Christmas: "That I got ya for fuckin Christmas," he said again, then laughed again, drank again.

It was no good – he couldn't understand why. She would sit all day like that and never move sometimes, and be dressed, her makeup on, her eyes flashing, and crying for no reason sometimes: "Because yer not workin," she said. "Get a job," she said: "Get yer own fuckin job." "All right I will – I'll go away and take Ronnie and me and Ronnie we'll go, and then I'll get a job." "Well, go then," he said.

But it was more than that and it made him uneasy to see her sitting there, sometimes dressed like that, and then crying besides. She took the car and went down again, he thought, Goddammit, he thought. "Goddamn bitch," he said. "Goddamn bitch."

But he stopped saying it – there was no more use in saying it anymore. The quiet. He put his hand through his hair down the back of his neck feeling the scald mark on the back of his neck, the thick disordered flesh. When he was a child: there was wind, and in the summer you felt it coming at you through the long grass in the fields when you lay there – the breeze off the water, and blueberries budding in the hot blueness and the sun dancing and glinting, and trees all of a colour in the distance like fine good smoke. Like fine good smoke rising with the dust created on the road and the slight wet smell of his shorts – and when he first saw Leah that time, her standing, the water smooth around her smoothness, the sand a fine brown hotness on his feet and she looked over at him, and then started talking to Mary – and he went to the edge of the beach, the breeze on the salt and on the charred log at the beach's edge. She kept talking to Mary – then she'd look over. He took a beer and sat on the log watching them in the water, knowing that in her head each time she went under, the good full shape of her in the waves, that she was thinking, Is he watching? Her youngness.

It was the good total youngness that she still had even now, even in the musk smell on the half-soiled bed, the sweat along her back at times mounting. Yes, even now sometimes in the shape of her legs when she moved, in the laughing. Yes, that day in the field with the breeze on her almost slight nakedness, and he over her and he had waited and waited.

"I love ya – I guess," he said.

"What?" she said.

"Ya – I guess." Then pain and stupidity hit him for saying it all, then the pain and stupidity left him and he felt better, he felt out of him rise a necessity to say it all, and he looked at her, her face expressionless because of what he said. "Ya I do, I guess," he said. But he felt he didn't want her to say it back, that he didn't want her to speak. When she did he became angry, not knowing why. He held her mouth so that she couldn't speak, laughing so that she wouldn't know why he didn't want her to say it, because it was not in him to have her say it – to ever have her say it; the day bright, the sun burning on his back. When she said it he laughed louder, stupidly:

"Sure ya do," he said.

"I do."

"Sure ya do."

"If you love me why can't I love you?"

"Sure ya do."

He picked up the bottle and drank from it. There was silence. He wasn't cursing her any more, in his mind the past – that day with her when she told him, something cold came over him. He cursed at it – at that feeling he had, at the day itself – and then at her again; leaving tonight to run down there; every goddamn chance she got to run down there.

Sometimes when he looked at her he felt that if he held her at that moment, at that precise moment, he would hold her forever, but then it would pass because she would turn and speak, or without even speaking ruin how she was at that precise moment – when he saw her in all the same substance of the gentle nakedness of that day – and then something cold would fill him, something bad in his taste and he wouldn't want to look at her. He'd look out and stare along the roadway. She'd say: "Cecil," and he wouldn't be able to answer, because of the badness that had replaced the moment itself: "Cecil!" she'd say: He wouldn't answer: "For Christ's sake – Cecil, will ya listen?"

"What the fuck ya want now?" he'd say, and it would be over, lost; the feeling and the badness both.

He rose and stood before it now, watching the same roadway, highway, he had watched for years. All the seasoned things in the air he knew, the bright golden weather filled with the touch of pollen, as if it rose, formed from the swollen grass; and then in the autumn, the ditch clay formed and hardened, the rock – sunken into the earth itself; earth into earth like some resemblance of a blotched face – his; and then in winter, *now*, at times the sky slate, coming down to touch the snow in the frozen fields, sometimes almost brilliant with the scent and the sense of cold. Darkness with the brilliant sense of cold. Between the distances of yellow light that fell from the roadlamps, the darkness. He drank from the bottle again.

He could stand there for hours – it didn't matter; what mattered was the sense at times of being completely alone, standing or sitting, staring into something, into nothing. It gave him that freedom which he could not understand or explain, a feeling which issued from within him. He would think of her when they were younger; her body never the same body, her smell never the same smell, and he would think always of holding her at that precise moment (sometimes it was Mary, in the water, sometimes he thought of her), yet what he thought of really was no one thing at all but timeless things – days when he lived on the settlement, when he knew her only as a young girl that lived below the bridge.

He had watched so many times from this position that he could, if he acknowledged it to himself, know every trace of sunlight and dampness that hit the road, and tell the season, day and hour just by that – just by the wind blowing the leaves and the way the sun spoke of them, just by the clotted dooryard mud in April, the way the heels of her shoes were scuffed by the mud or the film of dust they collected in June when she would walk up to Ronald's closing. The minute healing and bursting of the pavement and the blots of tar.

What was it? They were gone down again both of them, she leading him out of the house by the hand, saying, "And I won't be home tonight." "Fuck ya," he said. "Little Mommy's boy – little Mommy's boy," he said. "You leave him alone," she said. Ronnie said nothing. Then he said: "Well, that's what the Christ you're makin him – makin him think I'm the old scar-faced bastard, makin him think I'm the bastard."

"Feel sorry for yerself," she said.

"Fuck ya – fuck ya," he said.

At first it was just themselves, knowing what he had said and what she had repeated, it made him behave as if it could never be unsaid. He didn't know. It was as if because he had spoken *that*, the breeze on her almost slight nakedness, his large hand stroking along her shoulder, that all things followed. It was as if he was into it without even knowing or understanding. He cursed, the whisky burning at his insides every time he swallowed. Under the distant roadlamp a figure appeared walking toward him, then disappearing. "Christ – all I need," he thought. "All I goddamn well need."

They hiked to the dances and then home again. At first it was just themselves. It was her. And then it was what people said: "Oh Leah and Cecil, they'll be fightin to the altar – but they'll get to the altar" – and what people thought, and then it was the people's thoughts becoming their own thoughts without him knowing why. He didn't know.

He turned from the window and went to the kitchen sink. Maybe he wouldn't let the bastard in. It wasn't because when he said it he didn't mean it – it wasn't that; and her looking at him and him holding her mouth so she wouldn't say it back. It was because he could never say it again – never. She said: "Ya didn't ever love me." He never spoke. It was raining and they were standing against the rear door of the post office, and she was crying but he didn't answer her. He looked out to the rain, and the side-street littered, and in the air the full smell of oil and town vapour, the clinging of it to the buildings all along the side-street, to her wet thin summer skirt and blouse, and the dark brassière underneath. "Well, I don't care," she said. "I don't care," and in her eyes was the waiting for him to say it. The smell of oil and vapour with the rain. He watched it again – the town so quiet. "We better start hiking anyway," he said. The black thin strap of her undergarment showing, as if above the thin drenched material the breath heaving inward and outward in short quiet sobs. He started walking – looked back twice before she followed.

Shelby didn't knock. As he came under the kitchen window he saw Cecil, waved and then came in through the back porch without knocking. Cecil didn't turn to him when he entered, drank again from the bottle staring out to the road and field, ice-slate sky and reeling quiet of the darkness outside.

"What the hell ya doin in here with all the lights out?"

He didn't answer. There was a time that summer when he walked across the field, soaking from the after-rain and the field-wet, with the shot-gun. It was to scare her – to know himself that he could go out into that woods with the gun, and do it if he *wanted* to, with her or anyone else not being able to stop him. That he could, to let her know that, to say to her: "If ya don't stop bitchin cause ya haveta stop yer bitchin." Yet he knew, and she knew. When he threw the child he didn't mean to throw him, and when he grabbed the gun, went into the dooryard, the sun so bright his eyes squinted, so bright his scars burned with it, they both knew. She watching him from the window at the side.

Shelby snapped on the kitchen light. The presence of the small

man behind him made that oneness and quietness go – that goodness within him of being motionless in his own home; the lights out,
the road, the winter. Shelby was talking to him but he didn't
answer. He turned round, drank and handed the bottle over.

"Oh, ya got some," Shelby said. "What the hell ya doin in here
with the lights out?"

"Thinkin," Cecil said, taking the bottle back.

"Yer thinking, are ya?" Shelby said.

They sat at the kitchen table. It was as if Shelby brought into the
room, not the sky, nor the snow – but the place where he lived,
something of the smoke at the back of his shed that lingered there
with the undried pulp, the clinging of bad manure and soot and
particles of cinder in the ice. It reminded him of once, walking the
road to school and back and tasting it coming from the houses and
the air.

For a long time they were silent. He couldn't bring himself to talk,
to answer; the answers made by the passing of the bottle back and
forth.

For a long time they were silent, Shelby fidgeting. His hands were
skeletal, unclean, the bones protruding against the black-and-
reddish skin, the nails long. He moved them across the white
table-top in the cold room, reaching every now and then for the
bottle, Cecil watching them when he did so – the hands of a small
man moving that way. Then he took the bottle himself and finished
it.

"So yer thinking, are ya – what are ya thinkin about?"

The dim light, the sound of the small fridge, and inside her clothes
tossed across the bed.

Shelby unzipped his coat and leaned back.

"I brought some wine."

Cecil didn't answer.

"Well, what in hell are ya thinkin about?"

"Nothin."

"Nothin – nothin, ya bin sittin here for twenty minutes not
speakin, thinkin a nothin."

Cecil took the wine and drank from it. Then he passed it over and
stood, going back to the window again. It was the white; hands that
were drawn reddish over the white. He didn't want to look, didn't

want to speak to him. She wouldn't be home, he'd keep the door locked not to let her in, but she wouldn't be home. Going down there, always the same, Ronnie tugged along by her hand – her face tonight, the mascara dripping.

He went into the room, up behind her, just after supper. There was that damp warm heat from the stew that they had had, and her light neck felt warm when he put his large hand over it, and the skirt that she was zipping up the side, her naked thigh balanced in the thin twilight. "Leave me alone now," she said, "Come on," he said, trying to smile that way, his large hands on her. "Screw you," she said. The sun was low over the fields, glancing purple – the long winter emptiness on the road and the houses to the left, as if sleet had cut at their windows because of the reflection, because of the black cold glare the windows made. She straightened her stockings and he felt inside him, an emptiness running through him. He moved his hands along her shoulders downward. "Screw off now, I'm going ta bingo now." He wanted to come into the room after supper with her, wanted to have her lay in his arms, the softness of her heaving in his arms. He didn't know.

"Well, if ya ain't gonna talk to a man I may as well fuck off," Shelby said. He turned around and grunted. The wine was gone. In the room her clothes tossed on the bed, the yellowed walls, the white blind half-drawn to the outside night. Shelby lifted himself and went to the door, stood there, fidgeting, his tired small eyes staring.

"What the fuck ya starin at?"

"What the fuck were ya standin here in the dark for?"

"Nothin."

"For nothin?"

"Yes, for nothin."

"Well, yer fuckin crazy is what I say."

"You'll get a good swift kick is what I say."

Shelby opened the door and stood in it. He threw his fist out, yet Cecil did nothing – so he started cursing again. Cecil looked at him.

"And any time ya get around ta it ya owe me some money."

Cecil said nothing.

"Fuck-face."

"What did you call me?"

"You heard me."

Cecil started toward the door.

"You heard me," Shelby said, slamming it. Then he was out in the yard, throwing snow at the window. "And ya owe me money," he was saying. "And I'll get it from Leah."

He locked the door, turned the light off and went into the bedroom.

The bedroom was warm, silent. In here even the cars passing sounded distant. Or was it him, tonight? It didn't matter. He lay on the bed, a long time motionless. When a car did pass he could catch the walls, as they moved in shadow, the light glancing through the half-closed blind, the small light fixture over the bulb. She wouldn't be home – not tonight, he tagging behind her that way, not looking at him – never looking. "As if I'm the old scar-faced bastard," he said. "Feel sorry for yerself," she said.

What was it? It was Shelby. Because if a man ever said that to him he wouldn't take it – he'd lash out at the man, and yet Shelby tonight stood in the doorway cursing and he said nothing – he stood there watching and said nothing.

Because of that time, her warmth coming through her skirt when she ran into the water; the water to her waist and in the smoke on the shore the sand-gnats circling; the fire hot and red on his bared arms, the light of the fire in the darkened air. He sat listening to her voice out in it, the small happy voice echoing over the waves, and then her coming from the water and the skirt twisted to her legs, inward, her legs a fine shadow underneath.

"Good ass there," Niles said.

"What?" he said.

The water running from her legs into the dirt, the bared blouse soaked and her breath heaving.

"Good arse there," Niles said.

"What?" he said. The sand-gnats circling against her as she moved, her form uncovered to the smoke on the shore wind, to water on the shore wind – the fine thin undergarments that she wore.

Niles looked at him, then at her again, the steam rising from her clothes, the burned embers of the fire and the heated dying coals.

"Nothin," he said.

"What?" he said. The red coals of the fire glowing on her legs.

"I said *nothin*," Niles said.

"Fuck off," he said.

"Don't think yer the only one that's ever been into that," Niles said.

"What?" he said.

"Inta that bitch," Niles said.

They faced each other. It seemed that all strength left him and then when they started at each other all strength came back, and then when all strength returned, as if it rushed along his veins, he was swinging. As if swinging out at something, someone was the only outlet to the strength and anger that went through him. He couldn't see. Niles hit him four times and he went back, not seeing, the smoke and the sand-gnats circling in it, the darkness circling and Leah and Mary shouting. But he did not go down. Niles hit him four times without him ever once connecting and yet he didn't go down. Then he found himself, began to block away the punches. The sand wet and sinking, the smell of shore water on the shore night and the taste in the confusion of the fists against his head. Leah holding him, her drenched softness clinging to his left arm, so that Niles hit him again with him helpless, unable to swing out.

"Cecil!"

"You fuck off me now."

Because she was holding him, he couldn't swing. He kept blocking with his right. Niles swinging with his right so that it was hard to block and she on his arm that way.

"Yer gonna get hurt," he said.

"Cecil!"

"Yer gonna get hurt – take her off me, Shelby, take her off me."

"Cecil!" Her wetness pinned against his arm. Shelby did nothing, the smoke in his wizened face.

"Take her off me, for fuck sake, Shelby."

"Cecil."

"Yer gonna get hurt." He could see nothing; Shelby only a form, the smoke against him and the black flecks of sand-gnats above her head and her screaming. He threw out with his left and she went reeling. He didn't know if she was hurt. Then he began swinging, connecting with both right and left. It seemed as if Niles's face crumbled when he hit, he didn't know. He didn't know if she was hurt. Then when he thought Niles would go down, he didn't, and when he thought he had won he hadn't. He felt nothing of the blood running from the corner of his mouth, over his eye – saw or knew nothing of the blood on Niles's mouth or face.

"Cecil!"

He pushed her hard out of the way, swinging her in the direction of the water. Then he grabbed Niles around the neck and put him down. It was sheer weight that brought him down into the sand, wet and sinking, both of them, their hair and clothes mud-ridden, the stale smell of smoke and river.

"Cecil!"

He felt nothing inside. When she came back he felt nothing of her, heard nothing. He kept swinging, Niles's face bloody, his mouth opening and closing and he kept swinging.

Then Niles threw him off and stood. They faced each other again for a long time, his face stinging. He felt the blood now, saw the blood on Niles's face and mouth, an almost soundless ringing in his ear.

"Yer both crazy," Leah said. "Yer both crazy."

She walked along the shoreline to the bridge. In a moment Cecil followed, the streaks of blood from his mouth already hardening against his chin, and over his eye a blotched, oozing disquiet, a burning pain.

"Yer crazy."

"Next time you latch on to me in a fight you'll get a good swift kick in the arse."

"Ya well, I don't like fights," she said crying. "I don't like people fighting."

He lay back in the bed, his eyes open, her clothes scattered under him – the loose bed-garments on the floor. "Let her go," he thought. "Let her and him and anyone that wants ta go with them go – cause if it was up ta me they'd go."

There was silence in the house again, only the unquiet of his mind. He laughed again and cursed and then was silent, all this only half-realizing that he was speaking into nothing, only half-realizing that they were gone down there again for the night and that she wasn't in the room to hear what he was saying – to understand what it was that he was shouting. As if she was in the room with her hair down; with the mascara like it was this evening.

He continued talking for a long time, stopping at intervals to realize the silence itself. His arms were trembling without him knowing it, and he was cold now. It was as if she was in the room and he was saying everything and she was listening without saying a word; not able to say a word because everything that he said was true. "Sure ya do," he said. "Sure ya have everyone on this river thinking I'm the bastard that no one could live with – cause I'm so mean, and I beat the kid – *feel sorry for yerself, feel sorry for yerself,* yer the only bitch that does any feeling sorry for yerself around here – so ya can pack up and fuck off, pack up and fuck off any time ya like – ya know that, ya know that – then why the fuck do ya stay?"

He wished he'd taken more of Shelby's wine. Because there was nothing left now and a pain seemed to come over him while he was speaking, so that he stopped short and listened. Over his head when the cars passed the light reflected against the ceiling and the walls, against the mirror tilted on the dresser and the dresser drawers left open after she had changed again. Then her face came back – the way it looked – and he shut his eyes.

It was that she didn't even try to stop him, she just took no part. "I'm going to bingo now," she said. It was after supper – the wet warmth of the stew that they had eaten. In the room when he closed the door the thin cold winter light through the venetian blind drawing faint against the yellow walls. She didn't stop him, she took no part, lay motionless and removed upon the bed – her face looking up at him that way, her mouth twisted, a hollowness about it somehow that he had never seen before. It was because he had wanted her to stay soft and warm in his arms, because she looked at supper as she had looked before – the good total youngness of her movement and her form. "Christ Jesus," he said.

He brought a blanket around him and rolled on his side. It was that she took no part.

"For Christ sake woman," he said.

She looked at him, motionless and unmoving, her legs together almost rigid. Then he began to curse and she said nothing, and he felt inside all hatred and rage; something that he was powerless to control, powerless to stop himself from hurting her as if hurting her was the answer to what she was doing – as if hurting her that way was the answer to the way she looked, to the way her legs went rigid under his hands.

And it was his hands. All the time he was doing it he saw the scars; the stove again like that night when he went toward it, and then the black redness of not knowing once the stove blew, of being reeled backwards and feeling it, the endless desperate energy and heat – that when he fell that night he could feel through every second of his unconsciousness the blind dark redness of the heat.

She said nothing. Not once did she speak – not once did he think of anything but the stove and the flame, of finding himself being dragged from it. Only the knowledge that he was hurting her and cursing her and that he couldn't stop.

He was trembling under the blanket, a pain that went through him every time he thought of it, of her standing afterwards and going to the dresser to change, her fine legs almost sickly by the light through the blinds. She didn't cry – not even that. It was as if an emptiness came into the room and touched them and they couldn't speak. Then she turned and went to the door. She went outside and called Ronnie and when he came in she said:

"We're going down to see Irene."

Cecil came from the bedroom.

"Sure fly the hell down there," he said. "Great place ta go – and make sure ya tell them everything," he said.

"And we won't be home tonight," she said.

"Sure I'm the old scar-faced bastard – I'm the bastard, ya got him believin that so's he won't even come near me."

"Feel sorry for yerself," she said.

"Fuck ya, fuck ya," he said.

The Accident

JOYCE MARSHALL

In that last and most difficult of our three summers in the village, I see us as trailing around endlessly together in a little string. I can almost look down and find those children, purely, without the future – all I now know or surmise about Hilary and Laura and have learned or made of myself. I would like to really get back to them, just as they were, because then perhaps I could untangle the truth of what happened or just seemed to happen – events or fancies that are linked for me always with the picture of three children moving along unwillingly and rather slowly, never side by side as I remember them but one after one after one in the distinct shapes and sizes that spaced out the five years. We were two and a half years apart, so precisely that Laura, the youngest, shared my birthday. Which was just one of many things I held against her.

The youngest except for the baby. I should make that clear. The baby, not yet called Claudia because my parents were finding it harder even than usual to agree upon a name, was never a threat. The real warfare was between us older three. And it was warfare. It was relentless. It was bitter. Yet at the same time I speak of, before we were strong enough to break away (physically) from one another, we were tied together most of the day. For safety. We lived – or camped – that summer a long way back from the broadening of the St Lawrence River we called the lake on a dirt and pebble trail known somewhat grandly as St John's Road; for the twice daily swims that were ritual in our family we had to cross two sets of railway tracks – each with its little station, gate and roller-coaster hill – and later the main village street across to the lake side and the beginning of the gentle curve that led around to the beach.

In winter I had all the aloneness I could wish in my own class at school. And different fears and different learning. But memory is capricious. I seldom, when I look back at my childhood, connect the seasons, as if our twice yearly upheavals of dogs and cats and children split them apart. And when I think of the struggle with my sisters, I remember chiefly the summers, which were long in our family, slow similar days stretching from May until November. And of course, the road – that soft easy curve edging the lake. Is it still there, I wonder Or has it been swallowed up by the airport? I have never tried to know which. It remains My archetypal road that I dream of again and again in so many ways. I was there again last night but the lake had become an abyss, I was trying to throw an infant – a very large screaming infant – over the side; I woke in panic in what seemed for an instant an immense and hollow room. And because I dislike those murderous dreams, which I shouldn't need any more, I began to think instead of that other safer terror, the accident, and to ask myself, as I have done so many times, whether it really happened as I seem to remember it. Did the man exist, in fact? Can it be possible that I was allowed to stand so close to him leaning right over him as I seem to do, listening to words that like so many of my childhood words I have no means to understand? He seems real. At least the fear and horror do. Perhaps I have reached back to imagine him, harbinger. At times I can believe this and yet I do seem to see him clearly, lying there bleeding on the edge of that vanished road

I was nine that year. This I am sure of because the sister who would not become Claudia till ten minutes or so before our grand-father, alarming in canonical robes, splashed her with water and uttered the name, was still quite new When I see the man, I see her also, lying in her crouched baby position in our old straw carriage with its corduroy lining, under one of the trees in the bumpy ungrassed yard of that strange house. The first human being I loved. The emotion we feel for parents is a demanding, seeking. This new kind of love, which I found whole in me the moment the new little creature was laid on my arms, was a huge inner swelling almost cracking my ribs. Now I understand, I remember thinking, what they mean when they say: My heart swelled. A peremptory feeling, inexplicable, a bit frightening. I didn't know what I was going to do with it. But I rather liked it. It was magic. It still seems magic as I recall it. No later love has staled that first.

I tried to spend as much time as I could beside the baby. Serve her Just look at her. I ran and fetched. Kept lifting the green mosquito netting tacked over her carriage for a new careful study of the always astonishing line of the cheek, tiny token fingers, bluish eyelid shells. I told myself I would die for her, this small human I didn't have to try to please, who could do nothing for me. My mother, who was almost instinctively alarmed, at least troubled, by my behaviour a great part of the time, used to thrust me away when I poked my head too close as she changed or nursed the baby. Why when she was so busy was I suddenly always under her feet? Why was I so quiet? Why didn't I go and help Hilary, who was trying to teach Laura to skip hot pepper on the bit of level road in front of the house? Why didn't I have friends? (When she knew as well as I did that in this rickety farmhouse way back from the village and its few summer cottages there were no friends for me to have.)

I have called it a difficult summer. This was partly the house, not enough rooms for us and those too small, awkwardly cut up and confining with its little low windows and evil smells. And the presence of the farm's real owners in a shack at the end of the vegetable garden just back of the house. My parents, who were always slow about summer rentals, had taken the place at night, had not realized that the quarters to which the farm-family proposed to move for the summer were so close. It was disconcerting to have them all there weeding by day almost under our kitchen window and at night sitting in a row in front of their shack, rocking in unison, gazing at us. My mother, who was sociable, tried waving and gesticulating but, though they smiled and nodded always, it went no further; clearly they had a strong sense of bounds and when our dog went too close they shooed him back. There was quite a large family of half-grown children, including a girl of about my age

"Go and play with her, Martha," my mother said to me once "Maybe she'd like to. Poor little thing. Always working. She could help you with French. Show you the cows and chickens. Even if you can't talk much, you could . . . skip, play hopscotch."

The thought of approaching that thin fierce-looking dark girl, whose bed I perhaps slept in and who must hate me for it as I would have hated her in a similar case, filled me with terror but, because I didn't want to admit – and defend – my cowardice, I just said crossly that I didn't like her.

"Yes, she does look a bit common," my mother said.

Her answer, which should have made my not liking the girl all right, was merely puzzling. Did it mean that we were uncommon? And if so, why and how? I knew there was no use trying to find out. My mother was in a very bad mood, tied down almost all day in this poky house where diapers had to be boiled in pails on a wood-burning stove and spread over bushes and rocks to dry. She couldn't play tennis and seldom found time to wheel the carriage to the beach. No days could suddenly be declared too hot for anything but a picnic by the lake or a wild ramble across fields to find blueberries. My father was interested that year, I think, in a mining property in northern Ontario. He was away much of the time, not coming home at night to cool and calm us, change the atmosphere, sing us grand opera, substitute his sort of energy for our mother's. There wasn't even a maid to talk to. The one we'd brought with us had taken one sniff at the kitchen and, refusing even to be led up to examine the "dear little room under the eaves" where she was to sleep, demanded to be put on the next train back to Montreal. (Our maids often left abruptly. I can't remember even one who lasted a whole summer. We liked the maids, who had fascinating lives and discussed them with us.)

My mother couldn't understand, she kept saying with one of the sideways looks that seemed to discover us for the first time, why she had let this happen. "Why did I marry and have four children?" she asked again and again as if sooner or later she'd find a reason. "I should have been a business girl." We must take a lesson from her and all be business girls. She would see to this herself. I can't remember whether we answered. Mother often complained and in a very vocal, almost automatic way. I don't think we minded being lumped together as something deplorable she had permitted to happen to her one day when she was looking the wrong way. We were very solidly here; that was all that mattered. Our mother was quick and restless, her energies loose and untapped. In another time and place she would have been a magnificent suffragette. No force-feeding her. She would have starved to the death, no question about that. And whenever I read about Emmeline Pankhurst I see the red-gold hair, proud mouth and glinting eyes of my mother. Meanwhile we were all to be business girls, remote as that seemed. This summer we had other concerns.

The family was shifting again. I can say again, though this is the first of the shifts I really remember. We had always quarrelled, we three, sometimes savagely and physically, had fought as children have to do for position and space, had worked out certain niches for ourselves. Now there was a fourth and places no longer held. Not that we were aware of any of this except in some deep domain of blood and bone. We knew simply – at least I knew – that it was a difficult summer, hot, monotonous. This was my first experience of boredom; I hadn't known that days could simply go on and on, always very much the same. I recall them as hot and parched with a sound of rustling – from the corn perhaps, that rather spindly corn the farm-family weeded. Seldom raining but very often thundery. And no sight or sound or even smell of water. (We were water-creatures in our family, my father too. He had met my mother, we knew, in this very lake, had fallen in love with her sparkling face under the pompommed bathing-cap. We children were all carried into the water before we could walk. And to be in the country but dry, on a hill-top, with no liquid shimmer visible between trees to us was anguish.) And there my mother must stay most of the time with the occasional company of three bickering children who could seldom succeed in being what she frequently told us we ought to be, three dear little sisters. (She herself had been one of seven dear little sisters. We had seen their picture, standing in a close loving rank in front of our grandfather's old rectory at Bolton Centre, all very shiny and neat in high-necked dresses with a great many tucks. They were our despair. They had loved one another then and were still the best of friends, greeeting one another after weeks with cries of delight. Children who grew up in rectories were different, it seemed to me, loved automatically, big ones liked nothing better than taking care of little ones, no one ever bit her sister. I could never live up to them.)

I was skinny and long at nine, all knobs and angles. I did not find myself appealing, could not make myself look pretty even with constant practice at the mirror. Worse, my behaviour never came out quite as I wanted it to. Success in childhood, I see now, depends in large part on one's gifts as a mimic. I had none. And as I could seldom think quickly enough of a handy lie, I was obliged to try to say what I meant – and sound foolish. Hilary was an excellent mimic, stood watchful close to the grown-ups and learned to be charming. She was the chief of my enemies, the first usurper, rooting me out of a place I possessed and must long for still. (So that I murder her still in dreams. I'm sorry Hilary. It's a very impersonal murder.) Not till recently did it occur to me that I was also chief of Hilary's enemies, already firmly established when she came. So that she could only become my mirror? Was obliged to be good, docile and positive because I wasn't. Did I make Hilary too in part as I struggled to make myself? I can see her trotting about that summer, more docile than ever, helping and serving, busying herself with the sort of games adults find enchanting – tucked in some little corner playing house or teacher, dressing up the cat, cuddling Laura.

For Laura, that untested child, had turned fretful, Laura for whom everything had always come easily simply because she was beautiful, in the creamy dimpled way that is the only way for children to be beautiful, and with two expressions: a touching gravity, a beguiling smile. It was hard not to hate someone who just needed to exist to delight. What Hilary thought of her I do not know; this summer she had attached herself to Laura, crooned, protected, made beds for her out of chairs, pretended to feed her. I pinched, crowded, snatched. And Laura, who seldom cried, had never told tales, not even when a blow from my croquet mallet made her bite her tongue till it bled, was now always whimpering, saw threats in shadows, screamed at thunder so that she had to be taken out of bed, rocked, called darling baby. She was called darling baby far too often, I thought. Beguiling always, she was now, it seemed to me, learning to work at being beguiling. I resented this bitterly, wanting my treasure, the real baby, to have all the love, simply because she was my chosen one. I noticed that Laura seldom looked at the baby, didn't seem even to like her. Jealous for my darling, I saw any subtraction of love from her as an insult to me. It was a trying summer as we slowly became more and more ourselves and in new ways. If it was really quite that simple. I can't be sure because, when you get down to it, I remember very little. Just a general stormy sense – that rustle, all that growly thunder – an impression of pushing and pulling, of things that ought to be clear and easy not clear or easy

And though I would have preferred to stay at home with my darling, who was learning to smile when I lifted the netting to examine her, I was obliged to spend almost all those long summer days with two enemies. Walking with them through that village where no one ever spoke to us. Fairly well used, I suppose – and this may be a handy lesson to learn early – to a world in which many things and most people were indifferent. In the city during the winter I sometimes joined with my school-mates to throw stones at the French children. *Pea soup. Dirty French pea soup. French pea soup and Johnny cake make the Frenchie's belly ache.* I had learned these interesting taunts while I was learning "Come over, red rover" and "One two three alarie", and all were games, I thought. In this very small village, which I always recall as silent, almost painted because nothing I heard was comprehended, in some way so subtle and yet so clear I never tried to examine it, I was very definitely not at home. It must have been at about this time that I began to feel rather precarious, that finger and thumb could flick me away. (Even when I was running, pelting through fields, and should have felt most physical and real, I would begin to seem weightless, floaty.) But if we did not seem to be observed, except with some loose blanket disapproval – so much the same, always, it could be pretty well ignored – this had its good side too. We could go anywhere we liked. In a world where all the adults were enemies, leagued together by similar tastes and standards, it was a relief to find some who, however great their displeasure, would never tell our parents.

When I say we could go anywhere, I don't mean by this that there was anywhere much to go. We weren't given pocket-money, couldn't have kept track of it in our clutter of sand-pails, wadded towels, and rubber bathing-caps, and so couldn't go into the store – except on occasional Saturdays with my father – to brood over the huge glass jars that held all the marvellous candy that could be bought for a single cent. But because we were all irritable that summer we broke rules, almost without thinking. There weren't many. *Don't loiter or peer into the stores.* We loitered and peered. *Don't climb fences on St John's Road. You might meet a bull.* We climbed fences and picked flowers almost out of the mouths of the cows, examined bluebird's nests in rotting fence-posts, pulled long stalks of timothy to suck. And when there was a little gathering of people on the expanded sidewalk in front of the grocery-store or the butcher's, we walked right into it, trailed through it and, as it seemed, made no more impression than when we chopped through the water with

our bouncing and energetic breast-stroke at our little cove. Which is
why, I imagine, we could have managed, young and small as we
were, to get through to the front of the crowd that pressed that day
around the man who lay dying after the accident. The village
people simply didn't notice us; small alien figures always roaming
about.

I've thought of it all so many times, smudging it probably. But
always the same details come. And the same gaps. We were on our
way home from the beach, had passed the long fence of the magnificent house, fancily gabled behind trees – it had fifty-six rooms,
I'd heard – and there just ahead were all those people staring at
something in front of them. I suppose to us it was simply an
interesting sight. We were curious. So in we went, I first because
bigger and stronger, better at wriggling through, the others after.

There were often accidents at the sharp bend the road was forced
to take before it slipped into its slow curve. On the north side, the
side where we weren't allowed to walk, the corner of a white-
plastered, rather small house jutted through the sidewalk a foot or
two into the road. Some old witch-lady had lived there for years,
refusing to sacrifice part of her house or let it be moved back. She
believed, we had heard, that since she and her house had been
there when the road was just a track, they had a right to remain.
Cars often met head-on at that spot. The man in today's accident, I
learned from adult discussion later, had been speeding, had been
drunk, might have fallen asleep in the sun, at any rate had failed to
make the sudden veer. His car was on our side of the road, against
a telephone pole, he himself a few feet away. Someone must have
moved him for I see him as lying straight and tidy on his back, on
the grassy strip between the wooden sidewalk and the unrailed
gallery of a house. The village people looked down at him as if,
having done what they could, the necessary phone calls made,
they sensed that he wanted to be alone and let him be. I have an
impression of tremendous excitement and yet silence. He himself
was not silent. He was crying as I looked into his face, very close to
it, bent a little forward as I had had to do to work my way through
the crowd. He was calling someone, at least speaking the same few
syllables again and again. I think I imagined that he was calling a
name. Have I added the blood? Transported that broken bleeding

face from elsewhere? Normandy? Spain? I remember a great deal of blood, all very red. In his hair, running into his eyes. Perhaps coming from his eyes. (I seem to know that he couldn't see.) A red pool in the grass around his head as he went on calling in that very fast, bubbling sort of voice. I believe I simply stood there, stooping slightly, looking at him. Not wanting to. Unable to turn or move.

Then at some point an awareness of Laura. Right at my knee. Perhaps pulling at me, for I remember her hand, her battered yellow sand-pail and the little shovel with the paintless handle. (This must be real for I see her hand in the scale of those times, the top of her head with the glint of the sun on its crown.) She was behind me, trying to get past me, whimpering, frightened. (I asked her once. "Do you remember, Laura? A terrible accident – a man badly hurt when we were little?" "Oh yes," she said. "At one of those parades Dad used to take us to. A horse reared and fell back, crushing the rider." And looked so stricken, for Laura has grown up to be the most tender-hearted of us all, that I pressed no further. We lived different lives, our memories are loose in our own heads and seldom meet.) Hilary I haven't asked, for Hilary would maintain as she always does that she remembers nothing at all from before she was eight. Yet very clearly at my other side I can hear her high-pitched, very positive voice: "They're going to take him to the hospital. Don't worry, darling baby Laura. They're going to take him to the hospital and they're going to sew him all together again. Don't worry, Laura. They're going to–"

"Shut up," my own voice, "Oh shut up." And I looked down – again or still – at Laura's face just at my side, saw it for the first time as a human face detached from me, crumpling before something far too big for it. Saw all sorts of other things, whether or not I put them in words, and with that first sense of the true otherness of others just as themselves, had an inkling at least of all that would be required of me, willing or not, as I went on living – demands that are made of us that we must fulfil and love that can come, and does, in all sorts of forms, not only for the chosen.

I think I knew I had to get Laura away from there and did, took hold of that hand with the sand-pail and, twisting and turning as I had entered it, led her out of the crowd. But very little is sure in our memories. Of all our trudges home through the village, our walks up St John's Road, I cannot select that one from the others. It was a difficult and edgy summer. Always thundery, always very much the same.

Some Grist for Mervyn's Mill

MORDECAI RICHLER

Mervyn Kaplansky stepped out of the rain on a dreary Saturday afternoon in August to inquire about our back bedroom.

"It's twelve dollars a week," my father said, "payable in advance."

Mervyn set down forty-eight dollars on the table. Astonished, my father retreated a step. "What's the rush-rush? Look around first. Maybe you won't like it here."

"You believe in electricity?"

There were no lights on in our house. "We're not the kind to skimp," my father said. "But we're orthodox here. Today is *shabus*."

"No, no, no. Between people."

"What are you? A wise-guy."

"I do. And as soon as I came in here I felt the right vibrations. Hi kid." Mervyn grinned breezily at me, but the hand he mussed my hair with was shaking. "I'm going to love it here."

My father watched disconcerted but too intimidated to protest, as Mervyn sat down on the bed, bouncing a little to try the mattress. "Go get your mother right away," he said to me.

Fortunately, she had just entered the room. I didn't want to miss anything.

"Meet your new roomer," Mervyn said, jumping up.

"Hold your horses." My father hooked his thumbs in his suspenders. "What do you do for a living?" he asked.

"I'm a writer."

"With what firm?"

"No, no, no. For myself. I'm a creative artist."

My father could see at once that my mother was enraptured and so, reconciled to yet another defeat, he said, "Haven't you any . . . things?"

"When Oscar Wilde entered the United States and they asked him if he had anything to declare, he said, 'Only my genius.'"

My father made a sour face.

"My things are at the station," Mervyn said, swallowing hard. "May I bring them over?"

"Bring."

Mervyn returned an hour or so later with his trunk, several suitcases, and an assortment of oddities that included a piece of driftwood, a wine bottle that had been made into a lamp base, a collection of pebbles, a twelve-inch-high replica of Rodin's *The Thinker*, a bull-fight poster, a Karsh portrait of GBS, innumerable notebooks, a ball-point pen with a built-in flashlight, and a framed cheque for fourteen dollars and eighty-five cents from the *Family Herald & Weekly Star*.

"Feel free to borrow any of our books," my mother said.

"Well, thanks. But I try not to read too much now that I'm a wordsmith myself. I'm afraid of being influenced, you see."

Mervyn was a short, fat boy with curly black hair, warm wet eyes, and an engaging smile. I could see his underwear through the triangles of tension that ran from button to button down his shirt. The last button had probably burst off. It was gone. Mervyn, I figured, must have been at least twenty-three years old, but he looked much younger.

"Where did you say you were from?" my father asked.

"I didn't."

Thumbs hooked in his suspenders, rocking on his heels, my father waited.

"Toronto," Mervyn said bitterly. "Toronto the Good. My father's a bigtime insurance agent and my brothers are in ladies' wear. They're in the rat-race. All of them."

"You'll find that in this house," my mother said, "we are not materialists."

Mervyn slept in – or, as he put it, stocked the unconscious – until noon every day. He typed through the afternoon and then, depleted, slept some more, and usually typed again deep into the night. He was the first writer I had ever met and I worshipped him. So did my mother.

"Have you ever noticed his hands," she said, and I thought she was going to lecture me about his chewed-up fingernails, but what she said was, "They're artist's hands. Your grandfather had hands like that." If a neighbour dropped in for tea, my mother would whisper, "We'll have to speak quietly," and, indicating the tap-tap of the typewriter from the back bedroom, she'd add, "in there,

Mervyn is creating." My mother prepared special dishes for Mervyn. Soup, she felt, was especially nourishing. Fish was the best brain food. She discouraged chocolates and nuts because of Mervyn's complexion, but she brought him coffee at all hours, and if a day passed with no sound coming from the back room my mother would be extremely upset. Eventually, she'd knock softly on Mervyn's door. "Anything I can get you?" she'd ask.

"It's no use. It just isn't coming today. I go through periods like that, you know."

Mervyn was writing a novel, his first, and it was about the struggles of our people in a hostile society. The novel's title was, to begin with, a secret between Mervyn and my mother. Occasionally, he read excerpts to her. She made only one correction. "I wouldn't say 'whore'," she said. "It isn't nice, is it? Say 'lady of easy virtue'." The two of them began to go in for literary discussions. "Shakespeare," my mother would say, "Shakespeare knew everything." And Mervyn, nodding, would reply, "But he stole all his plots. He was a plagiarist." My mother told Mervyn about her father, the rabbi, and the books he had written in Yiddish. "At his funeral," she told him, "they had to have six motor-cycle policemen to control the crowds." More than once my father came home from work to find the two of them still seated at the kitchen table, and his supper wasn't ready or he had to eat a cold plate. Flushing, stammering apologies, Mervyn would flee to his room. He was, I think, the only man who was ever afraid of my father, and this my father found very heady stuff. He spoke gruffly, even profanely in Mervyn's presence, and called him Moitle behind his back. But, when you come down to it, all my father had against Mervyn was the fact that my mother no longer baked potato kugel. (Starch was bad for Mervyn.) My father began to spend more of his time playing cards at Tansky's Cigar & Soda, and when Mervyn fell behind with the rent, he threatened to take action.

"But you can't trouble him now," my mother said, "when he's in the middle of his novel. He works so hard. He's a genius maybe."

"He's peanuts, or what's he doing here?"

I used to fetch Mervyn cigarettes and headache tablets from the drugstore round the corner. On some days when it wasn't coming, the two of us would play casino and Mervyn, at his breezy best, used to wisecrack a lot. "What would you say," he said, "if I told you I aim to out-Emile Zola?" Once he let me read one of his stories, "Was The Champ A Chump?", that had been printed in magazines in Australia and South Africa. I told him that I wanted to be a writer too. "Kid," he said, "a word from the wise. Never become a wordsmith. Digging ditches would be easier."

From the day of his arrival Mervyn had always worked hard, but what with his money running low he was now so determined to get his novel done, that he seldom went out any more. Not even for a stroll. My mother felt this was bad for his digestion. So she arranged a date with Molly Rosen. Molly, who lived only three doors down the street, was the best looker on St Urbain, and my mother noticed that for weeks now Mervyn always happened to be standing by the window when it was time for Molly to pass on the way home from work. "Now you go out," my mother said, "and enjoy. You're still a youngster. The novel can wait for a day."

"But what does Molly want with me?"

"She's crazy to meet you. For weeks now she's been asking questions."

Mervyn complained that he lacked a clean shirt, he pleaded a headache, but my mother said, "Don't be afraid she won't eat you." All at once Mervyn's tone changed. He tilted his head cockily. "Don't wait up for me," he said.

Mervyn came home early. "What happened?" I asked.

"I got bored."

"*With* Molly?"

"Molly's an insect. Sex is highly over-estimated, you know. It also saps an artist's creative energies."

But when my mother came home from her Talmud Torah meeting and discovered that Mervyn had come home so early she felt that she had been personally affronted. Mrs Rosen was summoned to tea.

"It's a Saturday night," she said, "she puts on her best dress, and that cheapskate where does he take her? To sit on the mountain. Do you know that she turned down three other boys, including Ready-To-Wear's *only* son, because you made such a *gedille*?"

"With dumb-bells like Ready-To-Wear she can have dates any night of the week. Mervyn's a creative artist."

"On a Saturday night to take a beautiful young thing to sit on the mountain. From those benches you can get piles."

"Don't be disgusting."

"She's got on her dancing shoes and you know what's for him a date? To watch the people go by. He likes to make up stories about them he says. You mean it breaks his heart to part with a dollar."

"To bring up your daughter to be a gold-digger. For shame."

"All right. I wasn't going to blab, but if that's how you feel – modern men and women, he told her, experiment *before* marriage. And right there on the bench he tried dirty filthy things with her. He . . ."

"Don't draw me no pictures. If I know your Molly he didn't have to try so hard."

"How dare you! She went out with him it was a favour for the marble cake recipe. The dirty piker he asked her to marry him he hasn't even got a job. She laughed in his face."

Mervyn denied that he had tried any funny stuff with Molly – he had too much respect for womankind, he said – but after my father heard that he had come home so early he no longer teased Mervyn when he stood by the window to watch Molly pass. He even resisted making wisecracks when Molly's kid brother returned Mervyn's thick letters unopened. Once, he tried to console Mervyn. "With a towel over the face," he said gruffly, "one's the same as another."

Mervyn's cheeks reddened. He coughed. And my father turned away, disgusted.

"Make no mistake," Mervyn said with a sudden jaunty smile. "You're talking to a boy who's been around. We pen-pushers are notorious lechers."

Mervyn soon fell behind with the rent again and my father began to complain.

"You can't trouble him now," my mother said. "He's in agony. It isn't coming today."

"Yeah, sure. The trouble is there's something coming to me."

"Yesterday he read me a chapter from his book. It's so beautiful you could die." My mother told him that F.J. Kugelman, the Montreal correspondent of *The Jewish Daily Forward*, had looked at the book. "He says Mervyn is a very deep writer."

"Kugelman's for the birds. If Mervyn's such a big writer, let him make me out a cheque for the rent. That's my kind of reading, you know."

"Give him one week more. Something will come through for him, I'm sure."

My father waited another week, counting off the days. "E-Day minus three today," he'd say. "Anything come through for the genius?" Nothing, not one lousy dime, came through for Mervyn. In fact he had secretly borrowed from my mother for the postage to send his novel to a publisher in New York. "E-Day minus one today," my father said. And then, irritated because he had yet to be asked what the E stood for, he added, "E for Eviction."

On Friday my mother prepared an enormous potato kugel. But when my father came home, elated, the first thing he said was, "Where's Mervyn?"

"Can't you wait until after supper, even?"

Mervyn stepped softly into the kitchen. "You want me?" he asked.

My father slapped a magazine down on the table. *Liberty*. He opened it at a short story titled "A Doll For The Deacon". Mel Kane, Jr," he said, "isn't that your literary handle?"

"His *nom de plume*," my mother said.

"Then the story is yours." My father clapped Mervyn on the back. "Why didn't you tell me you were a writer? I thought you were a . . . well, a fruitcup. You know what I mean. A long-hair."

"Let me see that," my mother said.

Absently, my father handed her the magazine. "You mean to say," he said, "you made all that up out of your own head?"

Mervyn nodded. He grinned. But he could see that my mother was displeased.

"It's a top-notch story," my father said. Smiling, he turned to my mother. "All the time I thought he was a sponger. A poet. He's a writer. Can you beat that?" He laughed, delighted. "Excuse me," he said, and he went to wash his hands.

"Here's your story, Mervyn," my mother said. "I'd rather not read it."

Mervyn lowered his head.

"But you don't understand, Maw. Mervyn has to do that sort of stuff. For the money. He's got to eat too, you know."

My mother reflected briefly. "A little tip, then," she said to

Mervyn. "Better he doesn't know why . . . well, you understand."

"Sure I do."

At supper my father said, "Hey, what's your novel called, Mr Kane?"

"The Dirty Jews.'

"Are you crazy?'

"It's an ironic title," my mother said.

"Wow! It sure is."

"I want to throw the lie back in their ugly faces," Mervyn said.

"Yeah. Yeah, sure." My father invited Mervyn to Tansky's to meet the boys. "In one night there," he said, "you can pick up enough material for a book."

"I don't think Mervyn is interested."

Mervyn, I could see, looked dejected. But he didn't dare antagonize my mother. Remembering something he had once told me, I said, "To a creative writer every experience is welcome."

"Yes, that's true," my mother said. "I hadn't thought of it like that."

So my father, Mervyn and I set off together. My father showed *Liberty* to all of Tansky's regulars. While Mervyn lit one cigarette off another, coughed, smiled foolishly and coughed again, my father introduced him as the up-and-coming writer.

"If he's such a big writer what's he doing on St Urbain Street?"

My father explained that Mervyn had just finished his first novel. "When that comes out," he said, "this boy will be batting in the major leagues."

The regulars looked Mervyn up and down. His suit was shiny.

"You must understand," Mervyn said, "that, at the best of times, it's difficult for an artist to earn a living. Society is naturally hostile to us."

"So what's so special? I'm a plumber. Society isn't hostile to me, but I've got the same problem. Listen here, it's hard for anybody to earn a living."

"You don't get it," Mervyn said, retreating a step. "*I'm* in rebellion against society."

Tansky moved away, disgusted. "Gorki, there was a writer. This boy . . ."

Molly's father thrust himself into the group surrounding Mervyn. "You wrote a novel," he asked, "it's true?"

"It's with a big publisher in New York right now," my father said.

"You should remember," Takifman said menacingly, "only to write good things about the Jews."

Shapiro winked at Mervyn. The regulars smiled, some shyly, others hopeful, believing. Mervyn looked back at them solemnly. "It is my profound hope," he said, "that in the years to come our people will have every reason to be proud of me."

Segal stood Mervyn for a Pepsi and a sandwich. "Six months from now," he said, "I'll be saying I knew you when . . ."

Mervyn whirled around on his counter stool. "I'm going to out-Emile Zola," he said. He shook with laughter.

"Do you think there's going to be another war?" Perlman asked.

"Oh, lay off," my father said. "Give the man air. No wisdom outside of office hours, eh, Mervyn?"

Mervyn slapped his knees and laughed some more. Molly's father pulled him aside. "You wrote this story," he said, holding up *Liberty*, "and don't lie because I'll find you out."

"Yeah," Mervyn said, "I'm the grub-streeter who knocked that one off. But it's my novel that I really care about."

"You know who I am? I'm Molly's father. Rosen. Put it there, Mervyn. There's nothing to worry. You leave everything to me."

My mother was still awake when we got home. Alone at the kitchen table. "You were certainly gone a long time," she said to Mervyn.

"Nobody forced him to stay."

"He's too polite," my mother said, slipping her tooled leather bookmark between the pages of *Wuthering Heights*. "He wouldn't tell you when he was bored by such common types."

"Hey," my father said, remembering. "Hey, Mervyn. Can you beat that Takifman for a character?"

Mervyn started to smile, but my mother sighed and he looked away. "It's time I hit the hay," he said.

"Well," my father pulled down his suspenders. "If anyone wants to use the library let him speak now or forever hold his peace."

"*Please, Sam.* You only say things like that to disgust me. I know that."

My father went into Mervyn's room. He smiled a little. Mervyn waited, puzzled. My father rubbed his forehead. He pulled his ear.

"Well, I'm not a fool. You should know that. Life does things to you, but . . ."

"It certainly does, Mr Hersh."

"You won't end up a zero like me. So I'm glad for you. Well, good night."

But my father did not go to bed immediately. Instead he got out his collection of pipes, neglected all these years, and sat down at the kitchen table to clean and restore them. And, starting the next morning, he began to search out and clip items in the newspapers, human interest stories with a twist, that might be exploited by Mervyn. When he came home from work – early, he had not stopped off at Tansky's – my father did not demand his supper right off but, instead, went directly to Mervyn's room. I could hear the two men talking in low voices. Finally, my mother had to disturb them. Molly was on the phone.

"Mr Kaplansky. Mervyn. Would you like to take me out on Friday night? I'm free."

Mervyn didn't answer.

"We could watch the people go by. Anything you say, Mervyn."

"Did your father put you up to this?"

"What's the diff? You wanted to go out with me. Well, on Friday, I'm free."

"I'm sorry. I can't do it."

"Don't you like me any more?"

"I sure do. And the attraction is more than merely sexual. But if we go out together it will have to be because you so desire it."

"Mervyn, if you don't take me out on Friday he won't let me out to the dance Saturday night with Solly. Please, Mervyn."

"Sorry. But I must answer in the negative."

Mervyn told my mother about the telephone conversation and immediately she said, "You did right." But a few days later, she became tremendously concerned about Mervyn. He no longer slept in each morning. Instead, he was the first one up in the house, to wait by the window for the postman. After he had passed, however, Mervyn did not settle down to work. He'd wander sluggishly about the house or go out for a walk. Usually, Mervyn ended up at Tansky's. My father would be waiting there.

"You know," Sugarman said, "many amusing things have happened to me in my life. It would make *some* book."

The men wanted to know Mervyn's opinion of Sholem Asch, the red menace, and ungrateful children. They teased him about my father. "To hear him tell it you're a guaranteed genius."

"Well," Mervyn said, winking, blowing on his fingernails and rubbing them against his jacket lapel, "Who knows?"

But Molly's father said, "I read in the *Gazette* this morning where Hemingway was paid a hundred thousand dollars to make a movie from *one* story. A complete book must be worth at least five short stories. Wouldn't you say?"

And Mervyn, coughing, clearing his throat, didn't answer, but walked off quickly. His shirt collar, too highly starched, cut into the back of his hairless, reddening neck. When I caught up with him, he told me, "No wonder so many artists have been driven to suicide. Nobody understands us. We're not in the rat-race."

Molly came by at seven-thirty on Friday night.

"Is there something I can do for you?" my mother asked.

"I'm here to see Mr Kaplansky. I believe he rents a room here."

"Better to rent out a room than give fourteen ounces to the pound."

"If you are referring to my father's establishment then I'm sorry he can't give credit to everyone."

"We pay cash everywhere. Knock wood."

"I'm sure. Now, may I see Mr Kaplansky, *if you don't mind*?"

"He's still dining. But I'll inquire."

Molly didn't wait. She pushed past my mother into the kitchen. Her eyes were a little puffy. It looked to me like she had been crying. "Hi," she said. Molly wore her soft black hair in an upsweep. Her mouth was painted very red.

"Siddown," my father said. "Make yourself homely." Nobody laughed. "It's a joke," he said.

"Are you ready, Mervyn?"

Mervyn fiddled with his fork. "I've got work to do tonight," he said.

"I'll put up a pot of coffee for you right away."

Smiling thinly, Molly pulled back her coat, took a deep breath, and sat down. She had to perch on the edge of the chair either because of her skirt or that it hurt her to sit. "About the novel," she said, smiling at Mervyn, "congrats."

"But it hasn't even been accepted by a publisher yet."

"It's good, isn't it?"

"Of course it's good," my mother said.

"Then what's there to worry? Come on," Molly said, rising. "Let's skidaddle."

We all went to the window to watch them go down the street together.

"Look at her how she's grabbing his arm," my mother said. "Isn't it disgusting?"

"You lost by a TKO," my father said.

"*Thanks*," my mother said, and she left the room.

My father blew on his fingers. "Whew," he said. We continued to watch by the window. "I'll bet you she sharpens them on a grindstone every morning to get them so pointy, and he's such a shortie he wouldn't even have to bend over to . . ." My father sat down, lit his pipe, and opened *Liberty* at Mervyn's story. "You know, Mervyn's not *that* special a guy. Maybe it's not as hard as it seems to write a story."

"Digging ditches would be easier," I said.

My father took me to Tansky's for a Coke. Drumming his fingers on the counter, he answered questions about Mervyn. "Well, it has to do with this thing . . . The Muse. On some days, with the Muse, he works better. But on other days . . ." My father addressed the regulars with a daring touch of condescension; I had never seen him so assured before. "Well, that depends. But he says Hollywood is very corrupt."

Mervyn came home shortly after midnight.

"I want to give you a word of advice," my mother said. "That girl comes from very common people. You can do better, you know."

My father cracked his knuckles. He didn't look at Mervyn.

"You've got your future career to think of. You must choose a mate who won't be an embarrassment in the better circles."

"Or still better stay a bachelor," my father said.

"Nothing more dreadful can happen to a person," my mother said, "than to marry somebody who doesn't share his interests."

"Play the field a little," my father said, drawing on his pipe.

My mother looked into my father's face and laughed. My father's voice fell to a whisper. "You get married too young," he said, "and you live to regret it."

My mother laughed again. Her eyes were wet.

"I'm not the kind to stand by idly," Mervyn said, "while you insult Miss Rosen's good name."

My father, my mother, looked at Mervyn as if surprised by his presence. Mervyn retreated, startled. "*I mean that*," he said.

"Just who do you think you're talking to?" my mother said. She looked sharply at my father.

"Hey, there," my father said.

"I hope," my mother said, "success isn't giving you a swelled head."

"Success won't change me. I'm steadfast. But you are intruding into my personal affairs. Good-night."

My father seemed both dismayed and a little pleased that some-one had spoken up to my mother.

"And just what's ailing you?" my mother asked.

"Me? Nothing."

"If you could only see yourself. At your age. A pipe."

"According to the *Digest* it's safer than cigarettes."

"You know absolutely nothing about people. Mervyn would never be rude to me. It's only his artistic temperament coming out."

My father waited until my mother had gone to bed and then he slipped into Mervyn's room. "Hi." He sat down on the edge of Mer-vyn's bed. "Tell me to mind my own business if you want me to, but . . . well, have you had bad news from New York? The publisher?"

"*I'm still waiting to hear from New York.*"

"Sure," my father said, jumping up. "Sorry. Good-night." But he paused briefly at the door. "I've gone out on a limb for you. Please don't let me down."

Molly's father phoned the next morning "You had a good time Mervyn?"

"Yeah. Yeah, sure."

"Atta boy. That girl she's crazy about you. Like they say she's walking on air."

Molly, they said, had told the other girls in the office at Susy's Smart-Wear that she would probably soon be leaving for, as she put it, tropical climes. Gitel Shalinsky saw her shopping for beach wear on Park Avenue – in November, this – and the rumour was that Mervyn had already accepted a Hollywood offer for his book, a guaranteed best-seller. A couple of days later a package came for Mervyn. It was his novel. There was a printed form enclosed with it. The publishers felt the book was not for them.

"Tough luck," my father said.

"It's nothing," Mervyn said breezily. "Some of the best wordsmiths going have their novels turned down six-seven times before a publisher takes it. Besides, this outfit wasn't for me in the first place. It's a homosexual company. They only print the pretty-pretty prose boys." Mervyn laughed, he slapped his knees. "I'll send the book off to another publisher today."

My mother made Mervyn his favourite dishes for dinner. "You have real talent," she said to him, "and everything will come to you." Afterwards, Molly came by. Mervyn came home very late this time, but my mother waited up for him all the same.

"I'm invited to eat at the Rosens on Saturday night. Isn't that nice?"

"But I ordered something special from the butcher for us here."

"I'm sorry. I didn't know."

"So now you know. Please yourself, Mervyn. Oh, it's all right. I changed your bed. But you could have told me, you know."

Mervyn locked his hands together to quiet them. "Tell you what, for Christ's sake? There's nothing to tell."

"It's alright, *boyele*," my mother said. "Accidents happen."

Once more my father slipped into Mervyn's room. "It's OK," he said, "don't worry about Saturday night. Play around. Work the kinks out. But don't put anything in writing. You might live to regret it."

"I happen to think Molly is a remarkable girl."

"Me too. I'm not as old as you think."

"No, no, no. You don't understand."

My father showed Mervyn some clippings he had saved for him. One news story told of two brothers who had discovered each other by accident after twenty-five years, another was all about a funny day at court. He also gave Mervyn an announcement for the annual YHMA *Beacon* short-story contest. "I've got an idea for you," he said. "Listen, Mervyn, in the movies . . . well, when Humphrey Bogart, for instance, lights up a Chesterfield or asks for a Coke you think he doesn't get a nice little envelope from the companies concerned? Sure he does. Well, your problem seems to be money. So why couldn't you do the same thing in books? Like if your hero has to fly somewhere, for instance, why use an unnamed airline? Couldn't he go TWA because it's the safest, the best, and maybe he picks up a cutie-pie on board? Or if your central character is . . . well, a lush, couldn't he always insist on Seagram's because it's the greatest? Get the idea? I could write, say, TWA, Pepsi, Seagram's and Adam's Hats and find out how much a book plug is worth to them, and you . . . well, what do you think?"

"I could never do that in a book of mine, that's what I think. It would reflect on my integrity. People would begin to talk, see."

But people had already began to talk. Molly's kid brother told me Mervyn had made a hit at dinner. His father, he said, had told Mervyn he felt, along with the moderns, that in-laws should not live with young couples, not always, but the climate in Montreal was a real killer for his wife, and if it so happened that he ever had a son-in-law in, let's say, California . . . well, it would be nice to visit . . . and Mervyn agreed that families should be close-knit. Not all the talk was favourable, however. The boys on the street were hostile to Mervyn. An outsider, a Torontonian, they felt, was threatening to carry off our Molly.

"There they go," the boys would say as Molly and Mervyn walked hand-in-hand past the pool room, "Beauty and the Beast."

"All these years they've been looking, and looking, and looking, and there he is, the missing link."

Mervyn was openly taunted on the street.

"Hey, big writer. Lard-ass. How many periods in a bottle of ink?"

"Shakespeare, come here. How did you get to look like that, or were you paid for the accident?"

But Mervyn assured me that he wasn't troubled by the boys. "The masses," he said, "have always been hostile to the artist. They've driven plenty of our number to self-slaughter, you know. But I can see through them."

His novel was turned down again.

"It doesn't matter," Mervyn said. "There are better publishers."

"But wouldn't they be experts there," my father asked. "I mean maybe . . ."

"Look at this, will you? This time they sent me a personal letter! You know who this is from? It's from one of the greatest editors in all of America."

"Maybe so," my father said uneasily, "but he doesn't want your book."

"He admires my energy and enthusiasm, doesn't he?"

Once more Mervyn mailed off his novel, but this time he did not resume his watch by the window. Mervyn was no longer the same. I don't mean that his face had broken out worse than ever – it had, it's true, only that was probably because he was eating too many starchy foods again – but suddenly he seemed indifferent to his novel's fate. I gave birth, he said, sent my baby out into the world, and now he's on his own. Another factor was that Mervyn had become, as he put it, pregnant once more (he looks it too, one of Tansky's regulars told me): that is to say, he was at work on a new book. My mother interpreted this as a very good sign and she did her upmost to encourage Mervyn. Though she continued to change his sheets just about every other night, she never complained about it. Why, she even pretended this was normal procedure in our house. But Mervyn seemed perpetually irritated and he avoided the type of literary discussion that had formerly given my mother such deep pleasure. Every night now he went out with Molly and there were times when he did not return until four or five in the morning.

And now, curiously enough, it was my father who waited up for Mervyn, or stole out of bed to join him in the kitchen. He would make coffee and take down his prized bottle of apricot brandy. More than once I was awakened by his laughter. My father told Mervyn stories of his father's house, his boyhood, and the hard times that came after. He told Mervyn how his mother-in-law had been bedridden in our house for seven years, and with pride implicit in his every word – a pride that would have amazed and maybe even flattered my mother – he told Mervyn how my mother had tended to the old lady better than any nurse with umpteen diplomas. "To see her now," I heard my father say, "is like night and day. Before the time of the old lady's stroke she was no sour-puss. Well, that's life." He told Mervyn about the first time he had seen my mother, and how she had written him letters with poems by Shelley, Keats and Byron in them, when all the time he had lived only two streets away. But another time I heard my father say, "When I was a young man, you know, there were days on end when I never went to bed. I was so excited. I used to go out and walk the streets better than snooze. I thought if I slept maybe I'd miss something. Now isn't that crazy?" Mervyn muttered a reply. Usually, he seemed weary and self-absorbed. But my father was irrepressible. Listening to him, his tender tone with Mervyn and the surprise of his laughter, I felt that I had reason to be envious. My father had never talked like that to me or my sister. But I was so astonished to discover this side of my father, it was all so unexpected, that I soon forgot my jealousy.

One night I heard Mervyn tell my father, "Maybe the novel I sent out is no good. Maybe it's just something I had to work out of my system."

"Are you crazy it's no good? I told everyone you were a big writer."

"It's the apricot brandy talking," Mervyn said breezily. "I was only kidding you."

But Mervyn had his problems. I heard from Molly's kid brother that Mr Rosen had told him he was ready to retire. "Not that I want to be a burden to anybody," he had said. Molly had begun to take all the movie magazines available at Tansky's. "So that when I meet the stars face to face," she had told Gitel, "I shouldn't put my foot in it, and embarrass Merv."

Mervyn began to pick at his food, and it was not uncommon for him to leap up from the table and rush to the bathroom, holding his hand to his mouth. I discovered for the first time that my mother had bought a rubber sheet for Mervyn's bed. If Mervyn had to pass Tansky's, he no longer stopped to shoot the breeze. Instead, he would hurry past, his head lowered. Once, Segal stopped him. "What's a matter," he said, "you too good for us now?"

Tansky's regulars began to work on my father.

"All of a sudden, your genius there, he's such a BTO," Sugerman said, "that he has no time for us here."

"Let's face it," my father said. "You're zeros. We all are. But my friend Mervyn . . ."

"Don't tell me, Sam. He's full of beans. Baked beans."

My father stopped going to Tansky's altogether. He took to playing solitaire at home.

"What are you doing here?" my mother asked.

"Can't I stay home one night? It's my house too, you know."

"I want the truth, Sam."

"Aw, those guys. You think those cockroaches know what an

artist's struggle is?" He hesitated, watching my mother closely. "By them it must be that Mervyn isn't good enough. He's no writer."

"You know," my mother said, "he owes us seven weeks' rent now."

"The first day Mervyn came here," my father said, his eyes half-shut as he held his match to his pipe, "he said there was a kind of electricity between us. Well, I'm not going to let him down over a few bucks "

But something was bothering Mervyn. For that night and the next he did not go out with Molly. He went to the window to watch her pass again and then retreated to his room to do the crossword puzzles

"Feel like a casino?" I asked.

"I love that girl," Mervyn said. "I adore her."

"I thought everything was OK, but I thought you were making time."

"No, no, no. I want to marry her. I told Molly that I'd settle down and get a job if she'd have me."

"Are you crazy? A job? With your talent?"

"That's what she said."

"Aw, let's play casino. It'll take your mind off things."

"She doesn't understand. Nobody does. For me to take a job is not like some ordinary guy taking a job. I'm always studying my own reactions. I want to know how a shipper feels from the inside."

"You mean you'd take a job *as a shipper*?"

"But it's not like I'd really be a shipper. It would look like that from the outside, but I'd really be studying my co-workers all the time. I'm an artist, you know."

"Stop worrying, Mervyn. Tomorrow there'll be a letter begging you for your book."

But the next day nothing came. A week passed. Ten days.

"That's a very good sign," Mervyn said. "It means they are considering my book very carefully."

It got so we all waited around for the postman. Mervyn was aware that my father did not go to Tansky's any more and that my mother's friends had begun to tease her Except for his endless phone calls to Molly he hardly ever came out of his room. The phone calls were futile. Molly wouldn't speak to him

One evening my father returned from work, his face flushed

"Son-of-a-bitch," he said, "that Rosen he's a cockroach. You know what he's saying? He wouldn't have in his family a faker or a swindler. He said you were not a writer, Mervyn, but garbage." My father started to laugh. "But I trapped him for a liar. You know what he said? That you were going to take a job as a shipper. Boy, did I ever tell him."

"What did you say?" my mother asked.

"I told him good. Don't you worry. When I lose my temper, you know . . ."

"Maybe it wouldn't be such a bad idea for Mervyn to take a job. Better than go into debt he could –"

"You shouldn't have bragged about me to your friends so much," Mervyn said to my mother. "I didn't ask it."

"*I'm* a braggard? You take that back. You owe me an apology, I think. After all, *you're* the one who said you were such a big writer."

"My talent is unquestioned. I have stacks of letters from important people and –"

"I'm waiting for an apology, Sam?"

"I have to be fair. I've seen some of the letters, so that's true. But that's not to say Emily Post would approve of Mervyn calling you a –"

"My husband was right the first time. When he said you were a sponger, Mervyn."

"Don't worry," Mervyn said, turning to my father. "You'll get your rent back no matter what. Good-night."

I can't swear to it. I may have imagined it. But when I got up to go to the toilet late that night it seemed to me that I heard Mervyn sobbing in his room. Anyway, the next morning the postman rang the bell and Mervyn came back with a package and a letter.

"Not again," my father said.

"No. This happens to be a letter from the most important publisher in the United States. They are going to pay me 2,500 dollars for my book in advance against royalties."

"Hey. Lemme see that."

"Don't you trust me?"

"Of course we do." My mother hugged Mervyn. "All the time I knew you had it in you."

"This calls for a celebration," my father said, going to get the apricot brandy.

My mother went to phone Mrs Fisher. "Oh, Ida, I just called to say I'll be able to bake for the bazaar after all. No, nothing new here. Oh, I almost forgot. Remember Mervyn you were saying he was nothing but a little twerp? Well, he just got a fantastic offer for his book from a publisher in New York. No, I'm only allowed to say it runs into four figures. Excited? That one. I'm not even sure he'll accept."

My father grabbed the phone to call Tansky's.

"One minute. Hold it. Couldn't we keep quiet about this, and have a private sort of celebration?"

My father got through to the store. "Hello, Sugarman? Everybody come over here. Drinks on the house. Why, of Korsakov. No, wise-guy. She certainly isn't. At her age? It's Mervyn. He's considering a 5,000 dollar offer just to sign a contract for his book."

The phone rang an instant after my father had hung up.

"Well, hello Mrs Rosen," my mother said. "Well, thank you. I'll give him the message. No, no, why should I have anything against you we've been neighbours for years. No. Certainly not. It wasn't *me* you called a piker. Your Molly didn't laugh in my face."

Unnoticed, Mervyn sat down on the sofa. He held his head in his hands.

"There's the doorbell," my father said.

"I think I'll lie down for a minute. Excuse me."

By the time Mervyn came out of his room again many of Tansky's regulars had arrived. "If it had been up to me," my father said, "none of you would be here. But Mervyn's not the type to hold grudges."

Molly's father elbowed his way through the group surrounding Mervyn. "I want you to know," he said, "that I'm proud of you today. There's nobody I'd rather have for a son-in-law."

"You're sort of hurrying things. Aren't you?"

"What? Didn't you propose to her a hundred times she wouldn't have you? And now I'm standing here to tell you all right and you're beginning with the shaking in the pants. This I don't like."

Everybody turned to stare. There was some good-natured laughter.

"You wrote her such letters they still bring a blush to my face –"

"But they came back unopened."

Molly's father shrugged and Mervyn's face turned grey as a pencil eraser.

"But you listen here," Rosen said. "For Molly, if you don't mind, it isn't necessary for me to go begging."

"Here she is," somebody said.

The regulars moved in closer.

"Hi," Molly smelled richly of Lily of the Valley. You could see the outlines of her bra through her sweater (both were in Midnight Black, from Susy's Smart-Wear). Her tartan skirt was held together by an enormous gold-plated safety pin. "Hi, doll." She rushed up to Mervyn and kissed him. "Maw just told me." Molly turned to the others, her smile radiant. "Mr Kaplansky has asked for my hand in matrimony. We are engaged."

"Congratulations!" Rosen clapped Mervyn on the back. "The very best to you both."

There were whoops of approval all around.

"When it comes to choosing a bedroom set you can't go wrong with my son-in-law Lou."

"I hope," Takifman said sternly, "yours will be a kosher home."

"Some of the biggest crooks in town only eat kosher and I don't mind saying that straight to your face, Takifman."

"He's right, you know. And these days the most important thing with young couples is that they should be sexually compatible."

Mervyn, surrounded by the men, looked over their heads for Molly. He spotted her trapped in another circle in the far corner of the room. Molly was eating a banana. She smiled at Mervyn, she winked.

"Don't they make a lovely couple?"

"Twenty years ago they said the same thing about us. Does that answer your question?"

Mervyn was drinking heavily. He looked sick.

"Hey," my father said, his glass spilling over, "tell me, Segal, what goes in hard and stiff and comes out soft and wet?"

"Oh, for Christ's sake," I said. "Chewing gum. It's as old as the hills."

"You watch out," my father said. "You're asking for it."

"You know," Miller said. "I could do with something to eat."

My mother moved silently and tight-lipped among the guests collecting glasses just as soon as they were put down.

"I'll tell you what," Rosen said in a booming voice, "let's all go over to my place for a decent feed and some schnapps."

Our living room emptied more quickly than it had filled.

"Where's your mother?" my father asked, puzzled.

I told him she was in the kitchen and we went to get her. "Come on," my father said, "let's go to the Rosens."

"And who, may I ask, will clean up the mess you and your friends made here?"

"It won't run away."

"You have no pride."

"Oh, please. Don't start. Not today."

"Drunkard."

"Ray Milland, that's me. Hey, what's that coming out of the wall? A bat?"

"That poor innocent boy is being railroaded into a marriage he doesn't want and you just stand there."

"Couldn't you enjoy yourself *just once*?"

"You didn't see his face how scared he was? I thought he'd faint."

"Who ever got married he didn't need a little push? Why, I remember when I was a young man —"

"You go, Sam. Do me a favour. Go to the Rosens."

My father sent me out of the room.

"I'm not," he began, "well, I'm not always happy with you. Not day in and day out. I'm telling you straight."

"When I needed you to speak up for me you couldn't. Today courage comes in bottles. Do me a favour, Sam. Go."

"I wasn't going to go and leave you alone. I was going to stay. But if that's how you feel . . ."

My father returned to the living room to get his jacket. I jumped up.

"Where are *you* going?" he asked.

"To the party."

"You stay here with your mother you have no consideration."

"God damn it."

"You heard me." But my father paused for a moment at the door. Thumbs hooked in his suspenders, rocking to and fro on his heels, he raised his head so high his chin jutted out incongruously. "I wasn't always your father. I was a young man once."

"So?"

"Did you know," he said, one eye half-shut, "that LIVE spelled backwards is EVIL?"

I woke at three in the morning when I heard a chair crash in the living room; somebody fell, and this was followed by the sound of sobbing. It was Mervyn. Dizzy, wretched and bewildered. He sat on the floor with a glass in his hand. When he saw me coming he raised his glass. "The wordsmith's bottled enemy," he said, grinning.

"When you getting married?"

He laughed. I laughed too.

"I'm not getting married."

"Wha'?"

"Sh."

"But I thought you were crazy about Molly?"

"I was. I am no longer." Mervyn rose, he tottered over to the window.

"Have you ever looked up at the stars," he said, "and felt how small and unimportant we are?"

It hadn't occurred to me before.

"Nothing really matters. In terms of eternity our lives are shorter than a cigarette puff. Hey," he said. "Hey!" He took out his pen with the built-in flashlight and wrote something in his notebook. "For a writer," he said, "everything is grist to the mill. Nothing is humiliating."

"But what about Molly?"

"She's an insect. I told you the first time. All she wanted was my kudos. My fame . . . If you're really going to become a wordsmith remember one thing. The world is full of ridicule while you struggle. But once you've made it the glamour girls will come crawling."

He had begun to cry again. "Want me to sit with you for a while," I said.

"No. Go to bed. Leave me alone."

The next morning at breakfast my parents weren't talking. My mother's eyes were red and swollen and my father was in a forbidding mood. A telegram came for Mervyn.

"It's from New York," he said. "They want me right away. There's an offer for my book from Hollywood and they need me."

"You don't say?"

Mervyn thrust the telegram at my father. "Here," he said. "You read it."

"Take it easy. All I said was . . ." But my father read the telegram all the same. "Son-of-a-bitch," he said. "Hollywood."

We helped Mervyn pack.

"Shall I get Molly?" my father asked.

"No. I'll only be gone for a few days. I want to surprise her."

We all went to the window to wave. Just before he got into the taxi Mervyn looked up at us, he looked for a long while, but he didn't wave, and of course we never saw him again. A few days later a bill came for the telegram. It had been sent from our house. "I'm not surprised," my mother said.

My mother blamed the Rosens for Mervyn's flight, while they held us responsible for what they called their daughter's disgrace. My father put his pipes aside again and naturally he took a terrible ribbing at Tansky's. About a month later five-dollar bills began to arrive from Toronto. They came sporadically until Mervyn had paid up all his back rent. But he never answered any of my father's letters.

The Concert Stages of Europe

JACK HODGINS

Now I know Cornelia Horncastle would say I'm blaming the wrong person. I know that. I know too that she would say thirty years is a long time to hold a grudge, and that if I needed someone to blame for the fact that I made a fool of myself in front of the whole district and ruined my life in the process, then I ought to look around for the person who gave me my high-flown ideas in the first place. But she would be wrong; because there is no doubt I'd have led a different sort of life if it weren't for her, if it weren't for that piano keyboard her parents presented her with on her eleventh birthday. And everything – everything would have been different if that piano keyboard hadn't been the kind made out of stiff paper that you unfolded and laid out across the kitchen table in order to do your practising.

I don't suppose there would have been all that much harm in her having the silly thing, if only my mother hadn't got wind of it. What a fantastic idea, she said. You could learn to play without even making a sound! You could practise your scales without having to hear that awful racket when you hit a wrong note! A genius must have thought of it, she said. Certainly someone who'd read his Keats: *Heard melodies are sweet, but those unheard are sweeter.* "And don't laugh," she said, "because Cornelia Horncastle is learning to play the piano and her mother doesn't even have to miss an episode of *Ma Perkins* while she does it."

That girl, people had told her, would be giving concerts in Europe some day, command performances before royalty, and her parents hadn't even had to fork out the price of a piano. It was obvious proof, if you needed it, that a person didn't have to be rich to get somewhere in this world.

In fact, Cornelia's parents hadn't needed to put out even the small amount that paper keyboard would have cost. A piano teacher named Mrs Humphries had moved on to the old Dendoff place and, discovering that almost no one in the district owned a piano, gave the keyboard to the Horncastles along with a year's free lessons. It was her idea, apparently, that when everyone heard how quickly Cornelia was learning they'd be lining up to send her their children for lessons. She wanted to make the point that having no piano needn't stop anyone from becoming a pianist. No doubt she had a vision of paper keyboards in every house in Waterville, of children everywhere thumping their scales out on the kitchen table without offending anyone's ears, of a whole generation turning silently into Paderewskis without ever having played a note.

They would, I suppose, have to play a real piano when they went to her house for lessons once a week, but I was never able to find out for myself, because all that talk of Cornelia's marvellous career on the concert stages of Europe did not prompt my parents to buy one of those fake keyboards or sign me up for lessons with Mrs Humphries. My mother was born a Barclay, which meant she had a few ideas of her own, and Cornelia's glorious future prompted her to go one better. We would buy a *real* piano, she announced. And I would be sent to a teacher we could trust, not to that newcomer. If those concert stages of Europe were ever going to hear the talent of someone from the stump ranches of Waterville, it wouldn't be Cornelia Horncastle, it would be Barclay Desmond. Me.

My father nearly choked on his coffee. "But Clay's a boy!"

"So what?" my mother said. *All* those famous players used to be boys. What did he think Chopin was? Or Tchaikovsky?

My father was so embarrassed that his throat began to turn a dark pink. Some things were too unnatural even to think about.

But eventually she won him over. "Think how terrible you'd feel," she said, "if he ended up in the bush, like you. If Mozart's father had worked for the Comox Logging Company and thought piano-playing was for sissies, where would the world be today?"

My father had no answer to that. He'd known since before his marriage that though my mother would put up with being married to a logger, expecting every day to be made a widow, she wouldn't tolerate for one minute the notion that a child of hers would follow him up into those hills. The children of Lenora Barclay would enter the professions.

She was right, he had to agree; working in the woods was the last thing in the world he wanted for his sons. He'd rather they take up

ditch-digging or begging than have to work for that miserable logging company, or take their orders from a son-of-a-bitch like Tiny
Beechman, or get their skulls cracked open like Stanley Kirck. It was
a rotten way to make a living, and if he'd only had a decent education he could have made something of himself.

Of course, I knew he was saying all this for my mother's benefit.
He didn't really believe it for a minute. My father loved his work. I
could tell by the way he was always talking about Ab Jennings and
Shorty Cresswell, the men he worked with. I could tell by the
excitement that mounted in him every year as the time grew near for
the annual festival of loggers' sports where he usually won the
bucking contest. It was obvious, I thought, that the man really
wanted nothing more in this world than that one of his sons should
follow in his footsteps. And much as I disliked the idea, I was sure
that I was the one he'd set his hopes on. Kenny was good in school.
Laurel was a girl. I was the obvious choice. I even decided that what
he'd pegged me for was high-rigger. I was going to be one of those
men who risked their necks climbing hundreds of feet up the bare
lonely spar tree to hang the rigging from the top. Of course I would
fall and kill myself the first time I tried it, I knew that, but there was
no way I could convey my hesitation to my father since he would
never openly admit that this was really his goal for me.

And playing the piano on the concert stages of Europe was every
bit as unattractive. "Why not Kenny?" I said, when the piano had
arrived, by barge, from Vancouver.

"He's too busy already with his school work," my mother said.
Kenny was hoping for a scholarship, which meant he got out of just
about everything unpleasant.

"What about Laurel?"

"With her short fat fingers?"

In the meantime, she said, though she was no piano-player herself (a great sigh here for what might have been), she had no trouble
at all identifying which of those ivory keys was the all-important
Middle C and would show it to me, to memorize, so that I wouldn't
look like a total know-nothing when I showed up tomorrow for my
first lesson. She'd had one piano lesson herself as a girl, she told me,
and had learned all about Mister Middle C, but she'd never had a
second lesson because her time was needed by her father, outside,

helping with the chores. Seven daughters altogether, no sons, and she was the one who was the most often expected to fill the role of a boy. The rest of them had found the time to learn chords and chromatic scales and all those magic things she'd heard them practising while she was scrubbing out the dairy and cutting the runners off strawberry plants. They'd all become regular show-offs in one way or another, learning other instruments as well, putting on their own concerts and playing in dance bands and earning a reputation all over the district as entertaining livewires – The Barclay Sisters. And no one ever guessed that all the while she was dreaming about herself at that keyboard, tinkling away, playing beautiful music before huge audiences in elegant theatres.

"Then it isn't me that should be taking lessons," I said. "It's you."

"Don't be silly." But she walked to the new piano and pressed down one key, a black one, and looked as if I'd tempted her there for a minute. "It's too late now," she said. And then she sealed my fate: "But I just know that you're going to be a great pianist."

When my mother "just knew" something, that was as good as guaranteeing it already completed. It was her way of controlling the future and, incidentally, the rest of us. By "just knowing" things, she went through life commanding the future to fit into certain patterns she desired while we scurried around making sure that it worked out that way so she'd never have to be disappointed. She'd had one great disappointment as a girl – we were never quite sure what it was, since it was only alluded to in whispers with far-off looks – and it was important that it never happen again. I was trapped.

People were always asking what you were going to be when you grew up. As if your wishes counted. In the first six years of my life the country had convinced me it wanted me to grow up and get killed fighting Germans and Japanese. I'd seen the coils of barbed wire along the beach and knew they were there just to slow down the enemy while I went looking for my gun. The teachers at school obviously wanted me to grow up and become a teacher just like them, because as far as I could see nothing they ever taught me could be of any use or interest to a single adult in the world except someone getting paid to teach it to someone else. My mother was counting on my becoming a pianist with a swallow-tail coat and standing ovations. And my father, despite all his noises to the contrary, badly wanted me to climb into the crummy every morning with him and ride out those gravelly roads into mountains and risk my life destroying forests.

I did not want to be a logger. I did not want to be a teacher. I did not want to be a soldier. And I certainly did not want to be a pianist. If anyone had ever asked me what I did want to be when I grew up, in a way that meant they expected the truth, I'd have said quite simply that what I wanted was to be a Finn.

Our new neighbours, the Korhonens, were Finns. And being a Finn, I'd been told, meant something very specific. A Finn would give you the shirt off his back, a Finn was as honest as the day is long, a Finn could drink anybody under the table and beat up half a dozen Germans and Irishmen without trying, a Finn was not afraid of work, a Finn kept a house so clean you could eat off the floors. I knew all these things before ever meeting our neighbours, but as soon as I had met them I was able to add a couple more generalizations of my own to the catalogue: Finnish girls were blonde and beautiful and flirtatious, and Finnish boys were strong, brave, and incredibly intelligent. These conclusions were reached immediately after meeting Lilja Korhonen, whose turned-up nose and blue eyes fascinated me from the beginning, and Larry Korhonen, who was already a teenager and told me for starters that he was actually Superman, having learned to fly after long hours of practice off their barn roof. Mr and Mrs Korhonen, of course, fitted exactly all the things my parents had told me · about Finns in general. And so I decided my ambition in life was to be just like them.

I walked over to their house every Saturday afternoon and pretended to read their coloured funnies. I got in on the weekly steambath with Larry and his father in the sauna down by the barn. Mr Korhonen, a patient man whose eyes sparkled at my eager attempts, taught me to count to ten – *yksi, kaksi, kolme, nelja, viisi, kuusi, seitseman, kahdeksan, yhdeksan, kymmenen*. I helped Mrs Korhonen scrub her linoleum floors and put down newspapers so no one could walk on them, and I gorged myself on cinnamon cookies and *kala loota* and coffee sucked through a sugar cube. If there was something to be caught from just being around them, I wanted to catch it. And since being a Finn seemed to be a full-time occupation, I didn't have much patience with my parents, who behaved as if there were other things you had to prepare yourself for.

The first piano teacher they sent me to was Aunt Jessie, who lived in a narrow, cramped house up a gravel road that led to the mountains. She'd learned to play as a girl in Toronto, but she had no pretensions about being a real teacher, she was only doing this as a favour to my parents so they wouldn't have to send me to that Mrs Humphries, an outsider. But one of the problems was that Aunt Jessie – who was no aunt of mine at all, simply one of those family friends who somehow get saddled with an honorary family title – was exceptionally beautiful. She was so attractive, in fact, that even at the age of ten I had difficulty keeping my eyes or my mind on the lessons. She exuded a dreamy sort of delicate femininity; her soft, intimate voice made the hair on the back of my neck stand on end. Besides that, her own playing was so much more pleasant to listen to than my own stumbling clangs and clunks that she would often begin to show me how to do something and become so carried away with the sound of her own music that she just kept right on playing through the rest of my half-hour. It was a simple matter to persuade her to dismiss me early every week so that I'd have a little time to play in the creek that ran past the back of her house, poling a homemade raft up and down the length of her property while her daughters paid me nickels and candies for a ride. At the end of a year my parents suspected I wasn't progressing as fast as I should. They found out why on the day I fell in the creek and nearly drowned, had to be revived by a distraught Aunt Jessie, and was driven home soaked and shivering in the back seat of her old Hudson.

Mr Korhonen and my father were huddled over the taken-apart cream separator on the veranda when Aunt Jessie brought me up to the door. My father, when he saw me, had that peculiar look on his face that was half-way between amusement and concern, but Mr Korhonen laughed openly. "That boy lookit like a drowny rat."

I felt like a drowned rat too, but I joined his laughter. I was sure this would be the end of my piano career, and could hardly wait to see my mother roll her eyes to the ceiling, throw out her arms, and say, "I give up."

She did nothing of the sort. She tightened her lips and told Aunt

Jessie how disappointed she was. "No wonder the boy still stumbles around on that keyboard like a blindfolded rabbit; he's not going to learn the piano while he's out risking his life on the *river!*"

When I came downstairs in dry clothes Aunt Jessie had gone, no doubt wishing she'd left me to drown in the creek, and my parents and the Korhonens were all in the kitchen drinking coffee. The Korhonens sat at either side of the table, smoking hand-rolled cigarettes and squinting at me through the smoke. Mrs Korhonen could blow beautiful white streams down her nostrils. They'd left their gumboots on the piece of newspaper just inside the door, of course, and wore the same kind of grey work-socks on their feet that my father always wore on his. My father was leaning against the wall with both arms folded across his chest inside his wide elastic braces, as he sometimes did, swishing his mug gently as if he were trying to bring something up from the bottom. My mother, however, was unable to alight anywhere. She slammed wood down into the firebox of the stove, she rattled dishes in the sink water, she slammed cupboard doors, she went around the room with the coffee pot, refilling mugs, and all the while she sang the song of her betrayal, cursing her own stupidity for sending me to a friend instead of to a professional teacher, and suddenly in a flash of inspiration dumping all the blame on my father: "If you hadn't made me feel it was somehow pointless I wouldn't have felt guilty about spending more money!"

From behind the drifting shreds of smoke Mr Korhonen grinned at me. Sucked laughter between his teeth. "Yust *teenk*, boy, looks like-it you're saved!"

Mrs Korhonen stabbed out her cigarette in an ashtray, picked a piece of tobacco off her tongue, and composed her face into the most serious and ladylike expression she could muster. "Yeh! Better he learn to drive the tractor." And swung me a conspirator's grin.

"Not on your life," my mother said. Driving a machine may have been a good enough ambition for some people, she believed, but the Barclays had been in this country for four generations and she knew there were a few things higher. "What we'll do is send him to a real teacher. Mrs Greensborough."

Mrs Greensborough was well known for putting on a public recital in town once a year, climaxing the programme with her own rendition of Grieg's Piano Concerto – so beautiful that all went home, it was said, with tears in their eyes. The problem with Mrs Greensborough had nothing to do with her teaching. She was, as far as I could see, an excellent piano teacher. And besides, there was something rather exciting about playing on her piano, which was surrounded and nearly buried by a thousand tropical plants and dozens of cages full of squawking birds. Every week's lesson was rather like putting on a concert in the midst of the Amazon jungle. There was even a monkey that swung through the branches and sat on the top of the piano with the metronome between its paws. And Mrs Greensborough was at the same time warm and demanding, complimentary and hard to please – though given a little, like Aunt Jessie, to taking off on long passages of her own playing, as if she'd forgotten I was there.

It took a good hour's hard bicycling on uphill gravel roads before I could present myself for the lesson – past a dairy farm, a pig farm, a turkey farm, a dump, and a good long stretch of bush – then more washboard road through heavy timber where driveways disappeared into the trees and one dog after another lay in wait for its weekly battle with my right foot. Two spaniels, one Irish setter, and a bulldog. But it wasn't a spaniel or a setter or even a bulldog that met me on the driveway of the Greensboroughs" chicken farm, it was a huge German shepherd that came barking down the slope the second I had got the gate shut, and stuck its nose into my crotch. And kept it there, growling menacingly, the whole time it took me to back him up to the door of the house. There was no doubt in my mind that I would come home from piano lesson one Saturday minus a few parts. Once I had got to the house, I tried to get inside quickly and shut the door in his face, leaving him out there in the din of cackling hens; but he always got his nose between the door and the jamb, growled horribly and pushed himself inside so that he could lie on the floor at my feet and watch me hungrily the whole time I sat at the kitchen table waiting for Ginny Stamp to finish off her lesson and get out of there. By the time my turn came around my nerves were too frayed for me to get much benefit out of the lesson.

Still, somehow I learned. That Mrs Greensborough was a marvel- lous teacher, my mother said. The woman really knew her stuff.

And I was such a fast-learning student that it took less than two years for my mother to begin thinking it was time the world heard from me.

"Richy Ryder," she said, "is coming to town."

"What?"

"Richy Ryder, CJMT. *The Talent Show*."

I'd heard the programme. Every Saturday night Richy Ryder was in a different town somewhere in the province, hosting his one-hour talent contest from the stage of a local theatre and giving away free trips to Hawaii.

Something rolled over in my stomach.

"And here's the application form right here," she said, whipping two sheets of paper out of her purse to slap down on the table.

"No thank you," I said. If she thought I was going in it, she was crazy.

"Don't be silly. What harm is there in trying?" My mother always answered objections with great cheerfulness, as if they were hardly worth considering.

"I'll make a fool of myself."

"You play beautifully," she said. "It's amazing how far you've come in only two years. And besides, even if you don't win, the experience would be good for you."

"You have to go door-to-door ahead of time, begging for pledges, for money."

"Not begging," she said. She plunged her hands into the sink, peeling carrots so fast I couldn't see the blade of the vegetable peeler. "Just giving people a chance to vote for you. A dollar a vote." The carrot dropped, skinned naked, another one was picked up. She looked out of the window now toward the barn and, still smiling, delivered the argument that never failed. "I just know you'd win it if you went in, I can feel it in my bones."

"Not this time!" I shouted, nearly turning myself inside out with the terror. "Not this time. I just can't do it."

Yet somehow I found myself riding my bicycle up and down all the roads around Waterville, knocking at people's doors, explaining the contest, and asking for their money and their votes. I don't know why I did it. Perhaps I was doing it for the same reason I was tripping over everything, knocking things off tables, slamming my shoulder into door-jambs; I just couldn't help it, everything had gone out of control. I'd wakened one morning that year and found myself six feet two inches tall and as narrow as a fence stake. My feet were so far away they seemed to have nothing to do with me. My hands flopped around on the ends of those lanky arms like fish, something alive. My legs had grown so fast the bones in my knees parted and I had to wear elastic bandages to keep from falling apart. When I turned a corner on my bicycle, one knee would bump the handlebar, throwing me into the ditch. I was the same person as before, apparently, saddled with this new body I didn't know what to do with. Everything had gone out of control. I seemed to have nothing to do with the direction of my own life. It was perfectly logical that I should end up playing the piano on the radio, selling myself to the countryside for a chance to fly off to Hawaii and lie on the sand under the whispering palms.

There were actually two prizes offered. The all-expense, ten-day trip to Hawaii would go to the person who brought in the most votes for himself, a dollar a vote. But lest someone accuse the radio station of getting its values confused, there was also a prize for the person judged by the panel of experts to have the most talent. This prize, which was donated by Nelson's Hardware, was a leatherette footstool.

"It's not the prize that's important," people told me. "It's the chance to be heard by all those people."

I preferred not to think of all those people. It seemed to me that if I were cut out to be a concert pianist it would be my teacher and not my parents encouraging me in this thing. Mrs Greensborough, once she'd forked over her two dollars for two votes, said nothing at all. No doubt she was hoping I'd keep her name out of it.

But it had taken no imagination on my part to figure out that if I were to win the only prize worth trying for, the important thing was not to spend long hours at the keyboard, practising, but to get out on the road hammering at doors, on the telephone calling relatives, down at the General Store approaching strangers who stopped for gas. Daily piano practice shrank to one or two quick run-throughs of "The Robin's Return", school homework shrank to nothing at all, and home chores just got ignored. My brother and sister filled in for me, once in a while, so the chickens wouldn't starve to death and the woodbox would never be entirely empty, but they did it gracelessly. It was amazing, they said, how much time a great pianist had to spend out on the road, meeting his public. Becoming famous, they said, was more work than it was worth.

And becoming famous, I discovered, was what people assumed I was after. "You'll go places," they told me. "You'll put this place on the old map." I was a perfect combination of my father's down-to-earth get-up-and-go and my mother's finer sensitivity, they said. How wonderful to see a young person with such high ambition!

"I always knew this old place wouldn't be good enough to hold you," my grandmother said as she fished out a five-dollar bill from her purse. But my mother's sisters, who appeared from all parts of the old farmhouse in order to contribute a single collective vote, had some reservations to express. Eleanor, the youngest, said she doubted I'd be able to carry it off, I'd probably freeze when I was faced with a microphone, I'd forget what a piano was for. Christina announced she was betting I'd faint, or have to run out to the bathroom right in the middle of my piece. And Mabel, red-headed Mabel who'd played accordian once in an amateur show, said she remembered a boy who made such a fool of himself in one of these things that he went home and blew off his head. "Don't be so morbid," my grandmother said. "The boy probably had no talent. Clay here is destined for higher things."

From behind her my grandfather winked. He seldom had a chance to contribute more than that to a conversation. He waited until we were alone to stuff a five-dollar bill in my pocket and squeeze my arm.

I preferred my grandmother's opinion of me to the aunts'. I began to feed people lies so they'd think that about me – that I was destined for dizzy heights. I wanted to be a great pianist, I said, and if I won that trip to Hawaii I'd trade it in for the money so that I could go and study at the Toronto Conservatory. I'd heard of the Toronto Conservatory only because it was printed in big black letters on the front cover of all those yellow books of finger exercises I was expected to practise.

I don't know why people gave me their money. Pity, perhaps. Maybe it was impossible to say no to a six-foot-two-inch thirteen-year-old who trips over his own bike in front of your house, falls up your bottom step, blushes red with embarrassment when you open the door, and tells you he wants your money for a talent contest so he can become a Great Artist. At any rate, by the day of the contest I'd collected enough money to put me in the third spot. I would have to rely on pledges from the studio audience and phone-in pledges from the radio audience to rocket me up to first place. The person in second place when I walked into that theatre to take my seat down front with the rest of the contestants was Cornelia Horncastle.

I don't know how she managed it so secretly. I don't know where she found the people to give her money, living in the same community as I did, unless all those people who gave me their dollar bills when I knocked on their doors had just given her two the day before. Maybe she'd gone into town, canvassing street after street, something my parents wouldn't let me do on the grounds that town people already had enough strangers banging on their doors every day. Once I'd got outside the vague boundaries of Waterville I was to approach only friends or relatives or people who worked in the woods with my dad, or stores that had – as my mother put it – done a good business out of us over the years. Cornelia Horncastle, in order to get herself secretly into that second place, must have gone wild in town. Either that or discovered a rich relative.

She sat at the other end of the front row of contestants, frowning over the sheets of music in her hands. A short nod and a quick smile were all she gave me. Like the other contestants, I was kept busy licking my dry lips, rubbing my sweaty palms together, wondering if I should whip out to the bathroom one last time, and rubbernecking to get a look at people as they filled up the theatre behind us. Mrs Greensborough, wearing dark glasses and a big floppy hat, was jammed into the far corner at the rear, studying her programme. Mr and Mrs Korhonen and Lilja came partway down the aisle and found seats near the middle. Mr Korhonen winked at me. Larry, who was not quite the hero he had once been, despite the fact that he'd recently beat up one of the teachers and set fire to the bus shelter, came in with my brother Kenny – both of them looking uncomfortable – and slid into a back seat. My parents came all the way down front, so they could look back up the slope and pick out the seats they wanted. My mother smiled as she always did in public, as if she expected the most delightful surprise at any moment. They took seats near the front. Laurel was with them, reading a book.

My mother's sisters – with husbands, boyfriends, a few of my cousins – filled up the entire middle section of the back row. Eleanor, who was just a few years older than myself, crossed her eyes and stuck out her tongue when she saw that I'd turned to look. Mabel pulled in her chin and held up her hands, which she caused to tremble and shake. Time to be nervous, she was suggesting, in case I forgot. Bella, Christina, Gladdy, Frieda – all sat puffed up like members of a royal family, or the owners of this theatre, looking down over the crowd as if they believed every one of these people had come here expressly to watch their nephew and for no other reason. "Look, it's the Barclay girls," I heard someone behind me say. And someone else: "Oh, *them.*" The owner of the first voice giggled. "It's a wonder they aren't all entered in this thing, you know how they like to perform." A snort. "They *are* performing, just watch them." I could tell by the muffled "Shhh" and the rustling of clothing that one of them was nudging the other and pointing at me, at the back of my neck. "One of them's son." When I turned again, Eleanor stood up in the aisle by her seat, did a few steps of a tap dance, and quickly sat down. In case I was tempted to take myself seriously.

When my mother caught my eye, she mouthed a silent message: stop gawking at the audience, I was letting people see how unusual all this was to me, instead of taking it in my stride like a born performer. She indicated with her head that I should notice the stage.

As if I hadn't already absorbed every detail. It was exactly as she must have hoped. A great black concert grand with the lid lifted sat out near the front of the stage, against a painted backdrop of palm trees along a sandy beach, and – in great scrawled letters – the words "Richy Ryder's CJMT Talent Festival". A long blackboard leaned against one end of the proscenium arch, with all the contestants' names on it and the rank order of each. Someone named Brenda Roper was in first place. On the opposite side of the stage, a microphone seemed to have grown up out of a heap of pineapples. I felt sick.

Eventually Richy Ryder came out of whatever backstage room he'd been hiding in and passed down the row of contestants, identifying us and telling us to get up on to the stage when our turns came without breaking our necks on those steps. "You won't be nervous, when you get up there," he said. "I'll make you feel at ease." He was looking off somewhere else as he said it, and I could see his jaw muscles straining to hold back a yawn. And he wasn't fooling me with his "you won't be nervous" either, because I knew without a doubt that the minute I got up on that stage I would throw up all over the piano.

Under the spotlight, Richy Ryder acted like a different person. He did not look the least bit like yawning while he told the audience the best way to hold their hands to get the most out of applause, cautioned them against whistling or yelling obscenities, painted a glorious picture of the life ahead for the talented winner of this contest, complimented the audience on the number of happy, shiny faces he could see out there in the seats, and told them how lucky they were to have this opportunity of showing off the fine young talent of the valley to all the rest of the province. I slid down in my seat, sure that I would rather die than go through with this thing.

The first contestant was a fourteen-year-old girl dressed up like a gypsy, singing something in a foreign language. According to the blackboard she was way down in ninth place, so I didn't pay much attention until her voice cracked open in the middle of a high note and she clutched at her throat with both hands, a look of incredulous surprise on her face. She stopped right there, face a brilliant red, and after giving the audience a quick curtsy hurried off the stage. A great beginning, I thought. If people were going to fall to pieces like that through the whole show no one would even notice my upchucking on the Heintzman. I had a vision of myself dry-heaving the whole way through "The Robin's Return".

Number two stepped up to the microphone and answered all of Richy Ryder's questions as if they were some kind of test he had to pass in order to be allowed to perform. Yes sir, his name was Roger Casey, he said with a face drawn long and narrow with seriousness, and in case that wasn't enough he added that his father was born in Digby, Nova Scotia, and his mother was born Esther Romaine in a little house just a couple blocks up the street from the theatre, close to the Native Sons' Hall, and had gone to school with the mayor though she'd dropped out of Grade Eight to get a job at the Safeway cutting meat. And yes sir, he was going to play the saxophone because he'd taken lessons for four years from Mr D.P. Rowbottom on Seventh Street though he'd actually started out on the trumpet until he decided he didn't like it all that much. He came right out to the edge of the stage, toes sticking over, leaned back like a rooster about to crow, and blasted out "Softly As in a Morning Sunrise" so loud and hard that I thought his bulging eyes would pop right out of his head and his straining lungs would blast holes through that red-and-white shirt. Everyone moved forward, tense and straining, waiting for something terrible to happen – for him to fall off the stage or explode or go sailing off into the air from the force of his own fantastic intensity – but he stopped suddenly and everyone fell back exhausted and sweaty to clap for him.

The third contestant was less reassuring. A kid with talent. A smart-aleck ten-year-old with red hair, who told the audience he was going into show business when he grew up, started out playing "Swanee River" on his banjo, switched in the middle of a bar to a mouth organ, tap-danced across the stage to play a few bars on the piano, and finished off on a trombone he'd had stashed away behind the palm tree. He bowed, grinned, flung himself around the stage as if he'd spent his whole life on it, and looked as if he'd do his whole act again quite happily if the audience wanted him to. By the time the tremendous applause had died down my jaw was aching from the way I'd been grinding my teeth the whole time he was up there. The audience would not have gone quite so wild over him, I thought, if he hadn't been wearing a hearing aid and a leg brace.

Then it was my turn. A strange calm fell over me when my name was called, the kind of calm that I imagine comes over a person about to be executed when his mind finally buckles under the horror it has been faced with, something too terrible to believe in. I wondered for a moment if I had died. But no, my body at least hadn't died, for it transported me unbidden across the front of the audience, up the staircase (with only a slight stumble on the second step, hardly noticeable), and across the great wide stage of the theatre to stand facing Richy Ryder's enormous expanse of white smiling teeth, beside the microphone.

"And you are Barclay Philip Desmond," he said.

"Yes," I said.

And again "yes", because I realized that not only had my voice come out as thin and high as the squeal of a dry buzz-saw, but the microphone was at least a foot too low. I had to bend my knees to speak into it.

"You don't live in town, do you?" he said. He had no intention of adjusting that microphone. "You come from a place called ... Waterville. A logging and farming settlement?"

"Yes," I said.

And again "yes" because while he was speaking my legs had straightened up, I'd returned to my full height and had to duck again for the microphone.

He was speaking to me but his eyes, I could see, were busy keeping all that audience gathered together, while his voice and mind were obviously concentrated on the thousands of invisible people who were crouched inside that microphone, listening, the thousands of people who – I imagined now – were pulled up close to their sets all over the province, wondering if I was actually a pair of twins or if my voice had some peculiar way of echoing itself, a few tones lower.

"Does living in the country like that mean you have to milk the cows every morning before you go to school?"

"Yes."

And again "yes".

I could see Mrs Greensborough cowering in the back corner. I promise not to mention you, I thought. And the Korhonens, grinning. I had clearly passed over into another world they couldn't believe in.

"If you've got a lot of farm chores to do, when do you find the time to practise the piano?"

He had me this time. A "yes" wouldn't be good enough. "Right after school," I said, and ducked to repeat. "Right after school. As soon as I get home. For an hour."

"And I just bet," he said, throwing the audience an enormous wink, "that like every other red-blooded country kid you hate every minute of it. You'd rather be outside playing baseball."

The audience laughed. I could see my mother straining forward; she still had the all-purpose waiting-for-the-surprise smile on her lips but her eyes were frowning at the master of ceremonies. She did not approve of the comment. And behind that face she was no doubt thinking to herself "I just know he's going to win" over and over so hard that she was getting pains in the back of her neck. Beside her, my father had a tight grin on his face. He was chuckling to himself, and sliding a look around the room to see how the others were taking this.

Up at the back, most of my aunts – and their husbands, their boyfriends – had tilted their chins down to their chests, offering me only the tops of their heads. Eleanor, however, had both hands behind her neck. She was laughing harder than anyone else.

Apparently I was not expected to respond to the last comment, for he had another question as soon as the laughter had died. "How old are you, son?"

"Thirteen."

For once I remembered to duck the first time.

"Thirteen. Does your wife like the idea of your going on the radio like this?"

Again the audience laughed. My face burned. I felt tears in my eyes. I had no control over my face. I tried to laugh like everyone else but realized I probably looked like an idiot. Instead, I frowned and looked embarrassed and kicked at one shoe with the toe of the other.

"Just a joke," he said, "just a joke." The jerk knew he'd gone too far. "And now seriously, one last question before I turn you loose on those ivories over there."

My heart had started to thump so noisily I could hardly hear him. My hands, I realized, had gone numb. There was no feeling at all in my fingers. How was I ever going to play the piano?

"What are you going to be when you grow up?"

The thumping stopped. My heart stopped. A strange cold silence settled over the world. I was going to die right in front of all those people. What I was going to be was a corpse, dead of humiliation, killed in a trap I hadn't seen being set. What must have been only a few seconds crawled by while something crashed around in my head, trying to get out. I sensed the audience, hoping for some help from them. My mother had settled back in her seat and for the first time that surprise-me smile had gone. Rather, she looked confident, sure of what I was about to say.

And suddenly, I was aware of familiar faces all over that theatre. Neighbours. Friends of the family. My aunts. People who had heard me answer that question at their doors, people who thought they knew what I wanted.

There was nothing left of Mrs Greensborough but the top of her big hat. My father, too, was looking down at the floor between his feet. I saw myself falling from that spar tree, high in the mountains.

"Going to be?" I said, turning so fast that I bumped the microphone with my hand, which turned out after all not to be numb.

I ducked.

"Nothing," I said. "I don't know. Maybe . . . maybe nothing at all."

I don't know who it was that snorted when I screwed up the stool, sat down, and stood up to screw it down again. I don't know how well I played, I wasn't listening. I don't know how loud the audience clapped, I was in a hurry to get back to my seat. I don't know what the other contestants did, I wasn't paying any attention, except when Cornelia Horncastle got up on the stage, told the whole world she was going to be a professional pianist, and sat down to rattle off Rachmaninoff's Rhapsody on a Theme of Paganini as if she'd been playing for fifty years. As far as I know it may have been the first time she'd ever heard herself play it. She had a faint look of surprise on her face the whole time, as if she couldn't quite get over the way the keys went down when you touched them.

As soon as Cornelia came down off the stage, smiling modestly, and got back into her seat, Richy Ryder announced a fifteen-minute intermission while the talent judges made their decision and the studio audience went out into the lobby to pledge their money and their votes. Now that the talent had been displayed, people could spend their money according to what they'd heard rather than according to who happened to come knocking on their door. Most of the contestants got up to stretch their legs but I figured I'd stood up once too often that night and stayed in my seat. The lower exit was not far away; I contemplated using it; I could hitch-hike home and be in bed before any of the others got out of there.

I was stopped, though, by my father, who sat down in the seat next to mine and put a greasy carton of popcorn in my lap.

"Well," he said, "that's that."

His neck was flushed. This must have been a terrible evening for him. He had a carton of popcorn himself and tipped it up to gather a huge mouthful. I had never before in my life, I realized, seen my father eat popcorn. It must have been worse for him than I thought.

Not one of the aunts was anywhere in sight. I could see my mother standing in the far aisle, talking to Mrs Korhonen. Still smiling. She would never let herself fall apart in public, no matter what happened. My insides ached with the knowledge of what it must have been like right then to be her. I felt as if I had just betrayed her in front of the whole world. Betrayed everyone.

"Let's go home," I said.

"Not yet. Wait a while. Might as well see this thing to the end."

True, I thought. Wring every last drop of torture out of it.

He looked hard at me a moment, as if he were trying to guess what was going on in my head. And he did, he did, he always knew. "My old man wanted me to be a doctor," he said. "My mother wanted me to be a florist. She liked flowers. She thought if I was a florist I'd be able to send her a bouquet every week. But what does any of that matter now?"

Being part of a family was too complicated. And right then I decided I'd be a loner. No family for me. Nobody whose hearts could be broken every time I opened my mouth. Nobody *expecting* anything of me. Nobody to get me all tangled up in knots trying to guess who means what and what is it that's really going on inside anyone else. No temptations to presume I knew what someone else was thinking or feeling or hoping for.

When the lights had flickered and dimmed, and people had gone back to their seats, a young man with a beard came out on to the stage and changed the numbers behind the contestants' names. I'd dropped to fifth place, and Cornelia Horncastle had moved up to first. She had also, Richy Ryder announced, been awarded the judges' footstool for talent. The winner of the holiday in sunny Hawaii would not be announced until the next week, he said, when the radio audience had enough time to mail in their votes.

"And that," my mother said when she came down the aisle with her coat on, "is the end of a long and tiring day." I could find no disappointment showing in her eyes, or in the set of her mouth. Just relief. The same kind of relief that I felt myself. "You did a good job," she said, "and thank goodness it's over."

As soon as we got in the house I shut myself in the bedroom and announced I was never coming out. Lying on my bed, I tried to read my comic books but my mind passed from face to face all through the community, imagining everyone having a good laugh at the way my puffed-up ambition had got its reward. My face burned. Relatives, the aunts, would be ashamed of me. Eleanor would never let me forget. Mabel would remind me of the boy who'd done the only honourable thing, blown off his head. Why wasn't I doing the same? I lay awake the whole night, torturing myself with these thoughts. But when morning came and the hunger pains tempted me out of the bedroom as far as the breakfast table, I decided the whole wretched experience had brought one benefit with it: freedom from ambition. I wouldn't worry any more about becoming a pianist for my mother. Nor would I worry any more about becoming a high-rigger for my father. I was free at last to concentrate on pursuing the only goal that ever really mattered to me: becoming a Finn.

Of course I failed at that too. But then neither did Cornelia Horncastle become a great pianist on the concert stages of Europe. In fact, I understand that once she got back from her holiday on the beaches of Hawaii she announced to her parents that she was never going to touch a piano again as long as she lived, ivory, or cardboard, or any other kind. She had already, she said, accomplished all she'd ever wanted from it. And as far as I know, she's kept her word to this day.

I'm Dreaming of Rocket Richard

CLARK BLAISE

We were never quite the poorest people on the block, simply because I was, inexplicably, an only child. So there was more to go around. It was a strange kind of poverty, streaked with gentility (the kind that chopped you down when you least expected it); my mother would spend too much for long-range goals – Christmas clubs, reference books, even a burial society – and my father would drink it up or gamble it away as soon as he got it. I grew up thinking that being an only child, like poverty, was a blight you talked about only in secret. "Too long in the convent," my father would shout – a charge that could explain my mother's way with money or her favours – "there's ice up your cunt." An only child was scarcer than twins, maybe triplets, in Montreal just after the war. And so because I was an only child, things happened to me more vividly, without those warnings that older brothers carry as scars. I always had the sense of being the first in my family – which was to say the first of my people – to think my thoughts, to explore the parts of Montreal that we called foreign, even to question in an innocent way the multitudes of unmovable people and things.

When I went to the Forum to watch the Canadiens play hockey, I wore a Boston Bruins sweatshirt. That was way back, when poor people could get into the Forum, and when Rocket Richard scored fifty goals in fifty games. Despite the letters on the sweatshirt, I loved the Rocket. I loved the Canadiens fiercely. It had to do with the intimacy of old-time hockey, how close you were to the gods on the ice; you could read their lips and hear them grunt as they slammed the boards. So there I stood in my Boston Bruins shirt loving the Rocket. There was always that spot of perversity in the things I loved. In school the nuns called me "Curette" – "Little Priest".

I was always industrious. That's how it is with janitors' sons. I had to pull out the garbage sacks, put away tools, handle simple repairs, answer complaints about heat and water when my father was gone or too drunk to move. He used to sleep near the heating pipes on an inch-thick, rust-stained mattress under a Sally Ann blanket. He loved his tools; when he finally sold them I knew we'd hit the bottom.

Industriously, I built an ice surface, enclosed it with old doors from a demolished tenement. The goal mouth was a topless clothes-hamper I fished from the garbage. I battered it to splinters, playing. Luck of the only child: if I'd had an older brother, I'd have been put in goal. Luckily there was a younger kid on the third floor who knew his place and was given hockey pads one Christmas; his older brother and I would bruise him after school until darkness made it dangerous for him. I'd be in my Bruins jersey, dreaming of Rocket Richard.

Little priest that I was, I did more than build ice surfaces. In the mornings I would rise at a quarter to five and pick up a bundle of *Montreal Matin*s on the corner of Van Horne and Querbes. Seventy papers I had, and I could run with the last thirty-five, firing them up on second- and third-floor balconies, stuffing them into convenient grilles, and marking with hate all those buildings where the Greeks were moving in or the Jews had already settled and my papers weren't good enough to wrap their garbage in. There was another kid who delivered the morning *Gazette*s to part of my street – ten or twelve places that had no use for me. We were the only people yet awake, crisscrossing each other's paths, still in the dark, and way below zero, me with a *Matin* sack and he with his *Gazette*. Once, we even talked. We were waiting for our bundles under a street lamp in front of the closed tobacco store on the corner. It was about ten below and the sidewalks were uncleared from an all-night snow. He smoked one of my cigarettes and I smoked one of his and we found we didn't have anything to say to each other except *"merci"*. After half an hour I said "paper no come" and he agreed, so we walked away.

Later on more and more Greeks moved in; every time a vacancy popped up, some Greek would take it – they even made sure by putting only Greek signs in the windows – and my route was shrinking all the time. *Montreal Matin* fixed me up with a route much further east, off Rachel near St-André, and so I became the only ten-year-old in Montreal who'd wait at four-thirty in the morning for the first bus out of the garage to take him to his paper route. After a few days I didn't have to pay a fare. I'd take coffee from the driver's thermos, his cigarettes, and we'd discuss hockey from the night before. In return I'd give him a paper when he let me off. They didn't call me Curette for nothing.

The hockey, the hockey! I like all the major sports, and the setting of each one has its own special beauty – even old De Lorimier Downs had something of Yankee Stadium about it, and old Rocky Nelson banging out home runs from his rocking chair stance made me think of Babe Ruth, and who could compare to Jackie Robinson and Roberto Clemente when they were playing for us? Sundays in August with the Red Wings in town, you could always get in free after a couple of innings and see two great games. But the ice of big-time hockey, the old Forum, that went beyond landscape! Something about the ghostly white of the ice under those powerful lights, something about the hiss of the skates if you were standing close enough, the solid *pock-pock* of the rubber on a stick, and the low menacing whiz of a Rocket slap shot hugging the ice – there was nothing in any other sport to compare with the *spell* of hockey. Inside the Forum in the early fifties, those games against Boston (with the Rocket flying and a hated Boston goalie named Jack Gelineau in the nets) were evangelical, for truly we were *dans le cénacle* where everyone breathed as one.

The Bruins sweatshirt came from a cousin of mine in Manchester, New Hampshire, who brought it as a joke or maybe a present on one of his trips up to see us. I started wearing it in all my backyard practices and whenever I got standing room tickets at the Forum. Crazy, I think now; what was going on in me? Crying on all those few nights each winter when the Canadiens lost, quite literally throwing whatever I was holding high in the air whenever the Rocket scored – yet always wearing that hornet-coloured jersey? Anyone could see I was a good local kid; maybe I wanted someone to think I'd come all the way from Boston just to see the game, maybe I liked the good-natured kidding from my fellow standees ("'ey, you, Boston," they'd shout, "'oo's winning, eh?" and I'd snarl back after a period or two of silence, *"mange la baton, sac de marde . . .'*). I even used to wear that jersey when I delivered papers and I remember the pain of watching it slowly unravel in the cuffs and shoulders, hoping the cousin would come again. They were Schmitzes, my mother's sister had met him just after the war. Tante Lise and Uncle Howie.

I started to pick up English by reading a *Gazette* on my paper route, and I remember vividly one spring morning – with the sun coming up – studying a name that I took to be typically English. It began *Sch*, an odd combination, like my uncle's; then I suddenly thought of my mother's name – not mine – Deschenes, and I wondered: could it be? Hidden in the middle of my mother's name were those same English letters, and I began to think that we (tempting horror) were English too, that I had a right, a *sch*, to that Bruins jersey, to the world in the *Gazette* and on the other side of Atwater from the Forum. How I fantasized!

Every now and then the Schmitzes would drive up in a new car (I think now they came up whenever they bought a new car; I don't remember ever sitting in one of their cars without noticing a shred of plastic around the window-cranks and a smell of newness), and I would marvel at my cousins who were younger than me and taller ("they don't smoke," my mother would point out), and who whined a lot because they always wanted things (I never understood what) they couldn't get with us. My mother could carry on with them in English. I wanted to like them – an only child feels that way about his relatives, not having seen his genetic speculations exhausted, and tends to see himself refracted even into second and third cousins several times removed. Now I saw a devious link with that American world in the strange clot of letters common to my name and theirs, and that pleased me.

We even enjoyed a bout of prosperity at about that time. I was thirteen or so, and we had moved from Hutchison (where a Greek janitor was finally hired) to a place off St-Denis where my father took charge of a sixteen-apartment building; they paid him well and gave us a three-room place out of the basement damps. That was *bonheur* in my father's mind – moving up to the ground floor where the front door buzzer kept waking you up. It was reasonably new; he didn't start to have trouble with bugs and paint for almost a year. He even saved a little money.

At just about the same time, in the more spacious way of the Schmitzes, they packed up everything in Manchester (where Uncle Howie owned three dry-cleaning shops) and moved to North Hollywood, Florida. That's a fair proportion: Hutchison is to St-Denis what Manchester is to Florida. He started with one dry-cleaning shop and had three others within a year. If he'd really been one of us, we'd have been suspicious of his tactics and motives, we would have called him lucky and undeserving. But he was American, he had his *sch*, so whatever he did seemed blessed by a different branch of fate, and we wondered only how we could share.

It was the winter of 1952. It was a cold sunny time on St-Denis. I still delivered my papers (practically in the neighbourhood), my father wasn't drinking that much, and my mother was staying out of church except on Sunday – it was a bad sign when she started going on weekdays – and we had just bought a car. It was a used Plymouth, the first car we'd ever owned. The idea was that we should visit the Schmitzes this time in their Florida home for Christmas. It was even their idea, arranged through the sisters. My father packed his tools in the rear ("You never know, Mance; I'd like to show him what I can do . . ."). He moved his brother Real and family into our place – Real was handy enough, more affable, but an even bigger drinker. We left Montreal on 18 December and took a cheap and slow drive down, the pace imposed by my father, who underestimated the strain of driving, and by my mother, who'd read of speedtraps and tourists languishing twenty years in southern dungeons for running a stop sign. The drive was cheap because we were dependent on my mother for expense money as soon as we entered the States, since she was the one who could go into the motel office and find out the prices. It would be three or four in the afternoon and my father would be a nervous wreck; just as we were unloading the trunk and my father was checking the level of whisky in the glove compartment bottle, she'd come out announcing it was highway robbery, we couldn't stay here. My father would groan, curse, and slam the trunk. Things would be dark by the time we found a vacancy in one of those rows of one-room cabins, arranged like stepping stones or in a semicircle (the kind you still see nowadays out on the Gaspesie with boards on the windows and a faded billboard out front advertising "investment property"). My mother put a limit of three dollars a night on accommodations; we shopped in supermarkets for cold meat, bread, mustard, and Pepsis. My father rejoiced in the cheaper gas; my mother reminded him it was a smaller gallon. Quietly, I calculated the difference. Remember, no drinking after Savannah, my mother said. It was clear: he expected to become the manager of a Schmitz Dry Kleenery.

The Schmitzes had rented a spacious cottage about a mile from the beach in North Hollywood. The outside stucco was green, the roof tiles orange, and the flowers violently pink and purple. The shrubs looked decorated with little red Christmas bulbs; I picked one – gift of my cousin – bit, and screamed in surprise. Red chillies. The front windows were sprayed with Santa's sleigh and a snowy "Merry Christmas". Only in English, no "Joyeux Noël" like our greeting back home. That was what I'd noticed most all the way down, the incompleteness of the signs, the satisfaction that their version said it all. I'd kept looking on the other side of things – my side – and I'd kept twirling the radio dial, for an equivalence that never came.

It was Christmas week and the Schmitzes were wearing Bermuda shorts and T-shirts with sailfish on the front. Tante Lise wore coral earrings and a red halter, and all her pale flesh had freckled. The night we arrived, my father got up on a stepladder, anxious to impress, and strung coloured lights along the gutter while my uncle shouted directions and watered the lawn. Christmas – and drinking Kool-Aid in the yard! We picked chilli peppers and sold them to every West Indian cook who answered the back doorbell. At night I licked my fingers and hummed with the air-conditioning. My tongue burned for hours. That was the extraordinary part for me: that things as hot as chillies could grow in your yard, that I could bake in December heat, and that other natural laws remained the same. My father was still shorter than my mother, and his face turned red and blotchy here too (just as it did in August back home) instead of an even schmitzean brown, and when he took off his shirt, only a tattoo, scars, and angry red welts were revealed. Small and sickly he seemed; worse, mutilated. My cousins rode their chrome-plated bicycles to the beach, but I never owned a two-wheeler and this didn't seem the time to reveal another weakness. Give me ice, I thought, my stick and a puck and an open net. Some men were never meant for vacations in shirtless countries: small hairy men with dirty winter boils and red swellings that never became anything lanceable, and tattoos of celebrities in their brief season of fame, now forgotten. My father's tattoo was as long as my twelve-year-old hand, done in a waterfront parlour in Montreal the day he'd thought of enlisting. My mother had been horrified, more at the tattoo than the thought of his shipping out. The tattoo pictured a front-faced Rocket, staring at an imaginary goalie and slapping a rising shot through a cloud of ice chips. Even though I loved the Canadiens and the Rocket mightily, I would have preferred my father to walk shirtless down the middle of the street with a naked woman on his back than for him to strip for the Schmitzes and my enormous cousins, who pointed and laughed, while I could almost understand what they were laughing about. They thought his tattoo was a kind of tribal marking, like kinky hair, thin moustaches, and slanty eyes – that if I took off my shirt I'd have one too, only smaller. *Lacroix*, I said to myself: how could he and I have the same name? It was foreign. I was a Deschenes, a Schmitz in the making.

On Christmas Eve we trimmed a silvered little tree and my uncle played Bing Crosby records on the console hi-fi-shortwave-bookcase (the biggest thing going in Manchester, New Hampshire, before the days of television). It would have been longer than our living room in Montreal; even here it filled one wall. They tried to teach me to imitate Crosby's "White Christmas", but my English was hopeless. My mother and aunt sang in harmony; my father kept spilling his iced tea while trying to clap. It was painful. I waited impatiently to get to bed in order to cut the night as short as possible.

The murkiness of those memories! How intense, how foreign; it all happened like a dream in which everything follows logically from some incredible premise – that we should go to Florida, that it should be so hot in December, that my father should be on his best behaviour for nearly a month . . . that we could hope that a little initiative and optimism would carry us anywhere but deeper into debt and darkest despair . . .

I see myself as in a dream, walking the beach alone, watching the coarse brown sand fall over my soft white feet. I hear my mother and Tante Lise whispering together, yet they're five hundred feet ahead ("Yes," my mother is saying, "what life is there for him back there? You can see how this would suit him. To a T! To a T!" I'm wondering is it me, or my father, who has no future back there, and Tante Lise begins, "Of course, I'm only a wife. I don't know what his thinking is – "), but worse is the silent image of my father in his winter trousers rolled up to his skinny knees and gathered in folds by a borrowed belt (at home he'd always worn braces), shirtless, shrunken, almost running to keep up with my uncle who walks closer to the water, in Bermuda shorts. I can tell from the beaten smile on my father's lips and from the way Uncle Howie is talking (while looking over my father's head at the ships on the horizon), that what the women have arranged ("It would be good to have you so close, Mance . . . I get these moods sometimes, you know? And five shops are too much for Howie . . .") the men have made impossible. I know that when my father was smiling and his head was bobbing in agreement and he was running to keep up with someone, he was being told off, turned down, laughed at. And the next stage was for him to go off alone, then come back to us with a story that embarrassed us all by its transparency, and that would be the last of him, sober, for three, four, or five days . . . I can see all this and hear it, though I am utterly alone near the crashing surf and it seems to be night and a forgotten short-wave receiver still blasts forth on a beach blanket somewhere; I go to it hoping to catch something I can understand, a hockey game, the scores, but all I get wrenching the dial until it snaps is Bing Crosby dreaming of a white Christmas and Cuban music and indecipherable commentary from Havana, the dog races from Miami, *jai alai*.

That drive back to Montreal lasted almost a month. Our money ran out in Georgia and we had to wait two weeks in a shack in the negro part of Savannah, where a family like ours – with a mother who liked to talk, and a father who drank and showed up only to collect our rent, and a kid my age who spent his time caddying and getting up before the sun to hunt golf balls – found space for us in a large room behind the kitchen, recently vacated by a dead grandparent. There were irregularities, the used-car dealer kept saying, various legal expenses involved with international commerce between Canadian Plymouths and innocent Georgia dealers, and we knew not to act too anxious (or even give our address) for fear of losing whatever bit of money we stood to gain. Finally he gave us $75, and that was when my father took his tools out of the back and sold them at a gas station for $50. We went down to the bus station, bought three tickets to Montreal, and my father swept the change into my mother's pocketbook. We were dressed for the January weather we'd be having when we got off, and the boy from the house we'd been staying in, shaking his head as he watched us board, muttered, "Man, you sure is crazy." It became a phrase of my mother's for all the next hard years. "Man, you sure is crazy." I mastered it and wore it like a Bruins sweater, till it too wore out. I remember those nights on the bus, my mother counting the bills and coins in her purse, like beads on a rosary, the numbers a silent prayer.

Back on St-Denis we found Real and family very happily installed. The same egregious streak that sputtered in my father flowed broadly in his brother. He'd all but brought fresh fruit baskets to the sixteen residents, carried newspapers to their doors, repaired buzzers that had never worked, shovelled insanely wide swaths down the front steps, replaced lights in the basement lockers, oiled, painted, polished . . . even laid off the booze for the whole month we were gone (which to my father was the unforgivable treachery); in short, while we'd sunk all our savings and hocked all our valuables to launch ourselves in the dry-cleaning business, Real had simply moved his family three blocks into lifelong comfort and security. My father took it all very quietly; we thought he'd blow sky-high. But he was finished. He'd put up the best, and the longest, show of his life and he'd seen himself squashed like a worm underfoot. Maybe he'd had one of those hellish moments when he'd seen himself in his brother-in-law's sunglasses, running at his side, knowing that those sunglasses were turned to the horizon and not to him.

Be Fruitful and Multiply

MADELEINE FERRON
Translated by Sheila Watson

About eight o'clock they woke with a start. Amazed and confused, she shrank from the unexpectedness of her waking. She wasn't dreaming. It was true. She had been married the day before and was waking up with her husband in a bed in the neighbour's house. He was pushing back his hair and swearing as he painfully lifted his head. He had gone to bed dead drunk. "You cannot refuse," they said. "After all, you are the bridegroom."

Half-way through the evening he was drunk already and a shock of brown hair had fallen forward over his face without his making any effort at all to throw it back with a shake of his head as he usually did. Shifting from leg to leg, her senses blunted with sleep, she watched, heavy-eyed, the progress of the festivity, diverted from time to time by the almost wild pleasure he was taking in his own wedding feast.

Since it was her wedding too, she resolutely stayed awake, all the while envying her cousin who slept peacefully, her head against the corner of the wall. They were the same age – thirteen and a half. At that age sleep could be pardoned, she had heard them say again and again. Of course, but not on the night of one's wedding.

It was long after midnight when at last he signalled her to follow him. They went through the garden so that no one could see them or play mean tricks on them. She helped him to jump over the fence, to cross the ditch, and to climb the stairs. He fell across the bed and began to snore at once, his hands clenched like a child's. He was eighteen. She slept, curled round on an empty corner of the mattress.

They got up quickly as soon as they woke, ashamed to have stayed in bed so long. He ran to hitch up a buggy which he drove around in front of his in-laws" house. His wife's trunk was loaded on and he helped her up. He was formal, embarrassed; she, almost joyful. Then he turned the horse at a trot toward the property that had been prepared for them. He was to be the second neighbour down the road. She waved happily again and again and her mother, who was crying, kept watching, until they had rounded the corner, the blond braid that swung like a pendulum over the back of the buggy seat.

All day they worked eagerly getting settled. In the evening they went to bed early. He embraced her eagerly. Face to face with a heat that flamed and entangled her in its curious movement, she was frightened.

"What are you doing?" she asked.

He answered her quietly, "You are the sheep and I am the ram."

"Oh," she said. It was simple when one had a reference point.

On the first mornings of their life together, after he had left for the fields, she ran quickly to her mother's.

"Are you managing?" her mother always asked.

"Yes," the child replied smiling.

"Your husband, is he good to you?"

"Oh yes," she said. "He says I am a pretty sheep."

Sheep . . . sheep. The mother, fascinated, watched her daughter attentively but did not dare to question her further.

"Go back to your husband now," she said. "Busy yourself about the house and get his meal ready."

Since the girl hesitated uncertainly as if she did not understand, her mother sprinkled sugar on a slice of bread spread with cream, gave it to her and pushed her gently toward the door. The child went down the road eating her bread and the mother, reassured, leaned sadly against the wall of the house watching the thick swaying braid until the girl turned the corner of the road.

Little by little the young wife spaced her visits. In autumn when the cold rain began to fall, she came only on Sundays. She had found her own rhythm. Was she too eager, too ambitious? Perhaps she was simply inattentive. Her tempo was too swift. She always hurried now. She wove more bed covers than her chest could hold, cultivated more vegetables than they could eat, raised more calves than they knew how to sell.

And the children came quickly – almost faster than nature permits. She was never seen without a child in her arms, one in her belly, and another at her heels. She raised them well, mechanically, without counting them; accepted them as the seasons are accepted;

watched them leave; not with fatalism or resignation but steadfast and untroubled, face to face with the ineluctable cycle that makes the apple fall when it is ripe.

The simple mechanism she had set in motion did not falter. She was the cog wheel that had no right to oversee the whole machine. Everything went well. Only the rhythm was too fast. She outstripped the seasons. The begetting of her children pressed unreasonably on that of her grandchildren and the order was broken. Her daughters and her sons already had many children when she was still bearing others – giving her grandsons uncles who were younger than they were and for whom they could have no respect.

She had twenty-two children. It was extravagant. Fortunately, as one child was carried in the front door, beribboned and wailing, one went out the rear door alone, its knapsack on its back. Nevertheless, it was extravagant. She never realized it.

When her husband was buried and her youngest son married, she caught her breath, decided finally on slippers and a rocking chair. The mechanism could not adjust to a new rhythm. It broke down. She found herself disoriented, incapable of directing the stranger she had become, whom she did not know, who turned round and round with outstretched arms, more and more agitated.

"And if I should visit my family?" she asked her neighbour one day. She had children settled in the four corners of the province, some even exiled to the United States. She would go to take the census or, rather, she would go like a bishop to make the rounds of the diocese.

She had been seen leaving one morning, walking slowly. She had climbed into the bus, a small black cardboard suitcase in her hand. She had smiled at her neighbours but her eyes were still haggard.

She went first to the States. She was introduced to the wife of her grandson who spoke no French and to all the others whom she looked at searchingly.

"That one," she said, "is she my child or my child's child?"

The generations had become confused. She no longer knew.

She went back to Sept-Isles. One day, when she was rocking on the veranda with one of her sons, he pointed out a big dark-haired young man who was coming down the street.

"Look, mother," her son said. "He is my youngest." He was

eighteen and a shock of hair fell forward over his face. She began to cry.

"It is he," she said. "It is my husband."

The next day she was taken to the home of one of her daughters, whom she called by her sister's name. Her daughter took care of her for several days and then took her to the house of the other daughter who, after much kindness, took her to the home of one of the oldest of the grandsons. She asked no questions. She cried.

Finally, one of her boys, chaplain in a home for the aged, came to get her. She followed him obediently. When he presented her to the assembled community, she turned to him and said quietly, "Tell me, are all these your brothers?"

The Watcher

GUY VANDERHAEGHE

I suppose it was having a bad chest that turned me into an observer, a watcher, at an early age.

"Charlie has my chest," my mother often informed friends. "A real weakness there," she would add significantly, thumping her own wishbone soundly.

I suppose I had. Family lore had me narrowly escaping death from pneumonia at the age of four. It seems I spent an entire Sunday in delirium, soaking the sheets. Dr Carlyle was off at the reservoir rowing in his little skiff and couldn't be reached – something for which my mother illogically refused to forgive him. She was a woman who nursed and tenaciously held dark grudges. Forever after that incident the doctor was slightlingly and coldly dismissed in conversation as a "man who betrayed the public's trust".

Following that spell of pneumonia, I regularly suffered from bouts of bronchitis, which often landed me in hospital in Fortune, forty miles away. Compared with the oxygen tent and the whacking great needles that were buried in my skinny rump there, being invalided at home was a piece of cake. Coughing and hacking, I would leaf through catalogues and read comic books until my head swam with print-fatigue. My diet was largely of my own whimsical choosing – hot chocolate and graham wafers were supplemented by sticky sweet coughdrops, which I downed one after the another until my stomach could take no more, revolted, and tossed up the whole mess.

With the first signs of improvement in my condition my mother moved her baby to the living-room chesterfield, where she and the radio could keep me company. The electric kettle followed me and was soon burbling in the corner, jetting steam into the air to keep my lungs moist and pliable. Because I was neither quite sick nor quite well, these were the best days of my illnesses. My stay at home hadn't yet made me bored and restless, my chest no longer hurt when I breathed, and that loose pocket of rattling phlegm meant I didn't have to worry about going back to school just yet. So I luxuriated in this steamy equatorial climate, tended by a doting mother as if I were a rare tropical orchid.

My parents didn't own a television and so my curiosity and attention were focused on my surroundings during my illnesses. I tried to squeeze every bit of juice out of them. Sooner than most children I learned that if you kept quiet and still and didn't insist on drawing attention to yourself as many kids did, adults were inclined to regard you as being one with the furniture, as significant and sentient as a hassock. By keeping mum I was treated to illuminating glances into an adult world of conventional miseries and scandals.

I wasn't sure at the age of six what a miscarriage was, but I knew that Ida Thompson had had one and that now her plumbing was buggered. And watching old lady Kuznetzky hang her washing, through a living-room window trickling with condensed kettle steam, I was able to confirm for myself the rumour that the old girl eschewed panties. As she bent over to rummage in her laundry basket I caught a brief glimpse of huge, white buttocks that shimmered in the pale spring sunshine.

I also soon knew (how I don't remember exactly) that Norma Ruggs had business with the Liquor Board Store when she shuffled by our window every day at exactly 10.50 a.m. She was always at the store door at 11.00 when they unlocked and opened up for business. At 11.15 she trudged home again, a pint of ice cream in one hand, a brown paper bag disguising a bottle of fortified wine in the other, and her blotchy complexion painted a high colour of shame.

"Poor old girl," my mother would say whenever she caught sight of Norma passing by in her shabby coat and sloppy man's over-shoes. They had been in high school together, and Norma had been class brain and valedictorian. She had been an obliging, dutiful girl and still was. For the wine wasn't Norma's – the ice cream was her only vice. The booze was her husband's, a vet who had come back from the war badly crippled.

All this careful study of adults may have made me old before my time. In any case it seemed to mark me in some recognizable way as being "different" or "queer for a kid". When I went to live with my grandmother in July of 1959 she spotted it right away. Of course, she was only stating the obvious when she declared me skinny and delicate, but she also noted in her vinegary voice that my eyes had a bad habit of never letting her go, and that I was the worst case of little pitchers having big ears that she had ever come across.

I ended up at my grandmother's because in May of that year my mother's bad chest finally caught up with her, much to her and everyone else's surprise. It had been pretty generally agreed by all her acquaintances that Mabel Bradley's defects in that regard were largely imagined. Not so. A government-sponsored X-ray pro-gramme discovered tuberculosis, and she was packed off, pale and drawn with worry, for a stay in the sanatorium at Fort Qu'Appelle.

For roughly a month, until the school year ended, my father took charge of me and the house. He was a desolate, lanky, drooping weed of a man who had married late in life but nevertheless had been easily domesticated. I didn't like him much.

My father was badly wrenched by my mother's sickness and absence. He scrawled her long, untidy letters with a stub of gnawed pencil, and once he got shut of me, visited her every weekend. He was a soft and sentimental man whose eyes ran to water at the drop of a hat, or more accurately, death of a cat. Unlike his mother, my Grandma Bradley, he hadn't a scrap of flint or hard-headed common sense in him.

But then neither had any of his many brothers and sisters. It was as if the old girl had unflinchingly withheld the genetic code for responsibility and practicality from her pin-headed offspring. Life for her children was a series of thundering defeats, whirlwind cala-mities, or, at best, hurried strategic retreats. Businesses crashed and marriages failed, for they had – my father excepted – a taste for the unstable in partners marital and fiscal.

My mother saw no redeeming qualities in any of them. By and large they drank too much, talked too loudly, and raised ill-mannered children – monsters of depravity whose rudeness pro-vided my mother with endless illustrations of what she feared I might become. "You're eating just like a pig," she would say, "exactly like your cousin Elvin." Or to my father, "You're neglecting the belt. He's starting to get as lippy as that little snot Muriel."

And in the midst, in the very eye of this familial cyclone of mishap and discontent, stood Grandma Bradley, as firm as a rock. Troubles of all kinds were laid on her doorstep. When my cousin Criselda suddenly turned big-tummied at sixteen and it proved difficult to ascertain with any exactitude the father, or even point a finger of general blame in the direction of a putative sire, she was shipped off to Grandma Bradley until she delivered. Uncle Ernie dried out on Grandma's farm and Uncle Ed hid there from several people he had sold prefab, assemble-yourself, crop-duster airplanes to.

So it was only family tradition that I should be deposited there. When domestic duties finally overwhelmed him, and I complained too loudly about fried-egg sandwiches for dinner *again*, my father left the bacon rinds hardening and curling grotesquely on unwashed plates, the slut's wool eddying along the floor in the currents of a draft, and drove the one hundred and fifty miles to the farm, *right then and there*.

My father, a dangerous man behind the wheel, took any extended trip seriously, believing the highways to be narrow, unnavigable ribbons of carnage. This trip loomed so dangerously in his mind that, rather than tear a hand from the wheel, or an eye from the road, he had me, *chronic sufferer of lung disorders*, light his cigarettes and place them carefully in his dry lips. My mother would have killed him.

"You'll love it at Grandma's," he kept saying unconvincingly, "you'll have a real boy's summer on the farm. It'll build you up, the chores and all that. And good fun too. You don't know it now, but you are living the best days of your life right now. What I wouldn't give to be a kid again. You'll love it there. There's chickens and *everything*."

It wasn't exactly a lie. There were chickens. But the *everything* – as broad and overwhelming and suggestive of possibilities as my father tried to make it sound – didn't cover much. It certainly didn't comprehend a pony or a dog as I had hoped, chickens being the only livestock on the place.

It turned out that my grandmother, although she had spent most of her life on that particular piece of ground and eventually died there, didn't care much for the farm and was entirely out of sympathy with most varieties of animal life. She did keep chickens for the eggs, although she admitted that her spirits lifted considerably in the fall when it came time to butcher the hens.

Her flock was a garrulous, scraggly crew that spent their days having dust baths in the front yard, hiding their eggs, and, fleet and ferocious as hunting cheetahs, running down scuttling lizards which they trampled and pecked to death while their shiny, expressionless eyes shifted dizzily in their stupid heads. The only one of these birds I felt any compassion for was Stanley the rooster, a bedraggled male who spent his days tethered to a stake by a piece of bailer twine looped around his leg. Poor Stanley crowed heart-rendingly in his captivity: his comb drooped pathetically, and he was utterly crestfallen as he lecherously eyed his bantam beauties daintily scavenging. Grandma kept him in this unnatural bondage to prevent him fertilizing the eggs and producing blood spots in the yolks. Being a finicky eater I approved this policy, but nevertheless felt some guilt over Stanley.

No, the old Bradley homestead, all that encompassed by my father's *everything*, wasn't very impressive. The two-storey house, though big and solid, needed paint and shingles. A track had been worn in the kitchen linoleum clean through to the floorboards and a long rent in the screen door had been stitched shut with waxed thread. The yard was little more than a tangle of thigh-high ragweed and sowthistle to which the chickens repaired for shade. A windbreak of spruce on the north side of the house was dying from lack of water and the competition from Scotch thistle. The evergreens were no longer green; their sere needles fell away from the branches at the touch of a hand.

The abandoned barn out back was flanked by two mountainous rotted piles of manure which I remember sprouting button mushrooms after every warm soaker of a rain. That pile of shit was the only useful thing in a yard full of junk: wrecked cars, old wagon wheels, collapsing sheds. The barn itself was mightily decayed. The paint had been stripped from its planks by rain, hail, and dry, blistering winds, and the roof sagged like a tired nag's back. For a small boy it was an ominous place on a summer day. The air was still and dark and heavy with heat. At the sound of footsteps rats squeaked and scrabbled in the empty mangers, and the sparrows which had spattered the rafters white with their dung whirred about and fluted ghostly cries.

In 1959 Grandma Bradley would have been sixty-nine, which

made her a child of the gay nineties – although the supposed gaiety of that age didn't seem to have made much impress upon the development of her character. Physically she was an imposing woman. Easily six feet tall, she carried a hundred and eighty pounds on her generous frame without prompting speculation as to what she had against girdles. She could touch the floor effortlessly with the flat of her palms and pack an eighty-pound sack of chicken feed on her shoulder. She dyed her hair auburn in defiance of local mores, and never went to town to play bridge, whist, or canasta without wearing a hat and getting dressed to the teeth. Grandma loved card games of all varieties and considered anyone who didn't a mental defective.

A cigarette always smouldered in her trap. She smoked sixty a day and rolled them as thin as knitting needles in an effort at economy. These cigarettes were so wispy and delicate they tended to get lost between her swollen fingers.

And above all she believed in plain speaking. She let me know that as my father's maroon Meteor pulled out of the yard while we stood waving goodbye on the front steps.

"Let's get things straight from the beginning," she said without taking her eyes off the car as it bumped toward the grid road. "I don't chew my words twice. If you're like any of the rest of them I've had here, you've been raised as wild as a goddamn Indian. Not one of my grandchildren have been brought up to mind. Well, you'll mind around here. I don't jaw and blow hot air to jaw and blow hot air. I belted your father when he needed it, and make no mistake I'll belt you. Is that understood?"

"Yes," I said with a sinking feeling as I watched my father's car disappear down the road, swaying from side to side as its suspension was buffeted by potholes.

"These bloody bugs are eating me alive," she said, slapping her arm. "I'm going in."

I trailed after her as she slopped back into the house in a pair of badly mauled, laceless sneakers. The house was filled with a half-light that changed its texture with every room. The venetian blinds were drawn in the parlour and some flies carved Immelmanns in the dark air that smelled of cellar damp. Others battered their bullet bodies *tip-tap*, *tip-tap* against the window-panes.

In the kitchen my grandmother put the kettle on the stove to boil for tea. After she had lit one of her matchstick smokes, she inquired through a blue haze if I was hungry.

"People aren't supposed to smoke around me," I informed her. "Because of my chest. Dad can't even smoke in our house."

"That so?" she said genially. Her cheeks collapsed as she drew on her butt. I had a hint there, if I'd only known it, of how she'd look in her coffin. "You won't like it here then," she said. "I smoke all the time."

I tried a few unconvincing coughs. I was ignored. She didn't respond to the same signals as my mother.

"My mother has a bad chest, too," I said. "She's in a TB sanatorium."

"So I heard," my grandmother said, getting up to fetch the whistling kettle. "Oh, I suspect she'll be as right as rain in no time with a little rest. TB isn't what it used to be. Not with all these new drugs." She considered. "That's not to say though that your father'll ever hear the end of it. Mabel was always a silly little shit that way."

I almost fell off my chair. I had never thought I'd live to hear the day my mother was called a silly little shit.

"Drink tea?" asked Grandma Bradley, pouring boiling water into a brown teapot.

I shook my head.

"How old are you anyway?" she asked.

"Eleven."

"You're old enough then," she said, taking down a cup from the shelf. "Tea gets the kidneys moving and carries off the poisons in the blood. That's why all the Chinese live to be so old. They all live to be a hundred."

"I don't know if my mother would like it," I said. "Me drinking tea."

"You worry a lot for a kid," she said, "don't you?"

I didn't know how to answer that. It wasn't a question I had ever considered. I tried to shift the conversation.

"What's there for a kid to do around here?" I said in an unnaturally inquisitive voice.

"Well, we could play cribbage."

"I don't know how to play cribbage."

She was genuinely shocked. "What!" she exclaimed. "Why, you're eleven years old! Your father could count a cribbage hand when he was five. I taught all my kids to."

"I never learned how," I said. "We don't even have a deck of cards at our house. My father hates cards. Says he had too much of them as a boy."

At this my grandmother arched her eyebrows. "Is that a fact? Well, hoity-toity."

"So, since I don't play cards," I continued in a strained manner I imagined was polite, "what could I do – I mean, for fun?"

"Make your own fun," she said. "I never considered fun such a problem. Use your imagination. Take a broomstick and make like Nimrod."

"Who's Nimrod?" I asked.

"Pig ignorant," she said under her breath, and then louder, directly to me, "Ask me no questions and I'll tell you no lies. Drink your tea."

And that, for the time being, was that.

It's all very well to tell someone to make their own fun. It's the making of it that is the problem. In a short time I was a very bored kid. There was no one to play with, no horses to ride, no gun to shoot gophers, no dog for company. There was nothing to read except the *Country Guide* and *Western Producer*. There was nothing or nobody interesting to watch. I went through my grandmother's drawers but found nothing as surprising there as I had discovered in my parents'.

Most days it was so hot that the very idea of fun boiled out of me and evaporated. I moped and dragged myself listlessly around the house in the loose-jointed, water-boned way kids have when they can't stand anything, not even their precious selves.

On my better days I tried to take up with Stanley the rooster. Scant chance of that. Tremors of panic ran through his body at my approach. He tugged desperately on the twine until he jerked his free leg out from under himself and collapsed in the dust, his heart bumping the tiny crimson scallops of his breast feathers, the black pellets of his eyes glistening, all the while shitting copiously. Finally, in the last extremes of chicken terror, he would allow me to stroke his yellow beak and finger his comb.

I felt sorry for the captive Stanley and several times tried to take him for a walk, to give him a chance to take the air and broaden his limited horizons. But this prospect alarmed him so much that I was always forced to return him to his stake in disgust while he fluttered, squawked and flopped.

So fun was a commodity in short supply. That is, until something interesting turned up during the first week of August. Grandma Bradley was dredging little watering canals with a hoe among the corn stalks on a bright blue Monday morning, and I was shelling peas into a colander on the front stoop, when a black car nosed diffidently up the road and into the yard. Then it stopped a good twenty yards short of the house as if its occupants weren't sure of their welcome. After some time, the doors opened and a man and woman got carefully out.

The woman wore turquoise-blue pedal-pushers, a sloppy black turtleneck sweater, and a gash of scarlet lipstick swiped across her white, vivid face. This was my father's youngest sister, Aunt Evelyn.

The man took her gently and courteously by the elbow and balanced her as she edged up the front yard in her high heels, careful to avoid turning an ankle on a loose stone, or in an old tyre track.

The thing which immediately struck me about the man was his beard – the first I had ever seen. Beards weren't popular in 1959 – not in our part of the world. His was a randy, jutting, little goat's-beard that would have looked wicked on any other face but his. He was very tall and his considerable height was accented by a lack of corresponding breadth to his body. He appeared to have been racked and stretched against his will into an exceptional and unnatural anatomy. As he walked and talked animatedly, his free hand fluttered in front of my aunt. It sailed, twirled and gambolled on the air. Like a butterfly enticing a child, it seemed to lead her hypnotized across a yard fraught with perils for city-shod feet.

My grandmother laid down her hoe and called sharply to her daughter.

"Evvie!" she called. "Over here, Evvie!"

At the sound of her mother's voice my aunt's head snapped around and she began to wave jerkily and stiffly, striving to maintain a tottering balance on her high-heeled shoes. It wasn't hard to see that there was something not quite right with her. By the time my grandmother and I reached the pair, Aunt Evelyn was in tears, sobbing hollowly and jamming the heel of her palm into her front teeth.

The man was speaking calmly to her. "Control. Control. Deep, steady breaths. Think sea. Control. Control. Control. Think sea, Evelyn. Deep. Deep. Deep," he muttered.

"What the hell is the matter, Evelyn?" my grandmother asked sharply. "And who is *he*?"

"Evelyn is a little upset," the man said, keeping his attention focused on my aunt. "She's having one of her anxiety attacks. If you'd just give us a moment we'll clear this up. She's got to learn to handle stressful situations." He inclined his head in a priestly manner and said, "Be with the sea, Evelyn. Deep. Deep. Sink in the sea."

"It's her damn nerves again," said my grandmother.

"Yes," the man said benignly, with a smile of blinding condescension. "Sort of."

"She's been as nervous as a cut cat all her life," said my grandmother, mostly to herself.

"Momma," said Evelyn, weeping. "Momma."

"Slide beneath the waves, Evelyn. Down, down, down to the beautiful pearls," the man chanted softly. This was really something.

My grandmother took Aunt Evelyn by her free elbow, shook it, and said sharply, "Evelyn, shut up!" Then she began to drag her briskly toward the house. For a moment the man looked as if he had it in mind to protest, but in the end he meekly acted as a flanking escort for Aunt Evelyn as she was marched into the house. When I tried to follow, my grandmother gave me one of her looks and said definitely, "You find something to do out here."

I did. I waited a few minutes and then duck-walked my way under the parlour window. There I squatted with my knobby shoulder blades pressed against the siding and the sun beating into my face.

My grandmother obviously hadn't wasted any time with the social niceties. They were fairly into it.

"Lovers?" said my grandmother. "Is that what it's called now? Shack-up, you mean."

"Oh, Momma," said Evelyn, and she was crying, "it's all right. We're going to get married."

"You believe that?" said my grandmother. "You believe that geek is going to marry you?"

"Thompson," said the geek, "my name is Thompson, Robert Thompson, and we'll marry as soon as I get my divorce. Although Lord only knows when that'll be."

"That's right," said my grandmother, "Lord only knows." Then to her daughter, "You got another one. A real prize off the midway, didn't you? Evelyn, you're a certifiable lunatic."

"I didn't expect this," said Thompson. "We came here because Evelyn has had a bad time of it recently. She hasn't been eating or sleeping properly and consequently she's got herself run down. She finds it difficult to control her emotions, don't you, darling?"

I thought I heard a mild yes.

"So," said Thompson, continuing, "we decided Evelyn needs some peace and quiet before I go back to school in September."

"School," said my grandmother. "Don't tell me you're some kind of teacher?" She seemed stunned by the very idea.

"No," said Aunt Evelyn, and there was a tremor of pride in her voice that testified to her amazement that she had been capable of landing such a rare and remarkable fish. "Not a teacher. Robert's a graduate student of American Literature at the University of British Columbia."

"Hoity-toity," said Grandmother. "A graduate student. A graduate student of American Literature."

"Doctoral programme," said Robert.

"And did you ever ask yourself, Evelyn, what the hell this genius is doing with you? Or is it just the same old problem with you – elevator panties? Some guy comes along and pushes the button. Up, down. Up, down."

The image this created in my mind made me squeeze my knees together deliciously and stifle a giggle.

"Mother," said Evelyn, continuing to bawl.

"Guys like this don't marry barmaids," said my grandmother.

"Cocktail hostess," corrected Evelyn. "I'm a cocktail hostess."

"You don't have to make any excuses, dear," said Thompson pompously. "Remember what I told you. You're past the age of being judged."

"What the hell is that supposed to mean?" said my grandmother.

"And by the way, don't start handing out orders in my house. You won't be around long enough to make them stick."

"That remains to be seen," said Thompson.

"Let's go, Robert," said Evelyn nervously.

"Go on upstairs, Evelyn. I want to talk to your mother."

"You don't have to go anywhere," said my grandmother. "You can stay put."

"Evelyn, go upstairs." There was a pause and then I heard the sound of a chair creaking, then footsteps.

"Well," said my grandmother at last, "round one. Now for round two – get the hell out of my house."

"Can't do that."

"Why the hell not?"

"It's very difficult to explain," he said.

"Try."

"As you can see for yourself, Evelyn isn't well. She is very highly strung at the moment. I believe she is on the verge of a profound personality adjustment, a breakthrough." He paused dramatically. "Or breakdown."

"It's times like this that I wished I had a dog on the place to run off undesirables."

"The way I read it," said Thompson, unperturbed, "is that at the moment two people bulk very large in Evelyn's life. You and me. She needs the support and love of us both. You're not doing your share."

"I ought to slap your face."

"She has come home to try to get a hold of herself. We have to bury our dislikes for the moment. She needs to be handled very carefully."

"You make her sound like a trained bear. *Handled*. What that girl needs is a good talking to, and I am perfectly capable of giving her that."

"No, Mrs Bradley," Thompson said firmly in that maddeningly self-assured tone of his. "If you don't mind me saying so, I think that's part of her problem. It's important now for you to just let Evelyn *be*."

"Get out of my house," said my grandmother, at the end of her tether.

"I know it's difficult for you to understand," he said smoothly, "but if you understood the psychology of this you would see it's impossible for me to go; or for that matter, for Evelyn to go. If I leave she'll feel I've abandoned her. It can't be done. We're faced with a real psychological balancing act here."

"Now I've heard everything," said my grandmother. "Are you telling me you'd have the gall to move into a house where you're not wanted and just . . . just *stay there*?"

"Yes," said Thompson. "And I think you'll find me quite stubborn on this particular point."

"My God," said my grandmother. I could tell by her tone of voice that she had never come across anyone like Mr Thompson before. At a loss for a suitable reply, she simply reiterated, "My God."

"I'm going upstairs now," said Thompson. "Maybe you could get the boy to bring in our bags while I see how Evelyn is doing. The car isn't locked." The second time he spoke his voice came from further away; I imagined him paused in the doorway. "Mrs Bradley, please let's make this stay pleasant for Evelyn's sake."

She didn't bother answering him.

When I barged into the house some time later with conspicuous noisiness, I found my grandmother standing at the bottom of the stairs staring up the steps. "Well, I'll be damned," she said under her breath. "I've never seen anything like that. Goddamn freak." She even repeated it several times under her breath. "Goddamn freak. Goddamn freak."

Who could blame me if, after a boring summer, I felt my chest tighten with anticipation. Adults could be immensely interesting and entertaining if you knew what to watch for.

At first things were disappointingly quiet. Aunt Evelyn seldom set forth outside the door of the room she and her man inhabited by squatters" right. There was an argument, short and sharp, between Thompson and Grandmother over this. The professor claimed no one had any business prying into what Evelyn did up there. She was an adult and had the right to her privacy and her own thoughts. My grandmother claimed *she* had a right to know what was going on up there, even if nobody else thought she did.

I could have satisfied her curiosity on that point. Not much was

going on up there. Several squints through the keyhole had revealed
Aunt Evelyn lolling about the bedspread in a blue housecoat, eating
soda crackers and sardines, and reading a stack of movie magazines
she had had me lug out of the trunk of the car.

Food, you see, was beginning to become something of a problem
for our young lovers. Grandma rather pointedly set only three
places for meals, and Evelyn, out of loyalty to her boyfriend,
couldn't very well sit down and break bread with us. Not that
Thompson didn't take such things in his stride. He sauntered casually and conspicuously about the house as if he owned it, even
going so far as to poke his head in the fridge and rummage in it like
some pale, hairless bear. At times like that my grandmother was
capable of looking through him as if he didn't exist.

On the second day of his stay Thompson took up with me, which
was all right as far as I was concerned. I had no objection. Why he
decided to do this I'm not sure exactly. Perhaps he was looking for
some kind of an ally, no matter how weak. Most likely he wanted to
get under the old lady's skin. Or maybe he just couldn't bear not
having anyone to tell how wonderful he was. Thompson was that
kind of a guy.

I was certainly let in on the secret. He was a remarkable fellow. He
dwelt at great length on those things which made him such an
extraordinary human being. I may have gotten the order of pre-
cedence all wrong, but if I remember correctly there were three
things which made Thompson very special and different from all the
other people I would ever meet, no matter how long or hard I lived.

First, he was going to write a book about a poet called Allen
Ginsberg which was going to knock the socks off everybody who
counted. It turned out he had actually met this Ginsberg the summer
before in San Francisco and asked him if he could write a book about
him and Ginsberg had said, Sure, why the hell not? The way
Thompson described what it would be like when he published this
book left me with the impression that he was going to spend most of
the rest of his life riding around on people's shoulders and being
cheered by a multitude of admirers.

Second, he confessed to knowing a tremendous amount about
what made other people tick and how to adjust their mainsprings
when they went kaflooey. He knew all this because at one time his

own mainspring had gotten a little out of sorts. But now he was a fully integrated personality with a highly creative mind and a strong intuitive sense. That's why he was so much help to Aunt Evelyn in her time of troubles.

Third, he was a Buddhist.

The only one of these things which impressed me at the time was the bit about being a Buddhist. However, I was confused, because in the *Picture Book of the World's Great Religions* which we had at home, all the Buddhists were bald, and Thompson had a hell of a lot of hair, more than I had ever seen on a man. But even though he wasn't bald, he had an idol. A little bronze statue with the whimsical smile and slightly crossed eyes which he identified as Padma-sambhava. He told me that it was a Tibetan antique he had bought in San Fransisco as an object of veneration and an aid to his meditations. I asked him what a meditation was and he offered to teach me one. So I learned to recite with great seriousness and flexible intonation one of his Tibetan meditations, while my grandmother glared across her quintessentially Western parlour with unbelieving eyes.

I could soon deliver. "A king must go when his time has come. His wealth, his friends and his relatives cannot go with him. Wherever men go, wherever they stay, the effect of their past acts follows them like a shadow. Those who are in the grip of desire, the grip of existence, the grip of ignorance, move helplessly round through the spheres of life, as men or gods or as wretches in the lower regions."

Not that an eleven-year-old could make much of any of *that*.

Which is not to say that even an eleven-year-old could be fooled by Robert Thompson. In his stubbornness, egoism and blindness he was transparently un-Buddhalike. To watch him and my grandmother snarl and snap their teeth over that poor, dry bone, Evelyn, was evidence enough of how firmly bound we all are to the wretched wheel of life and its stumbling desires.

No, even his most effective weapon, his cool benevolence, that patina of patience and forbearance which Thompson displayed to Grandmother, could crack.

One windy day when he had coaxed Aunt Evelyn out for a walk I followed them at a distance. They passed the windbreak of spruce, and at the sagging barbed-wire fence he gallantly manipulated the wires while my aunt floundered over them in an impractical dress and crinoline. It was the kind of dippy thing she would decide to wear on a hike.

Thompson strode along through the rippling grass like a wading heron, his baggy pant-legs flapping and billowing in the wind. My aunt moved along gingerly behind him, one hand modestly pinning down her wind-teased dress in the front, the other hand plastering the back of it to her behind.

It was only when they stopped and faced each other that I realized that all the time they had been traversing the field they had been arguing. A certain vaguely communicated agitation in the attitude of her figure, the way his arm stabbed at the featureless wash of sky, implied a dispute. She turned toward the house and he caught her by the arm and jerked it. In a fifties calendar fantasy her dress lifted in the wind, exposing her panties. I sank in the grass until their seed tassels trembled against my chin. I wasn't going to miss watching this for the world.

She snapped and twisted on the end of his arm like a fish on a line. Her head was flung back in an exaggerated, antique display of despair; her head rolled grotesquely from side to side as if her neck were broken.

Suddenly Thompson began striking awkwardly at her exposed buttocks and thighs with the flat of his hand. The long, gangly arm slashed like a flail as she scampered around him, the radius of her escape limited by the distance of their linked arms.

From where I knelt in the grass I could hear nothing. I was too far off. As far as I was concerned there were no cries and no pleading. The whole scene, as I remember it, was shorn of any of the personal idiosyncrasies which manifest themselves in violence. It appeared a simple case of retribution.

That night, for the first time, my aunt came down to supper and claimed her place at the table with queenly graciousness. She wore shorts, too, for the first time, and gave a fine display of mottled, discoloured thighs which reminded me of bruised fruit. She made sure, almost as if by accident, that my grandmother had a good hard look at them.

Right out of the blue my grandmother said, "I don't want you hanging around that man any more. You stay away from him."

"Why?" I asked rather sulkily. He was the only company I had. Since my aunt's arrival Grandmother had paid no attention to me whatsoever.

It was late afternoon and we were sitting on the porch watching Evelyn squeal as she swung in the tyre swing Thompson had rigged up for me in the barn. He had thrown a length of stray rope over the runner for the sliding door and hung a tyre from it. I hadn't the heart to tell him I was too old for tyre swings.

Aunt Evelyn seemed to be enjoying it though. She was screaming and girlishly kicking up her legs. Thompson couldn't be seen. He was deep in the settled darkness of the barn, pushing her back and forth. She disappeared and reappeared according to the arc which she travelled through. Into the barn, out in the sun. Light, darkness. Light, darkness.

Grandma ignored my question. "Goddamn freak," she said, scratching a match on the porch rail and lighting one of her rollies. "Wait and see, he'll get his wagon fixed."

"Aunt Evelyn likes him," I noted pleasantly, just to stir things up a bit.

"Your Aunt Evelyn's screws are loose," she said sourly. "And he's the son of a bitch who owns the screwdriver that loosened them."

"He must be an awful smart fellow to be studying to be a professor at a university," I commented. It was the last dig I could chance.

"One thing I know for sure," snapped my grandmother. "He isn't smart enough to lift the toilet seat when he pees. There's evidence enough for that."

After hearing that, I took to leaving a few conspicuous droplets of my own as a matter of course on each visit. Every little bit might help things along.

I stood in his doorway and watched Thompson meditate. And don't think that, drenched in *satori* as he was, he didn't know it. He put on quite a performance sitting on the floor in his underpants. When he came out of his trance he pretended to be surprised to see me. While he dressed we struck up a conversation.

"You know, Charlie," he said while he put on his sandals (I'd never seen a grown man wear sandals in my entire life), "you remind me of my little Padma-sambhava," he said, nodding to the idol squatting on his dresser. "For while, you know, I thought it was the smile, but it isn't. It's the eyes."

"Its eyes are crossed," I said, none too flattered at the comparison.

"No they're not," he said good-naturedly. He tucked his shirt-tail into his pants. "The artist, the maker of that image, set them fairly close together to suggest – aesthetically speaking – the intensity of inner vision, its concentration." He picked up the idol and, looking at it, said, "These are very watchful eyes, very knowing eyes. Your eyes are something like that. From your eyes I could tell you're an intelligent boy." He paused, set Padma-sambhava back on the dresser, and asked. "Are you?"

I shrugged.

"Don't be afraid to say if you are," he said. "False modesty can be as corrupting as vanity. It took me twenty-five years to learn that."

"I usually get all A's on my report card," I volunteered.

"Well, that's something," he said, looking around the room for his belt. He picked a sweater off a chair and peered under it. "Then you see what's going on around here, don't you?" he asked. "You see what your grandmother is mistakenly trying to do?"

I nodded.

"That's right," he said. "You're a smart boy." He sat down on the bed. "Come here."

I went over to him. He took hold of me by the arms and looked into my eyes with all the sincerity he could muster. "You know, being intelligent means responsibilities. It means doing something worth while with your life. For instance, have you given any thought as to what you would like to be when you grow up?"

"A spy," I said.

The silly bugger laughed.

It was the persistent, rhythmic thud that first woke me, and once wakened, I picked up the undercurrent of muted clamour, of stifled struggle. The noise seeped through the beaverboard wall of the adjoining bedroom into my own, a storm of hectic urgency and violence. The floorboards of the old house squeaked; I heard what sounded like a strangled curse and moan, then a fleshy, meaty concussion which I took to be a slap. Was he killing her at last?

Choking her with the silent, poisonous care necessary to escape detection?

I remembered Thompson's arm flashing frenziedly in the sunlight. My aunt's discoloured thighs. My heart creaked in my chest with fear. And after killing her? Would the madman stop? Or would he do us all in, one by one?

I got out of bed on unsteady legs. The muffled commotion was growing louder, more distinct. I padded into the hallway. The door to their bedroom was partially open, and a light showed. Terror made me feel hollow; the pit of my stomach ached.

They were both naked, something which I hadn't expected, and which came as quite a shock. What was perhaps even more shocking was the fact that they seemed not only oblivious of me, but of each other as well. She was slung around so that her head was propped on a pillow resting on the footboard of the bed. One smooth leg was draped over the edge of the bed and her heel was beating time on the floorboards (the thud which woke me) as accompaniment to Thompson's plunging body and the soft, liquid grunts of expelled air which he made with every lunge. One of her hands gripped the footboard and her knuckles were white with strain.

I watched until the critical moment, right through the growing frenzy and ardour. They groaned and panted and heaved and shuddered and didn't know themselves. At the very last he lifted his bony, hatchet face with the jutting beard to the ceiling and closed his eyes; for a moment I thought he was praying as his lips moved soundlessly. But then he began to whimper and his mouth fell open and he looked stupider and weaker than any human being I had ever seen before in my life.

"Like pigs at the trough," my grandmother said at breakfast. "With the boy up there too."

My aunt turned a deep red, and then flushed again so violently that her thin lips appeared to turn blue.

I kept my head down and went on shovelling porridge. Thompson still wasn't invited to the table. He was leaning against the kitchen counter, his bony legs crossed at the ankles, eating an apple he had helped himself to.

"He didn't hear anything," my aunt said uncertainly. She

whispered conspiratorially across the table to Grandmother. "Not at that hour. He'd been asleep for hours."

I thought it wise, even though it meant drawing attention to myself, to establish my ignorance. "Hear what?" I inquired innocently.

"It wouldn't do any harm if he had," said Thompson, calmly biting and chewing the temptress's fruit.

"You wouldn't see it, would you?" said Grandma Bradley. "It wouldn't matter to you what he heard? You'd think that was manly."

"Manly has nothing to do with it. Doesn't enter into it," said Thompson in that cool way he had. "It's a fact of life, something he'll have to find out about sooner or later."

Aunt Evelyn began to cry. "Nobody is ever pleased with me," she spluttered. "I'm going crazy trying to please you both. I can't do it." She began to pull nervously at her hair. "He made me," she said finally in a confessional, humble tone to her mother.

"Evelyn," said my grandmother, "you have a place here. I would never send you away. I want you here. But he has to go. I want him to go. If he is going to rub my nose in it that way he has to go. I won't have that man under my roof."

"Evelyn isn't apologizing for anything," Thompson said. "And she isn't running away either. You can't force her to choose. It isn't healthy or fair."

"There have been other ones before you," said Grandma. "This isn't anything new for Evelyn."

"Momma!"

"I'm aware of that," he said stiffly, and his face vibrated with the effort to smile. "Provincial mores have never held much water with me. I like to think I'm above all that."

Suddenly my grandmother spotted me. "What are you gawking at!" she shouted. "Get on out of here!"

I didn't budge an inch.

"Leave him alone," said Thompson.

"You'll be out of here within a week," said Grandmother. "I swear."

"No," he said smiling. "When I'm ready."

"You'll go home and go with your tail between your legs. Last night was the last straw," she said. And by God you could tell she meant it.

Thompson gave her his beatific Buddha-grin and shook his head from side to side, very, very slowly.

A thunderstorm was brewing. The sky was a stew of dark, swollen cloud and a strange apple-green light. The temperature stood in the mid-nineties, not a breath of breeze stirred, my skin crawled and my head pounded above my eyes and through the bridge of my nose. There wasn't a thing to do except sit on the bottom step of the porch, keep from picking up a sliver in your ass, and scratch the dirt with a stick. My grandmother had put her hat on and driven into town on some unexplained business. Thompson and my aunt were upstairs in their bedroom, sunk in a stuporous, sweaty afternoon's sleep.

Like my aunt and Thompson, all the chickens had gone to roost to wait for rain. The desertion of his harem had thrown the rooster into a flap. Stanley trotted neurotically around his tethering post, stopping every few circuits to beat his bedraggled pinions and crow lustily in masculine outrage. I watched him for a bit without much curiosity, and then climbed off the step and walked toward him, listlessly dragging my stick in my trail.

"Here Stanley, Stanley," I called, not entirely sure how to summon a rooster, or instil in him confidence and friendliness.

I did neither. My approach only further unhinged Stanley. His stride lengthened, the tempo of his pace increased, and his head began to dart abruptly from side to side in furtive despair. Finally, in a last desperate attempt to escape, Stanley upset himself trying to fly. He landed in a heap of disarranged, stiff, glistening feathers. I put my foot on his string and pinned him to the ground.

"Nice pretty, pretty Stanley," I said coaxingly, adopting the tone that a neighbour used with her budgie, since I wasn't sure how one talked to a bird. I slowly extended my thumb to stroke his bright-red neck feathers. Darting angrily, he struck the ball of my thumb with a snappish peck and simultaneously hit my wrist with his heel spur. He didn't hurt me, but he did startle me badly. So badly I gave a little yelp. Which made me feel foolish and more than a little cowardly.

"You son of a bitch," I said, reaching down slowly and staring into one unblinking glassy eye in which I could see my face looming larger and larger. I caught the rooster's legs and held them firmly together. Stanley crowed defiantly and showed me his wicked little tongue.

"Now, Stanley," I said, "relax, I'm just going to stroke you. I'm just going to stroke you. I'm just going to pet Stanley."

No deal. He struck furiously again with a snake-like agility, and bounded in my hand, wings beating his poultry smell into my face. A real fighting cock at last. Maybe it was the weather. Perhaps his rooster pride and patience would suffer no more indignities.

The heat, the sultry menace of the gathering storm, made me feel prickly, edgy. I flicked my middle finger smartly against his tiny chicken skull, hard enough to rattle his pea-sized brain. "You like that, buster?" I asked him, and snapped him another one for good measure. He struck back again, his comb red, crested, and rubbery with fury.

I was angry myself. I turned him upside down and left him dangling, his wings drumming against the legs of my jeans. Then I righted him abruptly; he looked dishevelled, seedy and dazed.

"OK, Stanley," I said, feeling the intoxication of power. "I'm boss here, and you behave." There was a gleeful edge to my voice, which surprised me a little. I realized I was hoping this confrontation would escalate. Wishing that he would provoke me into something.

Strange images came into my head: the bruises on my aunt's legs; Thompson's face drained of life, lifted like an empty receptacle toward the ceiling, waiting to be filled, the tendons of his neck stark and rigid with anticipation.

I was filled with anxiety, the heat seemed to stretch me, to tug at my nerves and my skin. Two drops of sweat, as large and perfectly formed as tears, rolled out of my hairline and splashed on to the rubber toes of my runners.

"Easy, Stanley," I breathed to him, "easy," and my hand crept deliberately towards him. This time he pecked me in such a way, directly on the knuckle, that it actually hurt. I took up my stick and rapped him on the beak curtly, the prim admonishment of a school-marm. I didn't hit him very hard, but it was hard enough to split the length of his beak with a narrow crack. The beak fissured like the nib of a fountain pen. Stanley squawked, opened and closed his beak spasmodically, bewildered by the pain. A bright jewel of blood bubbled out of the split and gathered to a trembling bead.

"There," I said excitedly, "now you've done it. How are you going to eat with a broken beak? You can't eat anything with a broken beak. You'll starve, you stupid goddamn chicken."

A wind that smelled of rain had sprung up. It ruffled his feathers until they moved with a barely discernible crackle.

"Poor Stanley," I said, and at last, numbed by the pain, he allowed me to stroke the gloss of his lacquer feathers.

I wasn't strong enough or practised enough to do a clean and efficient job of wringing his neck, but I succeeded in finishing him off after two clumsy attempts. Then because I wanted to leave the impression that a skunk had made off with him, I punched a couple of holes in his breast with my jack knife and tried to dribble some blood on the ground. Poor Stanley produced only a few meagre spots; this corpse refused to bleed in the presence of its murderer. I scattered a handful of his feathers on the ground and buried him in the larger of the two manure piles beside the barn.

"I don't think any skunk got that rooster," my grandmother said suspiciously, nudging at a feather with the toe of her boot until, finally disturbed, it was wafted away by the breeze.

Something squeezed my heart. How did she know?

"Skunks hunt at night," she said. "Must have been somebody's barn cat."

"You come along with me," my grandmother said. She was standing in front of the full-length hall mirror, settling on her hat, a deadly-looking hat pin poised above her skull. "We'll go into town and you can buy a comic book at the drugstore."

It was Friday and Friday was shopping day. But Grandma didn't wheel her battered De Soto to the kerb in front of the Brite Spot Grocery, she parked it in front of Maynard & Pritchard, Barristers and Solicitors.

"What are we doing here?" I asked.

Grandma was fumbling nervously with her purse. Small-town people don't like to be seen going to the lawyer's. "Come along with me. Hurry up."

"Why do I have to come?"

"Because I don't want you making a spectacle of yourself for the half-wits and loungers to gawk at," she said. "Let's not give them too much to wonder about."

Maynard & Pritchard, Barristers and Solicitors, smelled of wax and varnish and probity. My grandmother was shown into an office with a frosted pane of glass in the door and neat gilt lettering that announced it was occupied by D.F. Maynard, QC. I was ordered to occupy a hard chair, which I did, battering my heels on the rungs briskly enough to annoy the secretary into telling me to stop it.

My grandmother wasn't closeted long with her Queen's Counsel before the door opened and he glided after her into the passageway. Lawyer Maynard was the neatest man I had ever seen in my life. His suit fit him like a glove.

"The best I can do," he said, "is send him a registered letter telling him to remove himself from the premises, but it all comes to the same thing. If that doesn't scare him off, you'll have to have recourse to the police. That's all there is to it. I told you that yesterday and you haven't told me anything new today, Edith, that would make me change my mind. Just let him know you won't put up with him any more."

"No police," she said. "I don't want the police digging in my family's business and Evelyn giving one of her grand performances for some baby-skinned constable straight out of the depot. All I need is to get her away from him for a little while, then I could tune her in. I could get through to her in no time at all."

"Well," said Maynard, shrugging, "we could try the letter, but I don't think it would do any good. He has the status of a guest in your home; just tell him to go."

My grandmother was showing signs of exasperation. "But he *doesn't* go. That's the point. I've told him and told him. But he *won't*."

"Mrs Bradley," said the lawyer emphatically, "Edith, as a friend, don't waste your time. The police."

"I'm through wasting my time," she said.

Pulling away from the lawyer's office, my grandmother began a spirited conversation with herself. A wisp of hair had escaped from under her hat, and the dye winked a metallic red light as it jiggled up and down in the hot sunshine.

"I've told him and told him. But he won't listen. The goddamn freak thinks we're involved in a christly debating society. He thinks I don't mean business. But I mean business. I do. There's more than one way to skin a cat or scratch a dog's ass. We'll take the wheels off his little red wagon and see how she pulls."

"What about my comic book?" I said, as we drove past the Rexall.

"Shut up."

Grandma drove the De Soto to the edge of town and stopped it at the Ogdens'' place. It was a service station, or rather had been until the BA company had taken out their pumps and yanked the franchise, or whatever you call it, on the two brothers. Since then everything had gone steadily downhill. Cracks in the window-panes had been taped with masking tape, and the roof had been patched with flattened tin cans and old licence plates. The building itself was surrounded by an acre of wrecks, sulking hulks rotten with rust, the guts of their upholstery spilled and gnawed by rats and mice.

But the Ogden brothers still carried on a business after a fashion. They stripped their wrecks for parts and were reputed to be decent enough mechanics whenever they were sober enough to turn a wrench or thread a bolt. People brought work to them whenever they couldn't avoid it, and the rest of the year gave them a wide berth.

The Ogdens were famous for two things: their meanness and their profligacy as breeders. The place was always aswarm with kids who never seemed to wear pants except in the most severe weather, and tottered about the premises, their legs smeared with grease, shit, or various combinations of both.

"Wait here," my grandmother said, slamming the car door loudly enough to bring the two brothers out of their shop. Through the open door I saw a motor suspended on an intricate system of chains and pulleys.

The Ogdens stood with their hands in the pockets of their bib overalls while my grandmother talked to them. They were quite a sight. They didn't have a dozen teeth in their heads between them, even though the oldest brother couldn't have been more than forty. They just stood there, one sucking on a cigarette, the other on a Coke. Neither one moved or changed his expression, except once, when a tow-headed youngster piddled too close to Grandma. He was lazily and casually slapped on the side of the head by the nearest brother and ran away screaming, his stream cavorting wildly in front of him.

At last, their business concluded, the boys walked my grandmother back to the car.

"You'll get to that soon?" she said, sliding behind the wheel.

"Tomorrow all right?" said one. His words sounded all slack and chewed, issuing from his shrunken, old man's mouth.

"The sooner the better. I want that seen to, Bert."

"What seen to?" I asked.

"Bert and his brother Elwood are going to fix that rattle that's been plaguing me."

"Sure thing," said Elwood. "Nothing but clear sailing."

"What rattle?" I said.

"What rattle? What rattle? The one in the glove compartment," she said, banging it with the heel of her hand. "That rattle. You hear it?"

Thompson could get very edgy some days. "I should be working on my dissertation," he said, coiled in the big chair. "I shouldn't be wasting my time in this shit-hole. I should be working!"

"So why aren't you?" said Evelyn. She was spool knitting. That and reading movie magazines were the only things she ever did.

"How the christ do I work without a library? You see a goddamn library within a hundred miles of this place?"

"Why do you need a library?" she said calmly. "Can't you write?"

"Write?" he said, looking at the ceiling. "Write, she says. What the hell do you know about it? What the hell do *you* know about it?"

"I can't see why you can't write."

"Before you write, you research. That's what you do, you *research*."

"So bite my head off. It wasn't my idea to come here."

"It wasn't me that lost my goddamn job. How the hell were we supposed to pay the rent?"

"You could have got a job."

"I'm a student. Anyway, I told you, if I get a job my wife gets her hooks into me for support. I'll starve to death before I support that bitch."

"We could go back."

"How many times does it have to be explained to you? I don't get my scholarship cheque until the first of September. We happen to be broke. Absolutely. In fact, you're going to have to hit the old lady up for gas and eating money to get back to the coast. We're stuck here. Get that into your empty fucking head. The Lord Buddha might have been able to subsist on a single bean a day; I can't."

My grandmother came into the room. The conversation stopped.

"Do you think," she said to Thompson, "I could ask you to do me a favour?"

"Why, Mrs Bradley," he said, smiling, "whatever do you mean?"

"I was wondering whether you could take my car into town to Ogdens' to get it fixed."

"Oh," said Thompson. "I don't know where it is. I don't think I'm your man."

"Ask anyone where it is. They can tell you. It isn't hard to find."

"Why would you ask me to do you a favour, Mrs Bradley?" inquired Thompson complacently. Hearing his voice was like listening to someone drag their nails down a blackboard.

"Well, you can be goddamn sure I wouldn't," said Grandma, trying to keep a hold of herself, "except that I'm right in the middle of doing my pickling and canning. I thought you might be willing to move your lazy carcass to do something around here. Every time I turn around I seem to be falling over those legs of yours." She looked at the limbs in question as if she would like to dock them somewhere in the vicinity of the knee.

"No, I don't think I can," said Thompson easily, stroking his goat beard.

"And why the hell can't you?"

"Oh, let's just say I don't trust you, Mrs Bradley. I don't like to leave you alone with Evelyn. Lord knows what ideas you might put in her head."

"Or take out."

"That's right. Or take out," said Thompson with satisfaction. "You can't imagine the trouble it took me to get them in there." He turned to Evelyn. "She can't imagine the trouble, can she, dear?"

Evelyn threw her spool knitting on the floor and walked out of the room.

"Evelyn's mad and I'm glad," shouted Thompson at her back. "And I know how to tease her!"

"Charlie, come here," said Grandma. I went over to her. She took me firmly by the shoulder. "From now on," said my grandma, "my family is off limits to you. I don't want to see you talking to Charlie here, or to come within sniffing distance of Evelyn."

"What do you think of that idea, Charlie?" said Thompson. "Are you still my friend or what?"

I gave him a wink my grandma couldn't see. He thought that was great; he laughed like a madman. "Superb," he said. "Superb. There's no flies on Charlie. What a diplomat."

"What the hell is the matter with you, Mr Beatnik?" asked Grandma, annoyed beyond bearing. "What's so goddamn funny?"

"Ha ha!" roared Thompson. "What a charming notion! Me a beatnik!"

Grandma Bradley held the mouthpiece of the phone very close to her lips as she spoke into it. "No, it can't be brought in. You'll have to come out here to do the job."

She listened with an intent expression on her face. Spotting me pretending to look in the fridge, she waved me out of the kitchen with her hand. I dragged myself out and stood quietly in the hallway.

"This is a party line," she said, "remember that."

Another pause while she listened.

"OK," she said and hung up.

I spent some of my happiest hours squatting in the corn patch. I was completely hidden in there; even when I stood, the maturing stalks reached a foot or more above my head. It was a good place. On the hottest days it was relatively cool in that thicket of green where the shade was dark and deep and the leaves rustled and scraped and sawed drily overhead.

Nobody ever thought to look for me there. They could bellow their bloody lungs out for me and I could just sit and watch them getting uglier and uglier about it all. There was some satisfaction in that. I'd just reach up and pluck myself a cob. I loved raw corn. The newly formed kernels were tiny, pale pearls of sweetness that gushed juice. I'd munch and munch and smile and smile and think, why don't you drop dead?

It was my secret place, my sanctuary, where I couldn't be found or touched by them. But all the same, if I didn't let them intrude on me – that didn't mean I didn't want to keep tabs on things.

At the time I was watching Thompson stealing peas at the other end of the garden. He was like some primitive man who lived in a gathering culture. My grandma kept him so hungry he was constantly prowling for food: digging in cupboards, rifling the refrigerator, scrounging in the garden.

Clad only in Bermuda shorts he was a sorry sight. His bones threatened to rupture his skin and jut out every which way. He sported a scrub-board chest with two old pennies for nipples, and a wispy garland of hair decorated his sunken breastbone. His legs looked particularly rackety; all gristle, knobs and sinew.

We both heard the truck at the same time. It came bucking up the approach, spurting gravel behind it. Thompson turned around, shaded his eyes and peered at it. He wasn't much interested. He couldn't get very curious about the natives.

The truck stopped and a man stepped out on to the runningboard of the '51 IHC. He gazed around him, obviously looking for something or someone. This character had a blue handkerchief sprinkled with white polka dots tied in a triangle over his face. Exactly like an outlaw in an Audie Murphy Western. A genuine goddamn Jesse James.

He soon spotted Thompson standing half-naked in the garden, staring stupidly at this strange sight, his mouth bulging with peas. The outlaw ducked his head back into the cab of the truck, said something to the driver, and pointed. The driver then stepped out on to his runningboard and, standing on tippy-toe, peered over the roof of the cab at Thompson. He too wore a handkerchief tied over his mug, but his was red.

Then they both got down from the truck and began to walk very quickly toward Thompson with long, menacing strides.

"Fellows?" said Thompson.

At the sound of his voice the two men broke into a stiff-legged trot, and the one with the red handkerchief, while still moving, stooped down smoothly and snatched up the hoe that lay at the edge of the garden.

"What the hell is going on here, boys?" said Thompson, his voice pitched high with concern.

The man with the blue mask reached Thompson first. One long arm, a dirty clutch of fingers on its end, snaked out and caught him by the hair and jerked his head down. Then he kicked him in the pit of the stomach with his work boots.

"OK, fucker," he shouted, "too fucking smart to take a fucking hint?" and he punched him on the side of the face with several short, snapping blows that actually tore Thompson's head out of his grip. Thompson toppled over clumsily and fell in the dirt. "Get fucking lost," Blue Mask said more quietly.

"Evelyn!" yelled Thompson to the house. "Jesus Christ, Evelyn!"

I crouched lower in the corn patch and began to tremble. I was certain they were going to kill him.

"Shut up," said the man with the hoe. He glanced at the blade for a second, considered, then rotated the handle in his hands and hit Thompson a quick chop on the head with the blunt side. "Shut your fucking yap," he repeated.

"Evelyn! Evelyn! Oh God!" hollered Thompson, "I'm being murdered! For God's sake, somebody help me!" The side of his face was slick with blood.

"I told you shut up, cock sucker," said Red Mask, and kicked him in the ribs several times. Thompson groaned and hugged himself in the dust.

"Now you get lost, fucker," said the one with the hoe, "because if you don't stop bothering nice people we'll drive a spike in your skull."

"Somebody help me!" Thompson yelled at the house.

"Nobody there is going to help you," Blue Mask said. "You're all on your own, smart arse."

"You bastards," said Thompson, and spat ineffectually in their direction.

For his defiance he got struck a couple of chopping blows with the hoe. The last one skittered off his collar-bone with a sickening crunch.

"That's enough," said Red Mask, catching the handle of the hoe. "Come on."

The two sauntered back toward the truck, laughing. They weren't in any hurry to get out of there. Thompson lay on his side staring at their retreating backs. His face was wet with tears and blood.

The man with the red mask looked back over his shoulder and wiggled his ass at Thompson in an implausible imitation of effeminacy. "Was it worth it, tiger?" he shouted. "Getting your ashes hauled don't come cheap, do it?"

This set them off again. Passing me they pulled off their masks and stuffed them in their pockets. They didn't have to worry about Thompson when they had their backs to him; he couldn't see their faces. But I could. No surprise. They were the Ogden boys.

When the truck pulled out of the yard, its gears grinding, I burst out of my hiding place and ran to Thompson, who had got to his knees and was trying to stop the flow of blood from his scalp with his fingers. He was crying. Another first for Thompson. He was the first man I'd seen cry. It made me uncomfortable.

"The sons of bitches broke my ribs," he said, panting with shallow breaths. "God, I hope they didn't puncture a lung."

"Can you walk?" I asked.

"Don't think I don't know who's behind this," he said, getting carefully to his feet. His face was white. "You saw them," he said. "You saw their faces from the corn patch. We got the bastards."

He leaned a little on me as we made our way to the house. The front door was locked. We knocked. No answer. "Let me in, you old bitch!" shouted Thompson.

"Evelyn, open the goddamn door!" Silence. I couldn't hear a thing move in the house. It was as if they were all dead in there. It frightened me.

He started to kick the door. A panel splintered. "Open this door! Let me in, you old slut, or I'll kill you!"

Nothing.

"You better go," I said nervously. I didn't like this one little bit. "Those guys might come back and kill you."

"Evelyn!" he bellowed. "Evelyn!"

He kept it up for a good five minutes, alternately hammering and kicking the door, pleading with and threatening the occupants. By the end of that time he was sweating with exertion and pain. He went slowly down the steps, sobbing, beaten. "You saw them," he said, "we have the bastards dead to rights."

He winced when he eased his bare flesh on to the hot seat-covers of the car.

"I'll be back," he said, starting the motor of the car. "This isn't the end of this."

When Grandma was sure he had gone, the front door was unlocked and I was let in. I noticed my grandmother's hands trembled a touch when she lit her cigarette.

"You can't stay away from him, can you?" she said testily.

"You didn't have to do that," I said. "He was hurt. You ought to have let him in."

"I ought to have poisoned him a week ago. And don't talk about things you don't know anything about."

"Sometimes," I said, "all of you get on my nerves."

"Kids don't have nerves. Adults have nerves. They're the only ones entitled to them. And don't think I care a plugged nickel what does, or doesn't, get on your nerves."

"Where's Aunt Evelyn?"

"Your Aunt Evelyn is taken care of," she replied.

"Why wouldn't she come to the door?"

"She had her own road to Damascus. She has seen the light. Everything has been straightened out," she said. "Everything is back to normal."

He looked foolish huddled in the back of the police car later that evening. When the sun began to dip, the temperature dropped rapidly, and he was obviously cold dressed only in his Bermuda shorts. Thompson sat all hunched up to relieve the strain on his ribs, his hands pressed between his knees, shivering.

My grandmother and the constable spoke quietly by the car for some time; occasionally Thompson poked his head out the car window and said something. By the look on the constable's face when he spoke to Thompson, it was obvious he didn't care for him too much. Thompson had that kind of effect on people. Several times during the course of the discussion the constable glanced my way.

I edged a little closer so I could hear what they were saying.

"He's mad as a hatter," said my grandmother. "I don't know anything about two men. If you ask me, all this had something to do with drugs. My daughter says that this man takes drugs. He's some kind of beatnik."

"Christ," said Thompson, drawing his knees up as if to scrunch himself into a smaller, less noticeable package, "the woman is insane."

"One thing at a time, Mrs Bradley," said the RCMP constable.

"My daughter is finished with him," she said. "He beats her, you know. I want him kept off my property."

"I want to speak to Evelyn," Thompson said. He looked bedraggled and frightened. "Evelyn and I will leave this minute if this woman wants. But I've got to talk to Evelyn."

"My daughter doesn't want to see you, mister. She's finished with you," said Grandma Bradley, shifting her weight from side to side. She turned her attention to the constable. "He beats her," she said, "bruises all over her. Can you imagine?"

"The boy knows," said Thompson desperately. "He saw them. How many times do I have to tell you?" He piped his voice to me. "Didn't you, Charlie? You saw them, didn't you?"

"Charlie?" said my grandmother. This was news to her.

I stood very still.

"Come here, son," said the constable.

I walked slowly over to them.

"Did you see the faces of the men?" the constable asked, putting a hand on my shoulder. "Do you know the men? Are they from around here?"

"How would he know?" said my grandmother. "He's a stranger."

"He knows them. At least he saw them," said Thompson. "My little Padma-sambhava never misses a trick," he said, trying to jolly me. "You see everything, don't you, Charlie? You remember everything, don't you?"

I looked at my grandmother, who stood so calmly and commandingly, waiting.

"Hey, don't look to her for the answers," said Thompson nervously. "Don't be afraid of her. You remember everything, don't you?"

He had no business begging me. I had watched their game from the sidelines long enough to know the rules. At one time he had imagined himself a winner. And now he was asking me to save him, to take a risk, when I was more completely in her clutches than he would ever be. He forgot I was a child. I depended on her.

Thompson, I saw, was powerless. He couldn't protect me. God, I remembered more than he dreamed. I remembered how his lips had moved soundlessly, his face pleading with the ceiling, his face blotted of everything but abject urgency. Praying to a simpering, cross-eyed idol. His arm flashing as he struck my aunt's bare legs. Crawling in the dirt, covered with blood.

He had taught me that "Those who are in the grip of desire, the grip of existence, the grip of ignorance, move helplessly round through the spheres of life, as men or gods or as wretches in the lower regions." Well, he was helpless now. But he insisted on fighting back and hurting the rest of us. The weak ones like Evelyn and me.

I thought of Stanley the rooster and how it had felt when the tendons separated, the gristle parted and the bones crunched under my twisting hands.

"I don't know what he's talking about," I said to the constable softly. "I didn't see anybody."

"Clear out," said my grandmother triumphantly. "Beat it."

"You dirty little son of a bitch," he said to me. "You mean little bugger."

He didn't understand much. He had forced me into the game, and now that I was a player and no longer a watcher he didn't like it. The thing was that I was good at the game. But he, being a loser, couldn't appreciate that.

Then suddenly he said, "Evelyn." He pointed to the upstairs window of the house and tried to get out of the back seat of the police car. But of course he couldn't. They take the handles off the back doors. Nobody can get out unless they are let out.

"Goddamn it!" he shouted. "Let me out! She's waving to me! She wants me!"

I admit that the figure was hard to make out at that distance. But any damn fool could see she was only waving goodbye.

Antigone

SHEILA WATSON

My father ruled a kingdom on the right bank of the river. He ruled it
with a firm hand and a stout heart though he was often more
troubled than Moses, who was simply trying to bring a stubborn and
moody people under God's yoke. My father ruled men who thought
they were gods or the instruments of gods, at very least, god-
afflicted and god-pursued. He ruled Atlas who held up the sky, and
Hermes who went on endless messages, and Helen who'd been
hatched from an egg, and Pan the gardener, and Kallisto the bear,
and too many others to mention by name. Yet my father had no
thunderbolt, no trident, no helmet of darkness. His subjects were
delivered bound into his hands. He merely watched over them as
the hundred-handed ones watched over the dethroned Titans so
that they wouldn't bother Hellas again.

Despite the care which my father took to maintain an atmosphere
of sober common sense in his whole establishment, there were
occasional outbursts of self-indulgence which he could not control.
For instance, I have seen Helen walking naked down the narrow
cement path under the chestnut trees for no better reason, I suppose, than that the day was hot and the white flowers themselves
lay naked and expectant in the sunlight. And I have seen Atlas
forget the sky while he sat eating the dirt which held him up. These
were the things which I was not supposed to see.

If my father had been as sensible through and through as he was
thought to be, he would have packed me off to boarding school
when I was old enough to be disciplined by men. Instead he kept me
at home with my two cousins who, except for the accident of birth,
might as well have been my sisters. Today I imagine people concerned with our welfare would take such an environment into
account. At the time I speak of most people thought us fortunate –
especially the girls whose fathers' affairs had come to an unhappy
issue. I don't like to revive old scandal and I wouldn't except to deny
it; but it takes only a few impertinent newcomers in any community

to force open cupboards which had been decently sealed by time. However, my father was so busy setting his kingdom to rights that he let weeds grow up in his own garden.

As I said, if my father had had all his wits about him he would have sent me to boarding school – and Antigone and Ismene too. I might have fallen in love with the headmaster's daughter and Antigone might have learned that no human being can be right always. She might have found out besides that from the seeds of eternal justice grow madder flowers than any which Pan grew in the gardens of my father's kingdom.

Between the kingdom which my father ruled and the wilderness flows a river. It is this river which I am crossing now. Antigone is with me.

How often can we cross the same river, Antigone asks.

Her persistence annoys me. Besides, Heraklitos made nonsense of her question years ago. He saw a river too – the Inachos, the Kephissos, the Lethaios. The name doesn't matter. He said: See how quickly the water flows. However agile a man is, however nimbly he swims, or runs, or flies, the water slips away before him. See, even as he sets down his foot the water is displaced by the stream which crowds along in the shadow of its flight.

But after all, Antigone says, one must admit that it is the same kind of water. The oolichan runs in it as they ran last year and the year before. The gulls cry above the same banks. Boats drift towards the Delta and circle back against the current to gather up the catch.

At any rate, I tell her, we're standing on a new bridge. We are standing so high that the smell of mud and river weeds passes under us out to the straits. The unbroken curve of the bridge protects the eye from details of river life. The bridge is foolproof as a clinic's passport to happiness.

The old bridge still spans the river, but the cat-walk with its cracks and knot-holes, with its gap between planking and hand-rail has been torn down. The centre arch still grinds open to let boats up and down the river, but a child can no longer be walked on it or swung out on it beyond the water-gauge at the very centre of the flood.

I've known men who scorned any kind of bridge, Antigone says. Men have walked into the water, she says, or, impatient, have jumped from the bridge into the river below.

But these, I say, didn't really want to cross the river. They went Persephone's way, cradled in the current's arms, down the long halls under the pink feet of the gulls, under the booms and towlines, under the soft bellies of the fish.

Antigone looks at me.

There's no coming back, she says, if one goes far enough.

I know she's going to speak of her own misery and I won't listen. Only a god has the right to say: Look what I suffer. Only a god should say: What more ought I to have done for you that I have not done?

Once in winter, she says, a man walked over the river.

Taking advantage of nature, I remind her, since the river had never frozen before.

Yet he escaped from the penitentiary, she says. He escaped from the guards walking round the walls or standing with their guns in the sentry-boxes at the four corners of the enclosure. He escaped.

Not without risk, I say. He had to test the strength of the ice himself. Yet safer perhaps than if he had crossed by the old bridge where he might have slipped through a knot-hole or tumbled out through the railing.

He did escape, she persists, and lived forever on the far side of the river in the Alaska tea and bulrushes. For where, she asks, can a man go further than to the outermost edge of the world?

The habitable world, as I've said, is on the right bank of the river. Here is the market with its market stalls – the coops of hens, the long-tongued geese, the haltered calf, the bearded goat, the shoving pigs, and the empty bodies of cows and sheep and rabbits hanging on iron hooks. My father's kingdom provides asylum in the suburbs. Near it are the convent, the churches, and the penitentiary. Above these on the hill the cemetery looks down and on the river itself.

It is a world spread flat, tipped up into the sky so that men and women bend forward, walking as men walk when they board a ship at high tide. This is the world I feel with my feet. It is the world I see with my eyes.

I remember standing once with Antigone and Ismene in the square just outside the gates of my father's kingdom. Here from a bust set high on a cairn the stone eyes of Simon Fraser look from his stone face over the river that he found.

It is the head that counts, Ismene said.

It's no better than an urn, Antigone said, one of the urns we see when we climb to the cemetery above.

And all I could think was that I didn't want an urn, only a flat green grave with a chain about it.

A chain won't keep out the dogs, Antigone said.

But his soul could swing on it, Ismene said, like a bird blown on a branch in the wind.

And I remember Antigone's saying: The cat drags its belly on the ground and the rat sharpens its tooth in the ivy.

I should have loved Ismene, but I didn't. It was Antigone I loved. I should have loved Ismene because, although she walked the flat world with us, she managed somehow to see it round.

The earth is an oblate spheroid, she'd say. And I knew that she saw it there before her comprehensible and whole like a tangerine spiked through and held in place while it rotated on the axis of one of Nurse's steel sock needles. The earth was a tangerine and she saw the skin peeled off and the world parcelled out into neat segments, each segment sweet and fragrant in its own skin.

It's the head that counts, she said.

In her own head she made diagrams to live by, cut and fashioned after the eternal patterns spied out by Plato as he rummaged about in the sewing basket of the gods.

I should have loved Ismene. She would live now in some prefabricated and perfect chrysolite by some paradigm which made love round and whole. She would simply live and leave destruction in the purgatorial ditches outside her own walled paradise.

Antigone is different. She sees the world flat as I do and feels it tip beneath her feet. She has walked in the market and seen the living animals penned and the dead hanging stiff on their hooks. Yet she defies what she sees with a defiance which is almost denial. Like Atlas she tries to keep the vaulted sky from crushing the flat earth. Like Hermes she brings a message that there is life if one can escape to it in the brush and bulrushes in some dim Hades beyond the river. It is defiance not belief and I tell her that this time we walk the bridge to a walled cave where we can deny death no longer.

Yet she asks her questions still. And standing there I tell her that

Heraklitos has made nonsense of her question. I should have loved Ismene for she would have taught me what Plato meant when he said in all earnest that the union of the soul with the body is in no way better than dissolution. I expect that she understood things which Antigone is too proud to see.

I turn away from her and flatten my elbows on the high wall of the bridge. I look back at my father's kingdom. I see the terraces rolling down from the red-brick buildings with their barred windows. I remember hands shaking the bars and hear fingers tearing up paper and stuffing it through the meshes. Diktynna, mother of nets and high leaping fear. O Artemis, mistress of wild beasts and wild men.

The inmates are beginning to come out on the screened verandas. They pace up and down in straight lines or stand silent like figures which appear at the same time each day from some depths inside a clock.

On the upper terrace Pan the gardener is shifting sprinklers with a hooked stick. His face is shadowed by the brim of his hat. He moves as economically as an animal between the beds of lobelia and geranium. It is high noon.

Antigone has cut out a piece of sod and has scooped out a grave. The body lies in a coffin in the shade of the magnolia tree. Antigone and I are standing. Ismene is sitting between two low angled branches of the monkey puzzle tree. Her lap is filled with daisies. She slits the stem of one daisy and pulls the stem of another through it. She is making a chain for her neck and a crown for her hair.

Antigone reaches for a branch of the magnolia. It is almost beyond her grip. The buds flame above her. She stands on a small fire of daisies which smoulder in the roots of grass.

I see the magnolia buds. They brood above me, whiteness feathered on whiteness. I see Antigone's face turned to the light. I hear the living birds call to the sun. I speak private poetry to myself: Between four trumpeting angels at the four corners of the earth a bride stands before the altar in a gown as white as snow.

Yet I must have been speaking aloud because Antigone challenges me: You're mistaken. It's the winds the angels hold, the four winds of the earth. After the just are taken to paradise the winds will destroy the earth. It's a funeral, she says, not a wedding.

She looks towards the building.

Someone is coming down the path from the matron's house, she says.

I notice that she has pulled one of the magnolia blossoms from the branch. I take it from her. It is streaked with brown where her hands have bruised it. The sparrow which she has decided to bury lies on its back. Its feet are clenched tight against the feathers of its breast. I put the flower in the box with it.

Someone is coming down the path. She is wearing a blue cotton dress. Her cropped head is bent. She walks slowing carrying something in a napkin.

It's Kallisto the bear, I say. Let's hurry. What will my father say if he sees us talking to one of his patients?

If we live here with him, Antigone says, what can he expect? If he spends his life trying to tame people he can't complain if you behave as if they were tame. What would your father think, she says, if he saw us digging in the Institution lawn?

Pan comes closer. I glower at him. There's no use speaking to him. He's deaf and dumb.

Listen, I say to Antigone, my father's not unreasonable. Kallisto thinks she's a bear and he thinks he's a bear tamer, that's all. As for the lawn, I say quoting my father without conviction, a man must have order among his own if he is to keep order in the state.

Kallisto has come up to us. She is smiling and laughing to herself. She gives me her bundle.

Fish, she says.

I open the napkin.

Pink fish sandwiches, I say.

For the party, she says.

But it isn't a party, Antigone says. It's a funeral.

For the funeral breakfast, I say.

Ismene is twisting two chains of daisies into a rope. Pan has stopped pulling the sprinkler about. He is standing beside Ismene resting himself on his hooked stick. Kallisto squats down beside her. Ismene turns away, preoccupied, but she can't turn far because of Pan's legs.

> Father said we never should
> Play with madmen in the wood.

I look at Antigone.

It's my funeral, she says.

I go over to Ismene and gather up a handful of loose daisies from her lap. The sun reaches through the shadow of the magnolia tree.

It's my funeral, Antigone says. She moves possessively towards the body.

An ant is crawling into the bundle of sandwiches which I've put on the ground. A file of ants is marching on the sparrow's box.

I go over and drop daisies on the bird's stiff body. My voice speaks ritual words: Deliver me, O Lord, from everlasting death on this dreadful day. I tremble and am afraid.

The voice of a people comforts me. I look at Antigone. I look her in the eye.

It had better be a proper funeral then, I say.

Kallisto is crouched forward on her hands. Tears are running down her cheeks and she is licking them away with her tongue.

My voice rises again: I said in the midst of my days, I shall not see –

Antigone just stands there. She looks frightened, but her eyes defy me with their assertion.

It's my funeral, she says. It's my bird. I was the one who wanted to bury it.

She is looking for a reason. She will say something which sounds eternally right.

Things have to be buried, she says. They can't be left lying around anyhow for people to see.

Birds shouldn't die, I tell her. They have wings. Cats and rats haven't wings.

Stop crying, she says to Kallisto. It's only a bird.

It has a bride's flower in its hand, Kallisto says.

We shall rise again, I mutter, but we shall not all be changed.

Antigone does not seem to hear me.

Behold, I say in a voice she must hear, in a moment, in the twinkling of an eye, the trumpet shall sound.

Ismene turns to Kallisto and throws a daisy chain about her neck.

Shall a virgin forget her adorning or a bride the ornament of her breast?

Kallisto is lifting her arms towards the tree.

The bridegroom has come, she says, white as a fall of snow. He stands above me in a great ring of fire.

Antigone looks at me now.

Let's cover the bird up, she says. Your father will punish us all for making a disturbance.

He has on his garment, Kallisto says, and on his thigh is written King of Kings.

I look at the tree. If I could see with Kallisto's eyes I wouldn't be afraid of death, or punishment, or the penitentiary guards. I wouldn't be afraid of my father's belt or his honing strap or his bedroom slipper. I wouldn't be afraid of falling into the river through a knot-hole in the bridge.

But, as I look, I see the buds falling like burning lamps and I hear the sparrow twittering in its box. Woe, woe, woe because of the three trumpets which are yet to sound.

Kallisto is on her knees. She is growling like a bear. She lumbers over to the sandwiches and mauls them with her paw.

Ismene stands alone for Pan the gardener has gone.

Antigone is fitting a turf in place above the coffin. I go over and press the edge of the turf with my feet. Ismene has caught me by the hand.

Go away, Antigone says.

I see my father coming down the path. He has an attendant with him. In front of them walks Pan holding the sprinkler hook like a spear.

What are you doing here? my father asks.

Burying a bird, Antigone says.

Here? my father asks again.

Where else could I bury it? Antigone says.

My father looks at her.

This ground is public property, he says. No single person has any right to an inch of it.

I've taken six inches, Antigone says. Will you dig the bird up again?

Some of his subjects my father restrained since they were moved to throw themselves from high places or to tear one another to bits from jealousy or rage. Others who disturbed the public peace he taught to walk in the airing courts or to work in the kitchen or in the garden.

If men live at all, my father said, it is because discipline saves their life for them.

From Antigone he simply turned away.

The Rain Child

MARGARET LAURENCE

I recall the sky that day – overcast, the flat undistinguished grey nearly forgotten by us here during the months of azure which we come to regard as rights rather than privileges. As always when the rain hovers, the air was like syrup, thick and heavily still, over-sweet with flowering vines and the occasional ripe paw-paw that had fallen and now lay yellow and fermented, a winery for ants.

I was annoyed at having to stay in my office so late. Annoyed, too, that I found the oppressive humidity just before the rains a little more trying each year. I have always believed myself particularly well-suited to this climate. Miss Povey, of course, when I was idiotic enough to complain one day about the heat, hinted that the change of life might be more to blame than the weather.

"Of course, I remember how bothersome you found the heat one season," I parried. "Some years ago, as I recollect."

We work well together and even respect one another. Why must we make such petty stabs? Sitting depressed at my desk, I was at least thankful that when a breeze quickened we would receive it here. Blessings upon the founders of half a century ago who built Eburaso Girls" School at the top of the hill, for at the bottom the villagers would be steaming like crabs in a soup pot.

My leg hurt more than it had in a long time, and I badly wanted a cup of tea. Typical of Miss Povey, I thought, that she should leave yet another parental interview to me. Twenty-seven years here, to my twenty-two, and she still felt acutely uncomfortable with African parents, all of whom in her eyes were equally unenlightened. The fact that one father might be an illiterate cocoa farmer, while the next would possibly be a barrister from the city – such distinctions made no earthly difference to Hilda Povey. She was positive that parents would fail to comprehend the importance of sending their little girls to school with the proper clothing, and she harped upon this subject in a thoroughly tedious manner, as though the essence of education lay in the possession of six pairs of cotton knickers. Malice refreshed me for a moment. Then, as always, it began to chill. Were we still women, in actuality, who could bear only grudges, make venom for milk? I exaggerated for a while in this lamentably oratorical style, dramatizing the trivial for lack of anything great. Hilda, in point of fact, was an excellent headmistress. Like a budgerigar she darted and fussed through her days, but underneath the twittering there was a strong disciplined mind and a heart more pious than mine. Even in giving credit to her, however, I chose words churlishly – why had I not thought "devout" instead of "pious", with its undertones of self-righteousness? What could she possibly have said in my favour if she had been asked? That I taught English competently, even sometimes with love? That my irascibility was mainly reserved for my colleagues? The young ones in Primary did not find me terrifying, once they grew used to the sight of the lady in stout white drill skirt and drab lilac smock faded from purple, her greying hair arranged in what others might call a *chignon* but for me could only be termed a "bun", a lady of somewhat uncertain gait, clumping heavily into the classroom with her ebony cane. They felt free to laugh, my forest children, reticent and stiff in unaccustomed dresses, as we began the alien speech. "What are we doing, class?" And, as I sat down clumsily on the straight chair, to show them, they made their murmured and mirthful response – "We ah siddeen." The older girls in Middle School also seemed to accept me readily enough. Since Miss Harvey left us to marry that fool of a government geologist, I have had the senior girls for English literature and composition. Once when we were taking "Daffodils", Kwaale came to class with her arms full of wild orchids for me. How absurd Wordsworth seemed here then. I spoke instead about Akan poetry, and read them the drum prelude *Anyaneanyane*, in their own tongue as well as the translation. Miss Povey, hearing of it, took decided umbrage. Well. Perhaps she would not have found much to say in my favour after all.

I fidgeted and perspired, beginning to wonder if Dr Quansah would show up that day at all. Then, without my having heard his car or footsteps, he stood there at my office door, his daughter Ruth beside him.

"Miss —" He consulted a letter which he held in his hand. "Miss Violet Nedden?"

"Yes." I limped over to meet him. I was, stupidly, embarrassed that he had spoken my full name. Violet, applied to me, is of course quite ludicrous and I detest it. I felt as well the old need to explain my infirmity, but I refrained for the usual reasons. I do not know why it should matter to me to have people realize I was not always like this, but it does. In the pre-sulpha days when I first came here, I developed a tropical sore which festered badly; this is the result. But if I mention it to Africans, they tend to become faintly apologetic, as though it were somehow their fault that I bear the mark of Africa upon myself in much the same way as an ulcerated beggar of the streets.

Dr Quansah, perhaps to my relief, did not seem much at ease either. Awkwardly, he transferred Miss Povey's typewritten instructions to his left hand in order to shake hands with me. A man in his middle fifties, I judged him to be. Thickly built, with hands which seemed too immense to be a doctor's. He was well dressed, in a beige linen suit of good cut, and there was about his eyes a certain calm which his voice and gestures lacked.

His daughter resembled him, the same strong coarse features, the same skin shade, rather a lighter brown than is usual here. At fifteen she was more plump and childish in figure than most of our girls her age. Her frock was pretty and expensive, a blue cotton with white daisies on it, but as she was so stocky it looked too old for her.

"I don't know if Miss Povey told you," Dr Quansah began, "but Ruth has never before attended school in this – in her own country."

I must have shown my surprise, for he hastened on. "She was born in England and has lived all her life there. I went there as a young man, you see, to study medicine, and when I graduated I had the opportunity to stay on and do malaria research. Ultimately my wife joined me in London. She – she died in England. Ruth has been in boarding schools since she was six. I have always meant to return here, of course. I had not really intended to stay away so long, but I was very interested in malaria research, and it was an opportunity that only comes once. Perhaps I have even been able to accomplish a certain amount. Now the government here is financing a research station, and I am to be in charge of it. You may have heard of it – it is only twenty miles from here."

I could see that he had had to tell me so I should not think it odd

for an African to live away from his own country for so many years.
Like my impulse to explain my leg. We are all so anxious that people
should not think us different. See, we say, I am not peculiar – wait
until I tell you how it was with me.

"Well," I said slowly, "I do hope Ruth will like it here at Eburaso."

My feeling of apprehension was so marked, I remember, that I
attempted exorcism by finding sensible reasons. It was only the
season, I thought, the inevitable tension before the rains, and perhaps the season of regrets in myself as well. But I was not convinced.

"I, too, hope very much she will like it here," Dr Quansah said.
He did not sound overly confident.

"I'm sure I shall," Ruth said suddenly, excitedly, her round face
beaming. "I think it's great fun, Miss Nedden, coming to Africa like
this."

Her father and I exchanged quick and almost fearful glances. She
had spoken, of course, as any English schoolgirl might speak, going
abroad.

I do not know how long Ruth Quansah kept her sense of adventure.
Possibly it lasted the first day, certainly not longer. I watched her as
carefully as I could, but there was not much I could do.

I had no difficulty in picking her out from a group of girls, although
she wore the same light green uniform. She walked differently,
carried herself differently. She had none of their easy languor. She
strode along with brisk intensity, and in consequence perspired a
great deal. At meals she ate virtually nothing. I asked her if she had no
appetite, and she looked at me reproachfully.

"I'm starving," she said flatly. "But I can't eat this food, Miss
Nedden. I'm sorry, but I just can't. That awful mashed stuff, sort of
greyish yellow, like some funny kind of potatoes – it makes me sick."

"I'm afraid you'll have to get used to cassava," I said, restraining a
smile, for she looked so serious and so offended. "African food is
served to the girls here, naturally. Personally I'm very fond of it,
groundnut stew and such. Soon you won't find it strange."

She gave me such a hostile glance that I wondered uneasily what
we would do if she really determined to starve herself. Thank heaven
she could afford to lose a few pounds.

Our girls fetched their own washing water in buckets from our wells. The evening trek for water was a time of singing, of shouted gossip, of laughter, just as it was each morning for their mothers in the villages, taking the water vessels to the river. The walk was not an easy one for me, but one evening I stumbled rather irritably and unwillingly down the stony path to the wells.

Ruth was there, standing apart from the others. Each of the girls in turn filled a bucket, hoisted it up on to her head and sauntered off, still chattering and waving, without spilling a drop. Ruth was left alone to fill her bucket. Then, carrying it with both her hands clutched around the handle, she began to struggle back along the path. Perhaps foolishly, I smiled. It was done only in encouragement, but she mistook my meaning.

"I expect it looks very funny," she burst out. "I expect they all think so, too."

Before I could speak she had swung the full bucket and thrown it from her as hard as she could. The water struck at the ground, turning the dust to ochre mud, and the bucket rattled and rolled, dislodging pebbles along its way. The laughter among the feathery *niim* trees further up the path suddenly stopped, as a dozen pairs of hidden eyes peered. Looking bewildered, as though she were surprised and shocked by what she had done, Ruth sat down, her sturdy legs rigid in front of her, her child's soft face creased in tears.

"I didn't know it would be like this, here," she said at last. "I didn't know at all."

In the evenings the senior girls were allowed to change from their school uniforms to African cloth, and they usually did so, for they were very concerned with their appearances and they rightly believed that the dark-printed lengths of mammy-cloth were more becoming to them than their short school frocks. Twice a week it was my responsibility to hobble over and make the evening rounds of the residence. Ruth, I noticed, changed into one of her English frocks, a different one each time, it appeared. Tact had never been my greatest strength, but I tried to suggest that it might be better if she would wear cloth like the rest.

"You father would be glad to buy one for you, I'm sure."

"I've got one – it was my mother's," Ruth replied. She frowned.

"I don't know how to put it on properly. They – they'd only laugh if I asked them. And anyway –"

Her face took on that defiance which is really a betrayal of uncertainty.

"I don't like those cloths," she said clearly. "They look like fancy-dress costumes to me. I'd feel frightfully silly in one. I suppose the people here haven't got anything better to wear."

In class she had no restraint. She was clever, and she knew more about English literature and composition than the other girls, for she had been taught always in English, whereas for the first six years of their schooling they had received most of their instruction in their own language. But she would talk interminably, if allowed, and she rushed to answer my questions before anyone else had a chance. Abenaa, Mary Ansah, Yaa, Kwaale and all the rest would regard her with eyes which she possibly took to be full of awe for her erudition. I knew something of those bland brown eyes, however, and I believed them to contain only scorn for one who would so blatantly show off. But I was wrong. The afternoon Kwaale came to see me, I learned that in those first few weeks the other girls had believed, quite simply, that Ruth was insane.

The junior teachers live in residence in the main building, but Miss Povey and I have our own bungalows, hers on one side of the grounds, mine on the other. A small grove of bamboo partially shields my house, and although Yindo the garden boy deplores my taste, I keep the great spiny clumps of prickly pear that grow beside my door. Hilda Povey grows zinnia and nasturtiums, and spends hours trying to coax an exiled rose-bush into bloom, but I will have no English flowers. My garden burns magnificently with jungle lily and poinsettia, which Yindo gently uproots from the forest and puts in here.

The rains had broken and the air was cool and lightened. The downpour began predictably each evening around dusk, so I was still able to have my tea outside. I was exceedingly fond of my garden chair. I discovered it years ago at Jillaram's Silk Palace, a tatty little Indian shop in the side streets of the city which I seldom visited. The chair was rattan with a high fan-shaped back like a throne or a peacock's tail, enamelled in Chinese red and decorated extravagantly with gilt. I had never seen anything so splendidly

garish, so I bought it. The red had since been subdued by sun and
the gilt was flaking, but I still sat enthroned in it each afternoon, my
ebony sceptre by my side.

I did not hear Kwaale until she greeted me. She was wearing her
good cloth, an orange one patterned with small black stars that
wavered in their firmament as she moved. Kwaale had never been
unaware of her womanhood. Even as a child she walked with that
same slow grace. We did not need to hope that she would go on and
take teacher training or anything of that sort. She would marry
when she left school, and I believed that would be the right thing for
her to do. But sometimes it saddened me to think of what life would
probably be for her, bearing too many children in too short a span of
years, mourning the inevitable deaths of some of them, working
bent double at the planting and hoeing until her slim straightness
was warped. All at once I felt ashamed in the presence of this young
queen, who had only an inheritance of poverty to return to,
ashamed of my comfort and my heaviness, ashamed of my decrepit
scarlet throne and trivial game.

"Did you want to see me, Kwaale?" I spoke brusquely.

"Yes." She sat down on the stool at my feet. At first they had
thought Ruth demented, she said, but now they had changed their
minds. They had seen how well she did on her test papers. She was
sane, they had decided, but this was so much the worse for her, for
now she could be held responsible for what she did.

"What does she do, Kwaale?"

"She will not speak with us, nor eat with us. She pretends not to
eat at all. But we have seen her. She has money, you know, from her
father. The big palm grove – she goes there, and eats chocolate and
biscuits. By herself. Not one to anyone else. Such a thing."

Kwaale was genuinely shocked. Where these girls came from,
sharing was not done as a matter of moral principle, but as a
necessary condition of life.

"If one alone eats the honey," Kwaale said primly in Twi, "it
plagues his stomach."

It was, of course, a proverb. Kwaale was full of them. Her father
was a village elder in Eburaso, and although he did precious little
work, he was a highly respected man. He spoke continuously in
proverbs and dispensed his wisdom freely. He was a charming

person, but it was his wife, with the cassava and peppers and medicinal herbs she sold in the market, who had made it possible for some of their children to obtain an education.

"That is not all," Kwaale went on. "There is much worse. She becomes angry, even at the younger ones. Yesterday Ayesha spoke to her, and she hit the child on the face. Ayesha – if it had been one of the others, even –"

Ayesha, my youngest one, who had had to bear so much. Tears of rage must have come to my eyes, for Kwaale glanced at me, then lowered her head with that courtesy of the heart which forbids the observing of another's pain. I struggled with myself to be fair to Ruth. I called to mind the bleakness of her face as she trudged up the path with the water bucket.

"She is lonely, Kwaale, and does not quite know what to do. Try to be patient with her."

Kwaale sighed. "It is not easy –"

Then her resentment gained command. "The stranger is like passing water in the drain," she said fiercely.

Another of her father's proverbs. I looked at her in dismay.

"There is a different saying on that subject," I said drily, at last. "We had it in chapel not so long ago – don't you remember? From Exodus. 'Thou shalt not oppress a stranger, for ye know the heart of a stranger, seeing ye were strangers in the land of Egypt.'"

But Kwaale's eyes remained implacable. She had never been a stranger in the land of Egypt.

When Kwaale had gone, I sat unmoving for a while in my ridiculous rattan throne. Then I saw Ayesha walking along the path, so I called to her. We spoke together in Twi, Ayesha and I. She had begun to learn English, but she found it difficult and I tried not to press her beyond her present limits. She did not even speak her own language very well, if it was actually her own language – no one knew for certain. She was tiny for her age, approximately six. In her school dress she looked like one of those stick figures I used to draw as a child – billowing garments, straight lines for limbs, and the same disproportionately large eyes.

"Come here, Ayesha."

Obediently she came. Then, after the first moment of watchful survey which she still found necessary to observe, she scrambled on to my lap. I was careful – we were all careful here – not to establish bonds of too-great affection. As Miss Povey was fond of reminding us, these were not our children. But with Ayesha, the rule was sometimes hard to remember. I touched her face lightly with my hand.

"Did an older girl strike you, little one?"

She nodded wordlessly. She did not look angry or upset. She made no bid for sympathy because she had no sense of having been unfairly treated. A slap was not a very great injury to Ayesha.

"Why?" I asked gently. "Do you know why she did that thing?"

She shook her head. Then she lifted her eyes to mine.

"Where is the monkey today?"

She wanted to ignore the slap, to forget it. Forgetfulness is her protection. Sometimes I wondered, though, how much could be truly forgotten and what happened to it when it was entombed.

"The monkey is in my house," I said. "Do you want to see her?"

"Yes." So we walked inside and brought her out into the garden, my small and regal Ankyeo who was named, perhaps frivolously, after a great queen mother of this country. I did not know what species of monkey Ankyeo was. She was delicate-boned as a bird, and her fur was silver. She picked with her doll fingers at a pink hibiscus blossom, and Ayesha laughed. I wanted to make Ankyeo perform all her tricks, in order to hear again that rare laugh. But I knew I must not try to go too fast. After a while Ayesha tired of watching the monkey and sat cross-legged beside my chair, the old look of passivity on her face. We would have to move indoors before the rain started, but for the moment I left her as she was.

Ruth did not approach silently, as Kwaale and Ayesha had done, but with a loud crunching of shoes on the gravel path. When she saw Ayesha she stopped.

"I suppose you know."

"Yes. But it was not Ayesha who told me."

"Who, then?"

Of course I would not tell her. Her face grew sullen.

"Whoever it was, I think it was rotten of her to tell –"

"It did not appear that way to the girl in question. She was protecting the others from you, and that is a higher good in her eyes than any individual honour in not tattling."

"Protecting – from me?" There was desolation in her voice, and I relented.

"They will change, Ruth, once they see they can trust you. Why did you hit Ayesha?"

"It was a stupid thing to do," Ruth said in a voice almost inaudible with shame, "and I felt awful about it, and I'm terribly sorry. But she – she kept asking me something, you see, over and over again, in a sort of whining voice, and I – I just couldn't stand it any more."

"What did she ask you?"

"How should I know?" Ruth said. "I don't speak Twi."

I stared at her. "Not – any? I thought you might be a little rusty, but I never imagined – my dear child, it's your own language, after all."

"My father has always spoken English to me," she said. "My mother spoke in Twi, I suppose, but she died when I was under a year old."

"Why on earth didn't you tell the girls?"

"I don't know. I don't know why I didn't –"

I noticed then how much thinner she had grown and how her expression had altered. She no longer looked like a child. Her eyes were implacable as Kwaale's.

"They don't know anything outside this place," she said. "I don't care if I can't understand what they're saying to each other. I'm not interested, anyway."

Then her glance went to Ayesha once more.

"But why were they so angry – about her? I know it was mean, and I said I was sorry. But the way they all looked –"

"Ayesha was found by the police in Lagos," I said reluctantly. "She was sent back to this country because one of the constables recognized her speech as Twi. We heard about her and offered to have her here. There are many like her, I'm afraid, who are not found or heard about. She must have been stolen, you see, or sold when she was very young. She has not been able to tell us much. But the Nigerian police traced her back to several slave-dealers. When they discovered her she was being used as a child prostitute. She was very injured when she came to us here."

Ruth put her head down on her hands. She sat without speaking. Then her shoulders, hunched and still, began to tremble.

"You didn't know," I said. "There's no point in reproaching yourself now."

She looked up at me with a kind of naïve horror, the look of someone who recognizes for the first time the existence of cruelty.

"Things like that really happen here?"

I sighed. "Not just here. Evil does not select one place for its province."

But I could see that she did not believe me. The wind was beginning to rise, so we went indoors. Ayesha carried the stool, Ruth lifted my red throne, and I limped after them, feeling exhausted and not at all convinced just then that God was in His heaven. What a mercy for me that the church in whose mission school I had spent much of my adult life did not possess the means of scrutinizing too precisely the souls of its faithful servants.

We had barely got inside the bungalow when Ayesha missed the monkey. She flew outside to look for it, but no amount of searching revealed Ankyeo. Certain the monkey was gone forever, Ayesha threw herself down on the damp ground. While the wind moaned and screeched, the child, who never wept for herself, wept for a lost monkey and would not be comforted. I did not dare kneel beside her. My leg was too unreliable, and I knew I would not be able to get up again. I stood there, lumpish and helpless, while Ruth in the doorway shivered in her thin and daisied dress.

Then, like a veritable angel of the Lord, Yindo appeared, carrying Ankyeo. Immediately I experienced a resurrection of faith, while at the same time thinking how frail and fickle my belief must be, to be influenced by a child and a silver-furred monkey.

Yindo grinned and knelt beside Ayesha. He was no more than sixteen, a tall thin-wristed boy, a Dagomba from the northern desert. He had come here when he was twelve, one of the scores of young who were herded down each year to work on the cocoa farms because their own arid land had no place for them. He was one of our best garden boys, but he could not speak to anyone around here except in hesitant pidgin English, for no one here knew his language. His speech lack never bothered him with Ayesha. The two communicated in some fashion without words. He put the monkey in her arms and she held Ankyeo closely. Then she made a slight and courtly bow to Yindo. He laughed and shook his head. Drawing from his pocket a small charm, he showed it to her. It was the dried head of a chameleon, with blue glass beads and a puff of unwholesome-looking fur tied around it. Ayesha understood at once that it was this object which had enabled Yindo to find the monkey. She made another and deeper obeisance and from her own pocket drew the only thing she had to offer, a toffee wrapped in silver foil which I had given her at least two weeks ago. Yindo took it, touched it to his talisman, and put both carefully away.

Ruth had not missed the significance of the ritual. Her eyes were dilated with curiosity and contempt.

"He believes in it, doesn't he?" she said. "He actually believes in it."

"Don't be so quick to condemn the things you don't comprehend," I said sharply.

"I think it's horrible." She sounded frightened. "He's just a savage, isn't he, just a –"

"Stop it, Ruth. That's quite enough."

"I hate it here!" she cried. "I wish I were back at home."

"Child," I said, "this is your home."

She did not reply, but the denial in her face made me marvel at my own hypocrisy.

Each Friday Dr Quansah drove over to see Ruth, and usually on these afternoons he would call in at my bungalow for a few minutes to discuss her progress. At first our conversations were completely false, each of us politely telling the other that Ruth was getting on reasonably well. Then one day he dropped the pretence.

"She is very unhappy, isn't she? Please – don't think I am blaming you, Miss Nedden. Myself, rather. It is too different. What should I have done, all those years ago?"

"Don't be offended, Dr Quansah, but why wasn't she taught her own language?"

He waited a long moment before replying. He studied the clear amber tea in his cup.

"I was brought up in a small village," he said at last. "English came hard to me. When I went to Secondary School I experienced great difficulty at first in understanding even the gist of the lectures. I was determined that the same thing would not happen to Ruth. I suppose I imagined she would pick up her own language easily, once she returned here, as though the knowledge of one's family tongue was inherited. Of course, if her mother had lived –"

He set down the teacup and knotted his huge hands together in an unexpressed anguish that was painful to see.

"Both of them uprooted," he said. "It was my fault, I guess, and yet –"

He fell silent. Finally, his need to speak was greater than his reluctance to reveal himself.

"You see, my wife hated England, always. I knew, although she never spoke of it. Such women don't. She was a quiet woman, gentle and – obedient. My parents had chosen her and I had married her when I was a very young man, before I first left this country. Our differences were not so great, then, but later in those years in London – she was like a plant, expected to grow where the soil is not suitable for it. My friends and associates – the places I went for dinner – she did not accompany me. I never asked her to entertain those people in our house. I could not – you see that?"

I nodded and he continued in the same low voice with its burden of self-reproach.

"She was illiterate," he said. "She did not know anything of my life, as it became. She did not want to know. She refused to learn. I was – impatient with her. I know that. But –"

He turned away so I would not see his face.

"Have you any idea what it is like," he cried, "to need someone to talk to, and not to have even one person?"

"Yes," I said. "I have a thorough knowledge of that."

He looked at me in surprise, and when he saw that I did know, he seemed oddly relieved, as though, having exchanged vulnerabilities, we were neither of us endangered. My ebony cane slipped to the ground just then, and Dr Quansah stooped and picked it up, automatically and casually, hardly noticing it, and I was startled at myself, for I had felt no awkwardness in the moment either.

"When she became ill," he went on, "I do not think she really cared whether she lived or not. And now, Ruth – you know, when she was born, my wife called her by an African name which means 'child of the rain'. My wife missed the sun so very much. The rain, too, may have stood for her own tears. She had not wanted to bear her child so far from home."

Unexpectedly, he smiled, the dark features of his face relaxing, becoming less blunt and plain.

"Why did you leave your country and come here, Miss Nedden? For the church? Or for the sake of the Africans?"

I leaned back in my mock throne and re-arranged, a shade ironically, the folds of my lilac smock.

"I thought so, once," I replied. "But now I don't know. I think I may have come here mainly for myself, after all, hoping to find a place where my light could shine forth. Not a very palatable admission, perhaps."

"At least you did not take others along on your pilgrimage."

"No. I took no one. No one at all."

We sat without speaking, then, until the tea grew cold and the dusk gathered.

It was through me that Ruth met David Mackie. He was an intent, lemon-haired boy of fifteen. He had been ill and was therefore out from England, staying with his mother while he recuperated. Mrs Mackie was a widow. Her husband had managed an oil palm plantation for an African owner, and when he died Clare Mackie had stayed on and managed the place herself. I am sure she made a better job of it than her husband had, for she was one of those frighteningly efficient women, under whose piercing eye, one felt, even the oil palms would not dare to slacken their efforts. She was slender and quick, and she contrived to look dashing and yet not unfeminine in her corded jodhpurs and open-necked shirt, which she wore with a silk paisley scarf at the throat. David was more like his father, thoughtful and rather withdrawn, and maybe that is why I had agreed to help him occasionally with his studies, which he was then taking by correspondence.

The Mackies' big whitewashed bungalow, perched on its cement pillars and fringed around with languid casuarina trees, was only a short distance from the school, on the opposite side of the hill to the village. Ruth came to my bungalow one Sunday afternoon, when I had promised to go to the Mackies', and as she appeared bored and despondent, I suggested she come along with me.

After I had finished the lesson, Ruth and David talked together amicably enough while Mrs Mackie complained about the inadequacies of local labour and I sat fanning myself with a palm leaf and feeling grateful that fate had not made me one of Clare Mackie's employees.

"Would you like to see my animals?" I heard David ask Ruth, his voice still rather formal and yet pleased, too, to have a potential admirer for his treasures.

"Oh yes." She was eager; she understood people who collected animals. "What have you got?"

"A baby crocodile," he said proudly, "and a cutting-grass – that's a bush rat, you know, and several snakes, non-poisonous ones, and a lot of assorted toads. I shan't be able to keep the croc long, of course. They're too tricky to deal with. I had a duiker, too, but it died."

Off they went, and Mrs Mackie shrugged.

"He's mad about animals. I think they're disgusting. But he's got to have something to occupy his time, poor dear."

When the two returned from their inspection of David's private zoo, we drove back to the school in the Mackies' bone-shaking jeep. I thought no more about the visit until late the next week, when I realized that I had not seen Ruth after classes for some days. I asked her, and she looked at me guilelessly, certain I would be as pleased as she was herself.

"I've been helping David with his animals," she explained enthusiastically. "You know, Miss Nedden, he wants to be an animal collector when he's through school. Not a hobby – he wants to work at it always. To collect live specimens, you see, for places like Whipsnade and Regent's Park Zoo. He's lent me a whole lot of books about it. It's awfully interesting, really it is."

I did not know what to say. I could not summon up the sternness to deny her the first friendship she had made here. But of course it was not "here", really. She was drawn to David because he spoke in the ways she knew, and of things which made sense to her. So she continued to see him. She borrowed several of my books to lend to him. They were both fond of poetry. I worried, of course, but not for what might be thought the obvious reasons. Both Ruth and David needed companionship, but neither was ready for anything more. I did not have the fears Miss Povey would have harboured if she had known. I was anxious for another reason. Ruth's friendship with David isolated her more than ever from the other girls. She made ever less effort to get along with them now, for David was sufficient company.

Only once was I alarmed about her actual safety, the time when Ruth told me she and David had found an old fishing pirogue and had gone on the river in it.

"The river – " I was appalled. "Ruth, don't you know there are crocodiles there?"

"Of course." She had no awareness of having done anything dangerous. "That's why we went. We hoped to catch another baby croc, you see. But we had no luck."

"You had phenomenal luck," I snapped. "Don't you ever do that again. Not ever."

"Well, all right," she said regretfully. "But it was great fun."

The sense of adventure had returned to her, and all at once I realized why. David was showing Africa to her as she wanted to be shown it – from the outside.

I felt I should tell Dr Quansah, but when I finally did he was so upset that I was sorry I had mentioned it.

"It is not a good thing," he kept saying. "The fact that this is a boy does not concern me half so much, to be frank with you, as the fact that he is European."

"I would not have expected such illogicalities from you, Dr Quansah." I was annoyed, and perhaps guilty as well, for I had permitted the situation.

Dr Quansah looked thoughtfully at me.

"I do not think it is that. Yes – maybe you are right. I don't know. But I do not want my daughter to be hurt by any – stupidity. I know that."

"David's mother is employed as manager by an African owner."

"Yes," Dr Quansah said, and his voice contained a bitterness I had not heard in it before, "but what does she say about him, in private?"

I had no reply to that, for what he implied was perfectly true. He saw from my face that he had not been mistaken.

"I have been away a long time, Miss Nedden," he said, "but not long enough to forget some of the things that were said to me by Europeans when I was young."

I should not have blurted out my immediate thought, but I did.

"You have been able to talk to me –"

"Yes." He smiled self-mockingly. "I wonder if you know how much that has surprised me?"

Why should I have found it difficult then, to look at him, at the face whose composure I knew concealed such aloneness? I took refuge, as so often, in the adoption of an abrupt tone.

"Why should it be surprising? You liked people in England. You had friends there."

"I am not consistent, I know. But the English at home are not the same as the English abroad – you must have realized that. You are not typical, Miss Nedden. I still find most Europeans here as difficult to deal with as I ever did. And yet – I seem to have lost touch with my own people, too. The young laboratory technicians at the station – they do not trust me, and I find myself getting so very impatient with them, losing my temper because they have not comprehended what I wanted them to do, and –"

He broke off. "I really should not bother you with all this."

"Oh, but you're not." The words came out with an unthinking swiftness which mortified me later when I recalled it. "I haven't so many people I can talk with, either, you know."

"You told me as much, once," Dr Quansah said gently. "I had not forgotten."

Pride has so often been my demon, the tempting conviction that one is able to see the straight path and to point it out to others. I was proud of my cleverness when I persuaded Kwaale to begin teaching Ruth Quansah the language of her people. Each afternoon they had lessons, and I assisted only when necessary to clarify some point of grammar. Ruth, once she started, became quite interested. Despite what she had said, she was curious to know what the other girls talked about together. As for Kwaale, it soothed her rancour to be asked to instruct, and it gave her an opportunity to learn something about Ruth, to see her as she was and not as Kwaale's imagination had distorted her. Gradually the two became, if not friends, at least reasonably peaceful acquaintances. Ruth continued to see David, but as her afternoons were absorbed by the language lessons, she no longer went to the Mackies' house quite so often.

Then came the Odwira. Ruth asked if she might go down to the village with Kwaale, and as most of the girls would be going, I agreed. Miss Povey would have liked to keep the girls away from the local festivals, which she regarded as dangerously heathen, but this quarantine had never proved practicable. At the time of the Odwira the girls simply disappeared, permission or not, like migrating birds.

Late that afternoon I saw the school lorry setting off for Eburaso, so I decided to go along. We swerved perilously down the mountain road, and reached the village just in time to see the end of the procession, as the chief, carried in palanquin under his saffron umbrella, returned from the river after the rituals there. The palm-wine libations had been poured, the souls of the populace cleansed. Now the Eburasahene would offer the new yams to the ancestors, and then the celebrations would begin. Drumming and dancing would go on all night, and the next morning Miss Povey, if she were wise, would not ask too many questions.

The mud and thatch shanties of the village were empty of inhabitants and the one street was full. Shouting, singing, wildly excited, they sweated and thronged. Everyone who owned a good cloth was wearing it, and the women fortunate enough to possess gold earrings or bangles were flaunting them before the covetous eyes of those whose bracelets and beads were only coloured glass. For safety I remained in the parked lorry, fearing my unsteady leg in such a mob.

I spotted Kwaale and Ruth. Kwaale's usual air of tranquillity had vanished. She was all sun-coloured cloth and whirling brown arms. I had never seen anyone with such a violence of beauty as she possessed, like surf or volcano, a spendthrift splendour. Then, out of the street's turbulence of voices I heard the low shout of a young man near her.

"Fire a gun at me."

I knew what was about to happen, for the custom was a very old one. Kwaale threw back her head and laughed. Her hands flicked at her cloth and for an instant she stood there naked except for the white beads around her hips, and her *amoanse*, the red cloth between her legs. Still laughing, she knotted her cloth back on again, and the young man put an arm around her shoulders and drew her close to him.

Ruth, tidy and separate in her frock with its pastel flowers, stared as though unable to believe what she had seen. Slowly she turned and it was then that she saw me. She began to force her way through the crowd of villagers. Instantly Kwaale dropped the young man's hand and went after her. Ruth stood beside the lorry, her eyes appealing to me.

"You saw – you saw what she –"

Kwaale's hand was clawing at her shoulder then, spinning her around roughly.

"What are you telling her? It is not for you to say!"

Kwaale thought I would be bound to disapprove. I could have explained the custom to Ruth, as it had been explained to me many years ago by Kwaale's father. I could have told her it used to be "Shoot an arrow", for Mother Nyame created the sun with fire, and arrows of the same fire were shot into the veins of mankind and became life-blood. I could have said that the custom was a reminder that women are the source of life. But I did not, for I was by no means sure that either Kwaale or the young man knew the roots of the tradition or that they cared. Something was permitted at festival time – why should they care about anything other than the beat of their own blood?

"Wait, Ruth, you don't understand –"

"I understand what she is," Ruth said distinctly. "She's nothing but a –"

Kwaale turned upon her viciously.

"Talk, you! Talk and talk. What else could you do? No man here would want you as his wife – you're too ugly."

Ruth drew away, shocked and uncertain. But Kwaale had not finished.

"Why don't you go? Take all your money and go! Why don't you?"

I should have spoken then, tried to explain one to the other. I think I did, after a paralysed moment, but it was too late. Ruth, twisting away, struggled around the clusters of people and disappeared among the trees on the path that led back to the mountain top.

The driver had trouble in moving the lorry through the jammed streets. By the time we got on to the hill road Ruth was not there. When we reached the school I got out and limped over to the Primary girls who were playing outside the main building. I asked if they had seen her, and they twirled and fluttered around me like green and brown leaves, each trying to outdo the others in impressing me with their display of English.

"Miss Neddeen, I seein' she. Wit' my eye I seein' she. She going deah –"

The way they pointed was the road to the Mackies' house.

I did not especially want the lorry to go roaring into the Mackies' compound as though the errand were urgent or critical, so when we sighted the casuarina trees I had the driver stop. I walked slowly past David's menagerie, where the cutting-grass scratched in its cage and the snakes lay in bright apathetic coils. Some sense of propriety made me hesitate before I had quite reached the house. Ruth and David were on the veranda, and I could hear their voices. I suppose it was shameful of me to listen, but it would have been worse to appear at that moment.

"If it was up to me –" David's voice was strained and tight with embarrassment. "But you know what she's like."

"What did she say, David? What did she say?" Ruth's voice, desperate with her need to know, her fear of knowing.

"Oh, well – nothing much."

"Tell me!"

Then David, faltering, ashamed, tactless.

"Only that African girls mature awfully young, and she somehow got the daft notion that – look here, Ruth, I'm sorry, but when she gets an idea there's nothing anyone can do. I know it's a lot of rot. I know you're not the ordinary kind of African. You're almost – almost like a – like us."

It was his best, I suppose. It was not his fault that it was not good enough. She cried out, then, and although the casuarina boughs hid the two from my sight, I could imagine their faces well enough, and David's astounded look at the hurt in her eyes.

"Almost –" she said. Then, with a fury I would not have believed possible, "No, I'm not! I'm not like you at all. I won't be!"

"Listen, Ruth –"

But she had thrust off his hand and had gone. She passed close to the place where I stood but she did not see me. Once again I watched her running. Running and running, into the forest where I could not follow.

*

I was frantic lest Miss Povey should find out and notify Dr Quansah before we could find Ruth. I had Ayesha go all through the school and grounds, for she could move more rapidly and unobtrusively than I. I waited, stumping up and down my garden, finally forcing myself to sit down and assume at least the appearance of calm. At last Ayesha returned. Only tiredness showed in her face, and my heart contracted.

"You did not find her, little one?"

She shook her head. "She is not here. She is gone."

Gone. Had she remained in the forest, then, with its thorns and strangular vines, its ferned depths that could hide death, its green silences? Or had she run as far as the river, dark and smooth as oil, deceptively smooth, with its saurian kings who fed off whatever flesh they could find? I dared not think.

I did something then that I had never before permitted myself to do. I picked up Ayesha and held the child tightly, not for her consoling but for my own. She reached out and touched a finger to my face.

"You are crying. For her?"

Then Ayesha sighed a little, resignedly.

"Come then," she said. "I will show you where she is."

Had I known her so slightly all along, my small Ayesha whose childhood lay beaten and lost somewhere in the shanties and brothels of Takoradi or Kumasi, the airless upper rooms of palm-wine bars in Lagos or Kaduna? Without a word I rose and followed her.

We did not have far to go. The gardeners' quarters were at the back of the school grounds, surrounded by *niim* trees and a few banana palms. In the last hut of the row, Yindo sat cross-legged on the packed-earth floor. Beside him on a dirty and torn grass mat Ruth Quansah lay, face down, her head buried in her arms.

Ayesha pointed. Why had she wanted to conceal it? To this day I do not really know, nor what the hut recalled to her, nor what she felt, for her face bore no more expression than a pencilled stick-child's, and her eyes were as dull as they had been when she first came to us here.

Ruth heard my cane and my dragged foot. I know she did. But she did not stir.

"Madam –" Yindo's voice was nearly incoherent with terror. "I beg you. You no give me sack. I Dagomba man, madam. No got bruddah dis place. I beg you, mek I no go lose dis job –"

I tried to calm him with meaningless sounds of reassurance. Then I asked him to tell me. He spoke in a harsh whisper, his face averted.

"She come dis place like she crez'. She say – do so." He gestured unmistakably. "I – I try, but I can no do so for she. I too fear."

He held out his hands then in an appeal both desperate and hopeless. He was a desert man. He expected no mercy here, far from the dwellings of his tribe.

Ruth still had not moved. I do not think she had even heard Yindo's words. At last she lifted her head, but she did not speak. She scanned slowly the mud walls, the tin basin for washing, the upturned box that served as table, the old hurricane lamp, and in a niche the grey and grinning head of the dead chameleon, around it the blue beads like naive eyes shining and beside it the offering of a toffee wrapped in grimy silver paper.

I stood there in the hut doorway, leaning on my ebony cane to support my cumbersome body, looking at the three of them but finding nothing simple enough to say. What words, after all, could possibly have been given to the outcast children?

I told Dr Quansah. I did not spare him anything, nor myself either. I imagined he would be angry at my negligence, my blundering, but he was not.

"You should not blame yourself in this way," he said. "I do not want that. It is – really, I think it is a question of time, after all."

"Undoubtedly. But in the meantime?"

"I don't know." He passed a hand across his forehead. "I seem to become tired so much more than I used to. Solutions do not come readily any more. Even for a father like myself, who relies so much on schools, it is still not such an easy thing, to bring up a child without a mother."

I leaned back in my scarlet chair. The old rattan received my head, and my absurdly jagged breath eased.

"No," I said. "I'm sure it can't be easy."

We were silent for a moment. Then with some effort Dr Quansah began to speak, almost apologetically.

"Coming back to this country after so long away – you know, I think that it is the last new thing I shall be able to do in my life. Does that seem wrong? When one grows older, one is aware of so many difficulties. Often they appear to outweigh all else."

My hands fumbled for my cane, the ebony that was grown and carved here. I found and held it, and it both reassured and mocked me.

"Perhaps," I said deliberately. "But Ruth –"

"I am taking her away. She wants to go. What else can I do? There is a school in the town where a cousin of mine lives."

"Yes. I see. You cannot do anything else, of course."

He rose. "Goodbye," he said, "and –"

But he did not finish the sentence. We shook hands, and he left.

At Eburaso School we go on as before. Miss Povey and I still snipe back and forth, knowing in our hearts that we rely upon our differences and would miss them if they were not there. I still teach my alien speech to the young ones, who continue to impart to it a kind of garbled charm. I grow heavier and I fancy my lameness is more pronounced, although Kwaale assures me this is not the case. In few enough years I will have reached retirement age.

Sitting in my garden and looking at the sun on the prickly pear and the poinsettia, I think of that island of grey rain where I must go as a stranger, when the time comes, while others must remain as strangers here.

The Man from Mars

MARGARET ATWOOD

A long time ago Christine was walking through the park. She was still wearing her tennis dress; she hadn't had time to shower and change, and her hair was held back with an elastic band. Her chunky reddish face, exposed with no softening fringe, looked like a Russian peasant's, but without the elastic band the hair got in her eyes. The afternoon was too hot for April; the indoor courts had been steaming, her skin felt poached.

The sun had brought the old men out from wherever they spent the winter: she had read a story recently about one who lived for three years in a manhole. They sat weedishly on the benches or lay on the grass with their heads on squares of used newspaper. As she passed, their wrinkled toadstool faces drifted towards her, drawn by the movement of her body, then floated away again, uninterested.

The squirrels were out, too, foraging; two or three of them moved towards her in darts and pauses, eyes fixed on her expectantly, mouths with the ratlike receding chins open to show the yellowed front teeth. Christine walked faster, she had nothing to give them. People shouldn't feed them, she thought; it makes them anxious and they get mangy.

Half-way across the park she stopped to take off her cardigan. As she bent over to pick up her tennis racquet again someone touched her on her freshly bared arm. Christine seldom screamed; she straightened up suddenly, gripping the handle of her racquet. It was not one of the old men, however: it was a dark-haired boy of twelve or so.

"Excuse me," he said, "I search for Economics Building. Is it there?" He motioned towards the west.

Christine looked at him more closely. She had been mistaken: he was not young, just short. He came a little above her shoulder, but then, she was above the average height; "statuesque", her mother called it when she was straining. He was also what was referred to in their family as "a person from another culture": oriental without a doubt, though perhaps not Chinese. Christine judged he must be a foreign student and gave him her official welcoming smile. In high school she had been president of the United Nations Club; that year her school had been picked to represent the Egyptian delegation at the Mock Assembly. It had been an unpopular assignment – nobody wanted to be the Arabs – but she had seen it through. She had made rather a good speech about the Palestinian refugees.

"Yes," she said, "that's it over there. The one with the flat roof. See it?"

The man had been smiling nervously at her the whole time. He was wearing glasses with transparent plastic rims, through which his eyes bulged up at her as though through a goldfish bowl. He had not followed where she was pointing. Instead he thrust towards her a small pad of green paper and a ball-point pen.

"You make map," he said.

Christine set down her tennis racquet and drew a careful map. "We are here," she said, pronouncing distinctly. "You go this way. The building is here." She indicated the route with a dotted line and an X. The man leaned close to her, watching the progress of the map attentively; he smelled of cooked cauliflower and an unfamiliar brand of hair grease. When she had finished Christine handed the paper and pen back to him with a terminal smile.

"Wait," the man said. He tore the piece of paper with the map off the pad, folded it carefully and put it in his jacket pocket; the jacket sleeves came down over his wrists and had threads at the edges. He began to write something; she noticed with a slight feeling of revulsion that his nails and the end of his fingers were so badly bitten they seemed almost deformed. Several of his fingers were blue from the leaky ball-point.

"Here is my name," he said, holding the pad out to her.

Christine read an odd assemblage of Gs, Ys and Ns, neatly printed in block letters. "Thank you," she said.

"You now write your name," he said, extending the pen.

Christine hesitated. If this had been a person from her own culture she would have thought he was trying to pick her up. But then, people from her own culture never tried to pick her up; she was too big. They only one who had made the attempt was the Moroccan waiter at the beer parlour where they sometimes went after meetings, and he had been direct. He had just intercepted her on the way to the Ladies' Room and asked and she said no; that had been that. This man was not a waiter though, but a student; she didn't want to offend him. In his culture, whatever it was, this exchange of names on pieces of paper was probably a formal politeness, like saying thank you. She took the pen from him.

"That is a very pleasant name," he said. He folded the paper and placed it in his jacket pocket with the map.

Christine felt she had done her duty. "Well, goodbye," she said. "It was nice to have met you." She bent for her tennis racquet but he had already stooped and retrieved it and was holding it with both hands in front of him, like a captured banner.

"I carry this for you."

"Oh no, please. Don't bother, I am in a hurry," she said, articulating clearly. Deprived of her tennis racquet she felt weaponless. He started to saunter along the path; he was not nervous at all now, he seemed completely at ease.

"*Vous parlez français?*" he asked conversationally.

"*Oui, un petit peu,*" she said. "Not very well." How am I going to get my racquet away from him without being rude? she was wondering.

"*Mais vous avez un bel accent.*" His eyes goggled at her through the glasses: was he being flirtatious? She was well aware that her accent was wretched.

"Look," she said, for the first time letting her impatience show, "I really have to go. Give me my racquet, please."

He quickened his pace but gave no sign of returning the racquet. "Where you are going?"

"Home," she said. "My house."

"I go with you now," he said hopefully.

"*No,*" she said: she would have to be firm with him. She made a lunge and got a grip on her racquet; after a brief tug of war it came free.

"Goodbye," she said, turning away from his puzzled face and setting off at what she hoped was a discouraging jog-trot. It was like walking away from a growling dog: you shouldn't let on you were frightened. Why should she be frightened anyway? He was only half her size and she had the tennis racquet, there was nothing he could do to her.

Although she did not look back she could tell he was still following. Let there be a streetcar, she thought, and there was one but it
was far down the line, stuck behind a red light. He appeared at her
side, breathing audibly, a moment after she reached the stop. She
gazed ahead, rigid.

"You are my friend," he said tentatively.

Christine relented: he hadn't been trying to pick her up after all,
he was a stranger, he just wanted to meet some of the local people;
in his place she would have wanted the same thing.

"Yes," she said, doling him out a smile.

"That is good," he said. "My country is very far."

Christine couldn't think of an apt reply. "That's interesting," she
said. "Très intéressant." The streetcar was coming at last; she opened
her purse and got out a ticket.

"I go with you now," he said. His hand clamped on her arm above
the elbow.

"You . . . stay . . . here," Christine said, resisting the impulse to
shout but pausing between each word as though for a deaf person.
She detached his hand – his hold was quite feeble and could not
compete with her tennis biceps – and leapt off the kerb and up the
streetcar steps, hearing with relief the doors grind shut behind her.
Inside the car and a block away she permitted herself a glance out a
side window. He was standing where she had left him; he seemed to
be writing something on his little pad of paper.

When she reached home she had only time for a snack, and even
then she was almost late for the Debating Society. The topic was,
"Resolved: That War Is Obsolete". Her team took the affirmative and
won.

Christine came out of her last examination feeling depressed. It was
not the exam that depressed her but the fact that it was the last one:
it meant the end of the school year. She dropped into the coffee shop
as usual, then went home early because there didn't seem to be
anything else to do.

"Is that you dear?" her mother called from the living room. She
must have heard the front door close. Christine went in and flopped
on the sofa, disturbing the neat pattern of cushions.

"How was your exam, dear?" her mother asked.

"Fine," said Christine flatly. It had been fine; she had passed. She was not a brilliant student, she knew that, but she was conscientious. Her professors always wrote things like "A serious attempt" and "Well thought out but perhaps lacking in élan" on her term papers; they gave her Bs, the occasional B+. She was taking Political Science and Economics, and hoped for a job with the government after she graduated; with her father's connections she had a good chance.

"That's nice."

Christine felt, resentfully, that her mother had only a hazy idea of what an exam was. She was arranging gladioli in a vase; she had rubber gloves on to protect her hands as she always did when engaged in what she called "housework". As far as Christine could tell her housework consisted of arranging flowers in vases: daffodils and tulips and hyacinths through gladioli, irises and roses, all the way to asters and mums. Sometimes she cooked, elegantly and with chafing-dishes, but she thought of it as a hobby. The girl did everything else. Christine thought it faintly sinful to have a girl. The only ones available now were either foreign or pregnant; their expressions usually suggested they were being taken advantage of somehow. But her mother asked what they would do otherwise; they'd either have to go into a Home or stay in their own countries, and Christine had to agree this was probably true. It was hard, anyway, to argue with her mother. She was so delicate, so preserved-looking, a harsh breath would scratch the finish.

"An interesting young man phoned today," her mother said. She had finished the gladioli and was taking off her rubber gloves. "He asked to speak with you and when I said you weren't in we had quite a little chat. You didn't tell me about him, dear." She put on the glasses which she wore on a decorative chain around her neck, a signal that she was in her modern, intelligent mood rather than her old-fashioned whimsical one.

"Did he leave his name?" Christine asked. She knew a lot of young men but they didn't often call her; they conducted their business with her in the coffee shop or after meetings.

"He's a person from another culture. He said he would call back later."

Christine had to think a moment. She was vaguely acquainted

with several people from other cultures, Britain mostly; they belonged to the Debating Society.

"He's studying Philosophy in Montreal," her mother prompted. "He sounded French."

Christine began to remember the man in the park. "I don't think he's French, exactly," she said.

Her mother had taken off her glasses again and was poking absentmindedly at a bent gladiolus. "Well, he sounded French." She meditated, flowery sceptre in hand. "I think it would be nice if you had him to tea."

Christine's mother did her best. She had two other daughters, both of whom took after her. They were beautiful; one was well married already and the other would clearly have no trouble. Her friends consoled her about Christine by saying, "She's not fat, she's just big-boned, it's the father's side," and "Christine is so healthy." Her other daughters had never gotten involved in activities when they were at school, but since Christine could not possibly ever be beautiful even if she took off weight, it was just as well she was so athletic and political, it was a good thing she had interests. Christine's mother tried to encourage her interests whenever possible. Christine could tell when she was making an extra effort, there was a reproachful edge to her voice.

She knew her mother expected enthusiasm but she could not supply it. "I don't know, I'll have to see," she said dubiously.

"You took tired, darling," said her mother. "Perhaps you'd like a glass of milk."

Christine was in the bathtub when the phone rang. She was not prone to fantasy but when she was in the bathtub she often pretended she was a dolphin, a game left over from one of the girls who used to bathe her when she was small. Her mother was being bell-voiced and gracious in the hall; then there was a tap at the door.

"It's that nice young French student, Christine," her mother said.

"Tell him I'm in the bathtub," Christine said, louder than necessary. "He isn't French."

She could hear her mother frowning. "That wouldn't be very polite, Christine. I don't think he'd understand."

"Oh, all right," Christine said. She heaved herself out of the bathtub, swathed her pink bulk in a towel and splattered to the phone.

"Hello," she said gruffly. At a distance he was not pathetic, he was a nuisance. She could not imagine how he had tracked her down: most likely he went through the phone book, calling all the numbers with her last name until he hit on the right one.

"It is your friend."

"I know," she said. "How are you?"

"I am very fine." There was a long pause, during which Christine had a vicious urge to say, "Well goodbye then," and hang up; but she was aware of her mother poised figurine-like in her bedroom doorway. Then he said, "I hope you also are very fine."

"Yes," said Christine. She wasn't going to participate.

"I come to tea," he said.

This took Christine by surprise. "You do?"

"Your pleasant mother ask me. I come Thursday, four o'clock."

"Oh," Christine said, ungraciously.

"See you then," he said, with the conscious pride of one who has mastered a difficult idiom.

Christine set down the phone and went along the hall. Her mother was in her study, sitting innocently at her writing desk.

"Did you ask him to tea on Thursday?"

"Not exactly, dear," her mother said. "I did mention he might come round to tea some time, though."

"Well, he's coming Thursday. Four o'clock."

"What's wrong with that?" her mother said serenely. "I think it's a very nice gesture for us to make. I do think you might try to be a little more co-operative." She was pleased with herself.

"Since you invited him," said Christine, "you can bloody well stick around and help me entertain him. I don't want to be left making nice gestures all by myself."

"Christine, dear," her mother said, above being shocked. "You ought to put on your dressing gown, you'll catch a chill."

After sulking for an hour Christine tried to think of the tea as a cross between an examination and an executive meeting: not enjoyable, certainly, but to be got through as tactfully as possible. And it was a nice gesture. When the cakes her mother had ordered arrived from The Patisserie on Thursday morning she began to feel slightly festive; she even resolved to put on a dress, a good one, instead of a skirt and blouse. After all, she had nothing against him, except the memory of the way he had grabbed her tennis racquet and then her arm. She suppressed a quick impossible vision of herself pursued around the living room, fending him off with thrown sofa cushions and vases of gladioli; nevertheless she told the girl they would have tea in the garden. It would be a treat for him, and there was more space outdoors.

She had suspected her mother would dodge the tea, would contrive to be going out just as he was arriving: that way she could size him up and then leave them alone together. She had done things like that to Christine before; the excuse this time was the Symphony Committee. Sure enough, her mother carefully mislaid her gloves and located them with a faked murmur of joy when the doorbell rang. Christine relished for weeks afterwards the image of her mother's dropped jaw and flawless recovery when he was introduced: he wasn't quite the foreign potentate her optimistic, veil-fragile mind had concocted.

He was prepared for celebration. He had slicked on so much hair cream that his head seemed to be covered with a tight black patent-leather cap, and he had cut the threads off his jacket sleeves. His orange tie was overpoweringly splendid. Christine noticed, however, as he shook her mother's suddenly braced white glove that the ball-point ink on his fingers was indelible. His face had broken out, possibly in anticipation of the delights in store for him; he had a tiny camera slung over his shoulder and was smoking an exotic-smelling cigarette.

Christine led him through the cool flowery softly padded living room and out by the french doors into the garden. "You sit here," she said. "I will have the girl bring tea."

This girl was from the West Indies: Christine's parents had been enraptured with her when they were down at Christmas and had brought her back with them. Since that time she had become pregnant, but Christine's mother had not dismissed her. She said she was slightly disappointed but what could you expect, and she didn't see any real difference between a girl who was pregnant before you hired her and one who got that way afterwards. She prided herself on her tolerance; also there was a scarcity of girls. Strangely enough, the girl became progressively less easy to get along with. Either she did not share Christine's mother's view of her own generosity, or she felt she had gotten away with something and was therefore free to indulge in contempt. At first Christine had tried to treat her as an equal. "Don't call me 'Miss Christine'," she had said with an imitation of light, comradely laughter. "What you want me to call you then?" the girl had said, scowling. They had begun to have brief, surly arguments in the kitchen, which Christine decided were like the arguments between one servant and another: her mother's attitude towards each of them was similar, they were not altogether satisfactory but they would have to do.

The cakes, glossy with icing, were set out on a plate and the teapot was standing ready; on the counter the electric kettle boiled. Christine headed for it, but the girl, till then sitting with her elbows on the kitchen table and watching her expressionlessly, made a dash and intercepted her. Christine waited until she had poured the water into the pot. Then, "I'll carry it out, Elvira," she said. She had just decided she didn't want the girl to see her visitor's orange tie; already, she knew, her position in the girl's eyes had suffered because no one had yet attempted to get *her* pregnant.

"What you think they pay me for, Miss Christine?" the girl said insolently. She swung towards the garden with the tray; Christine trailed her, feeling lumpish and awkward. The girl was at least as big as she was but in a different way.

"Thank you, Elvira," Christine said when the tray was in place. The girl departed without a word, casting a disdainful backward glance at the frayed jacket sleeves, the stained fingers. Christine was now determined to be especially kind to him.

"You are very rich," he said.

"No," Christine protested, shaking her head, "we're not." She had never thought of her family as rich; it was one of her father's sayings that nobody made any money with the government.

"Yes," he repeated, "you are very rich." He sat back in his lawn chair, gazing about him as though dazed.

Christine set his cup of tea in front of him. She wasn't in the habit of paying much attention to the house or the garden; they were nothing special, far from being the largest on the street; other people took care of them. But now she looked where he was looking, seeing it all as though from a different height: the long expanses, the border flowers blazing in the early-summer sunlight, the flagged patio and walks, the high walls and the silence.

He came back to her face, sighing a little. "My English is not good," he said, "but I improve."

"You do," Christine said, nodding encouragement.

He took sips of his tea, quickly and tenderly, as though afraid of injuring the cup. "I like to stay here."

Christine passed him the cakes. He took only one, making a slight face as he ate it; but he had several more cups of tea while she finished the cakes. She managed to find out from him that he had come over on a church fellowship – she could not decode the denomination – and was studying Philosophy or Theology, or possibly both. She was feeling well-disposed towards him: he had behaved himself, he had caused her no inconvenience.

The teapot was at last empty. He sat up straight in his chair, as though alerted by a soundless gong. "You look this way, please," he said. Christine saw that he had placed his miniature camera on the stone sundial her mother had shipped back from England two years before. He wanted to take her picture. She was flattered, and settled herself to pose, smiling evenly.

He took off his glasses and laid them beside his plate. For a moment she saw his myopic, unprotected eyes turned towards her, with something tremulous and confiding in them she wanted to close herself off from knowing about. Then he went over and did something to the camera, his back to her. The next instant he was crouched beside her, his arm around her waist as far as it could reach, his other hand covering her own hands which she had folded in her lap, his cheek jammed up against hers. She was too startled to move. The camera clicked.

He stood up at once and replaced his glasses, which glittered now with a sad triumph. "Thank you, miss," he said to her. "I go now." He slung the camera back over his shoulder, keeping his hand on it as though to hold the lid on and prevent escape. "I send to my family; they will like."

He was out the gate and gone before Christine had recovered; then she laughed. She had been afraid he would attack her, she could admit it now, and he had; but not in the usual way. He had raped, *rapeo, rapere, rapui, to seize and carry off*, not herself but her celluloid image, and incidentally that of the silver tea service, which glinted mockingly at her as the girl bore it away, carrying it regally, the insignia, the official jewels.

Christine spent the summer as she had for the past three years: she was the sailing instructress at an expensive all-girls camp near Algonquin Park. She had been a camper there, everything was familiar to her; she sailed almost better than she played tennis.

The second week she got a letter from him, postmarked Montreal and forwarded from her home address. It was printed in block letters on a piece of the green paper, two or three sentences. It began, "I hope you are well," then described the weather in mono-syllables and ended, "I am fine." It was signed, "Your friend." Each week she got another of these letters, more or less identical. In one of them a colour print was enclosed: himself, slightly cross-eyed and grinning hilariously, even more spindly than she remembered him against her billowing draperies, flowers exploding around them like firecrackers, one of his hands an equivocal blur in her lap, the other out of sight; on her own face, astonishment and outrage, as though he was sticking her in the behind with his hidden thumb.

She answered the first letter, but after that the seniors were in training for the races. At the end of the summer, packing to go home, she threw all the letters away.

When she had been back for several weeks she received another of the green letters. This time there was a return address printed at the top which Christine noted with foreboding was in her own city. Every day she waited for the phone to ring; she was so certain his first attempt at contact would be a disembodied voice that when he came upon her abruptly in mid-campus she was unprepared.

"How are you?"

His smile was the same, but everything else about him had deteriorated. He was, if possible, thinner; his jacket sleeves had sprouted a lush new crop of threads, as though to conceal hands now so badly bitten they appeared to have been gnawed by rodents. His hair fell over his eyes, uncut, ungreased; his eyes in the hol-lowed face, a delicate triangle of skin stretched on bone, jumped behind his glasses like hooded fish. He had the end of a cigarette in the corner of his mouth, and as they walked he lit a new one from it.

"I'm fine," Christine said. She was thinking, I'm not going to get involved again, enough is enough, I've done my bit for internationalism. "How are you?"

"I live here now," he said. "Maybe I study Economics."

"That's nice." He didn't sound as though he was enrolled anywhere.

"I come to see you."

Christine didn't know whether he meant he had left Montreal in order to be near her or just wanted to visit her at her house as he had done in the spring; either way she refused to be implicated. They were outside the Political Science Building. "I have a class here," she said. "Goodbye." She was being callous, she realized that, but a quick chop was more merciful in the long run, that was what her beautiful sisters used to say.

Afterwards she decided it had been stupid of her to let him find out where her class was. Though a timetable was posted in each of the colleges: all he had to do was look her up and record her every probable movement in block letters on his green notepad. After that day he never left her alone.

Initially he waited outside the lecture rooms for her to come out. She said hello to him curtly at first and kept on going, but this didn't work; he followed her at a distance, smiling his changeless smile. Then she stopped speaking altogether and pretended to ignore him, but it made no difference, he followed her anyway. The fact that she was in some way afraid of him – or was it just embarrassment? – seemed only to encourage him. Her friends started to notice, asking her who he was and why he was tagging along behind her; she could hardly answer because she hardly knew.

As the weekdays passed and he showed no signs of letting up, she began to jog-trot between classes, finally to run. He was tireless, and had an amazing wind for one who smoked so heavily: he would speed along behind her, keeping the distance between them the same, as though he were a pull-toy attached to her by a string. She was aware of the ridiculous spectacle they must make, galloping across campus, something out of a cartoon short, a lumbering elephant stampeded by a smiling, emaciated mouse, both of them locked in the classic pattern of comic pursuit and flight; but she found that to race made her less nervous than to walk sedately, the skin on the back of her neck crawling with the feel of his eyes on it. At least she could use her muscles. She worked out routines, escapes: she would dash in the front door of the Ladies' Room in the coffee shop and out the back door, and he would lose the trail, until he discovered the other entrance. She would try to shake him by detours through baffling archways and corridors, but he seemed as familiar with the architectural mazes as she was herself. As a last refuge she could head for the women's dormitory and watch from safety as he was skidded to a halt by the receptionist's austere voice: men were not allowed past the entrance.

Lunch became difficult. She would be sitting, usually with other members of the Debating Society, just digging nicely into a sandwich, when he would appear suddenly as though he'd come up through an unseen manhole. She then had the choice of barging out through the crowded cafeteria, sandwich half-eaten, or finishing her lunch with him standing behind her chair, everyone at the table acutely aware of him, the conversation stilting and dwindling. Her friends learned to spot him from a distance; they posted lookouts. "Here he comes," they would whisper, helping her collect her belongings for the sprint they knew would follow.

Several times she got tired of running and turned to confront him. "What do you want?" she would ask, glowering belligerently down at him, almost clenching her fists; she felt like shaking him, hitting him.

"I wish to talk with you."

"Well, here I am," she would say. "What do you want to talk about?"

But he would say nothing; he would stand in front of her, shifting his feet, smiling perhaps apologetically (though she could never pinpoint the exact tone of that smile, chewed lips stretched apart over the nicotine-yellowed teeth, rising at the corners, flesh held stiffly in place for an invisible photographer), his eyes jerking from one part of her face to another as though he saw her in fragments.

Annoying and tedious though it was, his pursuit of her had an odd result: mysterious in itself, it rendered her equally mysterious. No one had ever found Christine mysterious before. To her parents she was a beefy heavyweight, a plodder, lacking in flair, ordinary as bread. To her sisters she was the plain one, treated with an indulgence they did not give to each other: they did not fear her as a rival. To her male friends she was the one who could be relied on. She was helpful and a hard worker, always good for a game of tennis with the athletes among them. They invited her along to drink beer with them so they could get into the cleaner, more desirable Ladies and Escorts side of the beer parlour, taking it for granted she would buy her share of the rounds. In moments of stress they confided to her their problems with women. There was nothing devious about her and nothing interesting.

Christine had always agreed with these estimates of herself. In childhood she had identified with the false bride or the ugly sister; whenever a story had begun, "Once there was a maiden as beautiful as she was good," she had known it wasn't her. That was just how it was, but it wasn't so bad. Her parents never expected her to be a brilliant social success and weren't overly disappointed when she wasn't. She was spared the manoeuvring and anxiety she witnessed among others her age, and she even had a kind of special position among men: she was an exception, she fitted none of the categories they commonly used when talking about girls; she wasn't a cock-teaser, a cold fish, an easy lay or a snarky bitch; she was an honorary person. She had grown to share their contempt for most women.

Now, however, there was something about her that could not be explained. A man was chasing her, a peculiar sort of man, granted, but still a man, and he was without doubt attracted to her, he couldn't leave her alone. Other men examined her more closely than they ever had, appraising her, trying to find out what it was those twitching bespectacled eyes saw in her. They started to ask her out, though they returned from these excursions with their curiosity unsatisfied, the secret of her charm still intact. Her opaque dumpling face, her solid bearshaped body became for them parts of a riddle no one could solve. Christine sensed this. In the bathtub she no longer imagined she was a dolphin; instead she imagined she was an elusive water-nixie, or sometimes, in moments of audacity, Marilyn Monroe. The daily chase was becoming a habit; she even looked forward to it. In addition to its other benefits she was losing weight.

All these weeks he had never phoned her or turned up at the house. He must have decided however that his tactics were not having the desired result, or perhaps he sensed she was becoming bored. The phone began to ring in the early morning or late at night when he could be sure she would be there. Sometimes he would simply breathe (she could recognize, or thought she could, the quality of his breathing), in which case she would hang up. Occasionally he would say again that he wanted to talk to her, but even when she gave him lots of time nothing else would follow. Then he extended his range: she would see him on her streetcar, smiling at her silently from a seat never closer than three away; she could feel him tracking her down her own street, though when she would break her resolve to pay no attention and would glance back he would be invisible or in the act of hiding behind a tree or hedge.

Among crowds of people and in daylight she had not really been afraid of him; she was stronger than he was and he had made no recent attempt to touch her. But the days were growing shorter and colder, it was almost November. Often she was arriving home in twilight or a darkness broken only by the feeble orange streetlamps. She brooded over the possibility of razors, knives, guns; by acquiring a weapon he could quickly turn the odds against her. She avoided wearing scarves, remembering the newspaper stories about girls who had been strangled by them. Putting on her nylons in the morning gave her a funny feeling. Her body seemed to have diminished, to have become smaller than his.

Was he deranged, was he a sex maniac? He seemed so harmless, yet it was that kind who often went berserk in the end. She pictured those ragged fingers at her throat, tearing at her clothes, though she could not think of herself as screaming. Parked cars, the shrubberies near her house, the driveways on either side of it, changed as she passed them from unnoticed background to sinister shadowed foreground, every detail distinct and harsh: they were places a man might crouch, leap out from. Yet every time she saw him in the clear light of morning or afternoon (for he still continued his old methods of pursuit), his ageing jacket and jittery eyes convinced her that it was she herself who was the tormentor, the persecutor. She was in some sense responsible; from the folds and crevices of the body she had treated for so long as a reliable machine was emanating, against her will, some potent invisible odour, like a dog's in heat or a female moth's, that made him unable to stop following her.

Her mother, who had been too preoccupied with the unavoidable fall entertaining to pay much attention to the number of phone calls Christine was getting or to the hired girl's complaints of a man who hung up without speaking, announced that she was flying down to New York for the weekend; her father decided to go too. Christine panicked: she saw herself in the bathtub with her throat slit, the blood drooling out of her neck and running in a little spiral down the drain (for by this time she believed he could walk through walls, could be everywhere at once). The girl would do nothing to help; she might even stand in the bathroom door with her arms folded, watching. Christine arranged to spend the weekend at her married sister's.

When she arrived back Sunday evening she found the girl close to hysterics. She said that on Saturday she had gone to pull the curtain across the french doors at dusk and had found a strangely contorted face, a man's face, pressed against the glass, staring in at her from the garden. She claimed she had fainted and had almost had her baby a month too early right there on the living-room carpet. Then she had called the police. He was gone by the time they got there but she had recognized him from the afternoon of the tea; she had informed them he was a friend of Christine's.

They called Monday evening to investigate, two of them. They were very polite, they knew who Christine's father was. Her father greeted them heartily; her mother hovered in the background, fidgeting with her porcelain hands, letting them see how frail and worried she was. She didn't like having them in the living room but they were necessary.

Christine had to admit he'd been following her around. She was relieved he'd been discovered, relieved also that she hadn't been the one to tell, though if he'd been a citizen of the country she would have called the police a long time ago. She insisted he was not dangerous, he had never hurt her.

"That kind don't hurt you," one of the policemen said. "They just kill you. You're lucky you aren't dead."

"Nut cases," the other one said.

Her mother volunteered that the thing about people from another culture was that you could never tell whether they were insane or not because their ways were so different. The policemen agreed with her, deferential but also condescending, as though she was a royal halfwit who had to be humoured.

"You know where he lives?" the first policeman asked. Christine had long ago torn up the letter with his address on it; she shook her head.

"We'll have to pick him up tomorrow then," he said. "Think you can keep him talking outside your class if he's waiting for you?"

After questioning her they held a murmured conversation with her father in the front hall. The girl, clearing away the coffee cups, said if they didn't lock him up she was leaving, she wasn't going to be scared half out of her skin like that again.

Next day when Christine came out of her Modern History lecture he was there, right on schedule. He seemed puzzled when she did not begin to run. She approached him, her heart thumping with treachery and the prospect of freedom. Her body was back to its usual size; she felt herself a giantess, self-controlled, invulnerable.

"How are you?" she asked, smiling brightly.

He looked at her with distrust.

"How have you been?" she ventured again. His own perennial smile faded; he took a step back from her.

"This the one?" said the policeman, popping out from behind a notice board like a Keystone Cop and laying a competent hand on the worn jacket shoulder. The other policeman lounged in the background; force would not be required.

"Don't *do* anything to him," she pleaded as they took him away. They nodded and grinned, respectful, scornful. He seemed to know perfectly well who they were and what they wanted.

The first policeman phoned that evening to make his report. Her father talked with him, jovial and managing. She herself was now out of the picture; she had been protected, her function was over.

"What did they *do* to him?" she asked anxiously as he came back into the living room. She was not sure what went on in police stations.

"They didn't do anything to him," he said, amused by her concern. "They could have booked him for Watching and Besetting, they wanted to know if I'd like to press charges. But it's not worth a court case: he's got a visa that says he's only allowed in the country as long as he studies in Montreal, so I told them to just ship him down there. If he turns up here again they'll deport him. They went around to his rooming house, his rent's two weeks overdue; the landlady said she was on the point of kicking him out. He seems happy enough to be getting his back rent paid and a free train ticket to Montreal." He paused. "They couldn't get anything out of him though."

"*Out* of him?" Christine asked.

"They tried to find out why he was doing it; following you, I mean." Her father's eyes swept her as though it was a riddle to him also. "They said when they asked him about that he just clammed up. Pretended he didn't understand English. He understood well enough, but he wasn't answering."

Christine thought this would be the end, but somehow between his arrest and the departure of the train he managed to elude his escort long enough for one more phone call.

"I see you again," he said. He didn't wait for her to hang up.

Now that he was no longer an embarrassing present reality, he could be talked about, he could become an amusing story. In fact, he was the only amusing story Christine had to tell, and telling it preserved both for herself and others the aura of her strange allure. Her friends and the men who continued to ask her out speculated about his motives. One suggested he had wanted to marry her so he could remain in the country; another said that oriental men were fond of well-built women: "It's your Rubens quality."

Christine thought about him a lot. She had not been attracted to him, rather the reverse, but as an idea only he was a romantic figure, the one man who found her irresistible; though she often wondered, inspecting her unchanged pink face and hefty body in her full-length mirror, just what it was about her that had done it. She avoided whenever it was proposed the theory of his insanity: it was only that there was more than one way of being sane.

But a new acquaintance, hearing the story for the first time, had a different explanation. "So he got you, too," he said, laughing. "That has to be the same guy who was hanging around our day camp a year ago this summer. He followed all the girls like that, a short guy, Japanese or something, glasses, smiling all the time."

"Maybe it was another one," Christine said.

"There couldn't be two of them, everything fits. This was a pretty weird guy."

"What . . . *kind* of girls did he follow?" Christine asked.

"Oh, just anyone who happened to be around. But if they paid any attention to him at first, if they were nice to him or anything, he was unshakeable. He was a bit of a pest, but harmless."

Christine ceased to tell her amusing story. She had been one among many, then. She went back to playing tennis, she had been neglecting her game.

A few months later the policeman who had been in charge of the case telephoned her again.

"Like you to know, miss, that fellow you were having the trouble with was sent back to his own country. Deported."

"What for?" Christine asked. "Did he try to come back here?" Maybe she had been special after all, maybe he had dared everything for her.

"Nothing like it," the policeman said. "He was up to the same tricks in Montreal but he really picked the wrong woman this time – a Mother Superior of a convent. They don't stand for things like that in Quebec – had him out of here before he knew what happened. I guess he'll be better off in his own place."

"How old was she?" Christine asked, after a silence.

"Oh, around sixty, I guess."

"Thank you very much for letting me know," Christine said in her best official manner. "It's such a relief." She wondered if the policeman had called to make fun of her.

She was almost crying when she put down the phone. What *had* he wanted from her then? A Mother Superior. Did she really look sixty, did she look like a mother? What did convents mean? Comfort, charity? Refuge? Was it that something had happened to him, some intolerable strain just from being in this country; her tennis dress and exposed legs too much for him, flesh and money seemingly available everywhere but withheld from him wherever he turned, the nun the symbol of some final distortion, the robe and veil reminiscent to his near-sighted eyes of the women of his homeland, the ones he was able to understand? But he was back in his own country, remote from her as another planet; she would never know.

He hadn't forgotten her though. In the spring she got a postcard with a foreign stamp and the familiar block-letter writing. On the front was a picture of a temple. He was fine, he hoped she was fine also, he was her friend. A month later another print of the picture he had taken in the garden arrived, in a sealed manila enveloped otherwise empty.

Christine's aura of mystery soon faded; anyway, she herself no longer believed in it. Life became again what she had always expected. She graduated with mediocre grades and went into the Department of Health and Welfare; she did a good job, and was seldom discriminated against for being a woman because nobody thought of her as one. She could afford a pleasant-sized apartment, though she did not put much energy into decorating it. She played less and less tennis; what had been muscle with a light coating of fat turned gradually into fat with a thin substratum of muscle. She began to get headaches.

As the years were used up and the war began to fill the newspapers and magazines, she realized which Eastern country he had actually been from. She had known the name but it hadn't registered at the time, it was such a minor place; she could never keep them separate in her mind.

But though she tried, she couldn't remember the name of the city, and the postcard was long gone – had he been from the North or the South, was he near the battle zone or safely far from it? Obsessively she bought magazines and pored over the available photographs, dead villagers, soldiers on the march, colour blowups of frightened or angry faces, spies being executed; she studied maps, she watched the late-night newscasts, the distant country and terrain becoming almost more familiar to her than her own. Once or twice she thought she could recognize him but it was no use, they all looked like him.

Finally she had to stop looking at the pictures. It bothered her too much, it was bad for her; she was beginning to have nightmares in which he was coming through the french doors of her mother's house in his shabby jacket, carrying a packsack and a rifle and a huge bouquet of richly coloured flowers. He was smiling in the same way but with blood streaked over his face, partly blotting out the features. She gave her television set away and took to reading nineteenth-century novels instead; Trollope and Galsworthy were her favourites. When, despite herself, she would think about him, she would tell herself that he had been crafty and agile-minded enough to survive, more or less, in her country, so surely he would be able to do it in his own, where he knew the language. She could not see him in the army, on either side; he wasn't the type, and to her knowledge he had not believed in any particular ideology. He would be something nondescript, something in the background, like herself; perhaps he had become an interpreter.

Leaving This Island Place

AUSTIN CLARKE

The faces at the grilled windows of the parish almshouse were looking out, on this hot Saturday afternoon, on a world of grey-flannel and cricket and cream shirts, a different world, as they had looked every afternoon from the long imprisonment of the wards. Something in those faces told me they were all going to die in the almshouse. Standing on the cricket field I searched for the face of my father. I knew he would never live to see the sun of day again.

It is not cricket, it is leaving the island that makes me think about my father. I am leaving the island. And as I walk across the green playing field and into the driveway of the almshouse, its walkway speckled with spots of tar and white pebbles, and walk right up to the white spotless front of the building, I know it is too late now to think of saving him. It is too late to become involved with this dying man.

In the open veranda I could see the men, looking half-alive and half-dead, lying on the smudged canvas cots that were once white and cream as the cricketers' clothes, airing themselves. They have played, perhaps, in too many muddy tournaments, and are now soiled. But I am leaving. But I know before I leave there is some powerful tug which pulls me into this almshouse, grabbing me and almost swallowing me to make me enter these doors and slap me flat on the sore-back canvas cot beside a man in dying health. But I am leaving.

"You wasn't coming to visit this poor man, this poor father o' yourn?" It is Miss Brewster, the head nurse. She knew my father and she knew me. And she knew that I played cricket every Saturday on the field across the world from the almshouse. She is old and haggard. And she looks as if she has looked once too often on the face of death; and now she herself resembles a half-dead, dried-out flying fish, wrapped in the grease-proof paper of her nurse's uniform. "That man having fits and convulsions by the hour! Every day he asking for you. All the time, day in and day out. And you is such a poor-great, high-school educated bastard that you now acting *too proud* to come in here, because it is a almshouse and not a *private ward*, to see your own father! And you didn' even have the presence o' mind to bring along a orange, not even one, or a banana for that man, *your father!*"

She was now leading me through a long dark hallway, through rows of men on their sides, and some on their backs, lying like soldiers on a battlefield. They all looked at me as if I was dying. I tried to avoid their eyes, and I looked instead at their bones and the long fingernails and toenails, the thermometers of their long idle illness. The matted hair and the smell of men overdue for the bed-pan: men too weary now to raise themselves to pass water even in a lonely gutter. They were dying slowly and surely, for the almshouse was crowded and it did not allow its patients to die too quickly. I passed them, miles out of my mind: the rotting clothes and sores, men of all colours, all ages, dressed like women in long blue sail-cloth-hard shirts that dropped right down to the scales on their toothpick legs. One face smiled at me, and I wondered whether the smile meant welcome.

"Wait here!" It was Miss Brewster again who had spoken. She opened the door of a room and pushed me inside as you would push a small boy into the headmaster's office for a caning; and straightway the smell of stale urine and of sweat and faeces whipped me in the face. When the door closed behind me I was alone with the dead, with the smells of the almshouse.

I am frightened. But I am leaving. I find myself thinking about the trimmed sandwiches and the whisky-and-sodas waiting for me at the farewell party in honour of my leaving. Something inside me is saying I should pay some respect in my thoughts for this man, this dying man. I opened my eyes and thought of Cynthia. I thought of her beautiful face beside my father's face. And I tried to hold her face in the hands of my mind, and I squeezed it close to me and kept myself alive with the living outside world of cricket and cheers and "tea in the pavilion". There is death in this room and I am inside it. And Cynthia's voice is saying to me, Run run run! back through the smells, through the fallen lines of the men, through the front door and out into the green sunlight of the afternoon and the cricket and shouts; out into the applause.

"That's he laying-down there. Your father," the voice said. It was Miss Brewster. She too must have felt the power of death in the room, for she spoke in a whisper.

This is my father: more real than the occasional boundary hit by the cricket bat and the cheers that came with the boundary only. The two large eyeballs in the sunset of this room are my father.

"Boy?" It was the skeleton talking. I am leaving. He held out a hand to touch me. Dirt was under his fingernails like black moons. I saw the hand. A dead hand, a dirty hand, a hand of quarter-moons of dirt under the claws of its nails. ("You want to know something, son?" my godmother told me long ago. "I'll tell you something. That man that your mother tell you to call your father, he isn't your father, in truth. Your mother put the blame of your birth on him because once upon a time, long long ago in this island, that man was a man.")

I do not touch the hand. I am leaving this place.

And then the words, distant and meaningless from this departure of love because they come too late, began to turn the room on a side. Words and words and words. He must have talked this way each time he heard a door open or shut; or a footstep. ". . . is a good thing you going away, son, a good thing. I hear you going away, and that is a good thing . . . because I am going away . . . from this place . . . Miss Brewster, she . . . but I am sorry . . . cannot go with you . . ." (Did my mother hate this man so much to drive him here? Did she drive him to such a stick of love that it broke his heart; and made him do foolish things with his young life on the village green of cricket near his house, that made him the playful enemy of Barrabas the policeman, whose delight, my godmother told me, was to drag my father the captain of the village team away drunk from victory and pleasure to throw him into the crowded jail to make him slip on the cold floor fast as a new cricket pitch with vomit . . . ("And it was then, my child, after all those times in the jail, that your father contract that sickness which nobody in this village don't call by name. It is so horrible a sickness.") . . . and I remember now that even before this time I was told by my mother that my father's name was not to be mentioned in her house which her husband made for me as my stepfather. And she kept her word. For eighteen years. For eighteen years, his name was never mentioned; so he had died before this present visit. And there was not even a spasm of a reminiscence of his name. He was dead before this. But sometimes I would risk the lash of her hand and visit him, in his small shack on the fringe of Rudders Pasture where he lived out the riotous twenty-four years of middle life. ("Your mother never loved that bastard," my godmother said.) But I loved him, in a way. I loved him when he was rich enough to give me two shillings for a visit, for each visit. And although my mother had said he had come "from no family at-all, at-all", had had "no background", yet to me in those laughing days he held a family circle of compassion in his heart. I see him now, lying somewhere on a cot, and I know I am leaving this island. In those days of cricket when I visited him, I visited him in his house: the pin-up girls of the screen, white and naked; and the photographs of black women he had taken with a box camera (because "Your father is some kind o' genius, but in this island we call him a blasted madman, but he may be a real genius"), black women always dressed in their Sunday-best after church, dressed in too much clothes, and above them all, above all those pin-ups and photographs, the photographs of me, caught running in a record time, torn from the island's newspapers. And there was one of me he had framed, when I passed my examinations at Harrison College. And once, because in those days he was my best admirer, I gave him a silver cup which I had won for winning a race in a speed which no boy had done in twenty-five years, at the same school, in the history of the school. And all those women on the walls, and some in real life, looking at me, and whispering under their breath so I might barely hear it, "That's his son!"; and some looking at me as if I had entered their bedroom of love at the wrong moment of hectic ecstasy; and he, like a child caught stealing, would hang his father's head in shame and apologize for them in a whisper, and would beg the women in a loud voice, "You don't see I am with *my son*? You can't behave yourself in his presence?" And once, standing in his house alone, when he went to buy a sugar cake for me, I was looking at the photograph of a naked woman on the wall and my eyes became full of mists and I saw coming out of the rainwater of vision my mother's face, and her neck and her shoulders and her breasts and her navel. And I shut my eyes tight, tight, tight and ran into him returning with the sugar cake and ran screaming from his house.

That was my last visit. This is my first visit after that. And I am
leaving this island place. After that last visit I gave myself headaches
wondering if my mother had gone to his shack before she found
herself big and heavy with the burden of me in her womb. ("Child,
you have no idea what he do to that poor pretty girl, your mother,
that she hates his guts even to this day!") . . . and the days at
Harrison College when the absence of his surname on my report
card would remind me in the eyes of my classmates that I might be
the best cricketer and the best runner, but that I was after all, among
this cream of best blood and brains, only a bas—) ". . . this island is
only a place, one place," his voice was saying. "The only saving
thing is to escape." He was a pile of very old rags thrown around a
stunted tree. Then he was talking again, in a new way. "Son, do not
leave before you get somebody to say a prayer for me . . . somebody
like Sister Christopher from the Nazarene Church . . ."

But Sister Christopher is dead. Dead and gone five years now,
"When she was shouting at the Lord one night at a revival", my
godmother said.

"She's dead."

"Dead?"

"Five years."

"But couldn' you still ask her to come, ask Miss Christo, Sister
Christopher to come . . ."

There is no point listening to a dying man talk. I am going to
leave. No point telling him that Sister Christopher is alive, because
he is beyond that, beyond praying for, since he is going to die and
he never was a Catholic. And I am going to leave. For I cannot forget
the grey-flannel and the cream of the cricket field just because he is
dying, and the sharp smell of the massage and the cheers of the men
and women at the tape, which I have now made a part of my life.
And the Saturday afternoon matinées with the wealthy middle-class
girls from Queen's College, wealthy in looks and wealthy in books,
with their boyfriends the growing-up leaders of the island. Forget all
that? And forget the starched white shirt and the blue-and-gold
Harrison College tie? Forget all this because a man is dying and
because he tells you he is going to die?

Perhaps I should forget them. They form a part of the accident of
my life, a life which – if there were any logic in life – ought to have

been spent in the gutters round the Bath Corner, or in some foreign white woman's rose garden, or fielding tennis balls in the Garrison Savannah Tennis Club where those who played tennis could be bad tennis players but had to be white.

Let him die. I am leaving this island place. And let him die with his claim on my life. And let the claim be nailed in the coffin, which the poor authorities for the poor will authorize out of plain dealboard, without a minister or a prayer. And forget Sister Christopher who prefers to testify and shout on God; and call somebody else, perhaps, more in keeping with the grey-flannel and the cream of the cricket field and Saturday afternoon walks in the park and matinées at the Empire Theatre. Call a canon. Call a canon to bury a pauper, call a canon to bury a pauper, ha-ha-haaaa! . . .

Throughout the laughter and the farewell speeches and the drinks that afternoon, all I did hear was the slamming of many heavy oak doors of the rectory when I went to ask the canon to bury the pauper. And I tried to prevent the slamming from telling me what it was telling me: that I was out of place here, that I belonged with the beginning in the almshouse. Each giggle, each toast, each rattle of drunken ice cubes in the whirling glass pointed a finger back to the almshouse. "Man, you not drinking?" a wealthy girl said. "Man, what's wrong with you, at all?" And someone else was saying, "Have any of you remember Freddie?" But Briggs said, "Remember that bitch? The fellar with the girl with the biggest bubbies in the whole Caribbean? And who uses to . . . man, Marcus! Marcus, I calling you! God-blummuh, Marcus we come here to drink rum and you mean to tell me that you selling we *water*, instead o' rum?" And Joan Warton said, "But wait, look this lucky bastard though, saying he going up in Canada to university! Boy, you real lucky, in truth. I hear though that up there they possess some real inferior low-class rum that they does mix with water. Yak-yak-yak! From now on you'd be drinking Canadian rum-water, so stop playing the arse and drink this Bajan rum, man. We paying for this, yuh know!" I was leaving. I was thinking of tomorrow, and I was climbing the BOAC gangplank on the plane bound for Canada, for hope, for school, for glory; and the sea and the distance had already eased the pain of conscience; and there was already much sea between me and the cause of conscience . . .

And when the party was over, Cynthia was with me on the sands of
Gravesend Beach. And the beach was full of moonlight and love.
There was laughter too; and the laughter of crabs scrambling among
dead leaves and skeletons of other crabs caught unawares by someone running into the sea. And there was a tourist ship in the outer
harbour. "Write! write, write, write, write me every day of the week,
every week of the year, and tell me what Canada is like, and think of
me always, and don't forget to say nice things in your letters, and
pray for me every night. And write poems, love poems like the ones
you write in the college magazine; and when you write don't send the
letters to the Rectory, because father would, well . . . send them to
Auntie's address. You understand? You know how ministers and
canons behave and think. I have to tell father, I have to tell him I love
you, and that we are getting married when you graduate. And I shall
tell him about us . . . when you leave tomorrow." Watching the sea
and the moonlight on the sea; and watching to see if the sea was
laughing; and the scarecrows of masts on the fishing boats now
lifeless and boastless, taking a breather from the depths and the
deaths of fishing; and the large incongruous luxury liner drunk-full of
tourists. And all the time Cynthia chatting and chattering, ". . . but
we should have got married, even secretly and eloped somewhere,
even to Trinidad, or even to Tobago. Father won't've known, and
won't've liked it, but we would've been married . . . Oh hell, man!
this island stifles me, and I wish I was leaving with you. Sometimes
I feel like a crab in a crab hole with a pile o' sand in front . . ."

"Remember how we used to build sandcastles on bank holidays?"

"And on Sundays, far far up the beach where nobody came . . ."

"Cynthia?"

"Darling?"

"My Old Man, my Old Man is dying right now . . ."

"You're too philosophical! Anyhow, where? Are you kidding? I
didn't even know you had an Old Man." And she laughs.

"I was at the almshouse this afternoon, before the party."

"Is he really in the almshouse?"

"St Michael's almshouse, near . . ."

"You must be joking. You *must* be joking!" She turned her back to
me, and her face to the sea. "You aren't pulling my leg, eh?" she
said. And before I could tell her more about my father, who he was,

how kind a man he was, she was walking from me and we were in her father's Jaguar and speeding away from the beach.

And it is the next day, mid-morning, and I am sitting in the Seawell Airport terminal, waiting to be called to board the plane. I am leaving. My father, is he dead yet? A newspaper is lying on a bench without a man, or woman. Something advises me to look in the obituary column and see if ... But my mother had said, as she packed my valises, making sure that the fried fish was in my brief-case which Cynthia had bought for me as a going-away present, my mother had said, "Look, boy, leave the dead to live with the blasted dead, do! Leave the dead in this damn islan' place!"

And I am thinking now of Cynthia who promised ("I promise, I promise, I promise. Man, you think I going let you leave this place, *leave Barbados*? and I not going be there at the airport?") to come to wave goodbye, to take a photograph waving goodbye from the terminal and the plane, to get her photograph taken for the social column waving goodbye at the airport, to kiss, to say goodbye and promise return in English, and say "*au revoir*" in French because she was the best student in French at Queen's College.

A man looks at the newspaper, and takes it up, and gives it to a man loaded-down as a new-traveller for a souvenir of the island. And the friend wraps two large bottles of Goddards Gold Braid rum in it, smuggling the rum and the newspaper out of the island, in memory of the island. And I know I will never find out how he died. Now there are only the fear and the tears and the handshakes of other people's saying goodbye and the weeping of departure. "Come back real soon again, man!" a fat, sweating man says, "and next time I going take you to some places that going make your head *curl*! Man, I intend to show you the whole islan', and give you some dolphin steaks that is more bigger than the ones we eat down in Nelson Street with the whores last night!" An old woman, who was crying, was saying goodbye to a younger woman who could have been her daughter, or her daughter-in-law, or her niece. "Don't take long to return back, child! Do not tarry too long. Come back again soon ... and don't forget that you was borned right here, pon this rock, pon this island. This is a good decent island, so return back as soon as you get yuh learning, come back again soon, child ..."

The plane is ready now. And Cynthia is not coming through the car park in her father's Jaguar. She has not come, she has not come as she promised. And I am leaving the island.

Below me on the ground are the ants of people, standing at an angle, near the terminal. And I can see the architect-models of houses and buildings, and the beautiful quiltwork patches of land under the plough ... and then there is the sea, and the sea, and then the sea.

The Sins of Tomás Benares

MATT COHEN

A narrow, three-storey house near College Street had been the home of the Benares family since they arrived in Toronto in 1936. Beside the front door, bolted to the brick, was a brass name-plate that was kept polished and bright: DR TOMÁS BENARES.

Benares had brought the name-plate – and little else – with him when he and his wife fled Spain just before the Civil War. For twenty years it had resided on the brick beside the doorway. And then, after various happinesses and tragedies – the tragedies being unfortunately more numerous – it had been replaced triumphantly by a new name-plate: DR ABRAHAM BENARES. This son, Abraham, was the only child to have survived those twenty years.

Abraham had lost not only his siblings, but also his mother. The day his name-plate was proudly mounted Tomás could at last say to himself that perhaps his string of bad fortune had finally been cut, for despite everything he now had a son who was a doctor, like himself, and who was married with two children.

By 1960, the Benares household was wealthy in many ways. True, the family had not moved to the north of the city like many other immigrants who had made money, but during the era of the DR ABRAHAM BENARES name-plate the adjoining house was purchased to give space for an expanded office and to provide an investment for Abraham Benares' swelling income as a famous internist. The back yards of both houses were combined into one elegant lawn that was tended twice a week by a professional gardener, an old Russian Jew who Tomás Benares had met first in his office, then at the synagogue. He spent most of his time drinking tea and muttering about the injustices that had been brought upon his people, while Tomás himself, by this time retired, toothless, and bent of back, crawled through the flower beds on his knees, wearing the discarded rubber dishwashing gloves of his son's extraordinarily beautiful wife.

Bella was her name. On anyone else, such a name would have

been a joke; but Bella's full figure and dark, Mediterranean face glowed with such animal heat that from the first day he met her Tomás felt like an old man in her presence. Of this Bella seemed entirely unaware. After moving into the house she cooked for Tomás, pressed her scorching lips to his on family occasions, even hovered over him during meals, her fruity breath like a hot caress against his neck. After her children were born she began to refer to Tomás as grandfather, and sometimes while the infants played on the living-room floor she would stand beside Tomás with the full weight of her fleshy hand sinking into his arm. "Look at us," she said to Tomás once, "three generations."

A few years after the birth of his daughter, Abraham Benares was walking with her down to College Street, as he did every Saturday, to buy a newspaper and a bag of apples, when a black Ford car left the street and continued its uncontrolled progress along the sidewalk where Abraham was walking. Instinctively, Abraham scooped Margaret into his arms, but the car was upon him before he could move. Abraham Benares, forty-one years old and the former holder of the city intercollegiate record for the one hundred yard dash, had time only to throw his daughter on to the adjacent lawn while the car mowed him down.

The next year, 1961, the name-plate on the door changed again: DR TOMÁS BENARES reappeared. There had been no insurance policy and the old man, now seventy-four years of age but still a licensed physician, recommended the practice of medicine. He got the complaining gardener to redivide the yard with a new fence, sold the house next door to pay his son's debts, and took over the task of providing for his daughter-in-law and his two grandchildren.

Before reopening his practice, Tomás Benares got new false teeth and two new suits. He spent six months reading his old medical textbooks and walked several miles every morning to sweep the cobwebs out of his brain. He also, while walking, made it a point of honour never to look over his shoulder.

On the eve of his ninety-fourth birthday Tomás Benares was sixty-two inches tall and weighed one hundred and twelve pounds. These facts he noted carefully in a small diary. Each year, sitting in his third-floor bedroom-study, Tomás Benares entered his height and weight into the pages of this diary. He also summarized any medical problems he had experienced during the year past, and made his prognosis for the year to come. There had once been an essay-like annual entry in which he confessed his outstanding sins and moral omissions from the previous year and outlined how he could correct or at least repent them in the year to follow. These essays had begun when Tomás was a medical student, and had continued well past the year in which his wife died. But when he had retired the first time from practising medicine and had the time to read over the fifty years of entries, he had noticed that his sins grew progressively more boring with age. And so, after that, he simply recorded the number of times he had enjoyed sexual intercourse that year.

Now, almost ninety-four, Tomás Benares couldn't help seeing that even this simple statistic had been absent for almost a decade. His diary was getting shorter while his life was getting longer. His last statistic had been when he was eighty-six – one time; the year before – none at all. But in his eighty-fourth year there had been a dozen transgressions. Transgressions! They should have been marked as victories. Tomás brushed back at the wisps of white hair that still adorned his skull. He couldn't remember feeling guilty or triumphant, couldn't remember any detail at all of the supposed events. Perhaps he had been lying. According to the entry, his height during that erotic year had been sixty-four inches, and his weight exactly twice that – one hundred and twenty-eight pounds. In 1956, when he had begun compiling the statistics, there had been only one admission of intercourse, but his height had been sixty-five inches and his weight one hundred and forty.

Suddenly, Tomás had a vision of himself as an old-fashioned movie. In each frame he was a different size, lived a different life. Only accelerating the reel could make the crowd into one person.

He was sitting in an old blue armchair that had been in the living room when Marguerita was still alive. There he used to read aloud in English to her, trying to get his accent right, while in the adjacent kitchen she washed up the dinner dishes and called out his mistakes. Now he imagined pulling himself out of the armchair, walking to the window to see if his grandson Joseph's car was parked on the street below. He hooked his fingers, permanently curved, into the arms of his chair. And then he pulled. But the chair was a vacuum sucking him down with the gravity of age. Beside him was a glass of raspberry wine. He brought it to his lips, wet the tip of his tongue. He was on that daily two-hour voyage between the departure of his day nurse and the arrival of Joseph. Eventually, perhaps soon, before his weight and height had entirely shrunk away and there were no statistics at all to enter into his diary, he would die. He wanted to die with the house empty. That was the last wish of Tomás Benares.

But even while his ninety-fourth birthday approached, Tomás Benares was not worrying about dying. To be sure he had become smaller with each year, and the prospect of worthwhile sin had almost disappeared; but despite the day nurse and the iron gravity of his chair, Tomás Benares was no invalid. Every morning this whole summer – save the week he had the flu – his nurse, whose name was Elizabeth Rankin, had helped him down the stairs and into the yard where, on his knees, he tended his gardens. While the front of the house had been let go by his careless grandson, Joseph, the back was preserved in the splendour it had known for almost fifty years. Bordering the carefully painted picket fence that surrounded the small yard were banks of flowers, the old strawberry patch, and in one corner a small stand of raspberry canes that were covered by netting to keep away the plague of thieving sparrows.

This morning, too, the morning of his birthday, Elizabeth Rankin helped him down the stairs. Elizabeth Rankin had strong arms, but although he could hardly walk down the three flights of stairs by himself – let alone climb back up – he could think of his own father, who had lived to be one hundred and twenty-three and of his grandfather Benares, who had lived to the same age. There was, in fact, no doubt that this enormous number was fate's stamp on the brow of the Benares men, though even fate could not *always* cope with automobiles.

But, as his own father had told Tomás, the Benares were to consider themselves blessed because fate seemed to pick them out more frequently than other people. For example, Tomás's father, who was born in 1820, had waited through two wives to have children, and when one was finally born, a boy, he had died of an unknown disease that winter brought to the Jewish quarter of Kiev.

So frightened had he been by this show of God's spite that Tomás's father had sold the family lumbering business and rushed his wife back to Spain, the cradle of his ancestors, where she bore Tomás in 1884. Tomás's grandfather had, of course, been hale and hearty at the time: one hundred and four years old, he had lived on the top floor of the house just as Tomás now lived on the top floor of his own grandson's house.

That old man, Tomás's grandfather, had been a round, brown apple baked dry by the sun and surrounded by a creamy white fringe of beard. He had been born in 1780 and Tomás, bemoaning the emptiness of his diary on the occasion of his oncoming ninety-fourth, realized suddenly that he was holding two hundred years in his mind. His father had warned him: the Benares men were long-lived relics whose minds sent arrows back into the swamp of the past, so deep into the swamp that the lives they recalled were clamped together in a formless gasping mass, waiting to be shaped by those who remembered. The women were more peripheral: stately and beautiful they were easily extinguished: perhaps they were bored to death by the small, round-headed stubborn men who made up the Benares tribe.

"We were always Spaniards," the old man told Tomás, "stubborn as donkeys." *Stubborn as a donkey*, the child Tomás had whispered. Had his mother not already screamed this at him? And he imagined ancient Spain: a vast, sandy expanse where the Jews had been persecuted and in revenge had hidden their religion under prayer shawls and been stubborn as donkeys.

And they hadn't changed, Tomás thought gleefully, they hadn't changed at all; filled with sudden enthusiasm and the image of himself as a white-haired, virile donkey, he pulled himself easily out of his chair and crossed the room to the window where he looked down for Joseph's car. The room was huge: the whole third floor of the house save for an alcove walled off as a bathroom. Yet even in the afternoon the room was dark as a cave, shadowed by its clutter of objects that included everything from his marriage bed to the stand-up scale with the weights and sliding rule that he used to assess himself for his yearly entry.

From the window he saw that his grandson's car had yet to arrive. On the sidewalk instead were children travelling back and forth on tricycles, shouting to each other in a fractured mixture of Portuguese and English. As always, when he saw children on the sidewalk, he had to resist opening the window and warning them to watch out for cars. It had been Margaret, only four years old, who had run back to the house to say that "Papa is sick," then had insisted on returning down the street with Tomás.

Two hundred years: would Margaret live long enough to sit frozen in a chair and feel her mind groping from one century to the next? Last year, on his birthday, she had given him the bottle of raspberry wine he was now drinking. "Every raspberry is a blessing," she had said. She had a flowery tongue, like her brother, and when she played music Tomás could sense her passion whirling like a dark ghost through the room. What would she remember? Her mother who had run away; her grandmother whom she had never known; her father, covered by a sheet by the time she and Tomás had arrived, blood from his crushed skull seeping into the white linen.

They had come a long way, the Benares: from the new Jerusalem in Toledo to two centuries in Kiev, only to be frightened back to Spain before fleeing again, this time to a prosperous city in the New World. But nothing had changed, Tomás thought, even the bitterness over his son's death still knifed through him exactly as it had when he saw Margaret's eyes at the door, when Joseph, at the funeral, broke into a long, keening howl.

Stubborn as a donkey. Tomás straightened his back and walked easily from the window towards his chair. He would soon be ninety-four years old; and if fate was to be trusted, which it wasn't, there were to be thirty more years of anniversaries. During the next year, he thought, he had better put some effort into improving his statistics.

He picked up his dairy again, flipped the pages backward, fell into a doze before he could start reading.

On his ninety-fourth birthday Tomás slept in. This meant not waking until after eight o'clock; and then lying in bed and thinking about his dreams. In the extra hours of sleep Tomás dreamed that he was a young man again, that he was married, living in Madrid, and that at noon the bright sun was warm as he walked the streets from his office to the café where he took lunch with his cronies. But in this dream he was not a doctor but a philosopher; for some strange reason it had been given to him to spend his entire life thinking about oak trees, and while strolling the broad, leafy streets it was precisely this subject that held his mind. He had also the duty, of course, of supervising various graduate students, all of whom were writing learned dissertations on the wonders of the oak; and it often, in this dream, pleased him to spend the afternoon with these bright and beautiful young people, drinking wine and saying what needed to be said.

In the bathroom, Tomás shaved himself with the electric razor that had been a gift from Joseph. Even on his own birthday he no longer trusted his hand with the straight razor that still hung, with its leather strop, from a nail in the wall. This, he suddenly thought, was the kind of detail that should also be noted in his annual diary – the texture of his shrinking world. Soon everything would be forbidden to him, and he would be left with only the space his own huddled skeleton could occupy. After shaving, Tomás washed his face, noting the exertion that was necessary just to open and close the cold water tap, and then he went back to the main room where he began slowly to dress.

It was true, he was willing to admit, that these days he often thought about his own death; but such thoughts did not disturb him. In fact, during those hours when he felt weak and sat in his chair breathing slowly, as if each weak breath might be his last, he often felt Death sitting with him. A quiet friend, Death; one who was frightening at first, but now was a familiar companion, an invisible brother waiting for him to come home.

But home, for Tomás Benares, was still the world of the living. When Elizabeth Rankin came to check on him, she found Tomás dressed and brushed. And a few minutes later he was sitting in his own garden, drinking espresso coffee and listening to the birds fuss in the flowering hedges that surrounded his patio. There Tomás, at peace, let the hot sun soak into his face. Death was with him in the garden, in the seductive buzz of insects, the comforting sound of water running in the nearby kitchen. The unaccustomed long sleep only gave Tomás the taste for more. He could feel himself drifting off, noted with interest that he had no desire to resist, felt Death pull his chair closer, his breath disguised as raspberries and mimosa.

*

At seventy-four years of age, also on his birthday, Tomás Benares had gone out to his front steps, unscrewed his son's name-plate and reaffixed his own. In the previous weeks he had restored the house to the arrangement it had known before his original retirement.

The front hall was the waiting room. On either side were long wooden benches, the varnished oak polished by a generation of patients. This front hall opened into a small parlour that looked on to the street. In that room was a desk, more chairs for waiting, and the doctor's files. At first his wife ran that parlour; after her death, Tomás had hired a nurse.

Behind the parlour was the smallest room of all. It had space for an examination table, a glass cabinet with a few books and several drawers of instruments, and a single uncomfortable chair. On the ceiling was a fluorescent light, and the window was protected by venetian blinds made of heavy plastic.

After Abraham's death his widow, Bella, and the children had stayed on in the Benares household, and so on the morning of the reopening Tomás had gone into the kitchen to find Bella making coffee and feeding breakfast to Joseph and Margaret. He sat down wordlessly at the kitchen table while Bella brought him coffee and toast, and he was still reading the front section of the morning paper when the doorbell rang. Joseph leapt from the table and ran down the hall. Tomás was examining the advertisement he had placed to announce the recommencement of his practice.

"Finish your coffee," said Bella. "Let her wait. She's the one who needs the job."

But Tomás was already on his feet. Slowly he walked down the hall to the front parlour. He could hear Joseph chatting with the woman, and was conscious of trying to keep his back straight. He was wearing, for his new practice, a suit newly tailored. His old tailor had died, but his son had measured Tomás with the cloth tape, letting his glasses slide down to rest on the tip of his nose exactly like his father had. Now in his new blue suit, a matching tie, and one of the white linen shirts that Marguerita had made for him, Tomás stood in his front parlour.

"Doctor Benares, I am Elizabeth Rankin; I answered your advertisement for a nurse."

"I am pleased to meet you, Mrs Rankin."

"Miss Rankin." Elizabeth Rankin was then a young woman entering middle age. She had brown hair parted in the middle and then pulled back in a bun behind her neck, eyes of a darker brown in which Tomás saw a mixture of fear and sympathy. She was wearing a skirt and a jacket, but had with her a small suitcase in case it was necessary for her to start work right away.

"Would you like to see my papers, Doctor Benares?"

"Yes, if you like. Please sit down."

Joseph was still in the room and Tomás let him watch as Elizabeth Rankin pulled out a diploma stating that she had graduated from McGill University in the biological sciences, and another diploma showing that she had received her RN from the same university.

"I have letters of reference, Doctor Benares."

"Joseph, please get a cup of coffee for Miss Rankin. Do you –"

"Just black, Joseph."

They sat in silence until Joseph arrived with the coffee, and then Tomás asked him to leave and closed the door behind him.

"I'm sorry," Elizabeth Rankin said. "I saw the advertisement and . . ."

She trailed off. It was six months since Tomás had seen her, but he recognized her right away; she was the woman who had been driving the car that had killed his son. At the scene of the accident she had shivered in shock until the ambulance arrived. Tomás had even offered her some sleeping pills. Then she had reappeared to hover on the edge of the mourners at Abraham's funeral.

"You're a very brave woman, Miss Rankin."

"No, I . . ." Her eyes clouded over. Tomás, behind the desk, watched her struggle. When he had seen her in the hall, his first reaction had been anger.

"I thought I should do something," she said. "I don't need a salary of course, and I *am* a qualified nurse."

"I see that," Tomás said drily.

"You must hate me," Elizabeth Rankin said.

Tomás shrugged. Joseph came back into the room and stood beside Elizabeth Rankin. She put her hand on his shoulder and the boy leaned against her.

"You mustn't bother Miss Rankin," Tomás said, but even as he spoke he could see Elizabeth's hand tightening on the boy's shoulder.

"Call Margaret," Tomás said to Joseph, and then asked himself why, indeed, he should forgive this woman. No reason came to mind, and while Joseph ran through the house, searching for his sister, Tomás sat in his reception room and looked carefully at the face of Elizabeth Rankin. The skin below her eyes was dark, perhaps she had trouble sleeping; and though her expression was maternal she had a tightly drawn quality that was just below the surface, as though the softness were a costume.

He remembered a friend, who had been beaten by a gang of Franco's men, saying he felt sorry for them. When Tomás's turn came, he had felt no pity for his assailants. And although what Elizabeth Rankin had done was an accident, not a malicious act, she was still the guilty party. Tomás wondered if she knew what he was thinking, wondered how she could not. She was sitting with one leg crossed over the other, her eyes on the door through which the sounds of the children's feet now came. And when Margaret, shy, sidled into the room, Tomás made a formal introduction. He was thinking, as he watched Margaret's face, how strange it was that the victims must always console their oppressors.

Margaret, four years old, curtsied and then held out her hand. There was no horrified scream, no flicker of recognition.

"Miss Rankin will be coming every morning," Tomás announced. "She will help me in my office."

"You are very kind, Doctor Benares."

"We will see," Tomás said. It was then that he had an extraordinary thought, or at least a thought that was extraordinary for him. It occurred to him that Elizabeth Rankin didn't simply want to atone, or to be consoled. She wanted to be taken advantage of.

Tomás waited until the children had left the room, then closed the door. He stood in front of Elizabeth Rankin until she, too, got to her feet.

"Pig," Tomás Benares hissed; and he spat at her face. The saliva missed its target and landed, instead, on the skin covering her right collar-bone. There it glistened, surrounded by tiny beads, before gliding down the open V of her blouse.

The eyes of Elizabeth Rankin contracted briefly. Then their expression returned to a flat calm. Tomás, enraged, turned on his heel and walked quickly out of the room. When he came back fifteen minutes later, Elizabeth Rankin had changed into her white uniform and was sorting through the files of his son.

Bella said it wasn't right.

"That you should have *her* in the house," she said. "It's disgusting."

"She has a diploma," Tomás said.

"And how are you going to pay her? You don't have any patients."

This discussion took place in the second-floor sitting room after the children were asleep. It was the room where Bella and Abraham used to go to have their privacy.

"At first I thought maybe you didn't recognize her," Bella started again, "and so I said to myself, what sort of joke is this? Maybe she didn't get enough the first time, maybe she has to come back for more."

"It was an accident," Tomás said.

"So you forgive her?" Bella challenged. She had a strong, bell-like voice which, when she and Abraham were first married, had been a family joke, one even she would laugh at; but since his death the tone had grown rusty and sepulchral.

Tomás shrugged.

"I don't forgive her," Bella said.

"It was an accident," Tomás said. "She has to work it out of her system."

"What about me? How am I going to work it out of my system?"

At thirty, Bella was even more beautiful than when she had been married. The children had made her heavy, but grief had carved away the excess flesh. She had jet-black hair and olive skin that her children had both inherited. Now she began to cry and Tomás, as always during these nightly outbursts of tears, went to stand by the window.

"Well?" Bella insisted. "What do you expect me to do?"

When she had asked this question before, Tomás advised her to go to sleep with the aid of a pill. But now he hesitated. For how many months, for how many years could he tell her to obliterate her evenings in sleeping pills.

"You're the saint," Bella said. "You never wanted anyone after Marguerita."

"I was lucky," Tomás said. "I had a family."

"I have a family."

"I was older," Tomás said.

"So," Bella repeated dully, "you never did want anyone else."

Tomás was silent. When Abraham brought her home he had asked Tomás what he thought of her. "She's very beautiful," Tomás had said. Abraham had happily agreed. Now she was more beautiful but, Tomás thought, also more stupid.

"It is very hard," Tomás said, "for a man my age to fall in love."

"Your wife died many years ago . . ."

Tomás shrugged. "I always felt old," he said, "ever since we came to Canada." All this time he had been standing at the window, and now he made sure his back was turned so that she wouldn't see his tears. The day Abraham had been killed he had cried with her. Since then, even at the funeral, he had refused to let her see his tears. Why? He didn't know. The sight of her, even the smell of her walking into a room, seemed to freeze his heart.

"If there was –" Bella started. She stopped. Tomás knew that he should help her, that she shouldn't have to fight Abraham's ghost *and* his father, but he couldn't bring himself to reach out. It was like watching an ant trying to struggle its way out of a pot of honey.

"If there was someone else," Bella said. "Even a job."

"What can you do?" Thomas asked, but the question was rhetorical; Bella had married Abraham the year after she had finished high school. She couldn't even type.

"*I* could be your receptionist, instead of that –"

"Nurse," Tomás interrupted. "I need a nurse, Bella."

"I can put a thermometer in someone's mouth," Bella said. "Are people going to die while you're next door in the office?"

"A doctor needs a nurse," Tomás said. "I didn't invent the rules."

"There's a rule?"

"It's a custom, Bella."

He turned from the window.

"And anyway," Bella said, "who's going to take care of the children?"

"That's right, the children need a mother."

"We need Bella in the kitchen making three meals a day so at night she can cry herself to sleep – while the murderer is working off her guilt so at night she can go out and play with the boys, her conscience clean."

"You don't know what she does at night –"

"You're such a saint," Bella said suddenly. "You are such a saint the whole world admires you, do you know that?"

"Bella –"

"The holy Doctor Benares. At seventy-four years of age he ends his retirement and begins work again to provide for his widowed daughter and his two orphaned grandchildren. Has the world ever seen such a man? At the *shul* they're talking about adding a sixth book to the Torah." She looked at Tomás, and Tomás, seeing her go out of control, could only stand and watch. She was like an ant, he was thinking. Now the ant was at the lip of the pot. It might fall back into the honey, in which case it would drown; or it might escape after all.

"You're such a saint," Bella said in her knife-edge voice, "you're such a saint that you think poor Bella just wants to go out and get laid."

She was teetering on the edge now, Tomás thought.

"You should see your face now," Bella said. "*Adultery*, you're thinking. *Whore.*"

"It's perfectly normal for a healthy –"

"Oh, healthy *shit*!" Bella screamed. "I just want to go out. Out, out, *out*!"

She was standing in the doorway, her face beet-red, panting with her fury. Tomás, staying perfectly still, could feel his own answering blush searing the backs of his ears, surrounding his neck like a hot rope.

"Even the saint goes for a walk," Bella's voice had dropped again. "Even the saint can spend the afternoon over at Herman Levine's apartment, playing cards and drinking beer."

Tomás could feel his whole body burning and chafing inside his suit. *The saint*, she was calling him. And what had he done to her? Offered her and her family a home when they needed it. "Did I make Abraham stay here?" Tomás asked. And then realized, to his shame, that he had said the words aloud.

He saw Bella in the doorway open her mouth until it looked like the muzzle of a cannon. Her lips struggled and convulsed. The room filled with unspoken obscenities.

Tomás reached a hand to touch the veins in his neck. They were so engorged with blood he was choking. He tore at his tie, forced his collar open.

"Oh, God," Bella moaned.

Tomás was coughing, trying to free his throat and chest. Bella was in the corner of his hazed vision, staring at him in the same detached way he had watched her only a few moments before.

The saint, Tomás was thinking, *she calls me the saint*. An old compartment of his mind suddenly opened, and he began to curse at her in Spanish. Then he turned his back and walked upstairs to his third-floor bedroom.

In the small hours of the morning, Tomás Benares was lying in the centre of his marriage bed, looking up at the ceiling of the bedroom and tracing the shadows with his tired eyes. These shadows: cast by the streetlights they were as much a part of his furniture as was the big oak bed, or the matching dressers that presided on either side – still waiting, it seemed, for the miraculous return of Marguerita.

As always he was wearing pyjamas – sewing had been another of Marguerita's talents – and like the rest of his clothes they had been cleaned and ironed by the same Bella who had stood in the doorway of the second-floor living room and bellowed and panted at him like an animal gone mad. The windows were open and while he argued with himself Tomás could feel the July night trying to cool his skin, soothe him. But he didn't want to be soothed, and every half-hour or so he raised himself on one elbow and reached for a cigarette, flaring the light in the darkness and feeling for a second the distant twin of the young man who had lived in Madrid forty years ago, the young man who had taken lovers (all of them beautiful in retrospect), whispered romantic promises (all of them ridiculous), and then had the good fortune to fall in love and marry a woman so beautiful and devoted that even his dreams could never have imagined her. And yet it was true, as he had told Bella, that when he came to Canada his life had ended. Even lying with Marguerita in this bed he had often been unable to sleep, had often, with this very gesture, lit up a small space in the night in order to feel close to the young man who had been deserted in Spain.

Return? Yes, it had occurred to him after the war was finished. Of course, Franco was still in power then, but it was his country and there were others who had returned. And yet, what would have been the life of an exile returned? The life of a man keeping his lips perpetually sealed, his thoughts to himself; the life of a man who had sold his heart in order to have the sights and smells that were familiar.

Now, Tomás told himself wryly, he was an old man who had lost his heart for nothing at all. Somehow, over the years, it had simply disappeared; like a beam of wood being eaten from the inside, it had dropped away without him knowing it.

Tomás Benares, on his seventy-fourth birthday, had just put out a cigarette and lain back with his head on the white linen pillow to resume his study of the shadows, when he heard the footsteps on the stairs up to his attic. Then there was the creak of the door opening and Bella, in her nightgown and carrying a candle, tiptoed into the room.

Tomás closed his eyes.

The footsteps came closer, he felt the bed sag with her weight. He could hear her breathing in the night, it was soft and slow; and then, as he realized he was holding his own breath, he felt Bella's hand come to rest on his forehead.

He opened his eyes. In the light of the candle her face was like stone, etched and lined with grief.

"I'm sorry," Tomás said.

"I'm the sorry one. And imagine, on your birthday."

"That's all right. We've been too closed-in here, since –" Here he hesitated, because for some reason the actual event was never spoken. "Since Abraham died."

Bella now took her hand away, and Tomás was aware of how cool and soft it had been. Sometimes, decades ago, Marguerita had comforted him in this same way when he couldn't sleep. Her hand on his forehead, fingers stroking his cheeks, his eyes, soothing murmurs until finally he drifted away, a log face-down in the cool water.

"There are still lives to be lived," Bella was saying. "The children."

"The children," Tomás repeated. Not since Marguerita had there been a woman in this room at night. For many years he used to lock the door when he went to bed, and even now he would still lock it on the rare times he was sick in case someone – who? – should dare to come on a mission of mercy.

"I get tired," Bella said. Her head drooped and Tomás could see, beyond the outline of her nightdress, the curve of her breasts, the fissure between. A beautiful woman, he had thought before . . . He was not as saintly as Bella imagined. On certain of the afternoons Bella thought he was at Herman Levine's, Tomás had been visiting a different apartment, that of a widow who was once his patient. She, too, knew what it was like to look at the shadows on the ceiling for one year after another, for one decade after another.

Now Tomás reached out for Bella's hand. Her skin was young and supple, not like the skin of the widow, or his own. There came a time in every person's life, Tomás thought, when the inner soul took a look at the body and said: Enough, you've lost what little beauty you had and now you're just an embarrassment – I'll keep carrying you around, but I refuse to take you seriously. Tomás, aside from some stray moments of vanity, had reached that point long ago; but Bella, he knew, was still in love with her body, still wore her own bones and skin and flesh as a proud inheritance and not an ageing inconvenience.

"Happy birthday," Bella said. She lifted Tomás's hand and pressed it to her mouth. At first, what he felt was the wetness of her mouth. And then it was her tears that flowed in tiny, warm streams around his fingers.

She blew out the candle at the same time that Tomás reached for her shoulder; and then he drew her down so she was lying beside him – she on top of the covers and he beneath, her thick, jet hair folded into his neck and face, her perfume and the scent of her mourning skin wrapped around him like a garden. Chastely he cuddled her to him, her warm breath as soothing as Marguerita's had once been. He felt himself drifting into sleep and he turned towards the perfume, the garden, turned towards Bella to hold her in his arms the way he used to hold Marguerita in that last exhausted moment of waking.

Bella shifted closer, herself breathing so slowly that Tomás thought she must be already asleep. He remembered, with relief, that his alarm was set for six o'clock; at least they would wake before the children. Then he felt his own hand, as if it had a life of its own, slide in a slow caress from Bella's shoulder to her elbow, touching, in an accidental way, her sleeping breast.

Sleep fled at once, and Tomás felt the sweat spring to his skin. Yet Bella only snuggled closer, breasts and hips flooding through the

blanket like warm oceans. Tomás imagined reaching for and lighting
a cigarette, the darkness parting once more. A short while ago he
had been mourning his youth and now, he reflected, he was feeling
as stupid as he ever had. Even with the widow there had been no
hesitation. Mostly on his visits they sat in her living room and drank
tea; sometimes, by a mutual consent that was arrived at without
discussion, they went to her bedroom and performed sex like a
warm and comfortable bath. A bath, he thought to himself, that was
how he and Bella should become; chaste, warm, comforts to each
other in the absence of Abraham. It wasn't right, he now decided, to
have frozen his heart to this woman – his daughter-in-law, after all;
surely she had a right to love, to the warmth and affection due to a
member of the family. *Bella*, he was ready to proclaim, *you are the
mother of my grandchildren, the chosen wife of my son. And if you couldn't
help shouting, at least you were willing to comfort me.*

Tomás held Bella closer. Her lips, he became aware, were pressed
against the hollow of his throat, moving slowly, kissing the skin and
now sucking gently at the hairs that curled up from his chest. Tomás
let his hands find the back of her neck. There was a delicate valley
that led down from her skull past the thick, black hair. He would
never have guessed she was built so finely.

Now Bella's weight lifted away for a moment, though her lips
stayed glued to his throat, and then suddenly she was underneath
the covers, her leg across his groin, her hand sliding up his chest.

Tomás felt something inside of him break. And then, as he raised
himself on top of Bella the night, too, broke open; a gigantic black
and dreamless mouth, it swallowed them both. He kissed her, tore
at her nightgown to suck at her breast, penetrated her so deeply that
she gagged; yet though he touched and kissed her every private
place; though they writhed on the bed and he felt the cool sweep of
her lips as they searched out his every nerve; though he even
opened his eyes to see the pleasure on her face, her black hair spread
like dead butterflies over Marguerita's linen pillow, her mouth open
with repeated climax, the night still swallowed them, obliterated
everything as it happened, took them rushing down its hot and
endless gorge until Tomás felt like Jonah in the belly of the whale;
felt like Jonah trapped in endless flesh and juice. And all he had to
escape with was his own sex: like an old sword he brandished it in

the blackness, pierced open tunnels, flailed it against the wet walls
of his prison.

"Bella, Bella, Bella." He whispered her name silently. Every time
he shaped his lips around her name, he was afraid the darkness of
his inner eye would part, and Abraham's face would appear before
him. But it didn't happen. Even as he scratched Bella's back, bit her
neck, penetrated her from behind, he taunted himself with the idea
that somewhere in this giant night Abraham must be waiting. His
name was on Tomás's lips: Abraham his son. How many command-
ments was he breaking? Tomás wondered, pressing Bella's breasts
to his parched cheeks.

Tomás felt his body, like a starved man at a banquet, go out of
control. Kissing, screwing, holding, stroking: everything he did
Bella wanted, did back, invented variations upon. For one brief
second he thought that Marguerita had never been like this, then his
mind turned on itself and he was convinced that this *was* Marguerita, back from the dead with God's blessing to make up, in a few
hours, a quarter-century of lost time.

But as he kissed and cried over his lost Marguerita, the night
began to lift and the first light drew a grey mask on the window.

By this time he and Bella were lying on their stomachs, side by
side, too exhausted to move.

The grey mask began to glow, and as it did Tomás felt the dread
rising in him. Surely God Himself would appear to take His revenge,
and with that thought Tomás realized he had forgotten his own
name. He felt his tongue searching, fluttering between his teeth,
tasting again his own sweat and Bella's fragrant juices. He must be,
he thought, in Hell. He had died and God, to drive his wicked soul
crazy, had given him this dream of his own daughter-in-law, his
dead son's wife.

"Thank you, Tomás."

No parting kiss, just soft steps across the carpet and then one
creak as she descended the stairs. Finally, the face of his son
appeared. It was an infant's face, staring uncomprehendingly at its
father.

Tomás sat up. His back was sore, his kidneys felt trampled, one
arm ached, his genitals burned. He stood up to go to the bathroom
and was so dizzy that for a few moments he had to cling to the

bedpost with his eyes closed. Then, limping and groaning, he crossed the room. When he got back to the bed there was no sign that Bella had been there – but the sheets were soaked as they sometimes were after a restless night.

He collapsed on the covers and slept dreamlessly until the alarm went off. When he opened his eyes his first thought was of Bella, and when he swung out of bed there was a sharp sting in his groin. But as he dressed he was beginning to speculate, even hope, that the whole episode had been a dream.

A few minutes later, downstairs at breakfast, Tomás found the children sitting alone at the table. Between them was a sealed envelope addressed to "Dr Tomás Benares, MD".

"Dear Tomás," the letter read, "I have decided that it is time for me to seek my own life in another city. Miss Rankin has already agreed to take care of the children for as long as necessary. I hope you will all understand me and remember that I love you. As always, Bella Benares."

On his birthday, his garden always seemed to reach that explosive point that marked the height of summer. No matter what the weather, it was this garden that made up for all other deprivations, and the fact that his ninety-fourth birthday was gloriously warm and sunny made it doubly perfect for Tomás to spend the day outside.

Despite the perfect blessing of the sky, as Tomás opened his eyes from that long doze that had carried the sun straight into the afternoon, he felt a chill in his blood, the knowledge that Death, that companion he'd grown used to, almost fond of, was starting to play tricks. Because sitting in front of him, leaning towards him as if the worlds of waking and sleeping had been forced together, was Bella herself.

"Tomás, Tomás, it's good to see you. It's Bella."

"I know," Tomás said. His voice sounded weak and grumpy; he coughed to clear his throat.

"Happy birthday, Tomás."

He pushed his hand across his eyes to rid himself of this illusion.

"Tomás, you're looking so good."

Bella: her face was fuller now, but the lines were carved deeper, bracketing her full lips and corrugating her forehead. And yet she was still young, amazing: her movements were lithe and supple; her jet-black hair was streaked, but still fell thick and wavy to her shoulders; her eyes still burned, and when she leaned forward to take his hand between her own the smell of her, dreams and remembrances, came flooding back.

"Tomás, are you glad to see me?"

"You look so young, Bella." This in a weak voice, but Tomás's throat-clearing cough was lost in the rich burst of Bella's laughter. Tomás, seeing her head thrown back and the flash of her strong teeth, could hardly believe that he, a doddering old man, whose knees were covered by a blanket in the middle of summer, had only a few years ago actually made love to this vibrant woman. Now she was like a racehorse in voracious maturity.

"Bella, the children."

"I know, Tomás. I telephoned Margaret; she's here. And I telephoned Joseph, too. His secretary said he was at a meeting all afternoon, but that he was coming here for dinner."

"Bella, you're looking wonderful, truly wonderful." Tomás had his hand hooked into hers and, suddenly aware that he was half-lying in his chair, was using her weight to try to lever himself up.

Instantly Bella was on her feet, her arm solicitously around his back, pulling him into position. She handled his weight, Tomás thought, like the weight of a baby. He felt surrounded by her, overpowered by her smell, her vitality, her cheery goodwill. *Puta*, Tomás whispered to himself. What a revenge. Twenty years ago he had been her equal; and now, suddenly – what had happened? Death was in the garden: Tomás could feel his presence, the familiar visitor turned trickster. And then Tomás felt some of his strength returning, strength in the form of contempt for Bella, who had waited twenty years to come back to this house; contempt for Death, who waited until a man was an ancient, drooling husk to test his will.

"You're the marvel, Tomás. Elizabeth says you work every day in the garden. How do you do it?"

"I spit in Death's face," Tomás rasped. Now he was beginning to feel more himself again, and he saw that Bella was offering him a cup of coffee. All night he had slept, and then again in the daytime. What a way to spend a birthday! But coffee would heat the blood, make it run faster. He realized that he was famished.

Bella had taken out a package of cigarettes now, and offered one to Tomás. He shook his head, thinking again how he had declined in these last years. Now Joseph wouldn't let him smoke in bed, even when he couldn't sleep. He was only allowed to smoke when there was someone else in the room, or when he was outside in the garden.

"Tomás. I hope you don't mind I came back. I wanted to see you again while – while we could still talk."

Tomás nodded. So the ant had escaped the honey pot after all, and ventured into the wide world. Now it was back, wanting to tell its adventures to the ant who had stayed home. Perhaps they hadn't spent that strange night making love after all; perhaps in his bed they had been struggling on the edge of the pot, fighting to see who would fall back and who would be set free.

"So," Bella said. "It's been so long."

Tomás, watching her, refusing to speak, felt control slowly moving towards him again. He sat up straighter, brushed the blanket off his legs.

"Or maybe we should talk tomorrow," Bella said, "when you're feeling stronger."

"I feel strong." His voice surprised even himself – not the weak squawk it sometimes was now, a chicken's squeak hardly audible over the telephone, but firm and definite, booming out of his chest the way it used to. Bella: she had woken him up once, perhaps she would once more.

He could see her moving back, hurt; but then she laughed again, her rich throaty laugh that Tomás used to hear echoing through the house when his son was still alive. He looked at her left hand; Abraham's modest engagement ring was still in place, but beside it was a larger ring, a glowing bloodstone set in a fat gold band. "Tomás," Bella was saying, "you really are a marvel, I swear you're going to live to see a hundred."

"One hundred and twenty-three," Tomás said. "Almost all of the Benares men live to be one hundred and twenty-three."

For a moment, the lines deepened again in Bella's face, and Tomás wished he could someday learn to hold his tongue. A bad habit that should have long ago been entered in his diary.

"You will," Bella finally said. Her voice had the old edge. *"Two* hundred and twenty-three, you'll dance on all our graves."

"Bella."

"I shouldn't have come."

"The children –"

"They'll be glad to see me, Tomás, they always are."

"Always?"

"Of course. Did you think I'd desert my own children?"

Tomás shook his head.

"Oh, I left, Tomás, I left. But I kept in touch. I sent them letters and they wrote me back. That woman helped me."

"Elizabeth?"

"I should never have called her a murderer, Tomás. It was an accident."

"They wrote you letters without telling me?"

Bella stood up. She was a powerful woman now, full-fleshed and in her prime; even Death had slunk away in the force of her presence. "I married again, Tomás. My husband and I lived in Seattle. When Joseph went to university there, he lived in my home."

"Joseph lived with you?"

"My husband's dead now, Tomás, but I didn't come for your pity. Or your money. I just wanted you to know that I would be in Toronto again, seeing my own children, having a regular life."

"A regular life," Tomás repeated. He felt dazed, dangerously weakened. Death was in the garden again, he was standing behind Bella, peeking out from behind her shoulders and making faces. He struggled to his feet. Only Bella could save him now, and yet he could see the fear on her face as he reached for her.

"Tomás, I –"

"You couldn't kill me!" Tomás roared. His lungs filled his chest like an eagle in flight. His flowering hedges, his roses, his carefully groomed patio snapped into focus. He stepped towards Bella, his balance perfect, his arm rising. He saw her mouth open, her lips begin to flutter. Beautiful but stupid, Tomás thought; some things never change. At his full height he was still tall enough to put his arm around her and lead her to the house.

"It's my birthday." His voice boomed with the joke. "Let me offer you a drink to celebrate your happy return."

His hand slid from her shoulder to her arm: the skin was smooth as warm silk. Her face turned towards his: puzzled, almost happy, and he could feel the heat of her breath as she prepared to speak.

"Of course I forgive you," Tomás said.

An Intimate Death

MARIE-CLAIRE BLAIS
Translated by Ray Ellenwood

His books are still there, untouched, just as he arranged them on the shelves of his study, the books he read, the books he wrote, his papers, his notes are still spread over his worktable, because surely he still has lots of time to finish a novel, an essay, the pictures, the drawings he loved, are also untouched on the orange wall he'd just painted, one of those pictures that remind you of Gauguin, with brown bodies in the sun, is an allegory of the sensual, paradisiacal life a person can lead on an island where it's always sunny and hot, he'd hung the picture on the orange wall above the table at which he reads and writes all day, but when evening comes and his work is done you can hear him laughing with his friends, although it's a sober laugh even when he smokes the euphoriant cigarettes he offers to everyone in that hot, nocturnal, intoxicating air, because there's barely enough wind at night, a breath of cool on the back of the neck, there's nothing but intoxication on this terrace, in this garden and at night we can hear him wandering lazily through the streets of the town, yes him, the intellectual who used to be so reserved, so discreet he seemed almost haughty, letting himself go in the blissful listlessness of the island, gradually he succumbs to his voluptuous temptations because surely he still has lots of time ahead of him, later, when he doesn't have to teach at that hidebound university back there, he'll come and live here among his books and his friends, and suddenly, how did it happen, one April morning, they made up a hospital bed in his room, under the towering trees that cover the roof of the tropical house with their branches, their tangled leaves, and he's thinking under this nest of lianas and stifling vegetation, lying on his hospital bed of intense pain while air comes to him in a mask and nourishment percolates drop by drop through tubes attached to his weakened flesh, he is thinking, those trees should have been cut long ago, they're so bushy, huge, they block the light, and their laughter can be heard from the garden, or the terrace, Vic and Frank and now they're here in this room leaning over him, washing him, changing him, turning him in his bed, for a few weeks already they've been here at his bedside, at first they offered him a hash cigarette, slipping it between his lips, then he refused, didn't he once tell them discreetly during a meal that he'd lost his taste for spicy food, those flavours that used to burn his throat, from now on, in the evening air, it's time for that indispensable morphine, and isn't it true they had to get rid of the young male nurse who was stealing the drugs prescribed for terminal patients at the hospital, and what would become of that kid from the black ghetto? His papers are spread over the table, the writing on them having become illegible, with hunched, tortured letters, and now he sees the misty silhouettes of Vic and Frank who are folding him in their arms because they have to change him, wash him like a baby, yesterday, indescribable consolation, they put some toys in his bed, then they took them away from him again because any object could hurt him, even a plush teddy bear, weren't his arms and legs covered with bruises, things have changed since the time they could still give him refreshing baths, now they have to turn him in his bed, he hardly weighs anything, and always those hunched, tortured letters among the notes on the worktable, under the picture that was hung on the wall painted orange last year, he's strong enough to say in a tone of deprived, repressed rage, he wants them to listen this time when he says, yes, his voice rattling, in a kind of incoherent sigh, when will it all be over, anyway, when will it all be over? Because there's other proof that his time has come, he thinks, and that is the hibiscus Peter brought yesterday, the one with the yellow flowers just blooming, which stopped suddenly, the buds glossy in the light wouldn't open, there's the sign, he thinks vaguely, the sign of departure, the trees are too high, too bushy, no ray of sun can get through any more, it's a yellow, tepid light at this hour of the morning, what did he say, Frank and Vic could barely hear him, a little water, yes, for the past few hours the water couldn't get past his burning lips any more, they'd sat him up with great tenderness, helped him support his head against the pillow, but it was no use, the cool water no longer soothed him, all he could do was repeat, when will it all be over, my friends, when will it all be over? He loved parties so much, too bad he's not here this evening with his friends, his colleagues, a few distant relatives as well,

celebrating in this sumptuous historical house where Frank and Vic
have organized a banquet in his honour, the man who loved parties
so much is somewhere else, there in the Gulf of Mexico where his
ashes are cooling, they rented a boat, says David, and the green
waves rocked them, never saw so many ashes, says David, and the
boat skimmed over the green water, carrying all of them along with
the man who wouldn't return from the voyage, yes, but that night
during the banquet the hibiscus began to bloom once more even
though the air was glacial for this warm season, the hibiscus was
blooming again spreading its wide, yellow corollas, and it was Peter,
wasn't it, standing near the plant in shy silence, who noticed it first,
the hibiscus is blooming and the man who couldn't drink or eat any
more, never mind do what they asked and roll on to his side to
relieve the pain a little, he too had seen that vigorous plant, the
hibiscus Peter had brought him and at that moment he'd felt the
breathing grow slow in his chest, Peter and the plant were the
incarnation of that living beauty he would never attain again, even
by stretching out his hand, that emaciated hand opening in the void,
lots of time ahead of him, later on he'd come to rest and write in his
island house, he'll write still more books, be an editor and poet by
turns, he'll discover authors and make them known in foreign lands,
and suddenly, one morning in March a male nurse pushes his
wheelchair through the Miami airport and indeed it's him, the
sportsman, the athlete who only yesterday was diving in the ocean
waves, it is indeed him, so feeble today he can't walk any more, it is
indeed him they're pushing in the wheelchair from one airport to
another, under the pitying and fearful eyes of a crowd full of latent
hostility, because this man passing has a contagious disease, and the
contagion is formidable, it's a contagion of fear that nourishes prejudice, racism, hate he thinks while the crowd parts to let him
through and he shivers with cold in this oppressive heat, touching
his face and feeling the premature wrinkles under his trembling
fingers, the sky is blue and hot, Vic and Frank are waiting for him
there, feebly listless he'd let himself be dressed that morning in his
blue sweater and grey corduroy slacks, fully aware that the young
black male nurse was gradually stripping him of the morphine he'd
need later on, who knows, maybe in a few days, but feebly listless,
he'd let himself be dressed for the journey, but what did those

people in the crowd see, under his sweater, his slacks, the sores, the black stigmata, because no part of his body had been spared, he was suffering as much inside as out, his breath was short and constricted, his pink colouring had faded in a few weeks, and when would it all be over, anyway, when would it all be over, that secret fire that wind of putrefaction blowing over him? And in this historical house on the island they were celebrating glass in hand, celebrating the man who used to be strong and beautiful, vigorous and tender, the lover of life when life was no longer there, they were celebrating the man who would never come back from the Gulf of Mexico and in the plane that was taking him back to the island the male nurse had raised him in his seat so he could see the ocean and there was a glint of joy in his blue eyes and the glint quickly disappeared as his gaze with its stricken intelligence became fixed on the green water, he saw the island lost amid thick vegetation, his island, and that evening Frank and Peter admitted they'd hardly recognized him when they saw him at the airport with the male nurse pushing the wheelchair, and in Frank's car they'd toured the island, saw once more its houses, the gardens he'd never see again and he'd said, I feel better already, they'd toured the alleys and the streets of this town full of odours surrounded by ocean, and they remembered how he'd spoken then about his eyes, yes, his eyes were still good, his sight wasn't affected, he could still read and work, and his books, his papers with the illegible, hunched, tortured letters were still there in the house under the trees, and they held a banquet in his honour but he wasn't there any more, among his relatives, his friends, he couldn't feel the night wind pass over the back of his neck, couldn't see the starry sky, at the end, said David, he wasn't aware of much, fortunately, he no longer knew what was happening to him, like a baby being changed and swabbed, such a proud man but he wasn't aware and we've got to be thankful for that small mercy, he was sinking all alone into a shadowy despair, laughing and crying, and yet he said, my God, when will it all be over, anyway, and his blue, intelligent gaze wandered all around him, around his abandoned and damaged body, the glint in his eyes suddenly paralysed in the dawn light, and they each had a copy of that recent photo of him where the dazzling glint of his blue eyes had blazed for the last time in the faded pallor of his face, on that

day too he was wearing the grey corduroy slacks, the blue wool
sweater and looked as if he were resting nonchalantly in a red
canvas chair, holding his head in his left hand, he must have felt
good that day, they said to themselves while contemplating the shy
grace of his smile, and the sick man's head, so very frail, bending
towards the left hand which supported the frail head as if it were
about to fall, yes, that's right, said David, and they all stared at this
farewell snapshot, discovering in it the premature wrinkles on his
forehead, the melancholy of his smile, wasn't there a kind of
laziness in his pose that day, David was saying, a sweet nonchalance
like in the good old days when he used to smoke his intoxicating
cigarettes beside his friends, remember that night back when he
used to go bar hopping after dark and he met Lee, Lee, the Japanese
boy in the striped pullover roller-skating past the sidewalk bars that
night with a luminous green band around his close-cropped head
glowing like a dragonfly in the night, others said, there's a kind of
abandon in his smile and in that movement of the hand, and such
grace too, such extreme nonchalance, he used to work a lot, but
taking it easy, he also really liked doing nothing, just dreaming
through the sensual sluggishness of those apparently endless summer days. . . . Behind him in the photograph there's the landscape of
water and sand that belonged to him so many times, behind the man
nonchalantly seated, relaxed, ready to laugh his sober laugh in the
red canvas chair, he used to welcome his friends while resting in
that chair in the garden, writers who'd come from every corner of
the world and then they set up the hospital bed in the bedroom and
he'd noticed how the trees were so high and bushy against the sky,
no, the air couldn't get in any more and the sunlight, and the
hibiscus Peter had placed near his bed, the hibiscus with its yellow
flowers had suddenly stopped blooming as if it had been draped in a
shroud of frost or deprived of the sun's glare, overwhelmed by the
same contemptible, servile suffering he'd felt, even that night when
he'd told his friends he didn't like spicy food any more, the lightness
of his smile had faded, the cool water would no longer pass his
burning lips, because a putrid fire consumed his heart, his bowels,
and that devastated body was barely visible under the trembling
damp sheets, even if Vic changed the sheets constantly weren't they
always humid, oh! when will it all be over, anyway, when will it all

be over? And then at last that glint of fierce anxiety became fixed at dawn in his eyes, the hibiscus stopped blooming finally, and it was all over, and the boats went on gliding over the green water and when the wind became too strong, the young people on their sailboards were cast out by the waves, a cold wind passed furtively over the green water and the hibiscus stopped blooming for two days when the cold wind came and you could feel it cut through you like a knife, and that was the hour a young man died, still overflowing with vitality, his books and his writings still untouched in his study on the worktable where bills in sealed envelopes were also piling up, and they were celebrating him that night, but he wasn't there any more among his relatives, his friends, to feel the breath of wind on the back of his neck and Lee no longer appeared at night on roller skates with a luminous green band around his close-cropped head, they raised their glasses but the man they celebrated wasn't there any more, the man who'd loved parties so much.

Ghosts at Jarry

HUGH HOOD

Mario at the big O, a man who likes company. Squeezed into the 400 level up and in and remote from the *voltigeur de gauche*, not too many people near him in the four-dollar seats, filling for a cement sandwich, like being on a slab. Cold concrete. The 400 level is indeterminate space, neither a good seat nor a bad, too far away to hear the cries of the infielders like lonely birds swooping over green, too near to shave the price. That April afternoon he saw *les boucaniers de Pittsburgh* take the Expos as the home forces booted the ball repeatedly. Fresh from Florida the unmeshed infield found the home weather too cold for fumbling fingers, baseballs rolling hither and yon, none penetrating the 400 level. No *fausse balle* enlivened the narrow precinct. Mario decided not to sit there again; it would have to be *le niveau 200*, *Section 18*, *Section 20*, or nothing, and it would cost.

He looked for friends, found none, though they were there for sure. They had told him they were coming, Ti-cul, Kurt, Silvo, present but invisible. After the fourth inning he went in search of Silvo, who used to sit out past third base at field level, but there was nobody in his seat, only vast stretches of unoccupied metal pigeonholes, roomy, chilly, in their thousands. He couldn't find his way back upstairs; the arrows and signs confused him, and he watched the rest of the game from a vacant seat downstairs, not having paid the full price. He felt nervous and guilty but no cheerful attendant asked to see his stub; nobody banished him from the third base line. Mario never got away with anything because he never tried to. Nobody came around selling peanuts; the vendors seemed lost in the empty reaches. Parched at the seventh-inning stretch he quit his usurped bench and found a nearby kiosk where nobody stood in line. He was served immediately, then had to find a lavatory, luckily next door. Mario blessed the Régie des Installations Olympiques for wise care of their *concitoyens*, but found the lavatory a maze of reverse-swinging doors. He had a hard time escaping, a belated rally in progress along the basepaths. Cash scored, the home forces appeared ready to carry the day. Mario fought his way to freedom in time to see the *Devinez l'assistance* figures flashed on the big board: 21,063, 19,750, 18,322, 20,004.

He thought: those are mistaken. There can't be twenty thousand people here, or eighteen thousand. I would guess maybe seven, he thought, maybe eight thousand. There is nobody buying beer, nobody helped me when I called. I might have perished in there. The board flashed the official figure: *Assistance d'aujourd'hui, 19,750.* He peered around incredulously. Had they counted sold empty seats perhaps? At Jarry such a throng would have stretched services beyond capacity. He'd never have been able to walk straight to the counter and demand a beer, not even after the game was over. Here there was infinite space, and it unsettled him. The long eighth inning continued; extra innings impended; afternoon stretched into early evening; people began to leave; the big O emptied; Mario got frightened.

He wondered if he would come back. It was so close to home, that was the thing. For his whole life, he and Ti-cul and Silvo and Kurt had been hoping for something in the east-end besides the Angus shops. Now here it was, five minutes from Rosemont, and it gave him vertigo. He looked out, squinting through the late shadows, at what-the-hell-was-it, sward? Turf? He wasn't sure of the word. *Gazon*? *Domtarturf*? It wasn't anything like grass, being a bright emerald, a colour never seen in the natural world, out of a laboratory, bottled. Such green as might be seen in a film about the distant future. He could see where the individual rolls had been zippered together and laughed when a tenth-inning ground ball, out past Parrish, suddenly bounded into the air as it hit one of the zippered seams in the gleaming surface and assumed a long incredible arc, hurtling past the amazed left-fielder towards the warning track. Two runs scored. Expos failed to even the count in their half of the tenth, and the game ended that way towards six o'clock.

The players vanished like wraiths; never had Mario seen them disappear so fast. He used to stand close to the field after the final out, to watch the inept homesters make their exposed way out to the foul pole in left and into the clubhouse, exchanging discontented repartee with certain regular fans. Once that disgusting, off-speed-pitch-specialist, Howie Reed, had flipped a baseball into *les estrades populaires* as he sauntered, cursing freely and indecently in words Mario failed to recognize, into the sheltering clubhouse. There had been a scramble. Children had injured themselves. Such a thing would be impossible under the new dispensation, contact irretrievably lost. Mario felt specks and points tickling the curling hairs on his neck and looked up. Unbelievably a warm spring rain was finding its way to him from on high, hardly a rain, more a mist, spitting. Nobody was visible but a non-lingual youth who scuttled past turning seats up, mute arguably from birth: nobody could have decided on the evidence. He would have to look for Kurt and the others at the tavern; he was sure to find them there. He moved up the steps and in out of the rain; spring night enveloped him. In the dark, strange patterns defined themselves on the concrete walls as wetness slid down pocked textures.

Roofless, open, the giant structure admitted natural flow of water, perhaps its most grateful feature. He pondered this matter as he made for the main gates, wondering whether he should go home or go downtown to eat. What would the stadium be like in heavy rain, in snow, roofless or roofed? He had heard from a friend in the air-conditioning business that huge conduits, giant circulating pumps, were being installed in the building, which would in time be completed as an all-weather sports palace. But here imagination failed. How heat it in winter? Who would sit in caverns of ice to watch what? Should Expos ever make it into *la série mondiale* they would have to play night games in mid-October; his Mediterranean blood roiled and thickened at the thought. A roof would inhibit free circulation of air. How dank, how chilled it would be, pressed up against that cold stone in late autumn! What could be done about it? And he thought, as he thought most days about the way things went on, how fix?

His feet had decided for him, leading him down the tunnel towards the Métro station. Nobody on the first flight. Nobody on the second flight. Silence along the terraces, solitude beside the newsagents' stands. Inside a sandwich again, he thought, eaten by a giant. One solitary man in a glass booth opening a vacuum bottle. Steam escaped from its top, making him think of the roofless big O. In this rain, in these temperatures, there would be puffs of steam from the hole in the top, possibly even rings of vapour as if expelled from the cancered lungs of a colossal cigarette-smoker. He passed on to an almost silent train; a solitary passenger wasn't anybody he knew.

When he rose up out of the Métro at the Berri-De Montigny station, he found the same spring rain falling into the lights of evening. He thought of the plastic emerald rug; this rain would not promote its growth, false surface. He had heard that the players preferred true grass which grew long, sometimes giving them a break on a hot grounder. Long growth might then be cut to surprise visiting teams with porous infields, a bit of baseball larceny less and less available to canny groundskeepers. Too bright. Too green.

And then there was the look and feeling of the oddly shaped hole in the roof, a shape that made him peculiarly uncomfortable, something wrong about it. He wasn't a poet; he wasn't an architect; he had a labouring job and didn't want to know about art, but he knew that the hole in the sky was quietly askew, wrong. It shouldn't curve that way because there was nothing in the curve to remind him of women's bodies. If something curved, thought Mario, it ought to curve in a useful or encouraging way.

He wouldn't go back in there; it wasn't like the old park, which had been like a village, close, warming, with the usual run of village characters. There had been a man who brought his goat to twenty games a season, and the club management connived at the smelly invasion, to court press photographers. At the opening game of the 1971 season, Mario's children had carried a huge homemade sign into the bleachers: BIENVENUE À NOS AMOURS LES EXPOS. At two in the afternoon a pressman took a picture, which appeared in the final edition of the *Star* that same afternoon; neighbours phoned excitedly during dinner to tell the family about it. The children had remembered it ever since and there was a copy of the picture still pinned to his bedroom door.

There had been that man who sprang up in the middle of rallies and danced like a dervish up and down the steps of the grandstand, executing unheard-of jigs and reels to an accompaniment of hand-clapping from thousands of enthusiasts around him, a lean man, crazy-looking, known around the National League as "the Dancer" His steps could not have been danced at the Stade Olympique. The pitch of the seats was too gradual, the stairs insufficiently raked. Some sort of classical pavanne would suit them, not the gyrations of the native Québecker.

In the twentieth row of the bleachers, right behind the third base foul pole, had sat night after night an unspeaking man in a short-sleeved shirt, grey-headed, immobile, stumpy cigar always in place, not a word to say for himself but always there. No cheer escaped this man, no violation of the careful probabilities of baseball by fledgeling expansion team could make him wince. Mario missed him terribly, searched for him during intense moments at the big O, realizing finally that the man had gone forever. He might just possibly be seated somewhere in the new building in his perpetual Buddhist posture but this seemed against all odds, the betting prohibitive. What is to be done, Mario wondered, how can this be restored?

Ballplayers – on the whole an ungenerous group of men – had hated Jarry Park for sound professional reasons as well as from personal pique. Not really great and good ballplayers, most early Expos wished to avoid the inspection of nearby fans, disliked the trudge along the track to the clubhouse, finally prevailed upon management to erect a cement-block tunnel from dugout to club-house, rendering themselves unobservable, incorrigible. A very few who for reasons of their own wished to court public favour con-tinued to take the outside walk; but these were popular players apt to be fringe performers, a Ronnie Brand, a Marv Staehle, José Herrera.

The old park had the world's crappiest outfield, frost-humped, deceptively grassy, stippled with rabbit holes, hell to run on. It had no foul area; the bullpens were in the laps of the fans. Visiting relief pitchers endured coarse taunts during rare Expos rallies. Expos firemen grew accustomed to the stagey resignation of the home supporters.

"*Attention, Attention. Le numéro vingt-cinq, Dan McGinn, lance main-tenant pour les Expos.*"

At this ominous declaration, Ti-cul, Kurt, Silvo, and Mario would groan, make retching noises. The Buddha of the bleachers might shift one buttock's width to right or left or he might not.

I will go back and look at Jarry Park, Mario decided. He had clipped a panoramic view of the old place from some special issue of

Le Dimanche, park packed beyond capacity for some extraordinary occasion. Taken from an altitude of seven hundred and fifty feet, probably from a helicopter hovering above the parking lot to the north-east of the playing field, the photo emphasized the ramshackle, spurious, ad hoc, temporary, incredible cheapness of the silly building. It had cost three million dollars. But no public facility of the contemporary scene could possibly cost three million dollars, the thing was unheard-of. It was eight hundred million or zilch – there is no other way. When Jarry had been built, not all that long ago, Mario recollected, hardly a decade, there had been no cranes sitting idle on the site over weekends, at overtime rates approaching sixty thousand an hour. Overtime for idling cranes alone had cost more at the Olympic site than the entire cost of Jarry Park, three million. How fix?

The players hated it, and it made sense: two strikes. He thought he'd go and have a final look before they started to tear it down; there was no conceivable use for the facility. All he did was work. It looked horrible. The metal flooring of the stands had leaked copiously. If you stood under it during a rain-delay, the precipitation poured down your neck and into the dank bun of your hotdog. Those hotdogs had always been dung-like, inert, without form and void. Soggy, they constituted an offence against nature. No. There was nothing to be said for the former home of the Montréal National League Baseball Club Limited.

Somewhere around the house there was a portable radio, usable on house current or batteries, a discarded Christmas gift with exhausted power pack. Mario located it, dusted it off, supplied the requisite D batteries, and took it with him across town on an indifferent, coolish, Sunday afternoon with the Cards in town.

At fifteen hundred feet a familiar Cessna 150 banked, trailing a long streamer which delivered the Gospel according to Parkside. ALWAYS A BETTER DEAL AT PARKSIDE MOTORS. The plane hastened away as Mario squinted aloft. Perhaps the pilot had forgotten himself, returned to his old flyway mistaking the open space below for the true ballgame, then found it empty. The drone of the engine faded. Jarry was really desert.

He sidled towards the exiguous metal structure. One thing about it, though lonely, deserted, vacant, boarded over, it hadn't corroded. The metal façade shone dully, white in the uncertain atmosphere. It was an afternoon of ill-defined light, little sun, light overcast, a genuine Montréal uncertainty of observation. There was nobody in the park. He passed along the chain-link fencing looking for entry. Surely some boy or dog or vandal had effected the necessary hole – and there it was, back along the third-base side near the rickety ticket booths and the press gate, a gaping tear, edges bent backwards, big enough to drive a Jeep through. Somebody had been at work with a pair of wire-cutters. The edges of the severed strands were shiny-fresh and could hurt you. He passed inside.

What is quieter than an abandoned ballpark, unless the tomb? He shuddered to think where all the voices had gone. Once this place had shaken and resounded with the shrieks of fifteen thousand maddened kiddies on Bat Day, fifteen thousand miniature Louisville Sluggers pounding in unison on the metal flooring; it had been a hellish event. Householders for blocks around had complained to the authorities but the promotion had become a recurrent event. Bat Day at Jarry Park was like the Last Judgement, sounding, deeply impressive.

But unlike the judgement in this, that it was not still impending. He stole across the flat paved open area between the fence and the refreshment counters. A blue souvenir stand leaned ready to collapse, doors locked. From between the doors a feather protruded electric blue. Mario tugged at the feather end, and the whole article slid noiselessly from between the locked doors, a celebratory feather dyed red, white, and blue. The other end stuck in the door, perhaps attached to a hat inside, too big to fit through the crack. He could do nothing to release it and left it floating solemnly in the faint breeze, passed up a ramp and into the deserted third-base seats, once the best place in the city to see a game. He idled along towards the foul pole, clutching his radio. The day around him grew imperceptibly warmer, the grey lightened. Vacancy. The seats were all before him and he was at the extreme outfield end of the park, immediately over the gateway to the abandoned clubhouse. He sprawled in one seat, then stood up, chose another, put his legs out in front of him, and switched on the radio.

". . . and after the pre-game show we'll have all the action for you right here at Radio 600, the voice of Montréal Expos baseball. I'm

Dave Van Horne and I'll be right here with Duke Snider to keep you up-to-date on the out-of-town scores and the other developments around the majors, right after this message . . ."

The sun came out. Mario drowsed and listened. He saw that this was life as it ought to be lived. The game came to him with perfect clarity and form over the radio. With his eyes shut he could fancy the whole place alive around him. Nothing was gone. The Gautama of the bleachers would be right over there twenty rows up, if he happened to glance in that direction. If the Expos happened to get something going – as they did almost immediately that afternoon – the dancer would get his legs going too. The air would be filled with flying bags of peanuts. People would be passing hotdogs along the rows in a fine comradeship. All he had to do was listen, and keep his eyes shut tight.

". . . opened the inning with a single, went to second on Cromartie's roller to the right side. Valentine homered, his sixth home run of the season and his nineteenth and twentieth RBIs. Perez reached on an error . . ."

Expos won that first game in Mario's resurrected Jarry, a shutout victory for Rogers, and after that there could be no question of viewing the games in the flesh. He started to come to the old park all the time, nights and Saturdays as well as on the Sabbath. He felt in control, as though the whole happening was invented by him. The conviction grew on him that he could influence the course of the games by wishing, commanding in imagination. He knew that this was not strictly so, but all the same the home club seemed to rally more often when he really willed them to – balls found holes in infields, defensive replacements offered models of anticipation. Rookies blossomed – three of them, almost a miracle – all through closed eyes. He now began to think about bringing his portable Sanyo along. If the atmospherics were right and the power pack strong, he might be able to watch the games on TV, listen to the expert radio commentary, have his eyes opened. Would the TV picture be an adequate surrogate for all he could imagine?

Night games would tell; they were the best of all because the tall poles no longer supported myriads of hot arcs. All was still, but not dark. Those night games in May and June at Jarry, the longest evenings of the year, had always been vexed by the slow disappearance of the sun behind the bleachers to the north-west. He remembered Ron Fairly refusing to scamper on to the playing area when the umpire called "Play Ball!" because of that late sun, dead in the eyes of the first baseman. Fairly, always an intransigent ball-player, had been able to persuade Dick Stello to delay the game until the sun disappeared, an unlikely twenty minutes. At Midsummer Day it didn't get dark in the park until sixth inning or even later, while across town the actual play would be shadowed in shrouding concrete, no illumination relieving the cavernous gloom. Night games were best.

Just about Midsummer Day, with a long brilliant evening light promised, he brought the Sanyo along and sneaked into his usual spot. For a while he contented himself with the radio and the fading summer sun on his tight eyelids, but as the light waned he grew curious, and when darkness descended very late, past nine-thirty, he turned on the TV and focused his gaze on the small picture, like some mystic concentrating on his mandala:

CARTER. 11 HR. 29 RBI. .268

The emission of light from the small screen was the only sparkle in the park, thought Mario. He leaned forward, the sounds of the city in the night drifting almost inaudibly overhead. He watched the final three innings, willing them to win, and they did. And as he switched to the post-game show on the radio, just as he turned his TV off, he caught a gleam of light almost the mirror image of his own at the extreme other end of the stands, over by the first-base foul pole. A line drawn from where he was sitting through centre-field to the distant glimmer would form the base of an isosceles triangle whose equal sides would extend through first and third to home. He had no intention of launching himself into the deep well of darkness in centre. But he felt drawn along the shining metal gangway which ran the length of the grandstand.

The main bank of seats in Jarry was formed in the shape of an enormous letter L, the two equal sides of an isosceles triangle with its apex behind home plate. A fan sitting in Mario's position sensed this shape as a long line extending away towards home, with the other leg of the L running out of the corner of his eye in the direction of the visitors" dressing room under the first-base stands. The whole mass had something the look of an opened penknife, as used in the boy's game of "baseball" early in the century.

The distant figure on the other side of the park now followed Mario's lead and extinguished whatever light had been showing. The whole park lay under the night sky empty, glowing with night-shine off the aluminium seatbacks. A breeze moved quietly in the grass. Mario inched his way silently towards home in the darkness, and peering through the dark he had the sense that somebody else was coming in from right-field. A faint metallic sound drifted above the pitcher's mound, shoes on metal plating. Small shoes, by the sound.

He eased forward along the runway, which stretched out in front of him like a white dusty road in the country under starlight. The towers of extinct arc-lights stood up around the park like sentinels. There was the billboard advertising cigarettes, unreadable in the dark. Out to his left the old scoreboard, which had never worked properly, loomed with comforting familiarity. Clink of shoes on metal. He strained his eyes to see across the narrowing infield. Somebody was there. He caught a glimpse of a pale face in dim reflection. Then he heard swift footsteps and saw a slender form move in the dark like the ghost of a batboy. He ran along the third-base line, reaching home at the same moment as the ghostly figure. A girl in a dark blue halter and a pair of jeans threw herself unresistingly into his arms. This terrified him. Mario had held no girl but his wife in his arms at any time these twenty years. He drew back and tried to see her. Like himself, she carried a small portable TV and a radio.

"I thought you were a ghost," exclaimed this stranger. "Heavens, how you scared me."

"I thought so too," said Mario.

"That you were a ghost? How could you think that?"

"No. That *you* were."

"That's silly," said the girl scornfully. "Anybody can see that I'm not a ghost. I'm a very popular girl."

"I'm sure you are, Miss, but I can't see you very well in the dark."

"Why are you here?"

"I like it better here."

"Oh, so do I, so do I. I hate that other place with a passion."

"And so you started to come back here, just like me, to listen to the games and watch them on your TV. How long have you been coming?"

"This is my first time."

"I hope it won't be your last," said Mario with a gallantry which astounded himself. It would have astonished his wife too.

"But we're . . . all alone in here?"

"There's certainly nobody here now, not even a security guard."

"Would I be safe with you?"

"Would one Expos fan insult another? And besides, now that there are two of us, others will come. I'm certain of it."

"Oh, I hope you're right," said the girl in a beseeching tone.

"I know I'm right," said Mario. "This is exactly how a house gets to be haunted." Afterwards, when he recognized the supreme justice of this observation he wondered how he'd hit on it. He considered himself habitually, by a kind of unthinking reflex, to be a stupid unfeeling person, but in this adventure he had shown, he saw, powerful imagination.

Many came after that first encounter; they came by ones and twos, then in troops, finally in hundreds. The abandoned park sprang back to a loony bootleg life all the sunny summer. People would bring their own hotdogs and beer, their radios. Somehow a cap and souvenir vendor found out about the secret congregation, and he came too one July evening with a trayful of hats and dolls and pennants. Nobody bought anything from him; they were afraid he'd disappear. Obviously the Montréal National League Baseball Club Limited knew nothing about him, a phantom souvenir salesman with phantom goods.

None of them revisited the big O. Not ever. And in the earliest hints of autumn they would laugh, and people in neighbourhood apartment blocks would wonder where the laughing was coming from, as the plangent tones of the Duke of Fallbrook oozed from the radios collected at Jarry.

". . . now we know, Dave and I know, that the club is playing a bit off the pace, but really you know folks that doesn't explain the dropoff in attendance. There has to be a big audience for Expos baseball out there somewhere, and I'm appealing to you – it's the old Duker talking . . ."

"That's right, Duke," said the voice of Dave Van Horne, "we've got a great home stand going here, so come on out to the Olympic Stadium and watch the Expos try to play the role of spoilers in this season's tight race in the National League East. Hope to see you real soon, right, Duke?"

"Right, Dave!"

But the ghosts of Jarry merely guffawed, an immense throng they were by now. And the first of them looked again at the wide heavens. No, he would never go back. He would spend no second afternoon in mental trouble excited by that crater in the air, gazing through the gaping enormous ellipse – was it an ellipse? – in the sky.

The Moslem Wife

MAVIS GALLANT

In the south of France, in the business room of a hotel quite near to the house where Katherine Mansfield (whom no one in this hotel had ever heard of) was writing "The Daughters of the Late Colonel", Netta Asher's father announced that there would never be a man-made catastrophe in Europe again. The dead of that recent war, the doomed nonsense of the Russian Bolsheviks had finally knocked sense into European heads. What people wanted now was to get on with life. When he said "life", he meant its commercial business.

Who would have contradicted Mr Asher? Certainly not Netta. She did not understand what he meant quite so well as his French solicitor seemed to, but she did listen with interest and respect, and then watched him signing papers that, she knew, concerned her for life. He was renewing the long lease her family held on the Hotel Prince Albert and Albion. Netta was then eleven. One hundred years should at least see her through the prime of life said Mr Asher, only half-jokingly, for of course he thought his seed was immortal.

Netta supposed she might easily live to be more than a hundred – at any rate, for years and years. She knew that her father did not want her to marry until she was twenty-six and that she was then supposed to have a pair of children, the elder a boy. Netta and her father and the French lawyer shook hands on the lease, and she was given her first glass of champagne. The date on the bottle was 1909, for the year of her birth. Netta bravely pronounced the wine delicious, but her father said she would know much better vintages before she was through.

Netta remembered the handshake but perhaps not the terms. When the lease had eighty-eight years to run, she married her first cousin, Jack Ross, which was not at all what her father had had in mind. Nor would there be the useful pair of children – Jack couldn't abide them. Like Netta he came from a hotelkeeping family where the young were like blight. Netta had up to now never shown a scrap of maternal feeling over anything, but Mr Asher thought Jack might have made an amiable parent – a kind one, at least. She consoled Mr Asher on one count, by taking the hotel over in his lifetime. The hotel was, to Netta, a natural life; and so when Mr Asher, dying, said, "She behaves as I wanted her to," he was right as far as the drift of Netta's behaviour was concerned but wrong about its course.

The Ashers' hotel was not down on the seafront, though boats and sea could be had from the south-facing rooms.

Across a road nearly empty of traffic were handsome villas, and behind and to either side stood healthy olive trees and a large lemon grove. The hotel was painted a deep ochre with white trim. It had white awnings and green shutters and black iron balconies as lacquered and shiny as Chinese boxes. It possessed two tennis courts, a lily pond, a sheltered winter garden, a formal rose garden, and trees full of nightingales. In the summer dark, *belles-de-nuit* glowed pink, lemon, white, and after their evening watering they gave off a perfume that varied from plant to plant and seemed to match the petals' coloration. In May the nights were dense with stars and fireflies. From the rose garden one might have seen the twin pulse of cigarettes on a balcony, where Jack and Netta sat drinking a last brandy-and-soda before turning in. Most of the rooms were shuttered by then, for no traveller would have dreamed of being south except in winter. Jack and Netta and a few servants had the whole place to themselves. Netta would hire workmen and have the rooms that needed it repainted – the blue cardroom, and the red-walled bar, and the white dining room, where Victorian mirrors gave back glossy walls and blown curtains and nineteenth-century views of the Ligurian coast, the work of an Asher great-uncle. Everything upstairs and down was soaked and wiped and polished, and even the pictures were relentlessly washed with soft cloths and ordinary laundry soap. Netta also had the boiler overhauled and the linen mended and new monograms embroidered and the looking glasses resilvered and the shutters taken off their hinges and scraped and made spruce green again for next year's sun to fade, while Jack talked about decorators and expert gardeners and even wrote to some, and banged tennis balls against the large new garage. He also read books and translated poetry for its own sake and practised playing the clarinet. He had studied music once, and still thought that an important life, a musical life, was there in the middle distance. One summer, just to see if he could, he translated pages of St-John Perse, which were as blank as the garage wall to Netta, in any tongue.

Netta adored every minute of her life, and she thought Jack had a good life too, with nearly half the year for the pleasures that suited him. As soon as the grounds and rooms and cellar and roof had been put to rights, she and Jack packed and went travelling somewhere. Jack made the plans. He was never so cheerful as when buying Baedekers and dragging out their stickered trunks. But Netta was nothing of a traveller. She would have been glad to see the same sun rising out of the same sea from the window every day until she died. She loved Jack, and what she liked best after him was the hotel. It was a place where, once, people had come to die of tuberculosis, yet it held no trace or feeling of danger. When Netta walked with her workmen through sheeted summer rooms, hearing the cicadas and hearing Jack start, stop, start some deeply alien music (alien even when her memory automatically gave her a composer's name), she was reminded that here the dead had never been allowed to corrupt the living; the dead had been dressed for an outing and removed as soon as their first muscular stiffness relaxed. Some were wheeled out in chairs, sitting, and some reclined on portable cots, as if merely resting.

That is why there is no bad atmosphere here, she would say to herself. Death has been swept away, discarded. When the shutters are closed on a room, it is for sleep or for love. Netta could think this easily because neither she nor Jack was ever sick. They knew nothing about insomnia, and they made love every day of their lives – they had married in order to be able to.

Spring had been the season for dying in the old days. Invalids who had struggled through the dark comfort of winter took fright as the night receded. They felt without protection. Netta knew about this, and about the difference between darkness and brightness, but neither affected her. She was not afraid of death or of the dead – they were nothing but cold, heavy furniture. She could have tied jaws shut and weighted eyelids with native instinctiveness, as other women were born knowing the temperature for an infant's milk.

"There are no ghosts," she could say, entering the room where her mother, then her father had died. "If there were, I would know."

Netta took it for granted, now she was married, that Jack felt as she did about light, dark, death, and love. They were as alike in some ways (none of them physical) as a couple of twins, spoke much the same language in the same accents, had the same jokes – mostly about other people – and had been together as much as their families would let them for most of their lives. Other men seemed dull to Netta – slower, perhaps, lacking the spoken shorthand she had with Jack. She never mentioned this. For one thing, both of them had the idea that, being English, one must not say too much. Born abroad, they worked hard at an Englishness that was innocently inaccurate, rooted mostly in attitudes. Their families had been innkeepers along this coast for a century, even before Dr James Henry Bennet had discovered "the Genoese Rivieras". In one of his guides to the region, a "Mr Ross" is mentioned as a hotel owner who will accept English bank cheques, and there is a "Mr Asher", reliable purveyor of English groceries. The most trustworthy shipping agents in 1860 are the Montale brothers, converts to the Anglican Church, possessors of a British *laissez-passer* to Malta and Egypt. These families, by now plaited like hair, were connections of Netta's and Jack's and still in business from beyond Marseilles to Genoa. No wonder that other men bored her, and that each thought the other both familiar and unique. But of course they were unalike too. When once someone asked them, "Are you related to Montale, the poet?" Netta answered, "What poet?" and Jack said, "I wish we were."

There were no poets in the family. Apart from the great-uncle who had painted landscapes, the only person to try anything peculiar had been Jack, with his music. He had been allowed to study, up to a point; his father had been no good with hotels – had been a failure, in fact, bailed out four times by his cousins, and it had been thought, for a time, that Jack Ross might be a dunderhead too. Music might do him; he might not be fit for anything else.

Information of this kind about the meaning of failure had been gleaned by Netta years before, when she first became aware of her little cousin. Jack's father and mother – the commercial blunderers – had come to the Prince Albert and Albion to ride out a crisis. They were somewhere between undischarged bankruptcy and annihilation, but one was polite: Netta curtsied to her aunt and uncle. Her

eyes were on Jack. She could not read yet, though she could sift and
classify attitudes. She drew near him, sucking her lower lip, her
hands behind her back. For the first time she was conscious of the
beauty of another child. He was younger than Netta, imprisoned in
a portable-fence arrangement in which he moved tirelessly, crab-
wise, hanging on a barrier he could easily have climbed. He was as
fair as his Irish mother and sunburned a deep brown. His blue gaze
was not a baby's – it was too challenging. He was naked except for
shorts that were large and seemed about to fall down. The sunburn,
the undress were because his mother was reckless and rather odd.
Netta – whose mother was perfect – wore boots, stockings, a
longsleeved frock, and a white sun hat. She heard the adults laugh
and say that Jack looked like a prizefighter. She walked around his
prison, staring, and the blue-eyed fighter stared back.

The Rosses stayed for a long time, while the family sent telegrams
and tried to raise money for them. No one looked after Jack much.
He would lie on a marble step of the staircase watching the hotel
guests going into the cardroom or the dining room. One night, for a
reason that remorse was to wipe out in a minute, Netta gave him
such a savage kick (though he was not really in her way) that one of
his legs remained paralysed for a long time.

"*Why* did you do it?" her father asked her – this in the room where
she was shut up on bread and water. Netta didn't know. She loved
Jack, but who would believe it now? Jack learned to walk, then to
run, and in time to ski and play tennis; but her lifelong gift to him
was a loss of balance, a sudden lopsided bend of a knee. Jack's
parents had meantime been given a small hotel to run at Bandol. Mr
Asher, responsible for a bank loan, kept an eye on the place. He
went often, in a hotel car with a chauffeur, Netta perched beside
him. When, years later, the families found out that the devoted
young cousins had become lovers, they separated them without
saying much. Netta was too independent to be dealt with. Besides,
her father did not want a rift; his wife had died, and he needed
Netta. Jack whose claim on music had been the subject of teasing
until now, was suddenly sent to study in England. Netta saw that he
was secretly dismayed. He wanted to be almost anything as long as
it was impossible, and then only as an act of grace. Netta's father did
think it was his duty to tell her that marriage was, at its best, a

parched arrangement, intolerable without a flow of golden guineas and fresh blood. As cousins, Jack and Netta could not bring each other anything except stale money. Nothing stopped them: they were married four months after Jack became twenty-one. Netta heard someone remark at her wedding, "She doesn't need a husband," meaning perhaps the practical, matter-of-fact person she now seemed to be. She did have the dry, burned-out look of someone turned inward. Her dark eyes glowed out of a thin face. She had the shape of a girl of fourteen. Jack, who was large, and fair, and who might be stout at forty if he wasn't careful, looked exactly his age, and seemed quite ready to be married.

Netta could not understand why, loving Jack as she did, she did not look more like him. It had troubled her in the past when they did not think exactly the same thing at almost the same time. During the secret meetings of their long engagement she had noticed how even before a parting they were nearly apart – they had begun to "unmesh", as she called it. Drinking a last drink, usually in the buffet of a railway station, she would see that Jack was somewhere else, thinking about the next-best thing to Netta. The next-best thing might only be a book he wanted to finish reading, but it was enough to make her feel exiled. He often told Netta, "I'm not holding on to you. You're free," because he thought it needed saying, and of course he wanted freedom for himself. But to Netta "freedom" had a cold sound. Is that what I do want, she would wonder. Is that what I think he should offer? Their partings were often on the edge of parting forever, not just because Jack had said or done or thought the wrong thing but because between them they generated the high sexual tension that leads to quarrels. Barely ten minutes after agreeing that no one in the world could possibly know what they knew, one of them, either one, could curse the other out over something trivial. Yet they were, and remained, much in love, and when they were apart Netta sent him letters that were almost despairing with enchantment.

Jack answered, of course, but his letters were cautious. Her exploration of feeling was part of an unlimited capacity she seemed to have for passionate behaviour, so at odds with her appearance, which had been dry and sardonic even in childhood. Save for an erotic sentence or two near the end (which Netta read first) Jack's messages might have been meant for any girl cousin he particularly liked. Love was memory, and he was no good at the memory game; he needed Netta there. The instant he saw her he knew all he had missed. But Netta, by then, felt forgotten, and she came to each new meeting aggressive and hurt, afflicted with the physical signs of her doubts and injuries – cold sores, rashes, erratic periods, mysterious temperatures. If she tried to discuss it he would say, "We aren't going over all that again, are we?" Where Netta was concerned he had settled for the established faith, but Netta, who had a wilder, more secret God, wanted a prayer a minute, not to speak of unending miracles and revelations.

When they finally married, both were relieved that the strain of partings and of tense disputes in railway stations would come to a stop. Each privately blamed the other for past violence, and both believed that once they could live openly, without interference, they would never have a disagreement again. Netta did not want Jack to regret the cold freedom he had vainly tried to offer her. He must have his liberty, and his music, and other people, and, oh, anything he wanted – whatever would stop him from saying he was ready to let her go free. The first thing Netta did was to make certain they had the best room in the hotel. She had never actually owned a room until now. The private apartments of her family had always been surrendered in a crisis: everyone had packed up and moved as beds were required. She and Jack were hopelessly untidy, because both had spent their early years moving down hotel corridors, trailing belts and raincoats, with tennis shoes hanging from knotted strings over their shoulders, their arms around books and sweaters and grey flannel bundles. Both had done lessons in the corners of lounges, with cups and glasses rattling, and other children running, and English voices louder than anything. Jack, who had been vaguely educated, remembered his boarding schools as places where one had a permanent bed. Netta chose for her marriage a south-facing room with a large balcony and an awning of dazzling white. It was furnished with lemonwood that had been brought to the Riviera by Russians for their own villas long before. To the lemonwood Netta's mother had added English chintzes; the result, in Netta's eyes, was not bizarre but charming. The room was deeply mirrored; when the shutters were closed on hot afternoons a play of light became as green as a forest on the walls, and as blue as seawater in the glass. A quality of suspension, of disbelief in gravity, now belonged to Netta. She became tidy, silent, less introspective, as watchful and as reflective as her bedroom mirrors. Jack stayed as he was, luckily; any alteration would have worried her, just as a change in an often-read story will trouble a small child. She was intensely, almost unnaturally happy.

One day she overheard an English doctor, whose wife played bridge every afternoon at the hotel, refer to her, to Netta, as "the little Moslem wife". It was said affectionately, for the doctor liked her. She wondered if he had seen through walls and had watched her picking up the clothing and the wet towels Jack left strewn like clues to his presence. The phrase was collected and passed from mouth to mouth in the idle English colony. Netta, the last person in the world deliberately to eavesdrop (she lacked that sort of interest in other people), was sharp of hearing where her marriage was concerned. She had a special antenna for Jack, for his shades of meaning, secret intentions, for his innocent contradictions. Perhaps "Moslem wife" meant several things, and possibly it was plain to anyone with eyes that Jack, without meaning a bit of harm by it, had a way with women. Those he attracted were a puzzling lot, to Netta. She had already catalogued them – elegant elderly parties with tongues like carving knives; gentle, clever girls who flourished on the unattainable; untouchable-daughter types, canny about their virginity, wondering if Jack would be father enough to justify the sacrifice. There was still another kind – tough, sunburned, clad in dark colours – who made Netta think in the vocabulary of horoscopes. Her gem – diamonds. Her colour – black. Her language – worse than Netta's. She noticed that even when Jack had no real use for a woman he never made it apparent; he adopted anyone who took a liking to him. He assumed – Netta thought – a tribal, paternal air that was curious in so young a man. The plot of attraction interested him, no matter how it turned out. He was like someone reading several novels at once, or like someone playing simultaneous chess.

Netta did not want her marriage to become a world of stone. She said nothing except, "Listen, Jack, I've been at this hotel business longer than you have. It's wiser not to be too pally with the guests."

At Christmas the older women gave him boxes of expensive soap. "They must think someone around here wants a good wash," Netta remarked. Outside their fenced area of private jokes and private love was a landscape too open, too light-drenched, for serious talk. And then, when? Jack woke up quickly and early in the morning and smiled as naturally as children do. He knew where he was and the day of the week and the hour. The best moment of the day was the first cigarette. When something bloody happened, it was never before six in the evening. At night he had a dark look that went with a dark mood, sometimes. Netta would tell him that she could see a cruise ship floating on the black horizon like a piece of the Milky Way, and she would get that look for an answer. But it never lasted. His memory was too short to let him sulk, no matter what fragment of night had crossed his mind. She knew, having heard other couples all her life, that at least she and Jack never made the conjugal sounds that passed for conversation and that might as well have been bow-wow and quack quack.

If, by chance, Jack found himself drawn to another woman, if the tide of attraction suddenly ran the other way, then he would discover in himself a great need to talk to his wife. They sat out on their balcony for much of one long night and he told her about his Irish mother. His mother's eccentricity – "Vera's dottiness", where the family was concerned – had kept Jack from taking anything seriously. He had been afraid of pulling her mad attention in his direction. Countless times she had faked tuberculosis and cancer and announced her own imminent death. A telephone call from a hospital had once declared her lost in a car crash. "It's a new life, a new life," her husband had babbled, coming away from the phone. Jack saw his father then as beautiful. Women are beautiful when they fall in love, said Jack; sometimes the glow will last a few hours, sometimes even a day or two.

"You know," said Jack, as if Netta knew, "the look of amazement on a girl's face . . ."

Well, that same incandescence had suffused Jack's father when he thought his wife had died, and it continued to shine until a taxi deposited dotty Vera with her cheerful announcement that she had certainly brought off a successful April Fool. After Jack's father died she became violent. "Getting away from her was a form of violence in me," Jack said. "But I did it." That was why he was secretive; that was why he was independent. He had never wanted any woman to get her hands on his life.

Netta heard this out calmly. Where his own feelings were concerned she thought he was making them up as he went along. The garden smelled coolly of jasmine and mimosa. She wondered who his new girl was, and if he was likely to blurt out a name. But all he had been working up to was that his mother – mad, spoiled, devilish, whatever she was – would need to live with Jack and Netta, unless Netta agreed to giving her an income. An income would let her remain where she was – at the moment, in a Rudolf Steiner community in Switzerland, devoted to medieval gardening and to getting the best out of Goethe. Netta's father's training prevented even the thought of spending the money in such a manner.

"You won't regret all you've told me, will you?" she asked. She saw that the new situation would be her burden, her chain, her mean little joke sometimes. Jack scarcely hesitated before saying that where Netta mattered he could never regret anything. But what really interested him now was his mother.

"Lifts give her claustrophobia," he said. "She mustn't be higher than the second floor." He sounded like a man bringing a legal concubine into his household, scrupulously anxious to give all his women equal rights. "And I hope she will make friends," he said. "It won't be easy, at her age. One can't live without them." He probably meant that he had none. Netta had been raised not to expect to have friends: you could not run a hotel and have scores of personal ties. She expected people to be polite and punctual and to mean what they said, and that was the end of it. Jack gave his friendship easily, but he expected considerable diversion in return.

Netta said drily, "If she plays bridge, she can play with Mrs Blackley." This was the wife of the doctor who had first said "Moslem wife". He had come down here to the Riviera for his wife's health; the two belonged to a subcolony of flat-dwelling expatriates. His medical practice was limited to hypochondriacs and rheumatic patients. He had time on his hands: Netta often saw him in the hotel reading room, standing, leafing – he took pleasure in handling books. Netta, no reader, did not like touching a book unless it was new. The doctor had a trick of speech Jack loved to imitate: he would break up his words with an extra syllable, some words only, and at that not every time. "It is all a matter of stu-hyle," he said, for "style", or, Jack's favourite, "Oh, well, in the end it all comes down to su-hex." "Uh-hebb and flo-ho of hormones" was the way he once described the behaviour of saints – Netta had looked twice at him over that. He was a firm agnostic and the first person from whom Netta heard there existed a magical Dr Freud. When Netta's father had died of pneumonia, the doctor's "I'm su-horry, Netta" had been so heartfelt she could not have wished it said another way.

His wife, Georgina, could lower her blood pressure or stop her heartbeat nearly at will. Netta sometimes wondered why Dr Black-ley had brought her to a soft climate rather than to the man at Vienna he so admired. Georgina was well enough to play fierce bridge, with Jack and anyone good enough. Her husband usually came to fetch her at the end of the afternoon when the players stopped for tea. Once, because he was obliged to return at once to a patient who needed him, she said, "Can't you be competent about anything?" Netta thought she understood, then, his resigned repeti-tion of "It's all su-hex." "Oh, don't explain. You bore me," said his wife, turning her back.

Netta followed him out to his car. She wore an India shawl that had been her mother's. The wind blew her hair; she had to hold it back. She said, "Why don't you kill her?"

"I am not a desperate person," he said. He looked at Netta, she looking up at him because she had to look up to nearly everyone except children, and he said, "I've wondered why we haven't been to bed."

"Who?" said Netta. "You and your wife? Oh. You mean me." She was not offended, she just gave the shawl a brusque tug and said, "Not a hope. Never with a guest," though of course that was not the reason.

"You might have to, if the guest were a maharaja," he said, to make it all harmless. "I am told it is pu-hart of the courtesy they expect."

"We don't get their trade," said Netta. This had not stopped her liking the doctor. She pitied him, rather, because of his wife, and because he wasn't Jack and could not have Netta.

"I do love you," said the doctor, deciding finally to sit down in his car. "Ee-nee-ormously." She watched him drive away as if she loved him too, and might never see him again. It never crossed her mind to mention any of this conversation to Jack.

That very spring, perhaps because of the doctor's words, the hotel did get some maharaja trade – three little sisters with ebony curls, men's eyebrows, large heads, and delicate hands and feet. They had four rooms, one for their governess. A chauffeur on permanent call lodged elsewhere. The governess, who was Dutch, had a perfect triangle of a nose and said "whom" for "who", pronouncing it "whum". The girls were to learn French, tennis, and swimming. The chauffeur arrived with a hairdresser, who cut their long hair; it lay on the governess's carpet, enough to fill a large pillow. Their toe- and fingernails were filed to points and looked like kitten's teeth. They came smiling down the marble staircase carrying new tennis rackets, wearing blue linen skirts and navy blazers. Mrs Blackley glanced up from the bridge game as they went by the cardroom. She had been one of those opposed to their having lessons at the English Lawn Tennis Club, for reasons that were, to her, perfectly evident.

She said, loudly, "They'll have to be in white."

"End whay, pray?" cried the governess, pointing her triangle nose.

"They can't go on the courts except in white. It is a private club. Entirely white."

"Whum do they all think they are?" the governess asked, prepared to stalk on. But the girls, with their newly cropped heads, and their vulnerable necks showing, caught the drift and refused to go.

"Whom indeed," said Georgina Blackley, fiddling with her bridge hand and looking happy.

"My wife's seamstress could run up white frocks for them in a minute," said Jack. Perhaps he did not dislike children all that much.

"Whom could," muttered Georgina.

But it turned out that the governess was not allowed to choose their clothes, and so Jack gave the children lessons at the hotel. For six weeks they trotted around the courts looking angelic in blue, or hopelessly foreign, depending upon who saw them. Of course they fell in love with Jack, offering him a passionate loyalty they had nowhere else to place. Netta watched the transfer of this gentle, anxious gift. After they departed, Jack was bad-tempered for several evenings and then never spoke of them again; they, needless to say, had been dragged from him weeping.

When this happened the Rosses had been married nearly five years. Being childless but still very loving, they had trouble deciding which of the two would be the child. Netta overheard "He's a darling, but she's a sergeant major and no mistake. And so *mean*." She also heard "He's a lazy bastard. He bullies her. She's a fool." She searched her heart again about children. Was it Jack or had it been Netta who had first said no? The only child she had ever admired was Jack, and not as a child but as a fighter, defying her. She and Jack were not the sort to have animal children, and Jack's dotty mother would probably soon be child enough for any couple to handle. Jack still seemed to adopt, in a tribal sense of his, half the women who fell in love with him. The only woman who resisted adoption was Netta – still burned out, still ardent, in a manner of speaking still fourteen. His mother had turned up meanwhile, getting down from a train wearing a sly air of enjoying her own jokes, just as she must have looked on the day of the April Fool. At first she was no great trouble, though she did complain about an ulcerated leg. After years of pretending, she at last had something real. Netta's policy of silence made Jack's mother confident. She began to make a mockery of his music: "All that money gone for nothing!" Or else, "The amount we wasted on schools! The hours he's thrown away with his nose in a book. All that reading – if at least it had got him somewhere." Netta noticed that he spent more time playing bridge and chatting to cronies in the bar now. She thought hard, and decided not to make it her business. His mother had once been pretty; perhaps he still saw her that way. She came of a ramshackle family with a usable past; she spoke of the Ashers and the Rosses as if she had known them when they were tinkers. English residents who had a low but solid barrier with Jack and Netta were fences-down with his mad mother: they seemed to take her at her own word when it was about herself. She began then to behave like a superior sort of guest, inviting large parties to her table for meals, ordering special wines and dishes at inconvenient hours, standing endless rounds of drinks in the bar.

Netta told herself, Jack wants it this way. It is his home too. She began to live a life apart, leaving Jack to his mother. She sat wearing her own mother's shawl, hunched over a new, modern adding machine, punching out accounts. "Funny couple," she heard now. She frowned, smiling in her mind; none of these people knew what bound them, or how tied they were. She had the habit of dodging out of her mother-in-law's parties by saying, "I've got such an awful lot to do." It made them laugh, because they thought this was Netta's term for slave-driving the servants. They thought the staff did the work, and that Netta counted the profits and was too busy with bookkeeping to keep an eye on Jack – who now, at twenty-six, was as attractive as he ever would be.

A woman named Iris Cordier was one of Jack's mother's new friends. Tall, loud, in winter dully pale, she reminded Netta of a blonde penguin. Her voice moved between a squeak and a moo, and was a mark of the distinguished literary family to which her father belonged. Her mother, a Frenchwoman, had been in and out of nursing homes for years. The Cordiers haunted the Riviera with Iris looking after her parents and watching their diets. Now she lived in a flat somewhere in Roquebrune with the survivor of the pair – the mother, Netta believed. Iris paused and glanced in the business room where Mr Asher had signed the hundred-year lease. She was on her way to lunch – Jack's mother's guest, of course.

"I say, aren't you Miss Asher?"

"I was." Iris, like Dr Blackley, was probably younger than she looked. Out of her own childhood Netta recalled a desperate adolescent Iris with middle-aged parents clamped like handcuffs on her life. "How is your mother?" Netta had been about to say "How is Mrs Cordier?" but it sounded servile.

"I didn't know you knew her."

"I remember her well. Your father too. He was a nice person."

"And still is," said Iris, sharply. "He lives with me, and he always will. French daughters don't abandon their parents." No one had ever sounded more English to Netta. "And your father and mother?"

"Both dead now. I'm married to Jack Ross."

"Nobody told me," said Iris, in a way that made Netta think, Good Lord, Iris too? Jack could not possibly seem like a patriarchal figure where she was concerned; perhaps this time the game was reversed and Iris played at being tribal and maternal. The idea of Jack, or of any man, flinging himself on that iron bosom made Netta smile. As if startled, Iris covered her mouth. She seemed to be frightened of smiling back.

Oh, well, and what of it, Iris too, said Netta to herself, suddenly turning back to her accounts. As it happened, Netta was mistaken (as she never would have been with a bill). That day Jack was meeting Iris for the first time.

The upshot of these errors and encounters was an invitation to Roquebrune to visit Iris's father. Jack's mother was ruthlessly excluded, even though Iris probably owed her a return engagement because of the lunch. Netta supposed that Iris had decided one had to get past Netta to reach Jack – an inexactness if ever there was one. Or perhaps it was Netta Iris wanted. In that case the error became a farce. Netta had almost no knowledge of private houses. She looked around at something that did not much interest her, for she hated to leave her own home, and saw Iris's father, apparently too old and shaky to get out of his armchair. He smiled and he nodded, meanwhile stroking an ageing cat. He said to Netta, "You resemble your mother. A sweet woman. Obliging and quiet. I used to tell her that I longed to live in her hotel and be looked after."

Not by me, thought Netta.

Iris's amber bracelets rattled as she pushed and pulled everyone through introductions. Jack and Netta had been asked to meet a young American Netta had often seen in her own bar, and a couple named Sandy and Sandra Braunsweg, who turned out to be Anglo-Swiss and twins. Iris's long arms were around them as she cried to Netta, "Don't you know these babies?" They were, like the Rosses, somewhere in their twenties. Jack looked on, blue-eyed, interested, smiling at everything new. Netta supposed that she was now seeing some of the rather hard-up snobbish – snobbish what? "Intelligumhen-sia," she imagined Dr Blackley supplying. Having arrived at a word, Netta was ready to go home; but they had only just arrived. The American turned to Netta. He looked bored, and astonished by it. He needs the word for "bored", she decided. Then he can go home, too. The Riviera was no place for Americans. They could not sit all day waiting for mail and the daily papers and for the clock to show a respectable drinking time. They made the best of things when they were caught with a house they'd been rash enough to rent unseen. Netta often had them then *en pension* for meals: a hotel dining room was one way of meeting people. They paid a fee to use the tennis courts, and they liked the bar. Netta would notice then how Jack picked up any accent within hearing.

Jack was now being attentive to the old man, Iris's father. Though this was none of Mr Cordier's business, Jack said, "My wife and I are first cousins, as well as second cousins twice over."

"You don't look it."

Everyone began to speak at once, and it was a minute or two before Netta heard Jack again. This time he said, "We are from a family of great . . ." It was lost. What now? Great innkeepers? Worriers? Skinflints? Whatever it was, old Mr Cordier kept nodding to show he approved.

"We don't see nearly enough of young men like you," he said.

"True!" said Iris loudly. "We live in a dreary world of ill women down here." Netta thought this hard on the American, on Mr Cordier, and on the male Braunsweg twin, but none of them looked offended. "I've got no time for women," said Iris. She slapped down a glass of whisky so that it splashed, and rapped on a table with her knuckles. "Shall I tell you why? Because women don't tick over. They just simply don't tick over." No one disputed this. Iris went on: women were underinformed. One could have virile conversations only with men. Women were attached to the past through fear, whereas men had a fearless sense of history. "Men tick," she said, glaring at Jack.

"I am not attached to a past," said Netta, slowly. "The past holds no attractions." She was not used to general conversation. She thought that every word called for consideration and for an answer. "Nothing could be worse than the way we children were dressed. And our mothers – the hard waves of their hair, the white lips. I think of those pale profiles and I wonder if those women were ever young."

Poor Netta, who saw herself as profoundly English, spread consternation by being suddenly foreign and gassy. She talked the English of expatriate children, as if reading aloud. The twins looked shocked. But she had appealed to the American. He sat beside her on a scuffed velvet sofa. He was so large that she slid an inch or so in his direction when he sat down. He was Sandra Braunsweg's special friend: they had been in London together. He was trying to write.

"What do you mean?" said Netta. "Write what?"

"Well – a novel, to start," he said. His father had staked him to one year, then another. He mentioned all that Sandra had borne with, how she had actually kicked and punched him to keep him from being too American. He had embarrassed her to death in London by asking a waitress, "Miss, where's the toilet?"

Netta said, "Didn't you mind being corrected?"

"Oh, no. It was just friendly."

Jack meanwhile was listening to Sandra telling about her English forebears and her English education. "I had many years of undeniably excellent schooling," she said. "Mitten Todd."

"What's that?" said Jack.

"It's near Bristol. I met excellent girls from Italy, Spain. I took *him* there to visit," she said, generously including the American. "I said, 'Get a yellow necktie.' He went straight out and bought one. I wore a little Schiaparelli. Bought in Geneva but still a real . . . A yellow jacket over a grey . . . Well, we arrived at my excellent old school, and even though the day was drizzly I said, 'Put the top of the car back.' He did so at once, and then he understood. The interior of the car harmonized perfectly with the yellow and grey." The twins were orphaned. Iris was like a mother.

"When Mummy died we didn't know where to put all the Chippendale," said Sandra. "Iris took a lot of it."

Netta thought, She is so silly. How can he respond? The girl's dimples and freckles and soft little hands were nothing Netta could have ever described: she had never in her life thought a word like "pretty". People were beautiful or they were not. Her happiness had always been great enough to allow for despair. She knew that some people thought Jack was happy and she was not.

"And what made you marry your young cousin?" the old man boomed at Netta. Perhaps his background allowed him to ask impertinent questions; he must have been doing so nearly forever. He stroked his cat; he was confident. He was spokesman for a roomful of wondering people.

"Jack was a moody child and I promised his mother I would look after him," said Netta. In her hopelessly un-English way she believed she had said something funny.

At eleven o'clock the hotel car expected to fetch the Rosses was nowhere. They trudged home by moonlight. For the last hour of the evening Jack had been skewered on virile conversations, first with Iris, then with Sandra, to whom Netta had already given "Chippendale" as a private name. It proved that Iris was right about concentrating on men and their ticking – Jack even thought Sandra rather pretty.

"Prettier than me?" said Netta, without the faintest idea what she meant, but aware she had said something stupid.

"Not so attractive," said Jack. His slight limp returned straight out of childhood. *She* had caused his accident.

"But she's not always clear," said Netta. "Mitten Todd, for example."

"Who're you talking about?"

"Who are *you*?"

"Iris, of course."

As if they had suddenly quarrelled they fell silent. In silence they entered their room and prepared for bed. Jack poured a whisky, walked on the clothes he had dropped, carried his drink to the bathroom. Through the half-shut door he called suddenly, "Why did you say that asinine thing about promising to look after me?"

"It seemed so unlikely, I thought they'd laugh." She had a glimpse of herself in the mirrors picking up his shed clothes.

He said, "Well, is it true?"

She was quiet for such a long time that he came to see if she was still in the room. She said, "No, your mother never said that or anything like it."

"We shouldn't have gone to Roquebrune," said Jack. "I think those bloody people are going to be a nuisance. Iris wants her father to stay here, with the cat, while she goes to England for a month. How do we get out of that?"

"By saying no."

"I'm rotten at no."

"I told you not to be too pally with women," she said, as a joke again, but jokes were her way of having floods of tears.

Before this had a chance to heal, Iris's father moved in, bringing his cat in a basket. He looked at his room and said, "Medium large." He looked at his bed and said, "Reasonably long." He was, in short, daft about measurements. When he took books out of the reading room, he was apt to return them with "This volume contains about 70,000 words" written inside the back cover.

Netta had not wanted Iris's father, but Jack had said yes to it. She had not wanted the sick cat, but Jack had said yes to that too. The old man, who was lost without Iris, lived for his meals. He would appear at the shut doors of the dining room an hour too early, waiting for the menu to be typed and posted. In a voice that matched Iris's for carrying power, he read aloud, alone: "Consommé. Good Lord, again? Is there a choice between the fish and the cutlet? I can't possibly eat all of that. A bit of salad and a boiled egg. That's all I could possibly want." That was rubbish, because Mr Cordier ate the menu and more, and if there were two puddings, or a pudding and ice cream, he ate both and asked for pastry, fruit, and cheese to follow. One day, after Dr Blackley had attended him for faintness, Netta passed a message on to Iris, who had been back from England for a fortnight now but seemed in no hurry to take her father away.

"Keith Blackley thinks your father should go on a diet."

"He can't," said Iris. "Our other doctor says dieting causes cancer."

"You can't have heard that properly," Netta said.

"It is like those silly people who smoke to keep their figures," said Iris. "Dieting."

"Blackley hasn't said he should smoke, just that he should eat less of everything."

"My father has never smoked in his life," Iris cried. "As for his diet, I weighed his food out for years. He's not here forever. I'll take him back as soon as he's had enough of hotels."

He stayed for a long time, and the cat did too, and a nuisance they both were to the servants. When the cat was too ailing to walk, the old man carried it to a path behind the tennis courts and put it down on the gravel to die. Netta came out with the old man's tea on a tray (not done for everyone, but having him out of the way was a relief) and she saw the cat lying on its side, eyes wide, as if profoundly thinking. She saw unlicked dirt on its coat and ants exploring its paws. The old man sat in a garden chair, wearing a panama hat, his hands clasped on a stick. He called, "Oh, Netta, take her away. I am too old to watch anything die. I know what she'll do," he said, indifferently, his voice falling as she came near. "Oh, I know that. Turn on her back and give a shriek. I've heard it often."

Netta disburdened her tray on to a garden table and pulled the tray cloth under the cat. She was angered at the haste and indecency of the ants. "It would be polite to leave her," she said. "She doesn't want to be watched."

"I always sit here," said the old man.

Jack, making for the courts with Chippendale, looked as if the sight of the two conversing amused him. Then he understood and scooped up the cat and tray cloth and went away with the cat over his shoulder. He laid it in the shade of a Judas tree, and within an hour it was dead. Iris's father said, "I've got no one to talk to here. That's my trouble. That shroud was too small for my poor Polly. Ask my daughter to fetch me."

Jack's mother said that night, "I'm sure you wish that I had a devoted daughter to take me away too." Because of the attention given the cat she seemed to feel she had not been nuisance enough. She had taken to saying, "My leg is dying before I am," and imploring Jack to preserve her leg, should it be amputated, and make certain it was buried with her. She wanted Jack to be close by at nearly any hour now, so that she could lean on him. After sitting for hours at bridge she had trouble climbing two flights of stairs; nothing would induce her to use the lift.

"Nothing ever came of your music," she would say, leaning on him. "Of course, you have a wife to distract your now. I needed a daughter. Every woman does." Netta managed to trap her alone, and forced her to sit while she stood over her. Netta said, "Look Aunt Vera, I forbid you, I absolutely forbid you, do you hear, to make a nurse of Jack, and I shall strangle you with my own hands if you go on saying nothing came of his music. You are not to say it in my hearing or out of it. Is that plain?"

Jack's mother got up to her room without assistance. About an hour later the gardener found her on a soft bed of wallflowers. "An inch to the left and she'd have landed on a rake," he said to Netta.

She was still alive when Netta knelt down. In her fall she had crushed the plants, the yellow minted *giroflées de Nice*. Netta thought that she was now, at last, for the first time, inhaling one of the smells of death. Her aunt's arms and legs were turned and twisted; her skirt was pulled so that her swollen leg showed. It seemed that she had jumped carrying her walking stick – it lay across the path. She often slept in an armchair, afternoons, with one eye slightly open. She opened that eye now and, seeing she had Netta, said, "My son." Netta was thinking, I have never known her. And if I knew her, then it was Jack or myself I could not understand. Netta was afraid of giving orders, and of telling people not to touch her aunt before Dr Blackley could be summoned, because she knew that she had always been mistaken. Now Jack was there, propping his mother up, brushing leaves and earth out of her hair. Her head dropped on his shoulder. Netta thought from the sudden heaviness that her aunt had died, but she sighed and opened that one eye again, saying this time, "Doctor?" Netta left everyone doing the wrong things to her dying – no, her murdered – aunt. She said quite calmly into a telephone, "I'm afraid that my aunt must have jumped or fallen from the second floor."

Jack found a letter on his mother's night table that began, "Why blame Netta? I forgive." At dawn he and Netta sat at a card table with yesterday's cigarettes still not cleaned out of the ashtray, and he did not ask what Netta had said or done that called for for-giveness. They kept pushing the letter back and forth. He would read it and then Netta would. It seemed natural for them to be silent. Jack had sat beside his mother for much of the night. Each of them then went to sleep for an hour, apart, in one of the empty rooms, just as they had done in the old days when their parents were juggling beds and guests and double and single quarters. By the time the doctor returned for his second visit Jack was neatly dressed and seemed wide awake. He sat in the bar drinking black coffee and reading a travel book of Evelyn Waugh's called *Labels*. Netta, who looked far more untidy and underslept, wondered if Jack wished he might leave now, and sail from Monte Carlo on the *Stella Polaris*.

Dr Blackley said, "Well, you are a dim pair. She is not in pu-hain, you know." Netta supposed this was the roundabout way doctors have of announcing death, very like "Her sufferings have ended."

But Jack, looking hard at the doctor, had heard another meaning. "Jumped or fell," said Dr Blackley. "She neither fell nor jumped. She is up there enjoying a damned good thu-hing."

Netta went out and through the lounge and up the marble steps. She sat down in the shaded room on the chair where Jack had spent most of the night. Her aunt did not look like anyone Netta knew, not even like Jack. She stared at the alien face and said, "Aunt Vera, Keith Blackley says there is nothing really the matter. You must have made a mistake. Perhaps you fainted on the path, overcome by the scent of wallflowers. What would you like me to tell Jack?"

Jack's mother turned on her side and slowly, tenderly, raised herself on an elbow. "Well, Netta," she said, "I daresay the fool is right. But as I've been given quite a lot of sleeping stuff, I'd as soon stay here for now."

Netta said, "Are you hungry?"

"I should very much like a ham sandwich on English bread, and about that much gin with a lump of ice."

She began coming down for meals a few days later. They knew she had crept down the stairs and flung her walking stick over the path and let herself fall hard on a bed of wallflowers – had even plucked her skirt up for a bit of accuracy; but she was also someone returned from beyond the limits, from the other side of the wall. Once she said, "It was like diving and suddenly realizing there was no water in the sea." Again, "It is not true that your life rushes before your eyes. You can see the flowers floating up to you. Even a short fall takes a long time."

Everyone was deeply changed by this incident. The effect on the victim herself was that she got religion hard.

"We are all hopeless nonbelievers!" shouted Iris, drinking in the bar one afternoon. "At least, I hope we are. But when I see you, Vera, I feel there might be something in religion. You look positively temperate."

"I am allowed to love God, I hope," said Jack's mother.

Jack never saw or heard his mother anymore. He leaned against the bar, reading. It was his favourite place. Even on the sunniest of afternoons he read by the red-shaded light. Netta was present only because she had supplies to check. Knowing she ought to keep out

of this, she still said, "Religion is more than love. It is supposed to
tell you why you exist and what you are expected to do about it."

"You have no religious feelings at all?" This was the only serious
and almost the only friendly question Iris was ever to ask Netta.

"None," said Netta. "I'm running a business."

"I love God as Jack used to love music," said his mother. "At least
he said he did when we were paying for lessons."

"Adam and Eve had God," said Netta. "They had nobody *but*
God. A fat lot of good that did them." This was as far as their
dialectic went. Jack had not moved once except to turn pages. He
read steadily but cautiously now, as if every author had a design on
him. That was one effect of his mother's incident. The other was that
he gave up bridge and went back to playing the clarinet. Iris hammered out an accompaniment on the upright piano in the old music
room, mostly used for listening to radio broadcasts. She was the
only person Netta had ever heard who could make Mozart sound
like an Irish jig. Presently Iris began to say that it was time Jack gave
a concert. Before this could turn into a crisis Iris changed her mind
and said what he wanted was a holiday. Netta thought he needed
something: he seemed to be exhausted by love, friendship, by being
a husband, someone's son, by trying to make a world out of reading
and sense out of life. A visit to England to meet some stimulating
people, said Iris. To help Iris with her tiresome father during the
journey. To visit art galleries and bookshops and go to concerts. To
meet people. To talk.

This was a hot, troubled season, and many persons were planning
journeys – not to meet other people but for fear of a war. The hotel
had emptied out by the end of March. Netta, whose father had
known there would never be another catastrophe, had her workmen
come in, as usual. She could hear the radiators being drained and
got ready for painting as she packed Jack's clothes. They had never
been separated before. They kept telling each other that it was only
for a short holiday – for three or four weeks. She was surprised at
how neat marriage was, at how many years and feelings could be
folded and put under a lid. Once, she went to the window so that he
would not see her tears and think she was trying to blackmail him.
Looking out, she noticed the American, Chippendale's lover, idly
knocking a tennis ball against the garage, as Jack had done in the

early summers of their life; he had come round to the hotel looking for a partner, but that season there were none. She suddenly knew to a certainty that if Jack were to die she would search the crowd of mourners for a man she could live with. She would not return from the funeral alone.

Grief and memory, yes, she said to herself, but what about three o'clock in the morning?

By June nearly everyone Netta knew had vanished, or, like the Blackleys, had started to pack. Netta had new tablecloths made, and ordered new white awnings, and two dozen rose-bushes from the nursery at Cap Ferrat. The American came over every day and followed her from room to room, talking. He had nothing better to do. The Swiss twins were in England. His father, who had been backing his writing career until now, had suddenly changed his mind about it – now, when he needed money to get out of Europe. He had projects for living on his own, but they required a dose of funds. He wanted to open a restaurant on the Riviera where nothing but chicken pie would be served. Or else a vast and expensive café where people would pay to make their own sandwiches. He said that he was seeing the food of the future, but all that Netta could see was customers asking for their money back. He trapped her behind the bar and said he loved her; Netta made other women look like stuffed dolls. He could still remember the shock of meeting her, the attraction, the brilliant answer she had made to Iris about attachments to the past.

Netta let him rave until he asked for a loan. She laughed and wondered if it was for the chicken-pie restaurant. No – he wanted to get on a boat sailing from Cannes. She said, quite cheerfully, "I can't be Venus and Barclays Bank. You have to choose."

He said, "Can't Venus ever turn up with a letter of credit?"

She shook her head. "Not a hope."

But when it was July and Jack hadn't come back, he cornered her again. Money wasn't in it now: his father had not only relented but had virtually ordered him home. He was about twenty-two, she guessed. He could still plead successfully for parental help and for indulgence from women. She said, no more than affectionately, "I'm going to show you a very pretty room."

A few days later Dr Blackley came alone to say goodbye.

"Are you really staying?" he asked.

"I am responsible for the last eighty-one years of this lease," said Netta. "I'm going to be thirty. It's a long tenure. Besides, I've got Jack's mother and she won't leave. Jack has a chance now to visit America. It doesn't sound sensible to me, but she writes encouraging him. She imagines him suddenly very rich and sending for her. I've discovered the limit of what you can feel about people. I've discovered something else," she said abruptly. "It is that sex and love have nothing in common. Only a coincidence, sometimes. You think the coincidence will go on and so you get married. I suppose that is what men are born knowing and women learn by accident."

"I'm su-horry."

"For God's sake, don't be. It's a relief."

She had no feeling of guilt, only of amazement. Jack, as a memory, was in a restricted area – the tennis courts, the cardroom, the bar. She saw him at bridge with Mrs Blackley and pouring drinks for temporary friends. He crossed the lounge jauntily with a cluster of little dark-haired girls wearing blue. In the mirrored bedroom there was only Netta. Her dreams were cleansed of him. The looking glasses still held their blue-and-silver-water shadows, but they lost the habit of giving back the moods and gestures of a Moslem wife.

About five years after this, Netta wrote to Jack. The war had caught him in America, during the voyage his mother had so wanted him to have. His limp had kept him out of the Army. As his mother (now dead) might have put it, all that reading had finally got him somewhere: he had spent the last years putting out a two-pager on aspects of European culture – part of a scrupulous effort Britain was making for the West. That was nearly all Netta knew. A Belgian Red Cross official had arrived, apparently in Jack's name, to see if she was still alive. She sat in her father's business room, wearing a coat and a shawl because there was no way of heating any part of the hotel now, and she tried to get on with the letter she had been writing in her head, on and off, for many years.

"In June 1940, we were evacuated," she started, for the tenth or eleventh time. "I was back by October. Italians had taken over the hotel. They used the mirror behind the bar for target practice. Oddly enough it was not smashed. It is covered with spiderwebs, and the bullet hole is the spider. I had great trouble over Aunt Vera, who disappeared and was found finally in one of the attic rooms.

"The Italians made a pet of her. Took her picture. She enjoyed that. Everyone who became thin had a desire to be photographed, as if knowing they would use this intimidating evidence against those loved ones who had missed being starved. Guilt for life. After an initial period of hardship, during which she often had her picture taken at her request, the Italians brought food and looked after her, more than anyone. She was their mama. We were annexed territory and in time we had the same food as the Italians. The thin pictures of your mother are here on my desk.

"She buried her British passport and would never say where. Perhaps under the Judas tree with Mr Cordier's cat, Polly. She remained just as mad and just as spoiled, and that became dangerous when life stopped being ordinary. She complained about me to the Italians. At that time a complaint was a matter of prison and of death if it was made to the wrong person. Luckily for me, there was also the right person to take the message.

"A couple of years after that, the Germans and certain French took over and the Italians were shut up in another hotel without food or water, and some people risked their well-being to take water to them (for not everyone preferred the new situation, you can believe me). When she was dying I asked her if she had a message for one Italian officer who had made such a pet of her and she said, 'No, why?' She died without a word for anybody. She was buried as 'Rossini', because the Italians had changed people's names. She had said she was French, a Frenchwoman named Ross, and so some peculiar civil status was created for us – the two Mrs Rossinis.

"The records were topsy-turvy; it would have meant going to the Germans and explaining my dead aunt was British, and of course I thought I would not. The death certificate and permission to bury are for a Vera Rossini. I have them here on my desk for you with her pictures.

"You are probably wondering where I have found all this writing paper. The Germans left it behind. When we were being shelled, I took what few books were left in the reading room down to what used to be the wine cellar and read by candlelight. You are probably wondering where the candles came from. A long story. I even have paint for the radiators, large buckets that have never been opened.

"I live in one room, my mother's old sitting room. The business room can be used but the files have gone. When the Italians were here your mother was their mother, but I was not their Moslem wife, although I still had respect for men. One yelled *'Luce, luce'*, because your mother was showing a light. She said, 'Bugger you, you little toad.' He said, 'Granny, I said *"luce"* not *"Duce"*.'

"Not long ago we crept out of our shelled homes, looking like cave dwellers. When you see the hotel again, it will be functioning. I shall have painted the radiators. Long shoots of bramble come in through the cardroom windows. There are drifts of leaves in the old music room and I saw scorpions and heard their rustling like the rustle of death. Everything that could have been looted has gone. Sheets, bedding, mattresses. The neighbours did quite a lot of that. At the risk of their lives. When the Italians were here we had rice and oil. Your mother, who was crazy, used to put out grains to feed the mice.

"When the Germans came we had to live under Vichy law, which meant each region lived on what it could produce. As ours produces nothing, we got quite thin again. Aunt Vera died plump. Do you know what it means when I say she used to complain about me?

"Send me some books. As long as they are in English. I am quite sick of the three other languages in which I've heard so many threats, such boasting, such a lot of lying.

"For a time I thought people would like to know how the Italians left and the Germans came in. It was like this: They came in with the first car moving slowly, flying the French flag. The highest-ranking French official in the region. Not a German. No, just a chap getting his job back. The Belgian Red Cross people were completely uninterested and warned me that no one would ever want to hear.

"I suppose that you already have the fiction of all this. The fiction must be different, oh very different, from Italians sobbing with homesickness in the night. The Germans were not real, they were specially got up for the events of the time. Sat in the white dining room, eating with whatever plates and spoons were not broken or looted, ate soups that were mostly water, were forbidden to complain. Only in retreat did they develop faces and I noticed then that some were terrified and many were old. A radio broadcast from some untouched area advised the local population not to attack them as they retreated, it would make wild animals of them. But they were attacked by some young boys shooting out of a window and eight hostages were taken, including the son of the man who cut the maharaja's daughters' black hair, and they were shot and left along the wall of a café on the more or less Italian side of the border. And the man who owned the café was killed too, but later, by civilians – he had given names to the Gestapo once, or perhaps it was something else. He got on the wrong side of the right side at the wrong time, and he was thrown down the deep gorge between the two frontiers.

"Up in one of the hill villages Germans stayed till no one was alive. I was at that time in the former wine cellar, reading books by candlelight.

"The Belgian Red Cross team found the skeleton of a German deserter in a cave and took back the helmet and skull to Knokke-le-Zoute as souvenirs.

"My war has ended. Our family held together almost from the Napoleonic adventures. It is shattered now. Sentiment does not keep families whole – only mutual pride and mutual money."

This true story sounded so implausible that she decided never to send it. She wrote a sensible letter asking for sugar and rice and for new books; nothing must be older than 1940.

Jack answered at once: there were no new authors (he had been asking people). Sugar was unobtainable, and there were queues for rice. Shoes had been rationed. There were no women's stockings but lisle, and the famous American legs looked terrible. You could not find butter or meat or tinned pineapple. In restaurants, instead of butter you were given miniature golf balls of cream cheese. He supposed that all this must sound like small beer to Netta.

A notice arrived that a CARE package awaited her at the post office. It meant that Jack had added his name and his money to a mailing list. She refused to sign for it; then she changed her mind and discovered it was not from Jack but from the American she had once taken to such a pretty room. Jack did send rice and sugar and delicious coffee but he forgot about books. His letters followed;

sometimes three arrived in a morning. She left them sealed for days. When she sat down to answer, all she could remember were implausible things.

Iris came back. She was the first. She had grown puffy in England – the result of drinking whatever alcohol she could get her hands on and grimly eating her sweets allowance: there would be that much less gin and chocolate for the Germans if ever they landed. She put her now wide bottom on a comfortable armchair – one of the few chairs the first wave of Italians had not burned with cigarettes or idly hacked at with daggers – and said Jack had been living with a woman in America and to spare the gossip had let her be known as his wife. Another Mrs Ross? When Netta discovered it was dimpled Chippendale, she laughed aloud.

"I've seen them," said Iris. "I mean I saw them together. King Charles and a spaniel. Jack wiped his feet on her."

Netta's feelings were of lightness, relief. She would not have to tell Jack about the partisans hanging by the neck in the arches of the Place Masséna at Nice. When Iris had finished talking, Netta said, "What about his music?"

"I don't know."

"How can you not know something so important?"

"Jack had a good chance at things, but he made a mess of everything," said Iris. "My father is still living. Life really is too incredible for some of us."

A dark girl of about twenty turned up soon after. Her costume, a grey dress buttoned to the neck, gave her the appearance of being in uniform. She unzipped a military-looking bag and cried, in an unplaceable accent, "Hallo, hallo, Mrs Ross? A few small gifts for you," and unpacked a bottle of Haig, four tins of corned beef, a jar of honey, and six pairs of American nylon stockings, which Netta had never seen before, and were as good to have under a mattress as gold. Netta looked up at the tall girl.

"Remember? I was the middle sister. With," she said gravely, "the typical middle-sister problems." She scarcely recalled Jack, her beloved. The memory of Netta had grown up with her. "I remember you laughing," she said, without loving that memory. She was a severe, tragic girl. "You were the first adult I ever heard laughing. At night in bed I could hear it from your balcony. You sat smoking with, I suppose, your handsome husband. I used to laugh just to hear you."

She had married an Iranian journalist. He had discovered that political prisoners in the United States were working under lamentable conditions in tin mines. President Truman had sent them there. People from all over the world planned to unite to get them out. The girl said she had been to Germany and to Austria, she had visited camps, they were all alike, and that was already the past, and the future was the prisoners in the tin mines.

Netta said, "In what part of the country are these mines?"

The middle sister looked at her sadly and said, "Is there more than one part?"

For the first time in years, Netta could see Jack clearly. They were silently sharing a joke; he had caught it too. She and the girl lunched in a corner of the battered dining room. The tables were scarred with initials. There were no tablecloths. One of the great-uncle's paintings still hung on a wall. It showed the Quai Laurenti, a country road alongside the sea. Netta, who had no use for the past, was discovering a past she could regret. Out of a dark, gentle silence – silence imposed by the impossibility of telling anything real – she counted the cracks in the walls. When silence failed she heard power saws ripping into olive trees and a lemon grove. With a sense of deliverance she understood that soon there would be nothing left to spoil. Her great-uncle's picture, which ought to have changed out of sympathetic magic, remained faithful. She regretted everything now, even the three anxious little girls in blue linen. Every calamitous season between then and now seemed to descend directly from Georgina Blackley's having said "white" just to keep three children in their place. Clad in buttoned-up grey, the middle sister now picked at corned beef and said she had hated her father, her mother, her sisters, and most of all the Dutch governess.

"Where is she now?" said Netta.

"Dead, I hope." This was from someone who had visited camps. Netta sat listening, her cheek on her hand. Death made death casual: she had always known. Neither the vanquished in their flight nor the victors returning to pick over rubble seemed half so vindictive as a tragic girl who had disliked her governess.

*

Dr Blackley came back looking positively cheerful. In those days men still liked soldiering. It made them feel young, if they needed to feel it, and it got them away from home. War made the break few men could make on their own. The doctor looked years younger, too, and very fit. His wife was not with him. She had survived everything, and the hardships she had undergone had completely restored her to health – which had made it easy for her husband to leave her. Actually, he had never gone back, except to wind up the matter.

"There are things about Georgina I respect and admire," he said, as husbands will say from a distance. His war had been in Malta. He had come here, as soon as he could, to the shelled, gnawed, tarnished coast (as if he had not seen enough at Malta) to ask Netta to divorce Jack and to marry him, or live with him – anything she wanted, on any terms.

But she wanted nothing – at least not from him.

"Well, one can't defeat a memory," he said. "I always thought it was mostly su-hex between the two of you."

"So it was," said Netta. "So far as I remember."

"Everyone noticed. You would vanish at odd hours. Dis-huppear."

"Yes, we did."

"You can't live on memories," he objected. "Though I respect you for being faithful, of course."

"What you are talking about is something of which one has no specific memory," said Netta. "Only of seasons. Places. Rooms. It is as abstract to remember as to read about. That is why it is boring in talk except as a joke, and boring in books except for poetry."

"You never read poetry."

"I do now."

"I guessed that," he said.

"That lack of memory is why people are unfaithful, as it is so curiously called. When I see closed shutters I know there are lovers behind them. That is how the memory works. The rest is just convention and small talk."

"Why lovers? Why not someone sleeping off the wine he had for lunch?"

"No. Lovers."

"A middle-aged man cutting his toenails in the bathtub," he said with unexpected feeling. "Wearing bifocal lenses so that he can see his own feet."

"No, lovers. Always."

He said, "Have you missed him?"

"Missed who?"

"Who the bloody hell are we talking about?"

"The Italian commander billeted here. He was not a guest. He was here by force. I was not breaking a rule. Without him I'd have perished in every way. He may be home with his wife now. Or in that fortress near Turin where he sent other men. Or dead." She looked at the doctor and said, "Well, what would you like me to do? Sit here and cry?"

"I can't imagine you with a brute."

"I never said that."

"Do you miss him still?"

"The absence of Jack was like a cancer, which I am sure has taken root, and of which I am bound to die," said Netta.

"You'll bu-hury us all," he said, as doctors tell the condemned.

"I haven't said I won't." She rose suddenly and straightened her skirt, as she used to do when hotel guests became pally. "Conversation over," it meant.

"Don't be too hard on Jack," he said.

"I am hard on myself," she replied.

After he had gone he sent her a parcel of books, printed on greyish paper, in warped wartime covers. All of the titles were, to Netta, unknown. There was *Fireman Flower* and *The Horse's Mouth* and *Four Quartets* and *The Stuff to Give the Troops* and *Better Than a Kick in the Pants* and *Put Out More Flags*. A note added that the next package would contain Henry Green and Dylan Thomas. She guessed he would not want to be thanked, but she did so anyway. At the end of her letter was "Please remember, if you mind too much, that I said no to you once before." Leaning on the bar, exactly as Jack used to, with a glass of the middle sister's drink at hand, she opened *Better Than a Kick in the Pants* and read, ". . . two Fascists came in, one of them tall and thin and tough looking; the other smaller, with only one arm and an empty sleeve pinned up to his shoulder. Both of them were quite young and wore black shirts."

Oh, thought Netta, I am the only one who knows all this. No one will ever realize how much I know of the truth, the truth, the truth, and she put her head on her hands, her elbows on the scarred bar, and let the first tears of her after-war run down her wrists.

The last to return was the one who should have been first. Jack wrote that he was coming down from the north as far as Nice by bus. It was a common way of travelling and much cheaper than by train. Netta guessed that he was mildly hard up and that he had saved nothing from his war job. The bus came in at six, at the foot of the Place Masséna. There was a deep-blue late-afternoon sky and pale sunlight. She could hear birds from the public gardens nearby. The Place was as she had always seen it, like an elegant drawing room with a blue ceiling. It was nearly empty. Jack looked out on this sunlighted, handsome space and said, "Well, I'll just leave my stuff at the bus office, for the moment" – perhaps noticing that Netta had not invited him anywhere. He placed his ticket on the counter, and she saw that he had not come from far away: he must have been moving south by stages. He carried an aura of London pub life; he had been in London for weeks.

A frowning man hurrying to wind things up so he could have his first drink of the evening said, "The office is closing and we don't keep baggage here."

"People used to be nice," Jack said.

"Bus people?"

"Just people."

She was hit by the sharp change in his accent. As for the way of speaking, which is something else again, he was like the heir to great estates back home after a Grand Tour. Perhaps the estates had run down in his absence. She slipped the frowning man a thousand francs, a new pastel-tinted bill, on which the face of a calm girl glowed like an opal. She said, "We shan't be long."

She set off over the Place, walking diagonally – Jack beside her, of course. He did not ask where they were headed, though he did make her smile by saying, "Did you bring a car?", expecting one of the hotel cars to be parked nearby, perhaps with a driver to open the door; perhaps with cold chicken and wine in a hamper, too. He said, "I'd forgotten about having to tip for every little thing." He did not question his destination, which was no farther than a café at the far end of the square. What she felt at this instant was intense revulsion. She thought, I don't want him, and pushed away some invisible flying thing – a bat or a blown paper. He looked at her with surprise. He must have been wondering if hardship had taught Netta to talk in her mind.

This is it, the freedom he was always offering me, she said to herself, smiling up at the beautiful sky.

They moved slowly along the nearly empty square, pausing only when some worn-out Peugeot or an old bicycle, finding no other target, made a swing in their direction. Safely on the pavement, they walked under the arches where partisans had been hanged. It seemed to Netta the bodies had been taken down only a day or so before. Jack, who knew about this way of dying from hearsay, chose a café table nearly under a poor lad's bound, dangling feet.

"I had a woman next to me on the bus who kept a hedgehog all winter in a basketful of shavings," he said. "He can drink milk out of a wineglass." He hesitated. "I'm sorry about the books you asked for. I was sick of books by then. I was sick of rhetoric and culture and patriotic crap."

"I suppose it is all very different over there," said Netta.

"God, yes."

He seemed to expect her to ask questions, so she said, "What kind of clothes do they wear?"

"They wear quite a lot of plaids and tartans. They eat at peculiar hours. You'll see them eating strawberries and cream just when you're thinking of having a drink."

She said, "Did you visit the tin mines, where Truman sends his political prisoners?"

"*Tin* mines?" said Jack. "No."

"Remember the three little girls from the maharaja trade?"

Neither could quite hear what the other had to say. They were partially deaf to each other.

Netta continued softly, "Now, as I understand it, she first brought an American to London, and then she took an Englishman to America."

He had too much the habit of women, he was playing too close a game, to waste points saying, "Who? What?"

"It was over as fast as it started," he said. "But then the war came and we were stuck. She became a friend," he said. "I'm quite fond of her" – which Netta translated as, "It is a subterranean river that may yet come to light." "You wouldn't know her," he said. "She's very different now. I talked so much about the south, down here, she finally found some land going dirt cheap at Bandol. The mayor arranged for her to have an orchard next to her property, so she won't have neighbours. It hardly cost her anything. He said to her, 'You're very pretty.'"

"No one ever had a bargain in property because of a pretty face," said Netta.

"Wasn't it lucky," said Jack. He could no longer hear himself, let alone Netta. "The war was unsettling, being in America. She minded not being active. Actually she was using the Swiss passport, which made it worse. Her brother was killed over Bremen. She needs security now. In a way it was sorcerer and apprentice between us, and she suddenly grew up. She'll be better off with a roof over her head. She writes a little now. Her poetry isn't bad," he said, as if Netta had challenged its quality.

"Is she at Bandol now, writing poetry?"

"Well, no." He laughed suddenly. "There isn't a roof yet. And, you know, people don't sit writing that way. They just think they're going to."

"Who has replaced you?" said Netta. "Another sorcerer?"

"Oh, *he* . . . he looks like George II in a strong light. Or like Queen Anne. Queen Anne and Lady Mary, somebody called them." Iris, that must have been. Queen Anne and Lady Mary wasn't bad – better than King Charles and his spaniel. She was beginning to enjoy his story. He saw it, and said lightly, "I was too preoccupied with you to manage another life. I couldn't see myself going on and on away from you. I didn't want to grow middle-aged at odds with myself."

But he had lost her; she was enjoying a reverie about Jack now, wearing one of those purple sunburns people acquire at golf. She saw him driving an open car, with large soft freckles on his purple skull. She saw his mistress's dog on the front seat and the dog's ears flying like pennants. The revulsion she felt did not lend distance but brought a dreamy reality closer still. He must be thirty-four now, she said to herself. A terrible age for a man who has never imagined thirty-four.

"Well, perhaps you have made a mess of it," she said, quoting Iris.

"What mess? I'm here. *He* –"

"Queen Anne?"

"Yes, well, actually Gerald is his name; he wears nothing but brown. Brown suit, brown tie, brown shoes. I said, '*He* can't go to Mitten Todd. He won't match.'"

"Harmonize," she said.

"That's it. Harmonize with the –"

"What about Gerald's wife? I'm sure he has one."

"Lucretia."

"No, really?"

"On my honour. When I last saw them they were all together, talking."

Netta was remembering what the middle sister had said about laughter on the balcony. She couldn't look at him. The merest crossing of glances made her start laughing rather wildly into her hands. The hysterical quality of her own laughter caught her in mid-air. What were they talking about? He hitched his chair nearer and dared to take her wrist.

"Tell me, now," he said, as if they were to be two old confidence men getting their stories straight. "What about you? Was there ever . . ." The glaze of laughter had not left his face and voice. She saw that he would make her his business, if she let him. Pulling back, she felt another clasp, through a wall of fog. She groped for this other, invisible hand, but it dissolved. It was a lost, indifferent hand; it no longer recognized her warmth. She understood: He is dead . . . Jack, closed to ghosts, deaf to their voices, was spared this. He would be spared everything, she saw. She envied him his imperviousness, his true unhysterical laughter.

Perhaps that's why I kicked him, she said. I was always jealous. Not of women. Of his short memory, his comfortable imagination. And I am going to be thirty-seven and I have a dark, an accurate, a deadly memory.

He still held her wrist and turned it another way, saying, "Look, there's paint on it."

"Oh, God, where is the waiter?" she cried, as if that were the one important thing. Jack looked his age, exactly. She looked like a burned-out child who had been told a ghost story. Desperately seeking the waiter, she turned to the café behind them and saw the last light of the long afternoon strike the mirror above the bar – a flash in a tunnel; hands juggling with fire. That unexpected play, at a remove, borne indoors, displayed to anyone who could stare without blinking, was a complete story. It was the brightness on the looking glass, the only part of a life, or a love, or a promise, that could never be concealed, changed, or corrupted.

Not a hope, she was trying to tell him. He could read her face now. She reminded herself, if I say it, I am free. I can finish painting the radiators in peace. I can read every book in the world. If I had relied on my memory for guidance, I would never have crept out of the wine cellar. Memory is what ought to prevent you from buying a dog after the first dog dies, but it never does. It should at least keep you from saying yes twice to the same person.

"I've always loved you," he chose to announce – it really was an announcement, in a new voice that stated nothing except facts.

The dark, the ghosts, the candlelight, her tears on the scarred bar – *they* were real. And still, whether she wanted to see it or not, the light of imagination danced all over the square. She did not dare to turn again to the mirror, lest she confuse the two and forget which light was real. A pure white awning on a cross street seemed to her to be of indestructible beauty. The window it sheltered was hollowed with sadness and shadow. She said with the same deep sadness, "I believe you." The wave of revulsion receded, sucked back under another wave – a powerful adolescent craving for something simple, such as true love.

Her face did not show this. It was set in adolescent stubbornness, and this was one of their old, secret meetings when, sullen and hurt, she had to be coaxed into life as Jack wanted it lived. It was he same voyage, at the same rate of speed. The Place seemed to her to be full of invisible traffic – first a whisper of tyres, then a faint, high screeching, then a steady roar. If Jack heard anything, it could be only the blood in the veins and his loud, happy thought. To a practical romantic like Jack, dying to get Netta to bed right away, what she was hearing was only the uh-hebb and flo-ho of hormones, as Dr Blackley said. She caught a look of amazement on his face: *Now* he knew what he had been deprived of. *Now* he remembered. It had been Netta, all along.

Their evening shadows accompanied them over the long square. "I still have a car," she remarked. "But no petrol. There's a train." She did keep on hearing a noise, as of heavy traffic rushing near and tearing away. Her own quiet voice carried across it, saying, "Not a hope." He must have heard that. Why, it was as loud as a shout. He held her arm lightly. He was as buoyant as morning. This *was* his morning – the first light on the mirror, the first cigarette. He pulled her into an archway where no one could see. What could I do, she asked her ghosts, but let my arm be held, my steps be guided?

Later, Jack said that the walk with Netta back across the Place Masséna was the happiest event of his life. Having no reliable counter-event to put in its place, she let the memory stand.

Roget's Thesaurus

KEATH FRASER

I had begun my lists. Mother was always saying, "Peter, why not play outside like other boys?" Her patience with collectors was not prodigal; she didn't understand my obsession. I wanted to polish words like shells, before I let them in. Sometimes I tied on bits of string to watch them sway, bump maybe, like chestnuts. They were treasures these words. I could have eaten them had the idiom not existed, even then, to mean remorse. I loved the way they smelled, their inky scent of coal. Sniffing their penny notebook made me think of fire. (See FERVOUR.)

I fiddled with sounds and significations. No words could exist, even in their thousands, until I made them objects on paper: hairpins, lapis lazuli, teeth, fish hooks, dead bees . . . Later on my study became a museum for the old weapons poets had used. Mother would have died. By then, of course, she had; pleased I had grown up to become what she approved, a doctor.

My young wife died of tumours the size of apples. That I was a practitioner of healing seemed absurd. It smothered me like fog, her dying, her breath in the end so moist. When *his* wife died my uncle took a razor to his throat. (See DESPAIR, see INSANITY, see OMEGA.) He died disbelieving in the antidote of language. Oh, my wife, I have only words to play with.

When I retired it was because of deafness. My passion for travel spent, my sense of duty to the poor used up, I remembered listening for words everywhere. At the Athenaeum, among the dying in Millbank Penitentiary, after concerts, at the Royal Society, during sermons in St Pancras. I started to consolidate. At last I could describe – not prescribe. After fifty years I concluded synonyms were reductive, did not exist, were only analogous words. Unlike Dr Johnson I was no poet. My book would be a philosopher's tool, my soubriquet a thesaurus.

My contribution was to relationships. I created families out of ideas like Space and Matter and Affections. I grouped words in precisely a thousand ways: reacquainted siblings, introduced cousins, befriended black sheep, mediated between enemies. I printed place names and organized a banquet.

London had never seen anything quite like it. Recalcitrant louts, my words, they scented taxonomy and grew inebrious. Mother was well out of it.

She knew me for my polite accomplishments, my papers on optics, comparative anatomy, the poor, zoology, human ageing, mathematics, the deaf and dumb. I was a Renaissance man for I chewed what I bit off. Still, I was no more satisfied with my Bridgewater Treatise on the design of all natural history than with my report for the Water Commission on pollution in the Thames. Only less pessimistic. By the time Asiatic cholera broke out, and people were vomiting and diarrhoetic, my work had been forgotten. Not until I fathered my *Thesaurus* did I dream of prinking. Who knew, perhaps crazy poets would become Roget's trollops, when they discovered his interest in truth not eloquence.

My book appeared the same year as volumes by Dickens, Hawthorne, Melville – fabulators, all of us. (See FICTION.) I too dreamed of the unity of man's existence, and offered a tool for attacking false logic, truisms, jargon, sophism. Though any fretless voice can sing if words are as precise as notes, men in power often sound discordant. Music isn't accident, nor memory history. Language (like the violin) so long to learn.

There is no language, I used to say to Mother, like our own. Look how nations that we oppress trust it. It's the bridge we use to bring back silks and spices, tobacco leaves and cinnamon. Yet all one reviewer wrote of my work was it "made eloquence too easy for the lazy and ignorant". Eloquence I have always distrusted. Maybe this is why my *Thesaurus* has gone through twenty-eight editions.

Men are odd animals. I have never felt as at home around *them* as around their words; without these they're monkeys. (See TRUISM.) The other day I was going through my book and it struck me I have more words for Disapprobation than Approbation. Why is this?

So I spend my last days at West Malvern in my ninety-first year. I no longer walk in parks. I'm pleased I fear death, it makes me feel younger. Death is a poet's idiom to take the mind off complacency. (See SWAN SONG, see CROSSING THE BAR, see THE GREAT ADVENTURE.) I have never thought of death but that it has refurbished me.

The Search for Petula Clark
GLENN GOULD

Across the province of Ontario, which I call home, Queen's High-way No. 17 plies for some 1,100 miles through the pre-Cambrian rock of the Canadian Shield. With its east–west course deflected, where it climbs the north-east shore of Lake Superior, it appears in cartographic profile like one of those prehistoric airborne monsters which Hollywood promoted to star status in such late-late-show spine tinglers of the 1950s as *Blood Beast from Outer Space* or *Beak from the Beyond*, and to which the fuselage design of the XB15 paid the tribute of science borrowing from art.

Though its tail feathers tickle the urban outcroppings of Montreal and its beak pecks at the fertile prairie granary of Manitoba, No. 17 defines for much of its passage across Ontario the northernmost limit of agrarian settlement. It is endowed with habitation, when at all, by fishing villages, mining camps, and timber towns that straddle the highway every fifty miles or so. Among these, names such as Michipicoten and Batchawana advertise the continuing seg-regation of the Canadian Indian; Rossport and Jackfish proclaim the no-nonsense mapmaking of the early white settlers; and Marathon and Terrace Bay – "Gem of the North Shore" – betray the postwar influx of American capital. (Terrace is the Brasilia of Kimberley-Clark's Kleenex–Kotex operation in Ontario.)

The layout of these latter towns, set amidst the most beguiling landscape in central North America, rigorously subscribes to that concept of northern town planning which might be defined as 1984 Prefab and, to my mind, provides the source of so compelling an allegory of the human condition as might well have found its way into the fantasy prose of the late Karel Čapek.

Marathon, a timber town of some twenty-six hundred souls, clings to the banks of a fjord which indents the coast of Lake Superior. Due to a minor miscalculation by one of the company's engineers as to the probable course of the prevailing winds, the place has been overhung since its inception two decades ago with a pulp-and-paper stench that serves to proclaim the monolithic nature of the town's economy even as it discourages any supplemental income from the tourist trade. Real estate values, consequently, are relative to one's distance from the plant. At the boardwalk level, the company has located a barracks for unmarried and/or itinerant workers; up a block, hotel, cinema, chapel, and general store; at the next plateau, an assortment of prefabs; beyond them, at a further elevation, some split-levels for the junior execs; and, finally, with one more gentle ascent and a hard right turn, a block of paternalistic brick mansions which would be right at home among the more exclusive suburbs of Westchester County, New York. Surely the upward mobility of North American society can scarcely ever have been more persuasively demonstrated. "Gives a man something to shoot at," I was assured by one local luminary, whose political persuasion, it developed, was somewhere to the right of Prince Metternich.

A few hundred yards beyond Presidential Row, a bulldozed trail leads to the smog-free top of the fjord. But from this approach, one is held at bay by a padlocked gate bearing a sign from which, in the manner of those reassuring marquees once used to decorate the boarding ramps of Pan American Airways, one learns that "your company has now had one hundred and sixty-five accident-free work days" and that access to the top is prohibited. Up there, on that crest beyond the stench, one can see the two indispensable features of any thriving timber town – its log-shoot breaking bush back through the trackless terrain and an antenna for the low-power relay system of the Canadian Broadcasting Corporation.

These relay outlets, with their radius of three or four miles, serve only the immediate area of each community. As one drives along No. 17, encountering them every hour or so, they constitute the surest evidence that the "outside" (as we northerners like to call it) is with us still. In the outpost communities, the CBC's culture pitch (Boulez is very big in Batchawana) is supplemented by local pro-gramming which, in the imaginative traditions of commercial radio everywhere, leans toward a formula of news on the hour and fifty-five minutes of the pop picks from *Billboard* magazine. This happy ambivalence made my last trip along "17" noteworthy, for at that time, climbing fast on all the charts and featured hard upon the hour by most deejays was an item called "Who Am I?" The singer was Petula Clark; the composer and conductor, Tony Hatch.

I contrived to match my driving speed to the distance between relay outlets, came to hear it most hours and in the end to know it, if not better than the soloist, as least as well, perhaps, as most of the sidemen who were booked for the date. After several hundred miles of this exposure, I checked into the hotel at Marathon and made plans to contemplate Petula.

"Who Am I?" was the fourth in a remarkable series of songs which established the American career of Petula Clark. Released in 1966 and preceded the year before by "Sign of the Times" and "My Love", it laid to rest any uncharitable notion that her success with the ubiquitous "Downtown" of 1964 was a fluke. Moreover, this quartet of hits was designed to convey the idea that, bound as she might be by limitations of timbre and range, she would not accept any corresponding restrictions of theme and sentiment. Each of the four songs details an adjacent plateau of experience – the twenty-three months separating the release dates of "Downtown" and "Who Am I?" being but a modest acceleration of the American teenager's precipitous scramble from the parental nest.

And Pet Clark is in many ways the compleat synthesis of this experience. At thirty-four, with two children, with three distinct careers (in the forties she was the British cinema's anticipation of Annette Funicello, and a decade later a subdued chanteuse in Paris niteries), and with a voice, figure, and (at a respectable distance) face that betray few of the ravages of this experiential sequence, she is pop music's most persuasive embodiments of the Gidget syndrome. Her audience is large, constant, and possessed of an enthusiasm which transcends the generations. One recent visitor from the Netherlands, a gentleman in his sixties who had previously assured me that American pop trends were the corrupting inspiration behind last summer's "Provo" riots in that country, became impaled upon his grandchildren's enthusiasm for "My Love". He said it called to mind the spirit of congregational singing in the Dutch Reform church and asked to hear it once again.

Petula minimizes the emotional metamorphosis implicit in these songs, extracting from the text of each the same message of detachment and sexual circumspection. "Downtown", that intoxicated adolescent daydream –

> Things will be great when you're Downtown,
> Don't wait a minute, for Downtown,
> Everything's waiting for you.

– is as she tells it, but a step from "My Love", that vigorous essay in self-advertisement –

> My love is warmer than the warmest sunshine,
>   Softer than a sigh;
> My love is deeper than the deepest ocean,
>   Wider than the sky.

– and from the reconciliatory concession of "Sign of the Times" –

> I'll never understand the way you treated me,
> But when I hold your hand, I know you couldn't be the way you
>   used to be.

The sequence of events implicit in these songs is sufficiently ambiguous as to allow the audience dipping-in privileges. It's entirely possible to start with "Who Am I?" as I did, and sample "Downtown" later at one's leisure. But a well-ordered career in pop music should be conceived like the dramatis personae of soap opera – dipping in to "The Secret Storm" once every semester should tell you all you need to know about how things are working out for Amy Ames. And similarly, the title, tempo, and tonal range of a performer's hits should observe a certain bibliographic progression. (You thought Frankie had other reasons for "It's been a very good year"?) I'm inclined to suspect that had the sequence of her songs been reversed, Petula's American reputation might not have gained momentum quite so easily. There's an inevitability about that quartet with its relentless on-pressing to the experiences of adulthood or reasonable facsimile thereof. To a teenage audience whose social–sexual awareness dovetailed with their release dates, Petula in her well-turned-out Gidgetry would provide gratifying reassurance of postadolescent survival.

To her more mature public, she's a comfort of another kind. Everything about her onstage, on-mike manner belies the aggressive proclamations of the lyrics. Face, figure, discreet gyrations, but, above all, that voice, fiercely loyal to its one great octave, indulging none but the most circumspect slides and filigree, vibrato so tight and fast as to be nonexistent – none of that "here comes the fermata so hold on" tremolando with which her nibs Georgia Gibbs grated like squeaky chalk upon the exposed nerves of my generation – Petula panders to the wishful thinking of the older set that, style be hanged, modesty prevails. ("Leave the child be, Maw, it's just a touch of prickly heat.")

The gap between the demonstrative attitude of the lyrics and the restraint with which Petula ministers to their delivery is symptomatic of a more fundamental dichotomy. Each of the songs contrived for her by Tony Hatch emphasizes some aspect of that discrepancy between an adolescent's short-term need to rebel and a long-range readiness to conform. In each the score pointedly contradicts that broad streak of self-indulgence which permeates the lyrics. The harmonic attitude is, at all times, hymnal, upright, and relentlessly diatonic.

Well, come to that, almost all pop music today *is* relentlessly diatonic – the Max Reger–Vincent d'Indy chromatic bent which infiltrated big-band arranging in the late thirties and the forties ran its course when Ralph Flanagan got augmented sixths out of his system. But Tony Hatch's diatonicism, relative to Messrs. Lennon, McCartney, et al., is possessed of more than just a difference in kind. For the Beatles, a neotriadic persuasion is (was?) a guerrilla tactic – an instrument of revolution. Annexing such vox populi conventions of English folk harmony as the "Greensleeves"-type nonchalance of old Vaughan Williams's lethargic parallel fifths, the new minstrels turned this lovably bumbling plainspeech into a disparaging mimicry of upper-class inflection. They went about sabotaging the seats of tonal power and piety with the same opportunism that, in *Room at the Top*, motivated Laurence Harvey in his seduction of Sir Donald Wolfit's daughter.

Tonally, the Beatles have as little regard for the niceties of voice leading as Erik Satie for the anguished cross-relation of the German postromantics. Theirs is a happy, cocky, belligerently resourceless brand of harmonic primitivism. Their career has been one long send-up of the equation: sophistication = chromatic extension. The wilful, dominant prolongations and false tonic releases to which they subject us, "Michelle" notwithstanding, in the name of fore- ground elaboration, are merely symptomatic of a cavalier disincli- nation to observe the psychological properties of tonal background. In the Liverpudlian repertoire, the indulgent amateurishness of the musical material, though closely rivalled by the indifference of the performing style, is actually surpassed only by the ineptitude of the studio production method. ("Strawberry Fields" suggests a chance encounter at a mountain wedding between Claudio Monteverdi and a jug band.)

And yet, for a portion of the musical elite, the Beatles are, for this year at least, incomparably "in". After all, if you make use of sitars, white noise, and Cathy Berberian, you must have something, right? Wrong! The real attraction, concealed by virtue of that same adroit self-deception with which coffeehouse intellectuals talked them- selves into Charlie Parker in the forties and Lennie Tristano in the fifties, is the need for the common triad as purgative. After all, the central nervous system can accommodate only so many pages of persistent pianissimos, chord clusters in the marge, and tritones on the vibes. Sooner or later, the diet palls and the patient cries out for a cool draught of C major.

In filling this need, however, the Beatles are entirely incidental. They get the nod at the moment simply through that amateurish- ness which makes the whole phenomenon of *their* C major seem credible as an accident of overtone displacements, and through that avant-garde article of faith that nothing is more despicable than a professional triad tester. The Beatles "in" versus Petula's relative "out" can be diagnosed on the same terms and as part of that same syndrome of status quest that renders Tristano's *G minor Complex* arcane, Poulenc's Organ Concerto in the same key banal, the poetry of the Iglulik Eskimos absorbing, Sibelius's *Tapiola* tedious, and that drives those who feel diffident to buy Bentleys.

But for Tony Hatch, tonality is not a worked-out lode. It is a viable and continuing source of productive energy with priorities that demand and get, from him, attention. "Downtown" is the most affirmatively diatonic exhortation in the key of E major since the unlikely team of Felix Mendelssohn and Harriet Beecher Stowe pooled talents for

Still, still, with Thee, when purple morning breaketh
When the bird waketh and the shadows flee . . .

"Sign of the Times", on the other hand, admits one fairly sophisticated altercation between the tonic with its dominant, and the
minor–mediant relation, similarly embroidered, which twice under-
lines the idea that "Perhaps my lucky star is now beginning to
shine" – the harmonic overlay suggests that there is still sufficient
alto-stratus cloud cover to hamper visibility. "My Love", though,
remains firmly persuaded of its nonmodulating course. Throughout
its two minutes and forty-five seconds, the only extradiatonic event
which disturbs proceedings is the near-inevitable hookup to the
flattened supertonic for a final chorus – two neighbourly dominants
being the pivots involved. Indeed, only one secondary dominant,
which happens to coincide with the line "It shows how wrong we all
can be", compromises the virginal propriety of its responsibly con-
firming Fuxian basses, and none of those stray, flattened leading-
tones-as-root implies a moment's lack of resolution. It's all of a piece,
a proud, secure Methodist tract – preordained, devoid of doubt, admit-
ting of no compromise. And as legions of Petulas gyrate, ensnared
within its righteous euphony, galleries of oval-framed ancestors
peer down upon that deft deflation of the lyrics, and approve.

After the prevailing euphoria of the three songs which preceded
it, "Who Am I?" reads like a document of despair. It catalogues
those symptoms of disenchantment and ennui which inevitably
scuttle a trajectory of emotional escalation such as bound that trilogy
together. The singer's "Downtown'-based confidence in the thera-
peutic effect of "noise", "hurry", and "bright lights" has been shattered. Those alluring asphalt canyons, which promised "an escape
from that life which is making you lonely", have exacted a high price
for their gift of anonymity. For though she has now found a place
where "buildings reach up to the sky", where "traffic thunders on
the busy street", where "pavement slips beneath my feet", she
continues to "walk alone and wonder, Who Am I?"

Clearly, it's a question of identity crisis, vertiginous and claustro-
phobic, induced through the traumatic experience of a metropolitan
environment and, quite possibly, aggravated by sore feet. There is,
of course, the inevitable apotheosis, complete with falsetto C, in

behalf of the restorative therapy of amour. ("But I have something else entirely free, the love of someone close to me, and to question such good fortune, Who Am I?") Yet the prevailing dysphoria of that existentially questing title is not to be routed by so conventional and halfhearted an appendage.

Motivically, "Who Am I?" plays a similar game of reverse "Downtown"-ism. The principal motivic cell unit of that ebullient lied consisted of the interval of a minor third plus a major second, alternating, upon occasion, with a major third followed by a minor second. In "Downtown", the composite of either of these figures, the perfect fourth, became the title motive and the figures themselves were elongated by reiterated notes ("When/you're/a/lone/and/life/is"), shuffled by commas ("downtown, where") ("to help, I") (["Pret]-ty, how can"), and constantly elaborated by the sort of free-diatonic transpositioning which seems entirely consistent with the improvisory fantasies of youth.

In "Who Am I?", however, the same motive, though introduced and occasionally relieved by scale-step passages ("The build-ings-reach-up-to-the-sky"), is most often locked into a diatonic spiral – the notes F-E-C and C-A-G serving to underline "I walk alone and wonder, Who Am I?" Furthermore, the bass line at this moment is engaged with the notes D-G-E and G-E-A, a vertical synchronization of which would imply a harmonic composite of the title motive. Now, admittedly, such Shoenbergian jargon must be charily applied to the carefree creations of the pop scene. At all costs, one must avoid those more formidable precepts of Princetonian Babbittry such as "pitch class", which, since they have not yet forded the Hudson unchallenged, can scarcely be expected to have plied the Atlantic and to have taken Walthamstow studio without a fight. Nevertheless, "Downtown" and "Who Am I?" clearly represent two sides of the same much-minted coin. The infectious enthusiasm of the "Downtown" motive encounters its obverse in the somnambulistic systematization of the "Who Am I?" symbol, a unit perfectly adapted to the tenor of mindless confidence and the tone of slurred articulation with which Petula evokes the interminable mid-morning coffee-hour laments of all the secret sippers of suburbia.

Strictly speaking, the idea of suburbia is meaningless within the context of Marathon. From waterfront to Presidential Row is but five blocks, and beyond that elevation one can pick out only two symbols of urban periphery: the Peninsula Golf and Country Club (NO TRESPASSING – KEEP OFF THE GRASS – BEWARE THE DOG) and, as summer alternative, a small pond cared for by a local service club in lieu of the fjord, which was long ago rendered unfit for swimming. Both are well within range of the transmitter, though its power rapidly declines as one passes beyond the country club toward the highway, and consequently, whether via transistor or foyer PA, one remains exposed to the same single-channel news and music menu.

The problem for citizens of Marathon is that, however tacitly, a preoccupation with escalation and a concern with subsequent decline effectively cancel each other out. And the result, despite the conscientious stratification of the town, is a curiously compromised emotional unilaterality.

There are, of course, other ways to plan a town. Terrace Bay was designed two years after Marathon and apparently profited by the miscalculations which plagued its eastern neighbour. Wind direction (predominantly nor'westerly) was carefully plotted and the plant accordingly located to the north and east of the settlement. The town was designed around a shopping plaza and set on level ground two hundred feet above Lake Superior. The executives were encouraged to locate like den mothers, one to each prefab block. "Coddling the men don't work," Prince Metternich assured me. "Just robs them of incentive!" I resolved to have a look and set off at dusk for The Gem of the North Shore.

No. 17, patrolled at night, affords a remarkable auditory experience. The height of land in northern Ontario, a modest two thousand feet, is attained immediately north of Lake Superior. From beyond that point all water flows toward Hudson's Bay and, ultimately, the Arctic Sea. Traversing that promontory, after sundown, one discovers an astounding clarity of AM reception. All the accents of the continent are spread across the band, and, as one twiddles the dial to reap the diversity of that encounter, the day's auditory impressions with their hypnotic insularity recede, then re-emerge as part of a balanced and resilient perspective . . .

———————

This is London calling in the North American service of the BBC. Here is the news read by — . And it's forty-six chilly degrees in Grand Bend. Say there, Dad, if it's time for that second car you've been promising the little woman, how's about checking the bargains down at — ? Et maintenant, la symphonie numéro quarante-deux, Kochel sept-cent-vingt de Mozart, jouée par — . Okay, chickadees, here's the one you've been asking for and tonight it's specially dedicated to Paul from Doris, to Marianne from a secret admirer, and to all the men in special detention detail out at the Institute from Big Bertha and the gals of HMS Vagabond, riding at anchor just a cosy quarter-mile beyond the international limit – Pet Clark with that question we've all been asking . . . "I walk alone and wonder, Who Am I?"

The Naming of Albert Johnson

RUDY WIEBE

1. *The Eagle River, Yukon*
Wednesday 17 February 1932
Tuesday 16 February

There is arctic silence at last, after the long snarl of rifles. As if all the stubby trees within earshot had finished splitting in the cold. Then the sound of the airplane almost around the river's bend begins to return, turning as tight a spiral as it may up over bank and trees and back down, over the man crumpled on the bedroll, over the frantic staked dog teams, spluttering, down, glancing down off the wind-ridged river. Tail leaping, almost cartwheeling over its desperate roar for skis, immense sound rocketing from that bouncing black dot on the level glare but stopped finally, its prop whirl staggering out motionless just behind the man moving inevitably forward on snowshoes, not looking back, step by step up the river with his rifle ready. Hesitates, lifts one foot, then the other, stops, and moves forward again to the splotch in the vast whiteness before him.

The pack is too huge, and apparently worried by rats with very long, fine teeth. Behind it a twisted body. Unbelievably small. One outflung hand still clutching a rifle, but no motion, nothing, the airplane dead and only the distant sounds of dogs somewhere, of men moving at the banks of the river. The police rifle points down, steadily extending the police arm until it can lever the body, already stiffening, up. A red crater for hip. As if one small part of that incredible toughness had rebelled at last, exploded red out of itself, splattering itself with itself when everything but itself was at last unreachable. But the face is turning up. Rime, and clots of snow ground into whiskers, the fur hat hurled somewhere by bullets perhaps and the whipped cowlick already a mat frozen above half-open eyes showing only white, nostrils flared, the concrete face wiped clean of everything but snarl. Freezing snarl and teeth. As if the long clenched jaws had tightened down beyond some ultimate cog and openly locked their teeth into their own torn lips in one final wordlessly silent scream.

The pilot blunders up, gasping. "By God, we got the son, of a bitch!", stumbles across the back of the snowshoes and recovers beside the policeman. Gagging a little, "My G—" All that sudden colour propped up by the rifle barrel on the otherwise white snow. And the terrible face.

The one necessary bullet, in the spine where its small entry cannot be seen at this moment, and was never felt as six others were, knocked the man face down in the snow. Though that would never loosen his grip on his rifle. The man had been working himself over on his side, not concerned as it seemed for the bullets singing to him from the level drifts in front of him or the trees on either bank. With his left hand he was reaching into his coat pocket to reload his Savage .30-.30, almost warm on the inside of his other bare hand, and he knew as every good hunter must that he had exactly thirty-nine bullets left besides the one hidden under the rifle's butt plate. If they moved in any closer he also had the Winchester .22 with sixty-four bullets, and closer still there will be the sawed-off shotgun, though he had only a few shells left, he could not now be certain exactly how many. He had stuffed snow tight into the hole where one or perhaps two shells had exploded in his opposite hip pocket. A man could lose his blood in a minute from a hole that size but the snow was still white and icy the instant he had to glance at it, packing it in. If they had got him there before forcing him down behind his pack in the middle of the river, he could not have moved enough to pull out the pack straps, leave alone get behind it for protection. Bullets twitch it, whine about his tea tin like his axe handle snapping once at his legs as he ran from the eastern river bank too steep to clamber up, a very bad mistake to have to discover after spending several minutes and a hundred yards of strength running his snowshoes towards it. Not a single rock, steep and bare like polished planks. But he had gained a little on them, he saw that as he curved without stopping toward the centre of the river and the line of trees beyond it. That bank is easily climbed, he knows because he climbed it that morning, but all the dogs and men so suddenly around the hairpin turn surprised him toward the nearest bank, and he sees the teams spreading to outflank him, three toward the low west bank. And two of them bending over the one army radioman he got.

Instantly the man knew it was the river that had betrayed him. He had outlegged their dogs and lost the plane time and again on glare-ice and in fog and brush and between the endless trails of caribou herds, but the sluggish loops of this river doubling back on itself have betrayed him. It is his own best move, forward and then back, circle forward and further back, backwards, so the ones following his separate tracks will suddenly confront each other in cursing bewilderment. But this river, it cannot be named the Porcupine, has out-doubled him. For the dogs leaping toward him around the bend, the roaring radioman heaving at his sled, scrabbling for his rifle, this is clearly what he saw when he climbed the tree on the far bank; one of the teams he saw then across a wide tongue of land already ahead of him, as it seemed, and he started back to get further behind them before he followed and picked them off singly in whatever tracks of his they thought they were following. These dogs and this driver rounding to face him as he walks so carefully backwards in his snowshoes on the curve of his own tracks.

Whatever this river is spiralling back into the Yukon hills, his rifle will not betray him. Words are bellowing out of the racket of teams hurtling around the bend. His rifle speaks easily, wordlessly to the army radioman kneeling, sharpshooter position, left elbow propped on left knee. The sights glided together certain and deadly, and long before the sound had returned that one kneeling was already flung back clean as frozen wood bursting at his axe.

He has not eaten, he believes it must be two days, and the rabbit tracks are so old they give no hope for his snares. The squirrel burrow may be better. He is scraping curls from tiny spruce twigs, watching them tighten against the lard pail, watching the flames as it seems there licking the tin blacker with their gold tongues. The fire lives with him, and he will soon examine the tinfoil of matches in his pocket, and the tinfoil bundle in his pack and also the other two paper-wrapped packages. That must be done daily, if possible. The pack, unopened, with the .22 laced to its side is between his left shoulder and the snow hollow; the moose hides spread under and behind him; the snowshoes stuck erect into the snow on the right, the long axe lying there and the rifle also, in its cloth cover but on the moose-hide pouch. He has already worked carefully on his feet, kneading as much of the frost out of one and then the other as he can before the fire though two toes on the left are black and the heel of the right is rubbed raw. Bad lacing when he walked backwards, and too numb for him to notice. The one toe can only be kept another day, perhaps, but he has only a gun-oily rag for his heel. Gun oil? Spruce gum? Wait. His feet are wrapped and ready to move instantly and he sits watching warmth curl around the pail. Leans his face down into it. Then he puts the knife away in his clothes and pulls out a tiny paper. His hard fingers unfold it carefully, he studies the crystals a moment, and then as the flames tighten the blackened spirals of spruce he pours that into the steaming pail. He studies the paper, the brownness of it; the suggestion of a word beginning, or perhaps ending, that shines through its substance. He lowers it steadily then until it darkens, smiling as a spot of deep brown breaks through the possible name and curls back a black empty circle towards his fingers. He lets it go, feeling warmth like a massage in its final flare and dying. There is nothing left but a smaller fold of pepper and a bag of salt so when he drinks it is very slowly, letting each mouthful move for every part of his tongue to hold a moment this last faint sweetness.

He sits in the small yellow globe created by fire. Drinking. The wind breathes through the small spruce, his body rests motionlessly; knowing that dug into the snow with drifts and spruce tips above him they could see his smokeless fire only if they flew directly over him. And the plane cannot fly at night. They are somewhere very close now, and their plane less than a few minutes behind. It had flown straight in an hour, again and again, all he had overlaid with tangled tracks in five weeks, but the silent land is what it is. He is now resting motionlessly. And waiting.

And the whisky-jacks are suddenly there. He had not known them before to come after dark, but grey and white tipped with black they fluffed themselves at the grey edge of his light, watching, and then one hopped two hops. Sideways. The first living thing he had seen since the caribou. But he reaches for the bits of babiche he had cut and rubbed in salt, laid ready on the cloth of the riflebutt. He throws, the draggle-tail is gone but the other watches, head cocked,

then jumps so easily the long space his stiff throw had managed,
and the bit is gone. He does not move his body, tosses another bit,
and another, closer, closer and then draggle-tail is there scrabbling
for the bit, and he twitches the white string lying beside the bits of
babiche left by the rifle, sees the bigger piece tug from the snow and
draggle-tail leap to it. Gulp. He tugs, feels the slight weight as the
thread lifts from the snow in the firelight, and now the other is gone
while draggle-tail comes toward him inevitably, string pulling the
beak soundlessly agape, wings desperate in snow, dragged between
rifle and fire into the waiting claw of his hand. He felt the bird's
blood beat against his palm, the legs and tail and wings thud an
instant, shuddering and then limp between his relentless fingers.

Wings. Noiselessly he felt the beautiful muscles shift, slip over
bones delicate as twigs. He could lope circles around any dogs they
set on his trail but that beast labelled in letters combing the clouds,
staring everywhere until its roar suddenly blundered up out of a
canyon or over a ridge, laying its relentless shadow like words on
the world: he would have dragged every tree in the Yukon together
to build a fire and boil that. Steel pipes and canvas and wires and
name, that stinking noise. In the silence under the spruce he skims
the tiny fat bubbles from the darkening soup; watches them
coagulate yellow on the shavings. Better than gun oil, or gum. He
began to unwrap his feet again but listening, always listening. The
delicate furrow of the bird pointed toward him in the snow.

2. *The Richardson Mountains*, NWT
Tuesday 9 February 1932
Saturday 30 January

Though it means moving two and three miles to their one, the best
trail to confuse them in the foothill ravines was a spiral zigzag. West
of the mountains he has not seen them; he has outrun them so far in
crossing the Richardson Mountains during the blizzard that when
he reaches a river he thought it must be the Porcupine because he
seems at last to be inside something that is completely alone. But the
creeks draining east lay in seemingly parallel but eventually converging canyons with tundra plateaux glazed under wind between
them, and when he paused on one leg of his zag he sometimes saw

them, across one plateau or in a canyon, labouring with their dogs and sleds as it seems ahead of him. In the white scream of the mountain pass where no human being has ever ventured in winter he does not dare pause to sleep for two days and the long night between them, one toe and perhaps another frozen beyond saving and parts of his face dead, but in the east he had seen the trackers up close, once been above them and watched them coming along his trails toward each other unawares out of two converging canyons with their sleds and drivers trailing, and suddenly round the cliff to face each other in cursing amazement. He was far enough not to hear their words as they heated water for tea, wasting daylight minutes, beating their hands to keep warm.

The police drive the dog teams now, and the Indians sometimes; the ones who can track him on the glazed snow, through zags and bends, always wary of ambush, are the two army radiomen. One of the sleds is loaded with batteries when it should be food, but they sniff silently along his tracks, loping giant circles ahead of the heaving dogs and swinging arms like semaphores when they find a trail leading as it seems directly back toward the sleds they have just left. He would not have thought them so relentless at unravelling his trails, these two who every morning tried to raise the police on their frozen radio, and when he was convinced they would follow him as certainly as Millen and the plane roared up, dropping supplies, it was time to accept the rising blizzard over the mountains and find at last, for certain, the Porcupine River.

It is certainly Millen who brought the plane north just before the blizzard, and it was Millen who saw his smoke and heard him coughing, whistling in that canyon camp hidden in trees under a cliff so steep he has to chop handholds in the frozen rock to get out of there. Without dynamite again, or bombs, they could not dig him out; even in his unending alert his heart jerks at the sound of what was a foot slipping against a frozen tree up the ridge facing him. His rifle is out of its sheath, the shell racking home in the cold like precise steel biting. There is nothing more; an animal? A tree bursting? He crouches motionless, for if they are there they should be all around him, perhaps above on the cliff, and he will not move until he knows. Only the wind worrying spruce and snow, whining wordlessly. There, twenty yards away a shadow moves, Millen

certainly, and his shot snaps as his rifle swings up, as he drops.
Bullets snick from everywhere, their sound booming back and forth
along the canyon. He has only fired once and is down, completely
aware, on the wrong side of his fire and he shoots carefully again to
draw their shots and they come, four harmlessly high and nicely
spaced out: there are two – Millen and another – below him in the
canyon and two a bit higher on the right ridge, one of them that
slipped. Nothing up the canyon or above on the cliff. With that
knowledge he gathered himself and leaped over the fire against the
cliff and one on the ridge made a good shot that cut his jacket and he
could fall as if gut-shot in the hollow or deadfall. Until the fire died,
he was almost comfortable.

In the growing dusk he watches the big Swede, who drove dogs
very well, crawl toward Millen stretched out, face down. He
watches him tie Millen's legs together with the laces of his mukluks
and drag him backwards, plowing a long furrow and leaving the
rifle sunk in the snow. He wastes no shot at their steady firing, and
when they stop there are Millen's words still

You're surrounded. King isn't dead. Will you give

waiting, frozen in the canyon. He lay absolutely motionless behind
the deadfall against the cliff, as if he were dead, knowing they
would have to move finally. He flexed his feet continuously, and his
fingers as he shifted the rifle no more quickly than a clock hand,
moving into the position it would have to be when they charged
him. They almost outwait him; it is really a question between the
coming darkness and his freezing despite his invisible motions, but
before darkness Millen had to move. Two of them were coming and
he shifted his rifle slightly on the log to cover the left one – it must
have been the long cold that made him mistake that for Millen – who
dived out of sight, his shot thundering along the canyon, but Millen
did not drop behind anything. Simply down on one knee, firing.
Once, twice bullets tore the log and then he had his head up with
those eyes staring straight down his sights and he fired two shots so
fast the roar in the canyon sounded as one and Millen stood up, the
whole length over him, whirled in that silent unmistakable way and
crashed face down in the snow. He hears them dragging and chopping trees for a stage cache to keep the body, and in the darkness he

chops handholds up the face of the cliff, step by step as he hoists himself and his pack out of another good shelter. As he has had to leave others.

3. *The Rat River*, NWT
Saturday 10 January 1932
Thursday 31 December 1931
Tuesday 28 July

In his regular round of each loophole he peers down the promontory toward their fires glaring up from behind the river bank. They surround him on three sides, nine of them with no more than forty dogs, which in this cold means they already need more supplies than they can have brought with them. They will be making plans for something, suddenly, beyond bullets against his logs and guns and it will have to come soon. In the long darkness, and he can wait far easier than they. Dynamite. If they have any more to thaw out very carefully after blowing open the roof and stovepipe as darkness settled, a hole hardly big enough for one of them – a Norwegian, they were everywhere with their long noses – to fill it an instant, staring down at him gathering himself from the corner out of roof-sod and pipes and snow: the cabin barely stuck above the drifts but that one was gigantic to lean in like that, staring until he lifted his rifle and the long face vanished an instant before his bullet passed through that space. But the hole was large enough for the cold to slide down along the wall and work itself into his trench, which would be all that saved him when they used the last of their dynamite. He began to feel what they had stalked him with all day: cold tightening steadily as steel around toes, face, around fingers.

In the clearing still nothing stirs. There is only the penumbra of light along the circle of the bank as if they had laid a trenchfire to thaw the entire promontory and were soundlessly burrowing in under him. Their flares were long dead, the sky across the river flickering with orange lights to vanish down into spruce and willows again, like the shadow blotting a notch in the eastern bank and he thrust his rifle through the chink and had almost got a shot away when a projectile arced against the sky and he jerked the gun out, diving, into the trench deep under the wall among the moose hides that could not protect him from the roof and walls tearing apart so loud it seemed most of himself had been blasted to the farthest granules of sweet, silent earth. The sods and foot-thick logs he had built together where the river curled were gone and he would climb out and walk away as he always had, but first he pulled himself up and out between the splinters, still holding the rifle, just in time to see yellow light humpling through the snow toward him and he fired three times so fast it sounded in his ears as though his cabin was continuing to explode. The shadows around the light dance in one spot an instant but come on in a straight black line, lengthening down, faster, and the light cuts straight across his eyes and he gets away the fourth shot and the light tears itself into bits. He might have been lying on his back staring up into night and had the stars explode into existence above him. And whatever darkness is left before him then blunders away, desperately plowing away from him through the snow like the first one who came twice with a voice repeating at his door

I am Constable Alfred King, are you in there?

fist thudding the door the second time with a paper creaking louder than his voice so thin in the cold silence

I have a search warrant now, we have had complaints and if you don't open

and then plowing away in a long desperate scrabble through the sun-shot snow while the three others at the river bank thumped their bullets hopelessly high into the logs but shattering the window again and again until they dragged King and each other head first over the edge while he placed lead carefully over them, snapping willow bits on top of them and still seeing, strangely, the tiny hole that had materialized up into his door when he flexed the trigger, still hearing the grunt that had wormed in through the slivers of the board he had whipsawn himself. Legs and feet wrapped in moose hide lay a moment across his window, level in the snow, jerking as if barely attached to a body knocked over helpless, a face somewhere twisted in gradually developing pain that had first leaned against his door, fist banging while that other one held the dogs at the edge of the clearing, waiting

Hallo? Hallo? This is Constable Alfred King of the Royal Canadian Mounted Police. I want to talk to you. Constable Millen

and they looked into each other's eyes, once, through his tiny window. The eyes peering down into his – could he be seen from out of the blinding sun? – squinted blue from a boy's round face with bulging nose bridged over pale with cold. King, of the Royal Mounted. Like a silly book title, or the funny papers. He didn't look it as much as Spike Millen, main snooper and tracker at Arctic Red River who baked pies and danced, everybody said, better than any man in the north. Let them dance hipped in snow, get themselves dragged away under spruce and dangling traps, asking, laying words on him, naming things

You come across from the Yukon? You got a trapper's licence? The Loucheaux trap the Rat, up towards the Richardson Mountains. You'll need a licence, why not

Words. Dropping out of nothing into advice. Maybe he wanted a kicker to move that new canoe against the Rat River? Loaded down as it is. The Rat drops fast, you have to handline the portage anyway to get past Destruction City where those would-be Klondikers wintered in '98. He looked up at the trader above him on the wedge of gravel. He had expected at least silence. From a trader standing with a bulge of seven hundred dollars in his pocket; in the south a man could feed himself with that for two years. Mouths always full of words, pushing, every mouth falling open and dropping words from nothing into meaning. The trader's eyes shifted finally perhaps to the junction of the rivers behind them, south and west, the united river clicking under the canoe. As he raised his paddle. The new rifle oiled and ready with its butt almost touching his knees as he kneels, ready to pull the canoe around.

4. *Above Fort McPherson*, NWT
Tuesday 7 July 1931

The Porcupine River, as he thought it was then, chuckled between the three logs of his raft. He could hear that below him, under the mosquitoes probing the mesh about his head, and see the gold lengthen up the river like the canoe that would come toward him from the north where the sun just refused to open the spiky horizon. Gilded, hammered out slowly, soundlessly toward him the thick gold. He sat almost without breathing, watching it come like silence. And then imperceptibly the black spired riverbend grew pointed, stretched itself in a thin straight line double-bumped, gradually spreading a straight wedge below the sun through the golden river. When he had gathered that slowly into anger it was already too late to choke his fire; the vee had abruptly bent toward him, the bow man already raised his paddle; hailed. Almost it seemed as if a name had been blundered into the silence, but he did not move in his fury. The river chuckled again.

"... o-o-o-o ..." the point of the wedge almost under him now. And the sound of a name, that was so clear he could almost distinguish it. Perhaps he already knew what it was, had long since lived this in that endlessly enraged chamber of himself, even to the strange Indian accent mounded below him in the canoe bow where the black hump of the stern partner moved them straight toward him out of the fanned ripples, crumpling gold. To the humps of his raft below on the gravel waiting to anchor them.

"What d'ya want."

"You Albert Johnson?"

It could have been the sternman who named him. The sun like hatchet-strokes across slanted eyes, the gaunt noses below him there holding the canoe against the current, their paddles hooked in the logs of his raft. Two Loucheaux half-faces, black and red kneeling in the roiled gold of the river, the words thudding softly in his ears.

You Albert Johnson?

One midnight above the Arctic Circle to hear again the inevitability of name. He has not heard it in four years, it could be to the very day since that Vancouver garden, staring into the evening sun and hearing this quiet sound from these motionless – perhaps they are men kneeling there, perhaps waiting for him to accept again what has now been laid inevitably upon him, the name come to meet him in his journey north, come out of the north around the bend and against the current of the Peel River, as they name that too, to confront him on a river he thought another and aloud where he would have found after all his years, at long last, only nameless silence.

You Albert Johnson?

"Yes," he said finally.

And out of his rage he begins to gather words together. Slowly, every word he can locate, as heavily as he would gather stones on a Saskatchewan field, to hold them for one violent moment against himself between his two hands before he heaves them up and hurls them – but they are gone. The ripples of their passing may have been smoothing out as he stares at where they should have been had they been there. Only the briefly golden river lies before him, whatever its name may be since it must have one, bending back somewhere beyond that land, curling back upon itself in its giant, relentless spirals down to the implacable, and ice-choked, arctic sea.

King of the Raft

DANIEL DAVID MOSES

There was a raft in the river that year, put there, anchored with an anvil, just below a bend, by the one of the fathers who worked away in Buffalo, who could spend only every other weekend, if that, at home. The one of the mothers whose husband worked the land and came in from the fields for every meal muttered as she set the table that the raft was the only way the father who worked in the city was able to pretend he cared about his sons. Her husband, also one of the fathers, who had once when young gone across the border to work and then, unhappy there, returned, could not answer, soaking the dust of soil from his hands.

Most of the sons used that raft that was there just that one summer in the usually slow-moving water during the long evenings after supper, after the days of the fieldwork of haying and then combining were done. A few of them, the ones whose fathers and mothers practised Christianity, also used it in the afternoons on sunny Sundays after the sitting through church and family luncheons. And the one of the sons who had only a father who came and went following the work – that son appeared whenever his rare duties or lonely freedom became too much for him.

The sons would come to the raft in Indian file along a footpath the half mile from the road and change their overalls or jeans for swimsuits among the goldenrod and milkweed on the bank, quickly, to preserve modesty and their blood from the mosquitoes, the only females around. Then one of the sons would run down the clay slope and stumble in with splashing and a cry of shock or joy for the water's current temperature. The other sons would follow, and, by the time they all climbed out on to the raft out in the stream, through laughter would become boys again.

The boys used that raft in the murky green water to catch the sun or their breaths on or to dive from when they tried to touch the mud bottom. One of the younger ones also used to stand looking across the current to the other side, trying to see through that field of corn there, the last bit of land that belonged to the Reserve. Beyond it the highway ran, a border patrolled by a few cars flashing chrome in the sun or headlights through the evening blue like messages from the city. Every one of the boys used the raft several times that summer to get across the river and back, the accomplishment proof of their new masculinity. And once the younger one who spent time looking at that other land, crossed and climbed up the bank there and explored the shadows between the rows of corn, the leaves like dry tongues along his naked arms as he came to the field's far edge where the asphalt of that highway stood empty.

Toward the cool end of the evenings, any boy left out on the raft in the lapping black water would be too far from the shore to hear the conversations. They went on against a background noise of the fire the boys always built against the river's grey mist and mosquito lust, that they sometimes built for roasting corn, hot dogs, marshmallows. The conversations went on along with or over games of chess. Years later, one of the older boys, watching his own son play the game with a friend in silence, wondered if perhaps that was why their conversations that year of the raft about cars, guitars and girls – especially each other's sisters – about school and beer, always ended up in stalemate or check. Most of the boys ended up winning only their own solitariness from the conversations by the river. But the one who had only a father never even learned the rules of play.

One sunny Sunday after church late in the summer, the one who had only a father already sat on the raft in the river as the rest of the boys undressed. He smiled at the boy who had gone across through the corn, who made it into the water first. Then he stood up and the raft made waves as gentle as those in his blue-black hair – I'm the king of the raft, he yelled, challenging the boy who had seen the highway to win that wet wooden square. And a battle was joined, and the day was wet and fair, until the king of the raft, to show his strength to the rest of the boys still on shore, took a hank of the highway boy's straight hair in hand and held the highway boy underwater till the highway boy saw blue fire and almost drowned. The story went around among the mothers and the fathers and soon that son who had only a father found himself unwelcome. Other stories came around, rumours about his getting into fights or failing grades or how his father's latest girlfriend had dyed her Indian hair blond. And the boy who almost had drowned found he both feared the king of the raft and missed the waves in his blue-black hair.

One muggy evening when pale thunderheads growled in from the west, the boy who had almost drowned, who had the farthest to go to get home, left the raft and the rest by the river early. On the dark road he met the king, who had something to say. They hid together with a case of beer in a cool culvert under the road. The king of the raft was going away with his father to live in Buffalo in the United States and thought the boy who had almost drowned could use what was left of this beer the king's father would never miss. The boy who had almost drowned sipped from his bottle of sour beer and heard the rain beginning to hiss at the end of the culvert. He crawled and looked out in time to see the blue fire of lightning hit a tree. In the flash he saw again the waves in the king's blue-black hair, the grin that offered another beer. The boy who had almost drowned felt he was going down again, and, muttering some excuse, ran out into the rain. The king yelled after him that old insult boys use about your mother wanting you home.

The boy who had almost drowned found he could cross through the rain, anchored by his old running shoes to the ground, though the water came down like another river, cold and clear and wide as the horizon. He made it home and stood on the porch, waiting for the other side of the storm, hearing hail hitting the roof and water through the eaves filling up the cistern. Later, out of the storm, he could still hear far off a gurgling in the gully and a quiet roar as the distant river tore between its banks. The storm still growled somewhere beyond the eastern horizon.

The raft was gone the next evening when the boys came to the bank and the current was still too cold and quick to swim in. No one crossed the river for the rest of the summer. The king of the raft never appeared again anywhere. In the fall, a rumour came around about his going to work in the city and in the winter another one claimed he had died. The boy who had crossed through the rain thought about going down even quicker in winter river water. Then a newspaper confirmed the death. In a traffic accident, the rain boy read. None of the boys had even met that impaired driver, that one of the fathers, surviving and charged without a licence. One of the mothers muttered as she set another mother's hair about people not able to care even about their kids. The rain boy let the king of the raft sink into the river, washing him away in his mind and decided he would someday cross over and follow the highway through that land and find the city.

Kill Day on the Government Wharf

AUDREY THOMAS

"I only wish," she said, refilling his coffee mug, "that it was all a little more primitive."

The man, intent on his fried bread and tomato, did not hear or chose to ignore the wistfulness in her voice. Mouth full, he chuckled, and then, swallowing, "All what?"

"All *this*," she said impatiently, gesturing toward the inside of the little cabin. They were sitting by the window, having breakfast. It was nine o'clock on a Sunday morning and the sky outside bulged and sagged with heavy bundles of dirty-looking clouds. He wanted to get back out on the water before it rained.

"I thought you liked it here," he said, challenging her with a smile. She was playing games again.

"I do. I love it. I really don't ever want to go back. But," she said, looking at him over the rim of her mug, "seeing that the old man died only a few months later, don't you think it was rather unkind of Fate to have suggested plumbing and electricity to him? I mean," she added with a smile, "also seeing as how we were going to be the reluctant beneficiaries of all that expense."

"You may be reluctant," he said, wiping his mouth, "I'm not. I think we were damned lucky myself."

She shrugged and stood up to clear the table, rubbing the small of her back unconsciously. She had acquired a slight tan in the ten days she'd been away and he thought how well she looked. There was a sprinkling of pale greeny-coppery freckles across her nose and along her arms. She looked strong and self-reliant and almost pretty as she stood by the window with the stacked plates in her hand. It was not myth, he thought, or a white lie to make them feel better. Women really do look lovely when they're pregnant. Sometimes she would say to him, quite seriously,

"Tom, do you think I'm pretty?" or

"Tom, what would you say about me if you saw me across the room?"

Her questions made him impatient and embarrassed and he usually ended up by returning some smart remark because he was both a shy and a truthful man. He wished she would ask him now, but he did not volunteer his vision. Instead he got up and said,

"Where's Robert?"

"Right on the porch. I can see him. He has a dish full of oysters and clams and a hermit crab in a whelk shell. He's been fascinated by it for two days now. I didn't know," she added, "that barnacles were little creatures. They've got little hand-like things that come out and scoop the water looking for food."

"Yes, I believe those are actually their feet," he said. "My grandfather told me that years ago. They stand on their heads, once they become fixed, and kick the food into their mouths for the rest of their lives. Now *that's* primitive for you." He drew on his pullover again. "How would you feel if I had another little fish-around before it rains? Then I'll take Robert for a walk and let you have some peace."

"Oh he's all right, except sometimes when he wants to crawl all over me. He's actually better here than at home. Everything excites him. He could live here forever as well."

"You must go back soon," he reminded her gently, "whether you like it or not."

"I don't want to. I hate the city. And I like it better here now," she said, "than later on, when all the summer people come."

"You don't get lonely?"

"No, not at all." She was embarrassed to admit it and irritated he had asked. "I walk and sit and look and read my books at night or listen to the radio. And there's Robert of course. He's become afraid of the dark, though," she said thoughtfully. "I wonder why. He wakes me up at night."

"Weren't you?" he challenged. "I was."

She turned, surprised. She had been of course, but she was a very nervous, sickly child.

"Yes." She stood at the sink, soapy hands held out of the water, poised over a plate, remembering. "I used to lie very still because I was absolutely sure there was someone in the room. If he knew I was awake, or if I should call out, he would strangle me or slit my throat."

"Footsteps on stairs," he said, rolling a cigarette.

"Faces outside window-panes," she countered.

"And don't forget," he added, "the boy may actually have seen something. A deer, or even the Hooper's dog. I've seen him stand up and pull the curtain back after his nap. Leave the light on." He put the tobacco tin back on the window sill and got up. "Leave the bathroom light on. It won't break us."

"Won't that make him weak?" she cried. "Isn't that giving in to his fears?"

"Not really. He'll outgrow it. I think maybe that kind of strength comes from reassurance." He kissed the back of her hair. "See you later on."

"Bring us back a fish," she said, reminding him of his role as provider, knowing in her heart it was all one to him whether he landed a fish or not. She was jealous of his relationship with the little boat, the oars, the sea. He would come back with a look of almost sensual pleasure on his face.

He went out, banging the door, and she could hear him teasing the little boy, explaining something. She left the dishes to dry and poured herself another cup of coffee. The baby kicked and she patted her abdomen as if to reassure it. Boy or girl, dark or light, she wondered idly but not very earnestly. It was out of her hands, like the weather and the tides. But would she really like to have it out here, maybe alone, with Robert crying from the prison of his crib or huddled at the foot of her bed, marked and possibly scarred forever by the groaning and the blood? Robert had been quick, amazingly and blessedly quick for a first child; the doctor had told her this indicated a rapid labour for the second. In her own way she was shy, particularly about physical things. Could she really go along to old Mrs Hooper's and ask for help, or accept the possibility of being taken off the Island by one of the local fishing boats, observed by the taciturn, sun-baked faces of the men to whom she would be, if known at all, simply another of the summer folk.

It was easier in the old days, she felt, when there were no choices. She smiled at herself, for Tom, if he had been listening, would have added "and childbed fever, and babies dying, and women worn out before they'd hardly begun". He called her a romantic and accused her of never thinking things through. *He* was the one who could really have survived here without complaint, in the old days. He was the one who had the strength to drag up driftwood from the little rocky beach, and saw it up by hand, and the knowledge that enabled him to mend things or to start a perfect fire every time. He hauled his rowboat down to the wharf below their place on a triangular carrier he'd made from old wheels off a discarded pram, pulled it down the narrow ramp, which could be very steep when the tide was out, lowered it over the side, stepped in carefully and rowed away. When he was around she was jealous of his strength and his knowledge – he had grown up in the country and by the sea. She was a city girl and forever yearning after the names of things. She dreamed; he did. Her hands were clumsy, except when loving her husband or her son, and she often regretted that she had never learned to knit or weave or even to play an instrument. She liked to read and to walk and to talk and felt herself to be shallow and impractical.

Yet since they had found the cabin she had experienced a certain degree of content and growing self-respect. She had learned to bake good, heavy bread in the little two-burner hotplate/oven which she hoped to replace, eventually, with an old, iron, wood- or oil-burning stove; she had learned about ammonia for wasp stings and how to recognize the edible mushrooms that grew in profusion near the abandoned schoolhouse. She could even light a fire now, almost every time.

She had bought a booklet on edible plants and was secretly learning something about the sustaining nature of the various weeds and plants that grew so profusely around her. She had started an herb garden in an old bureau drawer and already had visions of bunches of herbs drying from the kitchen ceiling, jars of rose-hip and black-berry jam, mushrooms keeping in brine in heavy earthenware crocks. Things could be learned from books and by experiment. She got a pencil and jotted down on a piece of drawing paper a list:

cod	thistles	pick salad
salmon	stinging nettles	? maybe sell some of our apples
oysters	blackberries	? my bread
mussels	apples	
	mushrooms	
	dandelions	

plant a garden, make beer?, a goat and chickens for Robert and the baby.

Then she laughed and crumpled up the paper and threw it in the potbelly stove (her pride and joy and a present discovered for her by Tom) which heated the little kitchen. The fire was nearly out. She would set some bread and then take Robert down on the dock until Tom returned.

"Robbie," she called, knocking on the window, "d'you want to help me make bread?" From his expression she could tell he hadn't heard so she went to the other side of the room – Tom had knocked most of the wall out to make one big room out of two – and opened the front door. It was chilly and she shivered. "Hey, d'you want to help me make some bread?"

He nodded, sturdy and solemn like his father, but with her light skin and hair. She undid his jacket and kissed him. His cheeks were very red.

"Your ears are cold," she laughed, holding his head, like a ball between her hands. "And you smell like the sea. Where did you put your cap?"

"I dunno, I want some juice." He wriggled away from her and she thought with a stab of regret, "So soon?" and tried to fix him as he was at just that moment, red-cheeked and fat, with his bird-bright eyes and cool, sea-smelling skin, to remember him like that forever.

"Come on," he said, tugging at her skirt, "juice and cookies."

"Who said anything about cookies?" she asked in mock severity.

"Juice," he repeated, quite sure of himself. "And two cookies. I'm allowed two cookies."

"Says who?"

"Juice and two cookies," he said, climbing on to a chair by the kitchen table.

Afterward, after they had smelled the yeast and kneaded the dough and made a tiny loaf for Robert in a muffin tin, she covered the bread and left it near the still-warm stove and took the child down to the wharf to watch the fishermen. There were three boats in: the *Trincomali*, the *Sutil* and the *Mary T* and they jostled one another in the slightly choppy water. She looked toward the other islands for Tom, but couldn't see him. Then carefully she and the little boy went down the ramp to the lower dock, where most of the activity was taking place. A few of the Indians she knew by sight, had seen them along the road or in the little store which served that end of the Island; but most of the ten or so people on the dock or sitting on the decks of boats were strangers to her and she felt suddenly rather presumptuous about coming down at all, like some sightseer – which was, of course, exactly what she was.

"Do you mind if we come down?" she called above the noise of the hysterical gulls and a radio which was blaring in one of the cabins. Two young men in identical red-plaid lumberjackets were drinking beer and taking a break on the deck of the *Mary T*. They looked up at her as she spoke, looked without curiosity, she felt, but simply recognizing her as a fact, like the gulls or the flapping fish, of their Sunday morning.

"Suit yourself, Missus," said an older man who seemed to be in charge.

"But mind you don't slip on them boards."

She looked down. He was right, of course. The main part of the lower dock was, by now, viscous and treacherous with blood and the remains of fish gut. The men in their gumboots stepped carefully. The kill had been going on for at least an hour and the smell of fish and the cry of gulls hung thick in the heavy air. There was an almost palpable curtain of smell and sound and that, with the sight of the gasping fish, made her dizzy for a moment, turned the wharf into an old-fashioned wood-planked roundabout such as she had clung to, in parks, as a child, while she, the little boy, the Indians, the gulls, the small-eyed, gasping fish, the grey and swollen sky spun round and round in a cacophony of sound and smell and pure sensation. She willed herself to stop, but felt slightly sick – as she often had on the actual roundabouts of her childhood – and buried her face in the sweet-smelling hair of her child, as if he were a posy. She breathed deeply, sat up, and smiled. No one had seen – except perhaps the two young Indians. Everyone else was busy. She smiled and began to enjoy and register what she was seeing.

Everywhere there were fish in various stages of life or death. Live cod swam beneath the decks of the little boats, round and round, bumping into one another as though they were part of some mad children's game, seeking desperately for a way out to the open sea. Then one of the men, with a net, would scoop up a fish, fling it on to

the wharf where it would be clubbed by another man and disembowelled swiftly by a third, the guts flung overboard to the raucous
gulls. Often the fish were not dead when they were gutted. She
could see that, and it should have mattered. The whole thing should
have mattered: the clubbing, the disembowelling, the sad stupid
faces of the cod with their receding chins and silly Chinamen's
beards. Yet instead of bothering, it thrilled her, this strange Sunday
morning ritual of death and survival.

The fish were piled haphazardly in garbage cans, crammed in,
tails any old way, and carried up the ramp by two of the men to be
weighed on the scales at the top. The sole woman, also Indian and
quite young, her hair done up in curlers under a pale pink chiffon
scarf, carefully wrote down the weights as they were called out.
"Ninety-nine." "Seventy-eight." Hundreds of pounds of cod to be
packed in ice until the truck came and took them to the city on the
evening ferry boat. And at how much a pound, she wondered. Fish
was expensive in the city – too expensive, she thought – and wondered how much, in fact, went to these hardworking fishermen. But
she dared not ask. Their faces, if not hostile, were closed to her,
intent upon the task at hand. There was almost a rhythm to it, and
although they did not sing, she felt the instinctual lift and drop and
slice of the three who were actually responsible for the kill. If she
had been a composer she could have written it down. One question
from her and it might all be ruined. For a moment the sun slipped
out, and she turned her face upward, feeling very happy and alive
just to be there, on this particular morning, watching the hands of
these fishermen, hands that glittered with scales, like mica, in the
sunlight, listening to the thud of the fish, the creaking and wheeling
of the gulls. A year ago, she felt, the whole scene would have
sickened her – now, in a strange way, she understood and was part
of it. Crab-like, she could feel a new self forming underneath the
old, brittle shell – could feel herself expanding, breaking free. The
child kicked, as if in recognition – a crab within a crab. If only Tom –
but the living child tugged at her arm.

"I'm hungry."

"Ah, Robert. Wait a while." She was resentful. Sulky. He knew
how to beat her.

"I want to pee. I want to pee *and* poop," he added defiantly.

She sighed. "Okay you win. Let's go." She got up stiffly, from sitting in one position for so long. A cod's heart beat by itself just below the ramp. Carefully she avoided it, walking in a heavy dream up the now steeper ramp (the tide was going out already) and up the path to her cabin.

Still in a dream she cared for the child and wiped his bottom and punched the bread, turning the little oven on to heat. After the child had been given a sandwich she put him down for a nap and sat at the kitchen table, dreaming. The first few drops of rain began to fall but these she did not see. She saw Tom and a fishing boat and living out their lives together here away from the noise and the terror of the city. Fish – and apples – and bread. Making love in the early morning, rising to love with the sun, the two of them – and Robert – and the baby. She put the bread in the oven, wishing now that Tom would come back so she could talk to him.

"You only like the island," he had said, "because you know you can get off. Any time. You're playing at being a primitive. Like a still life of dead ducks or partridges or peonies with just one ant. Just let it be."

"What's wrong with wanting to be simple and uncluttered?" she had cried.

"Nothing," he had replied, "if that's what you really are."

She began a pie, suddenly restless, when there was a knock on the door. It startled her and the baby kicked again.

"Hello," she said, too conscious of her rolled-up sleeves and floury hands. "Can I help you?"

It was one of the young Indians.

"The fellows say you have a telephone Missus. Could I use it? My brother-in-law wuz supposed to pick us up and he ain't come."

"Of course. It's right there." She retreated to the kitchen and sliced apples, trying not to listen. But of course there was no wall. Short of covering her ears there was little she could do.

"Hey. Thelma. Is that you Thelma? Well where the hell is Joe? Yeah. All morning. Naw. I'm calling from the house up above. Oh yeah? Well tell him to get the hell up here quick. Yeah. Okay. Be seeing you."

She heard the phone replaced and then he came around the big fireplace, which, with the potbelly stove, divided the one large room partially into two. "Say," he said, "I got blood all over your phone. Have you got a rag?"

She looked at his hands, which were all scored with shallow cuts, she could see, and the blood still bright orange-red and seeping.

"You're hurt."

"Naw," he said proudly, standing with his weight on one leg, "It's always like that when we do the cod. The knives is too sharp. *You* know," he added with a smile, as if she really did. Little drops of blood fell as he spoke, spattering on the linoleum floor.

"Don't you want some Band-aids at least?"

"Wouldn't last two minutes in that wet," he said, "but give me a rag to clean up the phone."

"I'll do it," she said, bending awkwardly to one of the bottom cupboards to get a floor cloth. She preceded him into the living-room. He was right: the receiver was bright with blood, and some spots of blood decorated an air-letter, like notary's seals, which she had left open on the desk. Snow White in her paleness. He became Rose Red. "What am I thinking of?" she blushed.

"I sure am sorry," he said, looking at her with his dark bright eyes. "I didn't mean to mess up your things." She stood before him, the cloth bright with his blood, accepting his youth, his maleness, his arrogance. Her own pale blood drummed loudly in her ears.

"If you're positive you're all right," she managed.

"Yeah. Can't be helped. It'll heal over by next Sunday." He held his hands out to her and she could see, along with the seeping blood, the thin white wire-like lines of a hundred former scars. Slowly she reahed out and dipped two fingers in the blood, then raised them and drew them across her forehead and down across each cheek.

"Christ," he said softly, then took the clean end of the rag and spit on it and gently wiped her face. She was very conscious of her bigness and leaned slightly forward so he would not have to brush against her belly. What would *their* children have been like?

Then the spell broke and he laughed self-consciously and looked around.

"Sure is a nice place you've got here," but she was aware he didn't mean it. What would his ideal be? He was very handsome with his coarse dark hair and red plaid lumberjacket.

"Well," she said, with her face too open, too revealing.

"Well," he answered, eager now to go. "Yeah. See you around. Thanks for the use of your phone."

She nodded and he was gone.

When Tom returned the little house was rich with the smells of bread and rhubarb pie and coffee.

"Any luck?"

"Yes," he said, "and no. I didn't catch anything – but you did."

"I did?" she said, puzzled.

"Yeah. One of the fishermen gave me this for you. He said you let him use the phone. It was very nice of him, I must say."

And there, cleaned and filleted, presumably with the knife that had cut him so, was a beautiful bit of cod. She took it in her hands, felt the cool rasping texture of it, and wondered for an alien moment if his tongue would feel like that – cool, rough as a cat's tongue, tasting of fish.

"What did he say?" she asked, her back to the man.

"He said 'give this to the Missus'. Why?"

"Nothing. I thought he was kind of cheeky. He made me feel old."

Later that night on their couch before the fire, she startled him by the violence of her lovemaking. He felt somehow she was trying to possess him, devour him, maybe even exorcize him. And why hadn't she cooked the cod for supper? She had said that all of a sudden she didn't feel like fish. He stared at her, asleep, her full mouth slightly open, and felt the sad and immeasurable gulf between them, then sat up for a moment and pulled the curtain back, looking vainly for the reassurance of the moon behind the beaded curtain of the rain. The man shook his head. There were no answers, only questions. One could only live and accept. He turned away from his wife and dove effortlessly into a deep, cool, dreamless sleep. The rain fell on the little cabin, and on the trees and on the government wharf below, where, with persistence, it washed away all traces of the cod and the kill, except for two beer bottles, which lolled against the pilings as the two young Indians had lolled earlier that day. The rain fell; the baby kicked. The woman moaned a little in her sleep and moved closer to the reassuring back of the puzzle who was her husband. And still the rain fell on, and Sunday night – eventually – turned into Monday morning.

Arkendale

SEAN VIRGO

The Dutch barn stood out high behind the old farmhouse and the stone byres. It was almost empty now: the unused remnants of the winter hay lay trodden in a low heap by one of the corner posts. A few hens, white ones and brown, pecked and scratched in the earth floor. For the rest the house-martins owned it – they flashed under the hump of its eaves and swooped upwards on the other side: fluttering up, almost hovering before the flimsy clouds; twittering in the same rhythm as their rapid wings; and then plunging down again in zest or flirtation, to assert that the ground was their province too – transformed into low blue shadows gliding and it seemed running on their wings, too fast to pinpoint, darting like fish inches above the greening furrows.

High in the boat-hulled roof their nests clustered on the rusty girders – little honeycombs and termite humps, glued to the struts and feather-lined already, breast-warm. Battle raged in the colony. A complacent house-sparrow squatted in the entrance of a nest, puffing out his chest with its horseshoe sneer. He chirruped back at the furious, hovering builders and one egg, another, came out between his feet and shone for a moment in the afternoon light before slapping on the earth beside the hens. Dispossession was complete. The martins flew off to find more mud, more feathers, more horsehair. The cock sparrow quick-winged it out to the gutter. Moments later he was treading his mate, hopping off and on repeatedly, his eyes rolling at the sky. She grew bored and dropped down to compose herself with a dust bath among the chickens. He went back to his new home, prating to his immigrant neighbours with the glamour of a conqueror, the smugness of a native son.

A hundred yards down the road a tractor paused at the crossroads and the young man who vaulted from its fender picked out his haversack from among the milk-churns on the trailer and shouted his thanks. The tractor grumbled off, loosing jerky smoke signals against the long blue line of Melbeck Scar on the horizon. The young man did not trouble to shoulder his pack but carried it swinging by its strap, and set out striding toward the village. He half turned to wave again at the departing vehicle as its smoke stack vanished between the drystone walls of the Askrigg road.

He was perhaps twenty-two or -three, but in the elation of his mood he projected toward the houses an adolescent strut and ebullience. His shoulders were squared, he swung the green knapsack with gusto, he smiled – positively grinned – into the light moorland wind. After the precarious eight-mile drive up from Reeth over the tractor's wheel, he was glad to throw out his feet before him and he laughed for a moment at a vision of his platoon, goosestepping it on the drill square with such carefree zest.

He took to the turf verge of the road, springy under his feet. There was just a yard or so of grass and then the swift little beck that rushed down the village street by the house gates and out to the valley. He stooped for a moment above the water, catching the flickering drive of a hill trout for the shelter of a stone across its little pool. As a child he had often enough caught his family's breakfast in the hour after dawn, searching gently under bank or boulder for the nervous fish flesh there, soothing the hard, vibrant little body with his finger tips and scooping it suddenly on to the bank beside him.

Now he squatted and trailed his fingers, comb-like in the chill water. The current built up slightly against the back of his hand. A moment of complete delight came over him, a total sense of homecoming and being at home with people, animals, landscape. On patrol along the dusty ridge of Famagusta, or drinking on rare curfew-free evenings in the strained gloom of shabby Greek bars, he had constructed from this world of his school holidays a counterpoint of clarity and freedom. And it was real. He had set rowan ("the bead-bonny ash") springing from limestone clefts, against the dreadful patience of the olives and the tired, lifeless rocks; rabbit-stirred bracken against the goat-stunted bushes; tweed, crow's feet, blue-grey eyes against the loose cotton, slick skin, impossible mirror eyes of the Cypriots.

Today, after the endless disillusioning miles of railroad; the stale dirt; the obsessive passenger and newspaper chat of money, football, cars; and the whole stupefying extent of the brick-block ugliness that was England's lifeline, he had entered the dales at

Richmond and was entranced. It was real. The canny jesting driver on the ramshackle bus, the certainty of life which spoke through the clothes and speech of the other passengers. Quarter of a mile up the road out of Reeth he had been picked up, unsolicited, by the first farm vehicle to pass. The young driver, with no Greek nosiness, had nodded at him and grinned and then, perched bucolically on the juddering mudguard of the old tractor, he had been led slowly up the dale – almost at walking pace – seeing the land unfold around him over the grey stone walls, exactly as he had learned it in childhood by foot and bicycle. Exactly as he had promised himself of it in the hot prisoning days on the Med and before.

It was a hard land but not unyielding. Everything grew in measure, trees where they could find hold, lichen on the stones. The walls even and the whitewashed houses were in balance. They redefined the land but yielded to its contours. And, if nowhere else, around the farmhouses there were trees – sycamore, Scotch pine, even grey beeches – so that people declared themselves by oases, not scars. And by every church tower and rectory was a tall line of elms or ash trees, as though ordained for the raucous, nesting rooks.

So many of his memory pictures, he realized, had been vague where he had fancied them vivid. He could never have painted the strong short grass in the pastures, dinted everywhere by the constant treading of sheep. Or the thistles and dock clumps, randomly but justly spaced. There, now a straggling line of hawthorn trees bisected a larger field, the black ground along it bared by the daily tracking of the bullocks, the gnarled trunks rubbed smooth and tagged with sheep's wool. A vignette, then, of the dung and tread around a water trough. Today the full picture came back to reward him for the fragments of memories he had clutched, amulets and relics, to his exiled heart.

Now he was within ten miles of home he claimed kin with every grass-blade. He looked up toward the long, tall farmhouse that started the village, with its little cluster of byres and outbuildings and the high, red-roofed barn beyond. He marched toward it with a more thoughtful exuberance now. A gate beside the house led straight on to the yard from the road and he leaned over it as boys, their feet on the bottom rung, have always looked over gates, watching the martins cleave the air before him. The tag came to his mind, *they only nest on a happy house*, and, half-consciously, his eyes marked the row of nests along the house-eaves too.

The side door of the house stood open, and with the clatter of a pail a woman appeared, a young child clutching her hand and skirt. "You bide there now awhile," she said, and left the child on the step, clinging to the doorpost and swinging from foot to foot as he watched his mother. At the sound of the pail the chickens had jerked to attention; now as she appeared they came pell-mell from all sides of the yard, jostling like racehorses, their bodies shifting from one careering leg to another in absurd imbalance. The stranger laughed aloud at the old ladies" food-derby and the woman looked round.

"It's just the hens," he called. "I always thought them the stupidest creatures when they run."

She smiled, a bit uncertainly. But she'd a brisk air about her. "Aye, they're daft enough, p'raps," she said, "but they do what no human can do, and that's lay eggs." She dumped the bucket of pellets with a long sowing motion, and spread the food out a bit with her foot while her gloved hand scraped the pail clean. The birds were all around her in a mob, shouldering and pecking like an animated quilt in white and brown.

The toddler at the door had snatched his own handful from the bucket and was cramming the khaki crumbs at his mouth. Most of it fell on the step and two or three straggler hens pounced at his feet. He showed no fear of them, but made stabs at warding them off, swinging at them with open palm and open mouth, in surges of a child's anarchic violence. But the mother made it seem tame enough; she could contain it. "Let them be, Tommy," she laughed, and the humour retrieved his innocence in the stranger's eyes. "Thou's the size of elephant to them beggars."

"Could I get a glass of water from you?" the young man called.

She was refilling the chickens' water tower from a tap over the cattle trough. "You can surely," she said. "Come in. I'll see to it in a minute."

"I'll help myself," he said and vaulted over the gate. Tommy shrank for a moment at the big man crashing into his territory, but he was game. When the stranger reached the doorway, the little boy clenched his lips and set himself against the intruder's knees, pushing to keep him out. "Nah," he said, "Nah." He would not let him by.

The power of children. "I don't think he likes me." The mother was through with her work now and looked up at him: "Don't be taking that to heart," she said. The laugh-lines crinkled on her face, but her startling grey eyes were level and direct. "C'mon, Tommy, let the man be" – as calling off a dog.

In a flash the child's courage was gone and he ran against his mother's skirts. He sulked and would not look out, though a minute later his great blue eyes were teasing in the kitchen.

The woman moved the kettle across the hob. "You'll have a cup of tea," she said, reaching for a coronation caddy from the high mantel. It was almost an order. The kitchen was high, whitewashed, cool. In the ceiling were the old hooks for storing hams, though they were bare. A drying rack was hoisted above the old range, with children's clothes.

"Tommy's not your only child?" the stranger asked. She caught the direction of his eyes and laughed. "No, I've me hands full – our Pamela and young Stan will be in from school shortly."

Here in her special territory she was more relaxed. She sat him on the long settle against the wall and shooed Tommy away from the stove. "I hope I'm not keeping you from your work," said her guest.

She turned at the range and looked at him directly again. "You're a very polite young man," she said. She was laughing at him. He took her up on it and smiled back. They laughed. "Nay, don't fuss," she said. "The children always eat summat when they get home. Before they do their chores."

Tommy was determinedly trying to climb on a chair by the door where the rubber boots stood. His legs were not long enough: he'd get one knee over the edge and it would slip off from his weight. The young man got up and helped him on. The child allowed him but swiped at his arms once he was safe. "He *is* independent," the man laughed.

"Nowt wrong with that." The mother was setting cups and plates on the scrubbed deal table. "Just don't let him be saucy. He'll get used to you by and by. Won't you, pet?" And she handed the child a tin mug full of milk. The blue eyes watched them, owl-like, over the mug's rim.

She fetched a loaf of bread from the larder and a plate of griddle scones. It was too good to be true. The visitor grinned in exaggerated gratitude across the room: "Can I help?"

She ignored the gesture. "Passing through, are you?"

"Just as far as Hushgill," he said.

"D'you know folks there, then?"

"Oh it's my home," he said. He did not want to be thought a real stranger. And her manner did alter.

"I took you for a hiker. I don't recall seeing your face, though. Who're your people?"

"I've stayed at the rectory for years. Sort of an adopted son, I suppose."

"What, at Reverend Bullock's? Why, you must be the Palmer boy – Malcolm in't it?" He nodded. "I heard you were in t'Army, lad."

"I was, yes. I just got demobbed last week."

"Ah." She didn't pause for a second in her preparations. "Mrs Bullock will be happy to have you home. She's had problems with her leg, you know."

"Yes. I believe she's over it now."

"Aye. Well I don't get over there too often. Stanley does, of course – every other week or so." She rinsed the teapot with hot water. "And you were overseas were you – judging by your brown skin?"

"Yes. The last few months in Cyprus. Before that I was a year in Malaya."

"Cyprus. Oh we've read about that. Terrible things – shooting women and that."

Tommy hurled his mug clattering across the flagstoned floor and slithered from the chair, rushing out through the open door. "Ah, he's heard them coming," she said, imperturbably retrieving the mug. "He always meets them at the gate." She brought chairs to the table. "Stanley's got a Young Farmers' meeting in Keld after supper so you can stay and get a ride up."

"If it's no trouble . . ." His manners amused her no end.

A boy clumped in at the door, about eight years old, towheaded. Something of his mother about his jawline. Behind him his sister came lugging Tommy against her waist. Strange how the country girls are little women already, with so many of the attitudes and instinctive knowledge that town girls learn only after their adolescences. And strange, too, how in the country the girls take their mothers' looks, the boys more of their fathers'. Pamela's eyes are her mother's – at all points she is a miniature version. Perhaps through twenty generations of dales people this face, this body and personality can be handed down intact through mother and daughter, and the men simply intermediaries of need. For the men's line is not so pure. The women add something to that, too. Take something away. Perhaps in the thirteenth century, when Hushgill church was being built, there was another Pamela in the dale, knowing all that she knows now; another – what is the mother's name?

The children were aware of the stranger's cool gaze as his blue eyes took them in and passed for a moment to the mother, who stood poised. For a moment the old pendulum clock above the inside door stopped ticking.

"Say hello to Mr Palmer, on his way home to Hushgill," the mother said, taking the children's satchels and hanging them on the door pegs. "He's just back out of t'Army, been to foreign parts too. You dad'll be giving him a run up this evening." The boy watched covertly, the girl, half-smiling, direct. "And this is young Stan and this is Pamela."

Malcolm greeted them, but in their shyness they were talking – the boy especially – to their mother. The girl fussed with Tommy. He would have to speak first.

"Is Mr Metcalf still your teacher?" he asked the girl.

"He's *his*," she gestured at her brother. "We've got Miss Allison." The boy responded: "Do you know him, then?"

"Yes," Malcolm said. "We used to play cricket together."

The boy was scarlet-faced, "I forget his name, Mam," he hissed.

She laughed and ruffled his hair. "Mr Palmer, you noodle."

"Malcolm would be easier," said Malcolm.

"You're a soldier?" said young Stan, the ice broken.

"Well, I was. Not anymore."

"Who were you fighting, then?"

He hesitated. "Well we were just keeping the peace, you know. Not really fighting."

"Not ever?"

"Just once in a while."

"Don't fuss, Stan" – his mother, but the boy was finding himself.

"Did you kill anyone ever? Shoot them?"

Malcolm's eyes flickered to the mother at the table, then settled seriously on the boy's. "Oh no," he said, "no, I never had to do that." Something kept him from looking at the mother. But she divined the lie and yearned to him for it. She allowed herself to see him for the first time and a pang of loyalty and gratitude went out to him like a touch.

"Me dad did!" Young Stan's arms danced to his eyes' excitement. "Duzzens of Germans, wi' a machine gun. All in a row!"

She called them briskly to the table, and poured the thick tea from a pewter teapot. In the first home he had entered for two years, Malcolm was almost unbearably affected – by the family, the mother figure, the homely nostalgic foods. He smiled up gratefully and she, open now to his realities, responded with open face and eyes.

Pamela let out a little scream, just as young Stan blurted: "Did you ever see one of these?" The mother's reproof was cut off by the visitor's obvious delight. The boy held, laced between his fingers, a small snake above his plate. A slow-worm.

"Yes I did," and Malcolm held out his hand. The boy, delightedly, eased the gold and black lizard onto the stranger's palm. It locked around his wrist – the shining black eyes gazing straight ahead, the snake-tongue flicking once at his skin. "And I bet I know where you found him too."

"Where?"

"At Rigswell Crag, above the lead mines."

"That's right." They were firm friends. "Did you used to have them?"

"Quite a few, yes. What does this one eat?"

"Flies and moths mostly. What I can catch. Yours?"

"That kind of thing – they like fishing maggots too. You should try that."

"Ugh," said Pamela, "all that yellow stuff when you put the hook in."

Over their plate of slugs and snails and puppy dogs' tails, they winked in conspiracy. Why, this is the kind of happiness you should cling to, savouring it while it's happening, not in retrospect. The continuity, after the years at school and away, made another breach in the armour that the world and the army had wrought on him. Probably the boys still play the same games, tell the same jokes – and learn from them – fight the same fights. Without hesitation he began to sing softly as he spread thick raspberry jam on his scone:

> The Queen came down from Bolton's Kep
> And danced upon the Shaw

Stan joins in, overloud, scone crumbs flying:

> And when the warden stayed her hand
> She rapped him on the jaw

Then Pamela, too, and her mother in the chorus:

> Me jaw is in, me teeth are out
> I cannot get them mended

Tommy shrieking, banging upon the table . . .

> The Queen's rid off to Holy Road
> and there me story's ended.

"Oh my," said the mother, retrieving Tommy's debris, "I mind the lads singing that when I were Pam's age."

That wouldn't have been so long ago. He reckoned the years of her early school leaving added to his National Service. It was almost time enough for her to have borne her children. Her hands, out of the farmyard gauntlets, were fine, pale, and well-tended. He'd been responding to her only as a mother, but her self was breaking through that. And in her body, too, there was a pride that matched her eyes – there was no heaviness, no drudgery – he watched the woman, her poise within her work, and her limbs shifting through the loose apron, the heavy tweed skirt.

And she, in response, diverted him. "Stan, it's your turn at t'eggs. Pam, pet, you help prepare things for your father."

"Will you come out, Malcolm?" said the boy.

They crossed the yard to the stone outbuildings. In the late afternoon sun swallows streaked in all directions, chasing insects through the yard. The air was filled with the minute clicks their beaks made at every catch. Two martins fluttered up from a puddle gathering nest-mud, and a grey farm cat that had been watching them from the stable threshold slunk off thwarted. "Come and see the Broody," the boy said.

Inside the stable a big brown hen sat on a hayrack in the gloom, staring trancedly at them. It was quite dark inside and the segregated bird presided over the cool mystery of the place. Malcolm couldn't help his voice dropping to a whisper. "Have you got her on eggs?"

"No – just a pot egg to get her over it," and the boy pointed to the man-made sop to maternity in the straw. Malcolm reached over softly and touched it – it was blood hot from the barren impulse of the bird. In the next stall a pan clattered and a snout came wheezing and pushing at a crack in the boards.

"That's Sam Pig," said Stan proudly, "he's two hundred pound already."

"Hello Sam," Malcolm introduced himself. "Are they fattening you up then?"

"Sam, Sam, the Christmas ham," chanted the boy, pushing some grain from his pocket into the pig's dish.

"Won't you feel sorry when he's killed?"

"No," scornfully. "Our Pam always cries about it, but she eats him all the same. This year I'm allowed to help me dad butcher him. You should hear them squeal."

"I know," said Malcolm. "It's creepy."

The boy laughed. You have to learn about men gradually. He wouldn't boast anymore. This one was different from his father, but he was all right.

Malcolm eased the moment along. "We'd better get those eggs," he laughed, "before your dad gets home and chases me round the houses."

They stopped at the yard fence on their way to the tarred henhouses in the field. Malcolm leaned against the fence and the boy sat astride it. The shadows were longer now on the grass, the furrows beyond were black ruts, and the fence-posts stretched across the yard – the boy's perched shadow and the man's vaulting together almost to the house door. The day was beginning its comfortable drift into evening. A cow bellowed for her calf somewhere up the fields.

Over the outhouses a carrion crow with ragged wings came

beating steadily along. A swarm of house-martins rose shrilly from all sides and climbed, pestering and shearing around it. The crow stood on its wingtip toward the east, sideslipped away from them, and uttered one croak, harsh and contemptuous. When it had crossed the yard's boundaries the bird-mob came back to the barn, shrill with agitation.

Young Stan waved his arm after the crow: "I know where *he's* from," he cried. "He's nesting up in Yarby Gill – we been there last two years." Perched, with his arm outstretched and face alight, he reminded Malcolm irresistibly of the sailor in *The Boyhood of Ralegh*. The yarns. The world beyond. "It's a *blue* carrion" – the boy was afire with his knowledge.

"Blue? Oh, you mean the eggs. Really – I've never seen one, Stan."

"Aye, nearly pure blue and with funny pointed ends. We took a clutch three weeks back. They'll have laid again now."

Malcolm saw, as vividly as if the boy had led him there, the wind-turned Scotch pine, with the grey, twig-stacked nest on its single overhang. And saw the boy perched as now, but higher in the true wind, at the crow's-nest, a mariner questing for new lands. And what had Ralegh come to – the flower of chivalry who butchered a thousand unarmed men on Dingle strand and then, betrayed, rewrote the world's history in the Tower.

"I'll show you the eggs," Stan promised, "when we get back in."

Malcolm laughed – "What about the hens' eggs? Here's your sister come to chase us up."

The girl crossed the yard with a sack-lined bucket, bossily self-possessed. She clouted her brother on the arm and slipped easily out of his reach as he flailed back, shown up in front of his new friend. She contrived to make him look oafish, aggressive, without surrendering an ounce of her own serenity.

The three of them went together through the field, Malcolm deferring to the girl as though she were a woman, a lady, already. She accepted it with poise, her young voice quiet and factual, while young Stan clamoured shrilly for attention over her head. The man's laugh came back to the house as they walked.

The woman watched them from the bedroom window upstairs. Her mouth was smiling lightly, with the tolerant acceptance of a mother; her eyes were younger, bright with the innocence of an earlier time. The steady sweep of the brush through her hair tilted her face and her eyes half closed – as though mesmerized by the brush strokes – as her children moved with the man out of sight behind the sheds.

She stood for a long moment against the window, her hand arrested by her face, out of time. It was, she believed, her first private moment in so many years. Yet she had never missed it.

She laid her brush softly on the dresser and moved, barefoot, to the massive wardrobe across the room. Inside, her husband's better jackets hung with his suit, dwarfing her own clothes, palpable with his presence. Their twin, married aroma exhaled through the old wood, the hint of camphor. So a widow might see it. She deliberated for a few seconds, fiddling with a button on her cardigan, her lower lip pouting slightly, and then, swiftly but without haste, removed her outer garments. She let the skirt and slip lie pooled around her feet and dropped the cardigan behind her on the bed end. She was still undecided.

She watched herself, steadily, in the mirror inside the wardrobe door. She leaned forward toward her reflection, seeking to know her face better than the rituals of morning and night had taught her these last years. And she looked hard at the silvershine furrows at breast and hip where her motherhood spoke.

Something in her that she did not understand, that shamed her a little and was pushed down, wished that she could be younger, more beautiful for this stranger. Less masked by her role as mother and wife. She saw all of him, she believed, but she did not see through him. His being young, his being a man, did not reduce him. In the pride of her people she would not be ashamed, but she knew that she lacked the delicacy, the fineness that he would be accustomed to. She would not be ashamed, but she wished even so that she and her home and her clothes had those qualities.

And part of her meant none of these things and laughed at herself. She shook her head disbelievingly at this person in the mirror.

She heard their voices in the yard again and moved back round the bed to the window. Pamela saw her and pointed – Malcolm looked up and smiled. She waved. He saw her face at the glass, smiling serenely, her hand raised in brief acknowledgement. She, on the cool boards of her bedroom, stood almost naked and watched him pass below her.

She decided, and went briskly back to the wardrobe, reaching without hesitation for the pleated skirt. The lovat twinset would go with it. She shook her head at herself again, as at a wayward but harmless sister.

When she came down a few minutes later she stopped to look in at the little room over the stairs where Tommy lay sleeping in his crib. His fat cheek pressed against one of the bars; a small hand hung limply out from his cage. Her eyes softened: this, after all, was her. Pamela was scrubbing the eggs at the sink while Malcolm sat with young Stan on the settle sorting through the wild egg collection in the big cigar boxes.

The boy was holding up an almost circular, dull white egg: "That's a barn owl – it's right old. Me uncle Ned got that from t'church loft when he were a boy and the owl chased him all the way home." He looked up then: "Nearly five duzzen eggs, Mam," he announced. Pam, at the sink, grunted.

Her mother saw the smiling visitor's eyes stray from her face, taking in the fresh outfit and the person it revealed. She noted the tribute serenely. And Pam, when her mother came over, fingered the fine linen of the skirt wistfully. But young Stan was oblivious and continued with his catalogue. "I got this curlew's on a picnic at Fremington," and Malcolm, "I saw one hatch out once – you could see the little black beak chipping through the shell. But the mother was taking fits, so I didn't see it all."

The boy said seriously, "I wouldn't like to be cooped up inside an egg." The adults flashed a look of gay sympathy across the room. She looked fine. She was proud and womanly. Malcolm's eyes kept coming back to her, as she stood over the stove slicing puddings into the frying pan, pricking sausages, trimming the tiny lamb chops. The old smell of mixed grill filled the kitchen but even as he noted that with affection, he was imagining her in less homely settings.

"My, it's coming in dark early," she said, "I doubt we'll get rain by and by, thunder most likely."

"I seen lightning hit the church," Stan declared.

"You never did you liar," Pamela snapped and she and her

mother laughed together. The mother had such a way of taking the sting out of her children's aggressions.

There was a car outside, and a door slammed. "That's me dad," and young Stan hared off through the door. He called from outside, "He's got Uncle Ned wi' him."

The men stepped in. The leader was broad, florid-faced, bareheaded with a shock of black hair. His companion was slighter, cloth-capped, unmistakably the woman's brother, though much older. So the big man was the husband.

"Now Pam, now Stan," he grinned at the children. "Hello pet," to his wife. "Dressed up for company is it? Or are you gannin to t'whist drive tonight?"

"Get along wi' you," she laughed. "Stan, this is Malcolm Palmer from Hushgill – y'knows, what lives wi' t'Bullocks. Me husband, Stan, and me brother Edward."

"How do," each man nodded. "Back from t'wars are you?" said the husband.

"Back for good now."

"Aye? Well, none too soon, I imagine. I was in t'army mesen – in t'Desert and Italy."

"Yes, Stan here was telling me."

The man laughed shortly, "Oh aye, our Stan thinks 'tis all blood and glory, don't you lad?"

Malcolm did not take to the husband, it was hard to say why. Perhaps the huge, blunt hands or the coarsened red cheeks. The man had shrewd blue eyes, but it was the shrewdness of the cattle mart, not of insight. The brother was gentler, more humble.

"And where's t'young ruffian, Nell? Stan Shaw demanded.

She – Nell it was then, Helen, good – She said, "He's napping till supper. He were getting carried away."

"Aye, company'll do that to 'im. No offence –" the man nodded at Malcolm who smiled back.

"Well, I imagine you're waiting on a ride up t'dale wi' us," the man went on.

"If it's no trouble."

"Nay, course not, lad. Me and Ned'll get milking done now, before t'light's altogether gone, and we'll be off straight after supper."

"Shall I give you a hand?"

Again the shrewd, calculated look – perhaps doubting his fitness: "Nay, we doan't need a crowd. Howay, Stan, let's be off." And the boy shot out at the door where a big black and white collie was whimpering eagerly. They raced off together. "See you shortly," said the husband and the brother nodded shyly and let him out through the door first.

Was there a hint of defiance in the way the woman – Nell, Nell Shaw – looked at him now? The same look echoed by her daughter? Well, he would not judge – the man was kindly enough. But as he closed the lids carefully on young Stan's egg boxes, Malcolm had a quick, silly dream of the man being gone – dead or something – and himself giving the woman and her children another chance. Ah, he laughed at himself harshly, he'd have his own home to make.

The meal was all but ready now, waiting on the men. Nell Shaw went up to get Tommy, and Pamela sat down at the far end of the settle with a big leatherette book. A photograph album. There was something of the flirt in young Pam, or perhaps that was unfair, just childhood shyness. But she was inviting him to look at the pictures and to do so he would have to move along and sit beside her.

Once he did so she was entirely open again, laughing uninhibitedly at the childhood pictures of her brother and herself. The usual fat baby faces progressed through the pages and the years. The faces of now and the future grew sharper with each print, whereas with the mother and father it was the other way – Malcolm looked for the people they had been when they had drawn together.

In every photograph Nell looked steadily at the camera's eye, even in the pictures where she held her babies. She was watchful of what she would give and the effect was neutral, contained. But Stan Shaw would be grinning, out of focus as he turned to someone outside the picture, or blurring his hand as he brought a cigarette up to his face.

Pamela was in fits of laughter at the wedding shots when her mother came down with half-asleep Tommy. The child's flushed face peered crossly out at the world. "What is it then?" and she came over to see. "You and them old pictures – something to show to a guest, I must say." And though she laughed she clearly did feel exposed, yet there was no need.

Her face at the wedding, with the crowd of stiff relatives at the old church porch, was the same as in the other photos: direct, not challenging at all, but lightly smiling, concealing. While her husband, for all the awkward clothing, stared brazenly at the camera, at the future, fixing forever his pride of ownership, of a bargain well struck. Malcolm looked up at her, knowingly, for the first time. His insights, it seemed, gave him a kind of power. Did that man really value the bargain, did he know her?

Young Stan was back then at the door, the collie's great plume of a tail waving beside him. "You can put the eggs on now, Mam, they're almost through."

The boy came over to the settle and made a sudden grab for the album. He danced clear with it as Pamela protested, almost gabbling in his triumph. "I'll show you one, I'll show you one!" He dumped the album at the table, fending his sister off, and snatched out a few unmounted snaps from the end pages. He danced off again, shuffling through them and "Here it is," he shouted, "Malcolm, look at this now."

His mother turned to shush him and shook her head in wry vexation. The boy brought his prize over. It was a picture of Nell before she was married. A family joke, clearly. She was standing under the branch of an aspen tree, with a river and rocks behind, completely unaware of the camera. Her hair was longer than now, and her eyes seemed huge. They looked up and sideways through the leaves, almost afraid, and her lips were slightly apart, her hair loose on her young shoulders. It was the only photo where she did not stare back, matching the viewer's gaze.

Young Stan was almost beside himself. "Dad calls that the Great Gawk," he spluttered, "don't he, Gawk, I mean, Mam?" And Pamela, too, who had retrieved the album, was in convulsions beside him.

Malcolm looked at the picture and at Nell and, catching her eyes, said quietly, "It's lovely." The children hushed, puzzled at the change in the air. "It's lovely," he repeated, his eyes holding her. A light flush mantled upon her cheekbones. Under his gaze she could feel that hidden girl repossessing her. She turned away. "Nay," she murmured, smoothing her skirt at the hips.

And then the men were back. Tommy came to life and rushed to his father. And Malcolm returned the picture to Pamela who looked at him shrewdly before closing the album, with a quiet smile, and returning it to the shelf.

Stan Shaw was hurling Tommy as high as the ceiling, twisting and turning the child in his huge hands. The boy's eyes went almost up into his head at every toss, and he squealed in rapture each time he jolted back into his father's grip. "Shall we put you on t'hook. Shall we leave you up there. Shall we. Shall we." The child was near hysteria. But a soft, easy pride shone from the man's face and though his wife moved to still the violent sport, when he turned to her, his face flushed deeper and eyes glittering, a shaft of strong feeling passed from one to the other, their eyes knew each other, and Malcolm, watching, was ashamed. It was a real marriage then; he should not judge in haste. And in his shame he warmed to the man, who sensed the feeling across the room. He set the child gently back on a chair and joked with the stranger while he washed his hands beside his wife at the sink.

The meal was lavish, especially for Malcolm, coming so soon after the tea he'd been given. "Beats Naafi rations I reckon," said Edward, who was himself thawing out now, to the children and the company. They passed on news of the dales and Malcolm spoke of the troubles abroad that seemed no part of this England. He did not want to leave here, yet he knew he had been marked, perhaps finally set apart, by the hot places of the fading empire.

And suddenly, talking, easily joking with these people, he began to dread the short run that remained up the dale to his home. He foresaw, so predictable, Mr Bullock's gruff, undemonstrative affection; and then his wife's earnest seeking after news and understanding as she kept him late into the night sitting in her Windsor chair by the fire, her eyes fixed on him and full of faith in his destiny.

He had even let those good people down by declining a commission. He would have to tell all this news again and again, steadfastly talking only about himself, and he would be telling nothing, skirting whatever it was in himself that he sensed to be true, but which words just clouded.

Pamela was looking at him curiously, with something very like compassion. He knew she must be echoing her mother's awareness and felt for the first time underhand. He avoided looking over.

The energy of the long day was slipping from him and though the men talked on unconcerned he excused his stillness – "I must be getting tired I think."

"No wonder neither," Stan Shaw said cheerily, and he wiped his plate clean with a last slice of bread. "Let's be off, shall us, Ned?" And with little ado they scraped back their chairs and made for their boots and the door.

He wondered at the lack of thanks for the meal, at the man's leaving without touching his wife. He had not touched her since he came in. But she seemed content, it was their way. He must not judge. He picked up his own jacket at the door, and the rucksack. He wanted to give the woman something and for a moment had the impulse to unpack the filigree Malayan bracelet he had saved for Mrs Bullock. That would be wrong. He had little with him, and it was hard to give, but the impulse was strong. "Stan," he said, "Pamela, here's a little present for you both. They're from Malaya and you must be careful with them – they're just for decoration."

He unwrapped from their tissue wrappings the two inlaid brass pendants he had brought in Penang. The children came forward dutifully but perplexed until he drew out the concealed wings and the wicked, hinged knife blades slipped through. Young Stan's face went red with pleasure and his hand itched to take his, while Pamela blurted, "Oh thanks, they're smashin'." The father muttered, "Nay, you mustn't waste them on t'youngsters," and then, "Well mind you look after them." He was almost fierce with his children for what they'd been given. But their mother smiled over their heads. She knew the gift was hers.

The door was open and a circle of Ayrshire cows looked in on them from the dark yard. The dog got up from the step, stretched, and then cleared a path for the men. Malcolm used her name for the first time, holding her gaze as long as she'd allow it. "I'll be seeing you again soon I expect," he told the children. And her.

"Aye, likely," she said. "Goodbye then."

They moved to the gate through the staring crowd of dairy cows. The van waited by the road, backed in to the gate. Stan Shaw swung the back door open and the dog leaped in without hesitation, settling down at once on the sacks beside the spare wheel. It looked back out at them from its lair, the quick huffing of its breath almost the only sound on the dark road. Malcolm peered in over the dog's head and could just make out the single seats up front. "I'll ride in the back," he said quickly.

"Nay, no need for that," Stan Shaw lit up a cigarette and the three faces were clear for a moment. "We'll fit y'in somehow."

"No, I'll be fine in the back."

"Well, suit thesen. She's a right old bone-shaker, be warned – move t'dog over and get some sacking under you."

Malcolm scrambled through the narrow door and settled his back against the wheel hump. The dog nudged over and lay warm against his leg, and he stretched his arm across its back. The door slammed and the men walked round to the front. Stan Shaw started the motor and called back, "Are y'all reet, lad?"

"Fine thanks."

"Well, doan't lean against t'doors or y'll be flying out at next corner!"

The van moved out into the road and down the row of houses. Tyre-irons and cans rattled noisily and the exhaust pipe was loose. He would not have to attempt conversation. Up ahead the men's cigarettes glowed and the car's headlights lobbed against walls, trees, the signpost at the crossroads. Malcolm settled back again beside the dog, wedging his haversack behind his head. It was like a childhood ride on the verge of sleep – the little van rattling between the walls of the twisting dales road, down its own tunnel of light.

Occasionally the beams would reflect off something at a corner and throw the men's shadows back into the van, huge shouldered. Houselights and isolated road lamps cast beads of colour anti-clockwise round the interior, picking out the windows, the door latch, the dog's watchful eye. They plunged on down the lanes and the men's indistinct conversation blurred into the background with the engine and the hum of the tyres.

They left Pamela to listen for Tommy and went out into the dusky yard. Over to the left they could hear the beasts tramping into the byres where the light was, and the men's voices, the clash of cans. Young Stan's voice called out and then the steady throbbing of the milker cut in. Nell moved on, indistinctly, toward the low stone building on their right. She touched his arm, turning as if to guide him, and her hurricane lamp picked out her features eerily from below as she unlatched the shed door. He followed her into the animal closeness there – the pig's feet clattered for a moment and its breath came snuffling inquiringly through the boards of the stall.

"Canst reach yon hook?" Her voice was almost a whisper as his had been this afternoon. He took the lantern from her carefully and held it up as she pointed. A curved rusty spike projected from the low roof beam and he hung the lantern there swinging, casting dim vaults of light around the windowless, closed shed. He was aware then of the broody, clenched upon her fruitless nest in the straw, staring up at him.

The air in the place was heavy, tense with readiness. He did not move, nor she. They did not look toward each other. But the unspoken word filled the shed, waiting only for the one gesture to cross the border. The time was endless. By an effort of will Malcolm turned toward her – standing just beside him and watching him steadily. Her eyes were neither eloquent nor embarrassed, her rather square jaw was lifted slightly. He tried to speak, to cross the time, but it came out as a mumble, indistinct. It was enough, though. "Shall you kiss me?" she said quietly, never taking her eyes from his face.

He moved right against her, his arms by his sides. His eyes began to close as he touched her lips softly. For answer she laid her hand on his shoulder and leaned into him. His arms came up and around her back; her lips parted under his – the simple pressure given and returned. Then a kind of shudder passed through her and at once he was kissing her deeply, tasting the softness of her mouth while her breathing lifted her against him. His eyes opened for an instant and hers were looking darkly back at him, but then her hand began to tug at his neck and her eyelids came heavily down.

They moved against the hayrack and as their bodies parted slightly he slipped his hand upon her breast under her jersey. She reached back with a deft impatient movement and unhooked herself. A weak cry was dragged from him as he touched the fullness of her breasts, the heavy, mother's nipples revealed to him. He was admitted to a more special privacy than that of virginity. Their kissing went on, unbroken, pressing them closer if that were possible at each contact. Little sounds called like lost animals from their throats, while his hand was following the unspoken commands of her body, coming up at last upon the dizzying eager wetness that parted for him and came back like a lightning shock through his fingers and into the pit of his being. And her hand moved gently against his thigh, nudging his erectness, calling him almost unbearably.

He was not expert in his touching, he was a stranger to the needs of her body, but her wanting and her tenderness called him to her. It was him she wanted; she was not surrendering to herself. They slipped down upon the straw, their clothing coming free without a break in the spell. And she drew him into her in the shadow of the stalls, so that pleasure was the wrong word for it and the delicious grasp of her flesh around him was at work too upon his face and in the constant kneading of her hand upon his shoulderblade. She drew up his shirt, her sweater, so that their breasts might come together and arched against him at that first complete touch.

She was gone before him, but still so close. A sudden frightening summons spoke to his loins, a wildheart rhythm as if he would break right through beneath her skin seized them both. And they lay, under the still lantern, while his hand wonderingly stroked the generous softness of her thigh till she turned to him, her eyes dark, was it with tears? and whispered, "Go back to the house, my lad. I'll follow after."

She was taking no nonsense from the children. As the sound of the van faded she set the door firmly to. She chivvied them through their chores – Pam stacking the dishes, young Stan clearing back the chairs and sweeping up crumbs. They were loud and impulsive, infecting Tommy with their mood as he pranced, stamping round the stone floor, shouting out commands. "You've gone daft the lot of you," she snapped, only half amused. She wanted her private place again, if only for a moment.

She scraped all the meal scraps into the bucket with the peelings and bones and told the children to go feed the pig and lock up the hens. "Take Tommy wi' you," she said, "and get some steam out of him. He's driving me crackers."

Stan took down the lantern and led them out, bucket swinging, while Pamela romped with Tommy. The cows scattered at their shouts and then circled round to stare again. Nell closed the door and breathed deeply as the room settled in around her. It was what she must have sometimes, she saw that. She tugged her apron down from the drying rack and tied it around her. It amused her to be doing her chores in her good clothes. She ran water into the sink. It was a funny day all round.

A few minutes later she looked out into the mirror night of the small-paned window above the sink. Her own hand moved into the reflection there, looping the wrung dishcloth over the cold brass tap. The window was a crack open – a cool reminder of the real night through the mirror touched her wet forearm. One of the animals stumbled on a stone in the yard; the darkness, clouded with the herd's breath, seemed soft and protective to her home.

She stooped to see her face in the window, altered and refined by the dark shadows on the imperfect glass. She smiled quietly to herself, remembering the strange compliment again. "Luvleh," she murmured, lingering on the long northern vowels, and, in a kind of wonder, "Luvleh . . ."

Night Travellers

SANDRA BIRDSELL

"When a woman has intercourse," Mika told herself, "she thinks of what might happen." She climbed in the night the hill that led away from the river and James. She travelled in a black and white landscape because it was void of details that would have demanded her attention. And the night was also a cover. Above, the starlit summer sky served only to make God seem more remote, withdrawn. As she walked, she took comfort in the sound of the frogs in the moist ditches on either side of the road, the call of an owl hunting in the park below.

Men, she was certain, thinking of both James and Maurice, didn't think of such things as a seed piercing another seed and a baby growing instantly, latching itself fast to the sides of her life. Men were inside themselves when they shot their juices. It was just another trick that God played, to keep the babies coming. Replenish the earth. Well – she was doing her job.

She reached the top of the hill and then she stooped slightly, giving in to the weight of a stone which she cradled close to her breasts. If Maurice should ever think to ask, she would be able to say, "I was out gathering rocks for my rock garden. It's the only time I can go, when the children are sleeping." And she would still be telling the truth.

She stopped to catch her breath and turned to look back at the park beside the river. Lot's wife looking back with longing towards a forbidden city. But unlike Lot's wife, she did not become a pillar of salt. From among the trees in the park, light shone out from the tiny window in James's bunkhouse. He had turned on the lantern. Pride made her wish that he would have stood for a few decent moments and watched while she climbed the hill. For this reason she'd kept her back straight until she was certain he couldn't see her anymore. But already, he was stretched out, lost in one of the many books he kept on the floor beside the cot. What did she expect? That had been their agreement, not to look for anything from each other. She had

Maurice and the children. He had his dream of voyages in a sailboat.

At the top of the hill, the road stretched broad and straight, one half mile to the centre of town. She could see lights as cars on Main Street headed in and swiftly out of town. She passed by the grove of fruit trees that surrounded her parents' garden. The scent of ripe fruit carried across the road and she thought of the apples her mother had given to her, baskets of them, in the bottom of the cupboard. Her parents' white cottage stood beyond the garden in the darkness. I'm sorry, she said. I forgot about the apples. But with the children my hands are already full. She thought of the children, round cheeked and flushed with their dreams and her step quickened.

Beyond the ditch, there was a sudden rustling sound, like an animal rising up quickly. Mika, startled, stood still and listened. A dark figure stepped from the cover of the fruit trees on to the path that joined the cottage to the road.

"Who's there?" She heard movement, fabric rubbing against fabric. A dry cough. "Papa, is that you?"

Her father came forward in the darkness. Relief made her knees weak.

"Liebe, Mika. I was hoping, but I knew in my heart it was you."

Knew it was me, what? What did he know? "What are you doing up so late?" she asked instead. "The night air isn't good for your lungs."

"When one of my children is in trouble, I don't worry about such things."

"What's this, trouble?" she asked. She felt her heart jump against the stone she clutched tightly to her breast. As he turned towards her, he was illuminated by the moon and she saw that he'd pulled his pants on over his night clothes. His shirt lay open, exposing the onion-like skin on his chest to the cool breeze. She saw concern for her in the deep lines in his face. If only he would use anger, it would be easier to oppose him.

"Nah, you know of what I speak. I've seen your coming and going. I've seen him. I'm ashamed for you."

"What you've seen is me gathering rocks for a rock garden." She held up the stone. "I gather them from beneath the bridge."

"Mika." There was sorrow in his voice.

It was the same tone of voice he'd used on her all her life. It made her change her course of action because she didn't want to be responsible for his sorrow. It was the same thing with Maurice. Peace at all costs. Maurice had forced himself on her and she'd forgiven him because of an offer to build a new window in the kitchen. She hated that about herself.

"So, you've seen my coming and going and you're ashamed for me. I'm not."

He blocked her path. "Come to the house. We should talk and –"

She pushed around him and began to walk away. Talk? Talk about Maurice and his black night moods? About another baby coming in a house full of babies? No, we will talk about my responsibilities instead.

"Have you travelled that far then," she heard him call after her, "that you can now make excuses for your behaviour? What am I to tell the elders at church?"

Before her, silhouetted against the sky, the flutter of wedge-shaped wings, two bats feeding on insects. They would become entangled in her hair. She heard his light step on the road and then he walked beside her. "Why should you tell them anything?" she asked. "It's none of their concern. What I do is my own business."

"We're a community," he said. "People united by our belief, like a family. When one member hurts, the whole family suffers."

"A family. I'm not part of that family," Mika said. "I don't belong anywhere."

"How can you say that? The women welcome you into their homes. They pray for you."

"Oh, they welcome me, all right. I'm to be pitied, prayed for. It gives them something to do."

They walked for a few moments without speaking. He pulled at his thick white moustache, the way he did when he was deep in thought. She stopped, turned to him. "Look. Papa. You know they don't accept Maurice. Even if he wanted to go, they don't invite him into their homes. They don't really accept me, either. So, if you feel it's important to tell the elders, tell them. I don't care."

The bats – their flight was a dance, a sudden dipping, a flutter, a smooth glide and they swerved back in among the trees. Gone. She walked faster. "The children are alone," she said.

"Oh, so you think of the children at least?" he said.

"Of course I think of them. I need something for myself too."

He put his large cool hand on her arm and drew her to the side of the road. His sun-tinged complexion had paled and there was fear in his eyes. "But not this," he said. "Not this. What are you saying? You need to ask God to forgive you. The wages of sin is death."

Always, Bible verses, given in love but becoming brick walls, erected swiftly in her path. The hair on her arms and neck prickled. "Papa," she said. "It's my sin and it's my death. Leave me be." She lifted the stone up and away from her breast and slammed it into the ground. She turned from him quickly and ran with her hands pressed against her stomach.

She undressed quickly, her heart still pounding, and listened to their sounds, the children, breathing all through the house. She'd stood first in one doorway listening for them, then in another, and finally she'd bent over the baby in the crib at the foot of her bed. She'd felt for him in the dark, found a moist lump beneath the blankets. She'd changed his diaper without awaking him. Maurice was not home. He was still at the hotel. She waited for her heart to be still so that she could sleep. She rubbed her stomach gently. What would it be, she wondered, this one that she carried with her to James? Would it be touched or bent in any way by her anger? Below, a door opened. She stiffened, then rolled over and faced the wall as Maurice came up the stairs.

"What are you thinking?" James asked.

Mika swung her legs over the side of the cot and sat up. Her feet rested in a trapezoid of moonlight which shone through the small window of the bunkhouse. She'd been half-listening to James telling her about some one person he knew who had never let him down. His voice rose and fell in its strange British accent and she was able to think above it. Through the other small window at the end of the bunkhouse, she could see her parents' cottage, a white sentinel on a hill. It was in darkness once again, but she was certain her father's white face looked out from behind the lace curtains.

"Oh, I'm not thinking about any one thing in particular." But all day she'd been wondering, how could you be forgiven by God for something you'd done if you weren't sorry you'd done it?

He rose up on his elbow and ran his hand along her arm. The smell of the bunkhouse was his smell, faintly like nutmeg, the warmth of sun trapped in weathered grey planks and it was also the smell of the other men who had slept there; the men who had come to town as James had after the flood to help clean and rebuild it. She put her hand overtop his.

"God, you're beautiful," he said.

"Don't say that."

"What, not say you're beautiful?" He laughed and sat up beside her. He reached for his cigarettes on the window-sill. "You're a strange one."

He was tired of listening to himself talk and had drawn her in by saying, "You're beautiful." In the beginning, he'd pranced around her, so obviously delighted that he'd charmed her into coming away from the riverbank with him, through the park to this bunkhouse. He'd followed her about, picking up the clothing she'd shed, hanging it over a chair so she wouldn't look rumpled when she left. He was a meticulous love-maker. He began by kissing the bottoms of her feet, the backs of her knees, her belly, causing the swing of the pendulum inside her to pause for several seconds at midpoint, so that she was neither being repelled nor attracted but suspended and still.

"Why don't you want me to tell you that you're beautiful?" James asked.

Because she didn't think she was beautiful. There was nothing beautiful about a person who would come home swollen and moist from love-making into the bed of another man. But what Maurice had done was not beautiful either. Two wrongs don't make a right, she'd instruct her own children.

"No, what I meant was, don't say God. Don't bring God into this."

Their thighs touched as they sat on the edge of the cot and she was amazed at how quickly she had become accustomed to the touch and smell of another man. The flare of his match revealed his exquisitely ugly nose. It was a fleshy hook pitted with blackheads. His chin and the skin around his mouth were deeply scarred by acne. You're so ugly, she'd once told him. She'd watched for evidence of injury, a faltering of his tremendous self-confidence. He'd laughed at her attempt, saw through it. She saw him daily as he walked past the house and he was always in a hurry, loose-jointed and thin, moving towards some vision he had of himself and his future.

He held the lit cigarette up to his watch. "Shouldn't you think about heading back? It's almost twelve."

"I've still got time."

He got up from the cot and his tanned chest moved into the trapezoid of light and then his buttocks, pinched together, muscular as he walked to the table beneath the window. He gathered up her hairpins and dropped them into her lap. He never forgot. He made certain each time that she left exactly as she'd come. She scooped the pins up and put them into the pocket of her dress.

"Don't you think you should fix your hair?"

"It's all right. Maurice is never home before I am."

He leaned over her, kissed her forehead. He slipped his hand inside her unbuttoned dress and fondled her. "I love your breasts. I think that's what I'll miss the most about Canada, your beautiful sexy breasts."

She put her arms about his neck and drew him down on top of her. "Once I'm gone," he said into her neck, "if we ever meet again, it will be chance. You know that, don't you?"

"Yes." In another month he wouldn't want her anyway. Already she could feel the baby between them. She listened to the sound of his heart pushing against her chest. The wind had fallen and the silence in the park was complete, the river still. The moment passed. She fingered the hairpins in her pocket. She pulled them loose and scattered them into the folds of his blanket. He'd find them tomorrow. When he was making his bed, tight corners, planning his day, his mind leaping forward to the next event, he'd find her pins and he'd think of her for one second. She knew he wouldn't think of her longer than that, or wonder what she might be doing at that moment or try and recall her features as she did his; she even longed for the sight of his lanky body, his brown trousers flapping loosely about his ankles, the funny way he walked, arms swinging, leading with his ugly nose. I thought of you today, he'd said once, and I got this enormous stiff prick. I think of you too. She couldn't say, I love you.

"You'd better go," he said. "Before I change my mind and keep you here with me all night."

She pushed him from her, sat up and buttoned her dress. She used his comb and began combing her hair which was tangled and damp with sweat. The comb seemed to contain some residue of his energy, a reminder of the range of feelings she'd experienced only thirty minutes before. James got up, walked to the door and she followed him. He stood naked on the step. She gave him the comb. He plucked her dark hairs from its teeth and let the breeze catch them away. Above them, the stars were brilliant and clear. "Will you come tomorrow?" he asked.

"I don't know. If I can, I will."

"Try." He took her hand in his. He pressed the hairpins into her hand. "You've forgotten these."

Mika walked up the hill away from the park, the river, James. She heard nothing of the sounds of the night, the singing of insects, the owl hunting, nor did she see the phosphorus glow of fireflies among the tall grasses in the ditch. She was listening to the sound of her feet on the road, her heart beating, her breath labouring slightly as she climbed the hill and her thoughts. How could she be forgiven by God and brought to a state of serenity and continue to see James at the same time?

When she reached the top of the hill, her father waited on the path, pacing back and forth, swishing mosquitoes from his arms with a switch of leaves. Mika walked faster so that he would know she had no intention of stopping. He ceased pacing. She lifted her head and strode by him. She felt the sting of leaves on her legs. She stopped suddenly, her breath caught in her throat, and fought back anger. He threw the switch aside.

"Where is the stone you've been searching for tonight?" he asked.

"I have nothing to say. You can't make me argue with you. If you want to argue, then do it with yourself." Her voice did not betray her anger. She still felt the biting edge of the leaves on her skin. She walked away swiftly, and then faster until she was running from him. Her breath became tight and then a spot of fire burned in her centre. But she wouldn't stop running until she was home, safe, behind the door.

She sat at the kitchen table and pressed her face against the cool arborite. To be alone for once, just to be left alone. She listened to a fly buzzing against a window. The wind in the kitchen curtain swept against the potted plant. Water dripped into the sink. Something sticky against her arms – she sat up and frowned as her hand met toast crumbs and smears of jam left behind by one of the children. Her legs felt weak as she went over to the sink to stop the dripping of water and to get a cloth to wash the table. She reached to turn the light on above the sink and saw through the window her father entering the yard. She stood with her hands pressed to her face and waited. She wouldn't answer the door and he might think that she was upstairs, sleeping.

His light touch on the door, a gentle knock and – silence. Above her, the sound of electricity in the clock. He coughed twice. She could see him fumbling for his pocket, to spit his blood-flecked mucus into a handkerchief.

"Mika, I know you're there. Mika, open the door."

It wasn't locked, but she knew he wouldn't come in unless she opened it.

"You're causing much sorrow," he said. "Your mother has been crying most of the day."

Crying over children is a waste of time, Mika thought. In the end, they do what they want.

"She says for me to tell you, think of eternity."

The anger erupted. She stepped towards the closed door. "Eternity? Eternity? Papa. I've spent all my life preparing for eternity. No one tells me how to live each day. Right here, where I am."

She heard him sigh. "But when you think of it, we're here for such a little time when you consider all of eternity," he said.

"Yes, and it's my little time. Mine. Not yours."

He didn't speak for a few moments. She held her breath. She waited for him to leave. She sensed his wretched disappointment in her, his fading spirit. I can't help that, she told herself.

"Mika, one thing," he said. His voice was barely more than a whisper. "There's something wrong with your thinking. If we could just talk. I'm not well. I need to know before I –" He broke off and began to cough.

Before I die. She finished the sentence for him. She turned her back to the door and pressed her knuckles into her teeth and bit into them. Anger rose and grew until her fists were free and raised up. That he would try to use his illness against her. It's my life, she told herself. It's my life.

"Go away," she cried. She faced the door once again and stamped her foot. "Go away." She would tear the curtains from the windows, upset chairs, bring all the children running to stare at her anger. She would let them see what had been done to her, she would tell them, it's my life. She would – she gasped. A sharp kick in her belly, then a fluttering of a limb against her walls. Another movement, a sliding downward, a memory drawing her inside instantly like a flick of a knuckle against her temple. The baby. Like all the others asleep in the rooms upstairs, it travelled with her.

"Mika, please. I care for you."

She opened the door and stood before him, head bent and arms hanging by her sides. They faced each other. His shoulders sagged beneath his thin shirt. "Come in," she said. "I'll lend you one of Maurice's sweaters." She began to cry.

He stepped inside quickly and put his hand on her shoulder. "Yes, yes," he said. "That's it. You must cry over what you've done. It's the beginning of healing. God loves a meek and contrite heart."

She leaned into him, felt the sharpness of his rib cage beneath her arms. I cry because I can't have what I want. He's going away soon. I am meek and contrite because he doesn't want anything more than just a fleeting small part of what I am. I am filled with sorrow because I know myself too well. If I could have him, I wouldn't want him.

"It's over," he said. "You won't go and see that man again."

She heard the rasping sound of fluids in his chest. She loved him.

"No, I won't see him anymore."

She turned her face against his chest and stared into the night beyond him. She felt empty, barren, but at peace. In the garden, a bright glow flared suddenly and she thought, it's a cigarette. But the glow rose and fell among the vegetation and then became bead-shaped, blue, brighter, her desire riding the night up and up in a wide arc, soaring across the garden into the branches of thick trees. A firefly, Mika thought. And she watched it until it vanished.

By Grand Central Station I Sat Down and Wept

ELIZABETH SMART

I am standing on a corner in Monterey, waiting for the bus to come in, and all the muscles of my will are holding my terror to face the moment I most desire. Apprehension and the summer afternoon keep drying my lips, prepared at ten-minute intervals all through the five-hour wait.

But then it is her eyes that come forward out of the vulgar dis-embarkers to reassure me that the bus has not disgorged disaster: her madonna eyes, soft as the newly born, trusting as the untempted. And, for a moment, at that gaze, I am happy to forego my future, and postpone indefinitely the miracle hanging fire. Her eyes shower me with their innocence and surprise.

Was it for her, after all, for her whom I had never expected nor imagined, that there had been compounded such ruses of coincidence? Behind her he for whom I have waited so long, who has stalked so unbearably through my nightly dreams, fumbles with the tickets and the bags, and shuffles up to the event which too much anticipation has fingered to shreds.

For after all, it is all her. We sit in a café drinking coffee. He recounts their adventures and says, "It was like this, wasn't it, darling?," "I did well then, didn't I, dear heart?," and she smiles happily across the room with a confidence that appals.

How can she walk through the streets, so vulnerable, so unknowing, and not have people and dogs and perpetual calamity following her? But overhung with her vines of faith, she is protected from their gaze like the pools in Epping Forest. I see she can walk across the leering world and suffer injury only from the ones she loves. But I love her and her silence is propaganda for sainthood.

So we drive along the Californian coast singing together, and I entirely renounce him for only her peace of mind. The wild road winds round ledges manufactured from the mountains and cliffs. The Pacific in blue spasms reaches all its superlatives.

*

Why do I not jump off this cliff where I lie sickened by the moon? I know these days are offering me only murder for my future. It is not just the creeping fingers of the cold that dissuade me from action, and allow me to accept the hypocritical hope that there may be some solution. Like Macbeth, I keep remembering that I am their host. So it is tomorrow's breakfast rather than the future's blood that dictates fatal forbearance. Nature, perpetual whore, distracts with the immediate. Shifty-eyed with this fallacy, I plough back to my bed, up through the tickling grass.

So, through the summer days, we sit on the Californian coast, drinking coffee on the wooden steps of our cottages.

Up the canyon the redwoods and the thick leaf-hands of the castor-tree forbode disaster by their beauty, built on too grand a scale. The creek gushes over green boulders into pools no human ever uses down canyons into the sea.

But poison oak grows over the path and over all the banks, and it is impossible even to go into the damp overhung valley without being poisoned. Later in the year it flushes scarlet, both warning of and recording fatality.

Between the canyons the hills slide steep and cropped to the cliffs that isolate the Pacific. They change from gold to silver, grow purple and massive from a distance, and disintegrate downhill in avalanches of sand.

Round the doorways double-size flowers grow without encouragement: lilies, nasturtiums in a bank down to the creek, roses, geraniums, fuchsias, bleeding-hearts, hydrangeas. The sea blooms. The stream rushes loudly.

When the sea otters leave their playing under the cliff, the kelp in amorous coils appear to pin down the Pacific. There are rattlesnakes and widow-spiders and mists that rise from below. But the days leave the recollection of sun and flowers.

Day deceives, but at night no one is safe from hallucinations. The legends here are all of blood-feuds and suicide, uncanny foresight and supernatural knowledge. Before the convict workers put in the road, loneliness drove women to jump into the sea. Tales were told of the convicts: how some went mad along the coast, while others became hypnotized by it, and, when they were released, returned to marry local girls.

The long days seduce all thought away, and we lie like the lizards in the sun, postponing our lives indefinitely. But by the bathing pool, or on the sandhills of the beach, the Beginning lurks uncomfortably on the outskirts of the circle, like an unpopular person whom ignoring can keep away. The very silence, the very avoiding of any intimacy between us, when he, when he was only a word, was able to cause me sleepless nights and shivers of intimation, is the more dangerous.

Our seeming detachment gathers strength. I sit back impersonally and say, I see human vanity, or feel myself full of gladness because there is a gentleness between him and her, or even feel irritation because he lets her do too much of the work, sits lolling whilst she chops wood for the stove.

But he never passes anywhere near me without every drop of my blood springing to attention. My mind may reason that the tenseness only registers neutrality, but my heart knows no true neutrality was ever so full of passion. One day along the path he brushed my breast in passing, and I thought, Does this efflorescence offend him? And I went into the redwoods brooding and blushing with rage, to be stamped so obviously with femininity, and liable to humiliation worse than Venus's with Adonis, purely by reason of my accidental but flaunting sex.

Alas, I know he is the hermaphrodite whose love looks up through the appletree with a golden indeterminate face. While we drive along the road in the evening, talking as impersonally as a radio discussion, he tells me, "A boy with green eyes and long lashes, whom I had never seen before, took me into the back of a printshop and made love to me, and for two weeks I went around remembering the numbers on bus conductors' hats."

"One should love beings whatever their sex," I reply, but withdraw into the dark with my obstreperous shape of shame, offended with my own flesh which cannot metamorphose into a printshop boy with armpits like chalices.

Then days go by without even this much exchange of metaphor, and my tongue seems to wither in my throat from the unhappy silence, and the moons that rise and set unused, and the suns that melt the Pacific uselessly, drive me to tears and my cliff of vigil at the end of the peninsula. I do not beckon to the Beginning, whose advent will surely strew our world with blood, but I weep for such a waste of life lying under my thumb.

His foreshortened face appears in profile on the car window like the irregular graph of my doom, merciless as a mathematician, leering accompaniment to all my good resolves. There is no medicinal to be obtained from the dried herbs of any natural hills, for when I tread those upward paths, the lowest vines conspire to abet my plot, and the poison oak thrusts its insinuation under my foot.

From the corner where the hill turns from the sea and goes into the secrecy and damp air of forbidden things, I stand disinterestedly examining the instruments and the pattern of my fate. It is a slow-motion process of the guillotine in action, and I see plainly that no miracle can avert the imminent deaths. I see, measuring the time, regarding equably the appearance, but I am as detached as the statistician is when he lists his thousands dead.

When his soft shadow, which yet in the night comes barbed with all the weapons of guilt, is cast up hugely on the pane, I watch it as from a loge in the theatre, the continually vibrating I in darkness. Swearing invulnerability, I measure mercilessly his shortcomings, and with luxurious scorn, ask who could be ensnared there.

But that huge shadow is more than my only moon, more even than my destruction: it has the innocent slipping advent of the next generation, which enters in one night of joy, and leaves a meadow-ful of lamenting milkmaids when its purpose is grown to fruit.

Also, smoothed away from all detail, I see, not the face of a lover to arouse my coquetry or defiance, but the gentle outline of a young girl. And this, though shocking, enables me to understand, and myself rise as virile as a cobra, out of my loge, to assume control.

He kissed my forehead driving along the coast in evening, and now, wherever I go, like the sword of Damocles, that greater never-to-be-given kiss hangs above my doomed head. He took my hand between the two shabby front seats of the Ford, and it was dark, and I was looking the other way, but now that hand casts everywhere an octopus shadow from which I can never escape. The tremendous gentleness of that moment smothers me under; all through the night it is centaurs hoofed and galloping over my heart: the poison has got into my blood. I stand on the edge of the cliff, but the future is already done.

It is written. Nothing can escape. Floating through the waves with seaweed in my hair, or being washed up battered on the inaccessible rocks, cannot undo the event to which there were never any alternatives. O lucky Daphne, motionless and green to avoid the touch of a god! Lucky Syrinx, who chose a legend instead of too much blood! For me there was no choice. There were no crossroads at all.

I am jealous of the hawk because he can get so far out of the world, or I follow with passionate envy the seagull swooping to possible cessation. The mourning-doves mercilessly coo my sentence in the woods. They are the hangmen pronouncing my sentence in the suitable language of love. I climb above the possessive clouds that squat over the sea, but the poison spreads. Naked I wait . . .

I am over-run, jungled in my bed, I am infested with a menagerie of desires: my heart is eaten by a dove, a cat scrambles in the cave of my sex, hounds in my head obey a whip-master who cries nothing but havoc as the hours test my endurance with an accumulation of tortures. Who, if I cried, would hear me among the angelic orders?

I am far, far beyond that island of days where once, it seems, I watched a flower grow, and counted the steps of the sun, and fed, if my memory serves, the smiling animal at his appointed hour. I am shot with wounds which have eyes that see a world all sorrow, always to be, panoramic and unhealable, and mouths that hang unspeakable in the sky of blood.

How can I be kind? How can I find bird-relief in the nest-building of day-to-day? Necessity supplies no velvet wing with which to escape. I am indeed and mortally pierced with the seeds of love.

Then she leans over in the pool and her damp dark hair falls like sorrow, like mercy, like the mourning-weeds of pity. Sitting nymphlike in the pool in the late afternoon her pathetic slenderness is covered over with a love as gentle as trusting as tenacious as the birds who rebuild their continually violated nests. When she clasps her hands happily at a tune she likes, it is more moving than I can bear. She is the innocent who is always the offering. She is the goddess of all things which the vigour of living destroys. Why are her arms so empty?

In the night she moans with the voice of the stream below my window, searching for the child whose touch she once felt and can never forget: the child who obeyed the laws of life better than she. But by day she obeys the voice of love as the stricken obey their god, and she walks with the light step of hope which only the naïve and the saints know. Her shoulders have always the attitude of grieving, and her thin breasts are pitiful like Virgin Shrines that have been robbed.

How can I speak to her? How can I comfort her? How can I explain to her any more than I can to the flowers that I crush with my foot when I walk in the field? He also is bent towards her in an attitude of solicitude. Can he hear his own heart while he listens for the tenderness of her sensibilities? Is there a way at all to avoid offending the lamb of god?

Under the waterfall he surprised me bathing and gave me what I could no more refuse than the earth can refuse the rain. Then he kissed me and went down to his cottage.

Absolve me, I prayed, up through the cathedral redwoods, and forgive me if this is sin. But the new moss caressed me and the water over my feet and the ferns approved me with endearments: My darling, my darling, lie down with us now for you also are earth whom nothing but love can sow.

And I lay down on the redwood needles and seemed to flow down the canyon with the thunder and confusion of the stream, in a happiness which, like birth, can afford to ignore the blood and the tearing. For nature has no time for mourning, absorbed by the turning world, and will, no matter what devastation attacks her, fulfil in underground ritual, all her proper prophecy.

Gently the woodsorrel and the dove explained the confirmation and guided my return. When I came out of the woods on to the hill, I had pine-needles in my hair for a bridal-wreath, and the sea and the sky and the gold hills smiled benignly. Jupiter has been with Leda, I thought, and now nothing can avert the Trojan Wars. All legend will be born, but who will escape alive?

But what can the woodsorrel and the mourning-dove, who deal only with eternals, know of the thorny sociabilities of human living? Of how the pressure of the hours of waiting, silent and inactive, weighs upon the head with a physical force that suffocates? The simplest daily pleasantries are torture, and a samson effort is needed to avoid his glance that draws me like gravity.

For excuse, for our being together, we sit at the typewriter, pretending a necessary collaboration. He has a book to be typed, but the words I try to force out die on the air and dissolve into kisses whose chemicals are even more deadly if undelivered. My fingers cannot be martial at the touch of an instrument so much connected with him. The machine sits like a temple of love among the papers we never finish, and if I awake at night and see it outlined in the dark, I am electrified with memories of dangerous propinquity.

The frustrations of past postponement can no longer be restrained. They hang ripe to burst with the birth of any moment. The typewriter is guilty with love and flowery with shame, and to me it speaks so loudly I fear it will communicate its indecency to casual visitors.

How stationary life has become, and the hours impossibly elongated. When we sit on the gold grass of the cliff, the sun between us insists on a solution for which we search in vain, but whose urgency we unbearably feel. I never was in love with death before, nor felt grateful because the rocks below could promise certain death. But now the idea of dying violently becomes an act wrapped in attractive melancholy, and displayed with every blandishment. For there is no beauty in denying love, except perhaps by death, and towards love what way is there?

To deny love, and deceive it meanly by pretending that what is unconsummated remains eternal, or that love sublimated reaches highest to heavenly love, is repulsive, as the hypocrite's face is repulsive when placed too near the truth. Farther off from the centre of the world, of all worlds, I might be better fooled, but can I see the light of a match while burning in the arms of the sun?

No, my advocates, my angels with sadist eyes, this is the beginning of my life, or the end. So I lean affirmation across the café table, and surrender my fifty years away with an easy smile. But the surety of my love is not dismayed by any eventuality which prudence or pity can conjure up, and in the end all that we can do is to sit at the table over which our hands cross, listening to tunes from the wurlitzer, with love huge and simple between us, and nothing more to be said.

So hourly, at the slightest noise, I start, I stand ready to feel the roof cave in on my head, the thunder of God's punishment announcing the limit of his endurance.

She walks lightly, like the child whose dancing feet will touch off gigantic explosives. She knows nothing, but like autumn birds feels foreboding in the air. Her movements are nervous, there are draughts in every room, but less wise than the birds whom small signs send on 3,000-mile flights, she only looks vaguely out to the Pacific, finding it strange that heaven has, after all, no Californian shore.

I have learned to smoke because I need something to hold on to. I dare not be without a cigarette in my hand. If I should be looking the other way when the hour of doom is struck, how shall I avoid being turned into stone unless I can remember something to do which will lead me back to the simplicity and safety of daily living?

IT is coming. The magnet of its imminent finger draws each hair of my body, the shudder of its approach disintegrates kisses, loses wishes on the disjointed air. The wet hands of the castor-tree at night brush me and I shriek, thinking that at last I am caught up with. The clouds move across the sky heavy and tubular. They gather and I am terror-struck to see them form a long black rainbow out of the mountain and disappear across the sea. The Thing is at hand. There is nothing to do but crouch and receive God's wrath.

*

And so, returning to Canada through the fall sunshine, I look homeward now and melt, for though I am crowned and anointed with love and have obtained from life all I asked, what am I as I enter my parents" house but another prodigal daughter? I see their faces at which I shall never be free to look dispassionately. They gaze out of the window with eyes harassed by what they continually fear they see, like premature ghosts, straggling homeward over the plain.

And I, who have the world in my pocket, can bring them nothing to comfort their disappointment or reward their optimism, but supplicate again for the fatted calf which they killed so often before and so in vain. Parents' imaginations build frameworks out of their own hopes and regrets into which children seldom grow, but instead, contrary as trees, lean sideways out of the architecture, blown by a fatal wind their parents never envisaged.

But the old gold of the October trees, the stunted cedars, the horizons, the chilly gullies with their red willow whips, intoxicate me and confirm belief in what I have done, claiming me like an indisputable mother saying Whether or No, Whether or No, my darling. The great rocks rise up to insist on belief, since they remain though Babylon is fallen, being moulded, but never conquered, by time pouring from eternity. Can I expect less than sympathy from those who see such things when they draw aside their curtains in the mornings? Like Antaeus, when I am thrust against this earth, I bounce back recharged with hope. Every yellow or scarlet leaf hangs like a flag waving me on. The brown ones lie on the ground like a thousand thousand witnesses to the simplicity of truth.

So love may blind the expectation in my parents' eyes; or eloquence rise from my urgency and melt them too with ruth; understanding may now stalk down Sparks Street in every clerk, undoing wrongs begun before Wolfe; or in Honey Dew cafés a kind look glance towards me as I open the door.

Asking no one's forgiveness for sins I refuse to recognize, why do I cry then to be returning homeward through a land I love like a lover? From a long way off those faces with their prayers like wounds peer out of the window, stiff with anxiety, but ready to welcome me with love. The sound of their steps pacing before the fireplace voices all the pain of the turning world.

O Absalom, Absalom, melt, melt with ruth.

Coming from California, which is oblivious of regret, approaching November whips me with the passion of the dying year. And after the greed already hardening part of the American face into stone, I fancy I see kindness and gentleness looking out at me from train windows. Surely the porter carrying my bags has extracted a spiritual lesson from his hardship. Surely this acceptance of a mediocre role gives human dignity.

And over the fading wooden houses I sense the reminiscences of the pioneers' passion, and the determination of early statesmen who were mild but individual, and able to allude to Shakespeare while discussing politics under the elms. No great neon face has been superimposed over their minor but memorable history. Nor has the blood of the early settlers, spilt in feud and heroism, yet been bottled by a Coca-Cola firm and sold as ten-cent tradition.

The faces, the faded houses, the autumn air, everything is omens of promise to the prodigal. But leaning against the train window, drunk with the hope which anything so unbegun always instils, I remember my past returnings: keep that vision, I pray, pressing my forehead against the panes: the faces *are* kind; the people *have* reserve; the birds gather in groups to migrate, forecasting fatal change: remember, when your eyes shrivel aggrievedly because you notice the jealousy of those that stay at home, here is no underlining of an accidental picturesqueness, but a waiting, unselfconscious as the unborn's, for future history to be performed upon it.

Remember that although this initial intoxication disappears, yet these things in that hour moved you to tears, and made of an outward gaze through the dining-car window a plenitude not to be borne.

The Only Daughter

LEON ROOKE

The lane upon which the child walked was long and straight, with high red-dirt walls to either side, which sometimes she could see above and other times could not. It was more trench than road, wide enough perhaps for three people to walk abreast, perhaps wide enough for a wagon. Yes, for a wagon, for she could see in the slippery mud where one had come and gone, though not when. The walls were eroded by rain and where boulders were packed into the dirt scraggly bushes, leafless now, made vain attempts at renewal. She walked mostly in the lane's middle, trying to avoid the collected puddles, since her shoes were new, or newish, and she yet took some pride in them. Suitcases half her own height hung from each arm. She had started the day with a ribbon through her hair, tied at the top in a bow, but at some point several miles back the ribbon had come loose and now lay unmissed in the mud. She wore, in addition to the shoes and a thin cotton dress, a black coat that flopped unevenly around her heels. A circle of mud, steadily expanding, caked the hem and seemed to pull the coat further from her shoulders. From time to time, fretfully, she yanked it back. A single large button secured the coat; the button was ever travelling up to her throat; her heels were ever stepping on to the hem. The coat draped loosely on her, an adult's coat, inherited with something of that other person's shape still intact. The sleeves were twice folded at each wrist that her hands might be clear. It had had a belt once; she wished she had it now.

From time to time she paused and placed the suitcases on dry earth or on stumps, on weedy patches in the lane, and shook her arms until feeling returned to them.

She had been walking this lane since first light; she had traversed it for a portion of yesterday. Now the sun, although it brought no warmth, was directly overhead. It moved when she moved, and at what pace she moved, and stopped when she stopped. But she did not look often at the sun or sky; she kept her sight on the road, on her feet, for the lane was strewn with rock and brush, with brown puddles of varying size, with massive boulders that cropped up from floor and wall. Occasionally, where the land was flat, the woods encroached until the land all but disappeared. She went, at such times, the way the wheel tracks went, passing under pine and cedar, under hemlock and droopy locust, under willow and numerous other dusty, unswaying trees. Where red dirt receded, clumps of wild grass took over, competing with moss and clover, and here she took longer rests. With leaves and sticks she wiped new layers of mud from her shoes. Her feet were wet and cold, but she was accustomed to this and gave thought to it only when pebbles worked inside her shoes. She wore a grown woman's nylon stockings, which bunched at her ankles. Originally these had been retained by rubber bands just above her knees, but the bands, rotted already, had broken countless times and no longer held. One she sometimes chewed in her mouth, trudging along now at a diminishing pace.

Rests were more frequent now. Her shoulders ached. Her legs ached, and her arms and hands worst of all, though her feet ached too. Her shoes were too tight. The man at the store had told her they would loosen, but they hadn't. This morning they'd been stiff and hard, though still wet, and she'd opened a heel blister, getting them on. She'd bitten her lip and tears had come, but she'd kept them on. She was too cold to feel much anyhow. Her hands were blistered too. They were swollen some. The suitcase handles were sharp, like little razors. She'd tried wrapping leaves about the handles but they'd shredded in a minute. They'd been slippery too. Green stuff had got into her cuts and stung. Maybe it was her hands that hurt the most. She'd thought it was her hands, but she'd carried the cases a few feet and the ache had hit her shoulders again. She was hungry, but she wasn't going to think about that. The shoulder ache was worse. Pins and needles stabbed down from her neck; her neck was stiff. A stiff neck was nothing though. She could put up with a stiff neck. The shoulder ache made her groan; it made her grit her teeth. But after a while she'd decided it was her arms that hurt more, the bones stretched near to bursting. Nothing could hurt more than that. But she'd halt and put down the cases and dangle her arms and shake that pain away. She couldn't shake out the shoulder ache;

shoulder was worse. She was hungry, but she wasn't going to think about that. Heck with that. What was bad was the button, which kept crawling up, gnawing a hole at her throat, always in the same spot. Maybe that was worse. Like somebody digging at it with an ice pick or pinching that same spot over and over. This was the most maddening somehow, because such a little thing. You wouldn't believe a smooth button could be so sharp. The same place over and over, her skin raw. Like her heels. Her heels were bloody. These stockings were ruined. Well she didn't mind that; she had plenty more. Maybe a dozen pair. She had a hat too, but you didn't need a hat out here. A hat would be silly out here. Mud was on her coat, but she couldn't help that. Mud was nothing, you could wash out that. She hoped you could. This dress she had on, you could sure wash that. She'd done so herself, and ironed it too, not three days ago. Not that a person would know it now. It was her shoes she most cared about. They were pretty shoes. If she ruined them that would be her bad luck because she had no other pair. But how could you ruin cowhide? Cows got wet, they didn't ruin; no reason these would either. She was hungry, but she wasn't going to think about that. Thinking about it only made matters worse. Last night she'd thought about it anyway, but only for a little while. Then she'd slept and thought about her aches. About which was worse. It was awful, whichever way you thought, but she wasn't going to cry about it any more than she was going to sit down in this lane and quit. She didn't mean to walk this road forever; aches would mend, cuts and blisters heal. She'd been tired before, tired a thousand times. Hungry too. But she'd got over it. She would this time too. So she bit her lip and let her eyes stay wet as they wanted to; she laboured on. She'd be there pretty soon. This lane wasn't no endless highway going nowhere. She knew where it was going. Her instructions had been clear on that score. *Git out fast. Go to him. This is where he lives.*

Whenever she stopped now she would lay back if that were possible, and draw the big coat tight about herself, and close her eyes. She would doze. But always, after a minute or two she would bolt up as if from fright, and dig both hands into her coat pockets. The left pocket contained an unopened package of Luden's Wild Cherry cough drops, and five or six black hairpins when these did not happen to be in her hair. In the right pocket was a small leather change purse, much scarred. She would open it and empty it in her lap and count her money. Her fear was that she would lose this or that it somehow might be stolen. She feared pickpockets even here on this solitary lane, for long ago, in another place, her mother had screamed and yelled and cried because a pickpocket had got her money. She remembered that. She remembered her mother's alarm as she cried, "How can we live? Tell me how we can manage now!" She remembered her mother's alarm, and her own, but not how they had managed. She had noticed no difference in how they got along. They had moved, she remembered that. Her mother had been absent much of the time. This was because of the pickpocket. She knew that.

She had in her possession two quarters, three dimes, a nickel, and four pennies. Yesterday she had had more but the man on the bus had taken the dollar bill. He had taken the half-dollar too, and had seemed to want to take more, but she had bitten her lip, watching his every move, and thirty-nine cents had been miraculously returned to her palm. "How I know you're not cheatin' me?" she said. "How I know how much this bus trip is?" "You don't," he said. He'd had a cigarette dangling from his lips the whole time, and scabs on his hand. He'd had black hairs in his nose. "You don't. No, you don't. You don't know nothin', I expect." She'd not risen to this taunt. She'd kept her palm open, stretched out to him. "You want me to kiss it?" he said. "Maybe you want a glob of my spit?" She'd yanked her hand back, since it seemed no more change was forthcoming. She'd put the coins in her purse and the purse in her coat pocket, and staggered down the aisle with her two suitcases. She'd put the cases on a seat at the back where there was a big round hump in the floor. For resting your feet, she supposed. She climbed over them and sat at the window, which wouldn't open. "You see them racks?" he said. "Them racks is for the suitcases. Ain't you never travelled before?" He stood over her, his cigarette dangling, squinting at her. She'd thrown her body over the suitcases. "I ain't putting them nowhere," she said. "I ain't having my property stole."

He'd gone.

She talked to no one during the journey. The bus was nearly empty. A boy hardly out of diapers sat up front, making faces at her. She gave him her black look and kept her lips sewed tight. He came back once and said, "This ain't your bus. I never seen you on this bus before." When he went back to his seat his mother slapped him. She ought to have. She ought to have smacked him a dozen times. She curled up, making a careful, secret study of each inch of the interior. Cold wind came through the window. The tyres whined. The seats were hard and squared off at the back where there was a rod you could lean your head against. The bus had a flat roof with rounded edges. The floor was nothing but tin. The seats weren't yellow though, like the dinette she and her mother used to have. The terrain outside was mostly a blur, and she told herself it wasn't worth looking at. The window was smeary anyhow.

It wasn't worth a bit what she'd paid.

In the afternoon, and repeatedly after that, she moved up the aisle to remind the man with the cigarette where she wanted to get off and to wonder aloud if he hadn't passed it already.

"Nobody told me it was this far," she said.

"That's right," he said. "You're abducted. This here is John Dillinger at the wheel."

"I don't care who you are. You better stop at that crossroads I told you about."

"It ain't no crossroads," he said, "it ain't hardly nothing. Just a scratch in the woods, that's all it is."

"Says you," she said.

"This here bus is heated," he told her. "Supposing you take off that there hot coat and try to relax yourself." She held her hand clenched over the purse in her pocket while she talked to him. She had no faith in him. He was one of them smart talkers, those her mother said you had to look out for. He looked to her like an out-and-out damn fool, with his stubbly growth of beard, with his scabs and dangling cigarette and his eyes squinted up so tight it surprised her he could see the road.

"Who you visiting?" he asked, but she locked her lips and veered back to her seat.

If he didn't stop where he was supposed to she didn't know what she'd do. She wondered what a body was supposed to do when it had to go to the bathroom. The boy up front got smacked again.

"It's going to rain," somebody said.

Somebody was always saying that. They got their brains out of a marble jug.

The man nearest her was eating a white apple. She'd never seen no white apple before. It almost made her puke to watch him eat it. But she watched every bite he took, and when he had gnawed it down to seeds and core she saw him drop it on the floor. She wouldn't eat no white apple no matter how hungry she got. She wouldn't eat no turnips either, or spinach, or innards of any kind. She wouldn't eat no fatback either.

She had her cough drops, but she was saving them.

She gnawed her nails and kept her vigil; she didn't know when it was she fell asleep.

Near dark, the bus driver pulled to the side of the road. It was the bumps, and gravel hitting the underside, that woke her. "Somebody meeting you, I hope," he said. "I don't take no responsibility. This here bus line don't take none. Strange things go on in them woods. Wild animals, too. Naw sir, you wouldn't find me getting off at no godforsaken place like this. Not at nighttime no how."

This angered her. It angered her because his saying it scared her and because she knew he saw it.

"I don't see no crossroads," she said.

He offered to help with her suitcases, but she held tightly to them. The boy who'd made faces was asleep with his mouth open. He had a booger hanging from his nose and snot smeared across his cheek. The woman beside him was smoking, staring in a dull way at nothing. She didn't have no nice hose like her mother had worn. She didn't wear no rouge or lipstick either.

It was a real dumb load on that bus.

She followed the driver to the front of the bus. He put a foot on the bumper and leaned his elbow on his knee. His shirt was bunched up, and she could see his ugly naked skin. The air the bus lights shot through was smoky. It did little cartwheels in the beams. "There she is," he said, meaning the lane.

But she didn't see it.

"There ain't nothing," she said. "You've let me off at the wrong place." She wanted her money back, but didn't say it. He was still pointing. "It's there," he said. "You can call it a crossroads till gold comes out your behind, but your calling it so ain't going to change it none. It's that little lane you see yonder by the stump. It ain't hardly more than a red-dirt path and you can beat my rear end till dooms-day and I'd still stay ignorant of where it goes. There was a house there once, or a store. I never seen no traffic come up out of that lane. I never had nobody go down it before. Far as I know there ain't a soul lives down that lane. Maybe a few squirrels and rabbits, maybe snakes, if they's got souls. I hope you come for a long visit cause you going to be in no shape to leave if ever you get where you're going. Be solid night soon. Looks to me like you took the wrong time to pay a call. But that's the road you ask for. That's Spider's Lane. You ask me, you're going to wish you'd stayed where you was."

He was a big blabbermouth. She would have told him so, but he was wrestling the suitcases from her. He tugged them from her hands and crossed the highway and plonked them down on the other side. She saw the lane now. Vines grew over it at the mouth. She still didn't see no stump.

"There you go," he said. "Service with a smile. I come by first thing in the morning, you want to go back, but you got to wave me down. Ticket cost the same, coming or going."

She picked up her cases and started off.

"You're uppity," he said, pitching his live cigarette into the ditch. "But I don't hold it against you. I reckon you never had no one to show you how to behave."

She called him a son of a bitch, with her teeth together and her eyes slitted, just the way her mother would have.

He sauntered back to his driver's seat. Two or three faces were at the greasy windows, mutely studying her. She heard the gears grind. Groaning, its twin beams slicing the dark, the bus moved on and after interminable seconds disappeared around the curve, its four blinkers still flashing.

She didn't believe this was the right place. Crossroads was what she'd been told to head down. But the sign, rotted where it entered the ground and thrust back into the bushes, had the right words on it, splashed on in a faded paint. *"Spider's Lane. You go down Spider's Lane till you're about to drop. When you've dropped I guess you'll be near enough."*

"But I don't want to go."

" 'Want' ain't got britches no more she can wear. 'Want' is dropped dead. I can't look out for you no more. 'Looking out' has finally got the best of me. You go."

"Yes'm."

"Are you going?"

"Yes'm."

"Then pull the covers up and let me sleep. Tuck me in."

"Yes'm."

She'd spent the night on pine straw in a hollow about a hundred feet off the road, camouflaging herself under broken branches, the coat pulled up over her head, the money purse in a fist up under her chin. She chewed on bitter pine bark and once or twice swallowed some. Her stomach churned. It was like someone inside trying to talk to her, refusing to shut up.

"I can't let you sleep with me. You'd kick. Now wouldn't you?"

"Yes'm."

"Sit there a while. Hold my hand."

"I will, mama. You rest now."

In late afternoon this second day she came to a creek and crossed it, carrying her shoes in one hand, her coat pulled up and bunched at the waist. Then she came back and again forded the stream, one of the suitcases riding at perilous balance on her head. The muddy bottom sucked at her feet. Green slime covered the rocks; she tried to avoid them. The water turned a thick brown where she walked. It trickled politely over the stones; up there a ways a skinny tree was down and twigs and leaves snagged on the skinny tree in the making of a forlorn dam. The stream swept at a good pace around it. There wouldn't be no beavers here. Beavers had better sense than to be in a place miserable as this. The woods here were thick and scraggly. Vines swept up over everything and hung still as ragged curtains from the trees. The earth was shaded, with pock holes scattered all over, each filled with an inch or two of water, and the creek was dark too, of an amber colour. She got the second suitcase across, though she nearly lost it once when she slipped. Her grip gave way on the coat bunched at her waist and the coat got wet from the knees down; as she reached for it her sleeve unrolled and it too plopped into the water. At the bank she took off the coat and squeezed what she could from it. Then she put it on again. It was heavier now. The sleeve was cold and soggy against her wrist. She shivered, and stood a moment hugging herself.

Mud squished between her toes. She knelt at the water's edge and let the cool water flow over her feet. She put her hands under, marvelling at how the slow current wanted to carry her hands along. Her stomach rumbled. She felt a wave of dizziness and knew she'd have to eat something soon. She should have spent some of her money for beans or a can of potted meat, but she hadn't been able to part with it. The prices alone was enough to make your gorge rise.

She thought of the cough drops in her pocket. Although here was food of a kind, she refrained from reaching for them. She'd never have put out good money for these cough drops herself. They'd been in her mama's shoulder purse, along with the hairpins and rumpled tissues, along with the comb and the teensy mirror in the fold-up case. The change purse had two dollars in it then, plus the change. It had her pills too, in a tiny brown bottle, only six left. Six gone to waste. She'd tried selling these back to the pharmacy man on the corner but he'd laughed at her. "How do I know you ain't spiked them pills?" he said. "How I know where in thunderation they been?" She'd insisted but he hadn't wilted an inch. The skinflint. Yes, you paid good money for a thing, it cost you an arm and a leg, but when you tried selling it back to these devils you found out how worthless it was. Those pills hadn't helped her mama. She'd said so herself a million times.

But you never knew. Those pills were now back in her mama's shiny black shoulder purse and the purse back in the suitcase. If ever she got to feeling run down the way her mama did then maybe she'd take them herself. Maybe they'd pep her up.

She examined her feet in the running water and wondered if she shouldn't wash her stockings now. They were bunched up wet around her ankles. She pulled them high again. They were streaked with mud, and stiff, nothing but pudding where her heels had bled. They had a zillion snags and runs. But there was no use now in opening up a suitcase and getting out another pair. In ten minutes they'd be as bad off as these. Best to wait until she got where she was going.

She cupped her hands into the water and drank. It dribbled

between her fingers and down her chin. The water was cool, but tasted smoky somehow. It tasted burned. It didn't have the sparkle of city water. No telling what animals had dropped their leavings in it. Oh, but it was cool. She wiped wet hands over her face and neck and throat, for she was sweaty from all this carrying. Oh my, that felt good. Be nice to just dunk her head underwater. But the water stung her blisters; it pitched a fit at her sores. She winced, thinking maybe this was the worst pain. But it wasn't. The worse pain was all over now, including in her stomach where the water she'd drank weighed like an anvil.

She thought seriously about taking off her clothes and bathing herself all over; there might be some advantage in this. It didn't hurt you none, her mama said, to be clean. But the air had a nip in it. She didn't want to end up coughing and moaning the way her mama had. Her mama had smelled. She'd run the washcloth over her mama and pat on the pink powder but in a little while the smell came back again. A smell sort of like a hot ironing board. Her skin was dark too, like the cover you ironed on. Though her mama hadn't smelled it. She'd said, "No, no, don't open the window! Can't I at least rest in peace?"

Minnows swam at her feet. They'd shoot off a little way then stop dead still, then dart off again. They hardly paid any attention now to her wriggling toes. She lifted her arms and sniffed under the armpits the way she'd at times seen her mama do. She couldn't smell anything. She didn't need no bath. To bathe here naked in the open would be next to foolishness. First thing you knew somebody'd be flying over in an aeroplane. Or some thief coming along. Anyway she'd never in her life bathed in full daylight. Bathing was for nighttime so you could go to sleep clean and dream nice pictures and wake up in the morning spick-and-span.

She looked hard at the suitcases. They'd got so heavy. My lifely goods, she thought. They weigh more than me. She wondered if maybe she couldn't lighten her load, maybe hide some of it away up here. Maybe take out the best things from the one case and stuff them in the other and go on along with that. She strode out of the creek, searching about for a good place. Maybe over there by that rotted stump. She'd never seen a place with so many stumps, or with so much rot. Some of it was black, too, like there had been a fire through here at some time. Long long ago, probably before she was born. Probably before her mama was born too. Before anybody was. Before there was this poor excuse for a lane or even spiders you could name it after. Probably a zillion years ago.

She saw no wheel tracks here and for an instant felt alarm. Had she somehow got off the main path? The tracks had come to be like company to her. But no, there they were, there they had been all the time. One set going one way, one going another. You could tell by how the horse hooves, if horse it was – mule maybe – left their prints in the ground. The one going was deeper; it had been carrying something. She wondered who had rode that wagon. Wondered if maybe it wasn't him. *Him*, yes, but she wouldn't say his name. It scared her even to think of him. What would he say when he saw her? Would he chase her off with a stick? *"Don't let him,"* her mama had said. *"You stand right up to him. Call him a jackal to his face, if that's what's come of him."*

She knelt over the bag before opening it; she listened, breath held, for any sound. Far off she saw a bird going. There was another one up in the big tree. Funny she hadn't seen it before. But she hadn't and maybe that meant there was a lot else she hadn't seen. Peeping Toms. Maybe this minute somebody was off in the bushes spying. Maybe him. Aw, heck no. That was foolishness. It looked more to her like no one was within a million miles. No one knew whether she was living or dead.

Everything was so still. Still and near to dead. She was going to have a hard time getting used to a quiet place like this. Even the creek bed seemed to feel it; its trickles were like little whispers over the stones.

"It's going to try me to my very eyeballs," she said aloud, just to give a voice to the place. "I don't know I can." Her voice shook. She laughed at herself.

She dragged both cases to the bushes at the side of the lane. She worked carefully and quickly, sorting out the goods, exchanging articles contained in one for articles in the other. Her mama's high-heeled pumps delayed her a bit. She placed the soft leather up to her cheek, her eyes closed. Closed and wet. Her mama had loved these pumps. She'd hardly worn them at all, loving them that much. She had a dozen clear memories of her mama in these pumps. Her mama had such beautiful legs. Ankles thin as her wrists and her hips lovely as a moving picture lady. Your heart went up to your throat when you thought of mama in these pumps. You'd think heads would snap off the way men turned theirs when mama when by. "Oh, mama, damn you," she said. "Oh, damn you." She wiped the coat sleeve against her eyes and took bitter sight on these high heels. Her mama had bought these for dancing first: *"I needed new pumps to go with my dress. Do you like them? You don't mind my leaving you alone? You go to sleep early and I promise I'll tell you everything went on when I come in."* Her mama danced in these shoes, but only that once. They were hardly worn; not a scuff any place. She saw her mama at the long mirror, turning, looking down at one lifted leg. Then turning and lifting the other. *"Are they straight, honey? My seams? Aren't they pretty with these new pumps? Am I pretty enough, do you think, to be seen in this world? You can come with us if you want to. Monty won't mind."*

She bit her lips, told herself to stop this. "Stop it," she said. "Stop this snivelling like a backward child. You quit it right now."

She'd take these pumps with her. Best be on the safe side. She'd take this silver mirror too, and the jewel box. She'd take these framed pictures of herself and her mama. Take these fancy scarves. These white gloves that went all the way up to her elbow. In these gloves wasn't mama grand!

She crushed down the lid and after an effort got it snapped. Both sides were stuffed out fat. She couldn't lift the bag. Oh heavy, too heavy. She stood up straight, screeching silently at the weight. She kicked the ground in fury and tried again. She strained, applying both hands, tongue between her teeth, crossing her eyes, and got it an inch or two off the ground. Hopeless. How could a few doodads weigh so much? It beat her. "It beats me," she said. "I'm stumped." The attempt made her giddy. It made her pulse race. She felt a flush of scarlet on her face and half-sat, half-tumbled down. Her knees shook. She let her head fall between her legs; she watched the ground undulate. The taste of bile charged up her throat. She couldn't stop the quivering in her legs. Her eyes refused to focus. Her face was hot and she slapped a hand up over her eyes, thinking: I've got what mama had. I've got a fever to beat the band. Her head swam. Was this how mama had felt? Her heartbeat was racing, she could hear it going clippity clop. Yesterday? Was it yesterday morning she'd eaten the last dregs of what was in the icebox and poured out a bottle of milk that had turned? Gurgle-gurgle. She'd had saltine crackers and a smear of peanut butter left in the jar. She could see that clearly, the empty jar, but not where that was. She could see the man with the cigarette dangling and the four bus lights blinking against the dark. She could see the white apple the man across from her had and in her hunger she almost reached for it. *Did* reach for it, or for something, because a second later the apple spun away and bus too and in its place, head lowered between her legs, there was just her own hand wildly scratching in the dirt. I've slipped off the deep end, she thought, like that sister my daddy had. My yo-yo's come loose. Was she so hungry she'd now eat dirt? She half-remembered a time when she had. As a baby she had. So her mama said. "You and dirt! You'd have stuffed wiggling beetles in your jaws if I hadn't kept you from it!" "Where was *he*, then?" "Him? Your papa? He was long gone. Or I was. You'd have had to chain me up like a dog to keep me out there." "What's he like? Did you ever see him again?" "Oh, once or twice. He come around. But our feelings for each other were all dead and buried by that time. I didn't know him from Adam, and wanted him less." "Would he know me now?" "Know you? Well, maybe he would. When you cry, when you want something bad and can't have it, you both have that hungdog miserable look. I reckon he might recognize that."

She got the bags sorted to her satisfaction. That one she was leaving behind she carried up through the woods, over a marsh that slurped at her heels; she hid the case away behind bramble bushes at the edge of a wide, untended, gullied field. She threw dead brush up over the hiding place. The bag looked safe enough there. She circled the spot, eyeing it from every angle, and pronounced herself satisfied. "Take a hawk's eye to find it," she said. "Anyway, I don't mean it to stay for long."

Something pricked at her ankle. She looked down with a screech. A black tick had its nose buried in her flesh. She picked it off, then another between her toes and rubbed her toes over the earth to erase the itch. She felt something crawling lightly, ticklishy, over her neck and she whirled in a fury, clawing with her fingers there. In a moment she was scratching herself all over, scrambling back through the marsh, feeling ticks all over. They were black ugly

things and came loose with little tufts of white skin clinging to them.
A pair of startled quail shot up in a sudden flurry of wings, startling
her. In an instant other groups burst out of nearby bush and weed
and cut in a swift, curving line through the sky. They circled high
and disappeared. A crow cawed somewhere. She heard the rattle of
something else too, uneven and distant, an echo perhaps, and stood
stock-still, cupping hands to one ear. It came again, a rumble this
time. She darted free of the marsh, zigzagging out, the long coat
yanked up to her waist and flapping. She dropped quickly down
into a spread of weeds. It sounded like a wagon. It sounded like
someone coming, to her. "Goddamnit," she whimpered, "I ain't
ready yet."

For a long time, flat in the weeds, her head raised, she didn't
move but stayed alert to all sounds, her muscles taut, her breath
shallow and quick. What if it's him? she thought. What if he sees my
suitcase on that road? What if it's stole, or he's got a gun and shoots
me dead? She considered leaping up, racing back to the lane, yanking her suitcase off into the bush. But she couldn't take the chance.
She didn't want to meet him like this, not in no woods and looking
like a rat. She would meet him, had to, but not like this, like some
brainless waif hiding in the woods, not knowing doodly-squat.

No further sound came. There was only stillness over the place.
"There ain't nothing," she whispered at last. "I imagined that
noise." Finally she got up, dusted off her clothes, searched her legs
and arms for ticks, and returned in a run to the lane.

Nothing had changed. There her suitcase was and the babbling
creek, nothing coming either up or down the lane. I dreamt up that
wagon, she thought. I surely did. To calm herself she stepped her
bare feet into the creek's cold water. Her mama had told her how to go
about it: "You walk right up to his door," she said. "You hold your
head high, too; I don't want him thinking I didn't know how to raise
you. You watch out for dogs; he'll have those. You knock and when
he comes you tell him who you are. You tell him what's gone on here.
What's come of me. You tell him it's his turn now." She'd made it
sound so easy, her mama had. But she hadn't told her it would take
days and days and a million miles to get her there. She hadn't said
nothing about how soon a full belly could start rubbing backbone.
She'd have to eat something soon; she couldn't go on like his.

She stared down at the tranquil water at her feet. There was white sand washed up in this spot. The water was clear, numbing to her legs. Her legs looked split, like she'd stepped out of her bones. She flexed her toes, grimacing at the icy waves. "What if he don't want me?" she said. "What if he says I can go rot in hell?" Her mama hadn't answered that. Her mama, poor thing, had moaned and coughed and slept.

Minnows swam lazily at her feet, looking silvery in the light. Her body threw a zigzag shadow as she bent her face to the surface. A minnow was a fish. A person could eat fish. The minnows veered away as she lowered her hands into the water. Then they reassembled to drift somnolently between her fingers and legs. Her stomach growled; her mouth moistened. She reckoned people had eaten worse. Babies gnawed at crib paint and didn't always die from it. In the picture show, seated beside her mama, she'd seen ritzy people eating frog legs. That would be a whole lot worse. Once her own mama had cooked what she called brains, and made her taste it. She didn't reckon minnows could kill her.

She cupped her hands together and brought them up ever so slowly. Mostly they drifted free. Those few trapped in her hands shook their tails as the water dribbled away; then they stretched flat and still against her skin, looking so much smaller than they had in the water.

Eyes closed, making a face, she licked her palms clean. She swallowed without chewing and imagined she felt them flopping about inside her empty stomach.

She was stopping to gather up more when she heard the sudden clop of hooves, the creak of wagon wheels. She caught her breath and with a low cry dashed out of the water. She swept up her suitcase, swung it, and went tumbling behind it into the dense thicket at the side of the road. She burrowed herself down.

A wagon came into sight, empty and rattling, pulled by a mule, which walked with its head low and bobbing, bobbing and swaying. The mule was old and tired, dust-coloured, its knees bald; yellow pus dripped from its eyes; as it neared she could see flies crawling over the pus. It was chewing at the bit in its mouth and swishing its tail.

At the stream the mule stopped and drank. It made big slurping noises and once or twice flung its head around. One of its ears didn't stand up.

When it was done drinking it clumped in its traces, edging off twisty from the wagon to munch on tall weeds.

"Well, Buddyroll?" the man said.

He had a whispery, gentle voice.

The man in the wagon was standing, the reins secured by a hand tucked by thumb into his waist. He was idly surveying the stream, content apparently to let the animal loiter and graze. Was this him? She did not think it could be. Her mama had said he'd be a good height and thin and pretty nice-looking. He'd have a certain glint in his eyes that would make a woman go goose bumpy. He'd have a way about him that let you know he meant to get what he wanted and that you wouldn't mind it. *"That man whispered things in my ear I'll carry to my grave,"* her mama had said. *"I think sometimes of what he said to me and my hair still stands up. He could make a mummy's eyes pop out."* Mama must of been joshing, for this one was nothing. He was red-dirt nothing. He had a big fat gut and muscly arms all stubby. He wore a rumpled greasy felt hat pushed back on his head. You could see where the brim had shaded his face so the sun burned his nose and left red swatches all across his face. It was an ugly face. He had a stick in his mouth, moving it from side to side. He had bulgy jaws and meaty ears and a thick, streaked neck. His little pig eyes gleamed. No, this wasn't him. It couldn't be. Mama didn't have memory to beat a bat.

She saw him unbutton his pants and lift out his thing. He peed in a long wide arch into the stream. He had big calloused sunburned hands and sunburned arms and a red nose, but his weasel was puny and white. It looked like hardly nothing a human would want. He'd be better off not peeing at all than showing that thing. He shook it, bent his knees and loaded it back inside. Him? The idea was so funny she almost laughed out loud. He wouldn't have sense to beat a cockroach. Him! The likelihood was plain disgusting. Her mama would never have let herself curl up to nothing looking like that.

He said something in a low voice to the mule, which turned and looked at him coldly. He hopped down and removed the bit from the animal's mouth. The mule rippled its haunches and went back to its feeding. It ripped up a tall growth of grass by the roots and ate it down to the dirt. It scraped the dirt off against a bald knee, then ate the roots. The man knelt by the stream, lacing a hand through the water. He pulled a rag from his pocket and wet it. He wiped the rag behind and around his neck. He dipped the rag again into the water and crossed over to the mule. The mule had an open puckered sore high on a hind leg. The man cleansed it. The mule swished him in the face a time or two, and rippled his skin again, and again the man said something to him.

Buddyroll quit, it sound like.

He put the bit back into the animal's mouth and hopped up into the wagon. He gave a small shake to the reins and sluggishly the mule responded. The wagon rattling started again. The man took off his hat as they crossed the stream, and swatted it against his leg. Dust flew up. The hatband had cut a line in his forehead, leaving a strip of white skin there. White and freckly. He didn't have much hair. What there was was reddish. She felt her face heat up, noticing this. His red hair, if you could believe mama, was where she'd got hers. He was how come she'd got her freckles, too.

He seemed to be smiling at something as the wagon creaked by, the smile slack on his face, as if he didn't know it to be there.

Her stomach rumbled. She shifted in her hiding spot, ramming a fist up against her stomach to quieten the emptiness.

"Damn son of a bitch," she said. "If he's mine I don't claim him."

Ahead, the road dipped and curved; it rose on to higher ground. A bit yonder from that point, trailing at a distance, she saw the wagon turn into a rutted yard.

He went on down the path, through an open fence gate at the rear of the house, to a weathered, leaning barn.

The house was as her mama said it would be.

A wide porch extended over the full length of the two front rooms, with two worn cane-bottom chairs tilted to the wall, and a wooden swing on chains that, except in summer, lifted the swing up to the ceiling. Two windows faced the lane, divided in the middle by a sagging pinewood door, the screen part open. Behind the front rooms, he'd added a hallway and two other rooms. He'd lived here, so her mama said, with a sick sister who hadn't taken lightly another woman's presence on the place. But the sister had passed on, her mama said. She'd died of craziness, if not boredom. An old sycamore, with a maze of thick graceful limbs, shaded one half of the yard. A stump across from it showed where another had been. A stone chimney went up at the side, and a bent weather vane with a rooster at the top guarded the roof of the house. She saw how he'd patched the tin roof with flattened-out cans. He'd put in a new window-pane not long before.

The place had lights now; it hadn't had electricity in her mama's time.

She was about to step up on the porch and peek through the windows when she heard him coming. He was whistling. She ducked low over the grass, hit the lane, and took off running. For the balance of the day she searched out the place, avoiding open fields, steering wide of his house. In the afternoon she crawled up in a tangle of vines and slept, pulling the black coat up over her head. It seemed to her she slept a long time but when she rubbed her eyes awake the same bird was alight, alight but silent, preening its feathers, on the same high limb. It was so blessed still out here even the birds had caught it. You couldn't hardly breathe because the earth seemed to want to sop it up like gravy on a plate. Her body itched all over. Her flesh was covered with bites, with scratches and welts. Bruises, head to toe. She took off her shoes and picked briars off the bottoms of her feet. They were black and swollen up some. You couldn't even see any more where the blisters had been; it was all raw now. She rolled the stockings down, gritting her teeth, wincing, as she peeled them away from the dried blood on her heels. That was the worst pain, these heels. These feet. These scratches and cuts and being stuck out here. Standing, she felt dizzy, and had to sit down again. Her head swirled. I've got what mama had, she thought. I'm going to waste away in these ungodly woods and go to my grave out here. She picked a black tick out of her scalp and flattened it between her two thumbnails. When mama went down she'd wanted to go down with her. She'd wanted to be shut up with her and have the lid closed on them. They'd said no, no you can't, but it seemed to her this had happened anyway. It was happening now. The lid was closing, but mama wasn't raising her arms to welcome her. Mama was stretched out flat, not saying anything. Come along, child. Come along, child. Mama's back was turned or she wasn't there at all: black space, cold black air, that's all mama was. She hadn't cried then, with mama being lowered down. She could have and wanted to but she hadn't because mama made her so mad. She hadn't wanted to be mad, not at mama, but she was so she just bit her lip and hung on, and if anybody spoke to her or touched her she moved away from them. She hated how they whispered, as if her mama could hear. She kept moving away and they kept coming with her until more of them were huddled with her up by the tree than were down there by the tent where her mama was. She didn't know why they'd come in the first place. Nobody had asked them to. They had no right to be there. She shook when they touched her. She threw off their hands and had to edge away. She had to go on up as far as the tree, but still they kept coming with her. Snivelling, fluttering up little hankies to the nose. What she wanted was for her and her mama to be alone. Not being alone with mama, that last time, that was the worst pain. It was worse than bloody heels and that man on the bus with a cigarette dangling between his lips. It was worse than spending good money to come out here to this dismal daddy in this dismal place. In the end it was her mama alone. You couldn't blame mama for turning her back on her, for changing into black space, into cold black air that never answered a word you said. She felt dizzy now, and hot, and knew this was her mama's sweat on her brow. "I won't talk to you, child, but you can have that. I give my fever to you, along with everything else." Hunger wasn't doing this to her. Hunger wasn't worth talking about, because she had money in her pocket and could buy food, lots of it, any time she wanted to. She could eat weeds, like that mule. She could eat these cough drops in her coat pocket, but she wouldn't. Her mama had said, "Go to the store and buy me these cough drops to ease my throat, and get some little treat for yourself," and she'd done so, but her mama hadn't touched them. Her mama's eyes had rolled in her head. You could take her hand in your own hand and squeeze but her mama couldn't squeeze your own hand back. She'd sleep and you'd sit by the bed thinking how beautiful she was. You'd hold her hand and your own hand would burn. You'd watch her eyes move under the lids sunken and dark. You'd watch the tremor in her lips and dab a wet cloth over them for they were always dry. Sweat broke out on her brow and you could fold a cold wet cloth over her but the cloth got hot as fire in a minute and in the meantime the fever just went on elsewhere. She'd wake and cough and say, "I didn't doze off did I?" "Can you eat, mama?" you'd say, "Can I bring you anything? Are you feeling better?" She'd pat your hand and try to smile. It broke your heart how she tried to smile and that was the worst pain. It was worse than blisters or having your belly gnaw or coming this far for nothing. Worse was what was back there, though it wasn't back there but with you every minute, which was what made it worse. Worse was mama not squeezing your hand after you'd squeezed hers first and then that hand not being there to squeeze although you could still feel her hand in yours. Worse was waiting for the squeeze to come and knowing now it wouldn't. "Mama, can I fetch you something? Can I rub your back or freshen them sheets?"

"Not now, child."

"All right, mama."

"Don't you be weary on my account, baby."

"All right, mama."

You could put your hand behind mama's head and lift her up; you could put a spoon between her lips and feed her like a baby. I loved bathing mama's feet. You could run a damp, cool cloth between her toes and sometimes that would make her smile. "You can turn the light off now," she'd say, and you'd go over and pretend to do it, not letting her know it was plain daylight and no lamp burning. She'd lean on you those days when she could cross the room, and she'd lean on you, coming back. "My right arm," she'd say, "is a pretty little girl. She's my left arm, too." Her lips would tremble when the real pains came and she'd turn her face against the pillow so you couldn't see it. You couldn't get a doctor to come. You'd call up on the store phone and they'd say do this, do that, and you tore home and did it but it didn't help none. You fed her pills by the pail but that didn't help none. "Does it help, mama? Does it relax you? Can you sleep now?"

"Oh, child. Oh Oh Oh. Oh, I feel like I've gone in the oven headfirst. Pull me out now. Grab my legs and pull. Putting a body headfirst into the fiery furnace is the one sure way they've found of making sure no ghosts lag behind. I feel my ghost has burned and the rest has yet to follow. You take my coat. You take my purse and my nice scarves and my new shoes. You take all the fine stockings the navy sees fit to give me."

The navy. You had to smile, thinking about that. You had to laugh out loud. Even her mama in her worse sickness could. One of her mama's old boyfriends, Monty his name was, sent these stockings to her. He got them from Ship's Store or foreign ports or off the black market and in they came, regular as rainwater. "I'm being swept off my feet by nylons," her mama would say. "It beats me what men will do. Why I only went out with that sailorman once! I let him hold me tight on the dance floor, but dancing was all. I liked his arms around me. I let him kiss and hold me when his leave was up and I dashed down to see him when he left on the train. I pulled him back against the red-brick wall and I was the one held him that time. That time I was the one raining the kisses down. 'You come back,' I said. He said he'd write, but what I said was, 'Well you know how sailors are.' I should have given myself to him. God knows, it's little enough. If his ship goes down and he doesn't return I'll cry and wish a thousand times I had. I think of that each time his nylons come. I think of it each time I pull one on."

Men loved her mama. Two had fought over her once, but she'd never spoken to either again.

"I won't be treated like I'm a lump of clay that they can mould and take and have. I didn't care a snake for either of them and they'd of saved themselves a heap of bruised knuckles had they asked me first.

"Your father wasn't that way," she said. "He never fought for me or raised a word to stop me when I said I was leaving that place. It wasn't him I was leaving, as I saw it. Only that place. He never so much as said 'Please' or 'Don't do it.' I know he was unhappy and cried, because his sister, crazy as she was, came one day and told me. She said 'Come back and this time I'll try to be good.' But your father didn't try to sway me. You can't lock up wind, he said. He said he wouldn't try to tame it either."

Several times in her wanderings the girl caught sight of her father as he moved from barn to shed or shed to house. Once, she spotted him on the rear doorstep, calmly surveying the horizon. In late afternoon he came out and scattered feed from a bucket to a half-dozen chickens that flew down from trees. He appeared later with a pail and followed a footpath down to where two sows wallowed in muddy puddles inside a pen. Afterward, she saw him carrying in wood. Another time he was out by the fence gate, whittling on something.

She didn't see any dogs. She saw something streak across his yard once, but couldn't tell what it was.

For long intervals, when he disappeared inside the house, she lay flat in this or that field watching his back door.

Down beyond the fenced-off area was an orchard; she trampled about there, but what little fruit remained on the ground was wormy and rotten. A space of ground nearer the house had served as his garden in seasons past. She pulled a young carrot out of the soil and ate it quickly; she searched a long time for others but found nothing.

On toward nightfall, troubled by the rising cold, she followed what seemed to be an ancient path, trampled down in parts, in parts wild again, and eventually found herself regarding an abandoned, burned-out site inside a ring of scorched trees. Someone had lived here. Wrinkled sheets of tin roofing, blackened boards and black jackknife timbers covered the area. Bushes sprouted midst the rubble. In one corner, climbing up over a wall that remained partially intact, honeysuckle was taking over. She eyed that wall. She eyed the tin. She could fashion a roof of some kind where that wall was, and spend the night here.

She set to work clearing out that space. She worked on into dark, scarcely noticing she had.

The little room she erected was well-hidden; you'd have to stand right up on it to know it was there. She had room for her suitcases and room to stretch out, though not stand up. She put in an opening at the front big enough so that she might crawl through.

She could hide here, she thought, for a million years.

Afterward, she lugged her suitcases up from the woods. She rested then in the cramped shelter, peering up at the streaks and pinpoints of night sky. For a few minutes she slept, although she did not intend to.

Later in the night she worked her way down to the creek and there, trembling with cold, washed herself. Like ice, the water was. It made her teeth chatter and her bones crunch up tight. But it felt good to be clean. It was like heaven, getting the soot and filth off her. She slipped naked into her coat, rolling up the dirty clothes under her arm. She hastened back to her shelter among the ruins and for long minutes sat shivering, waiting for warmth to return. She didn't think about hunger now. Being cold is the worse ache, she told herself. I've never known nothing worse than cold. Being alone in the world was a glory ride compared to being cold. If I stop shivering it will just go away. But she couldn't stop shivering. Her skin was so white and shaky she could see it even in this black hole. Her scalp itched; her hair was grimy, too; tomorrow in fresh daylight she'd go and wash that.

She felt about inside the suitcase for a pair of stockings – a new pair – and pulled them on. "Bless the navy," she said, for this was what her mama liked to say. "Him with his nylons, going to sweep me off my feet." She drew the hose up over her hips and tucked the extra length inside her panties. Her mama had kept hers up with garter belts or she'd rolled and twisted them somehow and they'd stayed up. Beautiful legs, old mama had. She felt about for a sweater and skirt and slipped these on. She got out a comb and raked that through her tangly hair, making low cries as the comb pulled. She wondered where her bow had got to. She rubbed a finger over her teeth and moistened that finger and set a shape to her eyebrows. She painted her lips with the tube her mama had said she could have. She rouged her cheeks, the way her mama had showed her how.

She took out her money and hid it away inside a suitcase.

She hooked the purse over her arm and crawled out of her hole.

In the beginning the house was but a faint speck of yellow light low on the horizon, obscured now and then by the land's undulations. She crossed the fields with short bursts of speed, swinging her shoes in her hands, using his lighted window as her guide. Soon the house was outlined in full, with the sagging roof and the bent weather vane and the big sycamore at the front.

She crouched down where his last field stopped, from there inching her way forward. Smoke wafted up from the chimney; the light was flickering. He passed by the window once and she ducked down, holding her breath. She could hear faint sounds from inside and wondered whether he had visitors, maybe a woman. She wondered what her mama would say about that. Or maybe her mama was wrong about the sister being dead the way she was about him having dogs. But it sounded to her like music; it sounded like a radio.

She raised her eyes above the sill. He was seated on a log stool before the fire, whittling on a piece of wood, a carving of some kind. He was seated on a log although the room held plenty of nice easy chairs and an old settee that looked comfortable. It surprised her how clean and orderly everything was. The floor was of polished wood, a nice deep colour, with numerous old clocks on the wall and nice pictures, and lacy antimacassars on the arms of the settee and chairs. It was a whole lot better-looking place than she would have thought, and lots better and more roomy than the place she and her mama had. Her mama hadn't been one for keeping things straight, and she hadn't either.

She didn't see no sister. She didn't see no tramp layabout girl-friend either.

His shirt was unbuttoned. He had a curly ring of hair on his chest and clean hands and what looked to her like greenish eyes.

He had a drink in a glass down on the floor beside him and now he drank from that. He took three or four deep swallows.

An alcoholic, she thought. If he ain't alcoholic then my name is Clementine.

He was patting his foot to music. The music didn't come from a radio, but from an old Victrola over in the corner. The lid was up and she could see a fat silvery arm spinning over the phonograph record. She'd seen Victrolas like that in town with a big white spotted dog beside them.

She knew that song. It was an old one. Her mama had hummed it sometimes.

"You're his only daughter," her mama had said. "You go to him. I mean it, now."

She moved around the house and clumped noisily up on to the porch. She stretched up her stockings and brushed at her coat. She took a deep breath and knocked on his door.

"I'll try it," she said. "I'll give him twenty-four hours to prove himself."

Photograph

DIONNE BRAND

My grandmother has left no trace, no sign of her self. There is no photograph, except one which she took with much trouble for her identity card. I remember the day that she had to take it. It was for voting, when we got Independence; and my grandmother, with fear in her eyes, woke up that morning, got dressed, put on her hat and left. It was the small beige hat with the lace piece for the face. There was apprehension in the house. My grandmother, on these occasions, the rare ones when she left the house, patted her temples with limacol. Her smelling salts were placed in her purse. The little bottle with the green crystals and liquid had a pungent odour and a powerful aura for me until I was much older. She never let us touch it. She kept it in her purse, now held tightly in one hand, the same hand which held her one embroidered handkerchief.

That morning we all woke up and were put to work getting my grandmother ready to go to the identity card place.

One of us put the water to boil for my grandmother's bath; my big sister combed her hair and the rest of us were dispatched to get shoes, petticoat, or stockings. My grandmother's mouth moved nervously as these events took place and her fingers hardened over ours each time our clumsy efforts crinkled a pleat or spilled scent.

We were an ever-growing bunch of cousins, sisters and brothers. My grandmother's grandchildren. Children of my grandmother's daughters. We were seven in all, from time to time more, given to my grandmother for safekeeping. Eula, Kat, Ava and I were sisters. Eula was the oldest. Genevieve, Wil and Dri were sister and brothers and our cousins. Our mothers were away. Away-away or in the country-away. That's all we knew of them except for their photographs which we used tauntingly in our battles about whose mother was prettier.

Like the bottle of smelling salts, all my grandmother's things had that same aura. We would wait until she was out of sight, which only meant that she was in the kitchen since she never left the

house, and then we would try on her dresses or her hat, or open the
bottom drawer of the wardrobe where she kept sheets, pillow-cases
and underwear, candles and candlesticks, boxes of matches, pieces
of cloth for headties and dresses and curtains, black cake and
wafers, rice and sweet bread, in pillow-cases, just in case of an
emergency. We would unpack my grandmother's things down to
the bottom of the drawer, where she kept camphor balls, and touch
them over and over again. We would wrap ourselves in pieces of
cloth, pretending we were African queens; we would put on my
grandmother's gold chain, pretending we were rich. We would
pinch her black cakes until they were down to nothing and then we
would swear that we never touched them and never saw who did.
Often, she caught us and beat us, but we were always on the
lookout for the next chance to interfere in my grandmother's sacred
things. There was always something new there. Once, just before
Christmas, we found a black doll. It caused commotion and rare
dissension among us. All of us wanted it so, of course, my grandmother discovered us. None of us, my grandmother said, deserved
it and on top of that she threatened that there would be no Santa
Claus for us. She kept the doll at the head of her bed until she
relented and gave it to Kat, who was the littlest.

We never knew how anything got into the drawer, because we
never saw things enter the house. Everything in the drawer was
pressed and ironed and smelled of starch and ironing and newness
and oldness. My grandmother guarded them often more like burden
than treasure. Their depletion would make her anxious; their addition would pose problems of space in our tiny house.

As she rarely left the house, my grandmother felt that everyone
on the street where we lived would be looking at her, going to take
her picture for her identity card. We felt the same too and worried as
she left, stepping heavily, yet shakily down the short hill that led to
the savannah, at the far end of which was the community centre. My
big sister held her hand. We could see the curtains moving discreetly
in the houses next to ours, as my grandmother walked, head up,
face hidden behind her veil. We prayed that she would not fall. She
had warned us not to hang out of the windows looking at her. We,
nevertheless, hung out of the windows gawking at her, along with
the woman who lived across the street, whom my grandmother

thought lived a scandalous life and had scandalous children and a scandalous laugh which could be heard all the way up the street when the woman sat old blagging with her friends on her veranda. We now hung out of the windows keeping company with "Tante", as she was called, standing with her hands on her massive hips looking and praying for my grandmother. She did not stop, nor did she turn back to give us her look; but we knew that the minute she returned our ears would be burning, because we had joined Tante in disgracing my grandmother.

The photograph from that outing is the only one we have of my grandmother and it is all wrinkled and chewed up, even after my grandmother hid it from us and warned us not to touch it. Someone retrieved it when my grandmother was taken to the hospital. The laminate was now dull and my grandmother's picture was grey and creased and distant.

As my grandmother turned the corner with my sister, the rest of us turned to lawlessness, eating sugar from the kitchen and opening the new refrigerator as often as we wanted and rummaging through my grandmother's things. Dressed up in my grandmother's clothes and splashing each other with her limacol, we paraded outside the house where she had distinctly told us not to go. We waved at Tante, mincing along in my grandmother's shoes. After a while, we grew tired and querulous; assessing the damage we had done to the kitchen, the sugar bowl and my grandmother's wardrobe, we began assigning blame. We all decided to tell on each other. Who had more sugar than whom and who was the first to open the cabinet drawer where my grandmother kept our birth certificates.

We liked to smell our birth certificates, their musty smell and yellowing water-marked coarse paper was proof that my grandmother owned us. She had made such a fuss to get them from our mothers.

A glum silence descended when we realized that it was useless quarrelling. We were all implicated and my grandmother always beat everyone, no matter who committed the crime.

When my grandmother returned we were too chastened to protest her beating. We began to cry as soon as we saw her coming around the corner with my sister. By the time she hit the doorstep we were weeping buckets and the noise we made sounded like a wake, groaning in unison and holding on to each other. My grandmother, too tired from her ordeal at the identity card place, looked us scornfully and sat down. There was a weakness in her eyes which we recognized. It meant that our beating would be postponed for hours, maybe days, until she could regain her strength. She had been what seemed like hours at the identity card place. My grandmother had to wait, leaning on my sister and having people stare at her, she said. All that indignity and the pain which always appeared in her back at these moments, had made her barely able to walk back to the house. We, too, had been so distraught that we did not even stand outside the house jumping up and down and shouting that she was coming. So at least she was spared that embarrassment. For the rest of the day we quietly went about our chores, without being told to do them and walked lightly past my grandmother's room, where she lay resting in a mound, under the pink chenille.

We had always lived with my grandmother. None of us could recollect our mothers, except as letters from England or occasional visits from women who came on weekends and made plans to take us, eventually, to live with them. The letters from England came every two weeks and at Christmas with a brown box full of foreign-smelling clothes. The clothes smelled of a good life in a country where white people lived and where bad-behaved children like us would not be tolerated. All this my grandmother said. There, children had manners and didn't play in mud and didn't dirty everything and didn't cry if there wasn't any food and didn't run under the mango trees, grabbing mangoes when the wind blew them down and walked and did not run through the house like warrahoons and did not act like little old niggers. Eula, my big sister, would read the letters to my grandmother who, from time to time, would let us listen. Then my grandmother would urge us to grow up and go away too and live well. When she came to the part about going away, we would feel half-proud and half-nervous. The occasional visits made us feel as precarious as the letters. When we misbehaved, my grandmother often threatened to send us away-away, where white men ate black children, or to quite-too-quite in the country.

Passing by my grandmother's room, bunched up under the spread, with her face tight and hollow-cheeked, her mouth set against us, the spectre of quite-to-quite and white cannibals loomed brightly. It was useless trying to "dog back" to her she said, when one of my cousins sat close to her bed, inquiring if she would like us to pick her grey hairs out. That was how serious this incident was. Because my grandmother loved us to pick her grey hairs from her head. She would promise us a penny for every ten which we could get by the root. If we broke a hair, that would not count, she said. And, if we threw the little balls of her hair out into the yard for the wind, my grandmother became quite upset since that meant that birds would fly off with her hair and send her mad, send her mind to the four corners of the earth, or they would build a nest with her hair and steal her brain. We never threw hair in the yard for the wind, at least not my grandmother's hair and we took on her indignant look when we chastised each other for doing it with our own hair. My cousin Genevieve didn't mind though. She chewed her long front plait when she sucked on her thumb and saved balls of hair to throw to the birds. Genevieve made mudpies under the house, which we bought with leaf money. You could get yellow mudpies or brown mudpies or red mudpies, this depended on the depth of the hole under the house and the wash water which my grandmother threw there on Saturdays. We took my grandmother's word that having to search the four corners of the earth for your mind was not an easy task, but Genevieve wondered what it would be like.

There's a photograph of Genevieve and me and two of my sisters someplace. We took it to send to England. My grandmother dressed us up, put my big sister in charge of us, giving her 50 cents tied up in a handkerchief and pinned to the waistband of her dress, and warned us not to give her any trouble. We marched to Wong's Studio on the Coffee, the main road in our town, and fidgeted as Mr Wong fixed us in front of a promenade scene to take our picture. My little sister cried through it all and sucked her fingers. Nobody knows that it's me in the photograph, but my sisters and Genevieve look like themselves.

Banishment from my grandmother's room was torture. It was her room, even though three of us slept beside her each night. It was a small room with two windows kept shut most of the time, except every afternoon when my grandmother would look out of the front window, her head resting on her big arms, waiting for us to return from school. There was a bed in the room with a headboard where she kept the Bible, a bureau with a round mirror and a washstand with a jug and basin. She spent much of her time here. We too, sitting on the polished floor under the front window talking to her or against the foot of the bed, if we were trying to get back into her favour or beg her for money. We knew the smell of the brown varnished wood of her bed intimately.

My grandmother's room was rescue from pursuit. Anyone trying to catch anyone would pull up straight and get quiet, if you ducked into her room. We read under my grandmother's bed and, playing catch, we hid from each other behind the bulk of her body.

We never received that licking for the photograph day, but my grandmother could keep a silence that was punishment enough. The photograph now does not look like her. It is grey and pained. In real, she was round and comfortable. When we knew her she had a full lap and beautiful arms, her cocoa brown skin smelled of wood smoke and familiar.

My grandmother never thought that people should sleep on Saturday. She woke us up "peepee au jour" as she called it, which meant before it was light outside, and set us to work. My grandmother said that she couldn't stand a lazy house, full of lazy children. The washing had to be done and dried before three o'clock on Saturday when the baking would begin and continue until the evening. My big sister and my grandmother did the washing, leaning over the scrubbing board and the tub and when we others grew older we scrubbed the clothes out, under the eyes of my grandmother. We had to lay the soap-scrubbed clothes out on the square pile of stones so that the sun would bleach them clean, then pick them up and rinse and hang them to dry. We all learned to bake from the time that our chins could reach the table and we washed dishes standing on the bench in front of the sink. In the rainy season, the washing was done on the sunniest days. A sudden shower of rain and my grandmother would send us flying to collect the washing off the lines. We would sit for hours watching the rain gush through the drains which we had dug, in anticipation, around the flower garden in front of the house. The yellow brown water lumbered unsteadily through the drains rebuilding the mud and forming a lake at the place where our efforts were frustrated by a large stone.

In the rainy season, my big sister planted corn and pigeon peas on the right side of the house. Just at the tail end of the season, we planted the flower garden. Zinnias and jump-up-and-kiss-me, which grew easily and xora and roses which we could never get to grow. Only the soil on one side of the front yard was good for growing flowers or food. On the other side a sour-sop tree and an almond tree sucked the soil of everything, leaving the ground sandy and thin, and pushed up their roots, ridging the yard, into a hill. The almond tree, under the front window, fed a nest of ants which lived in one pillar of our house. A line of small red ants could be seen making their way from pillar to almond tree carrying bits of leaves and bark.

One Saturday evening, I tried to stay outside playing longer than allowed by my grandmother, leaning on the almond tree and ignoring her calls. "Laugh and cry live in the same house," my grandmother warned, threatening to beat me when I finally came inside. At first I only felt the bite of one ant on my leg but, no sooner, my whole body was invaded by thousands of little red ants biting my skin blue crimson. My sisters and cousins laughed, my grandmother, looking at me pitiably, sent me to the shower; but the itching did not stop and the pains did not subside until the next day.

I often polished the floor on Saturdays. At first, I hated the brown polish-dried rag with which I had to rub the floors, creeping on my hands and knees. I hated the corners of the room which collected fluff and dust. If we tried to polish the floor without first scrubbing it, my grandmother would make us start all over again. My grandmother supervised all these activities when she was ill, sitting on the bed. She saw my distaste for the rag and therefore insisted that I polish over and over again some spot which I was sure that I had gone over. I learned to look at the rag, to notice its layers of brown polish, its waxy shines in some places, its wetness when my grandmother made me mix the polish with kerosene to stretch its use. It became a rich object, all full of continuous ribbing and working, which my grandmother insisted that I do with my hands and no shortcuts of standing and doing it with the heel of my foot. We poor people had to get used to work, my grandmother said. After polishing, we would shine the floor with more rags. Up and down, until my grandmother was satisfied. Then the morris chairs, whose slats fell off every once in a while with our jumping, had to be polished and shined, and the cabinet, and all put back in their place.

She wasted nothing. Everything turned into something else when it was too old to be everything. Dresses turned into skirts and then into underwear. Shoes turned into slippers. Corn, too hard for eating, turned into meal. My grandmother herself never wore anything new, except when she went out. She had two dresses and a petticoat hanging in the wardrobe for those times. At home, she dressed in layers of old clothing, half-slip over dress, old socks, because her feet were always cold, and slippers, cut out of old shoes. A safety pin or two, anchored to the front of her dress or the hem of her skirt, to pin up our falling underwear or ruined zippers.

My grandmother didn't like it when we changed the furniture around. She said that changing the furniture around was a sign to people that we didn't have any money. Only people with no money changed their furniture around and around all the time. My grandmother had various lectures on money, to protect us from the knowledge that we had little or none. At night, we could not drop pennies on the floor, for thieves may be passing and think that we did have money and come to rob us.

My grandmother always said that money ran through your hands like water, especially when you had so many mouths to feed. Every two or three weeks money would run out of my grandmother's hands. These times were as routine as our chores or going to school or the games which we played. My grandmother had stretched it over stewed chicken, rice, provisions and macaroni pie on Sundays, split peas soup on Mondays, fish and bake on Tuesdays, corn meal dumplings and salt cod on Wednesdays, okra and rice on Thursdays, split peas, salt cod and rice on Fridays and pelau on Saturdays. By the time the third week of the month came around my grandmother's stretching would become apparent. She carried a worried look on her face and was more silent than usual. We understood this to be a sign of lean times and times when we could not bother my grandmother or else we would get one of her painful explanations across our ears. Besides it really hurt my grandmother not to give us what we needed, as we all settled with her into a depressive hungry silence.

At times we couldn't help but look accusingly at her. Who else could we blame for the gnawing pain in our stomachs and the dry corners of our mouths. We stared at my grandmother hungrily, while she avoided our eyes. We would all gather around her as she lay in bed, leaning against her or sitting on the floor beside the bed, all in silence. We devoted these silences to hope – hope that something would appear to deliver us, perhaps my grandfather, with provisions from the country – and to wild imagination that we would be rich some day and be able to buy pounds of sugar and milk. But sweet water, a thin mixture of water and sugar, was all the balm for our hunger. When even that did not show itself in abundance, our silences were even deeper. We drank water, until our stomachs became distended and nautical.

My little sister, who came along a few years after we had grown accustomed to the routine of hunger and silence, could never grasp the importance of these moments. We made her swear not to cry for food when there wasn't any and, to give her credit, she did mean it when she promised. But the moment the hungry silence set in, she began to cry, begging my grandmother for sweet water. She probably cried out of fear that we would never eat again, and admittedly our silences were somewhat awesome, mixtures of despair and grief, made potent by the weakness which the heavy hot sun brought on in our bodies.

We resented my little sister for these indiscretions. She reminded us that we were hungry, a thought we had been transcending in our growing asceticism, and we felt sorry for my grandmother having to answer her cries. Because it was only then that my grandmother relented and sent one of us to borrow a cup of sugar from the woman across the street, Tante. One of us suffered the indignity of crossing the road and repeating haltingly whatever words my grandmother had told her to say.

My grandmother always sent us to Tante, never to Mrs Sommard who was a religious woman and our next-door neighbour, nor to Mrs Benjamin who had money and was our other next-door neighbour. Mrs Sommard only had prayers to give and Mrs Benjamin, scorn. But Tante, with nothing, like us, would give whatever she could manage. Mrs Sommard was a Seventh Day Adventist and the only time my grandmother sent one of us to beg a cup of something, Mrs Sommard sent back a message to pray. My grandmother took it quietly and never sent us there again and told us to have respect for Mrs Sommard because she was a religious woman and believed that God would provide.

Mrs Sommard's husband, Mr Sommard, took two years to die. For the two years that he took to die the house was always brightly lit. Mr Sommard was so afraid of dying that he could not sleep and didn't like it when darkness fell. He stayed awake all night and all day for two years and kept his wife and daughter awake too. My grandmother said he pinched them if they fell asleep and told them that if he couldn't sleep, they shouldn't sleep either. How this ordeal squared with Mrs Sommard's religiousness, my grandmother was of two minds about. Either the Lord was trying Mrs Sommard's faith or Mrs Sommard had done some wickedness that the Lord was punishing her for.

The Benjamins, on the other side, we didn't know where they got their money from, but they seemed to have a lot of it. For Mrs Benjamin sometimes told our friend Patsy not to play with us. Patsy lived with Mrs Benjamin, her grandmother, Miss Lena, her aunt and her grandfather, Mr Benjamin. We could always smell chicken that Miss Lena was cooking from their pot, even when our house fell into silence.

The Benjamins were the reason that my grandmother didn't like us running down into the backyard to pick up mangoes when the wind blew them down. She felt ashamed that we would show such hunger in the eyes of people who had plenty. The next thing was that the Benjamins' rose mango tree was so huge, it spread half its body over their fence into our yard. We felt that this meant that any mangoes that dropped on our side belonged to us and Patsy Benjamin and her family thought that it belonged to them. My grandmother took their side, not because she thought that they were right, but she thought that if they were such greedy people, they should have the mangoes. Let them kill themselves on it, she said. So she made us call to Mrs Benjamin and give them all the rose mangoes that fell in our yard. Mrs Benjamin thought that we were doing this out of respect for their status and so she would often tell us with superiority to keep the mangoes, but my grandmother would decline. We, grudgingly, had to do the same and, as my grandmother warned us, without a sad look on our faces. From time to time, we undermined my grandmother's pride, by pretending not to find any rose mangoes on the ground, and hid them in a stash under the house or deep in the backyard under leaves. Since my grandmother never ventured from the cover and secrecy of the walls of the house, or that area in the yard hidden by the walls, she was never likely to discover our lie.

Deep in the backyard, over the drain which we called the canal, we were out of range of my grandmother's voice, since she refused to shout, and the palms of her hands, but not her eyes. We were out of reach of her broomstick which she flung at our fleeing backs or up into one of the mango trees where one of us was perched, escaping her beatings.

Deep in the back of the yard, we smoked sponge wood and danced in risqué fashion and uttered the few cuss words that we knew and made up calypsos. There, we pretended to be big people with children. We put our hands on our hips and shook our heads, as we had seen big people do, and complained about having so much children, children, children to feed.

My grandmother showed us how to kill a chicken, holding its body in the tub and placing the scrubbing board over it leaving the neck exposed, then with a sharp knife quickly cut the neck, leaving the scrubbing board over the tub. Few of us became expert at killing a chicken. The beating of the dying fowl would frighten us and the scrubbing board would slip whereupon the headless bird would escape, its warm blood still gushing, propelling its body around and around the house. My grandmother would order us to go get the chicken, which was impossible since the direction that the chicken took and the speed with which it ran were indeterminate. She didn't like us making our faces up in distaste at anything that had to do with eating or cleaning or washing. So, whoever let the chicken escape or whoever refused to go get it would have to stand holding it for five minutes until my grandmother made a few turns in the house, then they would have to pluck it and gut it and wrap the feathers and innards in newspaper, throwing it in the garbage. That person may well have to take the garbage out for a week. If you can eat, my grandmother would say, you can clean and you shouldn't scorn life.

One day we found a huge balloon down in the backyard. It was the biggest balloon we'd ever had and it wasn't even around Christmas time. Patsy Benjamin, who played through her fence with us, hidden by the rose mango tree from her aunt Lena, forgot herself and started shouting that it was hers. She began crying and ran complaining to her aunt that we had stolen her balloon. Her aunt dragged her inside and we ran around our house fighting and pulling at each other swearing that the balloon belonged to this one or that one. My grandmother grabbed one of us on the fourth or fifth round and snatched the balloon away. We never understood the cause of this, since it was such a find and never quite understood my grandmother muttering something about Tante's son leaving his "nastiness" everywhere. Tante herself had been trying to get our attention, as we raced round and round the house. This was our first brush with what was called "doing rudeness". Later, when my big sister began to menstruate and stopped hanging around with us, we heard from our classmates that men menstruated too and so we put two and two together and figured that Tante's son's nastiness must have to do with his menstruation.

On our way home from school one day, a rumour blazed its way through all the children just let out from school that there was a male sanitary napkin at the side of the road near the pharmacy on Royal Road. It was someone from the Catholic girls" school who started it and troupe after troupe of school children hurried to the scene, to see it. The rumour spread back and forth, along the Coffee, with school children corroborating and testifying that they had actually seen it. By the time we got there, we only saw an empty brown box which we skirted, a little frightened at first, then pressed in for a better view. There really wasn't very much more to see and we figured that someone must have removed it before we got there. Nevertheless, we swore that we had seen it and continued to spread the rumour along the way, until we got home, picking up the chant which was building as all the girls whipped their fingers at the boys on the street singing, "Boys have periods TOOOOOO!" We couldn't ask my grandmother if men had periods, but it was the source of weeks of arguing back and forth.

When my period came, it was my big sister who told me what to do. My grandmother was not there. By then, my mother had returned from England and an unease had fallen over us. Anyway, when I showed my big sister, she shoved a sanitary napkin and two pins at me and told me not to play with boys anymore and that I couldn't climb the mango tree anymore and that I shouldn't fly around the yard anymore either. I swore everyone not to tell my mother when she got home from work but they all did anyway and my mother with her air, which I could never determine since I never looked her in the face, said nothing.

My mother had returned. We had anticipated her arrival with a mixture of pride and fear. These added to an uncomfortable sense that things would not be the same, because in the weeks preceding her arrival my grandmother revved up the old warning about us not being able to be rude or disobey anymore, that we would have to be on our best behaviour to be deserving of this woman who had been to England, where children were not like us. She was my grandmother's favourite daughter too, so my grandmother was quite proud of her. When she arrived, some of us hung back behind my grandmother's skirt, embarrassing her before my mother who, my grandmother said, was expecting to meet well brought up children who weren't afraid of people.

To tell the truth, we were expecting a white woman to come through the door, the way my grandmother had described my mother and the way the whole street that we lived on treated the news of my mother's return, as if we were about to ascend in their respect. The more my grandmother pushed us forward to say hello to my mother, the more we clung to her skirts until she finally had to order us to say hello. In the succeeding months, my grandmother tried to push us toward my mother. She looked at us with reproach in her eyes that we did not acknowledge my mother's presence and her power. My mother brought us wieners and fried eggs and mashed potatoes, which we had never had before, and said that she longed for kippers, which we did not know. We enjoyed her strangeness but we were uncomfortable under her eyes. Her suitcase smelled strange and foreign and for weeks despite our halting welcome of her, we showed off in the neighbourhood that we had someone from away.

Then she began ordering us about and the wars began.

Those winters in England, when she must have bicycled to Hampstead General Hospital from which we once received a letter and a

postcard with her smiling to us astride a bicycle, must have hardened the smile which my grandmother said that she had and which
was dimly recognizable from the photograph. These winters, which
she wrote about and which we envied as my sister read them to us,
she must have hated. And the thought of four ungrateful children
who deprived her of a new dress or stockings to travel London,
made my mother unmerciful on her return.

We would run to my grandmother, hiding behind her skirt, or
dive for the sanctuary of my grandmother's room. She would enter,
accusing my grandmother of interfering in how she chose to discipline "her" children. We were shocked. Where my mother acquired
this authority we could not imagine. At first our grandmother let her
hit us, but finally she could not help but intervene and ask my
mother if she thought she was beating animals. Then my mother
would reply that my grandmother had brought us up as animals.
This insult would galvanize us all against my mother. A back answer
would fly from the child in question who would, in turn, receive a
slap from my grandmother, whereupon my grandmother would
turn on my mother with the length of her tongue. When my grandmother gave someone the length of her tongue, it was given in a
low, intense and damning tone, punctuated by chest beating and
the biblical, "I have nurtured a viper in my bosom."

My mother often became hysterical and left the house, crying
what my grandmother said were crocodile tears. We had never seen
an adult cry in a rage before. The sound in her throat was a gagging
yet raging sound, which frightened us, but it was the sight of her tall
threatening figure which cowed us. Later, she lost hope that we
would ever come around to her and she began to think and accuse
my grandmother of setting her children against her. I recall her
shoes mostly, white and thick, striding across the tiny house.

These accusations increased and my grandmother began to talk of
dying and leaving us. Once or twice, my mother tried to intervene
on behalf of one or the other of us in a dispute with my grandmother. There would be silence from both my grandmother and us,
as to the strangeness of this intervention. It would immediately
bring us on side to my grandmother's point of view and my mother
would find herself in the company of an old woman and some
children who had a life of their own – who understood their plays,

their dances, gestures and signals, who were already intent on one another. My mother would find herself standing outside these gestures into which her inroads were abrupt and incautious. Each foray made our dances more secretive, our gestures subterranean.

Our life stopped when she entered the door of the house, conversations closed in mid-sentence and elegant gestures with each other turned to sharp asexual movements.

My mother sensed these closures since, at first, we could not hide these scenes fast enough to escape her jealous glance. In the end, we closed our scenes ostentatiously in her presence. My grandmother's tongue lapping over a new story or embellishing an old one would become brusque in, "Tell your mother good evening." We, telling my grandmother a story or receiving her assurance that when we get rich we would buy a this or a that, while picking out her grey hairs, would fall silent. We longed for when my mother stayed away. Most of all, we longed for when she worked nights. Then we could sit all evening in the grand darkness of my grandmother's stories.

When the electricity went out and my grandmother sat in the rocking chair, the wicker seat bursting from the weight of her hips, the stories she spun, no matter how often we heard them, languished over the darkness whose thickness we felt, rolling in and out of the veranda. Some nights the darkness billowing about us would be suffused by the perfume of lady-of-the-night, a white, velvet, yellow, orchid-like flower which grew up the street in a neighbour's yard. My grandmother's voice, brown and melodic, about how my grandfather, "Yuh Papa, one dark night, was walking from Ortoire to Guayaguayare . . ."

The road was dark and my grandfather walked alone with his torchlight pointed toward his feet. He came to a spot in the road, which suddenly chilled him. Then, a few yards later, he came to a hot spot in the road, which made him feel for a shower of rain. Then, up ahead, he saw a figure and behind him he heard its footsteps. He kept walking, the footsteps pursuing him dragging a chain, its figure ahead of him. If he had stopped, the figure, which my grandfather knew to be a legahoo, would take his soul; so my grandfather walked steadily, shining his torchlight at his feet and repeating psalm twenty-three, until he passed the bridge by the sea

wall and passed the savannah, until he arrived at St Mary's, where
he lived with my grandmother.

It was in the darkness of the veranda, in the honey chuckle back of
my grandmother's throat, that we learned how to catch a soucouyant and a lajabless and not to answer to the "hoop! hoop! hoop!" of
duennes, the souls of dead children who were not baptized, come to
call living children to play with them. To catch a soucouyant, you
had to either find the barrel of rain water where she had left her skin
and throw pepper in it or sprinkle salt or rice on your doorstep so
that when she tried to enter the house to take your blood, she would
have to count every grain of salt or rice before entering. If she
dropped just one grain or miscounted, she would have to start all
over again her impossible task and in the morning she would be
discovered, distraught and without her skin on the doorstep.

When we lived in the country before moving to the street, my
grandmother had shown us, walking along the beach in back of the
house, how to identify a duenne foot. She made it with her heel in
the sand and then, without laying the ball of her foot down, imprin-
ted her toes in the front of the heel print.

Back in the country, my grandmother walked outside and up and
down the beach and cut coconut with a cutlass and dug, chip-chip,
on the beach and slammed the kitchen window one night just as a
madman leapt to it to try to get into the house. My grandmother said
that, as a child in the country, my mother had fallen and hit her
head, ever since which she had been pampered and given the best
food to eat and so up to this day she was very moody and could go
off her head at the slightest. My mother took this liberty whenever
she returned home, skewing the order of our routines in my grandmother.

It seemed that my grandmother had raised more mad children
than usual, for my uncle was also mad and one time he held up a gas
station which was only the second time that my grandmother had to
leave the house, again on the arm of my big sister. We readied my
grandmother then and she and my big sister and I went to the
courthouse on the Promenade to hear my uncle's case. They didn't
allow children in, but they allowed my big sister as my grandmother
had to lean on her. My uncle's case was not heard that morning, so
we left the court and walked up to the Promenade. We had only

gone a few steps when my grandmother felt faint. My sister held the smelling salts at her nostrils, as we slowly made our way as inconspicuously as we could to a bench near the bandstand. My grandmother cried, mopping her eyes with her handkerchief and talked about the trouble her children had caused her. We, all three, sat on the bench on the Promenade near the bandstand, feeling stiff and uncomfortable. My grandmother said my uncle had allowed the public to wash their mouth in our family business. She was tired by then and she prayed that my mother would return and take care of us, so that she would be able to die in peace.

Soon after, someone must have written my mother to come home, for we received a letter saying that she was finally coming.

We had debated what to call my mother over and over again and came to no conclusions. Some of the words sounded insincere and disloyal, since they really belonged to my grandmother, although we never called her by those names. But when we tried them out for my mother, they hung so cold in the throat that we were discouraged immediately. Calling my mother by her given name was too presumptuous, even though we had always called all our aunts and uncles by theirs. Unable to come to a decision we abandoned each other to individual choices. In the end, after our vain attempts to form some word, we never called my mother by any name. If we needed to address her we stood about until she noticed that we were there and then we spoke. Finally, we never called my mother.

All of the words which we knew belonged to my grandmother. All of them, a voluptuous body of endearment, dependence, comfort and infinite knowing. We were all full of my grandmother, she had left us full and empty of her. We dreamed in my grandmother and we woke up in her, bleary-eyed and gesturing for her arm, her elbows, her smell. We jockeyed with each other, lied to each other, quarrelled with each other and with her for the boon of lying close to her, sculpting ourselves around the roundness of her back. Braiding her hair and oiling her feet. We dreamed in my grandmother and we woke up in her, bleary-eyed and gesturing for her lap, her arms, her elbows, her smell, the fat flesh of her arms. We fought, tricked each other for the crook between her thighs and calves. We anticipated where she would sit and got there before her. We brought her achar and paradise plums.

My mother had walked the streets of London, as the legend went, with one dress on her back for years, in order to send those brown envelopes, the stamps from which I saved in an old album. But her years of estrangement had left her angry and us cold to her sacrifice. She settled into fits of fury. Rage which raised welts on our backs, faces and thin legs. When my grandmother had turned away laughing from us, saying there was no place to beat, my mother found room.

Our silences which once warded off hunger now warded off her blows. She took this to mean impudence and her rages whipped around our silences more furiously than before. I, the most ascetic of all, sustained the most terrible moments of her rage. The more enraged she grew, the more silent I became, the harder she hit, the more wooden, I. I refined this silence into a jewel of the most sacred sandalwood, finely grained, perfumed, mournful yet stoic. I became the only inhabitant of a cloistered place carrying my jewel of fullness and emptiness, voluptuousness and scarcity. But she altered the silences profoundly.

Before, with my grandmother, the silences had company, were peopled by our hope. Now, they were desolate.

She had left us full and empty of her. When someone took the time to check, there was no photograph of my grandmother, no figure of my grandmother in layers of clothing and odd-sided socks, no finger stroking the air in reprimand, no arm under her chin at the front window or crossed over her breasts waiting for us.

My grandmother had never been away from home for more than a couple of hours and only three times that I could remember. So her absence was lonely. We visited her in the hospital every evening. They had put her in a room with eleven other people. The room was bare. You could see underneath all the beds from the doorway and the floors were always scrubbed with that hospital smelling antiseptic which reeked its own sickliness and which I detested for years after. My grandmother lay in one of the beds nearest the door and I remember my big sister remarking to my grandmother that she should have a better room, but my grandmother hushed her saying that it was all right and anyway she wouldn't be there for long and the nurses were nice to her. From the chair beside my grandmother's bed in the hospital you could see the parking lot on

Chancery Lane. I would sit with my grandmother, looking out the window and describing the scene to her. You could also see part of the wharf and the gulf of Paria which was murky where it held to the wharf. And St Paul's Church, where I was confirmed, even though I did not know the catechism and only mumbled when Canon Farquar drilled us in it.

Through our talks at the window my grandmother made me swear that I would behave for my mother. We planned, when I grew up and went away, that I would send for my grandmother and that I would grow up to be something good, that she and I and Eula and Ava and Kat and Genevieve would go to Guayaguayare and live there forever. I made her promise that she would not leave me with my mother.

It was a Sunday afternoon, the last time that I spoke with my grandmother. I was describing a bicycle rider in the parking lot and my grandmother promised to buy one for me when she got out of hospital.

My big sister cried and curled herself up beneath the radio when my grandmother died. Genevieve's face was wet with tears, her front braid pulled over her nose, she, sucking her thumb.

When they brought my grandmother home, it was after weeks in the white twelve-storey hospital. We took the curtains down, leaving all the windows and doors bare, in respect for the dead. The ornaments, doilies, and plastic flowers were removed and the mirrors and furniture covered with white sheets. We stayed inside the house and did not go out to play. We kept the house clean and we fell into our routine of silence when faced with hunger. We felt alone. We did not believe. We thought that it was untrue. In disbelief, we said of my grandmother, "Mama can't be serious!"

The night of the wake, the house was full of strangers. My grandmother would never allow this. Strangers, sitting and talking everywhere, even in my grandmother's room. Someone, a great-aunt, a sister of my grandmother, whom we had never seen before, turned to me sitting on the sewing machine and ordered me in a stern voice to get down. I left the room, slinking away, feeling abandoned by my grandmother to strangers.

I never cried in public for my grandmother. I locked myself in the bathroom or hid deep in the backyard and wept. I had learned as my grandmother had taught me, never to show people your private business.

When they brought my grandmother home the next day, we all made a line to kiss her goodbye. My littlest sister was afraid; the others smiled for my grandmother. I kissed my grandmother's face hoping that it was warm.

Condolence Visit

ROHINTON MISTRY

Yesterday had been the tenth day, *dusmoo*, after the funeral of Minocher Mirza. *Dusmoo* prayers were prayed at the fire-temple, and the widow Mirza awaited with apprehension the visitors who would troop into the house over the next few weeks. They would come to offer their condolence, share her grief, poke and pry into her life and Minocher's with a thousand questions. And to gratify them with answers she would have to relive the anguish of the most trying days of her life.

The more tactful ones would wait for the first month, *maasiso*, to elapse before besieging her with sympathy and comfort. But not the early birds; they would come flocking from today. It was open season, and Minocher Mirza had been well known in the Parsi community of Bombay.

After a long and troubled illness, Minocher had suddenly eased into a condition resembling a state of convalescence. Minocher and Daulat had both understood that it was only a spurious convalescence, there would be no real recovery. All the same, they were thankful his days and nights passed in relative comfort. He was able to wait for death freed from the agony which had racked his body for the past several months.

And as it so often happens in such cases, along with relief from physical torment, the doubts and fears which had tortured his mind released their hold as well. He was at peace with his being which was soon to be snuffed out.

Daulat, too, felt at peace because her one fervent prayer was being answered. Minocher would be allowed to die with dignity, without being reduced to something less than human; she would not have to witness any more of his suffering.

Thus Minocher had passed away in his sleep after six days spent in an inexplicable state of grace and tranquillity. Daulat had cried for the briefest period; she felt it would be sinful to show anything but gladness when he had been so fortunate in his final days.

Now, however, the inescapable condolence visits would make her regurgitate months of endless pain, nights spent sleeplessly, while she listened for his breath, his sighs, his groans, his vocalization of the agony within. For bearers of condolences and sympathies she would have to answer questions about the illness, about doctors and hospitals, about nurses and medicines, about X-rays and blood reports. She would be requested (tenderly but tenaciously, as though it was their rightful entitlement) to recreate the hell her beloved Minocher had suffered, instead of being allowed to hold on to the memory of these final blessed six days. The worst of it would be the repetition of details for different visitors at different hours on different days, until that intensely emotional time she had been through with Minocher would be reduced to a dry and dull lesson learned from a textbook which she would parrot like a schoolgirl.

Last year, Daulat's nephew Sarosh, the Canadian immigrant who now answered to the name of Sid, had arrived from Toronto for a visit, after ten years. Why he had never gone back he would not say, nor did he come to see her any more. After all that she and Minocher had done for him. But he did bring her a portable cassette tape recorder from Canada, remembering her fondness for music, so she could tape her favourite songs from All India Radio's two Western music programmes: "Merry Go Round" and "Saturday Date". Daulat, however, had refused it, saying, "Poor Minocher sick in bed, and I listen to music? Never!" She would not change her mind despite Sarosh-Sid's recounting of the problems he had had getting it through Bombay customs.

Now she wished she had accepted the gift. It could be handy, she thought with bitterness, to tape the details, to squeeze all of her and Minocher's suffering inside the plastic case, and proffer it to the visitors who came propelled by custom and convention. When they held out their right hands in the condolence-handshake position (fingertips of left hand tragically supporting right elbow, as though the right arm, overcome with grief, could not make it on its own) she could have thrust towards them the cassette and recorder: "You have come to ask about my life, my suffering, my sorrow? Here, take and listen. Listen on the machine, everything is on tape. How my Minocher fell sick, where it started to pain, how much it hurt, what doctor said, what specialist said, what happened in hospital. This R button?

Is for Rewind. Some part you like, you can hear it again, hear it ten times if you want: how nurse gave wrong medicine but my Minocher, sharp even in sickness, noticed different colour of pills and told her to check; how wardboy always handled the bedpan savagely, shoving it underneath as if doing sick people a big favour; how Minocher was afraid when time came for sponge bath, they were so careless and rough – felt like number three sandpaper on his bedsores, my brave Minocher would joke. What? The FF button? Means Fast Forward. If some part bores you, just press FF and tape will turn to something else: like how in hospital Minocher's bedsores were so terrible it would bring tears to my eyes to look, all filled with pus and a bad smell on him always, even after sponge bath, so I begged of doctor to let me take him home; how at home I changed dressings four times a day using sulfa ointment, and in two weeks bedsores were almost gone; how, as time went by and he got worse, his friends stopped coming when he needed them most, friends like you, now listening to this tape. Huh? This letter P? Stands for Pause. Press it if you want to shut off machine, if you cannot bear to hear more of your friend Minocher's suffering . . ."

Daulat stopped herself. Ah, the bitter thoughts of a tired old woman. But of what use? It was better not to think of these visits which were as inevitable as Minocher's death. The only way out was to lock up the flat and leave Firozsha Baag, live elsewhere for the next few weeks. Perhaps at a boarding house in Udwada, town of the most sacrosanct of all fire-temples. But though her choice of location would be irreproachable, the timing of her trip would generate the most virulent gossip and criticism the community was capable of, to weather which she possessed neither the strength nor the audacity. The visits would have to be suffered, just as Minocher had suffered his sickness, with forbearance.

The doorbell startled Daulat. This early in the morning could not bring a condolence visitor. The clock was about to strike nine as she went to the door.

Her neighbour Najamai glided in, as fluidly as the smell of slightly rancid fat that always trailed her. The pounds shed by her bulk in recent years constantly amazed Daulat. Today the smell was supplemented by *dhansaak masala*, she realized, as the odours found and penetrated her nostrils. It was usually possible to tell what Najamai had been cooking, she carried a bit of her kitchen with her wherever she went.

Although about the same age as Daulat, widowhood had descended much earlier upon Najamai, turning her into an authority on the subject of Religious Rituals And The Widowed Woman. This had never bothered Daulat before. But the death of Minocher offered Najamai unlimited scope, and she had made the best of it, besetting and bombarding Daulat with advice on topics ranging from items she should pack in her valise for the four-day Towers Of Silence vigil, to the recommended diet during the first ten days of mourning. Her counselling service had to close, however, with completion of the death rituals. Then Daulat was again able to regard her in the old way, with a mixture of tolerance and mild dislike.

"Forgive me for ringing your bell so early in the morning but I wanted to let you know, if you need chairs or glasses, just ask me."

"Thanks, but no one will – "

"No no, you see, yesterday was *dusmoo*, I am counting carefully. How quickly ten days have gone by! People will start visiting from today, believe me. Poor Minocher, so popular, he had so many friends, they will all visit – "

"Yes, they will, and I must get ready," said Daulat, interrupting what threatened to turn into an early morning prologue to a condolence visit. She found it hard to judge her too harshly, Najamai had had her share of sorrow and rough times. Her Soli had passed away the very year after the daughters, Vera and Dolly, had gone abroad for higher studies. The sudden burden of loneliness must have been horrible to bear. For a while, her large new refrigerator had helped to keep up a flow of neighbourly companionship, drawn forth by the offer of ice and other favours. But after the Francis incident, that, too, ceased. Tehmina refused to have anything to do with the fridge or with Najamai (her conscience heavy and her cataracts still unripe), and Silloo Boyce downstairs had also drastically reduced its use (though her conscience was clear, her sons Kersi and Percy had saved the day).

So Najamai, quite alone and spending her time wherever she was tolerated, now spied Minocher's pugree. "Oh, that's so nice, so shiny and black! And in such good condition!" she rhapsodized.

It truly was an elegant piece of headgear, and many years ago Minocher had purchased a glass display case for it. Daulat had brought it out into the living room this morning.

Najamai continued: "You know, pugrees are so hard to find these days, this one would bring a lot of money. But you must never sell it. Never. It is your Minocher's, so always keep it." With these exhortatory words she prepared to leave. Her eyes wandered around the flat for a last-minute scrutiny, the sort that evoked mild dislike for her in Daulat.

"You must be very busy today, so I'll – " Najamai turned towards Minocher's bedroom and halted in mid-sentence, in consternation: "*O baap ré!* The lamp is still burning! Beside Minocher's bed – that's wrong, very wrong!"

"Oh, I forgot all about it," lied Daulat, feigning dismay. "I was so busy. Thanks for reminding, I'll put it out."

But she had no such intention. When Minocher had breathed his last, the *dustoorji* from A Block had been summoned and had given her careful instructions on what was expected of her. The first and most important thing, the *dustoorji* had said, was to light a small oil lamp at the head of Minocher's bed; this lamp, he said, must burn for four days and nights while prayers were performed at the Towers Of Silence. But the little oil lamp became a source of comfort in a house grown quiet and empty for the lack of one silent feeble man, one shadow. Daulat kept the lamp lit past the prescribed four days, replenishing it constantly with coconut oil.

"Didn't *dustoorji* tell you?" asked Najamai. "For the first four days the soul comes to visit here. The lamp is there to welcome the soul. But after four days prayers are all complete, you know, and the soul must now quickly-quickly go to the Next World. With the lamp still burning the soul will be attracted to two different places: here and the Next World. So you must put it out, you are confusing the soul," Najamai earnestly concluded.

Nothing can confuse my Minocher, thought Daulat, he will go where he has to go. Aloud she said, "Yes, I'll put it out right away."

"Good, good," said Najamai, "and oh, I almost forgot to tell you, I have lots of cold-drink bottles in the fridge, Limca and Goldspot, nice and chilled, if you need them. Few years back, when visitors were coming after Dr Mody's *dusmoo*, I had no fridge, and poor Mrs

Mody had to keep running to Irani restaurant. But you are lucky just come to me."

What does she think, I'm giving a party the day after *dusmoo*? thought Daulat. In the bedroom she poured more oil in the glass, determined to keep the lamp lit as long as she felt the need. Only, the bedroom door must remain closed, so the tug-of-war between two worlds, with Minocher's soul in the middle, would not provide sport for visitors.

She sat in the armchair next to what had been Minocher's bed and watched the steady, unflickering flame of the oil lamp. Like Minocher, she thought, reliable and always there; how lucky I was to have such a husband. No bad habits, did not drink, did not go to the racecourse, did not give me any trouble. Ah, but he made up for it when he fell sick. How much worry he caused me then, while he still had the strength to argue and fight back. Would not eat his food, would not take his medicine, would not let me help with anything.

In the lamp glass coconut oil, because it was of the unrefined type, rested golden-hued on water, a natant disc. With a pure sootless flame the wick floated, a little raft upon the gold. And Daulat, looking for answers to difficult questions, stared at the flame. Slowly, across the months, borne upon the flame-raft came the incident of the Ostermilk tin. It came without the anger and frustration she had known then, it came in a new light. And she could not help smiling as she remembered.

It had been the day of the monthly inspection for bedbugs. Due to the critical nature of this task, Daulat tackled it with a zeal unreserved for anything else. She worked side by side with the servant. Minocher had been comfortable in the armchair, and the mattress was turned over. The servant removed the slats, one by one, while Daulat, armed with a torch, examined every crack and corner, every potential redoubt. Then she was ready to spray the mixture of Flit and Tik-20, and pulled at the handle of the pump.

But before plunging in the piston she glimpsed, between the bedpost and the wall, a large tin of Ostermilk on the floor. The servant dived under to retrieve it. The tin was shut tight, she had to pry the lid open with a spoon. And as it came off, there rose a stench powerful enough to rip to shreds the hardy nostrils of a latrine-basket collector. She quickly replaced the lid, fanning the air vigorously with her hand. Minocher seemed to be dozing off, olfactory nerves unaffected. Was he trying to subdue a smile? Daulat could not be sure. But the tin without its lid was placed outside the back door, in hopes that the smell would clear in a while.

The bedbug inspection was resumed and the Flitting finished without further interruption. Minocher's bed was soon ready, and he fell asleep in it.

The smell of the Ostermilk tin had now lost its former potency. Daulat squinted at the contents: a greyish mass of liquids and solids, no recognizable shapes or forms among them. With a stick she explored the gloppy, sloppy mess. Gradually, familiar objects began to emerge, greatly transmogrified but retaining enough of their original states to agitate her. She was now able to discern a square of fried egg, exhume a piece of toast, fish out an orange pip. So! This is what he did with his food! How *could* he get better if he did not eat. Indignation drove her back to his bedroom. She refused to be responsible for him if he was gong to behave in this way. Sickness or no sickness, I will have to tell him straight.

But Minocher was fast asleep, snoring gently. Like a child, she thought, and her anger had melted away. She did not have the heart to waken him; he had spent all night tossing and turning. Let him sleep. But from now on I will have to watch him carefully at mealtimes.

Beside the oil lamp Daulat returned to the present. Talking to visitors about such things would not be difficult. But they would be made uncomfortable, not knowing whether to laugh or keep the condolence-visit grimness upon their faces. The Ostermilk tin would have to remain their secret, hers and Minocher's. As would the oxtail soup, whose turn it now was to sail silently out of the past, on the golden disc, on the flame-raft of Minocher's lamp.

At the butcher's, Daulat and Minocher had always argued about oxtail which neither had ever eaten. Minocher wanted to try it, but she would say with a shudder, "See how they hang like snakes. How can you even think of eating that? It will bring bad luck, I won't cook it."

He called her superstitious. Oxtail, however, remained a dream deferred for Minocher. After his illness commenced, Daulat shopped alone, and at the meat market she would remember Minocher's penchant for trying new things. She picked her way cautiously over the wet, slippery floors, weaving through the narrow aisles between the meat stalls, avoiding the importunating hands that thrust shoulders and legs and chops before her. But she forced herself to stop before the pendent objects of her dread and fix them with a long, hard gaze, as though to stare them down and overcome her aversion.

She was often tempted to buy oxtail and surprise Minocher – something different might revive his now almost-dead appetite. But the thought of evil and misfortune associated with all things serpentine dissuaded her each time. Finally, when Minocher had entered the period of his pseudo-convalescence, he awakened after a peaceful night and said, "Do me a favour?" Daulat nodded, and he smiled wickedly: "Make oxtail soup." And that day, they dined on what had made her cringe for years, the first hearty meal for both since the illness had commandeered the course of their lives.

Daulat rose from the armchair. It was time now to carry out the plan she had made yesterday, walking past the Old-Age Home For Parsi Men, on her way back from the fire-temple. If Minocher could, he would want her to. Many were the times he had gone through his wardrobe selecting things he did not need or wear any longer, wrapped them in brown paper and string, and carried them to the Home for distribution.

Beginning with the ordinary items of everyday wear, she started sorting them: *sudras*, underwear, two spare *kustis*, sleeping suits, light cotton shirts for wearing around the house. She decided to make parcels right away – why wait for the prescribed year or six months and deny the need of the old men at the Home if she could (and Minocher certainly could) give today?

When the first heap of clothing took its place upon brown paper spread out on his bed, something wrenched inside her. The way it had wrenched when he had been pronounced dead by the doctor. Then it passed, as it had passed before. She concentrated on the clothes; one of each in every parcel: *sudra*, underpants, sleeping suit, shirt, would make it easier to distribute.

Bent over the bed, she worked unaware of her shadow on the wall, cast by the soft light of the oil lamp. Though the curtainless window was open, the room was half-dark because the sun was on the other side of the flat. But half-dark was light enough in this room into which had been concentrated her entire universe for the duration of her and Minocher's ordeal. Every little detail in this room she knew intimately: the slivered edge of the first compartment of the chest of drawers where a *sudra* could snag, she knew to avoid; the little trick, to ease out the shirt drawer which always stuck, she was familiar with; the special way to jiggle the key in the lock of the Godrej cupboard she had mastered a long time ago.

The Godrej steel cupboard Daulat tackled next. This was the difficult one, containing the "going-out" clothes: suits, ties, silk shirts, fashionable bush shirts, including some foreign ones sent by their Canadian nephew, Sarosh-Sid, and the envy of Minocher's friends. This cupboard would be the hard one to empty out, with each garment holding memories of parties and New Year's Eve dances, weddings and *navjotes*. Strung out on the hangers and spread out on the shelves were the chronicles of their life together, beginning with the Parsi formal dress Minocher had worn on the day of their wedding: silk *dugli*, white silk shirt, and the magnificent pugree. And to commence her life with him all she had had to do was move from her parents" flat in A Block to Minocher's in C Block. Yes, they were the only childhood sweethearts in Firozsha Baag who had got married, all the others had gone their separate ways.

The pugree was in its glass case in the living room where Daulat had left it earlier. She went to it now and opened the case. It gleamed the way it had forty years ago. How grand he had looked then, with the pugree splendidly seated on his head! There was only one other occasion when he had worn it since, on the wedding of Sarosh-Sid, who had been to them the son they never had. Sarosh's papers had arrived from the Canadian High Commission in New Delhi, and three months after the wedding he had emigrated with his brand new wife. They divorced a year later because she did not like it in Canada. For the wedding, Minocher had wanted Sarosh to wear the pugree, but he had insisted (like the modern young man that he was) on an English styled double-breasted suit. So Minocher had worn it instead. Pugree-making had become a lost art due to modern young men like Sarosh, but Minocher had known how to take care of his. Hence its mint condition.

Daulat took the pugree and case back into the bedroom as she went looking for the advertisement she had clipped out of the *Jam-E-Jamshed*. It had appeared six days ago, on the morning after she had returned from the Towers Of Silence: "Wanted – a pugree in good condition. Phone no. — ." Yesterday, Daulat had dialled the number; the advertiser was still looking. He was coming today to inspect Minocher's pugree.

The doorbell rang. It was Najamai. Again. In her wake followed Ramchandra, lugging four chairs of the stackable type. The idea of a full-time servant who would live under her roof had always been disagreeable to Najamai, but she had finally heeded the advice of the many who said that a full-time servant was safer than an odd-job man, he became like one of the family, responsible and loyal. Thus Najamai had taken the plunge; now the two were inseparable.

They walked in, her rancid-fat-*dhansaak-masala* smell embroidered by the attar of Ramchandra's hair oil. The combination made Daulat wince.

"Forgive me for disturbing you again, I was just now leaving with Ramu, many-many things to do today, and I thought, what if poor Daulat needs chairs? So I brought them now only, before we left. That way you will . . ."

Daulat stopped listening. Good thing the bedroom door was shut, or Najamai would have started another oil lamp exegesis. Would this garrulous busybody never leave her alone? There were extra chairs in the dining room she could bring out.

With Sarosh's cassette recorder, she could have made a tape for Najamai too. It would be a simple one to make, with many pauses during which Najamai did all the talking: Neighbour Najamai Take One – "Hullo, come in" – (long pause) – "hmm, right" – (short pause) – "yes yes, that's OK" – (long pause) – "right, right." It would be easy, compared to the tape for condolence visitors.

". . . you are listening, no? So chairs you can keep as long as you like, don't worry, Ramchandra can bring them back after a month, two months, after friends and relatives stop visiting. Come on, Ramu, come on, we're getting late."

Daulat shut the door and withdrew into her flat. Into the silence of the flat. Where moments of life past and forgotten, moments lost, misplaced, hidden away, were all waiting to be recovered. They were like the stubs of cinema tickets she came across in Minocher's trouser pockets or jackets, wrung through the laundry, crumpled and worn thin but still decipherable. Or like the old programme for a concert at Scot's Kirk by the Max Mueller Society of Bombay, found in a purse fallen, like Scot's Kirk, into desuetude. On the evening of the concert Minocher, with a touch of sarcasm, had quipped: Indian audience listens to German musicians inside a church built by skirted men – truly Bombay is cosmopolitan. The encore had been *Für Elise*. The music passed through her mind now, in the silent flat, by the light of the oil lamp: the beginning in A minor, full of sadness and nostalgia and an unbearable yearning for times gone by; then the modulation into C major, with its offer of hope and strength and understanding. This music, felt Daulat, was like a person remembering – if you could hear the sound of the working of remembrance, the mechanism of memory, *Für Elise* was what it would sound like.

Suddenly, remembering was extremely important, a deep-seated need surfacing, manifesting itself in Daulat's flat. All her life those closest to her had reminisced about events from their lives; she, the audience, had listened, sometimes rapt, sometimes impatient. Grandmother would sit her down and tell stories from years gone by; the favourite one was about her marriage and the elaborate matchmaking that preceded it. Mother would talk about her Girl Guide days, with a faraway look in her eyes; she still had her dark blue Girl Guide satchel, faded and frayed.

When grandmother had died no music was allowed in the house for three months. Even the neighbours, in all three blocks, had silenced their radios and gramophones for ten days. No one was permitted to play in the compound for a month. In those old days, the compound was not flagstoned, and clouds of dust were raised by the boys of Firozsha Baag as they tore about playing their games. The greatest nuisance was, of course, to the ground floor: furniture dusted and cleaned in the morning was recoated by nightfall. The thirty-day interdiction against games was a temporary reprieve for those tenants. That month, membership in the Cawasji Framji Memorial Library rose, and grandmother's death converted several boys in the Baag to reading. During that time, Daulat's mother introduced her to the kitchen and cooking – there was now room for one more in that part of the flat.

Daulat had become strangers with her radio shortly after Minocher's illness started. But the childhood proscription against music racked her with guilt whenever a strand of melody strayed into her room from the outside world. Minocher's favourite song was "At the Balalaika". He had taken her to see *Balalaika* starring Nelson Eddy at a morning show. It was playing at the Eros Cinema, it was his fourth time, and he was surprised that she had never seen the film before. How did the song . . . she hummed it, out of tune: At the Balalaika, one summer night a table laid for two, was just a private heaven made for two . . .

The wick of the oil lamp crackled. It did this when the oil was low. She fetched the bottle and filled the glass, shaking out the last drop, then placed the bottle on the window-sill: a reminder to replenish the oil.

Outside the peripatetic vendors started to arrive, which meant it was past three o'clock. Between one and three was nap time, and the watchman at the gate of Firozsha Baag kept out all hawkers, according to the instructions of the management. The potato-and-onion man got louder as he approached now, "Onions rupee a kilo, potatoes two rupees," faded after he went past, to the creaky obligato of his thirsty-for-lubrication cart as it jounced through the compound. He was followed by the fishwalli, the eggman, the biscuitwalla; and the ragman who sang with a sonorous vibrato:

> Of old saris and old clothes I am collector
> Of new plates and bowls in exchange I am giver . . .

From time to time BEST buses thundered past and all sounds were drowned out. Finally came the one Daulat was waiting for. She waved the empty bottle at the oilwalla, purchased a quarter-litre, and arranged with him to knock at her door every alternate day. She was not yet sure when she would be ready to let the lamp go out.

The clock showed half past four when she went in with the bottle. Minocher's things lay in neat brown paper packages, ready for the Old-Age Home. She shut the doors of the cupboards now almost empty; the clothes it took a man a lifetime to wear and enjoy, she thought, could be parcelled away in hours.

The man would soon arrive to see Minocher's pugree. She wondered what it was that had made him go to the trouble of advertising. Perhaps she should never have telephoned. Unless he had a good reason, she was not going to part with it. Definitely not if he was just some sort of collector.

The doorbell. Must be him, she thought, and looked through the peephole.

But standing outside were second cousin Moti and her two grandsons. Moti had not been at the funeral. Daulat did not open the door immediately. She could hear her admonishing the two little boys: "Now you better behave properly or I will not take you anywhere ever again. And if she serves Goldspot or Vimto or something, be polite, leave some in the glass. Drink it all and you'll get a pasting when you get home."

Daulat had heard enough. She opened the door and Moti, laden with eau-de-Cologne, fell on her neck with properly woeful utterances and tragic tones. "O Daulat, Daulat! What an unfortunate thing to happen to you! O very wrong thing has come to pass! Poor Minocher gone! Forgive me for not coming to the funeral, but my Gustadji's gout was so painful that day. Completely impossible. I said to Gustadji, least I can do now is visit you as soon as possible after *dusmoo.*"

Daulat nodded, trying to look grateful for the sympathy Moti was so desperate to offer to fulfil her duties. It was almost time to reach for her imaginary cassette player.

"Before you start thinking what a stupid woman I am to bring two little boys to a condolence visit, I must tell you that there was no one at home they could stay with. And we never leave them alone. It is so dangerous. You heard about that vegetablewalla in Bandra? Broke into a flat, strangled a child, stole everything. Cleaned it out completely. *Parvar daegar!* Save us from such wicked madmen!"

Daulat led the way into the living room, and Moti sat on the sofa. The boys occupied Najamai's loaned chairs. The bedroom door was open just a crack, revealing the oil lamp with its steady unwavering flame. Daulat shut it quickly lest Moti should notice and comment about the unorthodoxy of her source of comfort.

"Did he suffer much before the end? I heard from Ruby – you know Ruby, sister of Eruch Uncle's son-in-law Shapur, she was at the funeral – that poor Minocher was in great pain the last few days."

Daulat reached in her mind for the start switch of the cassette player. But Moti was not yet ready: "Couldn't the doctors do something? From what we hear these days, they can cure almost anything."

"Well," said Daulat, "our doctor was very helpful, but it was a hopeless case, he told me, we were just prolonging the agony."

"You know, I was reading in the *Indian Express* last week that doctors in China were able to make" – here, Moti lowered her voice in case the grandsons were listening, shielded her mouth with one hand, and pointed to her lap with the other – "a man's Part. His girlfriend ran off with another man and he was very upset. So he chopped off" – in a whisper – "his own Part, in frustration, and flushed it down the toilet. Later, in hospital, he regretted doing it, and God knows how, but the doctors made for him" – in a whisper again – "a New Part, out of his own skin and all. They say it works and everything. Isn't that amazing?"

"Yes, very interesting," said Daulat, relieved that Moti had, at least temporarily, forsaken the prescribed condolence visit questioning.

The doorbell again. Must be the young man for the pugree this time.

But in stepped ever-solicitous Najamai. "Sorry, sorry. Very sorry, didn't know you had company. Just wanted to see if you were OK, and let you know I was back. In case you need anything." Then leaning closer conspiratorially, rancid-fat-*dhansaak-masala* odours overwhelming Daulat, she whispered, "Good thing, no, I brought the extra chairs."

Daulat calculated quickly. If Najamai stayed, as indeed she was eager to, Moti would drift even further from the purpose of her visit. So she invited her in. "Please come and sit, meet my second cousin Moti. And these are her grandsons. Moti was just now telling me a very interesting case about doctors in China who made" – copying Moti's whisper – "a New Part for a man."

"A new part? But that's nothing new. They do it here also now, putting artificial arms-legs and little things inside hearts to make blood pump properly."

"No, no," said Moti. "Not a new part. This was" – in a whisper, dramatically pointing again to her lap for Najamai's benefit – "a New Part! And he can do everything with it. It works. Chinese doctors made it."

"Oh!" said Najamai, now understanding. "A New Part!"

Daulat left the two women to ponder the miracle, and went to the kitchen. There was a bottle of Goldspot in the icebox for the children. The kettle was ready and she poured three cups of tea. The doorbell rang for the third time while she arranged the tray. She was about to abandon it and go to the door but Najamai called out, "It's all right, I'll open it, don't worry, finish what you are doing."

Najamai said: "Yes?" to the young man standing outside.

"Are you Mrs Mirza?"

"No no, but come in. Daulat, there's a young man asking for you."

Daulat settled the tray on the teapoy before the sofa and went to the door. "You're here to see the pugree. Please come in and sit." He took one of Najamai's loaned chairs.

Najamai and Moti exchanged glances. Come for the pugree? What was going on?

The young man noticed the exchange and felt obliged to say something. "Mrs Mirza is selling Mr Mirza's pugree to me. You see, my fiancée and I, we decided to do everything, all the ceremonies, the proper traditional way at our wedding. In correct Parsi dress and all."

Daulat heard him explain in the next room and felt relieved. It was going to be all right, parting with the pugree would not be difficult. The young man's reasons would have made Minocher exceedingly happy.

But Najamai and Moti were aghast. Minocher's pugree being sold and the man barely digested by vultures at the Towers Of Silence! Najamai decided she had to take charge. She took a deep breath and tilted her chin pugnaciously. "Look here, *bawa*, it's very nice to hear you want to do it the proper Parsi way. So many young men are doing it in suits and ties these days. Why, one wedding I went to, the boy was wearing a shiny black suit with lacy, frilly-frilly shirt and bow tie. Exactly like Dhobitalao Goan wedding of a Catholic it was looking! So believe me when I say that we are very happy about yours."

She paused, took another deep breath, and prepared for a fortissimo finale. "But this poor woman who is giving you the pugree, her beloved husband's funeral was only ten days ago. Yesterday was *dusmoo*, and her tears are barely dry! And today you are taking away his pugree. It is not correct! You must come back later!" Then Najamai went after Daulat, and Moti followed.

The young man could see them go into a huddle from where he sat, and could hear them as well. Moti was saying, "Your neighbour is right, this is not proper. Wait for a few days."

And Najamai was emboldened to the point of presenting one of her theories. "You see, with help of prayers, the soul usually crosses over after four days. But sometimes the soul is very attached to this world and takes longer to make the crossing. And as long as the soul is here, everything such as clothes, cup-saucer, brush-comb, all must be kept same way they were, exactly same. Or the soul becomes very unhappy."

The young man was feeling extremely uncomfortable. He, of course, had not known that Daulat had been widowed as recently as ten days ago. Once again he felt obliged to say something. He cleared his throat: "Excuse me." But it was washed away in the downpour of Najamai's words.

He tried again, louder this time: "Excuse me, please!"

Najamai and Moti turned around sharply and delivered a challenging "Yes?"

"Excuse me, but maybe I should come back later for the pugree, the wedding is three months away."

"Yes! Yes!" said Moti and Najamai in unison. The latter continued: "I don't want you thinking I'm stirring my ladle in your pot, but that would be much better. Come back next month, after *maasiso*. You can try it on today if you like, see if it fits. In that there is no harm. Just don't take it away from the place where the soul expects it to be."

"I don't want to give any trouble," said the young man. "It's all right, I can try it later, the wedding is three months away. I'm sure it will fit."

Daulat, with the pugree in her hands, approached the young man. "If you think it is bad luck to wear a recently dead man's pugree and you are changing your mind, that 's OK with me." The young man vigorously shook his head from side to side, protesting, as Daulat continued: "But let me tell you, my Minocher would be happy to give it to you if he were here. He would rejoice to see someone get married in his pugree. So if you want it, take it today."

The young man looked at Moti and Najamai's flabbergasted countenances, then at Daulat calmly waiting for his decision. The tableau of four persisted: two women slack-jawed with disbelief; another holding a handsome black pugree; and in the middle, an embarrassed young man pulled two ways, like Minocher's soul, a tug-of-war between two worlds.

The young man broke the spell. He reached out for the pugree and gently took it from Daulat's hands.

"Come," she smiled, and walked towards the bedroom, to the dressing table.

"Excuse me," he said to Najamai and Moti, who were glaring resentfully, and followed. He placed the pugree on his head and looked in the mirror.

"See, it fits perfectly," said Daulat.

"Yes," he answered, "it does fit perfectly." He took it off, caressed it for a moment, then asked hesitantly, "How much . . . ?"

Daulat held up her hand; she had prepared for this moment. Though she had dismissed very quickly the thought of selling it, she had considered asking for its return after the wedding. Now, however, she shook her head and took the pugree from the young man. Carefully, she placed it in the glass case and handed it back to him.

"It is yours, wear it in good health. And take good care of it for my Minocher."

"I will, oh thank you," said the young man. "Thank you very much." He waited for a moment, then softly, shyly added, "And God bless you."

Daulat smiled. "If you have a son, maybe he'll wear it, too, on his wedding." The young man nodded, smiling back.

She saw him to the door and returned to the living room. Moti and Najamai were sipping half-heartedly at their tea, looking somewhat injured. The children had finished their cold drink. They were swishing the shrunken ice-cubes around in the forbidden final quarter-inch of liquid, left in their glasses as they'd been warned to, to attest to their good breeding. An irretrievably mixed up and confusing bit of testimony.

A beggar was crying outside, "Firstfloorwalla *bai*! Take pity on the poor! Secondfloorwalla *bai*! Help the hungry!"

Presently Najamai rose. "Have to leave now, Ramchandra must be ready with dinner."

Moti took the opportunity to depart as well, offering the fidgetiness of the two little boys for an excuse.

Daulat was alone once more. Leaving the cups and glasses where they stood with their dregs of tea and Goldspot, she went into Minocher's room. It was dark except for the glow of the oil lamp. The oil was low again and she reached for the bottle, then changed her mind.

From under one of the cups in the living room she retrieved a saucer and returned to his room. She stood before the lamp for a moment, looking deep into the flame, then slid the saucer over the glass. She covered it up completely, the way his face had been covered with a white sheet ten days ago.

In a few seconds the lamp was doused, snuffed out. The afterglow of the wick persisted; then it, too, was gone. The room was in full darkness.

Daulat sat in the armchair. The first round, at least, was definitely hers.

Foreigners

ELISABETH HARVOR

The night staff in the Operating Room would set up strange ban-quets in the night – rows of scissors, blades, clamps – sterile surgical cutlery laid out on dull green tablecloths. And when they had finished setting up every table, every room, they would make them-selves coffee, using the Pyrex pot in the supervisors' kitchen. If they wanted a glass of milk as well, or a glass of orange juice, they could walk down the hall to Blood Bank. There was always a quart of milk and a bottle of orange juice in the refrigerator there, in with the bottles of blood. But usually they didn't. Coffee was the drink of hospitals and night. They could carry it into the stretcher room and sit on old office swivel chairs, their feet up on the stretchers, and drink cup after cup of it, black. Then the sun would rise and they would hear the kitchen help calling out to each other, far below them in the hospital courtyard, in Estonian and Italian and Por-tuguese.

At the end of her night duty in the Operating Room, Anna had two days off and so she decided to go home. But in the residence there was a message for her: she was to go over to Male Surgery to see Miss Killeen. She packed her nightgown and jeans in a suitcase and got into a skirt and blouse. I can't have done anything wrong, she thought. And besides, Killeen was her friend. (The year before, when Killeen had still been a student, she'd been the senior on a night duty they'd shared on Male Surgery, and from working with her then Anna liked her a lot.) But of course it wasn't true she hadn't done wrong. She had. They both had. The only two nurses for forty patients, they had faked graphs on temperature charts, skipped dressings, left comatose patients unwashed.

Anna took the elevator up to the fifth floor. When the doors parted she saw Killeen, over at the medicine cupboard, pouring pills into paper cups. In spite of her fondness for Killeen, in spite of the soft summer morning, she felt a surge of terror. Killeen turned around. "Oh, Annie," she said, "did I scare you, calling you over like this? I'm sorry, but they said you were coming off nights and I wanted to catch you before you took off. I've got a little problem here and I wondered if you could help me out."

"What is it?"

"They brought in this sailor a couple of nights ago," Killeen said. "Off a boat docked in the harbour. A Danish boat. He doesn't speak any English. We know what's wrong with him because we've been in contact with the doctor out there. But this morning I suddenly remembered, you come from a Danish family. I wondered if you'd go and talk to him a little."

"I don't speak much Danish," Anna said. Really, she didn't know much more than a few songs and jingles and silly things. Her parents had assimilated completely and spoke perfect English. The Danish language was only something her family made jokes about – they said it was not a language at all but a disease of the throat; they said it sounded like the baaing of sick sheep.

"Don't worry," said Killeen. "All we need is to have you say a few words to him in his native tongue, to cheer him up. And if you could find out if he has any problems or complaints."

Anna walked down the hall and into the sailor's room. There were three men in there who were sitting cranked up in their beds, eating their breakfast in the bright morning light.

"The Danish man?"

"Behind the curtain, Miss."

She parted the curtains and let herself in. He was about thirty-five, dark and taciturn-looking. She wished him good morning in Danish. The dark face broke into a slight but hopeful smile. You speak Danish, he said to her in Danish. In Danish she answered no. Yes you do, he said. He thought it was some kind of game. So she decided to show him what she knew, to make joke of it, to show him that all she could do was count to ten, wish him a merry Christmas, ask him how he felt (but not understand too elaborate an answer), and thank him a thousand times for the lovely evening. She hoped he would laugh but he did not. Then she remembered that the way to say "good luck" in Danish was *til lykke*, but after this she didn't dare to say it to him, she just put her hand on his shoulder as a way of saying goodbye. But it wasn't to be so simple as that. He grabbed her hand and brought it down between his blanketed thighs so that through the blankets she could feel what he wanted her to feel; he held her so hard by the wrist that it hurt. She just stood there, like someone doing penance. She didn't look at him so she didn't know if he was looking at her. And after a while he let her go. She walked out into the hall.

Killeen was at her desk. "Were you able to communicate with each other?"

"I think he's lonely," Anna said. She could feel herself blushing.

"Oh well, there's nothing much wrong with him anyway. We'll have him back on his boat in a couple of days."

"I don't really speak Danish at all," Anna said. "We never spoke it at home."

"Well, it seems you did okay, at least you were able to understand he was lonely," Killeen said. "So thanks a million for coming over."

The person Anna sat next to on the New Sharon bus was a woman in her sixties. Her hands were covered with liver spots and freckles and three of her fingers were fitted out with diamond rings. She had a smoker's cough and an American accent. It turned out she was a nurse too and had been born and raised in Canada, not far from the countryside they were at that moment travelling through. She had trained in Halifax. In 1933 she had moved to the States, had married there, and had ended up in Florida, where she was now, in 1957, the owner of a nursing home. She said she was very successful. She said she wasn't telling this to boast but only to show how it pays to stick to your training. Then she turned to Anna and took her by the sleeve as if she could read her mind. "Oh honey!" she cried. "I can see that you have doubts!"

"Yes," Anna said. "I'm thinking of giving it up."

"Oh, no," the old nurse said. "Oh, don't do that. Don't ever do that. Remember, it's always something to fall back on."

The strange thing was, a year ago Anna had been even closer to leaving than she was now. She had sat in her parents' car and cried and said that she wanted to give the whole thing up. They had persuaded her to stay until her third year. Then you will have tried everything, they said. You will have been to the Case Room and the Operating Room and Emergency. If you still want to leave then, after you've tried everything, then we won't argue with you.

When Anna got out of the bus at New Sharon, her hoarse and freckled Florida friend touched her arm again and said, "Now you remember what I told you, honey," and she told her she would. She made a good connection with the bus to Athens, and had plenty of time to think about her life on the long trip there. She thought of the first death she'd seen, the first birth, the first post-mortem. The first post-mortem had been easy, coming over a year after the first death. Six student nurses walked over to the morgue together and on the way there they met three interns. It was a hot afternoon, and there was the smell of tar in the ocean air. The morgue sat behind the hospital and looked like a garage; it was made of concrete blocks, painted white, and it had a big, garage-like door. The moment they got inside they saw the body, lying on a marble-topped table. It was a woman, past middle-age, with a look of authority about her. Anna imagined that she had once been head of something – the purse section of a department store, say, or maybe a business office. Maybe she had even been a nurse. She was glad she wasn't young.

One of the interns stretched. "Cooler in here, anyway," he said, and then the door opened and the chief pathologist came in. He was a Scotsman and small and quick, in a very clean white coat. "Good day," he said, and he picked up a scalpel and made a long vertical incision. Anna took a deep breath and made herself recall the definition of anatomy that they'd been given at the beginning of Anatomy and Physiology:

Anatomy is the science which deals with the structure of the bodies of men and animals. It is studied by the dissection of the bodies of those who die in hospitals and other institutions, unclaimed by relatives.

This woman had no one who cared for her, then.

"Ladies and gentlemen," said the chief pathologist. "Look at the lady's lungs." They all looked. They were very flecked with black. "A lifetime resident of this city," the pathologist said, and they all laughed. Then he started asking people to show him things. The Falciform ligament. The seventh costal cartilege. The interns did all the showing; they were good at it. And after a while the pathologist forgot about the nurses and addressed his remarks to the interns entirely. He pointed out a small globe of flesh deep within the abdominal cavity. "Who knows what this is?" he asked them. And he allowed his eyes to shine. He was sure, this time, he had them stumped. And in fact they seemed to be. But Anna was not. At the time they had studied it she had been infatuated with one of the orderlies on Male Surgery, a dark solid boy named Douglas Mac-Kinnon.

"The Pouch of Douglas?" she said.

The pathologist gave her a quick, sharp look.

"Dead right," he said.

As for the first birth, when she saw her first birth she had a sense that she'd never had before of the fierce beauty of life, of the logic of the mystery, a sense of the connection between tension and bringing forth, and at the same time the feeling of being in *good hands*; every death she saw after the first birth was easier to take, except for the deaths of a few children. But then she'd hated the children's ward anyway; it had almost done her in. The sunniest place in the whole hospital, walled with glass, everything else about it was desperate: the noise, the smell, the overcrowding – it was as noisy and smelly as a zoo set up in a greenhouse but without the blessing of green plants. But the crazy thing was, the odd silent wards were no better. Here a great many small children were in a state of shock from having been separated from their parents and sat, hardly moving, in pyjamas sporting pink lambs or pink poodles, their eyes as unseeing as black pools. And in the chronic wards there was a deceptive lightness – here the children smiled and joked and knew all the routines and all the nurses' names; but they were the worst of all – it was as if the bewitched monstrous children of German fables had been given medical verity. Here was what you found in the chronic ward: children whose legs had grown to different lengths; children who had got puffed up into strangers overnight – their eyes turned into slits by the held-in fluid; children with enormous circus heads; there were medical names for all of it. Anna got sick on the children's ward – diarrhoea, bronchitis, high child-style fevers – even though normally, like the others, she was immune to everything. The thing was, courage in very young children was a frightening thing – so pure, so absolute, so detached from the very experience that could give it meaning; she knew they would give up life as easily and naturally as they would take their medicine.

And the children's ward wasn't all; there had been other places, places where the students hadn't just been overworked, they'd been humiliated too – some of the older supervisors, especially, had taken pleasure in humiliating them. On certain night duties, where the supervisors coming on duty in the mornings had made them stay late doing things they said they'd left undone or threatened to take their free time away from them until it seemed to them that these supervisors held not only their freedom and self-respect, but even their whole lives in their hands, Anna had given up eating almost entirely, preferring to sleep instead. The new wing of the nurses' residence was under construction then, and every morning before she went off duty she'd fill up her pockets with sleeping pills, to blot out the sound of the drills. She felt she couldn't open her window either. Her best friend, Joan Cosman, would come up to her room around suppertime and let up the blind and open the window to show a part of the hospital wall going pinkly light from the last of the sun. Or was it the sunrise? Rising out of a drugged sleep, it was scary not to know which. "What time is it?" Anna would say, and she'd scrabble around on her dressing table, looking for her watch. "Six o'clock," Joan would say. But the words "six o'clock" wouldn't have any meaning to Anna; until she could remember where she was working, where she was supposed to be, she couldn't figure them out.

Joan would sit heavily down on the bed, smelling of the day's smells. She was working in the Case Room then; there was the sweet-sick blend of ether, Dettol, coffee. She'd take the food she'd brought Anna out of a paper bag: peanut butter sandwiches that she'd made up herself in the nurses' kitchen; bananas and cookies left over from supper in the cafeteria.

Eat, she would say.

I'm not hungry.

You've got to eat.

Maybe they'll notice how thin I'm getting and give me time off to rest up, Anna said to Joan on one of these evenings.

Do you think they give a good goddamn?

They make us weigh ourselves every month, don't they?

You're a dreamer. Eat.

*

During the time Anna was in training in Hocksville her cousin Kamille was living with her family in Athens, helping out with the housework. Anna's parents had invited Kamille out from Denmark to live with them for as long as she wanted to, but after she had been in Canada for a year she planned to leave for the States. She was twenty-two and came from Anna's mother's side of the family. She always dressed in black. Black pants, black T-shirts, black aprons, black umbrella. "Elegant," people said. "You can certainly tell she doesn't come from around *here*." Kamille was the most practical person her Canadian relatives had ever seen – she had sewn all her own black clothes with the exception of the umbrella, she could make men's jackets and coats, she could even upholster chairs and sofas.

When Anna got out of the bus on Victoria Street and started walking up the hill toward her house, she could see Kamille in the distance, up on the front steps in her black clothes, shelling or peeling something. Kamille looked classic, forebodingly right, against the great white backdrop of Anna's parents' Greek Revival house. Anna's parents bought the Athens place after she started her training. When they got it it was a hovel, but a hovel with grandeur – all partitioned and warped and cracked inside, but with a good foundation and a beautifully proportioned shell. They spent several thousand dollars fixing it up. They asked Anna if it would be okay if they took the two thousand dollars they'd kept in a fund for her education and used it for renovations for the house, and she said it would be fine. She liked denial; she believed her capacity for it made her a better person than Arnie and Chess, her brother and sister. It was why she had chosen to be a nurse. Hard work, doing good. She approached the point where the driveway split, sweeping up on either side of a great heart of green grass.

"Hello, Annie!" called Kamille. "We are having a party tonight! Chess has gone off to the liquor store. She has with her two missionaries."

Anna sat down on the steps beside Kamille. "Are there still missionaries in these parts?" she asked her.

"These boys are Mormons," Kamille said. "They come from America." Her voice sounded very tender when she said America.

"You should call it the States, Kamille."

"The States," Kamille said, tender again. "Utah. Wyoming."

"Wyoming," Anna said. "I read a book about Wyoming when I was little. *My Friend Flicka*. About a horse." And she told herself to be sure to remember to ask the Wyoming Mormon if he knew Cheyenne.

Then Chess came back with the boys and the liquor. She brought the two of them over to the front of the house to introduce them to Anna. Anna hoped Chess would not introduce her as her "little sister" as she sometimes did. The terrible part about this was that whenever Chess did it people always believed her. But she didn't. She just told her their names: Elder Rodale, Elder Cayton.

"Sometimes also known by the names Al and Gary," Chess said. "I'm trying to talk them into staying for the party night. I've even promised them apple juice instead of punch in their paper cups. And they have to promise not to try to convert people." She smiled. They both smiled back at her, although the one called Al looked a little uneasy. But Gary gave Chess a serious tender look. "We know how to behave," he said. "Help me take this stuff inside," she said to him then, and they went into the house together. Al stood on the porch a moment, looking unhappy, then he went inside too.

"God, that Gary guy really seems to like Chess," Anna said.

"I guess so," said Kamille. "The trouble is, Chess has invited an older man to this party. Someone she really likes. A Norwegian. She met him somewhere at someone's house. He's twenty-seven."

"What's his name?"

"Karl something."

"Oh him," Anna said, in the despairing voice people will use about someone they covet. "I thought that's who it would be." And she told Kamille everything she knew about this Karl. How he had come to Canada after the war and learned English in no time at all. How he had done so brilliantly in high school and on the junior matriculation exams that the *Hocksville Herald* had written a special editorial about him. How his father was a veterinarian and had once saved the life of their late dog Ted. How the first time Ted was almost dying, she and her mother had driven him all the way to the vet's place and how, while they were there, they saw this Karl (a college boy by now) and how, going back home in the car, she'd said to her mother, "That's the man I'm going to marry."

"Chess is very nervous," said Kamille.

*

At supper that night Chess flirted with Gary. Al continued to look unhappy. Anna asked him if he was the one who came from Wyoming. He said he was. She asked him if he'd read *My Friend Flicka*, and he said he had. She told him she'd read it when she was young, that she'd thought it was a very beautiful book. Al asked her if she'd read *The Book of Mormon*. She said no. "*The Book of Mormon* is a very beautiful book too," he said. "It's an even more beautiful book than *My Friend Flicka*." Everyone smiled. Except Kamille. She was banging lids on counters and slapping plates on the table. She said to the Mormons, "These girls! They are not very domesticated!" This was true, but it hadn't always been that way. At fourteen, fifteen, sixteen, Anna had worked as a cook in her mother's music camp, cooking meals for the campers. She'd made pails of puddings and basins of macaroni salad, and jugs of custard sauce to pour over Lemon Snow. In her spare time she read *Fanny Farmer's Boston Cooking School Cook Book*. On Sunday's she made Maryland Chicken and in the middle of the week she made something the mother of one of the campers had taught her to do: ham and pineapple slices fried together, then simmered in Coca-Cola. But then she went into training in Hocksville and learned what real work was. Real work wasn't anything like cooking for thirty children, real work was running from seven in the morning till seven at night; real work was something that made you too tired to read, or eat. They usually did have some time off in the middle of the day though, but only if they weren't too far behind in their work, and even then it was tied in with a lunch hour or a class they had to go to. These classes were given by the doctors in a classroom in the basement of the nurses" residence. One of these doctors, in a class on obstetrics and gynaecology, had distinguished himself by defining menstruation as "the weeping of the disappointed uterus". They had a lot of fun with that afterward. They would go around saying to each other, "Is your uterus disappointed? Has it wept yet?" Or: "Well my *uterus* may be disappointed, but I sure as hell am not."

While they were clearing the table Chess was describing Anna to Gary. "Anna is a sweet person," she said. "A gentle person. Always kind to everyone." There was something about this that made Anna uneasy but she wasn't sure what it was. After they'd done up the dishes she went into Chess's room. "What are you wearing tonight?" she asked her. Chess took out her red dress and laid it down on her bed.

"Can I wear the green one, then?"

Chess took out the green dress and laid it down on the bed beside the red one. Anna loved the green dress; it was almost exactly the colour of the gowns they used in the OR, but a little softer, embossed with little flowers that were also green but slightly lighter, almost silver. She held it up to herself in front of the mirror. It was a colour that went well with tanned skin.

"On second thought," said Chess, lifting the dress away from Anna, "I think I'll wear this one myself."

"What'll I wear then? I can't wear the red."

"Borrow something from Mother."

Anna went into their mother's dressing room. Everything in there was in zippered bags. Rich formal things – for winter and for her mother's piano recitals. She took out a black cocktail dress and put it on. She thought: black goes well with tanned skin. She looked in one of the shoe bags and found a pair of golden sandals. She put them on and went over to the dressing table in them. She unstoppered the perfumes and sniffed them. She put Tigress on her wrists and Fleures de Rocailles between her breasts. She felt uneasy with her mother, but not with her mother's clothes. Her mother never minded lending things; she had more clothes than anyone; not just clothes for concert tours but young clothes – plaid dresses, square dance skirts. Sometimes she would give Chess and Anna clothes too, things she'd simply got tired of wearing. There was a certain innocence about her mother – she was in so many ways innocent of the dull and thankless responsibilities of parenthood; when they were little children and she embraced them her embraces were almost never to pat or celebrate *them*, her children, they were rather entreaties to her children to endorse some fine quality in herself. She used to hug them and say, "Do you know how lucky you are to have a mother who doesn't smell? I never smell, do you realize that? I always smell sweet." They would wriggle away from her as soon as seemed decent. Or at least Anna would. She was self-centred herself.

Downstairs, the doorbell rang and Anna ran down to answer it. A lot of people she didn't know were standing there, a shy group, wondering who she was.

"Come in!" she said. "I'll call Chess."

Chess came down the stairs then and Kamille and the Mormons came down behind her.

The next time the doorbell rang Anna and Chess both ran to get it. And when they opened the door there were two men there – Karl and someone else. "I knew right away," Chess told Anna later. "Right there at the door I knew he was falling in love with you. He had such a dumb, enthralled look."

The next morning when Chess and Anna were in their bedroom, combing their hair before breakfast, Chess said to Anna: "Do you know what Gary said last night, about you?"

"You mean Gary the Mormon?"

"You don't have to keep calling him Gary the Mormon like that."

"I'm sorry. What did he say?"

"He said, 'Do you still think Anna is a sweet person and a gentle person and kind to everyone now?'"

Everyone was at the table when Chess and Anna came out to the kitchen. All the people who'd stayed the night – Karl, Gary and Al, two old friends of the family named Dorie and Kay. Karl fetched a chair for Anna and fitted it in beside his own. A picnic was being planned. They were all supposed to go to White Church River Cove in Dorie's car. Kamille had already made the sandwiches.

But then Gary and Al said they'd have to stay in town, calling on people. And Kay said she had a headache. This was the excuse Anna had planned to use and for a moment she felt confused. Then she said, "That's funny, I have a headache too," and everyone laughed. Karl leaned over and whispered, "But you're coming anyway, aren't you?" and she shook her head no. A few minutes later her mother excused herself from the table and a short time after that she called down to Anna from her room, telling her to come upstairs.

When Anna got up there her mother was in the little bathroom adjoining the bedroom, running a glass of water. She shook two aspirins out of a bottle and handed them and the drink to Anna. "Chess has had lots of boyfriends," she said. The terrible corollary to that hung unspoken between them. "Take these," she said. Anna took them. Why not? She wanted to go. She wanted to be *ordered to go*. Chess came into the room then and closed the door tightly behind her. "It's not fair if Anna comes," she said. "Chess darling," their mother said to her, "Don't take this too hard! You've had lots of boyfriends. And you'll have many more. But facts are facts, darling. Karl seems to care for Anna." Chess started to cry. And Anna stood and rubbed her thumb the length of the wide white window-sill; she felt amazed and uneasy.

Chess talked a great deal on the way there. And after they'd found a place to eat and had finished eating and had taken shelter in an old covered bridge to wait out the rain that they'd feared and predicted all the way there she started to sing. Songs from *South Pacific*, *Oklahoma*, *An American in Paris*. She sang well, in a light, sad, chanteusey voice, but it was clear (at least to Anna) that Karl didn't care for that kind of thing. And after Chess had been singing for a while, Anna leaned back against the wall of the bridge and closed her eyes.

In the middle of the following week Anna got a letter from Karl. He was coming to Hocksville two days later and wondered if he could see her. Maybe we could go to a beach, he wrote. He signed the letter love.

On the beach, Karl told Anna about his childhood in Norway, under the Germans, and about coming to Canada in 1945 when he was sixteen and about how people had laughed at him when he went out skating because he wore britches and knee-socks. He told her about going to school in Oslo in '42, '43, and about trying to get in the back end of the soup line so he could get more of the meat that sank to the soup pot's bottom. Anna found she liked him ever better for the romance and deprivations of his past. He told her that a Norwegian Nazi had been shot by someone from the Underground in the street right in front of his school. He said that at the end of the war the Americans wanted to make a goodwill gesture to the Norwegians (who had suffered so much). They hit on the idea of sending over a freighter filled with peanut butter. But the Norwegians had never seen peanut butter before, and they found it, when it arrived, to be revolting stuff – *they* thought the goodwill boat was filled with excrement. "The Norwegians were hungry," Karl said, "but they were not *that* hungry." Anna smiled. "Speaking of excrement," she said, "I should tell you about my life at the hospital." His turn to smile. But she only told him the funny things, she didn't want him to know she was thinking of leaving there. It was her secret. She would move when she was ready. She saw it happening on a clear, fall day. She saw herself decently, adultly concealing her pleasure at getting free. She saw herself walking out of the nurses' residence carrying a little red overnight case, her coat over her arm; she saw how her eyes would give the impression of being nobly infatuated with a far horizon, like the eyes of a Red Cross nurse in one of the wartime posters from her childhood.

In real life, she was transferred to the Emergency wing. She liked it there. It was the first place she'd worked where they weren't short-staffed. And she liked the people she was working with – Smitty, Jackson, Devine, Becky Agulnick. Her first day off Karl was able to get his father's car to drive down to see her. He could stay overnight so they drove out to the Stone Bay house where Anna was born, now used by her family as a summer house. Anna's mother was out there and was expecting them and seemed overjoyed to see them. She was wearing a pink towel, boxer-style, around her neck; she had just washed her hair. When she gave concerts she always did her hair up into a dignified confection of braids and buns – using her own young braids, kept in a hat box – but now it hung fair and fluffy down to her shoulders. She was barefoot, perfumed. She gave them each a hard, theatrical hug. She had hot drinks already fixed for them and a fire in the fireplace. Anna got the impression that her mother thought she'd dreamed them up, that they were her production. She wanted to say to her: Listen, this would have happened anyway. He's already told me that my coming on that picnic didn't make any difference, we would have seen each other again, he's crazy about me. And he never was interested in Chess, not seriously; he thinks she likes herself too much. Her mother took Karl on a tour of the house and showed him the paintings and the things from Europe and her "country piano". She said, "Later, if you would like, I will play for you." Karl said that would be marvellous. And when Karl and Anna went out for a walk after they'd done the dishes Anna's mother came with them. By then there were big clouds, thin as smoke, moving fast across the sky. It was the first night that summer seemed conclusively over. Even the river had got more wild and fall-like, they could hear the waves coming in harder against the beach. Karl held hands with Anna's mother. They swung their hands back and forth like two children. Anna's hand he lifted into his pocket with his own. He made love to her between all her fingers with his thumb. "Isn't this inspiring?" cried Anna's mother, sniffing the wind, inhaling the view of the sky and the river.

The next morning when Anna woke up she smelled coffee and breakfast cooking. She went downstairs in her nightgown. Her mother was standing at the stove, frowning. Her hair was brushed, tied back. She was wearing a sky blue sundress. She was frying french toast in one pan and scrambling eggs with chives in another. In the big black skillet bacon was cooking. She had also made muffins, put peach jam in a blue bowl and strawberry jam in a clear glass dish. She had picked fresh flowers for the table, poured orange juice into wine goblets, and made up pots of both coffee and tea.

"My God," Anna said. "This is fantastic."

"I suppose I better put all this in the oven to keep it warm," her mother said. She seemed to be cross about something.

Anna went up to her room and pulled off her nightgown. She inspected her tan, then washed and dressed. She rubbed cologne on her arms and neck and hand lotion on her hands and legs. She fastened on a pair of high-heeled sandals and put on two rings and a bracelet. Then she went down the hall and knocked on Karl's door. He told her to come in. She went in there and closed the door behind her. The whole house smelled of sleeping breath and sun on rugs and coffee. Karl yawned and stretched and then pulled her down on the bed.

Lying beside him she posed one leg in its sandal. "My mother's made a big breakfast," she whispered. And then she whispered, "Do you know what I think? I think my mother wants to marry you." And then she felt her face start to glow because she had come so dangerously close to saying, "I think my mother wants to marry you *herself*."

But Karl, instead of answering her (and maybe not even having heard her – what she'd said, what she'd stopped herself from saying), started using one of his fingers to trace the outline of her sandaled heel, calf, thigh. It was a phrase he was writing. When he got to her panties he put a period between her legs. She spread them a little.

"Children!" called her mother, in the musical voice she used for company.

Karl took his finger out from under Anna's dress and brought it up over her belly and then up over one breast. At the nipple he pressed in another period. Then he proceeded up her neck and around her chin. He outlined her mouth. She parted her lips. He put a period in her mouth. She bit his finger.

"Everything's going to get cold!" called her mother. Less music in the voice now.

"Coming!" Karl shouted in a cheerful, sing-song voice.

And then the finger started outlining Anna's nose. She hated that. Her nose was too big and had a bump in it. She believed it had ruined her life. "If we got married . . ." Karl said. The finger came down over her nose again, ". . . do you think our children would have big noses?"

She sat up. "We'd better get down there," she said, "or she's going to start to get angry."

At the end of that summer Karl was ready to leave for Toronto where he had a job waiting. He stretched the time out a little longer to coincide with Anna's coming off days in Emergency so that they could spend a last day together in Athens.

His bus came in two hours after Anna's, and when he arrived at the house, pale as a dying prince, they all went into the living room for cakes and tea. Kamille had left for the States by this time, but Anna's brother Arnie was at home and so was Chess. It was a cold, cloudy, fall day, and the house seemed very draughty and polished. Karl talked in a very informed way about the Royal Danish Ballet, and Chess asked him a lot of questions.

After they'd brought the tea things out to the kitchen Arnie took Anna aside and said, "Hey little sister, are you going to marry this Karl, with his clipped English?" She said maybe I will, I don't know yet. And then she started to help Chess with the dishes.

While Chess and Anna were alone out there, Chess said, "Everything Karl said about the ballet was very interesting, I thought."

Anna said she thought so too.

"He got it all out of *Time* magazine," Chess said. "All of it. I read the whole review when I came down here on the bus. Those opinions weren't his own."

"That can't be true." Anna said. "He doesn't even read *Time*. He's a socialist."

"I have it in my suitcase," Chess said. "I can show it to you."

"I've got better things to do," Anna said. But her heart felt like it was beating ten times faster than usual.

Karl left for Toronto and Anna went back to the hospital. She was transferred to Male Surgery and with the fair-minded Killeen in charge she didn't mind it too much there. A whole month went by. She was now into the third month of her third year. "What a pity you're leaving," she imagined people would say, "when you've only nine months left to go." And then she imagined the way their eyes would drop, quite understandably, down to her belly.

The first snow came. Karl and Anna wrote to each other every day. His letters made her ache they were so sweet, full of quotes from Andrew Marvell, full of missing her body. More snow came. The supervisors got out boxes of Christmas decorations and for part of one peaceful hospital afternoon they all unrolled bandage-sized rolls of red and green crêpe paper and decorated the nursing stations. People started talking about Christmas and New Year's and on some wards they started making trades. The patients' radios played Christmas carols. Then suddenly (and inexplicably, because she'd already worked a long stretch there before), Anna was transferred to 6E, the worst ward in the whole hospital, run by a supervisor who was considered, even by the other supervisors, to be a sadist. Her name was M. K. Howard. If she had a first name no one seemed to know what it was, although there was a rumour the M stood for Mary. Sometimes, in fact, she was called the Virgin Mary. ("Hear you're spending Christmas with the Virgin Mary, you poor bastard," a girl named Connors said to Anna one day in the cafeteria.) At the end of a week with Howard, Anna felt she was in hell. And in the middle of hell she got a letter from Karl. He'd been at a party where he'd met a lot of new people. He had dropped ice-cubes down a girl's back. She was an amusing girl, he wrote, very dark and lively. You would like her. He thought it would be a good idea if they occasionally went out with other people.

After this, Anna started having trouble sleeping. Her skin itched; she lay awake parts of every night, scratching, panicked. What if the lack of sleep made her make a mistake with the medicines? What if she gave someone someone else's injection? And during the days she felt herself in the grip of a secret rage. The patients" radios played the same carols over and over – bouncy barbershop renditions of songs about roasting chestnuts and Christmastime in the city. She did not hear from Karl again and she did not write to him; but sometimes, in the middle of passing out pills or giving the needles, her eyes would fill up with tears. Three nights after his letter she didn't sleep at all, but she made up her mind. She would phone home in the morning and tell them that she had broken up with Karl and that she was sick and wanted to come home. She knew her mother would be alarmed enough to come and get her; her mother would not want Karl to escape.

When she came off duty the night of her last day she found her room filled up with people. People from her own class, people from other years, other classes. They were everywhere: on the bed, on the desk, on chairs, on suitcases. It wasn't a popular move, leaving; it inspired envy. And it left yet another ward short-staffed. The traditional way to leave was to tell one or two friends, swear them to secrecy, leave when the night and day staffs were safely at work or at supper in the hospital cafeteria. And pregnancy was the traditional reason.

Someone asked her if she was pregnant. She said no. "As a matter of fact, I'm menstruating," she said.

"The weeping of the disappointed uterus," someone said, and there was a patch of uneasy laughter.

Connors said, "Let's undress her and see if she's lying," and Anna felt really scared then because technically, at least, she *was* lying. She had had cramps all day but nothing had happened yet.

"Anna's been wanting to leave here for more than a year," said Joan Cosman, her friend. And no move was made against her.

She started to pack. She gave away her cape, caps, textbooks, uniforms. Also her late-leave card, to be forged later.

A delegation came with her to the elevator. Smitty and Becky Agulnick kissed her goodbye. Jackson and Devine told her to write. Connors punched her on the shoulder and said, "No hard feelings, I hope." She said no. Joan loaded her stuff into the elevator.

Outside it was snowing again and Anna's mother's coat was turned into a fat fur bell by the wind. Anna hurried behind it down the wide concrete steps. She never expected her mother to refuse to speak to her, and yet it often happened; it was happening now. In silence they fitted the suitcases into the back seat and climbed into the front and closed themselves in. In silence they drove down Porter Street and in silence they left Hocksville and the ocean and the lights of Port Charlotte behind. At Black Bay the river had frozen and been snowed on, but a channel had been kept open for the ferry. They drove in silence on to the ferry, bumping over its wooden flap, and in silence watched the snow fall into its road of black water. On the other side of the river they drove up and down hills that seemed a little steeper with the new snow on them. But by then the snow had stopped. East of Bucksfield there was even some fog. Cedar trees stood in fog on white fields. Country schools and country churches appeared, ghostly close to the highway. Anna's mother drove slowly after this, through settlements and small towns named to hold the wilderness at bay – Richmond, Cambridge, Annetteville, New Sharon – and as they came into New Sharon she even spoke.

"I think you should know what Jack Kincaid said when he heard you were giving up," Anna's mother said. (Jack Kincaid, dead now, in those days owned the men's wear store in Athens. When he was trying to persuade someone to buy from his range of fur-lined suede gloves he would say, "Feel that. Softer than a mouse's titty.")

"What did he say?" Anna asked her mother. For some mad reason she expected good news.

"He said, 'What that girl needs is a good whipping.'"

Anna laughed a harsh, light laugh. "Oh, I would not put great stock in anything Jack Kincaid might say," she said. "I would not greatly respect any opinion Jack Kincaid might have."

"Someone who's done what you've done is hardly entitled to sit in judgement on other people," her mother said. "You turned your back on the sick," her mother said.

Anna turned and looked out the window and would not answer.

When Karl came down the following Easter (by Christmas already they had patched things up – Karl had written to her; she had answered him in the next mail) they spent a lot of their time together talking about Anna's mother. Anna found she could talk more easily to Karl than she'd ever been able to talk to anyone else. But still she was careful, settled for telling him the little irritations, not the dark things. She said, "When she comes back from the post office she tells me I didn't get any mail. Then two hours later, when we're all sitting down to supper, she lifts the cover off the casserole dish and there is your letter. I never know what piece of crockery I'm going to find a letter in next."

He looked startled. "But what if she decided not to even give you a letter at all?" he asked her. She could have said, "Oh, I came into her room one night and found her sitting up in bed reading a letter you'd sent to me," but it didn't seem wise to let him know that. How could he continue to write to her about the sweet weight of her breasts if he knew a thing like that? She could have said, "She tried to kill herself once, with me in the car." She could have said, "Once when she was having her nap, she called me in to her room to cover her with an extra blanket and later, when she woke up, she came out into the kitchen and said, 'You made me dream I was dead. You covered me with that heavy, heavy blanket, you made me dream I was dead.'" But there were things she didn't want him to know; for instance she didn't want him to know what her mother had shouted out to her the time they were in the car and her mother had threatened to kill herself. Her mother had shouted out to her, "You turn people on and off like a tap! You don't love anyone! I might as well kill myself if I'm not loved!" And then she had pressed the accelerator down to the floor and driven their decrepit old car as fast as it could go. Which was only about eighty and besides, the road, for the next ten or fifteen miles, was going to be straight. Still, Anna had finally shouted out, "Of course I love you!" to her mother, and this was somehow the most humiliating thing to remember of all.

*

One night in early spring when they were lying in front of the fireplace, late, after the others had all gone to bed, Karl said, "Do you know what really irritates me about her more than anything else?"

"What," she said dreamily. "What." Whatever it was, she was sure she would love to hear it.

"The way she comes up to me and looks up at me with those innocent big blue eyes of hers and says, 'Do you love little Annie? Do you love her very much?'"

Anna snorted, appreciative.

"The way she calls you *little Annie*," he said.

"Yeah," she said. "Little Orphan Annie."

"Do you know what I feel like answering her?" he asked her. "When she asks me if I love you?"

Anna felt delicious. Her whole belly was jelly, ready to laugh. She felt weakened and lulled by the coming laughter, by that and the uneven heat – half of her face and one thigh were all hot from the fire. "What?" she said.

"I feel like saying no," he said. "I feel like saying no, I don't love her."

She sat up at once and drew herself a little away from him. "Why would you want to say that?" she asked him. "Whatever would you want to say that for?"

"To shut her up," he said.

Dreams

TIMOTHY FINDLEY

For R. E. Turner

Doctor Menlo was having a problem: he could not sleep and his wife – the other Doctor Menlo – was secretly staying awake in order to keep an eye on him. The trouble was that, in spite of her concern and in spite of all her efforts, Doctor Menlo – whose name was Mimi – was always nodding off because of her exhaustion.

She had tried drinking coffee, but this had no effect. She detested coffee and her system had a built-in rejection mechanism. She also prescribed herself a week's worth of Dexedrine to see if that would do the trick. *Five mg at bedtime* – all to no avail. And even though she put the plastic bottle of small orange hearts beneath her pillow and kept augmenting her intake, she would wake half an hour later with a dreadful start to discover the night was moving on to morning.

Everett Menlo had not yet declared the source of his problem. His restless condition had begun about ten days ago and had barely raised his interest. Soon, however, the time spent lying awake had increased from one to several hours and then, on Monday last, to all-night sessions. Now he lay in a state of rigid apprehension – eyes wide open, arms above his head, his hands in fists – like a man in pain unable to shut it out. His neck, his back and his shoulders constantly harried him with cramps and spasms. Everett Menlo had become a full-blown insomniac.

Clearly, Mimi Menlo concluded, her husband was refusing to sleep because he believed something dreadful was going to happen the moment he closed his eyes. She had encountered this sort of fear in one or two of her patients. Everett, on the other hand, would not discuss the subject. If the problem had been hers, he would have said *such things cannot occur if you have gained control of yourself.*

Mimi began to watch for the dawn. She would calculate its approach by listening for the increase of traffic down below the bedroom window. The Menlos' home was across the road from The Manulife Centre – corner of Bloor and Bay streets. Mimi's first sight of daylight always revealed the high, white shape of its terraced storeys. Their own apartment building was of a modest height and colour – twenty floors of smoky glass and polished brick. The shadow of the Manulife would crawl across the bedroom floor and climb the wall behind her, grey with fatigue and cold.

The Menlo beds were an arm's length apart, and lying like a rug between them was the shape of a large, black dog of unknown breed. All night long, in the dark of his well, the dog would dream and he would tell the content of his dreams the way that victims in a trance will tell of being pursued by posses of their nameless fears. He whimpered, he cried and sometimes he howled. His legs and his paws would jerk and flail and his claws would scrabble desperately against the parquet floor. Mimi – who loved this dog – would lay her hand against his side and let her fingers dabble in his coat in vain attempts to soothe him. Sometimes, she had to call his name in order to rouse him from his dreams because his heart would be racing. Other times, she smiled and thought: *at least there's one of us getting some sleep*. The dog's name was Thurber and he dreamed in beige and white.

Everett and Mimi Menlo were both psychiatrists. His field was schizophrenia; hers was autistic children. Mimi's venue was the Parkin Institute at the University of Toronto; Everett's was the Queen Street Mental Health Centre. Early in their marriage they had decided never to work as a team and not – unless it was a matter of financial life and death – to accept employment in the same institution. Both had always worked with the kind of physical intensity that kills, and yet they gave the impression this was the only tolerable way in which to function. It meant there was always a sense of peril in what they did, but the peril – according to Everett – made their lives worth living. This, at least, had been the theory twenty years ago when they were young.

Now, for whatever unnamed reason, peril had become his enemy and Everett Menlo had begun to look and behave and lose his sleep like a haunted man. But he refused to comment when Mimi asked him what was wrong. Instead, he gave the worst of all possible answers a psychiatrist can hear who seeks an explanation of a patient's silence: he said there was *absolutely nothing wrong*.

"You're sure you're not coming down with something?"

"Yes."

"And you wouldn't like a massage?"

"I've already told you: no."

"Can I get you anything?"

"No."

"And you don't want to talk?"

"That's right."

"Okay, Everett . . ."

"Okay, what?"

"Okay, nothing. I only hope you get some sleep tonight."

Everett stood up. "Have you been spying on me, Mimi?"

"What do you mean by *spying*?"

"Watching me all night long."

"Well, Everett, I don't see how I can fail to be aware you aren't asleep when we share this bedroom. I mean – I can hear you grinding your teeth. I can see you lying there wide awake."

"When?"

"All the time. You're staring at the ceiling."

"I've never stared at the ceiling in my whole life. I sleep on my stomach."

"You sleep on your stomach *if* you sleep. But you have not been sleeping. Period. No argument."

Everett Menlo went to his dresser and got out a pair of clean pyjamas. Turning his back on Mimi, he put them on.

Somewhat amused at the coyness of this gesture, Mimi asked what he was hiding.

"Nothing!" he shouted at her.

Mimi's mouth fell open. Everett never yelled. His anger wasn't like that; it manifested itself in other ways, in silence and withdrawal, never shouts.

Everett was staring at her defiantly. He had slammed the bottom drawer of his dresser. Now he was fumbling with the wrapper of a pack of cigarettes.

Mimi's stomach tied a knot.

Everett hadn't touched a cigarette for weeks.

"Please don't smoke those," she said. "You'll only be sorry if you do."

"And you," he said, "will be sorry if I don't."

"But, dear . . ." said Mimi.

"Leave me for Christ's sake alone!" Everett yelled.

Mimi gave up and sighed and then she said: "All right. Thurber and I will go and sleep in the living room. Good-night."

Everett sat on the edge of his bed. His hands were shaking.

"Please," he said – apparently addressing the floor. "Don't leave me here alone. I couldn't bear that."

This was perhaps the most chilling thing he could have said to her. Mimi was alarmed; her husband was genuinely terrified of something and he would not say what it was. If she had not been who she was – if she had not known what she knew – if her years of training had not prepared her to watch for signs like this, she might have been better off. As it was, she had to face the possibility the strongest, most sensible man on earth was having a nervous break-down of major proportions. Lots of people have breakdowns, of course; but not, she had thought, the gods of reason.

"All right," she said – her voice maintaining the kind of calm she knew a child afraid of the dark would appreciate. "In a minute I'll get us something to drink. But first, I'll go and change . . ."

Mimi went into the sanctum of the bathroom, where her night-gown waited for her – a portable hiding-place hanging on the back of the door. "You stay there," she said to Thurber, who had padded after her. "Mama will be out in just a moment."

Even in the dark, she could gauge Everett's tension. His shadow – all she could see of him – twitched from time to time and the twitching took on a kind of lurching rhythm, something like the broken clock in their living room.

Mimi lay on her side and tried to close her eyes. But her eyes were tied to a will of their own and would not obey her. Now she, too, was caught in the same irreversible tide of sleeplessness that bore her husband backward through the night. Four or five times she watched him lighting cigarettes – blowing out the matches, courting disaster in the bedclothes – conjuring the worst of deaths for the three of them: a flaming pyre on the twentieth floor.

All this behaviour was utterly unlike him; foreign to his code of disciplines and ethics; alien to everything he said and believed. *Openness, directness, sharing of ideas, encouraging imaginative response to every problem. Never hide troubles. Never allow despair . . .* These were his directives in everything he did. Now, he had thrown them over.

One thing was certain. She was not the cause of his sleeplessness. She didn't have affairs and neither did he. He might be ill – but whenever he'd been ill before, there had been no trauma; never a trauma like this one, at any rate. Perhaps it was something about a patient – one of his tougher cases; a wall in the patient's condition they could not break through; some circumstance of someone's lack of progress – a sudden veering towards a catatonic state, for instance – something that Everett had not foreseen that had stymied him and was slowly . . . what? Destroying his sense of professional control? His self-esteem? His scientific certainty? If only he would speak.

Mimi thought about her own worst case: a child whose obstinate refusal to communicate was currently breaking her heart and, thus, her ability to help. If ever she had needed Everett to talk to, it was now. All her fellow doctors were locked in a battle over this child: they wanted to take him away from her. Mimi refused to give him up; he might as well have been her own flesh and blood. Everything had been done – from gentle holding sessions to violent bouts of manufactured anger – in her attempt to make the child react. She was staying with him every day from the moment he was roused to the moment he was induced to sleep with drugs.

His name was Brian Bassett and he was eight years old. He sat on the floor in the furthest corner he could achieve in one of the observation-isolation rooms where all the autistic children were placed when nothing else in their treatment – nothing of love or expertise – had managed to break their silence. Mostly, this was a signal they were coming to the end of life.

There in his four-square, glass-box room, surrounded by all that can tempt a child if a child can be tempted – toys and food and story-book companions – Brian Bassett was in the process, now, of fading away. His eyes were never closed and his arms were restrained. He was attached to three machines that nurtured him with all that science can offer. But of course, the spirit and the will to live cannot be fed by force to those who do not want to feed.

Now, in the light of Brian Bassett's utter lack of willing contact with the world around him – his utter refusal to communicate – Mimi watched her husband through the night. Everett stared at the ceiling, lit by the Manulife building's distant lamps, borne on his back further and further out to sea. She had lost him, she was certain.

When, at last, he saw that Mimi had drifted into her own and welcome sleep, Everett rose from his bed and went out into the hall, past the simulated jungle of the solarium, until he reached the dining room. There, all the way till dawn, he amused himself with two decks of cards and endless games of Dead Man's Solitaire.

Thurber rose and shuffled after him. The dining room was one of Thurber's favourite places in all his confined but privileged world, for it was here – as in the kitchen – that from time to time a hand descended filled with the miracle of food. But whatever it was that his master was doing up there above him on the table-top, it wasn't anything to do with feeding or with being fed. The playing cards had an old and dusty dryness to their scent and they held no appeal for the dog. So he once again lay down and he took up his dreams, which at least gave his paws some exercise. This way, he failed to hear the advent of a new dimension to his master's problem. This occurred precisely at 5.45 a.m. when the telephone rang and Everett Menlo, having rushed to answer it, waited breathless for a minute while he listened and then said: "yes" in a curious, strangulated fashion. Thurber – had he been awake – would have recognized in his master's voice the signal for disaster.

For weeks now, Everett had been working with a patient who was severely and uniquely schizophrenic. This patient's name was Kenneth Albright, and while he was deeply suspicious, he was also oddly caring. Kenneth Albright loved the detritus of life, such as bits of woolly dust and wads of discarded paper. He loved all dried-up leaves that had drifted from their parent trees and he loved the dead bees that had curled up to die along the window-sills of his ward. He also loved the spiderwebs seen high up in the corners of the rooms where he sat on plastic chairs and ate with plastic spoons.

Kenneth Albright talked a lot about his dreams. But his dreams had become, of late, a major stumbling block in the process of his recovery. Back in the days when Kenneth had first become Doctor Menlo's patient, the dreams had been overburdened with detail: "over-cast", as he would say, "with characters" and over-produced, again in Kenneth's phrase, "as if I were dreaming the dreams of Cecil B. de Mille."

Then he had said: "But a person can't really dream someone else's dreams. Or can they, Doctor Menlo?"

"No" had been Everett's answer – definite and certain.

Everett Menlo had been delighted, at first, with Kenneth Albright's dreams. They had been immensely entertaining – complex and filled with intriguing detail. Kenneth himself was at a loss to explain the meaning of these dreams, but as Everett had said, it wasn't Kenneth's job to explain. That was Everett's job. His job and his pleasure. For quite a long while, during these early sessions, Everett had written out the dreams, taken them home and recounted them to Mimi.

Kenneth Albright was a paranoid schizophrenic. Four times now, he had attempted suicide. He was a fiercely angry man at times – and at other times as gentle and as pleasant as a docile child. He had suffered so greatly, in the very worst moments of his disease, that he could no longer work. His job – it was almost an incidental detail in his life and had no importance for him, so it seemed – was returning reference books, in the Metro Library, to their places in the stacks. Sometimes – mostly late of an afternoon – he might begin a psychotic episode of such profound dimensions that he would attempt his suicide right behind the counter and even once, in the full view of everyone, while riding in the glass-walled elevator. It was after this last occasion that he was brought, in restraints, to be a resident patient at the Queen Street Mental Health Centre. He had slashed his wrists with a razor – but not before he had also slashed and destroyed an antique copy of *Don Quixote*, the pages of which he pasted to the walls with blood.

For a week thereafter, Kenneth Albright – just like Brian Bassett – had refused to speak or to move. Everett had him kept in an isolation cell, force-fed and drugged. Slowly, by dint of patience, encouragement and caring even Kenneth could recognize as genuine, Everett Menlo had broken through the barrier. Kenneth was removed from isolation, pampered with food and cigarettes, and he began relating his dreams.

At first there seemed to be only the dreams and nothing else in Kenneth's memory. Broken pencils, discarded toys and the telephone directory all had roles to play in these dreams but there were never any people. All the weather was bleak and all the landscapes were empty. Houses, motor cars and office buildings never made an appearance. Sounds and smells had some importance; the wind would blow, the scent of unseen fires was often described. Stairwells were plentiful, leading nowhere, all of them rising from a subterranean world that Kenneth either did not dare to visit or would not describe.

The dreams had little variation, one from another. The themes had mostly to do with loss and with being lost. The broken pencils were all given names and the discarded toys were given to one another as companions. The telephone books were the sources of recitations – hours and hours of repeated names and numbers, some of which – Everett had noted with surprise – were absolutely accurate.

All of this held fast until an incident one morning that changed the face of Kenneth Albright's schizophrenia forever: an incident that stemmed – so it seemed – from something he had dreamed the night before.

Bearing in mind his previous attempts at suicide, it will be obvious that Kenneth Albright was never far from sight at the Queen Street Mental Health Centre. He was, in fact, under constant observation: constant, that is, as human beings and modern technology can manage. In the ward to which he was ultimately consigned, for instance, the toilet cabinets had no doors and the shower-rooms had no locks. Therefore, a person could not ever be alone with water, glass or shaving utensils. (All the razors were cordless automatics.) Scissors and knives were banned, as were pieces of string and rubber bands. A person could not even kill his feet and hands by binding up his wrists or ankles. Nothing poisonous was anywhere available. All the windows were barred. All the double doors between this ward and the corridors beyond were doors with triple locks and a guard was always near at hand.

Still, if people want to die, they will find a way. Mimi Menlo would discover this to her everlasting sorrow with Brian Bassett. Everett Menlo would discover this to his everlasting horror with Kenneth Albright.

On the morning of 19 April, a Tuesday, Everett Menlo, in the best of health, had welcomed a brand-new patient into his office. This was

Anne Marie Wilson, a young and brilliant pianist whose promising career had been halted mid-flight by a schizophrenic incident involving her ambition. She was, it seemed, no longer able to play and all her dreams were shattered. The cause was simple, to all appearances: Anne Marie had a sense of how, precisely, the music should be and she had not been able to master it accordingly. "Everything I attempt is terrible," she had said – in spite of all her critical accolades and all her professional success. Other doctors had tried and failed to break the barriers in Anne Marie, whose hands had taken on a life of their own, refusing altogether to work for her. Now it was Menlo's turn and hope was high.

Everett had been looking forward to his session with this prodigy. He loved all music and had thought to find some means within its discipline to reach her. She seemed so fragile, sitting there in the sunlight, and he had just begun to take his first notes when the door flew open and Louise, his secretary, had said: "I'm sorry, Doctor Menlo. There's a problem. Can you come with me at once?"

Everett excused himself.

Anne Marie was left in the sunlight to bide her time. Her fingers were moving around in her lap and she put them in her mouth to make them quiet.

Even as he'd heard his secretary speak, Everett had known the problem would be Kenneth Albright. Something in Kenneth's eyes had warned him there was trouble on the way: a certain wariness that indicated all was not as placid as it should have been, given his regimen of drugs. He had stayed long hours in one position, moving his fingers over his thighs as if to dry them on his trousers; watching his fellow patients come and go with abnormal interest – never, however, rising from his chair. An incident was on the horizon and Everett had been waiting for it, hoping it would not come.

Louise had said that Doctor Menlo was to go at once to Kenneth Albright's ward. Everett had run the whole way. Only after the attendant had let him in past the double doors did he slow his pace to a hurried walk and wipe his brow. He didn't want Kenneth to know how alarmed he had been.

Coming to the appointed place, he paused before he entered, closing his eyes, preparing himself for whatever he might have to

see. *Other people have killed themselves: I've seen it often enough*, he was
thinking. *I simply won't let it affect me.* Then he went in.

The room was small and white – a dining room – and Kenneth was
sitting down in a corner, his back pressed out against the walls on
either side of him. His head was bowed and his legs drawn up and
he was obviously trying to hide without much success. An intern
was standing above him and a nurse was kneeling down beside him.
Several pieces of bandaging with blood on them were scattered near
Kenneth's feet and there was a white enamel basin filled with
pinkish water on the floor beside the nurse.

"Morowetz," Everett said to the intern. "Tell me what has happened here." He said this just the way he posed such questions
when he took the interns through the wards at examination time,
quizzing them on symptoms and prognoses.

But Morowetz the intern had no answer. He was puzzled. What
had happened had no sane explanation.

Everett turned to Charterhouse, the nurse.

"On the morning of 19 April, at roughly ten-fifteen, I found
Kenneth Albright covered with blood," Ms Charterhouse was to
write in her report. "His hands, his arms, his face and his neck were
stained. I would say the blood was fresh and the patient's clothing –
mostly his shirt – was wet with it. Some – a very small amount of it –
had dried on his forehead. The rest was uniformly the kind of blood
you expect to find free-flowing from a wound. I called for assistance
and meanwhile attempted to ascertain where Mister Albright might
have been injured. I performed this examination without success. I
could find no source of bleeding anywhere on Mister Albright's
body."

Morowetz concurred.

The blood was someone else's.

"Was there a weapon of any kind?" Doctor Menlo had wanted to
know.

"No, sir. Nothing," said Charterhouse.

"And was he alone when you found him?"

"Yes, sir. Just like this in the corner."

"And the others?"

"All the patients in the ward were examined," Morowetz told him.

"And?"

"Not one of them was bleeding."

Everett said: "I see."

He looked down at Kenneth.

"This is Doctor Menlo, Kenneth. Have you anything to tell me?"

Kenneth did not reply.

Everett said: "When you've got him back in his room and tranquillized, will you call me, please?"

Morowetz nodded.

The call never came. Kenneth had fallen asleep. Either the drugs he was given had knocked him out cold, or he had opted for silence. Either way, he was incommunicado.

No one was discovered bleeding. Nothing was found to indicate an accident, a violent attack, an epileptic seizure. A weapon was not located. Kenneth Albright had not a single scratch on his flesh from stem, as Everett put it, to gudgeon. The blood, it seemed, had fallen like the rain from heaven: unexplained and inexplicable.

Later, as the day was ending, Everett Menlo left the Queen Street Mental Health Centre. He made his way home on the Queen streetcar and the Bay bus. When he reached the apartment, Thurber was waiting for him. Mimi was at a goddamned meeting.

That was the night Everett Menlo suffered the first of his failures to sleep. It was occasioned by the fact that, when he wakened sometime after three, he had just been dreaming. This, of course, was not unusual – but the dream itself was perturbing. There was someone lying there, in the bright white landscape of a hospital dining room. Whether it was a man or a woman could not be told, it was just a human body, lying down in a pool of blood.

Kenneth Albright was kneeling beside this body, pulling it open the way a child will pull a Christmas present open – yanking at its strings and ribbons, wanting only to see the contents. Everett saw this scene from several angles, never speaking, never being spoken to. In all the time he watched – the usual dream eternity – the silence was broken only by the sound of water dripping from an unseen tap. Then, Kenneth Albright rose and was covered with blood, the way he had been that morning. He stared at Doctor Menlo, looked right through him and departed. Nothing remained in the dining room but plastic tables and plastic chairs and the bright red thing on the floor that once had been a person. Everett Menlo did not know

and could not guess who this person might have been. He only
knew that Kenneth Albright had left this person's body in Everett
Menlo's dream.

Three nights running, the corpse remained in its place and every
time that Everett entered the dining room in the nightmare he was
certain he would find out who it was. On the fourth night, fully
expecting to discover he himself was the victim, he beheld the face
and saw it was a stranger.

But there are no strangers in dreams; he knew that now after twenty
years of practice. *There are no strangers; there are only people in disguise.*

Mimi made one final attempt in Brian Bassett's behalf to turn away
the fate to which his other doctors – both medical and psychiatric –
had consigned him. Not that, as a group, they had failed to expend
the full weight of all they knew and all they could do to save him.
One of his medical doctors – a woman whose name was Juliet
Bateman – had moved a cot into his isolation room and stayed with
him twenty-four hours a day for over a week. But her health had
been undermined by this and when she succumbed to the Shanghai
flu she removed herself for fear of infecting Brian Bassett.

The parents had come and gone on a daily basis for months in a
killing routine of visits. But parents, their presence and their loving,
are not the answer when a child has fallen into an autistic state. They
might as well have been strangers. And so they had been advised to
stay away.

Brian Bassett was eight years old – *unlucky eight*, as one of his
therapists had said – and in every other way, in terms of physical
development and mental capability, he had always been a perfectly
normal child. Now, in the final moments of his life, he weighed a
scant thirty pounds, when he should have weighed twice that
much.

Brian had not been heard to speak a single word in over a year of
constant observation. Earlier – long ago as seven months – a few
expressions would visit his face from time to time. Never a smile –
but often a kind of sneer, a passing of judgement, terrifying in its
intensity. Other times, a pinched expression would appear – a signal
of the shyness peculiar to autistic children, who think of light as
being unfriendly.

Mimi's militant efforts in behalf of Brian had been exemplary. Her fellow doctors thought of her as *Bassett's crazy guardian angel*. They begged her to remove herself in order to preserve her health. Being wise, being practical, they saw that all her efforts would not save him. But Mimi's version of being a guardian angel was more like being a surrogate warrior: a hired gun or a samurai. Her cool determination to thwart the enemies of silence, stillness and starvation gave her strengths that even she had been unaware were hers to command.

Brian Bassett, seated in his corner on the floor, maintained a solemn composure that lent his features a kind of unearthly beauty. His back was straight, his hands were poised, his hair was so fine he looked the very picture of a spirit waiting to enter a newborn creature. Sometimes Mimi wondered if this creature Brian Bassett waited to inhabit could be human. She thought of all the animals she had ever seen in all her travels and she fell upon the image of a newborn fawn as being the most tranquil and the most in need of stillness in order to survive. If only all the natural energy and curiosity of a newborn beast could have entered into Brian Bassett, surely, they would have transformed the boy in the corner into a vibrant, joyous human being. But it was not to be.

On 29 April – one week and three days after Everett had entered into his crisis of insomnia – Mimi sat on the floor in Brian Bassett's isolation room, gently massaging his arms and legs as she held him in her lap.

His weight, by now, was shocking – and his skin had become translucent. His eyes had not been closed for days – for weeks – and their expression might have been carved in stone.

"Speak to me. Speak to me," she whispered to him as she cradled his head beneath her chin. "Please at least speak before you die."

Nothing happened. Only silence.

Juliet Bateman – wrapped in a blanket – was watching through the observation glass as Mimi lifted up Brian Bassett and placed him in his cot. The cot had metal sides – and the sides were raised. Juliet Bateman could see Brian Bassett's eyes and his hands as Mimi stepped away.

Mimi looked at Juliet and shook her head. Juliet closed her eyes and pulled her blanket tighter like a skin that might protect her from the next five minutes.

Mimi went around the cot to the other side and dragged the IV stand in closer to the head. She fumbled for a moment with the long plastic lifelines – anti-dehydrants, nutrients – and she adjusted the needles and brought them down inside the nest of the cot where Brian Bassett lay and she lifted up his arm in order to insert the tubes and bind them into place with tape.

This was when it happened – just as Mimi Menlo was preparing to insert the second tube.

Brian Bassett looked at her and spoke.

"No," he said. "Don't."

Don't meant death.

Mimi paused – considered – and set the tube aside. Then she withdrew the tube already in place and she hung them both on the IV stand.

All right, she said to Brian Bassett in her mind, *you win*.

She looked down then with her arm along the side of the cot – and one hand trailing down so Brian Bassett could touch it if he wanted to. She smiled at him and said to him: "Not to worry. Not to worry. None of us is ever going to trouble you again." He watched her carefully. "Goodbye, Brian," she said. "I love you."

Juliet Bateman saw Mimi Menlo say all this and was fairly sure she had read the words in Mimi's lips just as they had been spoken.

Mimi started out of the room. She was determined now there was no turning back and that Brian Bassett was free to go his way. But just as she was turning the handle and pressing her weight against the door – she heard Brian Bassett speak again.

"Goodbye," he said.

And died.

Mimi went back and Juliet Bateman, too, and they stayed with him another hour before they turned out his lights. "Someone else can cover his face," said Mimi. "I'm not going to do it." Juliet agreed and they came back out to tell the nurse on duty that their ward had died and their work with him was over.

On 30 April – a Saturday – Mimi stayed home and made her notes and she wondered if and when she would weep for Brian Bassett. Her hand, as she wrote, was steady and her throat was not constricted and her eyes had no sensation beyond the burning itch of fatigue. She wondered what she looked like in the mirror, but resisted that discovery. Some things could wait. Outside it rained. Thurber dreamed in the corner. Bay Street rumbled in the basement.

Everett, in the meantime, had reached his own crisis and because of his desperate straits a part of Mimi Menlo's mind was on her husband. Now he had not slept for almost ten days. *We really ought to consign ourselves to hospital beds*, she thought. Somehow, the idea held no persuasion. It occurred to her that laughter might do a better job, if only they could find it. The brain, when over-extended, gives us the most surprisingly simple propositions, she concluded. *Stop*, it says to us. *Lie down and sleep.*

Five minutes later, Mimi found herself still sitting at the desk, with her fountain pen capped and her fingers raised to her lips in an attitude of gentle prayer. It required some effort to re-adjust her gaze and re-establish her focus on the surface of the window glass beyond which her mind had wandered. Sitting up, she had been asleep.

Thurber muttered something and stretched his legs and yawned, still asleep. Mimi glanced in his direction. *We've both been dreaming*, she thought, *but his dream continues*.

Somewhere behind her, the broken clock was attempting to strike the hour of three. Its voice was dull and rusty, needing oil.

Looking down, she saw the words *BRIAN BASSETT* written on the page before her and it occurred to her that, without his person, the words were nothing more than extrapolations from the alphabet – something fanciful we call a "name" in the hope that, one day, it will take on meaning.

She thought of Brian Bassett with his building blocks – pushing the letters around on the floor and coming up with more acceptable arrangements: *TINA STERABBS . . . IAN BRETT BASS . . . BEST STAB the RAIN*: a sentence. He had known all along, of course, that *BRIAN BASSETT* wasn't what he wanted because it wasn't what he was. He had come here against his will, was held here against his better judgement, fought against his captors and finally escaped.

But where was here to Ian Brett Bass? Where was here to Tina Sterabbs? Like Brian Bassett, they had all been here in someone else's dreams, and had to wait for someone else to wake before they could make their getaway.

Slowly, Mimi uncapped her fountain pen and drew a firm, black line through Brian Bassett's name. *We dreamed him*, she wrote, *that's all. And then we let him go.*

Seeing Everett standing in the doorway, knowing he had just returned from another Kenneth Albright crisis, she had no sense of apprehension. All this was only as it should be. Given the way that everything was going, it stood to reason Kenneth Albright's crisis had to come in this moment. If he managed, at last, to kill himself then at least her husband might begin to sleep again.

Far in the back of her mind a carping, critical voice remarked that any such thoughts were *deeply unfeeling and verging on the barbaric.* But Mimi dismissed this voice and another part of her brain stepped forward in her defence. *I will weep for Kenneth Albright*, she thought, *when I can weep for Brian Bassett. Now, all that matters is that Everett and I survive.*

Then she strode forward and put out her hand for Everett's briefcase, set the briefcase down and helped him out of his topcoat. She was playing wife. It seemed to be the thing to do.

For the next twenty minutes Everett had nothing to say, and after he had poured himself a drink and after Mimi had done the same, they sat in their chairs and waited for Everett to catch his breath.

The first thing he said when he finally spoke was: "Finish your notes?"

"Just about," Mimi told him. "I've written everything I can for now." She did not elaborate. "You're home early," she said, hoping to goad him into saying something new about Kenneth Albright.

"Yes," he said. "I am." But that was all.

Then he stood up – threw back the last of his drink and poured another. He lighted a cigarette and Mimi didn't even wince. He had been smoking now three days. The atmosphere between them had been, since then, enlivened with a magnetic kind of tension. But it was a moribund tension, slowly beginning to dissipate.

Mimi watched her husband's silent torment now with a kind of clinical detachment. This was the result, she liked to tell herself, of her training and her discipline. The lover in her could regard Everett warmly and with concern, but the psychiatrist in her could also watch him as someone suffering a nervous breakdown, someone who could not be helped until the symptoms had multiplied and declared themselves more openly.

Everett went into the darkest corner of the room and sat down hard in one of Mimi's straight-backed chairs: the ones inherited from her mother. He sat, prim, like a patient in a doctor's office, totally unrelaxed and nervy; expressionless. Either he had come to receive a deadly diagnosis, or he would get a clean bill of health.

Mimi glided over to the sofa in the window, plush and red and deeply comfortable; a place to recuperate. The view – if she chose to turn only slightly sideways – was one of the gentle rain that was falling on to Bay Street. Sopping-wet pigeons huddled on the window-sill; people across the street in the Manulife building were turning on their lights.

A renegade robin, nesting in their eaves, began to sing.

Everett Menlo began to talk.

"Please don't interrupt," he said at first.

"You know I won't," said Mimi. It was a rule that neither one should interrupt the telling of a case until they had been invited to do so.

Mimi put her fingers into her glass so the ice-cubes wouldn't click. She waited.

Everett spoke – but he spoke as if in someone else's voice, perhaps the voice of Kenneth Albright. This was not entirely unusual. Often, both Mimi and Everett Menlo spoke in the voices of their patients. What was unusual, this time, was that, speaking in Kenneth's voice, Everett began to sweat profusely – so profusely that Mimi was able to watch his shirt front darkening with perspiration.

"As you know," he said, "I have not been sleeping."

This was the understatement of the year. Mimi was silent.

"I have not been sleeping because – to put it in a nutshell – I have been afraid to dream."

Mimi was somewhat startled by this. Not by the fact that Everett was afraid to dream, but only because she had just been thinking of dreams herself.

"I have been afraid to dream, because in all my dreams there have been bodies. Corpses. Murder victims."

Mimi – not really listening – idly wondered if she had been one of them.

"In all my dreams, there have been corpses," Everett repeated. "But I am not the murderer. Kenneth Albright is the murderer, and, up to this moment, he had left behind him fifteen bodies: none of them people I recognize.

Mimi nodded. The ice-cubes in her drink were beginning to freeze her fingers. Any minute now, she prayed, they would surely melt.

"I gave up dreaming almost a week ago," said Everett, "thinking that if I did, the killing pattern might be altered; broken." Then he said tersely: "It was not. The killings have continued . . ."

"How do you know the killings have continued, Everett, if you've given up your dreaming? Wouldn't this mean he had no place to hide the bodies?"

In spite of the fact she had disobeyed their rule about not speaking, Everett answered her.

"I know they are being continued because I have seen the blood."

"Ah, yes. I see."

"No, Mimi. No. You do not see. The blood is not a figment of my imagination. The blood, in fact, is the only thing not dreamed." He explained the stains on Kenneth Albright's hands and arms and clothes and he said: "It happens every day. We have searched his person for signs of cuts and gashes – even for internal and rectal bleeding. Nothing. We have searched his quarters and all the other quarters in his ward. His ward is locked. His ward is isolated in the extreme. None of his fellow patients was ever found bleeding – never had cause to bleed. There were no injuries – no self-inflicted wounds. We thought of animals. Perhaps a mouse – a rat. But nothing. Nothing. Nothing . . . We also went so far as to strip-search all the members of the staff who entered that ward and I, too, offered myself for this experiment. Still nothing. Nothing. No one had bled."

Everett was now beginning to perspire so heavily he removed his jacket and threw it on the floor. Thurber woke and stared at it, startled. At first, it appeared to be the beast that had just pursued him through the woods and down the road. But, then, it sighed and settled and was just a coat; a rumpled jacket lying down on the rug.

Everett said: "We had taken samples of the blood on the patient's hands – on Kenneth Albright's hands and on his clothing and we had these samples analysed. No. It was not his own blood. No, it was not the blood of an animal. No, it was not the blood of a fellow patient. No, it was not the blood of any members of the staff . . ."

Everett's voice had risen.

"Whose blood was it?" he almost cried. "Whose the hell was it?"

Mimi waited.

Everett Menlo lighted another cigarette. He took a great gulp of his drink.

"Well . . ." He was calmer now; calmer of necessity. He had to marshal the evidence. He had to put it all in order – bring it into line with reason. "Did this mean that – somehow – the patient had managed to leave the premises – do some bloody deed and return without our knowledge of it? That is, after all, the only possible explanation. Isn't it?"

Mimi waited.

"Isn't it?" he repeated.

"Yes," she said. "It's the only possible explanation."

"Except there is no way out of that place. There is absolutely no way out."

Now there was a pause.

"But one," he added – his voice, again, a whisper.

Mimi was silent. Fearful – watching his twisted face.

"Tell me," Everett Menlo said – the perfect innocent, almost the perfect child in quest of forbidden knowledge. "Answer me this – be honest: is there blood in dreams?"

Mimi could not respond. She felt herself go pale. Her husband – after all, the sanest man alive – had just suggested something so completely mad he might as well have handed over his reason in a paper bag and said to her, *burn this*.

"The only place that Kenneth Albright goes, I tell you, is into dreams," Everett said. "That is the only place beyond the ward into which the patient can or does escape."

Another – briefer – pause.

"It is real blood, Mimi. Real. And he gets it all from dreams. *My dreams*."

They waited for this to settle.

Everett said: "I'm tired. I'm tired. I cannot bear this any more. I'm tired . . ."

Mimi thought, *good. No matter what else happens, he will sleep tonight.*
He did. And so, at last, did she.

Mimi's dreams were rarely of the kind that engender fear. She
dreamed more gentle scenes with open spaces that did not
intimidate. She would dream quite often of water and of animals.
Always, she was nothing more than an observer; roles were not
assigned her; often, this was sad. Somehow, she seemed at times
locked out, unable to participate. These were the dreams she
endured when Brian Bassett died: field trips to see him in some
desert setting; underwater excursions to watch him floating amongst
the seaweed. He never spoke, and, indeed, he never appeared to be
aware of her presence.

That night, when Everett fell into his bed exhausted and she did
likewise, Mimi's dream of Brian Bassett was the last she would ever
have of him and somehow, in the dream, she knew this. What she
saw was what, in magical terms, would be called a disappearing act.
Brian Bassett vanished. Gone.

Sometime after midnight on May Day morning, Mimi Menlo awoke
from her dream of Brian to the sound of Thurber thumping the floor
in a dream of his own.

Everett was not in his bed and Mimi cursed. She put on her
wrapper and her slippers and went beyond the bedroom into the
hall.

No lights were shining but the street lamps far below and the
windows gave no sign of stars.

Mimi made her way past the jungle, searching for Everett in the
living room. He was not there. She would dream of this one day; it
was a certainty.

"Everett?"

He did not reply.

Mimi turned and went back through the bedroom.

"Everett?"

She heard him. He was in the bathroom and she went in through
the door.

"Oh," she said, when she saw him. "Oh, my God."

*

Everett Menlo was standing in the bathtub, removing his pyjamas. They were soaking wet, but not with perspiration. They were soaking wet with blood.

For a moment, holding his jacket, letting its arms hang down across his belly and his groin, Everett stared at Mimi, blank-eyed from his nightmare.

Mimi raised her hands to her mouth. She felt as one must feel, if helpless, watching someone burn alive.

Everett threw the jacket down and started to remove his trousers. His pyjamas, made of cotton, had been green. His eyes were blinded now with blood and his hands reached out to find the shower taps.

"Please don't look at me," he said. "I . . . Please go away."

Mimi said: "No." She sat on the toilet seat. "I'm waiting here," she told him, "until we both wake up."

Obasan

JOY KOGAWA

> To him that overcometh
> will I give to eat
> of the hidden manna
> and will give him
> a white stone
> and in the stone
> a new name written . . .
>
> The Bible

The ball I found under the cot that day was never lost again. Obasan keeps it in a box with Stephen's toy cars on the bottom shelf in the bathroom. The rubber is cracked and scored with a black lacy design, and the colours are dull, but it still bounces a little.

Sick Bay, I learned eventually, was not a beach at all. And the place they called the Pool was not a pool of water, but a prison at the exhibition grounds called Hastings Park in Vancouver. Men, women and children outside Vancouver, from the "protected area" – a hundred-mile strip along the coast – were herded into the grounds and kept there like animals until they were shipped off to road-work camps and concentration camps in the interior of the province. From our family, it was only Grandma and Grandpa Nakane who were imprisoned at the Pool.

Some families were able to leave on their own and found homes in British Columbia's interior and elsewhere in Canada. Ghost towns such as Slocan – those old mining settlements, sometimes abandoned, sometimes with a remnant community – were reopened, and row upon row of two-family wooden huts were erected. Eventually the whole coast was cleared and everyone of the Japanese race in Vancouver was sent away.

The tension everywhere was not clear to me then and is not much clearer today. Time has solved few mysteries. Wars and rumours of wars, racial hatreds and fears are with us still.

The reality of today is that Uncle is dead and Obasan is left alone.

Weariness has invaded her and settled in her bones. Is it possible that her hearing could deteriorate so rapidly in just one month? The phone is ringing but she does not respond at all.

Aunt Emily is calling from the airport in Calgary where she's waiting for Stephen's flight from Montreal. They'll rent a car and drive down together this afternoon.

"Did you get my parcel?" she asks.

The airport sounds in the background are so loud she can hardly hear me. I shout into the receiver but it's obvious she doesn't know what I'm saying.

"Is Obasan all right? Did she sleep last night?" she asks.

It's such a relief to feel her sharing my concern.

Obasan has gone into the bathroom and is sweeping behind the toilet with a whisk made from a toy broom.

"Would you like to take a bath?" I ask.

She continues sweeping the imaginary dust.

"Ofuro?" I repeat. "Bath?"

"Orai," she replies at last, in a meek voice. "All right."

I run the water the way she prefers it, straight from the hot-water tap. It's been a while since we bathed together. After this, perhaps she'll rest. Piece by piece she removes her layers of underclothes, rags held together with safety pins. The new ones I've bought for her are left unused in boxes under her bed. She is small and naked and bent in the bathroom, the skin of her buttocks loose and drooping in a fold.

"Aah," she exhales deeply in a half-groan as she sinks into the hot water and closes her eyes.

I rub the washcloth over her legs and feet, the thin purple veins a scribbled maze, a skin map, her thick toenails, ancient rock formations. I am reminded of long-extinct volcanoes, the crust and rivulets of lava scars, criss-crossing down the bony hillside. Naked as prehistory, we lie together, the steam from the bath heavily misting the room.

"Any day now is all right," she says. "The work is finished." She is falling asleep in the water.

"It will be good to lie down," I shout, rousing her and draining the tub. I help her to stand and she moves to her room, her feet barely leaving the floor. Almost before I pull the covers over her, she is asleep.

I am feeling a bit dizzy from the heat myself.

*

I am sometimes not certain whether it is a cluttered attic in which I sit, a waiting room, a tunnel, a train. There is no beginning and no end to the forest, or the dust storm, no edge from which to know where the clearing begins. Here, in this familiar density, beneath this cloak, within this carapace, is the longing within the darkness.

1942.

We are leaving the BC coast – rain, cloud, mist – an air overladen with weeping. Behind us lies a salty sea within which swim our drowning specks of memory – our small waterlogged eulogies. We are going down to the middle of the earth with pick-axe eyes, tunnelling by train to the Interior, carried along by the momentum of the expulsion into the waiting wilderness.

We are hammers and chisels in the hands of would-be sculptors, battering the spirit of the sleeping mountain. We are the chips and sand, the fragments of fragments that fly like arrows from the heart of the rock. We are the silences that speak from stone. We are the despised rendered voiceless, stripped of car, radio, camera and every means of communication, a trainload of eyes covered with mud and spittle. We are the man in the Gospel of John, born into the world for the sake of the light. We are sent to Siloam, the pool called "Sent". We are sent to the sending, that we may bring sight. We are the scholarly and the illiterate, the envied and the ugly, the fierce and the docile. We are those pioneers who cleared the bush and the forest with our hands, the gardeners tending and attending the soil with our tenderness, the fishermen who are flung from the sea to flounder in the dust of the prairies.

We are the Issei and the Nisei and the Sansei, the Japanese Canadians. We disappear into the future undemanding as dew.

The memories are dream images. A pile of luggage in a large hall. Missionaries at the railway station handing out packages of toys. Stephen being carried on board the train, a white cast up to his thigh.

It is three decades ago and I am a small child resting my head in Obasan's lap. I am wearing a wine-coloured dirndl skirt with straps that criss-cross at the back. My white silk blouse has a Peter Pan collar dotted with tiny red flowers. I have a wine-coloured sweater with ivory duck buttons.

Stephen sits sideways on a seat by himself opposite us, his huge white leg like a cocoon.

The train is full of strangers. But even strangers are addressed as "ojisan" or "obasan", meaning uncle or aunt. Not one uncle or aunt, grandfather or grandmother, brother or sister, not one of us on this journey returns home again.

The train smells of oil and soot and orange peels and lurches groggily as we rock our way inland. Along the window-ledge, the black soot leaps and settles like insects. Underfoot and in the aisles and beside us on the seats we are surrounded by odd bits of luggage – bags, lunch baskets, blankets, pillows. My red umbrella with its knobby clear red handle sticks out of a box like the head of an exotic bird. In the seat behind us is a boy in short grey pants and jacket carrying a wooden slatted box with a tabby kitten inside. He is trying to distract the kitten with his finger but the kitten mews and mews, its mouth opening and closing. I can barely hear its high steady cry in the clackity-clack and steamy hiss of the train.

A few seats in front, one young woman is sitting with her narrow shoulders hunched over a tiny red-faced baby. Her short black hair falls into her bird-like face. She is so young, I would call her "o-nesan", older sister.

The woman in the aisle seat opposite us leans over and whispers to Obasan with a solemn nodding of her head and a flicker of her eyes indicating the young woman.

Obasan moves her head slowly and gravely in a nod as she listens. "Kawaiso," she says under her breath. The word is used whenever there is hurt and a need for tenderness.

The young woman, Kuniko-san, came from Saltspring Island, the woman says. Kuniko-san was rushed on to the train from Hastings Park, a few days after giving birth prematurely to her baby.

"She has nothing," the woman whispers. "Not even diapers."

Aya Obasan does not respond as she looks steadily at the dirt-covered floor. I lean out into the aisle and I can see the baby's tiny fist curled tight against its wrinkled face. Its eyes are closed and its mouth is squinched small as a button. Kuniko-san does not lift her eyes at all.

"Kawai," I whisper to Obasan, meaning that the baby is cute.

Obasan hands me an orange from a wicker basket and gestures towards Kuniko-san, indicating that I should take her the gift. But I pull back.

"For the baby," Obasan says urging me.

I withdraw further into my seat. She shakes open a furoshiki – a square cloth that is used to carry things by tying the corners together – and places a towel and some apples and oranges in it. I watch her lurching from side to side as she walks towards Kuniko-san.

Clutching the top of Kuniko-san's seat with one hand, Obasan bows and holds the furoshiki out to her. Kuniko-san clutches the baby against her breast and bows forward twice while accepting Obasan's gift without looking up.

As Obasan returns towards us, the old woman in the seat diagonal to ours beckons to me, nodding her head, urging me to come to her, her hand gesturing downwards in a digging waving motion. I lean towards her.

"A baby was born," the old woman says. "Is this not so?"

I nod.

The old woman bumps herself forward and off the seat. Her back is as round as a church bell. She is so short that when she is standing, she is lower than when she was sitting. She braces herself against the seat and bends forward.

"There is nothing to offer," she says as Obasan reaches her. She lifts her skirt and begins to remove a white flannel underskirt, her hand gathering the undergarment in pleats.

"Ah, no no Grandmother," Obasan says.

"Last night it was washed. It is nothing, but it is clean."

Obasan supports her in the rock rock of the train and they sway together back and forth. The old woman steps out of the garment, being careful not to let it touch the floor.

"Please – if it is acceptable. For a diaper. There is nothing to offer," the old woman says as she hoists herself on to the seat again. She folds the undergarment into a neat square, the fingers of her hand stiff and curled as driftwood.

*

I have gathered all the stained cups and dishes, the serving bowls and the teapot, and am cleaning them, removing the stains and grease, soaking them in a sink full of hot sudsy water. When I am half-way through I hear the sounds of two cars entering the drive-way. The car doors close and there are voices in the yard. In a moment, there is a slow light rapping on the living-room door and Nakayama-sensei's voice calls "Gomen-nasai," announcing his arrival. He opens the door and calls "Gomen-nasai" again in a loud but gentle voice.

"O," Obasan says and begins to rise, holding the blue pages and the magnifying glass in her hands.

"Please, please." He comes into the room, removing his black felt hat and waving his hand in the rapid patting movement indicating that she should not get up. His thin hair is so white it is almost luminous against his prairie-darkened face. Over the years, Nakayama-sensei has managed to visit Granton about once a month or so, when he is not travelling elsewhere.

Aunt Emily and Stephen are directly behind Nakayama-sensei. I am surprised at the amount of grey hair Stephen has. There is not so much that it streaks but the white is definitely visible as a light spray. He seems also to be slightly heavier than he was before, his face more full.

"Stee-bu san?" Obasan says. She puts the papers and magnifying glass on the chesterfield and stands up tottering. With her two hands outstretched, she steps unsteadily towards him.

Steve bends over and holds her hands with one hand as he removes his shoes with the other. He has just come in the door, and he already looks as if he would like to run out. His light black coat is pocked by large raindrops.

Aunt Emily also removes her shoes, then puts one arm around Obasan's shoulders. Obasan touches Steve's coat where it is wet. "Is it raining?" she asks. Then she chuckles. "Even if there is rain or thunder, these ears cannot hear."

I take Aunt Emily's and Nakayama-sensei's wet coats and hang them on the hooks beside the kitchen, then pour water into the heavy kettle for green tea.

Stephen, still wearing his wet coat, is sitting in the armchair with his legs splayed out like splints.

"Everyone someday dies," Obasan is saying to him.

"What happened, Naomi?" he asks with his back to me.

"I don't know really," I answer. I am slicing the stone bread to serve with the green tea. "I haven't got the details from Dr Brace."

Aunt Emily puts her bag down behind the armchair and comes into the kitchen. She looks for a dish towel to wipe the teacups.

"The Barkers were here just a while ago."

"Yeah?" Stephen sits up and takes off his coat jerkily. He grunts as Obasan tries to help him with it. Stepehen has made himself altogether unfamiliar with speaking Japanese.

Nakayama-sensei has picked up the magnifying glass and paper that Obasan left on the chesterfield and is glancing at the top page when Aunt Emily goes into the living room with the tray of teacups.

She stops short when she sees what Sensei is holding. All the rest of her papers are piled up on one edge of the coffee table.

"Everyone someday dies," Obasan is saying again, softly to herself.

Nakayama-sensei puts the papers and magnifying glass on the coffee table, then leaning back and with his mouth close to Obasan's ear, he says, "Should there be prayer?"

Obasan replies by bending forward in a prolonged bow.

I come into the room with the plate of buttered bread and kneel beside the coffee table. Everyone's head is bowed and we sit together in the stillness for a long time.

At last Nakayama-sensei stands up. He begins a long prayer of thanks in Japanese.

Stephen has his elbows on his knees and is feeling his chin lightly with his fingertips as he listens with his eyes fixed on the floor. I also have my eyes open. At one point, Stephen takes a corner of bread and breaks it off, then changing his mind, he sticks it back on the slice. At the end of the prayer, Aunt Emily says "Amen," and we sit together in the silence once more.

When Nakayama-sensei sits down, Aunt Emily opens her eyes, but Obasan's head remains bowed.

"It is good you are here," Nakayama-sensei says to Aunt Emily and Stephen. "You have come well."

Aunt Emily nods and takes her papers off the coffee table, making room for the teacups. Sensei leans forward to help and removes the blue papers and magnifying glass.

"Letters from a long time ago," Aunt Emily says to Sensei.

"Is that so," Nakayama-sensei says, glancing down through the bottom of his bifocals. His lips gradually become pursed in concentration as he reads the top page. When he comes to the end of the page, he stops.

"About this, I had no knowledge," he says in a low voice.

"What is it, Sensei?" I ask.

He puts the first page aside and reads the next and the next groaning quietly. When he is finished he puts the papers down and addresses Aunt Emily.

"Has there been no telling?"

"No," Aunt Emily says quietly.

"It is better to speak, is it not? They are not children any longer."

Aunt Emily nods slowly. "Yes," she says softly. "We ought to tell them. I always thought we should. But . . . kodomo no tame –." She fingers the buttons on her sweater and looks at me apologetically. "There was so much sad news. Mark was dead. Father was ill. The first time I came to Granton I brought the letters thinking we should tell them everything, but we decided to respect Nesan's wishes."

"Please, Aunt Emily," I whisper as she turns aside. "Tell us."

Aunt Emily takes the letters and reads the pages, handing them back to Sensei when she is finished.

"What is written?" I ask again.

"A matter of a long time time ago," Sensei says.

"What matter?"

Nakayama-sensei clears his throat. "Senso no toki – in the time of the war – your mother. Your grandmother. That there is suffering and their deep love." He reads the letters in silence once more, then begins reading aloud. The letter is addressed to Grandpa Kato. It is clear as he reads that the letters were never intended for Stephen and me. They were written by Grandma Kato.

The sound of rain beats against the windows and the roof. The rain is collecting in the eaves and pouring in a thin stream into the rain barrel at the corner near the kitchen door. Tomorrow I will fill the plastic bucket and bring the soft frothy water in – use it to water the houseplants and wash my hair.

Sensei's faltering voice is almost drowned out by the splattering gusts against the window. I stare at the gauze-curtained windows and imagine the raindrops sliding down the glass, black on black. In the sound of the howling outside, I hear other howling.

Sensei pauses as he reads. "Naomi," he says softly, "Stephen, your mother is speaking. Listen carefully to her voice."

Many of the Japanese words sound strange and the language is formal.

*

There are only two letters in the grey cardboard folder. The first is a brief and emotionless statement that Grandma Kato, her niece's daughter, and my mother are the only ones in the immediate family to have survived. The second letter is an outpouring.

I remember Grandma Kato as thin and tough, not given to melo-drama or overstatement of any kind. She was unbreakable. I felt she could endure all things and would survive any catastrophe. But I did not then understand what catastrophes were possible in human affairs.

Here, the ordinary Granton rain slides down wet and clean along the glass leaving a trail on the window like the Japanese writing on the thin blue-lined paper – straight down like a bead curtain of asterisks. The rain she describes is black, oily, thick, and strange.

"In the heat of the August sun", Grandma writes, "however much the effort to forget, there is no forgetfulness. As in a dream, I can still see the maggots crawling in the sockets of my niece's eyes. Her strong intelligent young son helped me move a bonsai tree that very morning. There is no forgetfulness."

When Nakayama-sensei reaches the end of the page, he stops reading and folds the letter as if he has decided to read no more. Aunt Emily begins to speak quietly, telling of a final letter from the Canadian missionary, Miss Best.

How often, I am wondering, did Grandma and Mother waken in those years with the unthinkable memories alive in their minds, the visible evidence of horror written on their skin, in their blood, carved in every mirror they passed, felt in every step they took. As a child I was told only that Mother and Grandma Kato were safe in Tokyo, visiting Grandma Kato's ailing mother.

"Someday, surely, they will return," Obasan used to say.

The two letters that reached us in Vancouver before all communi-cation ceased due to the war told us that Mother and Grandma Kato had arrived safely in Japan and were staying with Grandma Kato's sister and her husband in their home near the Tokyo Gas Company. My great-grandmother was then seventy-nine and was not expected to live to be eighty but, happily, she had become so well that she had returned home from the hospital and was even able on occasion to leave the house.

Nakayama-sensei opens the letter again and holds it, reading silently. Then looking over to Stephen, he says, "It is better to speak, is it not?"

"They're dead now," Stephen says.

Sensei nods.

"Please read, Sensei," I whisper.

"Yes," Aunt Emily says. "They should know."

Sensei starts again at the beginning. The letter is dated simply 1949. It was sent, Sensei says, from somewhere in Nagasaki. There was no return address.

"Though it was a time of war," Grandma writes, "what happiness that January 1945, to hear from my niece Setsuko, in Nagasaki." Setsuko's second child was due to be born within the month. In February, just as American air raids in Tokyo were intensifying, Mother went to help her cousin in Nagasaki. The baby was born three days after she arrived. Early in March, air raids and alarms were constant day and night in Tokyo. In spite of all the dangers of travel, Grandma Kato went to Nagasaki to be with my mother and to help with the care of the new baby. The last day she spent with her mother and sister in Tokyo, she said they sat on the tatami and talked, remembering their childhood and the days they went chestnut-picking together. They parted with laughter. The following night, Grandma Kato's sister, their mother and her sister's husband died in the B-29 bombings of 9 March 1945.

From this point on, Grandma's letter becomes increasingly chaotic, the details interspersed without chronological consistency. She and my mother, she writes, were unable to talk of all the things that happened. The horror would surely die sooner, they felt, if they refused to speak. But the silence and the constancy of the nightmare had become unbearable for Grandma and she hoped that by sharing them with her husband, she could be helped to extricate herself from the grip of the past.

"If these matters are sent away in this letter, perhaps they will depart a little from our souls", she writes. "For the burden of these words, forgive me."

Mother, for her part, continued her vigil of silence. She spoke with no one about her torment. She specifically requested that Stephen and I be spared the truth.

In all my high-school days, until we heard from Sensei that her grave had been found in Tokyo, I pictured her trapped in Japan by government regulations, or by an ailing grandmother. The letters I sent to the address in Tokyo were never answered or returned. I could not know that she and Grandma Kato had gone to Nagasaki to stay with Setsuko, her husband who was a dentist, and their two children, four-year-old Tomio and the new baby, Chieko.

The baby, Grandma writes, looked so much like me that she and my mother marvelled and often caught themselves calling her Naomi. With her widow's peak, her fat cheeks and pointed chin, she had a heart-shaped face like mine. Tomio, however, was not like Stephen at all. He was a sturdy child, extremely healthy and athletic, with a strong will like his father. He was fascinated by his new baby sister, sitting and watching her for hours as she slept or nursed. He made dolls for her. He helped to dress her. He loved to hold her in the bath, feeling her fingers holding his fingers tightly. He rocked her to sleep in his arms.

The weather was hot and humid that morning of 9 August. The air-raid alerts had ended. Tomio and some neighbourhood children had gone to the irrigation ditch to play and cool off as they sometimes did.

Shortly after eleven o'clock, Grandma Kato was preparing to make lunch. The baby was strapped to her back. She was bending over a bucket of water beside a large earthenware storage bin when a child in the street was heard shouting, "Look at the parachute!" A few seconds later there was a sudden white flash, brighter than a bolt of lightning. She had no idea what could have exploded. It was as if the entire sky were swallowed up. A moment later she was hurled sideways by a blast. She had a sensation of floating tranquilly in a cool whiteness high above the earth. When she regained consciousness she was slumped forward in a sitting position in the water bin. She gradually became aware of the moisture, an intolerable heat, blood, a mountain of debris and her niece's weak voice sounding at first distant, calling the names of her children. Then she could hear the other sounds – the far-away shouting. Around her, a thick dust made breathing difficult. Cheiko was still strapped to her back, but made no sound. She was alive but unconscious.

It took Grandma a long time to claw her way out of the wreckage. When she emerged, it was into an eerie twilight formed of heavy dust and smoke that blotted out the sun. What she saw was incomprehensible. Almost all the buildings were flattened or in flames as far as she could see. The landmarks were gone. Tall columns of fire rose through the haze and everywhere the dying and the wounded crawled, fled, stumbled like ghosts among the ruins. Voices screamed, calling the names of children, fathers, mothers, calling for help, calling for water.

Beneath some wreckage, she saw first the broken arm, then the writhing body of her niece, her head bent back, her hair singed, both her eye sockets blown out. In a weak and delirious voice, she was calling Tomio. Grandma Kato touched her niece's leg and the skin peeled off and stuck to the palm of her hand.

It isn't clear from the letter but at some point she came across Tomio, his legs pumping steadily up and down as he stood in one spot not knowing where to go. She gathered him in her arms. He was remarkably intact, his skin unburned.

She had no idea where Mother was, but with the two children, she began making her way towards the air-raid shelter. All around her people one after another collapsed and died, crying for water. One old man no longer able to keep moving lay on the ground holding up a dead baby and crying, "Save the children. Leave the old." No one took the dead child from his outstretched hands. Men, women, in many cases indistinguishable by sex, hairless, half-clothed, hobbled past. Skin hung from their bodies like tattered rags. One man held his bowels in with the stump of one hand. A child whom Grandma Kato recognized lay on the ground asking for help. She stopped and told him she would return as soon as she could. A woman she knew was begging for someone to help her lift the burning beam beneath which her children were trapped. The woman's children were friends of Tomio's. Grandma was loath to walk past, but with the two children, she could do no more and kept going. At no point does Grandma Kato mention the injuries she herself must have sustained.

Nearing the shelter, Grandma could see through the greyness that the entrance was clogged with dead bodies. She remembered then that her niece's father-in-law lived on a farm on the hillside, and she began making her way back through the burning city towards the river she would have to cross. The water, red with blood, was a raft of corpses. Further upstream, the bridge was twisted like noodles. Eventually she came to a spot where she was able to cross and, still carrying the two children, Grandma Kato made her way up the hillside.

After wandering for some time, she found a wooden water pipe dribbling a steady stream. She held Tomio's mouth to it and allowed him to drink as much as he wished though she had heard that too much water was not good. She unstrapped the still unconscious baby from her back. Exhausted, she drank from the pipe, and gathering the two children in her arms, she looked out at the burning city and lapsed into a sleep so deep she believed she was unconscious.

When she awakened, she was in the home of her niece's relatives and the baby was being fed barley water. The little boy was nowhere.

Almost immediately, Grandma set off to look for the child. Next day she returned to the area of her niece's home and every day thereafter she looked for Mother and the lost boy, checking the lists of the dead, looking over the unclaimed corpses. She discovered that her niece's husband was among the dead.

One evening when she had given up the search for the day, she sat down beside a naked woman she'd seen earlier who was aimlessly chipping wood to make a pyre on which to cremate a dead baby. The woman was utterly disfigured. Her nose and one cheek were almost gone. Great wounds and pustules covered her entire face and body. She was completely bald. She sat in a cloud of flies and maggots wriggled among her wounds. As Grandma watched her, the woman gave her a vacant gaze, then let out a cry. It was my mother.

The little boy was never found. Mother was taken to a hospital and was expected to die, but she survived. During one night she vomited yellow fluid and passed a great deal of blood. For a long time – Grandma does not say how long – Mother wore bandages on her face. When they were removed, Mother felt her face with her fingers, then asked for a cloth mask. Thereafter she would not take off her mask from morning to night.

"At this moment", Grandma writes, "we are preparing to visit Chieko-chan in the hospital." Chieko, four years old in 1949, waited daily for their visit, standing in the hospital corridor, tubes from her wrist attached to a bottle that was hung above her. A small bald-headed girl. She was dying of leukaemia.

"There may not be many more days," Grandma concludes.

After this, what could have happened? Did they leave the relatives in Nagasaki? Where and how did they survive?

When Sensei is finished reading, he folds and unfolds the letter, nodding his head slowly.

I put my hands around the teapot, feeling its round warmth against my palms. My skin feels hungry for warmth, for flesh. Grandma mentioned in her letter that she saw one woman cradling a hot-water bottle as if it were a baby.

Sensei places the letter back in the cardboard folder and closes it with the short red string around the tab.

"That there is brokenness," he says quietly. "That this world is brokenness. But within brokenness is the unbreakable name. How the whole earth groans till Love returns."

I stand up abruptly and leave the room, going into the kitchen for some more hot water. When I return, Sensei is sitting with his face in his hands.

Stephen is staring at the floor, his body hunched forward motionless. He glances up at me then looks away swiftly. I sit on a stool beside him and try to concentrate on what is being said. I can hear Aunt Emily telling us about Mother's grave. Then Nakayama-sensei stands and begins to say the Lord's Prayer under his breath. "And forgive us our trespasses – forgive us our trespasses –" he repeats, sighing deeply, "as we forgive others . . ." He lifts his head, looking upwards. "We are powerless to forgive unless we first are forgiven. It is a high calling my friends – the calling to forgive. But no person, no people is innocent. Therefore we must forgive one another."

I am not thinking of forgiveness. The sound of Sensei's voice grows as indistinct as the hum of distant traffic. Gradually the room grows still and it is as if I am back with Uncle again, listening and listening to the silent earth and the silent sky as I have done all my life.

I close my eyes.

We Are All in the Ojibway Circle

JOHN KELLY

Mr Commissioner, welcome to the territory of Treaty No. 3. It has been a long time since a Commission came to this region. The last time was in the early 1870s. In 1873, those long-ago proceedings gave us Treaty No. 3 – a treaty that has never been kept.

Now, one hundred and four years later, we are visited by another Commission – a Royal Commission on the Northern Environment. I sincerely wish we could whole-heartedly applaud your activity. I genuinely would like to talk of happy things. I would love to be able to rejoice in great achievements and plan for greater successes in the future. Unfortunately, that is not yet possible. Time, history and the white man have made it so.

But we have learned from the past. We have been made wary of Commissions that show promise. Due to our bitter history my people feel we must be cautious about unreservedly endorsing your inquiry. Until we see the way in which your Commission is conducted, we must be hesitant in giving you our unqualified support.

Allow me to explain . . . The way the present situation has come about is something like this. An Indian was sitting on a log feeling very comfortable because he had all the room he needed. A white man came along and said that he had been running a long time and was terribly tired. The bishop's men wanted to burn him alive and the king's soldiers were chasing him with guns. Could he please have a little place on the log so that he might rest from his awful journey. The Indian willingly shared a piece of his log with the white man. But the white man felt like stretching himself and asked for a little more room. The Indian let him have a little more of his log. The white traveller was satisfied for a short while but then he felt he wanted some more space. The Indian gave it to him. Of course, the guest did not go hungry or cold. Like a decent host, the Indian shared his pemmican and furs with the poor, harassed foreigner. As the time passed, it just so happened that the stock of food and clothing came under the control of the white man; the Indian was cold and hungry and barely holding on to the end of the log. Now the white man did not at all fancy the idea of sharing his log with such a miserable and sickly creature. It deeply hurt his sense of propriety. So he told the Indian to get off the log, but in his vast charity he suggested that the Indian could sit on a stump further away in the bush. Since 1871, the Ojibway of north-western Ontario have been sitting on the stump. In the last few years, we have begun to panic because the white man on the log is casting his eyes on our stump. Granted, the stump is small and damn prickly but at least we have a place to sit and occasionally we have been able to grab a bit of game and cast the line for a fish.

These are the results of the last Commission which was sent to this part of the country. Our land and resources were stolen. You, Mr Commissioner, have a golden opportunity to recommend that some of what is ours must be returned.

The first Commission travelled here and convinced my forefathers to sign a treaty. At that time your government needed our land as a passageway to the prairies for troops to fight the *métis*. It was also needed as a route for the settlers and, most of all, for its rich natural resources. My people were not informed of the reasons why you wanted a treaty, and you did not give us an opportunity to research and determine exactly what was in our best interests. My forefathers signed the treaty. They were deceived about its contents. They were never told about its effect. They were convinced they had no choice but to sign. And, with trust in the good faith and intentions of the Treaty Commission, my forefathers signed that treaty in 1873.

Our research tells us that the early Treaty Commissioners indeed had good faith and intentions. Nevertheless, history must judge them as unwilling pawns in a process aimed at destroying the native poeple. We warn you, Mr Commissioner, to be wary of becoming another well-intentioned pawn – and an unwitting tool of rich and powerful interests. Many well-intentioned people will testify before you. Many well-intentioned people come before me and before the Band Chiefs of Treaty No. 3 all the time. But it is your duty to look behind the good intentions and understand the long historical process of which we are all merely a part.

Let me tell you what happened to us after the Treaty Commissioners went back to the government carrying the Xs of my forefathers on a treaty that my ancestors didn't understand. The Commissioners reported that they had secured a surrender of all Ojibway rights in the Treaty No. 3 area. They explained that, in return for that surrender, the government had made certain promises. The government was basically happy. It was pleased to have the land surrender. Land was all they wanted. However, the government was not pleased with the treaty promises and consequently only made half-hearted efforts to implement them.

In the meantime, the Ojibway Chiefs returned to their bands. The Chiefs reported they had agreed with the representatives of the benevolent white queen that the Ojibway people should not prevent the white man's access to, and passage over, Treaty No. 3 land. The Chiefs reported that the government's representatives had said the traditional Ojibway life would not be disturbed. The Chiefs told of the promises made by the white negotiators. From then on, the Ojibway ceased all resistance to white intrusion and were prepared to share their land with the white man. We knew we had given up much by allowing the white man to enter Ojibway territory and we, therefore, looked forward to receiving the benefits and guarantees promised by the Treaty Commissioners.

Briefly, let me tell you what happened. If the Treaty Commissioners could be here to listen to the outcome of their well-intentioned efforts they might feel as saddened and betrayed as we do.

Not long after the treaty was made, a dispute arose between the Federal government and the Provincial government as to which government had jurisdiction over the Treaty No. 3 territory. Ontario said its western borders included Treaty No. 3. Ottawa said no. Ottawa claimed Ontario did not extend as far west as Treaty No. 3. Do not forget, Mr Commissioner, that at that time there was still no so-called development here. While the governments were arguing about lines on a map, my people continued to go about their business of living comfortably and securely from the riches of the land.

The dispute between the governments was not settled until the question was put before the highest court of the time. That court ruled, in 1888, that Ontario's western boundary did include most of the Treaty No. 3 territory. We are told that the legal consequence of this decision (which we did not know had been rendered) was that the surrender of our land (which we did not know had taken place) was not to the government which we had been dealing with, but to a government in a place called Toronto. That was a government we had never met with nor had any particular desire to meet. We didn't know what was going on because no one informed us. And no one provided us with the resources we needed in order to inform ourselves. We only found out there was something drastically wrong when we became aware that the promises made to us by the Treaty Commissioners were largely unfulfilled.

Our recent research has disclosed what has happened to our sacred treaty. When the courts decided Treaty No. 3 was in Ontario, the Ontario government said it would have to examine the treaty promises made by the Federal government. Negotiations were held. We were not represented at these meetings. We were never even notified that these negotiations were taking place. At these negotiations, Ontario refused to fulfil all of the treaty promises. The Federal government representatives did not protect our rights. Consequently, we lost much of what had been promised to us by the Treaty Commissioners.

Let me give you but one example. When we selected the locations for our reserves, we always took into account the lakes and rivers from which much of our traditional livelihood was procured. Every reserve was located on the water. It was agreed that the reserves included all of the adjacent waters. This agreement was even admitted by the governments. These are their words of 1894:

> The waters within the lands laid out or to be laid out as Indian reserves . . . including the land covered with water lying between the projecting headlands of any lake or sheets of water, not wholly surrounded by an Indian reserve or reserves, shall be deemed to form part of such reserve . . .

In 1915 the province unilaterally changed the definition of reserves and at one stroke stole much of our wealth. This time I quote from legislation passed in 1915:

> . . . the land covered with water lying between the projecting headlands of any lake or sheets of water not wholly surrounded by an Indian reserve . . . shall not be deemed to form part of such reserve . . .

We were not consulted, or even advised that this was happening. While the Federal government stood by, we were knowingly robbed by the Ontario government. We shall never forget it. Neither shall we rest until we get back what is ours.

I should add that Ontario agreed during the negotiations with the Federal government on the fulfilment of treaty promises, that if Ontario refused to confirm reserve lands previously agreed to by the Federal government, Ontario would create a commission or commissions to determine the question.

Such a commission was never created. From this we learn an important lesson: governments create commissions only when they must. Governments then use commissions for their own purposes.

I have spent some time recounting a little of what transpired at, and following Treaty No. 3, because I wanted you to know that we have had considerable experience with commissions. Our experience has never been good. We welcome the possibility that yours will be a commission which benefits our people instead of yet another one which robs and deceives us. I have also recounted these things so you will understand that we have had much experience with governments – particularly the government of Ontario. Our experience with governments is much like our experience with commissions: in one four-letter word, foul.

By dwelling on the early years following the signing of the Treaty, I do not wish to suggest that our grievances all occurred many years ago. On the contrary. Despite being robbed time and again by government, and more recently by industry, we still possess certain things of value which the white man covets. We have learned through our experience that wherever Indians possess or control anything economically valuable, there will always be those who will attempt to steal it. But, worst of all, your society and the government which appointed you seem to encourage, or at least condone, the theft of Indian lands. Apparently Indian lands are fair game while white lands are protected by very strict laws.

Almost always what is stolen from us is what you call natural resources. We propose to itemize and particularize our concerns in relation to natural resources. Let me tell you of a legend that my father told to me. The legend will help us understand the present situation a little. One year, a long time ago, as the summer season was ripening into autumn, the land of the Ojibway was struck by a great gale. Day and night the wind blew with persistent power. The creatures of the land and water were driven into hiding, and every evening the men returned home empty-handed. Even the plants seemed to have lost their sense of time so that the berries would not ripen and the root of the wild potato was bitter and watery as in summer. There was indeed much hunger in the wigwams of the Ojibway.

Then, one day, there came a stranger from somewhere in the sunrise beyond the lakes. The stranger said that he was sorry to see the children dying from hunger, and the men and women moaning in weakness. He said that he was angry with the wind, and could cut off its arms and legs. Then there would be peace on lake and forest for all time. And so, on that night the wind softened and then turned utterly powerless and still. The fish came out of the water and gambolled with reckless spirit on the calm water, and herds of elk and moose munched on the foliage in the clearings. "LOOK," said the stranger, "I have mastered the wind. You no longer have to sharpen the spear and stretch the trap-line. Just pick the meat and fish because it is all around you." The women were also happy to see the fruit bursting with juice. It was a time of plenty, a time of unending repose and gluttony.

Then, as the years passed in windless tranquillity, a mysterious curse spread over the earth. The herds of elk and moose dwindled and disappeared. Even the chirping squirrels and mighty bear were nowhere to be seen. Lakes and streams were covered with a green scum. Those who ate fish trembled and chattered as if they had the devil inside them. This was a new famine, an unusual pestilence. The Ojibway spoke to their Midewiwin Elders and beseeched for help. For fourteen days the Elders sang and prayed in the medicine lodge. At the end of that time, there was a tumult mightier than all the storms that have clapped in the heavens since the beginning of time. And there arose a wind that shook the earth from its four corners. Day and night it rained until it seemed that the land would sink under the burden of the deluge. At the end of this fury of rain and wind, the Midewiwin Elder of the Fifth Order came and spoke to the Ojibway Nation: "Man may never try his wiles and power against the Spirit of the Universe, nor is it good to reap from the acts of those who pitch their minds against Manitou."

Mr Commissioner, it seems to me that the stranger from the sunrise beyond the lakes just keeps coming back. Each time he promises us perpetual repose and gluttony, and leaves us with famine and disease. It also appears that, as the years go by, the circle of the Ojibway gets bigger and bigger. Canadians of all colours and religions are entering that circle. You might feel that you have roots somewhere else, but in reality, you are right here with us. I do not know if you feel the throbbing of the land in your chest, and if you feel the bear is your brother with a spirit purer and stronger than yours, or if the elk is on a higher level of life than is man. You may not share my spiritual anguish as I see the earth ravaged by the stranger, but you can no longer escape my fate as the soil turns barren and the rivers poison. Much against my will, and probably yours, time and circumstance have put us together in the same circle. And so I come not to plead with you to save me from the monstrous stranger of capitalist greed and technology. I come to inform you that my danger is your danger too. My genocide is your genocide.

To commit genocide it is not necessary to build camps and ovens. All that is required is to remove the basis for a way of life. In the case of the Ojibway this basis is the natural produce of the boreal forest.

Over the past two months, senior and respected Chiefs from my organization have travelled to all of the reserves in Treaty No. 3 with a message. The message they conveyed is that the government has formed a commission which might be able to do something about their concerns. The people on the reserves were asked to express their concerns and the message came back loud and clear, meeting after meeting. The people of Treaty No. 3 are concerned first and foremost about natural resources. They are concerned that the basis for their way of life is being steadily eroded. The irony of the situation is that we find this problem at a time when your world is contemplating the inadequacies of its lifestyles and goals. Your leaders are telling you to prepare for a less wasteful and more natural existence, while at the same time destroying my people's efficient and non-destructive lifestyle.

When we visited the reserves, the first concern of the people was always "wild rice". Since time immemorial we have picked the rice in the late summer of every year. Until recently only people permitted by the bands could harvest this rice but now the Ontario government proposes to open up rice picking to non-natives. The government claims my people do not harvest enough wild rice. These claims are false and backed up by nothing but prejudice and ignorance. The white men also claimed that native people were not efficient at harvesting buffalo.

Closely following wild rice as an area of concern on the reserves is the question of fishing rights. My people believe that not only do they have a right to fish in all waters and not only do they depend strongly on the availability of fish to feed their families, but additionally their commercial fishery should be encouraged and strengthened. Instead, my people find themselves charged for fishing off the shores of the reserves and their equipment is confiscated when all they want is food for their families. Moreover, a strict quota is imposed on their allowable commercial fishing catch. All of this harassment is apparently intended to satisfy angler tourists, mainly from the United States. My people are asked to go hungry so overfed rich tourists can catch bigger fish to display on their walls. It is said that commercial fishing in this region is not efficient yet the Ojibway are fishermen just as the residents of Nova Scotia or British Columbia. The difference is that instead of the massive government subsidies which the coastal fishermen enjoy, we get massive government harassment and discouragement.

Government does not seem capable of understanding the difference between commercial fishing as carried out by my people and that which is engaged in by the non-native community. Where a commercial fishing licence may support one white family it often supports thirty or more families when issued to an Indian band. As well as providing a vital source of protein, the commercial fishing complements the rice harvest in providing a cash income which goes much further in providing support for native people than it does when expended elsewhere. And still we are to be subject to quotas which do not take into account these different circumstances and the enormous benefits which accrue to a people from a fishery which would provide a minimum contribution in a pure cash economy.

The people on the reserves also told us that they were worried about trapping. Trapping was once our main industry. For many years trap-lines were held exclusively by native families who harvested their own particular areas. Then the government came along and told us they were going to register trap-lines and manage the taking of furs. They said they were doing it for our own good. But it was not many years before trap-lines started to pass from the old native families to friends of government officials. The people on the reserves tell us that the government is now saying the same things about wild rice as it used to say about trapping.

I have briefly described what appears to be a calculated attempt by the government and industry to destroy the life of the Ojibway through limiting our access to the environment. This environment is turned over to commercial operations which have shown little interest and understanding of the environment. The government seems to think that our way of life is on the decline so they do not need to be concerned about the damage they are causing. This is not a new point of view.

At the time of the treaties, immigrant scholars and administrators from Europe were making prophecies of doom for us. They were describing us as a dying race, and predicting that our culture and lifestyle would disappear in a matter of a few decades. They were all wrong. We are here, more numerous than ever. More importantly, we still live by the fundamental values of our traditional culture. We may be using the articles of a new technology, but in our spirit and in our mind, in the way we treat each other, the way we deal with the land and the animals, in these important matters, we continue to be true to the roots of our civilization. We have shown that we can survive as a race. We have proved that we will not be assimilated. We have demonstrated that our culture has a vitality that cannot be suppressed.

The Indian lived on this continent in a style that was natural to this continent. He ate the kind of food that the land offered naturally. He built his home and changed his location according to the time of the year and the movements of animals and plants. He lived as naturally in this environment as the trees and plants and animals. It was an accomplishment of the most superb wisdom. Our ancestors had learned to live with nature, not against it. An elder once said to me: "Do not fight against the cold, or you will freeze." Our people had discovered how to live without destroying, to survive without exploiting, to flourish in every respect without depleting the sources from which they drew their strength. These are not solely my thoughts, but the thoughts of my people across North America. They are a part of our vision, an awareness, a new understanding of the style of life that sprang from the true character of this land. That style of life has hope and happiness.

Something very different has been happening on our land for the last few centuries. Our white brothers from across the ocean have been attempting to graft another system of life upon this continent. It is a system that pits man against nature, and turns life into a continual war with the environment. And what are the consequences of such a philosophy? The five great lakes of our land are dying. Water and air are being fast filled with industrial poison, and forests are being wiped out. The land is being rapidly covered with asphalt and concrete, and oil from the earth is being burnt to a finish. Of course, you do not see any signs of critical shortages as you look around. No, North America is having its last great joy ride. It is not my intention to criticize and condemn white society for its way of life. What I want to say is that Indians from shore to shore have a collective realization that if civilized life is to survive on this land, the Indian way must be adopted. The Indian way of natural living is the only way man can become a part of the circle of life. This is what I call the Indian Vision.

The Indian Vision is not naïve and romantic. We recognize that economic development of the European type is inevitable in certain respects. We want to participate in the planning and regulation of this development. We want to control our share of it, and we want to receive our share of its profits and benefits.

Let me take the forest industry as an example. We have always used the forest and to utilize trees for the creation of manufactured products is entirely consistent with our traditional values so long as waste and destruction are not the result. We wish to benefit from the forest industry but in the past native people have been rudely ignored in the approbation of cutting licences. We have been almost completely cut off from participation in the industry. Large commercial interests such as Reed Paper are reaping the benefits of this public domain at the expense of the resident people, native and non-native alike. These companies offer few opportunities to the native people and, in fact, often treat us with scorn and disrespect. Yet these same companies are destroying the forest upon which we have always relied. We do not come here begging to say: "Mr Commissioner, get us jobs in the paper-mills." Instead what we feel must be said is: "Mr Commissioner, give us some control over the paper-mills before they destroy our land and your land too."

We have much more to say about the use of natural resources, both traditional and non-traditional, but I will save this for a later time.

Now I wish to turn to a matter of local concern. It is also a matter of great import to the Commission. I speak of what has been called the Reed Proposal. I submit to you that the plan of the Reed Paper Company for northern Ontario is insidious and disastrous. It is insane and vicious in itself, and a catastrophic symbol of the direction in which our society is proceeding. It has taken nature millions of years to cover the hard rock of the Laurentian Plateau with a veneer of soil which is still very shallow and quite poor. The trees are low in height and stunted. In fact, it is miracle that the land is covered with a forest. But this miracle has taken a millennia to happen. It is absolutely the first stand of timber on God's earth; a virgin forest. Yet this forest has a character that the southern people cannot grasp. It has been a long time in the making – so long in fact, that it is an integral part of the soil, the water, the climate and the animal life. The industrial community and its allies in government who are bent on making the easy money, the fast buck, see it differently. They view it as 16,640,000 acres of unclaimed forest that they can log and turn to pulp. They do not realize that if you clear this forest, you destroy permanently a delicately balanced ecological system. This land is so unique, so intolerant of disturbance, that it seems blasphemous even to think of it as property. You take from it what it can give you freely and use it frugally. It cannot withstand the industrial assault of greed. Once this forest of stunted black spruce has been logged and turned into pulp, it will be gone forever. You cannot make these trees regenerate. What is now the glory and beauty of northern Ontario, an area the size of New Brunswick, will be converted into a desolate cold swamp.

Now, a word about the Reed Paper Company of Canada which is supported in its industrial scheme by the Ontario government. It is a wholly-owned subsidiary of Reed International Ltd which, in turn, is a British-based multinational giant with holdings in 88 countries. Reed Paper of Canada itself is no mean economic venture. In 1974, its after-tax profits were almost thirty-six and one-half million dollars. But I do not wish to burden you with statistics. They are readily available to interested parties, and are often used only to confuse the innocent. I have, of course, an intimate personal acquaintance with the Reed Company. It is the parent of the Dryden Paper and Dryden Chemical Companies that have dumped thousands of tons of mercury into the English–Wabigoon River system. One of the results of this immoral act is that two of my communities, Whitedog and Grassy Narrows, have been shattered socially and economically. It is evident to me that the Reed Company has neither a moral conscience nor a sense of social responsibility. Its only objective is to increase the value of its stock and to enhance its profits. It is a blind agent of the ledger book. Reed is as powerful and efficient as it is amoral.

We not only feel shocked and distressed by the Reed Proposal, but we are also very frustrated. What do we do when the shepherd sends invitations to the wolf to attack the flock? The shepherd I am talking about is our government of the province of Ontario. The government of Premier William Davis developed the entire scheme for the deforestation of northern Ontario with such secrecy and divulged the information in such clever little instalments, that we can only characterize this project as a conspiracy.

Mr Commissioner, we face a serious problem. The last frontier of the boreal forest in Ontario, the only stand of virgin timber in the province, is in imminent danger of destruction. It is not a matter of sentimental conservation, but a problem of permanent ecological damage. For our communities, it is also a personal and human problem.

Once again, the stranger in my father's legend is back among us. And remember, this time we are all in the same circle. We live or die together.

The History of Cambodia

KEATH FRASER

Clam holes. Peeping dunlins. The beached star. Yes she can remember freedom. She was a girl carrying her sand-pail over salt flats that an ebbing tide had rumpled. Nothing behind her mattered. In front of her light nipped the tide line. The flats dropped off sheer into water green enough for freighters from Asia. Ships had come to wait at anchor for food. Ships had come to be watched in the summering sea.

She was a mile from shore. When she turned she could see Spanish Banks rising up in clay, bluffs that her mother said were falling into the sea. Her mother said European longboats and Indian canoes had steered toward them once and attacked the trees for masts and refuge. Those Salish, were they crabbers? Had they lived on the beach and come from Asia too?

She was a sad, romantic little girl and daydreamed of the sun setting far off in the Gulf of Siam. She lifted her eyes from a dainty pair of broken pincers. Mountains across the bay really were the reclining woman her mother, pointing, claimed. In a kitchen-shaped cloud over the Sleeping Beauty's nose she heard her mother singing with Perry Como, of faraway places with strange-sounding names. The radio had hail in its voice, it scratched. She listened instead to her sand-pail for the sound of the tide. Her head stuck fast inside, she lost her balance and fell forward into the sand. Her nose popped in pain. Hours passed and the flooding tide floated her down a warm tide pool in her helmet. Into every runnel water nosed like a long thin animal sniffing its way. It was dark until the lifeguard gave her sight again. She lay like kelp in his brown arms, tasting blood. The same salt water he was standing in up to his knees was touching toes in Asia.

After five years of captivity in ruined temples what she has come to long for most (should she be ashamed to admit this?), what the cadres in this prison forbid her: to prink. Prink? She would settle for a bath.

By the left buttock Tan Vim had led her, his palm in her pants to the temple at Angkor, where she was placed upon a pedestal. The jungle encroached. Unlike the bosomy stone around her, she couldn't help the guerrillas salvage their cost of revolution, and so she sat, frightened and bored. She was yearning for home while these busty *devatas* were leaving theirs without demur. For five years she had watched pilasters and friezes hacked off and boxed, crated out to Siam, temples turned back into stone. Smuggled booty bound for her country, anyone's, for salt, medicine or currency, to help her captors hammer from the future a new past, stone without image. A new history, Angkar's history. And when Phnom Penh fell they brought her here to prison.

A march that barely survived an exodus of millions going the other way. Those black-pyjamaed guerrillas driving out everyone! Legless men, blind mothers, bodies on hospital beds, children bleeding into plastic bags, footless soldiers, families carrying their homes in gunny sacks, dogs. Her own little band of invaders seemed lost in the silent, dusty movement of feet, bicycles, Mercedes, rickshaws. As the city emptied she saw the flotsam of abandoned bodies, sandals and suitcases washed up on boulevards. She saw, or foresaw, executions by the thousands: she had already seen these carried out for the "purification" of villages. And this a city! What rot they were discovering here God only knew. Her captors nodded to their comrades at every checkpoint on Route 6 into Phnom Penh. Grim adolescent guerrillas, who had swept into the capital hours earlier, were removing watches from wrists to bury time; lifting glasses off noses to kill literacy. These citizens, these class enemies, as good as dead.

Tan Vim vanished when they brought her and her child down Monivong Boulevard, through side-streets full of bombax trees, to this old high school. Pavement again, kerbs. A teenager with his AK-47 told her he had orders to remove all infants to the health centre for medical inspection. She never saw her daughter again. Led into a building, she had her picture taken in front of a white sheet. There was a moth hole in the cotton. Dozens of anxious men, women, even children were standing behind her in a silent line. The photographer disappeared under his black tent, then re-emerged with a scab on his nose. It must have been there before, the scab, he was not a magician.

She remembers, months ago, lying at first in a classroom lined with cots and shackled, recumbent bodies. They lay there day and night. At night the light bulb flickered and went out with the generator. She was used to darkness from living in the jungle; but others wept. They still do. The school sounds like death squatting. Screams, sobs, abrupt silences. At dawn prisoners are led away for interrogation and torture, confession and death. New faces follow old, there is barely room to squeeze them in. After the first two weeks on her back, when they came for her, she couldn't walk. She couldn't even talk. Listening at night for traffic, she concluded Phnom Penh was as deserted as the ancient capital of Angkor had been for a thousand years. Citizens, claimed the loudspeaker in the school yard, had been "relocated" for "re-education" in the countryside. She lay there piecing together Angkar's familiar-sounding slogans, and no one spoke to her for two weeks.

The school has three buildings, and in this cell of her own in the middle building she continues to listen. The biographies of prisoners in this building evidently require special scrutiny, protracted inquisition. Her tiny cell is divided off from other cubicles in the same classroom by a brick partition, and like the other prisoners she is anchored by the leg to an iron block on the floor.

Thousands have gone through this prison and the world esses like a snake. Traitors, spies, collaborators: Angkar suspects shadows in any story not its own. No past passes unpunished. The school's prisoners are forced to sign absurd, seditious autobiographies, then they are taken outside and shot. "Hell" in their language, she remembers, is "*norok*".

At first the staircase they led her up for questioning smelled of chalk dust, as if from eraser clappings by monitors after school. Now everything smells of defecation. The questions are endless, but there's no learning going on. Tan Vim, about whom these men upstairs keep asking her, vanished the day of liberation, months ago, down a side-street. She recalls the sound of his broken sandal slapping softly away. Perhaps he feared reprisal for keeping her a secret.

Answering questions, she lapses into fragments, the pin that held her together in the jungle removed. Her rusting voice is shrapnel. She has dysentery and quaking bowels. And her daughter is dead.

She has asked them pointedly about her daughter, about the French, the Americans, the war, but they volunteer nothing.

Once long ago she had wished to write a story about the darkening weight of ignorance, about this civilization shrinking to density many times its light, dying in the last flare-up of civil war. She had the picture even before flying to Cambodia. The country in her story would be at war with its own heart. She knew, she was up on war. At her editor's pleasure she had flown here from Saigon merely to confirm it. Only after her capture did she discover how the nation's history was leaking out to museums of newer nations. Iconoclasts, the red Khmers were leaving nothing but black holes. Worse, they were bequeathing open graves. No one was up on murder.

What month is this? Something she never lost in the jungle was track of time. Now she is struggling just to keep her memory. No longer anyone's "femme", anyone's booty, she will surely die as she should have five years ago, before Tan Vim let lust overcome his duty and "married" her in his stronghold of temple mountains. She places her cheek against the chafing reed mattress and refuses to breathe the smell of her own waste. Their line of questioning has been diplomatic, they think, deft, but she understands the destination. She will put her signature on nothing. They are determined to have her pay both the price of spying and the cost of Tan Vim's betrayal of his duty.

Sometimes she allows herself to imagine what the surprise of the outside world would be if she should suddenly, a bundle of bones, arrive by foot into Thailand with a bundle (her daughter) in arms. She has kept count of the years. It is 1975, maybe 1976 already. She would tell her fellow correspondents the cats of Angkor gave of themselves that she and her child could live ("*chhama*", the Khmers call a cat).

"Les cœurs?"

"Oui."

"Les avez-vous mangés?"

"Les tous."

She would tell the press when rats overran them they began to eat dog. The rats were boring.

"How were you treated, Aletta?"

The clink clink clink clink clink bored too. Same old rhythms, their chisels on stone. Her captors had vandalized the stone their ancestors had made dance across friezes, tombs and gallery walls for deified kings. Her captors had thought that to invert time you got rid of space. They expunged the images of ancestors, decapitated statues and peed on heads to polish the stone.

"I was treated like a lump of shit."

Once it was always summer. There were picnics in the sand. You could hear coho gulls in the seaweed, seaplanes in the sky. A mist lay up the sound like smoke. She knew there had been a war. Around the point and under the bluffs was a pair of gun towers to blow the Japanese from the Gulf of Georgia, had they ever tried to enter. This is what her mother said. The war was long over but it had been a good test for free souls. Mother.

The towers smelled of piss. They would walk around the banks to them when the tide was low. The towers had mouths and no tongues. The guns were gone. Painted on and scratched into the concrete walls were hearts and words. Her mother said these were the pleadings of religious fanatics and zoot suiters. She read some aloud: "Jesus Loves You." "Lick This." Her mother laughed. RRRAAAAH . . . crows in the arching alders.

They found shells of wrinkled whelks and sniffed the salty chambers. Barnacles on the rocks made sucking sounds, the sea was a friendly mouth. A woman in a sari was flying a kite. They watched tugs on the booming grounds of the delta and scows full of wood chips pushing into the salt chuck. "The salt chuck," she said. Somehow the words made her feel older. "The spectacular vernacular," said her mother.

This was freedom and she never knew it. Her mother encouraged her as a right to shine and never set. She would grow up in the fullness of summer. It would always be summer. Her mother wished the season and the world at her daughter's feet. Her daughter was to go everywhere and be happy, happy.

They went to a tea-leaf reader in August and the woman in a lemon-coloured apron, frying liver in her kitchen, predicted summer too. Blond hair forever and a beach full of boys. "The coast is clear," she said, "of any clowns, Chinese hard rocks, or plumbers."

Angkar Leu, the Supreme Organization, has more eyes than a pineapple. Time, it declares over the loudspeaker, has now begun.

And who has grown this rotting fruit? Lest she forget, she mouths to herself names repeated among her jungle-creeping captors as their bearing grew more confident the last two years. Khieu Samphan, Saloth Sar, Ieng Sary, Khieu Thirith, Son Sen, Hu Nim . . . She met none of these commissars, for during their flying visits to Tan Vim's district around Siem Reap, Vim kept her hidden. He accepted their orders, made forays into villages and moved his band of guerrillas and her among the ruined temples of Angkor like a thimblerig in the jungle.

Today, in this country they call Kampuchea, the officers prink. Privileged in their offices upstairs, they are enjoying their assumption of power, sitting in chairs after years on stumps plotting ambushes on homemade maps. Here in the city it is "Angkar doit . . ." and "Angkar ordonne . . ." These upstairs inquisitors, these higher-ups, luxuriate in speaking French and are pleased with their colonial graces and Paris educations. They used to question her three times a day, as if at meals, pretending to consult their files, plotting or unplotting she couldn't tell. What unnatural law would become them more than the drip drip drip of Chinese water torture? Yet they prefer the still less messy methods of electricity and bullets. It is they who are elegant and she, a primitive, who has forgotten how to move her tongue.

Tan Tan my suntan. Tan Tan the also ran. Tan Tan my moving van.

She knew they were executioners and yet had hoped for freedom through co-operation. But they have refused to believe her story. They have no inclination to reason from details she gave them willingly and has repeated many times since her arrival. So she has stopped telling them anything. To keep her brain turning over she massages her forehead to remove the daily residue of their questions. It isn't information they seek but an erosion of the only thing she has: a past. Even the jungle is a past of sorts to keep her sane.

These others in leg irons and chains are also taken daily for questioning and some do not return. No prisoner is evidently special beyond a confession Angkar finds acceptable. Being special has no more future in it than the smell of this classroom, filling up with shit till it chokes each in her own effluence. The drowning is slow, for they are fed just enough to keep them alive for another day's, week's pumping.

To keep sane it helps her to recall what at least in the jungle had a law. Tam Vim "married" her before raping her, for instance. This she later decided was because of his "*hooer-som*" ("good manners"), she punned: to his bewilderment, the humourless soul. What carnal hands. To witness their betrothal he had ordered an older cadre and two young ones to stand at attention as in some ceremony he remembered, and spoke his vow to possess her utterly. The guerrillas were dressed in black pyjamas, checked scarves and sandals cut from truck tyres. Her Levis had not yet rotted from her limbs. After his solemn vow, spoken ludicrously with his eyes shut, the crewcut Vim took her back inside their current temple hideout and sat her down on a pedestal from which Parvati, or some other goddess that week, had been removed for export. Ficus roots poured over the crumbling walls like scaly crocodiles. Bat wings purred. Always she could smell the deep damp stone, though the wet season had yet to come.

"Sit there."

He spoke French to her. His nose needed blowing and the hairs in his nostrils to be removed. In his mid-thirties and squat, he thought he knew what Western women wanted.

His hand slid into her pants to softly squeeze a buttock growing bonier by the day. But he changed his mind and began instead with her feet, unsandalling them, sucking her filthy digits toe by toe, reaming each black nail with his tongue. Here was worship, she thought fleetingly, and refreshment. Bad teeth gnawed her nails and a tongue tickled her arch. He wanted her to believe they had had a normal Khmer betrothal. "Oui," he nodded. But he was as nervous as she. He got as high as her knees when she accidentally bloodied his nose. She had only wished to close her knees in protest at his spreading them, tongue-loosened and spit-flecked.

"*Khma*," he said. He was ashamed. But went right ahead with the justification he suddenly felt he had to revenge his wound. Oh, her prince got over his nerves.

Each prisoner has an ammunition tin to defecate into, provided the ankle chain is long enough. One woman has her ankle *hand*-cuffed to the cot and can only befoul her bed. She is somebody dangerous, they must think, because she used to have her hair done in the

French way and knew an American banker. A balding little man with bulging eyes winds along the floor to empty their tins once a day. He is deaf to their pleas or to any screams in the corridor from the torturing rooms.

On the floor of the office upstairs are bloodstains drying each time the ulcerated guard brings her in. Is she intended to notice these? Their questions are always the same. Who is she? Where did she come from? Who does she know? They appear neither to expect answers nor, worse, that there can be answers. Her silence does not appear to bother them. Meticulous and rococo, their French sounds ridiculous and feeds contentedly off itself. One of them has chipped front teeth and a high forehead; the other, stiff hair and liver spots on his face and hands. They are polite, certainly, with manners calculated to leave her hope. But their castle of living skeletons wrecks the strategy. Where have they taken her daughter? What's happened to Lon Nol? She no longer asks.

For months she has listened to men and women writhing on their cots, wailing out of hopelessness, former cadres, schoolteachers, wives of military officers, suspected black marketeers and courtesans from the Sihanouk years – anybody whose collaboration with the past makes them useful. For the Khmer Rouge want to extract confessions, autobiographies, that will justify their genocide. In the common cell where they first kept her she had heard the whispering at night, and in the morning pleas, cries not to be led away. The turnover in that building was higher than here. Here prisoners often return to their cells: men and women taken one at a time into classrooms where metal frame beds await them, and narrow-eyed, flop-eared men with canes and electrodes to jolt out confessions like blood or urine. You can hear *sssst* when the shock is induced. *Ssssst* scream *ssssst*. These quieter, snakelike sounds seem louder than the screams. She listens, unable to understand her own exemption so far from this application of wires.

In the beginning she could smell chalk and dry orange peels left over from pupils chanting lessons. Now the school smells of shit and echoes with screams; burning skin and shovels in the school yard. What sort of cleaning out is this that smells and sounds worse and worse? Like her, the rest of these prisoners are also foreigners in a place that recognizes no immunity: "Tuol Sleng", this prison's called.

Her child.

Did they cover her with a sheet or just pitch her in a pit?

She wonders what it ever meant "to cover" in the manner she once thought important enought to devote her life to it. She was free to fly after stories given out by press officers in Saigon, by sources not to be identified, by the President of South Vietnam, by tipsy colonels (US) and solicitous generals (ARVN). Still, the romance remained elsewhere. Whenever the war became routine, her fellow journalists from AP and Reuters went, as they called it, abroad. Side trips they worked in as holidays. To Laos, maybe, or Bangkok, to cover corruption (whether of opium or currency it never mattered, if the story seemed good) and apprise a public back home.

What was a story?

RE LBJ WESTMORELAND CONFAB STOP FOLLOW VISIT OUTSIDE SAIGON STOP COVER DETAILS TROOPS HECKLING PRESIDENT STOP

She answered an editor's cables with facts owned by a hundred other reporters. Her own stories, torn dutifully off the ends of telex machines, must have read like dog food. She cabled home reshaped and reattributed conversations, encapsulated press conferences, packaged phrases.

Nothing alive. She was a syndicated correspondent of growing reputation who had been scrupulous to write nothing of herself.

"Hey, you were a reporter, right? How about the straight goods?"

"Is that baby yours?"

"Yeah, give us the whole story."

As if such stories could be given. As if this shrapnel could be reunited into the menace she once was, or felt she was, to lying commanders and inept fellow correspondents. As if disintegration itself was not her story. In the years since coming upon this story she began to understand that such tales only existed in *dying* to be told. Never told except to children, these were deeper into the woods than war reports. "As time passed, it grew dark . . ." No newspaper printed fairy tales. Too depressing, too romantic maybe, experienced as sharply as through the ears and eyes of children. Those parts of her once valued, barbed tongue and prodding brain, lie in fragments now. She imagines her fellow journalists noting her arrival in Bangkok, her return to Canada, and at one last press conference looking for angles, neat sides, and writing nothing whole. Just catch-as-catch-can.

As the tide came in the lifeguard would pull his rowboat further up the beach to keep it from floating away. He stood looking at bodies in the sea. She sat watching waves wash up his keel, curved planks flecked with foam. The foam lit the white planks from below, a dark creamy light moving from bow to stern, stern to bow. The gleaming planks overlapped like scales on a fish.

What pleasure she felt staring at his rowboat leaning to port in the sand. The golden blades of his oars tipped outward in their locks like hands at the stretch of bronze arms. She could see brass screws biting into the wood of two varnished seats. The ribs were dark, bathhouse green, and a strip of paint as red as his T-shirt ran around the gunwhale. His calves bulged when he lifted his stern. A lath of copper preserved the keel from scraping sand. She adored everything about his boat, its planes, its oarlocks. The oarlocks were spiky bangles.

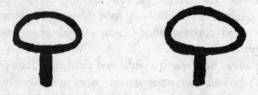

Surveying the sea, he looked taller than the Sleeping Beauty. Drowning bathers, invisible off beaches beneath the mountains, *he* could have swum across the bay to rescue. He need not even launch his boat to reach them with a long Australian crawl. How wonderful that sounded, a long Australian crawl. Australia was part of the empire, and her city that summer was holding the empire games. Australians came from the South Pacific and won the swimming medals because they knew the best way to crawl. They crawled up and down black lanes of the pool her mother encouraged her to watch on their new TV. Her mother hummed and drank Singapore Slings. She had a record on the hi-fi, not Perry Como but slow, sad music about swans, with the noise turned down on her shimmering screen.

*

OK SIEM REAP QUICKIE STOP BUT IS IT NEWS STOP CIA THE
TICKET STOP SMELL MISCHIEF VIENTIANE STOP BETTER STORY
THERE STOP WHY ART STOP

Her story was to be of the ravages of war on art, the year America
invaded the Parrot's Beak to drive the Vietcong from their sanctuaries and the Communists threatened to take refuge in the temples
of Angkor. Things weren't too good, they were even pretty bad. An
angle, it sounded fine, except maybe to a doubtful editor.

In an Air Vietnam jet her story began: "The rainy season drawing
near lets one sink to this destination turbulently. Below lie long
farms, then rising from acres of corrugated roofs the spire of a
cathedral and a golden stupa. At last bordering Phnom Penh's
avenues are flame trees and these have, even from the sky, the
panache of crimson scarves the soldiers wear . . ."

Dog food. From the airy heights.

Once upon a time, in 1970, she disappeared into the jungle at
Angkor Wat. She was captured by guerrillas. The ruins were full of
myths, pictured in bas-relief. Horses with fluted manes, nude dancing *apsaras*, marching spear carriers in earrings and topknots,
demons, wing-eared elephants, Bodhisattvas, spoke-wheeled char-
iots, reclining kings. At large in the world were cruelty and murder.

It so happened the murderers mocked the myths and sold them
abroad. In their place they substituted talismans to protect themselves from harm. The younger the murderers the more superstitions they wore, for Angkar expected them to do battle with Lon
Nol's men, who were children too and also scared.

These cadres stared at their prisoner. They could not understand
her reluctance to acquire talismans from a wandering monk, or from
a crow dropping purple pili nuts on a causeway to crack them open.
Around their necks they wore votive tablets, medals, pieces of
ribbon, odd-shaped seeds and pebbles. In their pockets they carried
miniature phalluses carved from bone. And on their belts they hung
dog foetuses.

In time, when Angkar denounced their jewelry as superstitious,
the guerrillas hid it in their mouths, sucking at invincibility. Stone
chips, bits of metal, tigers' teeth, boars' tusks, figurines carved
from fig trees and sandalwood. A statue of Vishnu came to lose each

of its four arms because the young warriors believed its fingers were suckable and sacred. Their iconoclasm was selective since the torso itself was salvaged for export.

She remembers the story.

She is filthy. Full of self-loathing, she wriggles on her cot in stains and fear. Self-loathing explains Angkar's own self-righteousness, its perversions its barbarism its murders. In Paris these leaders must have learned to hate themselves, giggling and self-conscious, outsiders within the navel of *haute couture*. Years later in the jungle, the centre once of Khmer *haute couture*, their cadres stripped the temples and defiled them with their excrement. Now in Phnom Penh, with its trappings of Paris, the Khmer Rouge are having further revenge. They swallow the city up like the jungle, the ficus roots, the weeds. No iconography like a blank frieze becomes them more. Cold black stone. Her own tombstone, too, she fears.

In 1970 she thought she understood cause and effect. She felt her bra scratch, so she took it off. She was eyed; she put it back on. If she planned ahead, yes, she would always succeed in stripping the veil from elusive truth. Correspondents who had talked to him said he wasn't worth the trouble, but she waited around the capital for Lon Nol anyway – to interview. She believed in questions, revelations: obfuscation, light: tyranny, redress. Sometimes, as with stories, she had discovered the way out before she understood or had even found the door in. Get rid of big cars, lavish spending, fat. Eliminate war. But flower power wasn't an answer. She had still believed in privacy, and communes she hated the thought of, yet captive in the jungle she soon learned private was public and that black and black was a far grimmer reality than black and white.

The colour of Angkar she learned was black.

And now Phnom Penh is as empty as Angkor. Someday will another amazed explorer like Henri Mouhot stumble upon it overgrown and squeezed by a fawning jungle?

Once upon a time she was happy here. Except for the nests of sandbags around banks and government buildings, for the barbed wire, this city was more peaceful than Bangkok. They drank chablis at La Taverne and sat around Madame Chantal's opium parlour talking to French and Australian diplomats, cadging rumours. The Americans, they speculated, were carrying out secret missions over remote parts of the country, dropping bombs. "Such missionaries," she sighed.

Journalists had loved Phnom Penh: French parks and sidewalk cafés, with flame trees and frangipani blossoms along the boulevards. A few reporters travelled to the front line in taxis. Only one or two never returned. Sitting around the little square in front of the post office, where civil servants ate couscous for lunch, visitors found it a more comfortable war than the Vietnamese variety. "A sideshow", as one English reporter put it. You loafed along the Mekong and sucked oranges. At night you went to the Café de Paris and La Cyrène to watch Lon Nol's corrupt generals emerge from their Mercedes trailing cologne and cigar ash.

Unlike Saigon there were no American GIs here to pester her, proposition her, impervious teenagers short on hair but long on gall. (Heaven for them was the forty-eight-hour furlough.)

From the Sukhalay Hotel she had watched Peugeots and *cyclo-pousses* weave down Monivong Boulevard. Heard horns and bicycle bells; observed a boy with coloured, gas-filled balloons standing regularly under a Pepsi sign on the corner of Kampuchea Krom. Usually she could count on someone's radio for the Fifth Dimension singing "Aquarius", which made her think of home. And in the evening from her balcony she watched a muscle man in a black bikini exercising in a rooftop garden. The Khmer sign advertising a body-building shop on a lower floor displayed the touched-up biceps of a man who was blond. The muscle man was dark.

In her mirror she'd prinked and gone to interview Lon Nol.

This radio. Its fustian voice, Angkar's parody of itself, haemorrhages from the loudspeaker outside like something dying. But it threatens all the same. It is a harsh woman's voice broadcasting Angkar's directions to hell. The gestures upstairs of the men who question her curl gracefully in the air like crocodile tails. These men, in Angkar's official posture, remain as disembodied as the radio, except their French stamps them aloof from the harsher urgings of the Khmer woman's voice. The voice hints that a paradise awaits those who commit themselves to hard work in the countryside. It is a voice pumped into hamlets like an irrigation canal delivering dry air, a treadmill once turned by an old woman's bare feet in the family field, now full of weeds and city strangers. Chipped Teeth's face has grown plumper. City food suits Liver Spots, too, judging by his jowls. To these men she has nothing anymore to say, for they regard the world as manipulative and accept only facts they have fashioned themselves. They have become the monstrous keepers of files and their own history.

Millions in the countryside won't hear the wailing at school that Angkar's voice can't drown.

Can't drown.

Her daughter had also wailed as if she knew the insult of being asked at birth to put up with the premise of a stone bed in a stone house. A recordless birth in a blank space. At her daughter's birth, Tan Vim hid them in a courtyard. He could justify none of his desires since her capture, and keeping her a secret from Angkar had only inflamed his lust. But having a child was the limit of his contempt of ideological duty, and he had tried to force upon her an abortion when he learned of the pregnancy. "We have painless ways. Easy, sure." Too late. She was past her own impulse of earlier months to abort this foetus. He tried losing his temper and his small eyes watered; when he switched from French into Khmer his voice rose and ran like a hot little river, full of dipping eddies and half-submerged roots. In full flood he was like the Tonle Sap. He inundated her in his flow of abuse. He curdled her blood when he roared. He pulled her down to levels of his own comprehension, made her tread water just to stay alive. And because she was taller than he, when he addressed her she was expected to be near a staircase and two steps lower. Still, as she grew thick and slow-moving with child, he began to forget he must dominate from the higher plane. More a risk than ever to him, if discovered, she seemed now to threaten him less – perhaps because she looked cowed. He would run his large hands over hers in calm moments and speak of the country they, the Khmer Rouge, would build compared to the corrupt colonial one he and others had suffered in: abuse, deprivation, imprisonment under Sihanouk. His wide face softened. He remembered to hold back his stinking breath. "Ma femme," he whispered, tugging her hair whose colour he loved, despite the oil and dirt. He would caress her tingling hands. He would vacillate from hatred to gentleness and back again like a steel swing in a sandlot. If he heard a comrade approaching, in any moment too vulnerable or tender, he would suddenly denounce her past. "You bitch!" he called her, pronouncing the "bit" in English with a vicious little puff he remembered to punctuate with a slap.

Slap.

She had felt her child trying to get out and failing to bore through her own years of boredom. The contracting pain was unlike any she'd imagined possible without her passing into a black hole forever. The instinct of creation must have kept her going. She had no drugs, no acupuncture, no herbal balms to link her with any history of gratefully relieved women. Only pain. She kept pushing, though the girl from a village near Banteay Samre, brought in as a midwife by Vim, kept telling her not to, wagging her forefinger. She didn't care. She pushed the pain south like a lunatic. The girl peered in between her legs like a child expecting something odd, a mulatto infant. The fingernails massaging her swollen stomach covered no skin, bitten down as they were to moons. To help herself forget the contractions, coming closer and closer together, she made this peasant girl's dirt-rimmed moons the ends of chocolate bars. She could always concentrate on food. Hunger had already been a four-year condition intensified by expectancy. Yet now when she required an appetite for something, anything, she felt none at all. She tried to remember the fragrance of sweet peas.

After her daughter's birth, for days, she felt more depressed than she thought the brain would allow anybody to feel before it closed down in despair. The cadres wanted her back at the fire as their cook. Yet she kept to her hammock in their temple at Preah Khan, listening to birds in the trees. Birds. She was nothing but Body, Cow, suckling her child with eyes round and unblinking at the sensation, like a bowel movement. She was stuck in the doldrums and sinking fast. Tan Vim sometimes brought her pilfered milk to drink, staring at his mulatto bastard with a smile. She had welts on her legs from spiders and mosquitoes; a prickling in her toes from bad circulation. She had no other way to countenance herself but to scratch. Instinct was trying to save her. She watched a coconut ripen, a cheeky crow, the angles of light changing in the *chum-sha* leaves: all the little ways used since her kidnapping to distract herself, seemed suddenly nauseous.

He put her to work packing empty mortar shells with nails, bicycle spokes, sharp stones, the redeemed amulets of dead cadres, glass. She carried her daughter around in a basket and steered clear of pits. She feared being clubbed on the back of the neck with an axe handle to fall forward and be buried alive. It was a custom she learned of with numbing knowledge: though at first she found excuses not to believe what she refused to witness. Tan said it was to save ammunition because the North Vietnamese, their mentors, hoarded ammunition and felt jealous of the Khmer Rouge. In their own country, he said, the Vietcong were still worried about victory. His job included bringing villages under Angkar's control: if need be to eliminate teachers, village chiefs, even monks. Any suspected spies. This *sdam*, said Vim, his face growing red and harsher. As the years passed the executions had increased. And he eventually forced her along to villages to bear witness, as if to shock the outside world through her.

He was interested in the world she had come from and in unguarded moments asked what she knew of Paris. He was pleased when she told him he knew Paris better than she, for he had studied there fourteen months. After fourteen months they sent him home. "Too smart," he said. Montreal, he wanted to know, was like Paris? Just as corrupt, she was careful to tell him, just as "prétentieuse".

Once he offered her pencil and paper, torn from a cheap notebook, as if daring her to draft a statement of the Khmer Rouge's benign treatment of these temples they inhabited at Angkor. To help the Khmer cause, he said. He had found out she was a journalist by going through her handbag. She agreed – perhaps too eagerly not to sound suspicious. "Even the minor temple, Prasat Kravanh", she wrote, "dedicated to Vishnu, still possesses the graceful lines of its incomparable god." Dog food. "The delicate inner sanctuary of Banteay Srei, the women's citadel, retains its sandstone pediments with nothing wiped out or spirited away." She was hoping the Supreme Organization would send her lies abroad. Lies in English from the jungle might have alerted her colleagues, her friends, her mother, that someone who knew idiomatic English was alive in a place like this. Of course Vim never intended to share her report with anyone.

Instead he drove out the few French archaeologists still at work on the monuments nearest Siem Reap. They were stooges of the Lon

Nol government, he insisted, easily scared away from their Western-esteemed wonder of the world. With them the last of the past's preservers vanished. Vim's band of guerrillas now controlled all of Angkor. Government troops, for a lark, attacked them once in the monuments with artillery fire and damaged the main wat where the Khmer Rouge flag flew from a tower. Lon Nol's soldiers then retired to town, satisfied (it seemed) with the status quo. Life was easier for them in Siem Reap; let the Americans, if they wished, bomb the Communists.

Tan Vim knew what to do with his hands around everything but people. The clink of hammers at Angkor Wat, the attempt to strip its history, began to resemble his other attempts at all the remoter temples. He ravished nymphs on pilasters as he had ravished his prisoner on a pedestal. And he couldn't wait to wipe out battle scenes depicting Indian epics. Stone men belonged to the past. As if preparing a stone rub, he patted those short wide hands on his breasts before attacking the walls.

She watched the backs of his knees where no hair grew in the smooth depressions. Yes, she would love a lifeguard, she would let one if he wished love her. She came with her friends to the beach while her mother took summer courses at the university. Her mother counted on her daughter's friendship with the best kinds of girls to save her from the solitary temptations of less fortunate girls (who had not been sent to a better school). But her friends knew when to get lost; they stepped on the gas of a white convertible; their strip of rubber was to wish her luck getting laid. "Or whatever," said the driver, smiling.

He noticed her alone on the sand and came over with an offer. She rubbed out the oarlocks and accepted. They ate his supper staring at the outline of the mountains. She lowered her eyes when he pointed

out the Sleeping Beauty, an anatomy he followed east with his own
eyes in the direction of Hope. Sand fleas bounced on her blanket as
if to see the sun banking under the horizon. She slapped the biters
among them and complained sweetly of friends who had left her
behind. He played along, this guard. He asked if she'd ever seen a
flea circus. A what? He was off duty so he showed her one.

Oh, she laughed. She tagged him with her sandal. Later she
helped him drag his rowboat high and dry. At dusk, when the
sandwiches were gone, they stood in the flood tide to watch Oriental men in hip waders unnetting oolichans. He took her hand in his
pink palm and swung it seaward to a freighter. He held the ship in
their hands. Listening, they heard an anchor lifting link by link
through an echoing scupper. The Great Chain of Being, he muttered
cleverly, without remembering what in the world he was repeating.
It sounded rusty she told him. Darryl, his name was Darryl, he was
in second-year arts.

They lay on her blanket by a barkless log. Fleas, tired of biting and
bouncing, slept, lights appeared on the far shore, stars peeped. You
could hear the stars in their spheres, he said impressively. She
studied the skin on his bronze arm, elbow to knuckles, and all the
golden hairs. Folds in his red trunks cupped the darkness like
ravines in the cliffs behind.

He was teaching her to kiss the way the school locker room had
prepared her. Except she drooled, no wonder, he was glued to her
mouth for as long as it took to drown her twitching. For second wind
she thought of grass hockey. He pulled up her sweater and undrew
her bathing-suit strap like a shoelace. This made a difference to how
the muscles of her neck settled back peacefully in his hands: she
knew how far she was going.

The constellations hung low, meteors showered, Perry Como
sang his casual, casual heart out. She had expected pain but not the
sheer love she felt for this boy who was raising her up.

A resurrection she cherished. Her mother encouraged any experience for the sake of its broadening ways. "It makes you forget the
deeper aches," she said, reddening her lips for class. Her mother
had used the fortune teller to map herself a promising course of study.

Afterward, on the beach, she lay with such a smell of salt in her
head it made her dizzy. This was the way warm wet fronts would

circle in from the south like redowas, arousing in those who loved that city a seasonal longing to deflower gardens for the sheer pleasure of bewitching a room. She remembers. That city. Her window west over tidal flats in full flood. Those Spanish Banks of gold.

This place must sound as Dachau did. The mistake has been to break her vow of silence and say so. Liver Spots, surprised to hear her squawk come back, immediately loses his temper. "Partez!" The guard with sores on his lip enters smartly and digs his rifle into her hip. He too loathes the way she smells. He keeps making phewing noises and jabbing her to move. The guard dog in the corridor shows its teeth and she realizes for the first time that not all Khmer dogs have been eaten. She can see its ribs.

The thought of food makes her sicker. Maybe the reason they now make her swallow green pills is because her dysentery embarrasses them. Or maybe it's to keep her alive a little longer for the satisfaction of tormenting a foreigner. They keep telling her no more foreigners live in Kampuchea. Is it because she's an endangered species, then, they refuse to let her die? They seem unwilling to believe she could have been a prisoner without their knowledge for five years. But clearly Tan Vim fascinates them. Did he talk about Vietnam? CIA? Treason? They relish her symbolic presence, rotting from the bowels out, a vanquished colonial cancer. Canadian, American – what's the difference to them?

In her bricked-in cubicle she listens to other prisoners being kept alive like herself. The rusty springs of their cots, their little wails and moans, the way they gnash their teeth. And their sighs, more frightening than death rattles. Prohibited by threat of instant execution is whispering, yet the urge to communicate is irresistible. The actress alongside her with lightened hair is a prisoner for no other reason than bringing joy to life. "I sing," she whispers. To this actress in her cell Flop Ears, an inquisitor with a classroom of his own, has come at last to deliver a confession he wishes her to sign. Has he kept this actress alive till now just to prod and tease her beauty like some boy a maimed bird? He decides to slap the sense of it into her. The sound of popping skin is telegraphed across the ceiling of their partitioned room. "Sign!" he's telling her.

Even former cadres of the Khmer Rouge have suddenly discovered themselves prisoners of the revolution they helped to kindle. Suspected now as spies, they're paying the inevitable price for solidarity with ideological purity. What they never realized is how much this purity develops an appetite for self-examination and purging. It feeds on paranoia. It is like an obsession with bowels. Something every day has to be expelled. And so a former information officer for the Khmer Rouge (thus the rumour as it sweeps through these little cells) now faces the same interrogation as they. He lies broken in his cell, buried by the movement, nauseated by the stench of his rotting zeal. And Tan Vim, who thought death a small price for eradicating the past, wouldn't have received the big-city welcome he envisioned after years in the bush. Probably Liver Spots and Chipped Teeth pretend to know nothing of his whereabouts just to resavour the details of their own suspicions, months ago, when they ordered him exterminated for the crime he was observed entering the city with. Her.

Arrivals continue, netted in the flow of people from the city, and in more recent months from dragnets in the countryside, young and zealous bands of cadres in search of collaborators, sceptics, counter-revolutionaries. She recalls her own teenage captors and their pitiful allegiance to Vim's harsh discipline. In the school yard hundreds of voices are hushed on command, new prisoners made to lie on the ground till cots inside are freed or the photographer's film replaced. She listens. They've started to use the school's third building for the unexpected overflow. Thousands murdered, the sheer numbers of fresh collaborators are curtailing the pleasure of Angkar's inquisitors in drawing out their tortures here in building number two. Flop Ears and company will be needed elsewhere. The circles of hell are meant to lap into one another at an efficient rate, but these devils at their desk are clumsy copiers of the sins they extract. The poor arrivals, once willing like this actress to confess to any sin as a sign of party loyalty, now with death in all their nostrils have learned, after photographing and processing, to welcome torture as a way of staying alive. The welcome is short-lived. By the sound of this school's turnover its graduates are signing confessions fast.

These flies, she thinks. This inconceivable stench.

*

The evening after her interview with Lon Nol she had walked down Kampuchea Krom alone. Women were selling white and blue lottery tickets, pieces of fried pork, pineapples. The dogs went their own ways, of odd pedigrees, descendants of imported French poodles whose love lives had taken new, less than cosmopolitan turns with local Khmer mongrels. And so her story went. Boys in sampots playing a street game with bare feet, trying to keep a shuttlecock in the air without using their hands; one had no hands. This shuttlecock was a symbol of Phnom Penh's spirit, fragile and gay, waiting to tumble when some boy, caught by surprise, spun too late to save the bird from falling. She had asked the prime minister about his boy soldiers that afternoon.

In his office near the French embassy, wearing a pink ascot with an embroidered *apsara*, Lon Nol looked rheumy-eyed and distracted, staring out his window on to the purple bougainvillaea. His face resembled plasticine. Maybe he knew that the Americans and not he were running his country. And these journalists seemed to have pipelines he didn't. There were cheques at his elbow, cheques across his desk; a well-paid army, he gestured, as if anticipating her question about warlord officers and unpaid soldiers with families in tow. "Regardez-vous."

"Pour les petits garçons?" she asked bluntly.

The general refused to be drawn. Pointing to his ear and grinning, he signalled trouble with her accent. He was pretending to enjoy himself.

With just five minutes allotted to her she would have to lead him up carefully to the monuments at Angkor Wat and his military intentions toward them. She wanted a nice quotation to hang him with, for she had already decided he deserved to hang. Incidentally, were American army rations for sale on the street here in Phnom Penh, she asked him, to the general's mind the worst abuse of the black market?

"Il en est de même partout." His nostrils, like the womanly hips on his ascot, flared. Tricky questions, he joked, didn't bother him. Why were foreign journalists always looking for bad things to report. "Ce n'est pas si mal." He had never even seen for sale one tin of American apple sauce. She wondered if he was blind to the uniforms from the States, the boots, the field-pack radios, watches, ammunition tins. Maybe he never walked the streets. The rumour was you could custom-order a Cadillac in the Mekong Delta.

As if as an afterthought in leaving, she had asked if he would bother to protect Angkor Wat from the reported pillage and occupation by the Communists. This was her tricky question.

"Naturellement. Nos richesses nationales."

What else could he say but deny to the other side in this civil war their common heritage? No matter who got killed and what treasures were destroyed, his own complicity in obliterating history, by using it as an excuse to attack his enemies, would be denied.

He was looking at his watch. "I hope you will not come to regret your journey," he added, in English. He said there were no more tourists at Angkor, he'd been talking to his commander in the district there. Therefore few guides, little Western food, maybe no hotel. Still, he hoped she would find pleasant things to say of Kambuja in a difficult time. He had used the Khmer word for his nation. The speech limped from his mouth like a stroke victim's. Not like an orator's, or any national leader's, for apart from his ascot no one could accuse him of flamboyance as they had the overthrown prince. She was ushered to the door.

He said, "I have no concern what you will write about me." She believed him. He was complacent, impervious, already dead.

Next morning on the tarmac was proof of his recent ascent to power. ROYAL AIR CAMBODGE said the letters of her plane to Siem Reap, with each letter of the first word slashed through with paint. Maintenance men bore similar deletions on their overalls.

The plane itself was an empty freight car with seats. It took off late in the afternoon, flying at an angle, always seeking altitude. Air pockets sucked down most of the way, through clouds the colour of prunes. To the west, embers of sunlight burned between black holes; to the east, lightning. A story so far with the expected unexpected flashes of colour: a routine article with enough of the unknown to hold her readers.

Her plane had made a smooth landing after dark with the humidity high and stars dim. The little bus to Siem Reap picked its way through barricades set up by soldiers who peered down the neck of her yellow blouse. The other two passengers were boys who worked at the airfield – still civilians because they hadn't volunteered for Lon Nol's army. They seemed anxious for news from Phnom Penh and put aside their English grammars full of excerpts, she saw, from Dickens.

At the dilapidated Hotel de la Paix the fan squeaked like a bed-spring. After he switched it on the bellboy went to fetch a thermos of water and, returning, wondered if he should bring up some food. Or something else? A kiss maybe? "Je suis très bon." (He meant "wicked".)

Crickets the size of fingers flew against the walls and landed on her bed where bedbugs made journeys of their own. Downstairs she had *poulet aux bananes* in the empty restaurant and went out to write up a touristless town.

Here, soldiers in Australian bush hats drank beer under striped canopies. Women were buying prawns and pineapples from stalls lit by bulbs on a wire. She noticed diners in dingy restaurants, neglectful of the threat of war, and courting teenagers dressed in jeans. Shops with locked metal shutters lined the arcades and in the side-streets sat families outside their shacks, or stretched out on low wooden beds, spiritless from the heat. She hid her notebook.

Lon Nol was wrong. She had no trouble finding food nor, it appeared, a guide.

A man in brown shorts, grinning, beckoned from his pedicab at the kerb. "For tomorrow? Three dollar for Angkor Thom morning come back lunch then Angkor Wat afternoon. OK?" He was open to offers, any means of selling his allegiance to the highest bidder, of whom there appeared to be few. "Change money?" For doing this he had a friend at the Grand Hotel who knew "people" in Hong Kong. (Why hadn't she remembered the Grand had been closed?) He slid a 500-riel note into her blouse pocket and said she could pay him in dollars tomorrow. She returned the note and wished him good-night. He had the saggiest nose she had ever seen, broken more than once, and violently.

She slept at odd angles, half-listening to drums and a saxophone inside some hall of laughing voices. Wind and rain lashed the Hotel of Peace, crickets flew, bugs tramped in the dark across her skin. She woke up to a pricking in her hand.

He was there talking in whispers to the bellboy at breakfast. So she bargained over the cost of his pedicab and drove with him out of

Siem Reap, a wagon towed by a bicycle. At each pedal's descent his thighs bulged and his calves hardened, the going down harder work than the coming up. Veins on his legs looked like Himalayan streams. Twenty-seven and looking forty, he had been a driver for fifteen or twenty years, he said, whatever the age of his contraption. He still couldn't afford to marry.

They drove down the Rue Charles de Gaulle, past old villas, along the little river with its bridges clotted with soldiers and barbed wire. Flame trees dripped blossoms on to the current where families bathed and did laundry.

Outside of town the jungle thickened, though in a glade, in training, were Lon Nol's volunteers. Officers shouted, volunteers crawled, recruits learned to point rifles, which they pointed at the pedicab and didn't shoot. Mere children crawling on their arms in the dirt; crimson scarves aflame at their throats.

Nearer the ruins they stopped at a house on stilts, where her driver climbed up a ladder to talk to a man whose black T-shirt was stuck with little burry pods and stamped with a single Chinese character. She could remember another man in a sampot herding his elephant down the road and shouting at some monkeys in a tree. The scene reminded her of Brueghel in the tropics. Children crowded around her pedicab to practise French and English greetings; a girl at the village pop stand, flaunting mangoes stuffed inside her blouse for the fun of two friends, sold Jew's harps to tourists who no longer came.

Closer to their destination the sun grew hotter and cicadas rang from the jungle like tiny telephones no one answered. They stopped at the end of a thin dirt road, listening, she remembers, for what?

Then this unattractive man with varicose veins and the saggy nose whistled. With a wooden whistle from his pocket, sharply.

He turned in the cracked saddle and stared, deep into her blouse, slack-mouthed and conspiratorially.

Suddenly the jungle around them was alive with eyes, men, walking on pieces of rubber tyre.

Chipped Teeth and Liver Spots have stopped asking for her so she wonders how long until she, too, is taken out to a classroom for torture and perhaps death. How to let them know the colour of her skin and hair is the colour of the true north strong and free? Fight for any possible immunity. Live.

Her cot stinks and the chain on her ankle has rubbed her skin raw. The little salamander of a man who empties her slops pretends to smell nothing, hear nothing. The eyes bulge unnaturally in his head and stare off in directions other than where he bends with his pail to empty her waste. Having eaten nothing since her dysentery grew worse, her body continues to heave. What it expels must be the remains of her soul.

She still dreams of immunity. Has refused to sign any confession they could use as posthumous justification for executing her as a spy. But should they begin to torture her as they do their countrymen, what then, would the suffering be worse than scribbling her signature and dying fast?

What a reversal of natural law their thinking is, like the Mekong pouring full of silt to the sea – only to reverse itself as happens during the monsoon, and flood backward up the Tonle Sap, ominously, into the Great Lake. It happens. Angkar's attempt at purification is full of sewage and bloating corpses.

These suspected collaborators chained in their cells, you can tell the way they stumble myopically to Flop Ears or some other inquisitor what bewilderment is. Logic and decency have gone out the door. Bled of its population, the city has no resistance left to fight this dark tumour in its anatomy. School flourishes toward a novel end. Angkar's lessons encourage fresh, seditious memories. Its new history is rooted in events these pupils have never witnessed, in cooked-up confessions, predictable outcomes. You watch. Suicide.

You have no tears for the desperate loneliness you feel. Like your bowels, the tear ducts are empty, but keep draining from spasms and fear. You hear prisoners being led away and the lucky ones returning, wet, drenched with a pail of water to have made the electric shock spread smoothly across their skins. Their screaming seems as much a crying out for other prisoners to rebel as a corroboration of hell's inside circle. Others do not return and new prisoners are herded into their cells like livestock.

"*Chveng, Sdam*": Angkar's voice marches from the loudspeaker for hours on end. Sometimes she listens to the phrases and tries to puzzle out their meanings. "Renunciation . . . farm work . . .

Angkar's blessings." Radio Phnom Penh, if it is listened to where people are sane, must sound like a washerwoman on her knees claiming to be the Blessed Virgin.

Scrub my hole with a ten-foot pole and crawl back down with a Tootsie Roll.

Angkar makes up its utopia out of propaganda and lies, refusing to accept any facts not its own. Her own story, if her inquisitors had been interested in hearing it whole, couldn't have been made up. She had witnessed too much for it to be fraudulent, which must be the reason for their not wanting to listen.

In the forest no one started starving till villages in the "liberated zones" caved in to the pressures of war – and with them the guerrillas" own food supply. Tan Vim was a better destroyer than organizer; and he divided his talent between villages and temples. In charge of "rescuing" ancient monuments from feudal passivity, he thought he understood how to deal with stone, how to "rehabilitate" this worn-out Khmer art. When he determined she'd come to Angkor as a pilgrim and not a spy he scoffed and boasted to her of the extent of his domain: 600 temples spread out over 150 square miles of forest, and he just thirty-four. He could make any claim. In the early years he left her in the securer temples to which he would return with booty that someone else's unit would bicycle out in sacks to the Thai border.

Sometimes he allowed her to bathe in a moat, if they had taken her along to raid a large, still unsecured wat like Angkor itself. She forgot to consider the advantages of drowning. She just lapsed alone on her back among the lotus and hyacinths. The muggy night would have cooled by then, the tapping coppersmith birds of the jungle gone to sleep. She would try lapsing into nirvana, using the perfumed blossoms to rub the boredom and coarseness from her life. This was before she began to understand the meaning of "*norok*". "Hell". And before she had a child.

One dawn, returning to a remoter temple, they were ambushed on the road near Angkor Thom. Caught in a crossfire, ten cadres, half Vim's unit, died. Village boys she had cooked for and known. Superstitious urchins working for a deadly Fagan, picking the pockets of the past, their brown liquid eyes frozen open in shock. The rest crawled into an ancient irrigation ditch, unable to return fire; no one dared stick his head out of the ditch. The government soldiers threw half a dozen grenades and melted away.

Tan Vim was enraged. Not because ten boys died, but because they were killed by tactics poached from the Khmer Rouge. He kicked one of the dead boys in the forehead. The head snapped back and stayed back, in the dirt. Punishment for getting killed.

She shook like a dog trying to clean herself, having lain in the ditch two hours. The sight of the dead boys made her vomit an undigested mango. Weeks passed. The anguish that lasted was her own filth, the lack of some clean centre in her soul.

"*Khma*", she learned to say. I!

She picked up what Khmer she could by listening and asking. This amused the adolescent cadres, who smelled as bad as she. "*Barang cheh khmy*" ("Frenchwoman speaks Khmer"). She asked them for lessons and received two. Once to learn "*chveng*" ("left"), once "*sdam*" ("right"). Vim explained these politics of direction to her in French. He made them sound so straightforward she finally asked him the direction of hell.

"*Norok*?" He beeped when he spoke, like a Renault horn. He wiped a hand over his stubbly hair. In Paris, studying to be an electrical engineer, he'd never finished. "Les professeurs," he claimed, by way of excuse. Older than she, he pretended to a political sophistication that rejected, along with colonialism, a religion he had learned as a boy from monks.

"Many hells," he said, "for different sins." This was what the politically naïve Buddhist believed, and the common man: hells within hells, each hotter and more severe than the last. Vim plugged one gummy nostril with his thumb to purge the other. He spat. A hell for thieves whose backs were beaten with wire. A hell for adulterers who got crushed by an iron mountain. The hottest hell was reserved for merchants who sold alcohol, drugs, animal traps. He said she could view all this nonsense for herself the next time they visited the gallery walls of Angkor Wat. Crushed bodies, scorched stomachs, dagger-leafed lotuses, severed heads, disembowelled stomachs: all shiny from the touch of a thousand visitors' hands. This stuff was "une histoire" the Khmers were glad to get rid of. Religion and art ("les enfers") were making for "la nouvelle réalité".

His hands on her body were damp. Like the stone faces of the surrounding friezes, which resembled his own slanted forehead, curling lips and flat nose, his hands felt cold and bloodless. He wasn't a man whom hell could have burned.

Sihanouk must have felt the same, when he paid his former enemies, the Khmer Rouge, a flying visit from Peking, and Vim in turn treated him like a prisoner, patronizing and uncivil. The prince's hand pulled away from Vim's. He giggled nervously. He was supposed to be rallying his new allies against Lon Nol, but sounded absurd congratulating Vim's unit on destroying his ancestors" shrines. Vim had had no time to hide her when Sihanouk dropped in unexpectedly from the jungle, accompanied by his small entourage. She actually tried to attract the prince's attention, first with glances and then a sudden question in English about the war, but the little monarch carefully ignored her. She wanted him to remark her existence, to mention seeing a Western woman when he left the country. Perhaps he was afraid to rescue her, this prince. He just gazed wistfully at the head of Vishnu in a sack; through her to the blank friezes. Nodding dutifully in agreement with Vim, he moved like the puppets his royal stone ancestors had become.

Afterward, Vim told her "cette merde" had killed many comrades in the sixties, ambushed them in the jungle with government soldiers, then strung up their bodies as examples to other freedom fighters and slit open their stomachs. He, for one, did not agree with Angkar's line of leaving villagers" illusions about their old monarch unchallenged.

Shortly thereafter Tan Vim returned from a foray with an object held high on a stick. High-pitched, manic giggling preceded the guerrillas and she, cooking their rice in the sanctuary of the same temple Sihanouk had visited, stirring her pot with a stick, saw the head of a man – a village chief, they told her, who had offered them everything but his own "self-criticism". His open eyes were saffron-coloured and disbelieving.

When she watched the submarine races the head in her hands was warm. Its tongue touched hers, her fingers slid under its hair, she closed her eyes then opened them to enjoy its pleasure. Spanish Banks after dark was where you went alone with a boy for an hour a week. You chewed Dentyne, or dabbed your tongue with Gold

Spot, between hamburgers at the White Spot and this sex at the beach. The Point Atkinson lighthouse blipped in the darkness. The headlights of cars leaving and arriving raked shadows over your dash. She sat through seasons, through boys, who rolled their windows up and down in accordance with the weather. Winter heaters steamed up their windshields, or was it her tropical breath against cold glass? These beautiful boys came up for air to wipe away the moisture. Trying out her larger desires, she would whisper to them of places there might be in the world to visit. Most boys groaned at the thought of a future anywhere but here and tried to bury her world in theirs: a tonsil-massaging tongue, fingers inside her pants, mouths on nipples. She gave them her body, its pleasures of the moment, but her mother's song kept her hope in the future firm. She tiddled her own yearning to travel. Her boyfriends wanted nothing but to sit pat; they liked local highways and fast cars. As domestic dreamers as any were the lifeguards who gazed all day out to sea, dreaming of surfboards and California.

Necklaces of light, the ski lift down the Sleeping Beauty's breast on Grouse, the forecastle and threaded cranes of anchored freighters luciferous with diamonds.

Sometimes fog rolled down the sound and the lighthouse disappeared. The fog-horn came on like aural braille to guide creeping freighters into port. A boyfriend would moan his satisfaction, already on his way to summer, though she remembered it was always summer if you knew where to go. She wanted to go west.

Her mother sent her east, to Montreal, because she had relatives there, even an ex-husband. Before deciding what to do with her life she listened to her father, who told her to take a degree in something useless at Laval. So she studied history and hated it. "Perfect," he said. She felt hemmed in by a lack of mountains. She missed the Pacific and ships, the beach and tides. Montreal was neither a strange-sounding name nor very far away. She would talk it over with her mother long distance. "I felt much nearer the faraway," she said, "at home."

Once upon a time the villagers had welcomed them. She could overhear Vim on his radio congratulating his cadres in the liberated zones for their kindness to the old and encouragement to the young.

He sounded false. As time passed and Angkar shifted its line, he grew clipped and she couldn't follow the instructions he barked to his fighters. He didn't want her to.

One day he forced her to join them on a march that took all night and all day, to a village close to Battambang. He didn't know she was already three months pregnant, otherwise he might have understood her trying to outmarch the rest of them in the hope of losing his child. He would have approved.

Village life under Angkar looked strange to her. Men, women and children lived in segregated houses and sex was forbidden. Monks, dismissed as parasites, pulled plows in the rice paddies. She never saw any group larger than two people talking. Vim called the village a *phum* and made a speech to its committee. He wanted to know why they were growing no more guavas, mangoes, pomegranates or breadfruit. The chief of the collective answered with a rehearsed bitterness. He spat into the palm of his hand. He blamed the Americans, and looked at her. The villagers, he said, were frightened of being bombed and were running away with whatever food they could carry. He rubbed his hand across a scar on his knee.

"Lon Nol and his henchmen," announced Tan Vim, "are the lackeys and valets of the American imperialists. Puppets, murderers, black marketeers. We must learn to resist them. You all must learn."

Veins cropped up in his eyes, acne scars reappeared on his cheeks and his crewcut stood straight up again when he trimmed himself in the mirror. He looked colder than usual, hard, stiffened by his imported ideology to a rod.

Fly-eyed children were starving. Families fleeing. Village life was breaking down.

Vim must have thought more executions would harden the collective resolve.

In another village, where the people had allowed government soldiers to encourage in them a sense of immunity from the Khmer Rouge, a row of men was asked to dig an irrigation ditch and then blindfolded and shot. Except for one old man. He was still standing there. He had started to laugh. Drily, in and out of his stomach like a coughing dog. He thought it was a joke and didn't want to be gulled before the village. He wanted to believe it was all a joke. His blindfold made him think he was being taught a lesson for some minor transgression like hoarding an orange. No one had died. All the other men were still standing there, he imagined, as he was.

As she was. Vim told her to move. She couldn't. She couldn't help it, her bowels let go instead.

A cadre went over to the old man and told him to kneel. He did. Swinging his rifle butt, the teenager drove the man's head into the ditch. Wood on bone. A second time: it sounded like a cricket bat against a cantaloupe.

"Voilà," said Vim.

They had no excuse for not at least shooting him like the others. With victory by the Khmer Rouge more and more likely, the North Vietnamese were now shipping them tons of ammunition.

Wives keened, their full and beautiful lips stretched in grim circles, howls, wails.

Today she has been taken upstairs again, still wearing the stinking black pyjamas given her in the jungle, and told her "file" is now closed. How queer their interest in her: taken upstairs every day for weeks at a time; then neglected in a state of boredom that allows her to think of immunity; followed by renewed interrogation. The pattern is established. But this time it has changed. She must sign a confession, says Liver Spots, she has no choice. He sounds matter-of-fact and preoccupied. He asks her politely to read two badly typed pages of English. Someone other than him or Chipped Teeth must have written it, for these men profess to speak no English. She stands there shaking from lack of food. The confession claims that she, Aletta Macvey, has worked demoniacally for the CIA in Phnom Penh; that her stark father was a CIA boss in Los Angeles, dwelling in vertigo; and that she has aided in channelling American dollars to the murderer Lon Nol, which allowed him to escape Kampuchea and the blood and pestilence of his crimes. This is its thrust, written in a high-flown English out of the last century, but ungrammatical and a caricature of formal language. No mention of her being a Canadian journalist, held in the jungle at Angkor for five years, or that a Khmer Rouge officer, now vanished, had made her his prostitute and fathered her child. (Or that among the people this officer had practised treachery and butchery.)

She says nothing.

When she continues to stand there, shaking, making no move to pick up the ballpoint pen, Liver Spots motions to the guard to take her away.

But not back to her cell, for this time she is taken to one of the torturers' classrooms and met by the tallest, thinnest Cambodian she has ever seen. He is leaning forward as if in need of a pole to rest his frame against. Ageless, he stands behind the teacher's desk with a small hill in his spine and glasses wired to his nose. A metal frame bed with dangling leather straps squats on the floor by his desk. The man does not greet her but instead whisks the air past her face with a bamboo cane.

Phhuuuuuh . . .

"Read!" he commands her.

On the blackboard are written seven English instructions underneath seven Khmer instructions.

1. You must answer in conformity and consultation with the questions I ask you, Sir. Do not try to turn away my question.
2. Do not try to escape by making pretexts according to your hypocritical ideas and botherations.
3. Do not be a fool for you are a chap who dares to thwart the revolution.
4. You must immediately answer my questions without wasting time to reflect in agitation and sentimentality.
5. During the bastinado or the electrisization you must not cry loudly.
6. Do sit down quietly. Wait in patience for the orders. If there are no orders do nothing. If I ask you to do something you must immediately do it without protestation.
7. If you disobey every point of my regulations you will get either ten strokes of the whip or five shocks of electric discharge.

"Sign this," he tells her, producing the same two pages she has left lying on the blotter upstairs.

She looks up into his eyes and says nothing. His eyes are like two beans gone black with age. They actually show surprise. He is used to prisoners staring at the floor and not up at him; he expects conduct in accord with his instructions.

"Sit down," he orders.

When she does not obey he motions with his cane, the guard comes over and presses down on her shoulders. Her knees lock, then buckle.

"Lie down," orders Bean Pole.

The guard pushes her flat on the wet, stinking mattress. Dark bloodstains glue the fabric to her hair; against her cheek the blood feels like putty. He straps her arms and legs to the metal, then notches a large strap across her waist.

Ffftttttt

The cane flicks down across her mouth without a word. She hasn't expected its suddenness and it shocks her more than anything since coming to this school. Unlike the shock of electrodes that she can see dangling from the light socket, this pain arrives out of the blue. *Ffttt-FFFtttttttt- FffTTTT-* With a different sound each time, whimsically, his cane scorches her body from abrupt angles. He seems to enjoy her inability to anticipate where the burning will come from next: face, thighs, soles of her feet, neck, arms, breasts . . .

She is crying when the guard walks over with a black handkerchief. Bean Pole goes back to his desk to write something in a notebook. The guard winds the hanky around her head as a blindfold. Against this darkness she keeps trying to pull her arms free of the straps, but exhaustion overwhelms her. Blind, she can smell herself powerfully now and realizes her bowels have been discharging whatever liquid remains in her body.

Afterward she remembers a pair of hands, long smooth hands, fumbling with her genitals, attaching cold metal that pinched like tweezers. Then a pail of water. This is the last thing she remembers, a pail of water.

What year is this?

The rainy season has begun again. So will the darkness.

She wakes up wet in her cell hating the monsoon. It reminds her: its mud, its days on end of misery, the chills it brought moving through the *maquis* like the plague: these obscure punishments for Vim's atrocities committed in the dry season. It reminds her of shivering in stone porticoes, surrounded by frozen statues as old and once as permanent as Chartres's. Of dripping vaulted roofs and slimy *nagas*. Of Vim, with nothing better to do than paw her thighs like an adolescent, smiling stupidly, waiting for the sun to return. And of being anchored forever inland, she thought ruefully once, at Angkor.

This rain in Phonm Penh falling like the sound of applause would bear no comparing to the drizzle of her own city. Here is no ocean to catch dripping cedars, falling maple leaves, overextended sails. At Angkor the sheets of rain had actually enshrouded the brocade steps and pillars, lintels and eaves. Fires went out, she couldn't cook, there was nothing *to* cook. The rain just hung around like hunger. Mornings and afternoons were worst; nothing ever dried out, least of all the stone they lived inside and on top of, waiting.

The teenage cadres spent days on end concocting feasts in their heads. Kilos of ducks, coconuts, Chinese vermicelli, pork, peaches, betel leaves, prawns, Battambang plums, aerated drinks, betrothal cakes, pigs" trotters, sweetmeats, rice served in bamboo shafts, beer, Chinese wine, cigarettes. Vim would translate their dream dishes into French if she couldn't guess their Khmer words. Sometimes they laughed at her quickness. When the villages could no longer be counted on to produce more than ideological platitudes, these gourmet guerrillas would bring her insects, dog carcasses, snails, tree bark, shot cats, leaves and buffalo skin to add to her boiling stew. She was a witch on her knees keeping them all alive, they knew, by keeping herself from starving.

Her milk was as thin as her child. These ogres would have drunk that too.

Still, when the sun returned with the butterflies and parakeets, malnourishment never seemed to have had any weakening effect on vandalism and the revolution. It was as if the divine King Jayavarman's smile, carved into four sides of each tower of the Bayon, had been built to mock the Khmer Rouge's new reality, and so the guerrillas were determined to help the jungle erase it. They even talked of blowing up any towers too large for export. Vim acknowledged the truth of what she'd read before her flight from Saigon, that Jayavarman had driven out the invading Chams, performed acts of charity and built the greatest capital in Indochina. All this the Khmer Rouge would repeat in their own time, he said, but the irony was lost on him. Even the Bayon's carvings of warriors and common people, the record of Jayavarman's victory over barbarism, he had orders in the name of the present struggle to dismantle for profit. Cooks, masons, acrobats: the diversity of characters was the glory of the art. Vim went so far as to order his own warriors to defecate on the stone they sent into exile.

Entering Angkor Wat for the first time, in the moonlight a month after her capture, she had strolled in awe down the causeway for hundreds of yards, entering sanctuaries piled on top of each other, as on a wedding cake, to the stars. Vim must have considered it ideologically correct never to look impressed by any temple mountain created to commemorate ancestors. As she looked down from two hundred feet at the wizened palms, reflecting moonlight from their fronds, he was moved to pee inside an alcove, then squeeze her breast and dare her to object. He said she reminded him of the celestial dancers on the bas-relief.

She said if *that* was the case she wished he would export her too.

That was when she remembered the Sleeping Beauty for the first time in ages, mountains predating Angkor and commemorating woman, not man. She knew mountains couldn't be exported any more than heaven imported, as these men seemed to think possible. She felt homesick.

His piss soured fast in the alcove.

Flies crawl across her face, but she has forgotten how to mind. How to mind the way she smells. The longing to prink has vanished with her sense of decency, which was the last thing holding these threadless rags together. The ache in her groin, the welts on her face and body, make it impossible to sleep.

Radio Phnom Penh goes on spluttering words like *Mayaguez*, a Spanish word, why? It sounds like the ship of death the way it anchors these repetitive broadcasts. Perhaps it is a ship. Word by word, she tries to fathom a voice that speaks only in phrases. Packaged dog food. Slogans.

Knowing she has no resistance left is calming, except one man won't let her alone, plucking her sleeve to sign the badly typed pages and threatening to strap her again to the metal bed and attach his rusty electrodes. It's his pride. He doesn't wish to proceed if he can elicit her signature without force. By the sheer hint of his power.

He has already demonstrated his power and is trying more teacherly persuasion.

Phhuuuuuh . . .

Nothing.

Ffftttttt . . .

Is it his superiors upstairs he wishes to please? A day passes, then three more. He has grown impatient and aches to uncurl himself to full height. No matter how useful she may be to Angkar's paranoia, he has other inquisitions to attend. *Sssssst*: does she understand that headlong sound he remonstrates? The plunder possible among present company? The termination? He speaks in a strange, melodramatic English, his eyes ossified behind their oval wire lenses. His is the first continuous English she has heard in years and the sound is familiar, though the cadences Khmer. How long will his supercilious patience last until he reverts to the methods he prefers using, the lessons he would rather teach? His bamboo swishes the air, stings her cheeks, urging her to reread his chalked instructions and the story on paper she refuses to acknowledge as her own.

The rain keeps up like the mosquitoes and flies. The boarded-up windows let in little daylight and she no longer hears the screams. Notices them but does not hear them. Notices the daylight but can't understand what day really means. The rain washes down roof tiles and ssshhhes to the ground. At night, when the generator's shut down, blackness is absolute and she begins to see. She feels like some starving beggar in an Oxfam ad covering her own starvation. It isn't a story the radio's voice cares about.

Angkar thinks its woman's voice will disarm opposition, but news wrapped in the repetitive harpings of any amplified tonsils is bound to ring false. Broadcasts go out into the countryside where millions must be huddled in mud, misery, starvation: people separated by sex and age, crippled or already dead from digging roads, fields, their own graves. Angkar's work camps have replaced farms; its death camps, schools.

"Farm Work is the Only Work!"

"You are Happy!"

"Now you are Free of Inequality, Exploitation, Corruption, Oppression, Feudalism, Superstition, Hunger, Poverty, Suffering, Lies!"

"Renounce your own Selfishness! Believe in Angkar! Trust Angkar!"

The voice encourages informers and other guardians of the revolution. The voice tells children to parade vigilantly.

But not her child who would still, if living, be spending time in this crook of space she used to call arms. These sticks.

This time.

Odd, but her own mother would be past her death, over it by now, the way she had once got over her husband's leaving them for a ballet dancer from Winnipeg, before he had actually gone! She found rumours in his pockets, confirmation in his diary. He was a dentist, a gentle driller, who in the end bought his way out handsomely.

Once upon a time the fog-horn came on in August. She asked her mother why, if it was clear over the bay, should they be hearing the fog-horn.

"Maybe they're testing it for winter."

It sounded like a funeral. And in the sunshine, when it started to flash, the lighthouse looked like an ambulance.

Heat wavered up over the salt flats. The anchored freighters seemed to float on a mirage that stretched to faraway places.

"He won't come back to us," said her mother. Her daughter thought she meant the lifeguard.

She was waiting for winter the way a bird is tricked to its nest by an eclipse of the sun. She felt desolate on her blanket with nothing to do but listen to seasons change.

"You could have drowned," said her mother. She wiped the blood from her daughter's nose. "You walked out too far. I lost sight of you, wandering."

Salt chuck. Siam.

In this school no one departs for a better place. To hang on by denial is something, even life. It transcends the filth. Used to blackness she keeps her mind clean, the crow rinsing the clam.

Is she going blind?

What she sees isn't what her eyes lean on anymore, a brick or a roach, but the recollection of a life constant in its yearning. This is what they would switch out of her now with a cane and wires.

Cleanliness she can feel growing in her corpse like a cell: a bright mirage to soften death. It would be something to make dying an art.

"The inversion may be explainable by scientists," said her mother, watching the fog roll in off the gulf. "But the feeling it gives you is magical."

A kind of love for the body being left behind. Years later in their arms she was already leaving boys the moment she got intimate in the front seat of an Olds or in the sand by a log. Memories of their smell, taste and touch were already more potent than their presence. Raphael-Dennis-Peter-Tom – their requests got plainer with the names. She enshrined each boy in his own body for an hour but rarely went all the way with anybody who did not know one far-away place from another. And few of them knew much geography.

Neither has she given Liver Spots, Chipped Teeth or Bean Pole the pleasure of what is in her power to refuse. To help them rewrite the scrap of history they think she represents. They have her body, but want the mind. She would have given her mind to lifeguards but they just wanted the body. Is the state of yearning, its loneliness, being in the wrong place at the wrong time? A condition she'd tried in herself to combat by becoming a foreign correspondent. Reports cabled the story of *norok* to editors every day from wars around the world, but never succeeded in telling it. Never from very far inside the woods. Death was as whimsical as fog, as selfish as a child. It needed to be touched.

Trying to make a myth of ideology, a new history out of ashes, her tormentors have separated comrades from spies, the future from the present. They have a death wish. They have made ideology retroactive and cleaned the life out of dream. Emptying the city of its citizens, they're now purging the city from its citizens, this country of its heart.

Bean Pole is asking for her again, this time to inquire about Tan Vim. He asks her to identify a man she has never seen in her life, draped before the blackboard like a washcloth on a hook. He might be a man she has passed in the corridor upstairs, recently an officer of some standing, now broken in spirit and abject in confession.

"You know this man?"

You shake your head.

"This is the man of which you have spoken of?"

You shake your head.

You feel stronger now. The inquisitor cannot understand this growing absence of fear unaccompanied by resignation. Well, you are determined to have a point of view and welcome the fog with little cakes and wine. You can do nothing to save a scapegoat.

Sssssssst . . . before your eyes.

Lying in your cot you make the fog-horn moan in memory of the August sun still shining on your skin. The peaks of the Sleeping Beauty are above the fog, her nose, chin and breasts where the sky is blue. You are a romantic little girl heartened by God's sculpture. Emerging from the fog bank, outside the tidemark, are echoes of a sailor tapping rust from a flag-drooping stern. What a lonely man. What a wonderful knowledge he has brought to port.

O my love

The Management of Grief

BHARATI MUKHERJEE

A woman I don't know is boiling tea the Indian way in my kitchen. There are a lot of women I don't know in my kitchen, whispering, and moving tactfully. They open doors, rummage through the pantry, and try not to ask me where things are kept. They remind me of when my sons were small, on Mother's Day or when Vikram and I were tired, and they would make big, sloppy omelettes. I would lie in bed pretending I didn't hear them.

Dr Sharma, the treasurer of the Indo-Canada Society, pulls me into the hallway. He wants to know if I am worried about money. His wife, who has just come up from the basement with a tray of empty cups and glasses, scolds him. "Don't bother Mrs Bhave with mundane details." She looks so monstrously pregnant her baby must be days overdue. I tell her she shouldn't be carrying heavy things. "Shaila," she says, smiling, "this is the fifth." Then she grabs a teenager by his shirt-tails. He slips his Walkman off his head. He has to be one of her four children, they have the same domed and dented foreheads. "What's the official word now?" she demands. The boy slips the headphones back on. "They're acting evasive, Ma. They're saying it could be an accident or a terrorist bomb."

All morning, the boys have been muttering, Sikh Bomb, Sikh Bomb. The men, not using the word, bow their heads in agreement. Mrs Sharma touches her forehead at such a word. At least they've stopped talking about space debris and Russian lasers.

Two radios are going in the dining room. They are tuned to different stations. Someone must have brought the radios down from my boys' bedrooms. I haven't gone into their rooms since Kusum came running across the front lawn in her bathrobe. She looked so funny, I was laughing when I opened the door.

The big TV in the den is being whizzed through American networks and cable channels.

"Damn!" some man swears bitterly. "How can these preachers carry on like nothing's happened?" I want to tell him we're not that important. You look at the audience, and at the preacher in his blue robe with his beautiful white hair, the potted palm trees under a blue sky, and you know they care about nothing.

The phone rings and rings. Dr Sharma's taken charge. "We're with her," he keeps saying. "Yes, yes, the doctor has given calming pills. Yes, yes, pills are having necessary effect." I wonder if pills alone explain this calm. Not peace, just a deadening quiet. I was always controlled, but never repressed. Sound can reach me, but my body is tensed, ready to scream. I hear their voices all around me. I hear my boys and Vikram cry, "Mommy, Shaila!" and their screams insulate me, like headphones.

The woman boiling water tells her story again and again. "I got the news first. My cousin called from Halifax before 6 a.m., can you imagine? He'd gotten up for prayers and his son was studying for medical exams and he heard on a rock channel that something had happened to a plane. They said first it had disappeared from the radar, like a giant eraser just reached out. His father called me, so I said to him, what do you mean 'something bad'? You mean a hijacking? And he said, *bebn*, there is no confirmation of anything yet, but check with your neighbours because a lot of them must be on that plane. So I called poor Kusum straightaway. I knew Kusum's husband and daughter were booked to go yesterday."

Kusum lives across the street from me. She and Satish had moved in less than a month ago. They said they needed a bigger place. All these people, the Sharmas and friends from the Indo-Canada Society, had been there for the housewarming. Satish and Kusum made homemade tandoori on their big gas grill and even the white neighbours piled their plates high with that luridly red, charred, juicy chicken. Their younger daughter had danced, and even our boys had broken away from the Stanley Cup telecast to put in a reluctant appearance. Everyone took pictures for their albums and for the community newspapers – another of our families had made it big in Toronto – and now I wonder how many of those happy faces are gone. "Why does God give us so much if all along He intends to take it away?" Kusum asks me.

I nod. We sit on carpeted stairs, holding hands like children. "I never once told him that I loved him," I say. I was too much the well brought up woman. I was so well brought up I never felt comfortable calling my husband by his first name.

"It's all right," Kusum says. "He knew. My husband knew. They felt it. Modern young girls have to say it because what they feel is fake."

Kusum's daughter, Pam, runs in with an overnight case. Pam's in her McDonald's uniform. "Mummy! You have to get dressed!" Panic makes her cranky. "A reporter's on his way here."

"Why?"

"You want to talk to him in your bathrobe?" She starts to brush her mother's long hair. She's the daughter who's always in trouble. She dates Canadian boys and hangs out in the mall, shopping for tight sweaters. The younger one, the goody-goody one according to Pam, the one with a voice so sweet that when she sang *bhajans* for Ethiopian relief even a frugal man like my husband wrote out a hundred-dollar cheque, *she* was on that plane. *She* was going to spend July and August with grandparents because Pam wouldn't go. Pam said she'd rather waitress at McDonald's. "If it's a choice between Bombay and Wonderland, I'm picking Wonderland," she'd said.

"Leave me alone," Kusum yells. "You know what I want to do? If I didn't have to look after you now, I'd hang myself."

Pam's young face goes blotchy with pain. "Thanks," she says, "don't let me stop you."

"Hush," pregnant Mrs Sharma scolds Pam. "Leave your mother alone. Mr Sharma will tackle the reporters and fill out the forms. He'll say what has to be said."

Pam stands her ground. "You think I don't know what Mummy's thinking? *Why her*? that's what. That's sick! Mummy wishes my little sister were alive and I were dead."

Kusum's hand in mine is trembly hot. We continue to sit on the stairs.

She calls before she arrives, wondering if there's anything I need. Her name is Judith Templeton and she's an appointee of the provincial government. "Multiculturalism?" I ask, and she says, "Partially," but her mandate is bigger. "I've been told you knew many people on the flight," she says. "Perhaps if you'd agree to help us reach the others . . .?"

She gives me time at least to put on tea water and pick up the mess in the front room. I have a few *samosas* from Kusum's housewarming that I could fry up, but then I think, Why prolong this visit?

Judith Templeton is much younger than she sounded. She wears a blue suit with a white blouse and a polka dot tie. Her blond hair is cut short, her only jewelry is pearl drop earrings. Her briefcase is new and expensive looking, a gleaming cordovan leather. She sits with it across her lap. When she looks out the front windows on to the street, her contact lenses seem to float in front of her light blue eyes.

"What sort of help do you want from me?" I ask. She has refused the tea, out of politeness, but I insist, along with some slightly stale biscuits.

"I have no experience," she admits. "That is, I have an MSW and I've worked in liaison with accident victims, but I mean I have no experience with a tragedy of this scale –"

"Who could?" I ask.

"– and with the complications of culture, language, and customs. Someone mentioned that Mrs Bhave is a pillar – because you've taken it more calmly."

At this, perhaps, I frown, for she reaches forward, almost to take my hand. "I hope you understand my meaning, Mrs Bhave. There are hundreds of people in Metro directly affected, like you, and some of them speak no English. There are some widows who've never handled money or gone on a bus, and there are old parents who still haven't eaten or gone outside their bedrooms. Some houses and apartments have been looted. Some wives are still hysterical. Some husbands are in shock and profound depression. We want to help, but our hands are tied in so many ways. We have to distribute money to some people, and there are legal documents – these things can be done. We have interpreters, but we don't always have the human touch, or maybe the right human touch. We don't want to make mistakes, Mrs Bhave, and that's why we'd like to ask you to help us."

"More mistakes, you mean," I say.

"Police matters are not in my hands," she answers.

"Nothing I can do will make any difference," I say. "We must all grieve in our own way."

"But you are coping very well. All the people said, Mrs Bhave is the strongest person of all. Perhaps if the others could see you, talk with you, it would help them."

"By the standards of the people you call hysterical, I am behaving very oddly and very badly, Miss Templeton." I want to say to her, *I wish I could scream, starve, walk into Lake Ontario, jump from a bridge*. "They would not see me as a model. I do not see myself as a model."

I am a freak. No one who has ever known me would think of me reacting this way. This terrible calm will not go away.

She asks me if she may call again, after I get back from a long trip that we all must make. "Of course," I say. "Feel free to call, anytime."

Four days later, I find Kusum squatting on a rock overlooking a bay in Ireland. It isn't a big rock, but it juts sharply out over water. This is as close as we'll ever get to them. June breezes balloon out her sari and unpin her knee-length hair. She has the bewildered look of a sea creature whom the tides have stranded.

It's been one hundred hours since Kusum came stumbling and screaming across my lawn. Waiting around the hospital, we've heard many stories. The police, the diplomats, they tell us things thinking we're strong, that knowledge is helpful to the grieving, and maybe it is. Some, I know, prefer ignorance, or their own versions. The plane broke in two, they say. Unconsciousness was instantaneous. No one suffered. My boys must have just finished their breakfasts. They loved eating on planes, they loved the smallness of plates, knives, and forks. Last year they saved the airline salt and pepper shakers. Half an hour more and they would have made it to Heathrow.

Kusum says that we can't escape our fate. She says that all those people – our husbands, my boys, her girl with the nightingale voice, all those Hindus, Christians, Sikhs, Muslims, Parsis, and atheists on that plane – were fated to die together off this beautiful bay. She learned this from a swami in Toronto.

I have my Valium.

Six of us "relatives" – two widows and four widowers – choose to spend the day today by the waters instead of sitting in a hospital room and scanning photographs of the dead. That's what they call us now: relatives. I've looked through twenty-seven photos in two days. They're very kind to us, the Irish are very understanding. Sometimes understanding means freeing a tourist bus for this trip to the bay, so we can pretend to spy our loved ones through the glassiness of waves or in sun-speckled cloud shapes.

I could die here, too, and be content.

"What is that, out there?" She's standing and flapping her hands and for a moment I see a head shape bobbing in the waves. She's standing in the water, I on the boulder. The tide is low, and a round, black, head-sized rock has just risen from the waves. She returns, her sari end dripping and ruined and her face is a twisted remnant of hope, the way mine was a hundred hours ago, still laughing but inwardly knowing that nothing but the ultimate tragedy could bring two women together at six o'clock on a Sunday morning. I watch her face sag into blankness.

"That water felt warm, Shaila," she says at length.

"You can't," I say. "We have to wait for our turn to come."

I haven't eaten in four days, haven't brushed my teeth.

"I know," she says. "I tell myself I have no right to grieve. They are in a better place than we are. My swami says I should be thrilled for them. My swami says depression is a sign of our selfishness."

Maybe I'm selfish. Selfishly I break away from Kusum and run, sandals slapping against stones, to the water's edge. What if my boys aren't lying pinned under the debris? What if they aren't stuck a mile below that innocent blue chop? What if, given the strong currents . . .

Now I've ruined my sari, one of my best. Kusum has joined me, knee-deep in water that feels to me like a swimming pool. I could settle in the water, and my husband would take my hand and the boys would slap water in my face just to see me scream.

"Do you remember what good swimmers my boys were, Kusum?"

"I saw the medals," she says.

One of the widowers, Dr Ranganathan from Montreal, walks out to us, carrying his shoes in one hand. He's an electrical engineer. Someone at the hotel mentioned his work is famous around the world, something about the place where physics and electricity come together. He has lost a huge family, something indescribable. "With some luck," Dr Ranganathan suggests to me, "a good swimmer could make it safely to some island. It is quite possible that there may be many many microscopic islets scattered around."

"You're not just saying that?" I tell Dr Ranganathan about Vinod, my elder son. Last year he took diving as well.

"It's a parent's duty to hope," he says. "It is foolish to rule out possibilities that have not been tested. I myself have not surrendered hope."

Kusum is sobbing once again. "Dear lady," he says, laying his free hand on her arm, and she calms down.

"Vinod is how old?" he asks me. He's very careful, as we all are. *Is*, not was.

"Fourteen. Yesterday he was fourteen. His father and uncle were going to take him down to the Taj and give him a big birthday party. I couldn't go with them because I couldn't get two weeks off from my stupid job in June." I process bills for a travel agent. June is a big travel month.

Dr Ranganathan whips the pockets of his suit jacket inside out. Squashed roses, in darkening shades of pink, float on the water. He tore the roses off creepers in somebody's garden. He didn't ask anyone if he could pluck the roses, but now there's been an article about it in the local papers. When you see an Indian person, it says, please give him or her flowers.

"A strong youth of fourteen," he says, "can very likely pull to safety a younger one."

My sons, though four years apart, were very close. Vinod wouldn't let Mithun drown. *Electrical engineering*, I think, foolishly perhaps: this man knows important secrets of the universe, things closed to me. Relief spins me lightheaded. No wonder my boys" photographs haven't turned up in the gallery of photos of the recovered dead. "Such pretty roses," I say.

"My wife loved pink roses. Every Friday I had to bring a bunch home. I used to say, Why? After twenty odd years of marriage you're still needing proof positive of my love?" He has identified his wife and three of his children. Then others from Montreal, the lucky ones, intact families with no survivors. He chuckles as he wades back to shore. Then he swings around to ask me a question. "Mrs Bhave, you are wanting to throw in some roses for your loved ones? I have two big ones left."

But I have other things to float: Vinod's pocket calculator; a half-painted model B-52 for my Mithun. They'd want them on their island. And for my husband? For him I let fall into the calm, glassy waters a poem I wrote in the hospital yesterday. Finally he'll know my feelings for him.

"Don't tumble, the rocks are slippery," Dr Ranganathan cautions. He holds out a hand for me to grab.

Then it's time to get back on the bus, time to rush back to our waiting posts on hospital benches.

Kusum is one of the lucky ones. The lucky ones flew here, identified in multiplicate their loved ones, then will fly to India with the bodies for proper ceremonies. Satish is one of the few males who surfaced. The photos of faces we saw on the walls in an office at Heathrow and here in the hospital are mostly of women. Women have more body fat, a nun said to me matter-of-factly. They float better.

Today I was stopped by a young sailor on the street. He had loaded bodies, he'd gone into the water when – he checks my face for signs of strength – when the sharks were first spotted. I don't blush, and he breaks down. "It's all right," I say. "Thank you." I had heard about the sharks from Dr Ranganathan. In his orderly mind, science brings understanding, it holds no terror. It is the shark's duty. For every deer there is a hunter, for every fish a fisherman.

The Irish are not shy; they rush to me and give me hugs and some are crying. I cannot imagine reactions like that on the streets of Toronto. Just strangers, and I am touched. Some carry flowers with them and give them to any Indian they see.

After lunch, a policeman I have gotten to know quite well catches hold of me. He says he thinks he has a match for Vinod. I explain what a good swimmer Vinod is.

"You want me with you when you look at photos?" Dr Ranganathan walks ahead of me into the picture gallery. In these matters, he is a scientist, and I am grateful. It is a new perspective. "They have performed miracles," he says. "We are indebted to them."

The first day or two the policemen showed us relatives only one picture at a time; now they're in a hurry, they're eager to lay out the possibles, and even the probables.

The face on the photo is of a boy much like Vinod; the same intelligent eyes, the same thick brows dipping into a V. But this boy's features, even his cheeks, are puffier, wider, mushier.

"No." My gaze is pulled by the other pictures. There are five other boys who look like Vinod.

The nun assigned to console me rubs the first picture with a fingertip. "When they've been in the water for a while, love, they look a little heavier." The bones under the skin are broken, they said on the first day – try to adjust your memories. It's important.

"It's not him. I'm his mother. I'd know."

"I know this one!" Dr Ranganathan cries out suddenly from the back of the gallery. "And this one!" I think he senses that I don't want to find my boys. "They are the Kutty brothers. They were also from Montreal." I don't mean to be crying. On the contrary, I am ecstatic. My suitcase in the hotel is packed heavy with dry clothes for my boys.

The policeman starts to cry. "I am so sorry, I am so sorry, ma'am. I really thought we had a match."

With the nun ahead of us and the policeman behind, we, the unlucky ones without our children's bodies, file out of the makeshift gallery.

From Ireland most of us go on to India. Kusum and I take the same direct flight to Bombay, so I can help her clear customs quickly. But we have to argue with a man in uniform. He has large boils on his face. The boils swell and glow with sweat as we argue with him. He wants Kusum to wait in line and he refuses to take authority because his boss is on a tea break. But Kusum won't let her coffins out of sight, and I shan't desert her though I know that my parents, elderly and diabetic, must be waiting in a stuffy car in a scorching lot.

"You bastard!" I scream at the man with the popping boils. Other passengers press closer. "You think we're smuggling contraband in those coffins!"

Once upon a time we were well brought up women; we were dutiful wives who kept our heads veiled, our voices shy and sweet.

In India, I become, once again, an only child of rich, ailing parents. Old friends of the family come to pay their respects. Some are Sikh, and inwardly, involuntarily, I cringe. My parents are progressive people; they do not blame communities for a few individuals.

In Canada it is a different story now.

"Stay longer," my mother pleads. "Canada is a cold place. Why would you want to be all by yourself?" I stay.

Three months pass. Then another.

"Vikram wouldn't have wanted you to give up things!" they protest. They call my husband by the name he was born with. In Toronto he'd changed to Vik so the men he worked with at his office would find his name as easy as Rod or Chris. "You know, the dead aren't cut off from us!"

My grandmother, the spoiled daughter of a rich *zamindar*, shaved her head with rusty razor blades when she was widowed at sixteen. My grandfather died of childhood diabetes when he was nineteen, and she saw herself as the harbinger of bad luck. My mother grew up without parents, raised indifferently by an uncle, while her true mother slept in a hut behind the main estate house and took her food with the servants. She grew up a rationalist. My parents abhor mindless mortification.

The zamindar's daughter kept stubborn faith in Vedic rituals; my parents rebelled. I am trapped between two modes of knowledge. At thirty-six, I am too old to start over and too young to give up. Like my husband's spirit, I flutter between worlds.

*

Courting aphasia, we travel. We travel with our phalanx of servants and poor relatives. To hill stations and to beach resorts. We play contract bridge in dusty gymkhana clubs. We ride stubby ponies up crumbly mountain trails. At tea dances, we let ourselves be twirled twice around the ballroom. We hit the holy spots we hadn't made time for before. In Varanasi, Kalighat, Rishikesh, Hardwar, astrologers and palmists seek me out and for a fee offer me cosmic consolations.

Already the widowers among us are being shown new bride candidates. They cannot resist the call of custom, the authority of their parents and older brothers. They must marry; it is the duty of a man to look after a wife. The new wives will be young widows with children, destitute but of good family. They will make loving wives, but the men will shun them. I've had calls from the men over crackling Indian telephone lines. "Save me," they say, these substantial, educated, successful men of forty. "My parents are arranging a marriage for me." In a month they will have buried one family and returned to Canada with a new bride and partial family.

I am comparatively lucky. No one here thinks of arranging a husband for an unlucky widow.

Then, on the third day of the sixth month into this odyssey, in an abandoned temple in a tiny Himalayan village, as I make my offering of flowers and sweetmeats to the god of a tribe of animists, my husband descends to me. He is squatting next to a scrawny *sadhu* in moth-eaten robes. Vikram wears the vanilla suit he wore the last time I hugged him. The *sadhu* tosses petals on a butter-fed flame, reciting Sanskrit mantras and sweeps his face of flies. My husband takes my hands in his.

You're beautiful, he starts. Then, *What are you doing here?*

Shall I stay? I ask. He only smiles, but already the image is fading. *You must finish alone what we started together.* No seaweed wreathes his mouth. He speaks too fast just as he used to when we were an envied family in our pink split-level. He is gone.

In the windowless altar room, smoky with joss sticks and clarified butter lamps, a sweaty hand gropes for my blouse. I do not shriek. The *sadhu* arranges his robe. The lamps hiss and sputter out.

When we come out of the temple, my mother says, "Did you feel something weird in there?"

My mother has no patience with ghosts, prophetic dreams, holy men, and cults.

"No," I lie. "Nothing."

But she knows that she's lost me. She knows that in days I shall be leaving.

Kusum's put her house up for sale. She wants to live in an ashram in Hardwar. Moving to Hardwar was her swami's idea. Her swami runs two ashrams, the one in Hardwar and another here in Toronto.

"Don't run away," I tell her.

"I'm not running away," she says. "I'm pursuing inner peace. You think you or that Ranganathan fellow are better off?"

Pam's left for California. She wants to do some modelling, she says. She says when she comes into her share of the insurance money she'll open a yoga-cum-aerobics studio in Hollywood. She sends me postcards so naughty I daren't leave them on the coffee table. Her mother has withdrawn from her and the world.

The rest of us don't lose touch, that's the point. Talk is all we have, says Dr Ranganathan, who has also resisted his relatives and returned to Montreal and to his job, alone. He says, whom better to talk with than other relatives? We've been melted down and recast as a new tribe.

He calls me twice a week from Montreal. Every Wednesday night and every Saturday afternoon. He is changing jobs, going to Ottawa. But Ottawa is over a hundred miles away, and he is forced to drive two hundred and twenty miles a day. He can't bring himself to sell his house. The house is a temple, he says; the king-sized bed in the master bedroom is a shrine. He sleeps on a folding cot. A devotee.

*

There are still some hysterical relatives. Judith Templeton's list of those needing help and those who've "accepted" is in nearly perfect balance. Acceptance means you speak of your family in the past tense and you make active plans for moving ahead with your life. There are courses at Seneca and Ryerson we could be taking. Her gleaming leather briefcase is full of college catalogues and lists of cultural societies that need our help. She has done impressive work, I tell her.

"In the textbooks on grief management," she replies – I am her confidante, I realize, one of the few whose grief has not sprung bizarre obsessions – "there are stages to pass through: rejection, depression, acceptance, reconstruction." She has compiled a chart and finds that six months after the tragedy, none of us still reject reality, but only a handful are reconstructing. "Depressed Acceptance" is the plateau we've reached. Remarriage is a major step in reconstruction (though she's a little surprised, even shocked, over *how* quickly some of the men have taken on new families). Selling one's house and changing jobs and cities is healthy.

How do I tell Judith Templeton that my family surrounds me, and that like creatures in epics, they've changed shapes? She sees me as calm and accepting but worries that I have no job, no career. My closest friends are worse off than I. I cannot tell her my days, even my nights, are thrilling.

She asks me to help with families she can't reach at all. An elderly couple in Agincourt whose sons were killed just weeks after they had brought their parents over from a village in Punjab. From their names, I know they are Sikh. Judith Templeton and a translator have visited them twice with offers of money for air fare to Ireland, with bank forms, power-of-attorney forms, but they have refused to sign, or to leave their tiny apartment. Their sons' money is frozen in the bank. Their sons' investment apartments have been trashed by tenants, the furnishings sold off. The parents fear that anything they sign or any money they receive will end the company's or the country's obligations to them. They fear they are selling their sons for two airline tickets to a place they've never seen.

The high-rise apartment is a tower of Indians and West Indians, with a sprinkling of Orientals. The nearest bus stop kiosk is lined with women in saris. Boys practise cricket in the parking lot. Inside the building, even I wince a bit from the ferocity of onion fumes, the distinctive and immediate Indianness of frying *ghee*, but Judith Templeton maintains a steady flow of information. These poor old people are in imminent danger of losing their place and all their services.

I say to her, "They are Sikh. They will not open up to a Hindu woman." And what I want to add is, as much as I try not to, I stiffen now at the sight of beards and turbans. I remember a time when we all trusted each other in this new country, it was only the new country we worried about.

The two rooms are dark and stuffy. The lights are off, and an oil lamp sputters on the coffee table. The bent old lady has let us in, and her husband is wrapping a white turban over his oiled, hip-length hair. She immediately goes to the kitchen, and I hear the most familiar sound of an Indian home, tap water hitting and filling a teapot.

They have not paid their utility bills, out of fear and the inability to write a cheque. The telephone is gone; electricity and gas and water are soon to follow. They have told Judith their sons will provide. They are good boys, and they have always earned and looked after their parents.

We converse a bit in Hindi. They do not ask about the crash and I wonder if I should bring it up. If they think I am here merely as a translator, then they may feel insulted. There are thousands of Punjabi-speakers, Sikhs, in Toronto to do a better job. And so I say to the old lady, "I too have lost my sons, and my husband, in the crash."

Her eyes immediately fill with tears. The man mutters a few words which sound like a blessing. "God provides and God takes away," he says.

I want to say, But only men destroy and give back nothing. "My boys and my husband are not coming back," I say. "We have to understand that."

Now the old woman responds. "But who is to say? Man alone does not decide these things." To this her husband adds his agreement.

Judith asks about the bank papers, the release forms. With a stroke of a pen, they will have a provincial trustee to pay their bills, invest their money, send them a monthly pension.

"Do you know this woman?" I ask them.

The man raises his hand from the table, turns it over and seems to regard each finger separately before he answers. "This young lady is always coming here, we make tea for her and she leaves papers for us to sign." His eyes scan a pile of papers in the corner of the room. "Soon we will be out of tea, then will she go away?"

The old lady adds, "I have asked my neighbours and no one else gets *angrezi* visitors. What have we done?"

"It's her job," I try to explain. "The government is worried. Soon you will have no place to stay, no lights, no gas, no water."

"Government will get its money. Tell her not to worry, we are honourable people."

I try to explain the government wishes to give money, not take. He raises his hand. "Let them take," he says. "We are accustomed to that. That is no problem."

"We are strong people," says the wife. "Tell her that."

"Who needs all this machinery?" demands the husband. "It is unhealthy, the bright lights, the cold air on a hot day, the cold food, the four gas rings. God will provide, not government."

"When our boys return," the mother says. Her husband sucks his teeth. "Enough talk," he says.

Judith breaks in. "Have you convinced them?" The snaps on her cordovan briefcase go off like firecrackers in that quiet apartment. She lays the sheaf of legal papers on the coffee table. "If they can't write their names, an X will do – I've told them that."

Now the old lady has shuffled to the kitchen and soon emerges with a pot of tea and two cups. "I think my bladder will go first on a job like this," Judith says to me, smiling. "If only there was some way of reaching them. Please thank her for the tea. Tell her she's very kind."

I nod in Judith's direction and tell them in Hindi, "She thanks you for the tea. She thinks you are being very hospitable but she doesn't have the slightest idea what it means."

I want to say, Humour her. I want to say, My boys and my husband are with me too, more than ever. I look in the old man's eyes and I can read his stubborn, peasant's message: *I have protected this woman as best I can. She is the only person I have left. Give to me or take from me what you will, but I will not sign for it. I will not pretend that I accept.*

In the car, Judith says, "You see what I'm up against? I'm sure they're lovely people, but their stubbornness and ignorance are driving me crazy. They think signing a paper is signing their sons" death warrants, don't they?"

I am looking out the window. I want to say, *In our culture, it is a parent's duty to hope.*

"Now Shaila, this next woman is a real mess. She cries all day and night, and she refuses all medical help. We may have to –"

"– Let me out at the subway," I say.

"I beg your pardon?" I can feel those blue eyes staring at me.

It would not be like her to disobey. She merely disapproves, and slows at a corner to let me out. Her voice is plaintive. "Is there anything I said? Anything I did?"

I could answer her suddenly in a dozen ways, but I choose not to. "Shaila? Let's talk about it," I hear, then slam the door.

A wife and mother begins her new life in a new country, and that life is cut short. Yet her husband tells her: Complete what we have started. We who stayed out of politics and came half-way around the world to avoid religious and political feuding have been the first in the New World to die from it. I no longer know what we started, nor how to complete it. I write letters to the editors of local papers and to members of Parliament. Now at least they admit it was a bomb. One MP answers back, with sympathy, but with a challenge. You want to make a difference? Work on a campaign. Work on mine. Politicize the Indian voter.

My husband's old lawyer helps me set up a trust. Vikram was a saver and a careful investor. He had saved the boys" boarding school and college fees. I sell the pink house at four times what we paid for it and take a small apartment downtown. I am looking for a charity to support.

We are deep in the Toronto winter, grey skies, icy pavements. I stay indoors, watching television. I have tried to assess my situation, how best to live my life, to complete what we began so many years ago. Kusum has written me from Hardwar that her life is now serene. She has seen Satish and has heard her daughter sing again. Kusum was on a pilgrimage, passing through a village when she heard a young girl's voice, singing one of her daughter's favourite *bhajans*. She followed the music through the squalor of a Himalayan village, to a hut where a young girl, an exact replica of her daughter, was fanning coals under the kitchen fire. When she appeared, the girl cried out, "Ma!" and ran away. What did I think of that?

I think I can only envy her.

Pam didn't make it to California, but writes me from Vancouver. She works in a department store, giving make-up hints to Indian and Oriental girls. Dr Ranganathan has given up his commute, given up his house and job, and accepted an academic position in Texas where no one knows his story and he has vowed not to tell it. He calls me now once a week.

I wait, I listen, and I pray, but Vikram has not returned to me. The voices and the shapes and the nights filled with visions ended abruptly several weeks ago.

I take it as a sign.

One rare, beautiful, sunny day last week, returning from a small errand on Yonge Street, I was walking through the park from the subway to my apartment. I live equidistant from the Ontario Houses of Parliament and the University of Toronto. The day was not cold, but something in the bare trees caught my attention. I looked up from the gravel, into the branches and the clear blue sky beyond. I thought I heard the rustling of larger forms, and I waited a moment for voices. Nothing.

"What?" I asked.

Then as I stood in the path looking north to Queen's Park and west to the university, I heard the voices of my family one last time. *Your time has come*, they said. *Go, be brave*.

I do not know where this voyage I have begun will end. I do not know which direction I will take. I dropped the package on a park bench and started walking.

Scenes

CAROL SHIELDS

In 1974 Frances was asked to give a lecture in Edmonton, and on the way there her plane was forced to make an emergency landing in a barley field. The man sitting next to her – they had not spoken – turned and asked if he might put his arms around her. She assented. They clung together, her size 12 dress and his wool suit. Later, he gave her his business card.

She kept the card for several weeks poked in the edge of her bedroom mirror. It is a beautiful mirror, a graceful rectangle in a pine frame, and very, very old. Once it was attached to the back of a bureau belonging to Frances's grandmother. Leaves, vines, flowers and fruit are shallowly carved in the soft wood of the frame. The carving might be described as primitive – and this is exactly why Frances loves it, being drawn to those things that are incomplete or in some way flawed. Furthermore, the mirror is the first thing she remembers seeing, *really* seeing, as a child. Visiting her grandmother, she noticed the stiff waves of light and shadow on the frame, the way square pansies interlocked with rigid grapes, and she remembers creeping out of her grandmother's bed where she had been put for an afternoon nap and climbing on a chair so she could touch the worked surface with the flat of her hand.

Her grandmother died. It was discovered by the aunts and uncles that on the back of the mirror was stuck a piece of adhesive tape and on the tape was written: "For my vain little granddaughter Frances." Frances's mother was affronted, but put it down to hardening of the arteries. Frances, who was only seven, felt uniquely, mysteriously honoured.

She did not attend the funeral; it was thought she was too young, and so instead she was taken one evening to the funeral home to bid goodbye to her grandmother's body. The room where the old lady lay was large, quiet, and hung all around with swags of velvet. Frances's father lifted her up so she could see her grandmother, who was wearing a black dress with a white crêpe jabot, her powdered face pulled tight as though with a drawstring into a sort of grimace. A lovely blanket with satin edging covered her trunky legs and torso. Laid out, calm and silent as a boat, she looked almost generous.

For some reason Frances was left alone with the casket for a few minutes, and she took this chance – she had to pull herself up on tiptoe – to reach out and touch her grandmother's lips with the middle finger of her right hand. It was like pressing in the side of a rubber ball. The lips did not turn to dust – which did not surprise Frances at all, but rather confirmed what she had known all along. Later, she would look at her finger and say to herself, "This finger has touched dead lips." Then she would feel herself grow rich with disgust. The touch, she knew, had not been an act of love at all, but only a kind of test.

With the same middle finger she later touched the gelatinous top of a goldfish swimming in a little glass bowl at school. She touched the raised mole on the back of her father's white neck. Shuddering, she touched horse turds in the back lane, and she touched her own urine springing on to the grass as she squatted behind the snowball bush by the fence. When she looked into her grandmother's mirror, now mounted on her own bedroom wall, she could hardly believe that she, Frances, had contravened so many natural laws.

The glass itself was bevelled all the way around, and she can remember that she took pleasure in lining up her round face so that the bevelled edge split it precisely in two. When she was fourteen she wrote in her diary, "Life is like looking into a bevelled mirror." The next day she crossed it out and, peering into the mirror, stuck out her tongue and made a face. All her life she'd had this weakness for preciosity, but mainly she'd managed to keep it in check.

She is a lithe and toothy woman with strong, thick, dark-brown hair, now starting to grey. She can be charming. "Frances can charm the bees out of the hive," said a friend of hers, a man she briefly thought she loved. Next year she'll be forty-five – terrible! – but at least she's kept her figure. A western sway to her voice is what people chiefly remember about her, just as they remember other people for their chins or noses. This voice sometimes makes her appear inquisitive, but, in fact, she generally hangs back and leaves it to others to begin a conversation.

Once, a woman got into an elevator with her and said, "Will you forgive me if I speak my mind. This morning I came within an inch of taking my life. There was no real reason, only everything had got suddenly so dull. But I'm all right now. In fact, I'm going straight to a restaurant and treat myself to a plate of french fries. Just fries, not even a sandwich to go with them. I was never allowed to have french fries when I was a little girl, but the time comes when a person should do what she wants to do."

The subject of childhood interests Frances, especially its prohibitions, so illogical and various, and its random doors and windows which appear solidly shut, but can, in fact, be opened easily with a touch or a password or a minute of devout resolution. It helps to be sly, also to be quick. There was a time when she worried that fate had pencilled her in as "debilitated by guilt", but mostly she takes guilt for what it is, a kind of lover who can be shrugged off or greeted at the gate. She looks at her two daughters and wonders if they'll look back resentfully, recalling only easy freedoms and an absence of terror – in other words, meagreness – and envy her for her own stern beginnings. It turned out to have been money in the bank, all the various shames and sweats of growing up. It was instructive; it kept things interesting; she still shivers, remembering how exquisitely sad she was as a child.

"It's only natural for children to be sad," says her husband, Theo, who, if he has a fault, is given to reductive statements. "Children are unhappy because they are inarticulate and hence lonely."

Frances can't remember being lonely, but telling this to Theo is like blowing into a hurricane. She was spoiled – a lovely word, she thinks – and adored by her parents, her plump, white-faced father and her skinny, sweet-tempered mother. Their love was immense and enveloping like a fall of snow. In the evenings, winter evenings, she sat between the two of them on a blue nubby sofa, listening to the varnished radio and taking sips from their cups of tea from time to time or sucking on a spoonful of sugar. The three of them sat enthralled through "Henry Aldrich" and "Fibber Magee and Molly", and when Frances laughed they looked at her and laughed too. Frances has no doubt that those spoonfuls of sugar and the roar of Fibber Magee's closet and her parents" soft looks were taken in and preserved so that she, years later, boiling an egg or making love or digging the garden, is sometimes struck by a blow of sweetness that seems to come out of nowhere.

The little brown house where she grew up sat in the middle of a block crowded with other such houses. In front of each lay a tiny lawn and a flower bed edged with stones. Rows of civic trees failed to flourish, but did not die either. True, there was terror in the back lane where the big boys played with sticks and jackknives, but the street was occupied mainly by quiet, hard-working families, and in the summertime hopscotch could be played in the street, there was so little traffic.

Frances's father spent his days "at the office". Her mother stayed at home, wore bib aprons, made jam and pickles and baked custard, and every morning before school brushed and braided Frances's hair. Frances can remember, or thinks she can remember, that one morning her mother walked as far as the corner with her and said, "I don't know why, but I'm so full of happiness today I can hardly bear it." The sun came fretting through the branches of a scrubby elm at that minute and splashed across her mother's face, making her look like someone in a painting or like one of the mothers in her school reader.

Learning to read was like falling into a mystery deeper than the mystery of airwaves or the halo around the head of the baby Jesus. Deliberately she made herself stumble and falter over the words in her first books, trying to hold back the rush of revelation. She saw other children being matter-of-fact and methodical, puzzling over vowels and consonants and sounding out words as though they were dimes and nickels that had to be extracted from the slot of a bank. She felt suffused with light and often skipped or hopped or ran wildly to keep herself from flying apart.

Her delirium, her failure to ingest books calmly, made her suspect there was something wrong with her or else with the world, yet she deeply distrusted the school librarian who insisted that a book could be a person's best friend. (Those subject to preciosity instantly spot others with the same affliction.) This librarian, Miss Mayes, visited all the classes. She was tall and soldierly with a high, light voice. "Boys and girls," she cried, bringing large red hands together, "a good book will never let you down." She went on; books could take you on magic journeys; books could teach you where the rain came from or how things used to be in the olden days. A person who truly loved books need never feel alone.

But, she continued, holding up a finger, there are people who do shameful things to books. They pull them from the shelves by their spines. They turn down the corners of pages; they leave them on screened porches where the rain and other elements can warp their covers; and they use curious and inappropriate objects as bookmarks.

From a petit-point bag she drew a list of objects that had been wrongly, criminally inserted between fresh clean pages: a blue-jay feather, an oak leaf, a matchbook cover, a piece of coloured chalk and, on one occasion – "on one occasion, boys and girls" – a *strip of bacon*.

A strip of bacon. In Frances's mind the strip of bacon was uncooked, cold and fatty with a pathetic streaking of lean. Its oil would press into the paper, a porky abomination, and its ends would flop out obscenely. The thought was thrilling: someone, someone who lived in the same school district, had had the audacity, the imagination, to mark the pages of a book with a strip of bacon. The existence of this person and his outrageous act penetrated the fever that had come over her since she'd learned to read, and she began to look around again and see what the world had to offer.

Next door lived Mr and Mrs Shaw, and upstairs, fast asleep, lived Louise Shaw, aged eighteen. She had been asleep for ten years. A boy across the street named Jackie McConnell told Frances that it was the sleeping sickness, that Louise Shaw had been bitten by the sleeping sickness bug, but Frances's mother said no, it was the coma. One day Mrs Shaw, smelling of chlorine bleach and wearing a flower-strewn housedress, stopped Frances on the sidewalk, held the back of her hand to the side of Frances's face and said, "Louise was just your age when we lost her. She was forever runningor skipping rope or throwing a ball up against the side of the garage. I used to say to her, don't make such a ruckus, you'll drive me crazy. I used to yell all the time at her, she was so full of beans and such a chatterbox." After that Frances felt herself under an obligation to Mrs Shaw, and whenever she saw her she made her body speed up and whirl on the grass or do cartwheels.

A little later she learned to negotiate the back lane. There, between board fences, garbage cans, garage doors and stands of tough weeds, she became newly nimble and strong. She learned to swear – damn, hell and dirty bastard – and played piggy-move-up and spud and got herself roughly kissed a number of times, and then something else happened: one of the neighbours put up a basketball hoop. For a year, maybe two – Frances doesn't trust her memory when it comes to time – she was obsessed with doing free throws. She became known as the queen of free throws; she acquired status, even with the big boys, able to sink ten out of ten baskets, but never, to her sorrow, twenty out of twenty. She threw free throws in the morning before school, at lunchtime, and in the evening until it got dark. Nothing made her happier than when the ball dropped silently through the ring without touching it or banking on the board. At night she dreamed of these silky baskets, the rush of air and the sinuous movement of the net, then the ball striking the pavement and returning to her hands. ("Sounds a bit Freudian to me," her husband, Theo, said when she tried to describe for him her time of free-throw madness, proving once again how far apart the two of them were in some things.) One morning she was up especially early. There was no one about. The milkman hadn't come yet, and there was dew shining on the tarry joints of the pavement. Holding the ball in her hands was like holding on to a face, it was so dearly familiar with its smell of leather and its seams and laces. That morning she threw twenty-seven perfect free throws before missing. Each time the ball went through the hoop she felt an additional oval of surprise grow round her body. She had springs inside her, in her arms and in the insteps of her feet. What stopped her finally was her mother calling her name, demanding to know what she was doing outside so early. "Nothing," Frances said, and knew for the first time the incalculable reward of self-possession.

There was a girl in her sewing class named Pat Leonard. She was older than the other girls, had a rough pitted face and a brain pocked with grotesqueries. "Imagine," she said to Frances, "sliding down a banister and suddenly it turns into a razor blade." When she trimmed the seams of the skirt she was making and accidentally cut through the fabric, she laughed out loud. To amuse the other girls she sewed the skin of her fingers together. She told a joke, a long story about a pickle factory that was really about eating excrement. In her purse was a packet of cigarettes. She had a boyfriend who went to the technical school, and several times she'd reached inside his pants and squeezed his thing until it went off like a squirt gun. She'd flunked math twice. She could hardly read. One day she wasn't there, and the sewing teacher said she'd been expelled. Frances felt as though she'd lost her best friend, even though she wouldn't have been seen dead walking down the hall with Pat Leonard. Melodramatic tears swam into her eyes, and then real tears that wouldn't stop until the teacher brought her a glass of water and offered to phone her mother.

Another time, she was walking home from a friend's in the early evening. She passed by a little house not far from her own. The windows were open and, floating on the summer air, came the sound of people speaking in a foreign language. There seemed to be a great number of them, and the conversation was very rapid and excited. They might have been quarrelling or telling old stories; Frances had no idea which. It could have been French or Russian or Portuguese they spoke. The words ran together and made queer little dashes and runs and choking sounds. Frances imagined immense, wide-branching grammars and steep, stone streets rising out of other centuries. She felt as though she'd been struck by a bolt of good fortune, and all because the world was bigger than she'd been led to believe.

At university, where she studied languages, she earned pocket money by working in the library. She and a girl named Ursula were entrusted with the key, and it was their job to open the library on Saturday mornings. During the minute or two before anyone else came, the two of them galloped at top speed through the reference room, the periodical room, the reading room, up and down the rows of stacks, filling that stilled air with what could only be called primal screams. Why this should have given Frances such exquisite pleasure she couldn't have said, since she was in rebellion against nothing she knew of. By the time the first students arrived, she and Ursula would be standing behind the main desk, date stamp in hand, sweet as dimity.

One Saturday, the first person who came was a bushy-headed, serious-minded zoology student named Theodore, called Theo by his friends. He gave Frances a funny look, then in a cracked, raspy voice asked her to come with him later and have a cup of coffee. A year later he asked her to marry him. He had a mind unblown by self-regard and lived, it seemed to Frances, in a nursery world of goodness and badness with not much room to move in between.

It's been mainly a happy marriage. Between the two of them, they've invented hundreds of complex ways of enslaving each other, some of them amazingly tender. Like other married people, they've learned to read each other's minds. Once Theo said to Frances as they drove around and around, utterly lost in a vast treeless suburb, "In every one of these houses there's been a declaration of love," and this was exactly the thought Frances had been thinking.

She has been faithful. To her surprise, to everyone's surprise, she turned out to have an aptitude for monogamy. Nevertheless, many of the scenes that have come into her life have involved men. Once she was walking down a very ordinary French street on a hot day. A man, bare-chested, drinking Perrier at a café table, sang out, "*Bonjour.*" Not "*bonjour, Madame*" or "*bonjour, Mademoiselle*" just "*bonjour.*" Cheeky. She was wearing white pants, a red blouse, a straw hat and sunglasses. "*Bonjour,*" she sang back and gave a sassy little kick, which became the start of a kind of dance. The man at the table clapped his hands over his head to keep time as she went dancing by.

Once she went to the British Museum to finish a piece of research. There was a bomb alert just as she entered, and everyone's shopping bags and briefcases were confiscated and searched. It happened that Frances had just bought a teddy bear for the child of a friend she was going to visit later in the day. The guard took it, shook it till its eyes rolled, and then carried it away to be X-rayed. Later he brought it to Frances, who was sitting at a table examining a beautiful old manuscript. As he handed her the bear, he kissed the air above its fuzzy head, and Frances felt her mouth go into the shape of a kiss, too, a kiss she intended to be an expression of her innocence, only that. He winked. She winked back. He leaned over and whispered into her ear a suggestion that was hideously, comically, obscene. She pretended not to hear, and a few minutes later she left, hurrying down the street full of cheerful shame, her work unfinished.

These are just some of the scenes in Frances's life. She thinks of them as scenes because they're much too fragmentary to be stories and far too immediate to be memories. They seem to bloom out of nothing, out of the thin, uncoloured air of defeats and pleasures. A curtain opens, a light appears, there are voices or music or sometimes a wide transparent stream of silence. Only rarely do they point to anything but themselves. They're difficult to talk about. They're useless, attached to nothing, can't be traded in or shaped into instruments to prise open the meaning of the universe.

There are people who think such scenes are ornaments suspended from lives that are otherwise busy and useful. Frances knows perfectly well that they are what a life is made of, one fitting against the next like English paving stones.

Or sometimes she thinks of them as little keys on a chain, keys that open nothing, but simply exist for the beauty of their toothed edges and the way they chime in her pocket.

Other times she is reminded of the Easter eggs her mother used to bring out every year. These were real hens' eggs with a hole poked in the top and bottom and the contents blown out. The day before Easter, Frances and her mother always sat down at the kitchen table with paint brushes, a glass of water and a box of watercolours. They would decorate half-a-dozen eggs, maybe more, but only the best were saved from year to year. These were taken from a cupboard just before Easter, removed from their shoebox, and carefully arranged, always on the same little pewter cake stand. The eggs had to be handled gently, especially the older ones.

Frances, when she was young, liked to pick up each one in turn and examine it minutely. She had a way of concentrating her thoughts and shutting everything else out, thinking only of this one little thing, this little egg that was round like the world, beautiful in colour and satin to the touch, and that fit into the hollow of her hand as though it were made for that very purpose.

Miles City, Montana

ALICE MUNRO

My father came across the field carrying the body of the boy who
had been drowned. There were several men together, returning
from the search, but he was the one carrying the body. The men
were muddy and exhausted, and walked with their heads down, as
if they were ashamed. Even the dogs were dispirited, dripping from
the cold river. When they all set out, hours before, the dogs were
nervy and yelping, the men tense and determined, and there was a
constrained, unspeakable excitement about the whole scene. It was
understood that they might find something horrible.

The boy's name was Steve Gauley. He was eight years old. His
hair and clothes were mud-coloured now and carried some bits of
dead leaves, twigs, and grass. He was like a heap of refuse that had
been left out all winter. His face was turned in to my father's chest,
but I could see a nostril, an ear, plugged up with greenish mud.

I don't think so. I don't think I really saw all this. Perhaps I saw
my father carrying him, and the other men following along, and the
dogs, but I would not have been allowed to get close enough to see
something like mud in his nostril. I must have heard someone
talking about that and imagined that I saw it. I see his face unaltered
except for the mud – Steve Gauley's familiar, sharp-honed, sneaky-
looking face – and it wouldn't have been like that; it would have
been bloated and changed and perhaps muddied all over after so
many hours in the water.

To have to bring back such news, such evidence, to a waiting
family, particularly a mother, would have made searchers move
heavily, but what was happening here was worse. It seemed a worse
shame (to hear people talk) that there was no mother, no woman at
all – no grandmother or aunt, or even a sister – to receive Steve
Gauley and give him his due of grief. His father was a hired man, a
drinker but not a drunk, an erratic man without being entertaining,
not friendly but not exactly a troublemaker. His fatherhood seemed
accidental, and the fact that the child had been left with him when

the mother went away, and that they continued living together, seemed accidental. They lived in a steep-roofed, grey-shingled hillbilly sort of house and that was just a bit better than a shack – the father fixed the roof and put supports under the porch, just enough and just in time – and their life was held together in a similar manner; that is, just well enough to keep the Children's Aid at bay. They didn't eat meals together or cook for each other, but there was food. Sometimes the father would give Steve money to buy food at the store, and Steve was seen to buy quite sensible things, such as pancake mix and macaroni dinner.

I had known Steve Gauley fairly well. I had not liked him more often than I had liked him. He was two years older than I was. He would hang around our place on Saturdays, scornful of whatever I was doing but unable to leave me alone. I couldn't be on the swing without him wanting to try it, and if I wouldn't give it up he came and pushed me so that I went crooked. He teased the dog. He got me into trouble – deliberately and maliciously, it seemed to me afterward – by daring me to do things I wouldn't have thought of on my own: digging up the potatoes to see how big they were when they were still only the size of marbles, and pushing over the stacked firewood to make a pile we could jump off. At school, we never spoke to each other. He was solitary, though not tormented. But on Saturday mornings, when I saw his thin, self-possessed figure sliding through the cedar hedge, I knew I was in for something and he would decide what. Sometimes it was all right. We pretended we were cowboys who had come to tame wild horses. We played in the pasture by the river, not far from the place where Steve drowned. We were horses and riders both, screaming and neighing and bucking and waving whips of tree branches beside a little nameless river that flows into the Saugeen in southern Ontario.

The funeral was held in our house. There was not enough room at Steve's father's place for the large crowd that was expected because of the circumstances. I have a memory of the crowded room but no picture of Steve in his coffin, or of the minister, or of wreaths of flowers. I remember that I was holding one flower, a white narcissus, which must have come from a pot somebody forced indoors, because it was too early for even the forsythia bush or the trilliums and marsh marigolds in the woods. I stood in a row of children, each of us holding a narcissus. We sang a childen's hymn, which somebody played on our piano: "When He Cometh, When He Cometh, to Make Up His Jewels". I was wearing white ribbed stockings, which were disgustingly itchy, and wrinkled at the knees and ankles. The feeling of these stockings on my legs is mixed up with another feeling in my memory. It is hard to describe. It had to do with my parents. Adults in general but my parents in particular. My father, who had carried Steve's body from the river, and my mother, who must have done most of the arranging of this funeral. My father in his dark-blue suit and my mother in her brown velvet dress with the creamy satin collar. They stood side by side opening and closing their mouths for the hymn, and I stood removed from them, in the row of children, watching. I felt a furious and sickening disgust. Children sometimes have an access of disgust concerning adults. The size, the lumpy shapes, the bloated power. The breath, the coarseness, the hairiness, the horrid secretions. But this was more. And the accompanying anger had nothing sharp and self-respecting about it. There was no release, as when I would finally bend and pick up a stone and throw it at Steve Gauley. It could not be understood or expressed, though it died down after a while into a heaviness, then just a taste, an occasional taste − a thin, familiar misgiving.

*

Twenty years or so later, in 1961, my husband, Andrew, and I got a brand-new car, our first − that is, our first brand-new. It was a Morris Oxford, oyster-coloured (the dealer had some fancier name for the colour) − a big small car, with plenty of room for us and our two children. Cynthia was six and Meg three and a half.

Andrew took a picture of me standing beside the car. I was wearing white pants, a black turtleneck, and sunglasses. I lounged against the car door, canting my hips to make myself look slim.

"Wonderful," Andrew said. "Great. You look like Jackie Kennedy." All over this continent probably, dark-haired, reasonably slender young women were told, when they were stylishly dressed or getting their pictures taken, that they looked like Jackie Kennedy.

Andrew took a lot of pictures of me, and of the children, our house, our garden, our excursions and possessions. He got copies made, labelled them carefully, and sent them back to his mother and his aunt and uncle in Ontario. He got copies for me to send to my father, who also lived in Ontario, and I did so, but less regularly than he sent his. When he saw pictures he thought I had already sent lying around the house, Andrew was perplexed and annoyed. He liked to have this record go forth.

That summer, we were presenting ourselves, not pictures. We were driving back from Vancouver, where we lived, to Ontario, which we still called "home", in our new car. Five days to get there, ten days there, five days back. For the first time, Andrew had three weeks" holiday. He worked in the legal department at B C Hydro.

On a Saturday morning, we loaded suitcases, two thermos bottles – one filled with coffee and one with lemonade – some fruit and sandwiches, picture books and colouring books, crayons, drawing pads, insect repellent, sweaters (in case it got cold in the mountains), and our two children into the car. Andrew locked the house, and Cynthia said ceremoniously, "Goodbye, house."

Meg said, "Goodbye, house." Then she said, "Where will we live now?"

"It's not goodbye forever," said Cynthia. "We're coming back. Mother! Meg thought we weren't ever coming back!"

"I did not," said Meg, kicking the back of my seat.

Andrew and I put on our sunglasses, and we drove away, over the Lions Gate Bridge and through the main part of Vancouver. We shed our house, the neighbourhood, the city, and – at the crossing point between Washington and British Columbia – our country. We were driving east across the United States, taking the most northerly route, and would cross into Canada again at Sarnia, Ontario. I don't know if we chose this route because the Trans-Canada Highway was not completely finished at the time or if we just wanted the feeling of driving through a foreign, a very slightly foreign, country – that extra bit of interest and adventure.

We were both in high spirits. Andrew congratulated the car several times. He said he felt so much better driving it than our old car, a 1951 Austin that slowed down dismally on the hills and had a fussy-old-lady image. So Andrew said now.

"What kind of image does this one have?" said Cynthia. She

listened to us carefully and liked to try out new words such as "image". Usually she got them right.

"Lively," I said. "Slightly sporty. It's not show-off."

"It's sensible, but it has class," Andrew said. "Like my image."

Cynthia thought that over and said with cautious pride, "That means like you think you want to be, Daddy?"

As for me, I was happy because of the shedding. I loved taking off. In my own house, I seemed to be more often looking for a place to hide – sometimes from the children but more often from the jobs to be done and the phone ringing and the sociability of the neighbourhood. I wanted to hide so that I could get busy at my real work, which was a sort of wooing of distant parts of myself. I lived in a state of siege, always losing just what I wanted to hold on to. But on trips there was no difficulty. I could be talking to Andrew, talking to the children and looking at whatever they wanted me to look at – a pig on a sign, a pony in a field, a Volkswagen on a revolving stand – and pouring lemonade into plastic cups, and all the time those bits and pieces would be flying together inside me. The essential composition would be achieved. This made me hopeful and light-hearted. It was being a watcher that did it. A watcher, not a keeper.

We turned east at Everett and climbed into the Cascades. I showed Cynthia our route on the map. First I showed her the map of the whole United States, which showed also the bottom part of Canada. Then I turned to the separate maps of each of the states we were going to pass through. Washington, Idaho, Montana, North Dakota, Minnesota, Wisconsin. I showed her the dotted line across Lake Michigan, which was the route of the ferry we would take. Then we would drive across Michigan to the bridge that linked the United States and Canada at Sarnia, Ontario. Home.

Meg wanted to see, too.

"You won't understand," said Cynthia. But she took the road atlas into the back seat.

"Sit back," she said to Meg. "Sit still. I'll show you."

I could hear her tracing the route for Meg, very accurately, just as I had done it for her. She looked up all the states" maps, knowing how to find them in alphabetical order.

"You know what that line is?" she said. "It's the road. That line is the road we're driving on. We're going right along this line."

Meg did not say anything.

"Mother, show me where we are right this minute," said Cynthia.

I took the atlas and pointed out the road through the mountains, and she took it back and showed it to Meg. "See where the road is all wiggly?" she said. "It's wiggly because there are so many turns in it. The wiggles are the turns." She flipped some pages and waited a moment. "Now," she said, "show me where we are." Then she called to me, "Mother, she understands! She pointed to it! Meg understands maps!"

It seems to me now that we invented characters for our children. We had them firmly set to play their parts. Cynthia was bright and diligent, sensitive, courteous, watchful. Sometimes we teased her for being too conscientious, too eager to be what we in fact depended on her to be. Any reproach or failure, any rebuff, went terribly deep with her. She was fair-haired, fair-skinned, easily showing the effects of the sun, raw winds, pride, or humiliation. Meg was more solidly built, more reticent – not rebellious but stubborn sometimes, mysterious. Her silences seemed to us to show her strength of character, and her negatives were taken as signs of imperturbable independence. Her hair was brown, and we cut it in straight bangs. Her eyes were a light hazel, clear and dazzling.

We were entirely pleased with these characters, enjoying the contradictions as well as the confirmations of them. We disliked the heavy, the uninventive, approach to being parents. I had a dread of turning into a certain kind of mother – the kind whose body sagged, who moved in woolly-smelling, milky-smelling fog, solemn with trivial burdens. I believed that all the attention these mothers paid, their need to be burdened, was the cause of colic, bed-wetting, asthma. I favoured another approach – the mock desperation, the inflated irony of the professional mothers who wrote for magazines. In those magazine pieces, the children were splendidly self-willed, hard-edged, perverse, indomitable. So were the mothers, through their wit, indomitable. The real-life mothers I warmed to were the sort who would phone up and say, "Is my embryo Hitler by any chance over at your house?" They cackled clear above the milky fog.

We saw a dead deer strapped across the front of a pickup truck.

"Somebody shot it," Cynthia said. "Hunters shoot the deer."

"It's not hunting season yet," Andrew said. "They may have hit it on the road. See the sign for deer crossing?"

"I would cry if we hit one," Cynthia said sternly.

I had made peanut-butter-and-marmalade sandwiches for the children and salmon-and-mayonnaise for us. But I had not put any lettuce in, and Andrew was disappointed.

"I didn't have any," I said.

"Couldn't you have got some?"

"I'd have had to buy a whole head of lettuce just to get enough for sandwiches, and I decided it wasn't worth it."

This was a lie. I had forgotten.

"They're a lot better with lettuce."

"I didn't think it made that much difference." After a silence, I said, "Don't be mad."

"I'm not mad. I like lettuce on sandwiches."

"I just didn't think it mattered that much."

"How would it be if I didn't bother to fill up the gas tank?"

"That's not the same thing."

"Sing a song," said Cynthia. She started to sing:

> Five little ducks went out one day,
> Over the hills and far away.
> One little duck went
> "Quack-quack-quack."
> Four little ducks came swimming back.

Andrew squeezed my hand and said, "Let's not fight."

"You're right. I should have got lettuce."

"It doesn't matter that much."

I wished that I could get my feelings about Andrew to come together into a serviceable and dependable feeling. I had even tried writing two lists, one of things I liked about him, one of things I disliked – in the cauldron of intimate life, things I loved and things I hated – as if I hoped by this to prove something, to come to a conclusion one way or the other. But I gave it up when I saw that all it proved was what I already knew – that I had violent contradictions. Sometimes the very sound of his footsteps seemed to me tyrannical, the set of his mouth smug and mean, his hard, straight body a barrier interposed – quite consciously, even dutifully, and with a nasty pleasure in its masculine authority – between me and whatever joy or lightness I could get in life. Then, with not much warning, he became my good friend and most essential companion. I felt the sweetness of his light bones and serious ideas, the vulnerability of his love, which I imagined to be much purer and more straightforward than my own. I could be greatly moved by an inflexibility, a harsh propriety, that at other times I scorned. I would think how humble he was, really, taking on such a ready-made role of husband, father, breadwinner, and how I myself in comparison was really a secret monster of egotism. Not so secret, either – not from him.

At the bottom of our fights, we served up what we thought were the ugliest truths. "I know there is something basically selfish and basically untrustworthy about you," Andrew once said. "I've always known it. I also know that that is why I fell in love with you."

"Yes," I said, feeling sorrowful but complacent.

"I know that I'd be better off without you."

"Yes. You would."

"You'd be happier without me."

"Yes."

And finally – finally – racked and purged, we clasped hands and laughed, laughed at those two benighted people, ourselves. Their grudges, their grievances, their self-justification. We leap-frogged over them. We declared them liars. We would have wine with dinner, or decide to give a party.

I haven't seen Andrew for years, don't know if he is still thin, has gone completely grey, insists on lettuce, tells the truth, or is hearty and disappointed.

We stayed the night in Wenatchee, Washington, where it hadn't rained for weeks. We ate dinner in a restaurant built about a tree – not a sapling in a tub but a tall, sturdy cottonwood. In the early-morning light, we climbed out of the irrigated valley, up dry, rocky, very steep hillsides that would seem to lead to more hills, and there on the top was a wide plateau, cut by the great Spokane and Columbia rivers. Grainland and grassland, mile after mile. There were straight roads here, and little farming towns with grain elevators. In fact, there was a sign announcing that this county we

were going through, Douglas County, had the second-highest
wheat yield of any county in the United States. The towns had
planted shade trees. At least, I thought they had been planted,
because there were no such big trees in the countryside.

All this was marvellously welcome to me. "Why do I love it so
much?" I said to Andrew. "Is it because it isn't scenery?"

"It reminds you of home," said Andrew. "A bout of severe nostalgia." But he said this kindly.

When we said "home" and meant Ontario, we had very different
places in mind. My home was a turkey farm, where my father lived
as a widower, and though it was the same house my mother had
lived in, had papered, painted, cleaned, furnished, it showed the
effects now of neglect and of some wild sociability. A life went on in
it that my mother could not have predicted or condoned. There were
parties for the turkey crew, the gutters and pluckers, and sometimes
one or two of the young men would be living there temporarily,
inviting their own friends and having their own impromptu parties.
This life, I thought, was better for my father than being lonely, and I
did not disapprove, had certainly no right to disapprove. Andrew
did not like to go there, naturally enough, because he was not the
sort who could sit around the kitchen table with the turkey crew,
telling jokes. They were intimidated by him and contemptuous of
him, and it seemed to me that my father, when they were around,
had to be on their side. And it wasn't only Andrew who had trouble.
I could manage those jokes, but it was an effort.

I wished for the days when I was little, before we had the turkeys.
We had cows, and sold the milk to the cheese factory. A turkey farm
is nothing like as pretty as a dairy farm or a sheep farm. You can see
that the turkeys are on a straight path to becoming frozen carcasses
and table meat. They don't have the pretence of a life of their own, a
browsing idyll, that cattle have, or pigs in the dappled orchard.
Turkey barns are long, efficient buildings – tin sheds. No beams or
hay or warm stables. Even the smell of guano seems thinner and
more offensive than the usual smell of stable manure. No hints there
of hay coils and rail fences and songbirds and the flowering hawthorn. The turkeys were all let out into one long field, which they
picked clean. They didn't look like great birds there but like fluttering laundry.

Once, shortly after my mother died, and after I was married – in fact, I was packing to join Andrew in Vancouver – I was at home alone for a couple of days with my father. There was a freakishly heavy rain all night. In the early light, we saw that the turkey field was flooded. At least, the low-lying parts of it were flooded – it was like a lake with many islands. The turkeys were huddled on these islands. Turkeys are very stupid. (My father would say, "You know a chicken? You know how stupid a chicken is? Well, a chicken is an Einstein compared with a turkey.") But they had managed to crowd to higher ground and avoid drowning. Now they might push each other off, suffocate each other, get cold and die. We couldn't wait for the water to go down. We went out in the old rowboat we had. I rowed and my father pulled the heavy, wet turkeys into the boat and we took them to the barn. It was still raining a little. The job was difficult and absurd and very uncomfortable. We were laughing. I was happy to be working with my father. I felt close to all hard, repetitive, appalling work, in which the body is finally worn out, the mind sunk (though sometimes the spirit can stay marvellously light), and I was homesick in advance for this life and this place. I thought that if Andrew could see me there in the rain, red-handed, muddy, trying to hold on to turkey legs and row the boat at the same time, he would only want to get me out of there and make me forget about it. The raw life angered him. My attachment to it angered him. I thought that I shouldn't have married him. But who else? One of the turkey crew?

And I didn't want to stay there. I might feel bad about leaving, but I would feel worse if somebody made me stay.

Andrew's mother lived in Toronto, in an apartment building looking out on Muir Park. When Andrew and his sister were both at home, his mother slept in the living room. Her husband, a doctor, had died when the children were still too young to go to school. She took a secretarial course and sold her house at Depression prices, moved to this apartment, managed to raise her children, with some help from relatives – her sister Caroline, her brother-in-law Roger. Andrew and his sister went to private schools and to camp in the summer.

"I suppose that was courtesy of the Fresh Air fund?" I said once, scornful of his claim that he had been poor. To my mind, Andrew's

urban life had been sheltered and fussy. His mother came home
with a headache from working all day in the noise, the harsh light of
the department-store office, but it did not occur to me that hers was
a hard or admirable life. I don't think she herself believed that she
was admirable – only unlucky. She worried about her work in the
office, her clothes, her cooking, her children. She worried most of all
about what Roger and Caroline would think.

Caroline and Roger lived on the east side of the park, in a handsome stone house. Roger was a tall man with a bald, freckled head, a
fat, firm stomach. Some operation on his throat had deprived him of
his voice – he spoke in a rough whisper. But everybody paid attention. At dinner once in the stone house – where all the dining-room
furniture was enormous, darkly glowing, palatial – I asked him a
question. I think it had to do with Whittaker Chambers, whose story
was then appearing in the *Saturday Evening Post*. The question was
mild in tone, but he guessed its subversive intent and took to calling
me Mrs Gromyko, referring to what he alleged to be my "sympathies". Perhaps he really craved an adversary, and could not find one.
At that dinner, I saw Andrew's hand tremble as he lit his mother's
cigarette. His Uncle Roger had paid for Andrew's education, and
was on the board of directors of several companies.

"He is just an opinionated old man," Andrew said to me later.
"What is the point of arguing with him?"

Before we left Vancouver, Andrew's mother had written, "Roger
seems quite intrigued by the idea of your buying a small car!" Her
exclamation mark showed apprehension. At that time, particularly
in Ontario, the choice of a small European car over a large American
car could be seen as some sort of declaration – a declaration of
tendencies Roger had been sniffing after all along.

"It isn't that small a car," said Andrew huffily.

"That's not the point," I said. "The point is, it isn't any of his
business!"

We spent the second night in Missoula. We had been told in
Spokane, at a gas station, that there was a lot of repair work going
on along Highway 2, and that we were in for a very hot, dusty drive,
with long waits, so we turned on to the interstate and drove through
Coeur d'Alene and Kellogg into Montana. After Missoula, we

turned south toward Butte, but detoured to see Helena, the state capital. In the car, we played Who Am I?

Cynthia was somebody dead, and an American, and a girl. Possibly a lady. She was not in a story. She had not been seen on television. Cynthia had not read about her in a book. She was not anybody who had come to the kindergarten, or a relative of any of Cynthia's friends.

"Is she human?" said Andrew, with a sudden shrewdness.

"No! That's what you forgot to ask!"

"An animal," I said reflectively.

"Is that a question? Sixteen questions!"

"No, it is not a question. I'm thinking. A dead animal."

"It's the deer," said Meg, who hadn't been playing.

"That's not fair!" said Cynthia. "She's not playing!"

"What deer?" said Andrew.

I said, "Yesterday."

"The day before," said Cynthia. "Meg wasn't playing. Nobody got it."

"The deer on the truck," said Andrew.

"It was a lady deer, because it didn't have antlers, and it was an American and it was dead," Cynthia said.

Andrew said, "I think it's kind of morbid, being a dead deer."

"I got it," said Meg.

Cynthia said, "I think I know what morbid is. It's depressing."

Helena, an old silver-mining town, looked forlorn to us even in the morning sunlight. Then Bozeman and Billings, not forlorn in the slightest – energetic, strung-out towns, with miles of blinding tinsel fluttering over used-car lots. We got too tired and hot even to play Who Am I? These busy, prosaic cities reminded me of similar places in Ontario, and I thought about what was really waiting there – the great tombstone furniture of Roger and Caroline's dining room, the dinners for which I must iron the children's dresses and warn them about forks, and then the other table a hundred miles away, the jokes of my father's crew. The pleasures I had been thinking of – looking at the countryside or drinking a Coke in an old-fashioned drugstore with fans and a high, pressed-tin ceiling – would have to be snatched in between.

"Meg's asleep," Cynthia said. "She's so hot. She makes me hot in the same seat with her."

"I hope she isn't feverish," I said, not turning around.

What are we doing this for, I thought, and the answer came – to show off. To give Andrew's mother and my father the pleasure of seeing their grandchildren. That was our duty. But beyond that we wanted to show them something. What strenuous children we were, Andrew and I, what relentless seekers of approbation. It was as if at some point we had received an unforgettable, indigestible message – that we were far from satisfactory, and that the most commonplace success in life was probably beyond us. Roger dealt out such messages, of course – that was his style – but Andrew's mother, my own mother and father couldn't have meant to do so. All they meant to tell us was "Watch out. Get along." My father, when I was in high school, teased me that I was getting to think I was so smart I would never find a boyfriend. He would have forgotten that in a week. I never forgot it. Andrew and I didn't forget things. We took umbrage.

"I wish there was a beach," said Cynthia.

"There probably is one," Andrew said. "Right around the next curve."

"There isn't a curve," she said, sounding insulted.

"That's what I mean."

"I wish there was some more lemonade."

"I will just wave my magic wand and produce some," I said. "Okay, Cynthia? Would you rather have grape juice? Will I do a beach while I'm at it?"

She was silent, and soon I felt repentant. "Maybe in the next town there might be a pool," I said. I looked at the map. "In Miles City. Anyway, there'll be something cool to drink."

"How far is it?" Andrew said.

"Not so far," I said. "Thirty miles, about."

"In Miles City," said Cynthia, in the tones of an incantation, "there is a beautiful blue swimming pool for children, and a park with lovely trees."

Andrew said to me, "You could have started something."

But there was a pool. There was a park, too, though not quite the oasis of Cynthia's fantasy. Prairie trees with thin leaves – cotton-woods and poplars – worn grass, and a high wire fence around the pool. Within this fence, a wall, not yet completed, of cement blocks. There were no shouts or splashes; over the entrance I saw a sign that said the pool was closed every day from noon until two o'clock. It was then twenty-five after twelve.

Nevertheless I called out, "Is anybody there?" I thought somebody must be around, because there was a small truck parked near the entrance. On the side of the truck were these words: "We have Brains, to fix your Drains. (We have Roto-Rooter too.)"

A girl came out, wearing a red lifeguard's shirt over her bathing suit. "Sorry, we're closed."

"We were just driving through," I said.

"We close every day from twelve until two. It's on the sign." She was eating a sandwich.

"I saw the sign," I said. "But this is the first water we've seen for so long, and the children are awfully hot, and I wondered if they could just dip in and out – just five minutes. We'd watch them."

A boy came into sight behind her. He was wearing jeans and a T-shirt with the words "Roto-Rooter" on it.

I was going to say that we were driving from British Columbia to Ontario, but I remembered that Canadian place names usually meant nothing to Americans. "We're driving right across the country," I said. "We haven't time to wait for the pool to open. We were just hoping the children could get cooled off."

Cynthia came running up barefoot behind me. "Mother, Mother, where is my bathing suit?" Then she stopped, sensing the serious adult negotiations. Meg was climbing out of the car – just wakened, and her top pulled up and her shorts pulled down, showing her pink stomach.

"Is it just those two?" the girl said.

"Just the two. We'll watch them."

"I can't let any adults in. If it's just the two, I guess I could watch them. I'm having my lunch." She said to Cynthia, "Do you want to come in the pool?"

"Yes, please," said Cynthia firmly.

Meg looked at the ground.

"Just a short time, because the pool is really closed," I said. "We appreciate this very much," I said to the girl.

"Well, I can eat my lunch out there, if it's just the two of them."

She looked toward the car as if she thought I might try to spring some more children on her.

When I found Cynthia's bathing suit, she took it into the changing room. She would not permit anybody, even Meg, to see her naked. I changed Meg, who stood on the front seat of the car. She had a pink cotton bathing suit with straps that crossed and buttoned. There were ruffles across the bottom.

"She *is* hot," I said. "But I don't think she's feverish."

I loved helping Meg to dress or undress, because her body still had the solid unself-consciousness, the sweet indifference, something of the milky smell, of a baby's body. Cynthia's body had long ago been pared down, shaped and altered, into Cynthia. We all liked to hug Meg, press and nuzzle her. Sometimes she would scowl and beat us off, and this forthright independence, this ferocious bashfulness, simply made her more appealing, more apt to be tormented and tickled in the way of family love.

Andrew and I sat in the car with the windows open. I could hear a radio playing, and thought it must belong to the girl or her boyfriend. I was thirsty, and got out of the car to look for a concession stand, or perhaps a soft-drink machine, somewhere in the park. I was wearing shorts, and the backs of my legs were slick with sweat. I saw a drinking fountain at the other side of the park and was walking toward it in a roundabout way, keeping to the shade of the trees. No place became real till you got out of the car. Dazed with the heat, with the sun on the blistered houses, the pavement, the burned grass, I walked slowly. I paid attention to a squashed leaf, ground a Popsicle stick under the heel of my sandal, squinted at a trash can strapped to a tree. This is the way you look at the poorest details of the world resurfaced, after you've been driving for a long time – you feel their singleness and precise location and the forlorn coincidence of your being there to see them.

Where are the children?

I turned around and moved quickly, not quite running, to a part of the fence beyond which the cement wall was not completed. I could see some of the pool. I saw Cynthia, standing about waist-deep in the water, fluttering her hands on the surface and discreetly watching something at the end of the pool, which I could not see. I thought by her pose, her discretion, the look on her face, that she must be watching some byplay between the lifeguard and her boyfriend. I couldn't see Meg. But I thought she must be playing in the shallow water – both the shallow and deep ends of the pool were out of my sight.

"Cynthia!" I had to call twice before she knew where my voice was coming from. "Cynthia! Where's Meg?"

It always seems to me, when I recall this scene, that Cynthia turns very gracefully toward me, then turns all around in the water – making me think of a ballerina on point – and spreads her arms in a gesture of the stage. "Dis-ap-peared!"

Cynthia was naturally graceful, and she did take dancing lessons, so these movements may have been as I have described. She did say "Disappeared" after looking all around the pool, but the strangely artificial style of speech and gesture, the lack of urgency, is more likely my invention. The fear I felt instantly when I couldn't see Meg – even while I was telling myself she must be in the shallower water – must have made Cynthia's movements seem unbearably slow and inappropriate to me, and the tone in which she could say "Disappeared" before the implications struck her (or was she covering, at once, some ever-ready guilt?) was heard by me as quite exquisitely, monstrously self-possessed.

I cried out for Andrew, and the lifeguard came into view. She was pointing toward the deep end of the pool, saying, "What's that?"

There, just within my view, a cluster of pink ruffles appeared, a bouquet, beneath the surface of the water. Why would a lifeguard stop and point, why would she ask what that was, why didn't she just dive into the water and swim to it? She didn't swim; she ran all the way around the edge of the pool. But by that time Andrew was over the fence. So many things seemed not quite plausible – Cynthia's behaviour, then the lifeguard's – and now I had the impression that Andrew jumped with one bound over this fence, which seemed about seven feet high. He must have climbed it very quickly, getting a grip on the wire.

I could not jump or climb it, so I ran to the entrance, where there was a sort of lattice gate, locked. It was not very high, and I did pull myself over it. I ran through the cement corridors, through the disinfectant pool for your feet, and came out on the edge of the pool.

The drama was over.

Andrew had got to Meg first, and had pulled her out of the water. He just had to reach over and grab her, because she was swimming somehow, with her head underwater – she was moving toward the edge of the pool. He was carrying her now, and the lifeguard was trotting along behind. Cynthia had climbed out of the water and was running to meet them. The only person aloof from the situation was the boyfriend, who had stayed on the bench at the shallow end, drinking a milkshake. He smiled at me, and I thought that unfeeling of him, even though the danger was past. He may have meant it kindly. I noticed that he had not turned the radio off, just down.

Meg had not swallowed any water. She hadn't even scared herself. Her hair was plastered to her head and her eyes were wide open, golden with amazement.

"I was getting the comb," she said. "I didn't know it was deep."

Andrew said, "She was swimming! She was swimming by herself. I saw her bathing suit in the water and then I saw her swimming."

"She nearly drowned," Cynthia said. "Didn't she? Meg nearly drowned."

"I don't know how it could have happened," said the lifeguard. "One moment she was there, and the next she wasn't."

What had happened was that Meg had climbed out of the water at the shallow end and run along the edge of the pool toward the deep end. She saw a comb that somebody had dropped lying on the bottom. She crouched down and reached in to pick it up, quite deceived about the depth of the water. She went over the edge and slipped into the pool, making such a light splash that nobody heard – not the lifeguard, who was kissing her boyfriend, or Cynthia, who was watching them. That must have been the moment under the trees when I thought, Where are the children? It must have been the same moment. At that moment, Meg was slipping, surprised, into the treacherously clear blue water.

"It's okay," I said to the lifeguard, who was nearly crying. "She can move pretty fast." (Though that wasn't what we usually said about Meg at all. We said she thought everything over and took her time.)

"You swam, Meg," said Cynthia, in a congratulatory way. (She told us about the kissing later.)

"I didn't know it was deep," Meg said. "I didn't drown."

*

We had lunch at a take-out place, eating hamburgers and fries at a picnic table not far from the highway. In my excitement, I forgot to get Meg a plain hamburger, and had to scrape off the relish and mustard with plastic spoons, then wipe the meat with a paper napkin, before she would eat it. I took advantage of the trash can there to clean out the car. Then we resumed driving east, with the car windows open in front. Cynthia and Meg fell asleep in the back seat.

Andrew and I talked quietly about what had happened. Suppose I hadn't had the impulse just at that moment to check on the children? Suppose we had gone uptown to get drinks, as we had thought of doing? How had Andrew got over the fence? Did he jump or climb? (He couldn't remember.) How had he reached Meg so quickly? And think of the lifeguard not watching. And Cynthia, taken up with the kissing. Not seeing anything else. Not seeing Meg drop over the edge.

Disappeared.

But she swam. She held her breath and came up swimming.

What a chain of lucky links.

That was all we spoke about – luck. But I was compelled to picture the opposite. At this moment, we could have been filling out forms. Meg removed from us, Meg's body being prepared for shipment. To Vancouver – where we had never noticed such a thing as a graveyard – or to Ontario? The scribbled drawings she had made this morning would still be in the back seat of the car. How could this be borne all at once, how did people bear it? The plump, sweet shoulders and hands and feet, the fine brown hair, the rather satisfied, secretive expression – all exactly the same as when she had been alive. The most ordinary tragedy. A child drowned in a swimming pool at noon on a sunny day. Things tidied up quickly. The pool opens as usual at two o'clock. The lifeguard is a bit shaken up and gets the afternoon off. She drives away with her boyfriend in the Roto-Rooter truck. The body sealed away in some kind of shipping coffin. Sedatives, phone calls, arrangements. Such a sudden vacancy, a blind sinking and shifting. Waking up groggy from the pills, thinking for a moment it wasn't true. Thinking if only we hadn't stopped, if only we hadn't taken this route, if only they hadn't let us use the pool. Probably no one would ever have known about the comb.

There's something trashy about this kind of imagining, isn't there?

Something shameful. Laying your finger on the wire to get the safe shock, feeling a bit of what it's like, then pulling back. I believed that Andrew was more scrupulous than I about such things, and that at this moment he was really trying to think about something else.

When I stood apart from my parents at Steve Gauley's funeral and watched them, and had this new, unpleasant feeling about them, I thought that I was understanding something about them for the first time. It was a deadly serious thing. I was understanding that they were implicated. Their big, stiff, dressed-up bodies did not stand between me and sudden death, or any kind of death. They gave consent. So it seemed. They gave consent to the death of children and to my death not by anything they said or thought but by the very fact that they had made children – they had made me. They had made me, and for that reason my death – however grieved they were, however they carried on – would seem to them anything but impossible or unnatural. This was a fact, and even then I knew they were not to blame.

But I did blame them. I charged them with effrontery, hypocrisy. On Steve Gauley's behalf, and on behalf of all children, who knew that by rights they should have sprung up free, to live a new, superior kind of life, not to be caught in the snares of vanquished grown-ups, with their sex and funerals.

Steve Gauley drowned, people said, because he was next thing to an orphan and was let run free. If he had been warned enough and given chores to do and kept in check, he wouldn't have fallen from an untrustworthy tree branch into a spring pond, a full gravel pit near the river – he wouldn't have drowned. He was neglected, he was free, so he drowned. And his father took it as an accident, such as might happen to a dog. He didn't have a good suit for the funeral, and he didn't bow his head for the prayers. But he was the only grown-up that I let off the hook. He was the only one I didn't see giving consent. He couldn't prevent anything, but he wasn't implicated in anything, either – not like the others, saying the Lord's Prayer in their unnaturally weighted voices, oozing religion and dishonour.

At Glendive, not far from the North Dakota border, we had a choice – either to continue on the interstate or head north-east, toward

Williston, taking Route 16, then some secondary roads that would get us back to Highway 2.

We agreed that the interstate would be faster, and that it was important for us not to spend too much time – that is, money – on the road. Nevertheless we decided to cut back to Highway 2.

"I just like the idea of it better," I said.

Andrew said, "That's because it's what we planned to do in the beginning."

"We missed seeing Kalispell and Havre. And Wolf Point. I like the name."

"We'll see them on the way back."

Andrew's saying "on the way back" was a surprising pleasure to me. Of course, I had believed that we would be coming back, with our car and our lives and our family intact, having covered all that distance, having dealt somehow with those loyalties and problems, held ourselves up for inspection in such a foolhardy way. But it was a relief to hear him say it.

"What I can't get over," said Andrew, "is how you got the signal. It's got to be some kind of extra sense that mothers have."

Partly I wanted to believe that, to bask in my extra sense. Partly I wanted to warn him – to warn everybody – never to count on it.

"What I can't understand," I said, "is how you got over the fence."

"Neither can I."

So we went on, with the two in the back seat trusting us, because of no choice, and we ourselves trusting to be forgiven, in time, for everything that had first to be seen and condemned by those children: whatever was flippant, arbitrary, careless, callous – all our natural, and particular, mistakes.

L'envoi. The Train to Mariposa

STEPHEN LEACOCK

It leaves the city every day about five o'clock in the evening, the train for Mariposa.

Strange that you did not know of it, though you come from the little town – or did, long years ago.

Odd that you never knew, in all these years, that the train was there every afternoon puffing up steam in the city station, and that you might have boarded it any day and gone home. No, not "home" – of course you couldn't call it "home" now; "home" means that big red sandstone house of yours in the costlier part of the city. "Home" means, in a way, this Mausoleum Club where you sometimes talk with me of the times that you had as a boy in Mariposa.

But of course "home" would hardly be the word you would apply to the little town, unless perhaps, late at night, when you'd been sitting reading in a quiet corner somewhere such a book as the present one.

Naturally you don't know of the Mariposa train now. Years ago, when you first came to the city as a boy with your way to make, you knew of it well enough, only too well. The price of a ticket counted in those days, and though you knew of the train you couldn't take it, but sometimes from sheer homesickness you used to wander down to the station on a Friday afternoon after your work, and watch the Mariposa people getting on the train and wish that you could go.

Why, you knew that train at one time better, I suppose, than any other single thing in the city, and loved it too for the little town in the sunshine that it ran to.

Do you remember how when you first began to make money you used to plan that just as soon as you were rich, really rich, you'd go back home again to the little town and build a great big house with a fine veranda – no stint about it, the best that money could buy, planed lumber, every square foot of it, and a fine picket fence in front of it.

It was to be one of the grandest and finest houses that thought could conceive; much finer, in true reality, than that vast palace of sandstone with the *porte-cochère* and the sweeping conservatories that you afterwards built in the costlier part of the city.

But if you have half-forgotten Mariposa, and long since lost the way to it, you are only like the greater part of the men here in this Mausoleum Club in the city. Would you believe it that practically every one of them came from Mariposa once upon a time, and that there isn't one of them that doesn't sometimes dream in the dull quiet of the long evening here in the club, that some day he will go back and see the place.

They all do. Only they're half-ashamed to own it.

Ask your neighbour there at the next table whether the partridge that they sometimes serve to you here can be compared for a moment to the birds that he and you, or he and someone else, used to shoot as boys in the spruce thickets along the lake. Ask him if he ever tasted duck that could for a moment be compared to the black ducks in the rich marsh along the Ossawippi. And as for fish, and fishing – no, don't ask him about that, for if he ever starts telling you of the chub they used to catch below the mill dam and the green bass that used to lie in the water-shadow of the rocks beside the Indian's Island, not even the long dull evening in this club would be long enough for the telling of it.

But no wonder they don't know about the five o'clock train for Mariposa. Very few people know about it. Hundreds of them know that there is a train that goes out at five o'clock, but they mistake it. Ever so many of them think it's just a suburban train. Lots of people that take it every day think it's only the train to the golf grounds, but the joke is that after it passes out of the city and the suburbs and the golf grounds, it turns itself little by little into the Mariposa train thundering and pounding towards the north with hemlock sparks pouring out into the darkness from the funnel of it.

Of course you can't tell it just at first. All those people that are crowding into it with golf-clubs, and wearing knickerbockers and flat caps, would deceive anybody. That crowd of suburban people going home on commutation tickets and sometimes standing thick in the aisles, those are, of course, not Mariposa people. But look round a little bit and you'll find them easily enough. Here and there in the crowd those people with the clothes that are perfectly all right and yet look odd in some way, the women with the peculiar hats and the – what do you say? – last year's fashions? Ah yes, of course, that must be it.

Anyway, those are the Mariposa people all right enough. That man with the two-dollar panama and the glaring spectacles is one of the greatest judges that ever adorned the bench of Missinaba County. That clerical gentleman with the wide black hat, who is explaining to the man with him the marvellous mechanism of the new air brake (one of the most conspicuous illustrations of the divine structure of the physical universe), surely you have seen him before. Mariposa people! Oh yes, there are any number of them on the train every day.

But of course you hardly recognize them while the train is still passing through the suburbs and the golf district and the outlying parts of the city area. But wait a little, and you will see that when the city is well behind you, bit by bit the train changes its character. The electric locomotive that took you through the city tunnels is off now and the old wood engine is hitched on in its place. I suppose, very probably, you haven't seen one of these wood engines since you were a boy forty years ago – the old engine with a wide top like a hat on its funnel, and with sparks enough to light up a suit for damages once in every mile.

Do you see, too, that the trim little cars that came out of the city on the electric suburban express are being discarded now at the way stations, one by one, and in their place is the old familiar car with the stuff cushions in red plush (how gorgeous it once seemed!) and with a box stove set up in one end of it? The stove is burning furiously at its sticks this autumn evening, for the air sets in chill as you get clear away from the city and are rising up to the higher ground of the country of the pines and the lakes.

Look from the window as you go. The city is far behind now and right and left of you there are trim farms with elms and maples near them and with tall windmills beside the barns that you can still see in the gathering dusk. There is a dull red light from the windows of the farmstead. It must be comfortable there after the roar and clatter of the city, and only think of the still quiet of it.

As you sit back half-dreaming in the car, you keep wondering why it is that you never come up before in all these years. Ever so many times you planned that just as soon as the rush and strain of business eased up a little, you would take the train and go back to the little town to see what it was like now, and if things had changed much since your day. But each time when your holidays came, somehow you changed your mind and went down to Narragansett or Nagahuckett or Nagasomething, and left over the visit to Mariposa for another time.

It is almost night now. You can still see the trees and the fences and the farmsteads, but they are fading fast in the twilight. They have lengthened out the train by this time with a string of flat cars and freight cars between where we are sitting and the engine. But at every crossway we can hear the long muffled roar of the whistle, dying to a melancholy wail that echoes into the woods; the woods, I say, for the farms are thinning out and the track plunges here and there into great stretches of bush – tall tamarack and red scrub willow and with a tangled undergrowth of brush that has defied for two generations all attempts to clear it into the form of fields.

Why, look, that great space that seems to open out in the half-dark of the falling evening – why, surely yes, Lake Ossawippi, the big lake, as they used to call it, from which the river runs down to the smaller lake – Lake Wissanotti – where the town of Mariposa has lain waiting for you there for thirty years.

This is Lake Ossawippi surely enough. You would know it any-where by the broad, still, black water with hardly a ripple, and with the grip of the coming frost already on it. Such a great sheet of blackness it looks as the train thunders along the side, swinging the curve of the embankment at a breakneck speed as it rounds the corner of the lake.

How fast the train goes this autumn night! You have travelled, I know you have, in the Empire State Express, and the New Limited and the Maritime Express that holds the record of six hundred whirling miles from Paris to Marseilles. But what are they to this, this mad career, this breakneck speed, this thundering roar of the Mar-iposa local driving hard to its home! Don't tell me that the speed is only twenty-five miles an hour. I don't care what it is. I tell you, and you can prove it for yourself if you will, that that train of mingled flat cars and coaches that goes tearing into the night, its engine whistle shrieking out its warning into the silent woods and echoing over the dull still lake, is the fastest train in the whole world.

Yes, and the best too – the most comfortable, the most reliable, the most luxurious and the speediest train that ever turned a wheel.

And the most genial, the most sociable too. See how the passengers all turn and talk to one another now as they get nearer and nearer to the little town. That dull reserve that seemed to hold the passengers in the electric suburban has clean vanished and gone. They are talking – listen – of the harvest, and the late election, and of how the local member is mentioned for the cabinet and all the old familiar topics of the sort. Already the conductor has changed his glazed hat for an ordinary round Christie and you can hear the passengers calling him and the brakeman "Bill" and "Sam" as if they were all one family.

What is it now – nine thirty? Ah, then we must be nearing the town – this big bush that we are passing through, you remember it surely as the great swamp just this side of the bridge over the Ossawippi? There is the bridge itself, and the long roar of the train as it rushes sounding over the trestle work that rises above the marsh. Hear the clatter as we pass the semaphores and the switch lights! We must be close in now!

What? it feels nervous and strange to be coming here again after all these years? It must indeed. No, don't bother to look at the reflection of your face in the window-pane shadowed by the night outside. Nobody could tell you now after all these years. Your face has changed in these long years of money-getting in the city. Perhaps if you had come back now and again, just at odd times, it wouldn't have been so.

There – you hear it? – the long whistle of the locomotive, one, two, three! You feel the sharp slackening of the train as it swings round the curve of the last embankment that brings it to the Mariposa station. See, too, as we round the curve, the row of the flashing lights, the bright windows of the depot.

How vivid and plain it all is. Just as it used to be thirty years ago. There is the string of the hotel buses drawn up all ready for the train, and as the train rounds in and stops hissing and panting at the platform, you can hear above all other sounds the cry of the brakemen and the porters:

"MARIPOSA! MARIPOSA!"

And, as we listen, the cry grows fainter and fainter in our ears and we are sitting here again in the leather chairs of the Mausoleum Club, talking of the little Town in the Sunshine that once we knew.

The Closing Down of Summer

ALISTAIR MACLEOD

It is August now, towards the end, and the weather can no longer be
trusted. All summer it has been very hot. So hot that the gardens
have died and the hay has not grown and the surface wells have
dried to dampened mud. The brooks that flow to the sea have dried
to trickles and the trout that inhabit them and the inland lakes are
soft and sluggish and gasping for life. Sometimes they are seen
floating dead in the over-warm water, their bodies covered with fat
grey parasites. They are very unlike the leaping, spirited trout of
spring, battling and alive in the rushing, clear, cold water; so elec-
trically filled with movement that it seems no parasite could ever
lodge within their flesh.

The heat has been bad for fish and wells and the growth of green
but for those who choose to lie on the beaches of the summer sun
the weather has been ideal. This is a record year for tourists in Nova
Scotia, we are constantly being told. More motorists have crossed
the border at Amherst than ever before. More cars have landed at
the ferry docks in Yarmouth. Motels and campsites have been filled
to capacity. The highways are heavy with touring buses and camper
trailers and cars with the inevitable lobster traps fastened to their
roofs. Tourism is booming as never before.

Here on this beach, on Cape Breton's west coast, there are no
tourists. Only ourselves. We have been here for most of the summer. Surprised at the endurance and consistency of the heat.
Waiting for it to break and perhaps to change the spell. At the end of
July we said to ourselves and to each other, "The August gale will
come and shatter all of this." The August gale is the traditional storm
that comes each August, the forerunner of the hurricanes that will
sweep up from the Caribbean and beat and lash this coast in the
months of autumn. The August gale with its shrieking winds and
crashing muddied waves has generally signalled the unofficial end
of summer and it may come in August's very early days. But, this
year, as yet, it has not come and there are only a few days left. Still

we know that the weather cannot last much longer and in another week the tourists will be gone and the schools will reopen and the pace of life will change. We will have to gather ourselves together then in some way and make the decisions that we have been postponing in the back of our minds. We are perhaps the best crew of shaft and development miners in the world and we were due in South Africa on the seventh of July.

But as yet we have not gone and the telegrams from Renco Development in Toronto have lain unanswered and the telephone calls have been unreturned. We are waiting for the change in the weather that will make it impossible for us to lie longer on the beach and then we will walk, for the final time, the steep and winding zigzagged trail that climbs the rocky face of Cameron's Point. When we reach the top of the cliff we will all be breathing heavily and then we will follow the little path that winds northward along the cliff's edge to the small field where our cars are parked, their hoods facing out to sea and their front tyres scant feet from the cliffside's edge. The climb will take us some twenty minutes but we are all still in good shape after a summer of idleness.

The golden little beach upon which we lie curves in a crescent for approximately three-quarters of a mile and then terminates at either end in looming cliffs. The north cliff is called Cameron's Point after the family that once owned the land, but the south cliff has no name. Both cliffs protect the beach, slowing the winds from both north and south and preserving its tranquillity.

At the south cliff a little brook ends its journey and plummets almost vertically some fifty feet into the sea. Sometimes after our swims or after lying too long in the sand we stand underneath its fall as we would a shower, feeling the fresh water fall upon our heads and necks and shoulders and running down our bodies" lengths to our feet which stand within the sea.

All of us have stood and turned our naked bodies unknown, unaccountable times beneath the spraying shower nozzles of the world's mining developments. Bodies that when free of mud and grime and the singed-hair smell of blasting powder are white almost to the colour of milk or ivory. Perhaps of leprosy. Too white to be quite healthy, for when we work we are often twelve hours in the shaft's bottom or in the development drifts and we do not often feel the sun. All summer we have watched our bodies change their colour and seen our hair grow bleached and ever lighter. Only the scars that all of us bear fail to respond to the healing power of the sun's heat. They seem to stand out even more vividly now, long running pink welts that course down our inner forearms or jagged saw-tooth ridges on the taut calves of our legs.

Many of us carry one shoulder permanently lower than the other where we have been hit by rock falls or the lip of the giant clam that swings down upon us in the narrow closeness of the shaft's bottom. And we have arms that we cannot raise above our heads and touches of arthritis in our backs and in our shoulders, magnified by the water that chills and falls upon us in our work. Few of us have all our fingers and some have lost either eyes or ears from falling tools or discharged blasting caps or flying stone or splintering timbers. Yet it is damage to our feet that we fear most of all. For loss of toes or damage to the intricate bones of heel or ankle means that we cannot support our bodies for the gruelling twelve-hour stand-up shifts. And injury to one foot means that the other must bear double its weight, which it can do for only a short time before poor circulation sets in to numb the leg and make it too inoperative. All of us are big men, over six feet tall and near two hundred pounds, and our feet have at the best of times a great deal of pressure bearing down upon them.

We are always intensely aware of our bodies and the pains that course and twinge through them. Even late at night when we would sleep they jolt us unexpectedly as if from an electric current, bringing tears to our eyes and causing our fists to clench in the whiteness of knuckles and the biting of nails into palms. At such times we desperately shift our positions or numb ourselves from the tumblers of alcohol we keep close by our sides.

Lying now upon the beach we see the external scars on ourselves and on each other and are stirred to the memories of how they occurred. When we are clothed the price we pay for what we do is not so visible as it is now.

Beside us on the beach lie the white Javex containers filled with alcohol. It is the purest of moonshine made by our relatives back in the hills and is impossible to buy. It comes to us only as a gift or in exchange for long-past favours: bringing home of bodies, small loans of forgotten dollars, kindnesses to now-dead grandmothers. It is as clear as water, and a teaspoonful of it when touched by a match will burn with the low blue flame of a votive candle until it is completely consumed, leaving the teaspoon hot and totally dry. When we are finished here we will pour what remains into forty-ounce vodka bottles and take it with us on the long drive to Toronto. For when we decide to go we will be driving hard and fast and all of our cars are big: Cadillacs with banged-in fenders and Lincolns and Oldsmobiles. We are often stopped for speeding on the stretch outside Mt Thom, or going through the Wentworth Valley, or on the narrow road to Fredericton, or on the fast straight road that leads from Rivière du Loup to Lévis, sometimes even on the 401. When we say that we must leave for Africa within hours we are seldom fined or in odd instances allowed to pay our speeding fines upon the spot. We do not wish to get into the entanglement of moonshine brought across provincial lines and the tedium that accompanies it. The fine for open commercial liquor is under fifteen dollars in most places and the transparent vodka bottles both show and keep their simple secret.

But we are not yet ready to leave and in the sun we pour the clear white fluid into styrofoam cups and drink it in long burning swallows, sometimes following such swallows with mouthfuls of Teem or Sprite or Seven-Up. No one bothers us here because we are so inaccessible. We can see any figure that would approach us from more than a mile away, silhouetted on the lonely cliff and the rocky and treacherous little footpath that is the only route to where we are. None of the RCMP who police this region are in any way local and it is unlikely that they even know this beach exists. And in the legal sense there is no public road that leads to the cliff where our cars now stand. Only vague paths and sheep trails through the burnt-out grass and around the clumps of alders and blueberry bushes and protruding stones and rotted stumps. The resilient young spruce trees scrape against the mufflers and oil pans of our cars and scratch against the doors. Hundreds of miles hence when we stop by the roadsides in Quebec and Ontario we will find small sprigs of this same spruce still wedged within the grillwork of our cars or stuck beneath the headlight bulbs. We will remove them and take them with us to Africa as mementoes or talismans or symbols of identity.

Much as our Highland ancestors, for centuries, fashioned crude badges of heather or of whortleberries to accompany them on the battlefields of the world. Perhaps so that in the closeness of their work with death they might find nearness to their homes and an intensified realization of themselves. We are lying now in the ember of summer's heat and in the stillness of its time.

Out on the flatness of the sea we can see the fishermen going about their work. They do not make much money anymore and few of them take it seriously. They say that the grounds have been over-fished by the huge factory fleets from Russia, Spain and Portugal. And it is true that on the still warm nights we can see the lights of such floating factories shining brightly off the coast. They appear as strange, movable, brilliant cities and when they are far out their blazing lights seem to mingle with those of the stars. The fishermen before us are older men or young boys. Grandfathers with their grandsons acting out their ancient rituals. At noon or at one or two before they start for home they will run their little boats into our quiet cove until their bows are almost touching the sand. They will toss us the gleaming blue-black mackerel and the silver herring and the brown-and-white striped cod and talk to us for a while, telling us anything that they think we should know. In return we toss them the whitened Javex bottles so that they may drink the pure clear contents. Sometimes the older men miss the toss and the white cylindrical bottles fall into the sea where they bob and toss like marker buoys or a child's duck in the bathtub until they are gaffed by someone in the boat or washed back in to shore. Later we cook the fish over small, crackling driftwood fires. This, we know too, cannot go on much longer.

In the quiet graveyards that lie inland the dead are buried. Behind the small white wooden churches and beneath the monuments of polished black granite they take their silent rest. Before we leave we will visit them to pray and take our last farewell. We will perhaps be afraid then, reading the dates of our brothers and uncles and cousins, recalling their youth and laughter and the place and man-ner of each death.

Death in the shafts and in the drifts is always violent and very often the body is so crushed or so blown apart that it cannot be reassembled properly for exposure in the coffin. Most of us have accompanied the grisly remains of such bodies trussed up in plastic bags on trains and planes and automobiles and delivered them up to the local undertaker. During the two or three days of the final wake and through the lonely all-night vigils kept in living rooms and old-fashioned parlours only memories and youthful photographs recall the physical reality that lies so dismembered and disturbed within each grey, sealed coffin. The most flattering photograph is placed upon the coffin's lid in an attempt to remind us of what was. I am thinking of this now, of the many youthful deaths I have been part of, and of the long homeward journeys in other seasons of other years. The digging of graves in the bitterness of February's cold, the shovelling of drifts of snow from the barren earth, and then the banging of the pick into the frozen ground, the striking of sparks from steel on stone and the scraping of shovels on earth and rock.

Some twenty years ago when first I went to the uranium shafts of Ontario's Elliot Lake and short-lived Bancroft we would have trouble getting our dead the final few miles to their high white houses. Often, in winter, we would have to use horses and sleighs to get them up the final hills, standing in chest-high snow, taking out window casings so that we might pass the coffin in and then out again for the last time. Or sometimes in the early spring we would again have to resort to horses when the leaving of the frost and the melting of the winter snow turned the brooks into red and roiling rivers and caused the dirt roads that led into the hills to become greasy and impassable. Sometimes in such seasons the underground springs beneath such roads erupt into tiny geysers, shooting their water upward and changing the roadbeds around them into quivering bogs that bury vehicles up to their hubs and axles.

And in November the rain is chill and cold at the graveside's edge. It falls upon our necks and splatters the red mud upon our gleaming shoes and on the pantlegs of our expensive suits. The bagpiper plays "Flowers of the Forest", as the violinist earlier played his haunting laments from the high choir loft. The music causes the hair to bristle on the backs of our necks and brings out the wildness of our grief and dredges the depths of our dense dark sorrow. At the graveside people sometimes shout farewells in Gaelic or throw themselves into the mud or upon the coffin as it is being lowered on its straps into the gaping earth.

Fifteen years ago when the timbers gave way in Springdale, Newfoundland, my younger brother died, crushed and broken amidst the constant tinkle of the dripping water and lying upon a bed of tumbled stone. We could not get him up from the bottom in time, as his eyes bulged from his head and the fluids of his body seeped quietly on to the glistening rock. Yet even as we tried we realized our task was hopeless and that he would not last, even on the surface. Would not last long enough for any kind of medical salvation. And even as the strength of his once-powerful grip began to loosen on my hand and his breath to rattle in his throat, we could see the earthly road that stretched before us as the witnesses and survivors of his death: the report to the local authorities, the statements to the company, to the police, to the coroner and then the difficult phone calls made on badly connected party lines or failing those the more efficient and more impersonal yellow telegrams. The darkness of the midnight phone call seems somehow to fade with the passing of time, or to change and be recreated like the ballads and folktales of the distant lonely past. Changing with each new telling as the tellers of the tales change, as they become different, older, more bitter or more serene. It is possible to hear descriptions of phone calls that you yourself have made some ten or fifteen years ago and to recognize very little about them except the undeniable kernel of truth that was at the centre of the messages they contained. But the yellow telegram is more blunt and more permanent in the starkness of its message and it is never, ever thrown away. It is kept in vases and in Bibles and in dresser drawers beneath white shirts and it is stumbled upon sometimes unexpectedly, years later, sometimes by other hands, in little sandalwood boxes containing locks of the baby's hair or tucked inside the small shoes in which he learned to walk. A simple obituary of a formal kind.

When my brother died in Springdale, Newfoundland, it was the twenty-first of October and when we brought his body home we were already deep into fall. On the high hardwood hills the mountain ash and the aspen and the scarlet maple were ablaze with colour beneath the weakened rays of the autumn sun. On alternate days the rain fell, sometimes becoming sleet or small hard hailstones. Sometimes the sun would shine in the morning, giving way to the vagaries of precipitation in the afternoon. And sometimes the cloud cover would float over the land even as the sun shone, blocking the sun out temporarily and casting shadows as if a giant bird were passing overhead. Standing beneath such a gliding cloud and feeling its occasional rain we could see the sun shining clearly at a distance of only a mile away. Seeing warmth so reachably near while feeling only the cold of the icy rain. But at the digging of his grave there was no sun at all. Only the rain falling relentlessly down upon us. It turned the crumbling clay to the slickest of mud, as slippery and glistening as that of the potter's wheel but many times more difficult to control. When we had dug some four feet down, the earthen walls began to slide and crumble and to give way around us and to fall upon our rubber boots and to press against the soaking pant legs that clung so clammily to our blue-veined legs. The deeper we dug the more intensely the rain fell, the drops dripping from our eyebrows and from our noses and the icy trickles running down the backs of our necks and down our spines and legs and into our squishing and sucking boots. When we had almost reached the required depth one of the walls that had been continuously crumbling and falling suddenly collapsed and with a great whoosh rolled down upon us. We were digging in our traditional family plot and when the wall gave way it sent the box that contained my father's coffin rolling down upon us. He had been dead for five years then, blown apart in Kirkland Lake, and at the time of his burial his coffin had been sealed. We were wildly and irrationally frightened by the slide and braced our backs against the splintered and disintegrating box, fearful lest it should tip and fall upon us and spill and throw whatever rotting relics remained of that past portion of our lives. Of little flesh but maybe green decaying bones or strands of silver matted hair.

We had held it there, braced by our backs in the pouring rain, until timbers were brought to shore up the new grave's side and to keep the past dead resting quietly. I had been very frightened then, holding the old dead in the quaking mud so that we might make room for the new in that same narrow cell of sliding earth and cracking wood. The next day at his funeral the rain continued to fall and in the grave that received him the unsteady timbers and the ground they held so temporarily back seemed but an extension of those that had caused his life to cease.

Lying now in the precarious heat of this still and burning summer I would wish that such thoughts and scenes of death might rise like the mists from the new day's ocean and leave me dry and somehow emptied on this scorching fine-grained sand.

In Africa it will be hot too, in spite of the coming rainy season, and on the veldt the heat will shimmer and the strange, fine-limbed animals will move across it in patterns older than memory. The nomads will follow their flocks of bleating goats in their constant search for grass and moisture and the women will carry earthen jars of water on their heads or baskets of clothes to slap against the rocks where the water is found.

In my own white house my wife does her declining wash among an increasingly bewildering battery of appliances. Her kitchen and her laundry room and her entire house gleam with porcelain and enamel and an ordered cleanliness that I can no longer comprehend. Little about me or about my work is clean or orderly and I am always mildly amazed to find the earnings of the violence and dirt in which I make my living converted into such meticulous brightness. The lightness of white and yellow curtains rustling crisply in the breeze. For us, most of our working lives is spent in rough, crude bunk-houses thrown up at the shafthead's site. Our bunks are made of two-by-fours sometimes roughly hammered together by ourselves and we sleep two men to a room or sometimes four or sometimes in the development's early stages in the vast "ram pastures" of twenty or thirty or perhaps even forty men crowded together in one vast, rectangular, unpartitioned room. Such rooms are like hospital wards without the privacy of the dividing curtains and they are filled, constantly, day and night, with the sounds of men snoring and coughing or spitting into cans by their bedsides, the incoherent moans and mumbles of uneasy sleepers and the thuds of half-conscious men making groaning love to their passive pillows. In Africa we will sleep, mostly naked, under incongruous structures of mosquito netting, hearing the sometimes rain on the roofs of corrugated iron. In the near 24-hour winter darkness of the Yukon, we have slept in sleeping bags, weighted down with blankets and surrounded by various heaters, still to wake to our breath as vapour in the coldness of the flashlight's gleam.

It is difficult to explain to my wife such things and we have grown more and more apart with the passage of the years. Meeting infrequently now almost as shy strangers, communicating mostly over vast distances through ineffectual say-nothing letters or cheques that substitute money for what once was conceived as love. Sometimes the cheques do not even come from me for in the developing African nations the political situation is often uncertain and North American money is sometimes suddenly and almost whimsically "frozen" or "nationalized", making it impossible to withdraw or remove. In times and places of such uneasiness, shaft crews such as ours often receive little or no actual money, only slips of paper to show our earnings, which are deposited in the metropolitan banks of New York or Toronto or London and from which our families are issued monthly cheques.

I would regain what was once real or imagined with my wife. The long nights of passionate lovemaking that seemed so short, the creating and birth of our seven children. Yet I was never home for the birth of any of my children, only for their fathering. I was not home when two of them died so shortly after birth and I have not been home to participate or to share in many of the youthful accomplishments of the other five. I have attended few parents' nights or eighth-grade graduations or father-and-son hockey banquets, and broken tricycle wheels and dolls with crippled limbs have been mended by other hands than mine.

Now my wife seems to have gone permanently into a world of avocado appliances and household cleanliness and the vicarious experiences provided by the interminable soap operas that fill her television afternoons. She has perhaps gone as deeply into that life as I have into the life of the shafts, seeming to tunnel ever downward and outward through unknown depths and distances and to become lost and separated and unavailable for communication. Yet we are not surprised or critical of each other for she too is from a mining family and grew up largely on funds sent home by an absentee father. Perhaps we are but becoming our previous generation.

And yet there are times, even now, when I can almost physically feel the summer of our marriage and of our honeymoon and of her singing the words of the current popular songs into my then-attentive ears. I had been working as part of a crew in Uranium City all winter and had been so long without proper radio reception that I knew nothing of the music of that time's hit parade. There was always a feeling of mild panic then, on hearing whole dance floors of people singing aloud songs that had come and flourished since my departure and which I had never heard. As if I had been on a journey to the land of the dead.

It would be of little use now to whisper popular lyrics into my ears for I have become partially deaf from the years of the jackleg drill's relentless pounding into walls of constant stone. I cannot hear much of what my wife and children say to me and communicate with the men about me through nods and gestures and the reading of familiar lips. Musically, most of us have long abandoned the modern hit parades and have gone, instead, back to the Gaelic songs remembered from our early youth. It is these songs that we hum now on the hotness of this beach and which we will take with us on our journey when we go.

We have perhaps gone back to the Gaelic songs because they are so constant and unchanging and speak to us as the privately familiar. As a youth and as a young man I did not even realize that I could understand or speak Gaelic and entertained a rather casual disdain for those who did. It was not until the isolation of the shafts began that it started to bubble up somehow within me, causing a feeling of unexpected surprise at finding it there at all. As if it had sunk in unconsciously through some strange osmotic process while I had been unwittingly growing up. Growing up without fully realizing the language of the conversations that swirled around me. Now in the shafts and on the beach we speak it almost constantly though it is no longer spoken in our homes. There is a "Celtic Revival" in the area now, fostered largely by government grants, and the younger children are taught individual Gaelic words in the classrooms for a few brief periods during each month. It is a revival that is very different from our own and it seems, like so much else, to have little relevance for us and to have largely passed us by. Once, it is true, we went up to sing our Gaelic songs at the various Celtic concerts which have become so much a part of the summer culture and we were billed by the bright young schoolteachers who run such things as MacKinnon's Miners' Chorus; but that too seemed as lonely and irrelevant as it was meaningless. It was as if we were parodies of ourselves, standing in rows, wearing our miners' gear, or being asked to shave and wear suits, being plied with rum while waiting for our turn on the programme, only then to mouth our songs to batteries of tape recorders and to people who did not understand them. It was as if it were everything that song should not be, contrived and artificial and non-spontaneous and lacking in communication.

I have heard and seen the Zulus dance until they shook the earth. I have seen large splendid men leap and twist and bend their bodies to the hard-baked flatness of the reddened soil. And I have followed their gestures and listened to their shouts and looked into their eyes in the hope that I might understand the meaning of their art. Hoping to find there a message that is recognizable only to primitive men. Yet, though I think I have caught glimpses of their joy, despair or disdain, it seems that in the end they must dance mainly for themselves. Their dancing speaks a language whose true meaning will elude me forever; I will never grasp the full impact of the subtleties and nuances that are spoken by the small head gesture or the flashing fleck of muscle.

I would like to understand more deeply what they have to say in the vague hope that it might be in some way akin to what is expressed in our own singing. That there might be some message that we share. But I can never enter deeply enough into their experience, can never penetrate behind the private mysteries of their eyes. Perhaps, I think sometimes, I am expecting too much. Yet on those occasions when we did sing at the concerts, I would have liked to reach beyond the tape recorders and the faces of the uninvolved to something that might prove to be more substantial and enduring. Yet in the end it seemed we too were only singing to ourselves. Singing songs in an archaic language as we too became more archaic and recognizing the nods of acknowledgement and shouted responses as coming only from our own friends and relatives. In many cases the same individuals from whom we had first learned our songs. Songs that are for the most part local and private and capable of losing almost all of their substance in translation. Yet in the introduction to the literature text that my eldest daughter brings home from the university it states that "the private experience, if articulated with skill, may communicate an appeal that is universal beyond the limitations of time or landscape." I have read that over several times and thought about its meaning in relation to myself.

When I was a boy my father told me that I would never understand the nature of sex until I had participated in it in some worthwhile way, and that there was little point in trying to grasp its meaning through erotic reading or looking at graphic pictures or listening to the real or imagined experiences of older men. As if the written or the spoken word or the mildly pornographic picture were capable of reaching only a small portion of the distance it might hope to journey on the road to understanding. In the early days of such wistful and exploratory reading the sexual act seemed most frequently to be described as "like flying". A boggling comparison at the time to virginal young men who had never been airborne. In the future numbness of our flight to Africa we will find little that is sexual if it is to be like our other flights to such distant destinations.

We will not have much to say about our flight to those we leave behind and little about our destinations when we land. Sending only the almost obligatory postcards that talk about the weather continents and oceans away. Saying that "things are going as expected", "going well". Postcards that have as their most exciting feature the exotic postage stamps sought after by the younger children for games of show and tell.

I have long since abandoned any hope of describing the sexual act or having it described to me. Perhaps it is enough to know that it is not at all like flying, though I do not know what it is really like. I have never been told, nor can I, in my turn, tell. But I would like somehow to show and tell the nature of my work and perhaps some of my entombed feelings to those that I would love, if they would care to listen.

I would like to tell my wife and children something of the way my years pass by on the route to my inevitable death. I would like to explain somehow what it is like to be a gladiator who fights always the impassiveness of water as it drips on darkened stone. And what it is like to work one's life in the tightness of confined space. I would like somehow to say how I felt when I lost my father in Kirkland

Lake or my younger brother in Springdale, Newfoundland. I would like to say how frightened I am sometimes of what I do. And of how I lie awake at night aware of my own decline and of the diminishing of the men around me. For all of us know we will not last much longer and that it is unlikely we will be replaced in the shaft's bottom by members of our own flesh and bone. For such replacement, like our Gaelic, seems to be of the past and now largely over.

Our sons will go to the universities to study dentistry or law and to become fatly affluent before they are thirty. Men who will stand over six feet tall and who will move their fat, pudgy fingers over the limited possibilities to be found in other people's mouths. Or men who sit behind desks shuffling papers relating to divorce or theft or assault or the taking of life. To grow prosperous from pain and sorrow and the desolation of human failure. They will be far removed from the physical life and will seek it out only through jogging or golf or games of handball with friendly colleagues. They will join expensive private clubs for the pleasures of perspiration and they will not die in falling stone or chilling water or thousands of miles from those they love. They will not die in any such manner, partially at least because we have told them not to and have encouraged them to seek out other ways of life which lead, we hope, to gentler deaths. And yet because it seems they will follow our advice instead of our lives, we will experience, in any future that is ours, only an increased sense of anguished isolation and an ironic feeling of confused bereavement. Perhaps it is always so for parents who give the young advice and find that it is followed. And who find that those who follow such advice must inevitably journey far from those who give it to distant lonely worlds which are forever unknowable to those who wait behind. Yet perhaps those who go find in the regions to which they travel but another kind of inarticulate loneliness. Perhaps the dentist feels mute anguish as he circles his chair, and the lawyer who lives in a world of words finds little relationship between professional talk and what he would hope to be true expression. Perhaps he too in his quiet heart sings something akin to Gaelic songs, sings in an old archaic language private words that reach to no one. And perhaps both lawyer and dentist journey down into an Africa as deep and dark and distant as ours. I can but vaguely imagine what I will never know.

I have always wished that my children could see me at my work. That they might journey down with me in the dripping cage to the shaft's bottom or walk the eerie tunnels of the drifts that end in walls of staring stone. And that they might see how articulate we are in the accomplishment of what we do. That they might appreciate the perfection of our drilling and the calculation of our angles and the measuring of our powder, and that they might understand that what we know through eye and ear and touch is of a finer quality than any information garnered by the most sophisticated of mining engineers with all their elaborate equipment.

I would like to show them how professional we are and how, in spite of the chill and the water and the dark and the danger, there is perhaps a certain eloquent beauty to be found in what we do. Not the beauty of stillness to be found in gleaming crystal or in the polished hardwood floors to which my wife devotes such care but rather the beauty of motion on the edge of violence, which by its very nature can never long endure. It is perhaps akin to the violent motion of the huge professional athletes on the given days or nights of their many games. Men as huge and physical as are we, polished and eloquent in the propelling of their bodies towards their desired goals and in their relationships and dependencies on one another but often numb and silent before the microphones of sedentary interviewers. Few of us get to show our children what we do on national television; we offer only the numbness and silence by itself. Unable either to show or tell.

I have always wished to be better than the merely mediocre and I have always wanted to use the power of my body in the fulfilling of such a wish. Perhaps that is why I left the university after only one year. A year which was spent mainly as an athlete and as a casual reader of English literature. I could not release myself enough physically and seemed always to be constricted and confined. In sleeping rooms that were too low, by toilet stalls that were too narrow, in lecture halls that were too hot, even by the desks in those lecture halls, which I found always so difficult to get in and out of. Confined too by bells and buzzers and curfews and deadlines, which for me had little meaning. I wanted to burst out, to use my strength in some demanding task that would allow me somehow to feel that I was breaking free. And I could not find enough release in the muddy wars on the football field or in the thudding contact of the enclosed and boarded rink. I suppose I was drawn too by the apparent glamour of the men who followed the shafts. Impressed by their returning here in summer with their fast cars and expensive clothes, also by the fact that I was from a mining family that has given itself for generations to the darkened earth.

I was aware even then of the ultimate irony of my choice. Aware of how contradictory it seemed that someone who was bothered by confinement should choose to spend his working days in the most confined of spaces. Yet the difference seems to be that when we work we are never still. Never merely entombed like the prisoner in the passive darkness of his solitary confinement. For we are always expanding the perimeters of our seeming incarceration. We are always moving downward or inward or forward or in the driving of our raises even upward. We are big men engaged in perhaps the most violent of occupations and we have chosen as our adversary walls and faces of massive stone. It is as if the stone of the spherical earth has challenged us to move its weight and find its treasure and we have accepted the challenge and responded with drill and steel and powder and strength and all our ingenuity. In the chill and damp we have given ourselves to the breaking down of walls and barriers. We have sentenced ourselves to enclosures so that we might taste the giddy joy of breaking through. Always hopeful of breaking through though we know we never will break free.

Drilling and hammering our way to the world's resources, we have left them when found and moved on. Left them for others to expand or to exploit and to make room for the often stable communities that come in our wake: the sewer lines and the fire hydrants and the neat rows of company houses, the over-organized athletic leagues and the ever-hopeful schools, the Junior Chambers of Commerce. We have moved about the world, liberating resources, largely untouched by political uncertainties and upheavals, seldom harmed by the midnight plots, the surprising coups and the fast assassinations. We were in Haiti with Duvalier in 1960 and in Chile before Allende and in the Congo before it became associated with Zaïre. In Bolivia and Guatemala and in Mexico and in a Jamaica that the tourists never see. Each segment of the world aspires to the treasure, real or imagined, that lies encased in its vaults of stone, and those who would find such booty are readily admitted and handsomely paid, be they employed by dictator or budding democracy or capitalists expanding their holdings and their wealth. Renco Development on Bay Street will wait for us. They will endure our summer on the beach and our lack of response to their seemingly urgent messages. They will endure our Toronto drunkenness and pay our bail and advance us personal loans. And when we go they will pay us thousands of dollars for our work, optimistically hoping that they may make millions in their turn. They will wait for us because they know from years of many contracts that we are the best bet to deliver for them in the end.

There are two other crews in Canada as strong, perhaps even stronger than we are. They are in Rouyn-Noranda; and as our crew is known as MacKinnon, theirs are known by the names of Lafrenière and Picard. We have worked beside them at various times, competed with them and brawled with them in the hall-like beer parlours of Malartic and Temiskaming, and occasionally we have saved one another's lives. They will not go to Africa for Renco Development because they are imprisoned in the depths of their language. And because they speak no English they will not move out of Quebec or out of northern or north-eastern Ontario. Once there was also the O'Leary crew, who were Irish Newfoundlanders. But many of them were lost in a cave-in in India, and of those who remained most have gone to work with their relatives on high-steel construction in New York. We see them sometimes, now, in the bars of Brooklyn or sometimes in the summers at the ferry terminal in North Sydney before they cross to Port-aux-Basques. Iron work, they say, also pays highly for the risk to life; and the long fall from the towering, swaying skyscrapers can occur for any man but once. It seems, for them, that they have exchanged the possibility of being fallen upon for that of falling itself. And that after years of dodging and fearing falling objects from above, they have become such potential objects themselves. Their loss diminishes us too because we know how good they were at what they did, and know too that the mangled remnants of their dead were flown from India in sealed containers to lie on such summer days as these beneath the nodding wild flowers that grow on outport graves.

I must not think too much of death and loss, I tell myself

repeatedly. For if I am to survive I must be as careful and calculating with my thoughts as I am with my tools when working so far beneath the earth's surface. I must always be careful of sloppiness and self-indulgence lest they cost me dearly in the end.

Out on the ocean now it is beginning to roughen and the south-west wind is blowing the smallish waves into larger versions of themselves. They are beginning to break upon the beach with curling whitecaps at their crests and the water that they consist of seems no longer blue but rather a dull and sombre grey. There are no longer boats visible on the once-flat sea, neither near at hand nor on the horizon's distant line. The sun no longer shines with the fierceness of the earlier day and the sky has begun to cloud over. Evening is approaching. The sand is whipped by the wind and blows into our faces and stings our bodies as might a thousand pinpricks or the tiny tips of many scorching needles. We flinch and shake ourselves and reach for our protective shirts. We leave our prone positions and come restlessly to our feet, coughing and spitting and moving uneasily like nervous animals anticipating a storm. In the sand we trace erratic designs and patterns with impatient toes. We look at one another, arching our eyebrows like bushy question marks. Perhaps this is what we have been waiting for? Perhaps this is the end of the beginning?

And now I can feel the eyes of the men upon me. They are waiting for me to give interpretations of the signals, waiting for my sign. I hesitate for a moment, running my eyes along the beach, watching water touching sand. And then I nod my head. There is almost a collective sigh that is more sensed than really heard. Almost like distant wind in far-off trees. Then suddenly they begin to move. Rapidly they gather their clothes and other belongings, shaking out the sand, folding and packing. Moving swiftly and with certainty they are closing down their summer even as it is closing down on them. MacKinnon's miners are finished now and moving out. We are leaving the beach of the summer sun and perhaps some of us will not see it anymore. For some of us may not return alive from the Africa for which we leave.

We begin to walk. First along the beach towards the north cliff of Cameron's Point, and then up the steep and winding zigzagged trail that climbs its face. When I am half-way up I stop and look back at the men strung out in single file behind me. We are mountain climbers in our way though bound together by no physical ropes of any kind. They stop and look back too, back and down to the beach we have so recently vacated. The waves are higher now and are breaking and cresting and rolling farther in. They have obliterated the outlines of our bodies in the sand and our footprints of brief moments before already have been washed away. There remains no evidence that we have ever been. It is as if we have never lain, nor ever walked nor ever thought what thoughts we had. We leave no art or mark behind. The sea has washed its sand slate clean.

And then the rain begins to fall. Not heavily but almost hesitantly. It is as if it has been hot and dry for so long that the act of raining has almost been forgotten and has now to be slowly and almost painfully relearned.

We reach the summit of the cliff and walk along the little path that leads us to our cars. The cars are dusty and their metal is still hot from the earlier sun. We lean across their hoods to lift the windshield wipers from the glass. The rubber of the wiper blades has almost melted into the windshields because of heat and long disuse, and when we lift them slender slivers of rubber remain behind. These blades will have to be replaced.

The isolated raindrops fall alike on windshield and on roof, on hood and trunk. They trace individual rivulets through the layers of grime and then trickle down to the parched and waiting earth.

And now it is two days later. The rain has continued to fall and in it we have gone about preparing and completing our rituals of farewell. We have visited the banks and checked out all the dates on our insurance policies. And we have gathered our working clothes, which when worn continents hence will make us loom even larger than we are in actual life. As if we are Greek actors or mastodons of an earlier time. Soon to be replaced or else perhaps to be extinct.

We have stood bareheaded by the graves and knelt in the mud by the black granite stones. And we have visited privately and in tiny self-conscious groups the small white churches which we may not see again. As we have become older it seems we have become strangely more religious in ways that border close on superstition. We will take with us worn family rosaries and faded charms and loop ancestral medals and crosses of delicate worn fragility around our scar-lashed necks and about the thickness of our wrists, seemingly unaware of whatever irony they might project. This too seems but a further longing for the past, far removed from the "rational" approaches to religion that we sometimes encounter in our children.

We have said farewells to our children too and to our wives and I have offered kisses and looked into their eyes and wept outwardly and inwardly for all I have not said or done and for my own clumsy failure at communication. I have not been able, as the young say, "to tell it like it is", and perhaps now I never shall.

By four o'clock we are ready to go. Our cars are gathered with their motors running and we will drive them hard and fast and be in Toronto tomorrow afternoon. We will not stop all night except for a few brief moments at the gleaming service stations and we will keep one sober and alert driver at the wheel of each of our speeding cars. Many of the rest of us will numb ourselves with moonshine for our own complex and diverse reasons: perhaps to loosen our thoughts and tongues or perhaps to deaden and hold them down, perhaps to be as the patient who takes an anaesthetic to avoid operational pain. We will hurtle in a dark night convoy across the landscapes and the borders of four waiting provinces.

As we move out, I feel myself a figure in some medieval ballad who has completed his formal farewells and goes now to meet his fatalistic future. I do not particularly wish to feel this way and again would shake myself free from thoughts of death and self-indulgence.

As we gather speed the land of the seacoast flashes by. I am in the front seat of the lead car, on the passenger side next to the window. In the side mirror I can see the other cars stretched out behind us. We go by the scarred and abandoned coal workings of our previous generations and drive swiftly westward into the declining day. The men in the back seat begin to pass around their moonshine and attempt to adjust their long legs within the constricted space. After a while they begin to sing in Gaelic, singing almost unconsciously the old words that are so worn and so familiar. They seem to handle them almost as they would familiar tools. I know that in the other cars they are doing the same even as I begin to silently mouth the words myself. There is no word in Gaelic for goodbye, only for farewell.

More than a quarter of a century ago in my single year at the university, I stumbled across an anonymous lyric from the fifteenth century. Last night while packing my clothes I encountered it again, this time in the literature text of my eldest daughter. The book was very different from the one that I had so casually used, as different perhaps as is my daughter from me. Yet the lyric was exactly the same. It had not changed at all. It comes to me now in this speeding car as the Gaelic choruses rise around me. I do not particularly welcome it or want it and indeed I had almost forgotten it. Yet it enters now regardless of my wants or wishes, much as one might see out of the corner of the eye an old acquaintance one has no wish to see at all. It comes again, unbidden and unexpected and imperfectly remembered. It seems borne up by the mounting, surging Gaelic voices like the flecked white foam on the surge of the towering, breaking wave. Different yet similar, and similar yet different, and in its time unable to deny:

> I wend to death, knight stith in stour;
> Through fight in field I won the flower;
> No fights me taught the death to quell –
> I wend to death, sooth I you tell.

> I wend to death, a king iwis;
> What helpes honour or worlde's bliss?
> Death is to man the final way –
> I wende to be clad in clay.

Notes on Contributors

MARGARET ATWOOD (b. 1939), although best known as a novelist, has also written ten books of poetry, two short-story collections and two children's books. She has also edited *The Oxford Book of Canadian Verse* (1982), *The Oxford Book of Canadian Short Stories in English* (1986) and *Best American Short Stories of 1989* (1989). Her novels include *The Edible Woman* (1969), *Surfacing* (1972), *The Handmaid's Tale* (1985) and *Cat's Eye* (1988). Books of poetry include *The Circle Game, You Are Happy* and *Interlunar*. "The Boys' Own Annual, 1911" appears in *Murder in the Dark*.

SANDRA BIRDSELL (b. 1942) is a native of Manitoba. Her stories about the fictional town of Agassiz began appearing in the 1970s. They are collected in *Night Travellers* (1982) and *Ladies of the House* (1984). Her first novel is *The Missing Child* (1989).

MARIE-CLAIRE BLAIS (b. 1939) received a convent education in Quebec city. Her works include *La Belle Bête* (1959; *Mad Shadows*, 1960), *Une saison dans la vie d'Emmanuel* (1965; *A Season in the Life of Emmanuel*, 1966), *Anna's World* (1984) and *Sommeil d'Hiver* (1986).

CLARK BLAISE (b. 1940) was born in Fargo, North Dakota, to a French-Canadian father and an English-Canadian mother. He moved to Montreal and became a Canadian citizen in 1966. His first book of stories, *A North American Education* (1973), was followed by *Tribal Justice* (1974). Blaise has written two novels, *Lunar Attractions* (1979) and *Lusts* (1983), as well as two non-fiction works co-authored with his wife Bharati Mukherjee. His latest book, *Resident Alien* (1986), is a collection of autobiographical short stories.

GEORGE BOWERING (b. 1935) was born and raised in the Okanagan Valley of British Columbia. Before attending university he was an RCAF aerial photographer. Bowering's poetry collections include *Rocky Mountain Foot, The Gangs of Kosmos, The Catch* and *Kerrisdale Elegies*, and his fiction includes *A Short Sad Book, Caprice* and *Burning*

Water, from which "Bring Forth a Wonder" is taken.

DIONNE BRAND (b. 1953) was born in the Caribbean and has lived in Toronto for the past twenty years. She studied English and philosophy at the University of Toronto. Her books of poetry include *Chronicles of the Hostile Sun* and *No Language is Neutral* (1990). Her poetry has appeared in various anthologies including *The Penguin Book of Caribbean Verse*. She has authored a non-fiction work, *Rivers Have Sources, Trees Have Roots – Speaking of Racism*. She has also made documentary films. "Photograph" is taken from her first collection of stories, *Sans Souci* (1988).

AUSTIN CLARKE (b. 1934) emigrated to Toronto from Barbados in 1955 to study economics and political science at the University of Toronto. In 1974–5, Clarke was cultural and press attaché to the Barbadian Embassy in Washington, DC. Before his return to Canada, he served as the general manager of the Caribbean Broadcasting Corporation. Best known for his trilogy of immigrant life in Toronto, Clarke has also written many short stories and an autobiography, *Growing Up Stupid Under the Union Jack* (1980). "Leaving This Island Place" appears in *When He Was Free and Young and He Used to Wear Silks*.

MATT COHEN (b. 1942) grew up in Ottawa, coming to Toronto for university studies. He has published four collections of short fiction, including *Café le Dog* (1983), from which "The Sins of Tomás Benares" is taken, and *Living in Water* (1988), and a children's book, *The Leaves of Louise* (1978). The fictional Ontario town of Salem is the setting for four of his novels, *The Disinherited* (1974), *The Colours of War* (1977), *The Sweet Second Summer of Kitty Malone* (1979) and *The Flowers of Darkness* (1981). Cohen has also published an historical novel, *The Spanish Doctor* (1984), and his latest novel is *Nadine* (1986).

JACQUES FERRON (1921–85), writer, physician and politician, was influenced as a child by a Jesuit education and his father's involvement with the Liberal Party. This early commitment to socialist principles was expressed in his work for left-wing magazines and in his lifelong dedication to the practice of medicine among the poor of Quebec. The author of some twenty plays, many works of fiction (including *Contes du pays incertain*, 1962; *Tales from the Uncertain*

Country) and countless articles, Ferron ran as a CCF candidate in the 1958 Federal election, organized the Rhinoceros Party in 1963 and was consulted by both the FLQ and Pierre Trudeau during the October Crisis in 1970. In 1980 he organized Regroupement des Ecrivains pour le OUI.

MADELEINE FERRON (b. 1922), the sister of writer Jacques Ferron, has lived most of her life in the rural Quebec of which she writes. Ferron has written both short stories and novels, including *Le baron écarlate* (1971), and *Sur le chemin Craig* (1983). With her late husband, Robert Cliche, Ferron has written two volumes of history of the Beauce county region of Quebec. Her latest collections of short stories, *Un singulier amour* (1987) and *Le Grand Théâtre* (1989), were inspired by urban life in Quebec City, where she now lives.

TIMOTHY FINDLEY (b. 1930) had a successful career as an actor before he began writing. His first novel, *The Last of the Crazy People*, was published in 1967. Other novels include *The Wars* (1977) and *Famous Last Words* (1981). His short stories have been collected in two volumes, *Dinner Along the Amazon* (1984) and *Stones* (1988), from which "Dreams" is taken.

KEATH FRASER (b. 1944) has published his work in many literary magazines and is the author of two collections of short fiction, *Taking Cover* (1982) and *Foreign Affairs* (1985). He lives in Vancouver and is currently working on a novel. He has recently edited an anthology, *The Fortunate Traveller: Writers' Worst Journeys*.

ALICE FRENCH (b. 1930) was born on Baillie Island in the Northwest Territories. Her parents were Alaskan Eskimo. Her father worked for the Canalaskan Trading Company (later the Hudson's Bay Company). Her account of her life in the Arctic, *My Name is Masak*, was published in 1976, and "Spring and Summer" is excerpted from that work.

MAVIS GALLANT (b. 1922) was born in Montreal, attended seventeen schools in Canada and the USA and worked as a reporter for the *Montreal Standard*. In 1950 she moved to Paris, where she has lived ever since. In 1951 she published her first story with *The New Yorker*. Her collections of stories include *My Heart is Broken* (1964), *From the*

Fifteenth District (1979), *Home Truths: Selected Canadian Stories* (1981), *Overhead in a Balloon: Stories of Paris* (1985), and *In Transit* (1988).

GLENN GOULD (1932–82) was born and raised in Toronto, and made his début as soloist with the Toronto Symphony at the age of fourteen. His brilliant débuts in Washington, DC, and New York brought him international attention in 1955. His first recording, Bach's "Goldberg Variations", became an instant classic, as did his second recording of the same music in 1981. In 1964, Gould retired from the concert circuit to devote himself to the art and technology of recording. He wrote television and radio documentaries and contributed to the *Globe and Mail*, the *New York Times Magazine* and *High Fidelity*. His writing is collected in *The Glenn Gould Reader* (1984), edited by Tim Page.

ELISABETH HARVOR (b. 1936) was born to Danish immigrant parents in Saint John, New Brunswick, and grew up on the Kingston Peninsula. Her stories have appeared in *The New Yorker* and *Saturday Night*, and have been collected in *Women and Children* (1973) and *If Only We Could Drive Like This Forever* (1988).

ANNE HÉBERT (b. 1916) was born at Sainte-Catherine de Fossambault, Quebec. She now lives in France. Her novels include *Le torrent* (1950; *The Torrent*, 1973); *Les chambres de bois* (1958; *The Silent Rooms*, 1974); *Les enfants du sabbat* (1975; *Children of the Black Sabbath*, 1977); *Les fous de bassan* (1982; *In the Shadow of the Wind*, 1983); and *Le premier jardin* (1988), from which this excerpt is taken.

JACK HODGINS (b. 1938) was born and raised in the Comox Valley on Vancouver Island, an area which he continues to celebrate in his fiction. His first collection of stories, *Spit Delaney's Island*, appeared in 1976. His novels include *The Invention of the World* (1978) and *The Resurrection of Joseph Bourne* (1978). Another collection of linked stories, *The Barclay Family Theatre*, was published in 1981.

HUGH HOOD (b. 1928) had his first collection of short stories, *Flying a Red Kite*, published in 1962, followed by a novel, *White Figure, White Ground* (1964). A prolific writer, Hood is in the middle of a projected twelve-volume series of novels.

JOHN KELLY (b. 1939) was born in Rainy River, Ontario, and raised on the Onigaming Reserve. He completed his undergraduate work at Lakehead University in 1970, and went on to earn a Masters degree in education at the University of Manitoba. Through the 1960s he taught at various schools on reserves in northern Ontario. In the 1970s he turned his attention to researching and analysing the educational needs of native Indians, designing and implementing many innovative educational programmes, and advising Band Councils on curriculum and planning. From 1977 to 1980 he served as Grand Chief, Grand Council Treaty No. 3 in Kenora, Ontario. It was during his tenure as Chief that he delivered this speech to the Royal Commission on the Northern Environment.

JOY KOGAWA (b. 1935) was interned with her family in British Columbia and Alberta during the Second World War. Kogawa would later write of her experience in her 1981 novel, *Obasan*, afterwards becoming politically active in fighting, successfully, for the redress of Japanese-Canadians. The author of several volumes of poetry, Kogawa has also written a children's book, *Naomi's Road* (1986).

MARGARET LAURENCE (1926–87) was born in Neepawa, Manitoba, and educated at United College, Winnipeg. Laurence spent several years in Africa, where her experiences provided the background for a novel, *This Side Jordan* (1960), a collection of short stories, *The Tomorrow Tamer* (1963), from which "The Rain Child" is taken, and a memoir, *The Prophet's Camel Bell* (1963). She is best known for her Manawaka novels and stories (*The Stone Angel*, 1964; *A Jest of God*, 1966; *The Fire Dwellers*, 1969; *A Bird in the House*, 1970; and *The Diviners*, 1974).

STEPHEN LEACOCK (1869–1944) was born in Swanmore, England, the son of a farmer who moved his family to Lake Simcoe, Ontario, in the late 1800s. Leacock was the author of over sixty books, including *Sunshine Sketches of a Little Town* (1912) and *Arcadian Adventures with the Idle Rich* (1914).

HUCH MACLENNAN (b. 1907) was born at Glace Bay on Cape Breton Island and moved to Halifax in 1915. Two years later he witnessed the Halifax explosion, an event which dominates his first published novel, *Barometer Rising* (1941). His later novels include *Two Solitudes* (1945) and *The Watch That Ends the Night* (1959). He is also well known as an essayist.

ALISTAIR MACLEOD (b. 1936) was born in North Battleford, Saskatchewan, to fifth-generation Cape Bretoners. After ten years on the prairies, the MacLeod family returned to Inverness County, Nova Scotia. In 1968 his story "The Boat" was published in the *Massachusetts Review* and went on to be reprinted in *Best American Short Stories*, 1969, among other anthologies. His first collection of short stories, *The Lost Salt Gift of Blood*, was published in 1976. His second collection, *As Birds Bring Forth the Sun*, was published in 1986.

JOYCE MARSHALL (b. 1913) has written novels (*Presently Tomorrow*, 1946; *Lovers and Strangers*, 1957), and short stories (*A Private Place*, 1975). She is the translator of three Gabrielle Roy books, *The Road Past Altamont*, *Windflower* and *Enchanted Summer*. Her collected stories will be appearing in 1990.

ROHINTON MISTRY (b. 1952) was born in Bombay. He emigrated to Canada in 1975 and began working at a bank. His first collection of stories, published in 1987, was *Tales from Firozsha Baag*. He is now working on a novel.

DANIEL DAVID MOSES (b. 1952) was born on the Six Nations Reserve near Brantford, Ontario. He is a member of Native Earth Performing Arts Inc. in Toronto. He has published a volume of poetry, *Delicate Bodies* (1980), and a play, *Coyote City* (1990).

BHARATI MUKHERJEE (b. 1940) was born in Calcutta, India, and was educated in India, England, Switzerland, and the United States. She is now professor of English at the University of California at Berkeley. Her earlier novels include *The Tiger's Daughter* (1972) and *Wife* (1975). *Days and Nights in Calcutta* (1977) and *The Sorrow and the Terror* (1987) were co-authored with her husband, Clark Blaise. Her most recent books are *Darkness* (1985), *The Middlemen and Other Stories* (1988), and *Jasmine* (1989), a novel.

ALICE MUNRO (b. 1931) began writing at fifteen, but it was not until 1968 that her first collection, *Dance of the Happy Shades*, brought her national acclaim. In 1972, after nine years in British Columbia and the publication of her second highly successful collection, *The Lives of Girls and Women* (1971), Munro returned to the rural Ontario of her childhood. Munro's stories appear regularly in *The New Yorker*. Her recent collections are *Who Do You Think You Are?* (1978), *The Progress of Love* and *Friend of My Youth* (1990).

DAVID ADAMS RICHARDS (b. 1950) was born in the Maritimes, and still lives in and writes about the Miramichi Valley of New Brunswick. His novels include *The Coming of Winter* (1974), *Blood Ties* (1976) and *Nights Below Station Street* (1987). His short stories have been collected in *Dancers at Night* (1978).

MORDECAI RICHLER (b. 1931) spent his first twenty years in Montreal, and then went to Europe, where he lived in France and Spain before settling in England in 1954, when his first novel, *The Acrobats*, was published. Before his return to Canada in 1972, Richler wrote novels, a memoir, and satirical journalism. His books include *The Apprenticeship of Duddy Kravitz* (1959), *Cocksure* (1968), *Hunting Tigers Under Glass* (1968) and *The Street* (1969), from which "Some Grist for Mervyn's Mill" is taken. He has written several film scripts and children's books. His latest novel, published in 1989, is *Solomon Gursky Was Here*.

CHARLES RITCHIE (b. 1906) has been Canada's ambassador to Germany, the UN, the USA and NATO, and he has also served as high commissioner to the UK. After his retirement he published four volumes of diplomatic journals, of which *The Siren Years* is perhaps the best known. *My Grandfather's House*, a memoir of Ritchie's youth in Halifax, was published in 1987.

LEON ROOKE (b. 1934) was born in Roanoke Rapids, North Carolina. He moved to Victoria, British Columbia, in 1969. He is the author of eight collections of short stories, and his novels include *Fat Woman* (1980) and *Shakespeare's Dog* (1983). He now lives in Eden Mills, Ontario. His short-story collections include *A Bolt of White Cloth* and *Saving the Province*. His latest novel is *A Good Baby*.

JOE ROSENBLATT (b. 1933) was born and raised in Toronto. His books of poetry include *Top Soil*, *Brides of the Stream*, and *Poetry Hotel: Selected Poems 1963–1985* (1985). He has also written two volumes of memoirs, *Escape from the Glue Factory* (1985), from which "The Lake" is taken, and *The Kissing Gold Fish of Siam* (1989).

SINCLAIR ROSS (b. 1908) is a native of Wild Rose, Saskatchewan. He worked as a bank clerk until his retirement. His novels include *As For Me and My House* (1957), *The Well* (1957), *Whir of Gold* (1970) and *Sawbones Memorial* (1974). Among his collections of stories are *The Lamp at Noon and Other Stories* (1968) and *The Race and Other Stories* (1983).

GABRIELLE ROY (1909–83) was born to Québécois parents in Saint-Boniface, Manitoba, youngest of eight children. Her first novel, *Bonheur d'occasion* (*The Tin Flute*), was published in 1945. Other works include a collection of semi-autobiographical stories, *Rue Deschambault* (1955; *Street of Riches*, 1957), from which "The Well of Dunrea" is taken; and *La route d'Altamont* (1966; *The Road Past Altamont*, 1966). The autobiography of her first thirty years was published posthumously as *La détresse et l'enchantement* (1984; *Enchantment and Sorrow*, 1987).

CAROL SHIELDS (b. 1935) came to Canada in 1957 and studied at the University of Ottawa. Published as a poet in the early 1970s, Shields gained critical attention for her first novel, *Small Ceremonies* (1976). She has since written four novels, including *Swann, a Mystery* (1988), and her collections of short stories include *Various Miracles* (1985), from which "Scenes" is taken, and *The Orange Fish* (1989).

ELIZABETH SMART (1913–86) was born in Ottawa and educated in Cobourg, Ontario. She lived most of her later life in England. In 1945 her highly acclaimed short novel, *By Grand Central Station I Sat Down and Wept*, was published – a part of which is excerpted here. *The Assumption of Rogues and Rascals*, a prose poem, was published in 1977, and her journals, edited by Alice van Wart, were published in 1986 under the title *Necessary Secrets*.

WALLACE STEGNER (b. 1909) was born in Lake Mills, Iowa, but lived from 1914 to 1920 in Saskatchewan. He spent the rest of his childhood in North Dakota, Washington, Montana and Utah. Stegner has written many novels, including *The Big Rock Candy Mountain* (1943) and *Angle of Repose* (1971), as well as two biographies, three collections of articles and essays and many short stories. An ardent conservationist, Stegner collaborated with his son Page and with photographer Eliot Porter on *American Places*. *Wolf Willow*

(1962) is his childhood memoir of Saskatchewan. His latest novel is *Crossing to Safety* (1987).

AUDREY THOMAS (b. 1935) was born in Binghamton, New York. She came to Canada in 1959. Her collections of stories include *Ten Green Bottles* (1967) and *Goodbye Harold Good Luck* (1986). She has written many novels, among them *Mrs Blood* (1975) and *Intertidal Life* (1984).

GUY VANDERHAEGHE (b. 1951) is a native of Saskatchewan. He worked as an archivist and teacher until the early 1980s, when he began to write full time. His first collection of stories was *Man Descending* (1982). He has since written another collection of stories, *The Trouble with Heroes* (1983), and two novels, *My Present Age* (1984) and *Homesick* (1989).

SEAN VIRGO (b. 1940) was born in Malta and came to Canada in 1966. He has published four books of poetry, a novel, *Selakhi* (1987), and three collections of short stories, *White Lies* (1980), *Wormwood* (1989) and *Through the Eyes of a Cat*.

SHEILA WATSON (b. 1909) was born in New Westminster, British Columbia, and she studied with Marshall McLuhan at the University of Toronto. Watson drew on her early teaching experience in the BC interior for the setting of her first novel, *The Double Hook* (1959). She has one collection of short stories, *Five Stories* (1984).

RUDY WIEBE (b. 1934) was born in Saskatchewan to a German-speaking Mennonite family. Wiebe's first novel was *Peace Shall Destroy Many* (1962). In 1966 Wiebe visited Mennonite communities in Paraguay and subsequently wrote of the experience in his 1970 novel *The Blue Mountains of China*. His other novels include *The Temptations of Big Bear* (1973), *The Scorched Wood People* (1977) and *My Lovely Enemy* (1983). *Playing Dead: A Contemplation Concerning the Arctic* (1989) is his most recent work. "The Naming of Albert Johnson" appears in his 1974 short-story collection, *Where is the Voice Coming From?*

ETHEL WILSON (1888–1980) was born in Port Elizabeth, South Africa. Her parents died when Wilson was ten, and she was sent to Vancouver to live with her maternal grandparents. Her short stories appear in *Mrs Golightly* (1961). Her novels include *Hetty Dorval* (1947), and *Swamp Angel* (1952) – the first chapter of which is excerpted here.